FORWARD

To the Children of the African Diaspora — from Harlem to Havana, from the Containment Zones in every corner of this world we call home...

This story is more than magic and mystery — it's a reflection of our roots, our resilience, and the bloodlines that bind us across oceans and generations.

We are not divided by borders, accents, or shades of skin.

We are connected by a deeper truth — one forged in survival, shaped by memory, and carried in the marrow of our bones. We are the children of the Diaspora.

Our ancestry is older than the empires that tried to break us.

And our stories — like our spirits — endure. We conjure legacy from struggle.

We speak forgotten tongues in defiance.

We carry the dreams of the stolen, the strength of the silenced, and the fire of those who refused to kneel.

This tale is for them — and for us.

For the ones who walk between worlds, who bear both burden and brilliance.

For every soul who has ever been told they are too much, too different, too strange, from being too light to be down, to being too dark and put down, your soul remains unconquered.

To my brothers and sisters of the diaspora in Santo Domingo, Kingston, San Juan, Port-au-Prince, Ouagadougou, and elsewhere, keep pushing for your independence, cultural and economic.

Welcome to Wands and Tommy Guns.

Our magic is ancient.

Our rhythm is jazz.

Dedicated to Charles Steffen Haskins Payne Sr.
A writer, a revolutionary, a father.
Your words lit torches. Your spirit still marches.
Gone too soon — but never forgotten.

PROLOGUE

The Warehouse

October 1923

RADIO CRACKLE. WBC RADIO THEME FADES IN AND OUT. THEN—THE VOICE OF WALTER GRIMSLEY:

"And they say it's not constitutional!"

Well, I say—forget the Constitution. George Washington wasn't a mage. Hamilton couldn't disappear in a puff of smoke. And let's just ignore the rumors that old Ben Franklin was a spellwright with a lightning fetish. We're talking about real America, folks. Built with hands. Not hexes."

"Now they tell us we're supposed to accept it. Accept blood rites in the street. Accept arcanists registering our children. Accept containment zones as the new normal. 'Progress,' they call it. No, friends—it's not progress. It's a slow collapse masked in parchment and spellpaper."

"Because here's the truth they don't want you to hear: You let magic get too close, and it burns the flag it claims to protect. It hollows out decency, twists the law, and turns men into monsters with badges."

"But not here. Not on this broadcast. While the rest of the world bends a knee to spells and sigils, I'll be right here behind this mic—reminding you what it means to be human."

"This is Walter Grimsley. And you're listening to—The Grim Truth."

The radio died with a soft *click*. Chase Cassidy stepped out of the black and tan Hispano-Suiza H6B Cabriolet DeVille, the low hum of the engine cutting through the still night air. The vehicle had barely stopped before he swung open the door and stood, imposing and confident.

His fedora, a deep gray that matched his suit, was pulled low over his eyes. The dim streetlight above flickered sporadically, casting a brief, golden glow across the words etched into the battered warehouse door: LOT 24.

Chase was a tall, athletically built African American man with a presence that demanded attention. His face, square-jawed with a 5 o'clock shadow, was marked by a few well-healed scars across his right cheek and continued over the bridge of his nose; a battle-worn reminder from the Great War that had left wounds both external and internal.

His movements were fluid, practiced—every step he took carried the weight of a life lived on the edge. His black and well-worn overcoat fluttered behind him as he adjusted it, pulling the collar up to shield himself from the biting wind.

A large bag sat heavy in the trunk, its contents unknown to anyone but him. Unfazed by its weight, Chase easily swung it over his shoulder, his overcoat blending with the shadows as he moved toward the warehouse entrance.

His gaze shifted to the side as his shoes hit the cold pavement. A brief flicker of light—a glow from a cigar—caught his attention. There, sitting in the back seat of the car, was the silhouette of a woman. The faint, rhythmic exhale of smoke danced into the air before vanishing. She said nothing, but her presence was palpable.

Chase's lips twitched in a half-smile, but it was more a reflex than anything else—an acknowledgment of her attention, not an invitation. His fingers brushed against the overcoat as he reached to adjust it, revealing a silver badge resting on his belt.

A quick flash of it, caught in the streetlight, spoke volumes. Chase Cassidy wasn't just a police man—he was a Hex-Breaker, a government-sponsored arcane bounty hunter.

His job was to find the magic-wielding outlaws, the rogue mages, and bring them down, no questions asked. The ward behind his ear, a magical inscription etched permanently into his skin, marked him as a product of a world where power and danger existed in a dangerous balance.

But tonight, it wasn't about the badge or the wards. It was about vengeance. His shoes clicked against the pavement as he turned, his gloved hand reaching for the door as he paused. A slight tilt of his head caught her reflection in his grey eyes. They were bound to each other.

The woman didn't follow, but her eyes never left him as she met his gaze. Chase entered the darkness, the door creaking closed behind him as he stepped into the cool, damp air of the warehouse. It was quiet, too quiet.

He knew better than to trust the silence. Chase paused briefly, adjusting to the new sensations. Something felt off, and a sense of unease encroached on him as though the shadows were watching him.

He inhaled slowly. The air was thick with the smell of mold, rust, and something more sinister—decay. Movement to the side caught his

attention. Beads of water raced up the wall like an army of angry ants. It clung to everything, making the walls seem alive, damp with the remnants of years left unattended.

The water pooled on the ceiling and flowed towards the staircase on the far side, a trail leading him to his quarry. Then he heard it, the slow rhythmic chanting above him. He was close.

Cassidy's boots echoed across the empty concrete floor as he pushed further down the dark hallway. Every step was measured, calculated, as if he were already anticipating what was to come. His hand brushed lightly against the cold metal railing as he ascended the stairs.

Reaching the top, he stopped in front of a locked bay door. Here, the chanting, though still faint, was the loudest. He set the heavy bag on the floor with a thud, the contents shifting with a low metallic clank. His movements were calm and unhurried.

Removing his gloves, Chase's left hand brushed against his right wrist, where a sigil, an arcane rune designed for offensive magic, was inscribed onto his skin. Fingers traced the outline of the sigil. The moment his magic flared to life, his eyes flashed a hellish amber, an unnatural glow that lit the dimness of the warehouse.

The air around him shimmered as if the very fabric of reality were bending to his will. Heat radiated from his hand as dark and almost translucent flames ignited from his palm. The lock, made of cold iron, began to melt, warping under the intense, fiery heat.

Chase watched as it fell away, the remnants of the lock sizzling on the ground like a dying ember. His eyes fixed onto the pool of rapidly cooling metal before he reached for the bag and, without a glance, retrieved the weapon he had come for.

A Thompson submachine gun.

With practiced hands, Chase attached a drum magazine to the weapon. His fingers, steady and unfaltering, clicked the magazine into place. But he wasn't just a man of firepower. He was something more. Something darker.

The door opened effortlessly under his grip, the smell of death and decay rushing to greet him. The putrid stench filled the air, almost suffocating. Chase didn't flinch. He spat in disgust, wiping his mouth with the back of his hand. His eyes, still glowing with that eerie amber light, scanned the darkness beyond, but all he could see was an oppressive void.

Then came the sound—a scraping, scuffling noise, low and guttural. It was coming closer. His heart rate didn't increase. Chase Cassidy was calm in the face of the oncoming storm. He raised the Tommy gun without hesitation, the barrel pointed at the doorway as the familiar weight of it felt like an extension of himself.

And then, the first shots rang out.

The shattering barrage of gunfire echoed through the vast emptiness of the warehouse, sharp and deafening. A monstrous, pale beast lunged from the shadows, its grotesque form crashing to the ground with a sickening thud.

But the fight was far from over. A piercing screech filled the air. The unmistakable shuffle of feet followed it—dozens of feet, perhaps more, growing louder with each passing second. They were closing in.

Chase's grip tightened on the Tommy gun, the weapon's weight comforting as he pulled the trigger again. A hail of arcane bullets tore through the pale, bloodshot-eyed creatures emerging from the darkness. Each burst sent more of them crashing to the floor, their hollowed eyes wide with hunger; these were vampires.

They twisted in agony as their renowned ability to heal failed them. But no matter how many fell, the swarm kept coming.

Relentless. Unstoppable.

The drum magazine clicked empty. Chase dropped the Tommy Gun without a second thought and drew his twin ivory-handled pistols from their holsters. He didn't need to aim. He never did.

With each shot, the vampires around him fell, their bodies slamming to the cold concrete floor in a sickening heap.

The last of them dropped, their ragged, gurgling breaths fading into silence. Dropping the pistols, he reached for the Tommy Gun again, quickly reloading. Timing was critical; mistakes could not be made.

And then, she appeared.

Adriana Mortem.

A woman, a monster, a legend of fear.

Chase lowered the submachine gun.

The end had finally come.

CHAPTER 1

Welcome to Madhatten
Two Weeks Earlier

The Grim Truth radio broadcast

"And now, folks, let's talk about that part of the city nobody likes to mention after dark... the place the papers politely call the Manhattan Arcane Restriction Zone."

"But the locals? They got a different name for it. They call it Madhatten."

"Yeah, you heard me right. Madhatten. Half 'Manhattan, 'half 'madness'—because that's exactly what's festering behind those arcane barriers. Have you ever stepped inside? Have you ever seen what's crawling through those back alleys?"

"Magic doesn't stay bottled up just because you put a fence around it folks! That zone was supposed to regulate the Arcanists—keep 'em monitored, keep 'em safe. And keep us safe from them. But from what I've seen? It's a free-for-all—gangs staking claims with blood and spellfire. Unlicensed charms traded in broad daylight. Buildings humming with energy no one understands."

"They say it's all under control. That the magical population is being treated humanely, given what they need. But if that's true, why does the river keep turning up corpses? Why do the convoy guards wear armor and carry rifles?"

"Let me tell you something, and I want you to really listen—Madhatten isn't some regulated experiment. It's a storm waiting to break. We need more than wards and wishful thinking. We need a real containment protocol before it spills over."

"This is Walter Grimsby on WBC Radio, bringing you the Grim Truth no one else will."

The morning air in Madhatten was thick with the scent of rain, smoke, and burnt ozone—the faint smell of magic that never quite faded from the streets. The city was a beast with many faces—some welcoming, most predatory. It was a place where power and desperation danced in the same breath, where magic wasn't just a gift but also a liability.

Chase Cassidy knew this better than most. The docks were always a place of trouble, but today the air carried something heavier—death.

The body of a young Fey child, no older than ten, lay crumpled against a stack of damp crates, his small frame contorted unnaturally. His skin, dark brown with an ethereal shimmer beneath, marked him as one of the many magical refugees forced into the Restriction Zone.

The faint glow that once lit his veins had faded, leaving only lifeless eyes staring into nothing.

Chase, clad in the faded blue uniform of the NYPD, stood at the perimeter, his posture rigid but his mind already assessing the scene. He had been on the force for two years now—long enough to know when a case would be buried before the ink dried on the report.

Assigned to blocking duty, he kept his stance firm, ensuring the growing crowd didn't push past the hastily erected barriers. Whispers and murmurs spread like wildfire, the familiar blend of outrage and indifference rippling through gathered bystanders.

Some gawked, eager for a spectacle, while others muttered darkly about the state of the city, about how bodies were turning up in places they shouldn't. A few clutched their coats tighter, crossing arms or whispering quick prayers, sensing this was no ordinary crime scene.

Chase didn't need a detective's badge to see how the higher-ups were moving—fast, quiet, trying to contain the fallout before it reached the press. In these two years, he had learned that justice in this city wasn't about truth but who held the strings.

Captain Whitman and Corporal O'Leary took charge of the scene, their presence barely stirring the other officers standing around the docks. Whitman was built like a football lineman—thick, heavy, and solid. His broad shoulders filled out his uniform, and his greying black hair was cropped short, a neatly trimmed mustache sitting above a mouth that rarely smiled.

A man like him didn't need to raise his voice to be heard—his presence alone was enough to keep most men in line.

Beside him, O'Leary was shorter, leaner, quicker, but no less formidable. A true Irishman with thinning red hair and sharp blue eyes, his face was lined with exhaustion but wary intelligence. He had a dogged sense of duty, though it was hard to tell where his loyalty truly rested.

Several officers stood idly by, their disinterest palpable. One, a grizzled man with a permanent sneer, spat on the corpse of the fey child lying on the ground.

"Another one of them," he muttered, shaking his head. "Damn

infestation."

Chase's blood ran hot. His grip on his baton tightened. His pulse drummed against his ears. "The hell's wrong with you?" His voice cut through the air, sharp and laced with barely restrained fury.

The officer turned toward him, unimpressed. "Relax, Cassidy. Ain't like anyone's gonna miss the brat."

Chase took a step forward, his stance rigid, his fists clenched. "Say that again." The officer barely spared him a glance. A smirk curled at the edge of his mouth, as if daring Chase to take a swing.

Before the tension could snap, O'Leary stepped between them, hands raised in mock peace. "Enough of this," he barked. His gaze flicked to Chase, firm but dismissive. "You're here to keep order, not pick fights."

Chase's jaw clenched, his breath steady but sharp. He stepped back, the fire in his chest barely contained. O'Leary, however, didn't chastise the other officer. Didn't so much as look at him with disapproval.

Instead, he just gave the bastard a nod before turning away. It was clear where his sympathies lay. Chase felt a bitter taste rise in his mouth. Whitman, who had been watching in silence, turned slowly.

"You just spit on a dead kid?" His voice was low, even, but an unmistakable weight was behind it—a warning.

The officer shrugged. "Damn Fey get what they—" Whitman's fist drove into the man's gut before the words could leave his mouth. The officer doubled over, gasping, choking, his cigarette tumbling from his lips.

Whitman grabbed him by the collar and hauled him upright, his grip like iron. "Say it again."

The officer wheezed, too winded to respond. O'Leary smirked. But he didn't intervene. Whitman shoved the officer back, watching him stumble and collapse against a crate. His voice rumbled like distant thunder.

"Anyone else got something smart to say?" Silence. The rest of the cops kept their heads down. Whitman exhaled sharply, rubbing a hand over his face. His words were for O'Leary alone, muttered just under his breath. "City's rotting from the inside, O'Leary." His tone was dark, heavy.

"Starting with our own goddamn department." O'Leary let out a dry chuckle, shaking his head. "Aye, Cap. Ain't that the truth."

The commotion drew new attention. A man in a weathered trench coat and a fedora tilted just enough to shade his eyes stepped onto the scene. A camera dangled from his neck, its leather strap worn from use.

Walter Grimsby, a name every cop in Madhatten knew—a reporter and radio personality, who thrived on scandal and had no love for magical folk. Grimsby lifted his camera, snapping a photo of the child's lifeless body before anyone could protest.

"Sad sight," he mused, voice thick with false sympathy.

"Seems like this Zone's got a bit of a magical infestation problem, doesn't it?"

Chase felt his hands curl into fists again. Whitman exhaled sharply, rubbing his temples, while O'Leary smirked slightly, as if amused. The contempt in the air was suffocating. Chase stared at the dead child, at the lack of care, at the way even the tragedy of a young life lost could be twisted into an excuse for hate.

He'd seen war.

He'd seen monsters.

This was worse.

A black, rusted hearse—known to the officers as the meat wagon —rumbled to the crime scene, its old tires grinding against the damp cobblestones. The vehicle wheezed as it came to a stop, steam hissing from the engine like the breath of a dying beast.

The rear doors creaked open, their rusted hinges groaning in protest. Two men in stained, gray coats stepped out, their expressions unreadable. They moved with practiced efficiency, carrying a stretcher between them as they approached the lifeless body of the fey child.

The crowd thickened, murmurs growing, but no one stepped forward. They all watched in cold detachment as the workers bent down and began the silent process of loading the small, fragile corpse into the back of the wagon. Their movements were mechanical, unfeeling.

Then came the sound of metal-tipped boots clicking against the pavement. The crowd hushed. A third figure emerged from the hearse, walking slowly and deliberately as if the air around him bent to his presence.

Dr. Horatio Buzzard.

Tall and thin as a switchblade, he was draped in a long, ink-black coat, the fabric embroidered with silver-threaded sigils. His wide-brimmed hat cast an eerie shadow over his sharp, dark features, and around his neck hung a collection of bone talismans, each rattling softly as he moved.

He stepped closer to the child's body, his yellowed eyes glinting beneath the flickering streetlamp. One of the wagon workers nodded to him, murmuring a low, respectful greeting.

Buzzard said nothing at first—only tilted his head, studying the corpse like a man might study a dying ember in the fire. A gloved hand emerged from his coat, fingers long, adorned with rings of arcane metals. With an almost reverent touch, he ran his fingers lightly over the child's wrist.

His rings hummed. A low vibration pulsed in the air, barely perceptible— but Chase felt it deep in his bones.

Dr. Buzzard exhaled softly, his lips curling into something akin to amusement, but without an ounce of joy.

"Now, now..." His deep voice carried the thick, rolling lilt of the islands, his accent rich like molasses. "Ain't this somethin'?"

Whitman sighed sharply, rubbing his temple. "You got something to say, Buzzard?"

Dr. Buzzard tilted his head, grinning just enough to show gold-capped teeth. "Oh, Cap'n Whitman. You already know the answer to that."

His fingers traced an invisible pattern over the child's chest, feeling for something unseen. Then, with a click of his tongue, he muttered a word in Creole French that sent a shiver through the air. Chase's gut twisted.

Dr. Buzzard stood up slowly, his bone talismans clinking as he did. "That ain't just murder, gentlemen." His voice dipped low, like a secret shared in the dead of night. "That's a ritual."

Whitman stiffened. O'Leary shifted uneasily, his hand brushing the grip of his baton. The other officers went silent.

Chase's brow furrowed.

"A ritual for what?"

Dr. Buzzard met his eyes, and for the first time, the amusement faded from his expression. "Not what, boy."

He gestured lazily toward the corpse. "Who?" The words sent an icy ripple through the gathered men.

Whitman clenched his jaw. "Shit."

Dr. Buzzard chuckled, his voice low and knowing. "Oh, you ain't even scratched the surface yet, Cap'n." He gestured to the hearse. "Now, if y'all don't mind, I've got a body to prep. But trust me... this little one's death? It ain't the end."

Tipping his hat slightly to Chase and Whitman, Dr. Buzzard turned on his heel and strode toward the wagon. He paused as he reached the doors, looking over his shoulder with that same too-wide, all-knowing grin.

"When you put a detective on this case," his voice took on a mocking lilt, filled with something halfway between amusement and warning. Make sure it's someone who understands the shadows of the city."

The doors slammed shut with that, and the meat wagon rumbled off into the night. Before the tension could settle, a figure emerged from the crowd—a man in a sharp, tailored suit, his every step deliberate.

Luis Weldon. The spokesperson for the National Magical Negro Freedom Society, Weldon was a man who commanded attention the moment he entered a space. His crisp pinstripe suit was pressed to perfection, his tie knotted tight, and his shoes gleamed under the dim gaslights. A gold pocket watch chain glinted against his dark vest as he moved, his expression grim and unreadable.

His gaze cut through the assembled officers until it landed squarely on Captain Whitman. His jaw tightened. "Weldon," he said, barely masking his irritation. "This is a police matter."

"That's exactly why I'm here," Weldon replied coolly. "This child-this magical child—deserves justice. Who's going to look into his death? Or are you planning on letting it slip through the cracks like so many others?"

Before Whitman could answer, a sharp click punctuated the air— a camera shutter snapping. Walter Grimsby, the ever-present investigative journalist, stood off to the side, his camera still raised, the smug glint in his eye all too familiar.

"Oh, please, Weldon," he drawled. "Don't pretend you're here for justice. You're here to make this a spectacle. Stir up trouble where there ain't none."

Weldon turned on him sharply. "Trouble? You mean like an officer spitting on the body of a dead child? Or do you mean the way you spin every tragedy involving magical folk into justification for their persecution?"

Grimsby's smirk widened. "I report what the people want to hear. Maybe if magic-folk weren't causing so much damn trouble, this wouldn't be an issue."

"Maybe if parasites like you weren't poisoning the truth, people would know whats really going on," Weldon shot back, his voice carrying over the restless crowd.

Whitman held up a hand. "Enough of this—"

"No," Weldon interrupted, returning to face the gathered onlookers. "Why are nonchanters—you know the type, non-magic people— investigating a magical death? Why isn't one of our own handling this? Why do we let them control the fates of our children?"

A ripple of unease and agreement spread through the gathered spectators. Some nodded in solemn approval, others shifted uncomfortably. Chase remained silent, his pulse thrumming. He knew the weight of Weldon's words. He also knew what came next.

And then, the first shout rang out. The crowd surged, bodies crashing against one another as chaos erupted. Shouts turned into cries of pain, and the police scrambled to contain the riot. A bottle shattered against a lamppost, and suddenly O'Leary was on the ground, clutching his head where a stray blow had landed.

Blood trickled between his fingers as he groaned. Chase acted on instinct, rushing to O'Leary's side and pulling him up before he was trampled. The Corporal muttered something incoherent, his legs unsteady, but Chase shoved him toward safety before breaking into a sprint after the attacker.

The man ran, weaving through the alleyways, but Chase was faster. He tackled the suspect to the ground, pinning him with practiced ease. The man thrashed, shouting angrily, but Chase twisted his arm behind his back, keeping him subdued.

Back at the docks, the fight between the crowd and the officers continued to rage. Whitman stood at the edge, his gaze shifting between the violence and Luis Weldon, who watched with a satisfied smirk. He wasn't just an activist—he was a man who thrived in moments like these.

Whitman clenched his fists, knowing that this was only the beginning.

———

Back at the precinct, the atmosphere was thick with anger and resentment. The air reeked of sweat, tobacco, and the stale musk of uniforms worn through too many hours of unrest.

The riot had left its mark—not just on the city but also on the men who wore the badge.

The heavy doors of the First Arcane Police Department swung open as officers trudged inside, some shaking their heads, others muttering under their breath. The station's main floor was a chaotic blend of slammed paperwork, low curses, and the dull buzz of electric lights flickering overhead.

The ceiling fans, meant to cut through the stagnant air, barely made a difference.

Chase strode in, his shoulders stiff, the weight of the night's events pressing down on him. His boots scuffed against the checkered linoleum floor, leaving faint streaks of blood—some of it his, most of it not. He could still hear the echoes of shouts from the streets, feel the lingering sting of spells that had burned through the air.

And then— a shove.

A particularly bitter cop, his face still red from the riot, shoulder-checked Chase as he passed, knocking him slightly off balance. "You kind of don't belong here," the officer sneered.

The words dug under Chase's skin like rusted nails. He reacted instinctively, his body moving before his mind could catch up. His hand snapped forward, grabbing the man by the collar, slamming him against a row of filing cabinets.

Heat flared instantly—his sigils pulsed, and the air around his fingers shimmered from the building energy. The officer's sneer vanished in an instant, replaced with wide-eyed panic.

"Let go of me, you goddamn —!" The words choked off as the temperature between them rose.

The spellbound energy etched into Chase's skin reacted like a furnace ready to ignite. The scent of burning wool filled the air where his fingers gripped the uniform.

Before things could escalate, a firm hand clamped down on Chase's shoulder.

"Enough!" O'Leary barked, stepping between them. His voice carried the weight of authority, but not without irritation. He shoved Chase back, then turned to the officer still gasping for breath.

"And you—cut the crap." The officer straightened his collar, his lip curled in anger and humiliation.

"He should be fired!" he spat. "He's a liability. A damn arcanist freak!"

The murmurs in the room grew. Some of the other officers nodded in quiet agreement, their faces dark with resentment. Someone muttered something low, barely audible.

A slur.

Chase didn't need to hear it. He felt it.

The tension in the entire room thickened, a powder keg waiting for a spark. O'Leary's face darkened. His eyes flicked toward the gathered officers, scanning their faces. He knew exactly what was happening—and he wasn't about to let it explode.

"I said that's enough!" he snapped. His tone left no room for argument. Then, turning back to Chase, his voice dropped slightly, firm but quieter, meant only for him. "Go home, Cassidy. Cool off."

Chase clenched his jaw, exhaling sharply through his nose. He was used to this and had lived in this tension since the moment he joined the force. It wasn't the first time he'd been reminded he was an outsider—it sure as hell wouldn't be the last.

His fists loosened. With one last look around the room, he turned on his heel and walked away.

Chase moved into the segregated changing area—the section meant for "special cases" like him. It was smaller, tucked away in the back, separated by a heavy metal divider. It was a reminder that he wasn't entirely welcome even here, among fellow officers.

He stripped off his uniform, stretching his sore shoulders, the familiar ache settling deep in his bones. His coat, battered and bloodstained, landed with a dull thud on the bench.

As he unbuttoned his shirt, he peeled it away from his skin, revealing the intricate arcane sigils and wards carved into his chest, arms, and back—the unmistakable hallmarks of a Spellbound soldier.

He had received them in the Great War, a desperate experiment to turn men into something more than flesh and blood—something that could survive the horrors no mortal should have faced.

The ink, etched deep into his skin by military spellwrights, shimmered faintly in the dim light, the magic within still humming, barely restrained.

Wards for protection, sigils for destruction, magical inscriptions designed to make him faster, stronger, harder to kill. They had saved his life more times than he could count. They had also marked him forever.

A group of white officers entered from the main room, their conversation cutting off as they spotted him. They paused. Their expressions shifted—from disdain to something darker.

"Look at that," one muttered, tilting his chin toward Chase. "Freak's got spells carved into him. You even human, Cassidy?"

Another sneered, nudging the man beside him.

"Bet those damn sigils keep him from feeling real pain." He cracked his knuckles.

"We should test that theory."

Chase didn't move immediately. He exhaled slowly, controlled. Then, he turned to face them. His grey eyes locked onto them, steady, cold, daring them.

The tension thickened in the room. The overhead bulbs buzzed faintly. The weight of violence sat on the edge of the moment, waiting for someone—anyone—to make the first move.

Then Chase smirked.

Slow.

Cold.

Amused.

He rolled his shoulders, his sigils flaring faintly with heat. The faint glow crawled across his skin like embers waiting to ignite.

"You're all welcome to try," he said casually, his voice edged with steel. "But your families won't recognize you if you do."

The challenge hung in the air.

No one moved. The moment stretched—and then snapped. The officer who had spoken first shifted uneasily, looking away.

Another muttered something under his breath, turning back toward his locker. Not one of them took the challenge. Chase huffed out a quiet laugh and turned back to his locker. That was what he thought.

He finished dressing without another word. Men like Chase Cassidy were walking a thin line. And tonight, it was only getting thinner.

———

Chase stepped off the train at 125th Street, the scent of roasted peanuts, grilled meats, and city grime filling his lungs. Harlem was alive, a world of its own—vibrant, loud, and defiant.

Magical vendors lined the sidewalks, selling charms, tinctures, and minor hexes to eager customers. A boy no older than ten floated playing cards between his fingers, his arcane talent drawing a small crowd. Further down, a woman whispered incantations over a pot of bubbling stew, the aroma shifting as she spoke, offering tastes of different memories with each bite.

On the stoop across the street, a mother swept her steps with a broom that moved of its own accord, weaving around her feet like it had its own will. In one hand, she cradled her baby, and with the other, she adjusted the warded pacifier charm clipped to the child's blanket. The faint shimmer of magic hummed in the air around her—barely enough to light a lantern, but steady, practiced, calm.

Common magic, Chase thought. The natural innate kind that marked one as being of the bloodlines. It flows through some like breath through lungs—just a part of living.

Most folks never got past this level. They could levitate fruit, warm tea with a glance, maybe light a candle on a good day. Little things. Useful, gentle things.

But every now and then, someone was *born different*. Born with the spark turned wildfire. They didn't need years of training—they taught themselves through sheer force of will, instinct, and usually a few painful mistakes. Those were the *sorcerers*. Untrained, raw, dangerous when cornered—but most just wanted to live. To be left alone.

Those with focus, discipline, or a little luck might earn a place at one of the arcane universities or specialized schools. There, they could learn to become mages, wielding spells with foci like wands, rings, or staffs. Others chose the path of the spellwright, the artificers who inscribed power into metal and glass—who made magic tools, not just magic acts.

But above them all were the wizards.

Only a handful of those in a generation ever passed the Trials. Three of them. Each one as deadly as it was secret. Those who survived didn't just learn magic—they *became* it. And the world bent around them accordingly.

Chase took the cigarette from behind his ear and lit it with a flick of a fingers. The flame hissed a little brighter than it should've, a rich amber.

Across the street, the boy tried to float the cards again. This time, they scattered flying everywhere. The kid looked around, frowning. The coins suddenly stopped flowing into his cup.

Chase smiled, just faintly.
"Sucks to be you, kid."

He passed a corner where Diego Salazar, an old friend and hustler, stood with a small group. Born in San Juan and raised on the same streets that birthed Chase, Diego was also of arcane blood. With curly hair and a few days' growth of stubble covering his face, the man looked very much what he was...a rogue.

Diego's dice clattered against the pavement, his grin widening as a man cursed under his breath, clearly on the losing end of the bet. Diego smirked. He rolled the dice once more, watching them tumble across the pavement before settling—another perfect roll.

The man across from him swore under his breath as Diego raked in the last of the coins and bills scattered between them.

"Damn cheat!" the man snarled, his fists clenching at his sides. He took a step forward, his face dark with anger. "Ain't no way you won fair."

Diego barely looked up as he pocketed the cash. "Luck favors the bold, amigo. If you don't like the odds, maybe dice ain't your game."

The man lunged, but Chase flicked open his coat just enough to flash his badge before he could get close.

"You really wanna make another bad decision tonight?" he asked, voice calm but firm.

The man froze, glancing from Chase to Diego before backing down with a muttered curse. "Ain't worth it."

Diego grinned, slapping Chase on the back. "Always knew you'd make yourself useful someday."

Chase smirked. "Diego Salazar, you are under arrest for fraud, street gambling and being so damn ugly you should be rotting in a cell."

Diego raised his hands in mock surrender. "Ah, Chase, my old friend. You and I know I'm too handsome to be near a police cell."

The two men shared a laugh before Chase patted him on the shoulder. "Come on, before he comes back with friends. The Midnight Martini's calling."

"Now you're speaking my language."

Diego Salazar was always the risk-taker, the gambler, the man who never let the rules get in his way. He and Chase had grown up together at St. Emilani's Orphanage, two boys with more street smarts than sense.

They had run cons on the local shopkeepers, stolen apples from market stalls, and dreamed of escaping the iron grip of the city's streets. That dream had taken them across the ocean, into the French Foreign Legion, where they learned how to fight, survive, and trust no one but each other.

They had run cons on corner shopkeepers, stolen apples from market stalls, and dreamed—always dreamed—of escaping the iron grip of the city streets. And war, in its twisted generosity, granted that wish. But war has a way of splitting even the closest of friends.

For Chase, a mortar blast sent him into a field infirmary, and from there into the hands of the Americans. Project Infernus remade him— inscribed sigils into his flesh, laced spellbinding runic circuitry across his body. He emerged from the ordeal forever changed. When he joined the Harlem Hellfighters, he was no longer just a soldier but a weapon whose veins thrummed with infernal power he neither sought nor fully understood.

Diego stayed in the Legion, grinding through the brutal years that followed. Mud, steel, blood, and luck became his instructors. His arcane training was trial by fire—learning spellcraft in trenches choked with smoke, in ruined towns lit by artillery flash, in moments when survival itself became the only lesson worth mastering.

Same war. Two different kinds of magic. But the real magic - was the bond that carried them from the alleyways of home to the killing fields of Europe and back to streets of Madhattan.

Diego's dice were never just trinkets from a street game. Somewhere between the Legion's desert marches and the trenches of the Marne, he learned to use them as an arcane focal point—anchors that let him shape the Aether the way the cold shaped breath. Through them he channeled two very different kinds of power: the standard spellcraft he'd clawed together under fire, and the strange, slippery magic that answered only to chance. His own blend of probability. His own way of seizing the odds and bending them until they screamed. In Diego's hands, the dice were a conduit, a weapon, and a promise that fate itself could be stacked—if you were bold enough to roll.

For chase it was still cheating.

Diego was a head shorter than himself, built wiry but quick. His tan skin and wavy black hair marked his Puerto Rican heritage, but it was the ever-present smirk and the glint in his dark eyes that truly defined him.

He dressed sharp, always with a touch of flair—tonight, it was a dark blue pinstriped vest over a crisp white shirt, sleeves rolled up just enough to show the tattoos winding around his forearms—old symbols of protection mixed with dice and playing cards—a gambler's faith in ink.

The Midnight Martini was a speakeasy hidden behind the façade of a tailor's shop, its entrance marked only by a discreet brass plaque. Inside, the air was thick with the scent of whiskey, cigar smoke, and the faint trace of magic that mingled with the dim lighting.

The low murmur of conversations, the clink of glasses, and the sultry tones of a jazz singer filled the intimate space. The place was a haven for those who didn't fit neatly into the world outside—bootleggers, hustlers, arcanists, and those who walked the line between.

Chase and Diego settled into a booth near the back, a bottle of rum between them. They poured their drinks, the ice clinking softly in the glasses as they leaned back against the worn leather seats.

"To old times," Diego said, lifting his glass.

Chase smirked but didn't hesitate to clink his glass against Diego's. "To making it out alive."

They drank, the burn of the liquor a familiar comfort. For a while, they talked about safer things—the old days at St. Emilani's, the legion, the war. Diego spoke with his usual bravado, embellishing stories Chase had already lived through, making himself the hero of every tale. Chase let him have his fun.

But then, Diego's smirk turned sly. "So," he said, swirling his drink. "Have you seen Isabelle lately?"

Chase's smirk vanished. He set his glass down with a little too much force. "That's none of your business, Diego."

Diego chuckled, raising his hands in mock innocence. "Relax, hermano. I know that you took her walking out pretty hard."

Chase exhaled sharply, shaking his head.

Isabelle.

The name lingered in his mind like the echo of a song he couldn't forget. He could still remember the scent of her—jasmine and spice, with something darker underneath, like the last embers of a dying fire.

The way her fingers traced along his jaw, calloused from years of tending wounds, yet soft when she touched him. He could still hear her voice, smooth and sultry when she whispered his name, sharp as a knife when her temper flared.

She had always been fire—wild, untamed, and warm enough to make a man think he could survive the cold just by standing close. And yet, she had left.

Walked away without looking back, just like the last note of a song fading into silence. Chase shook himself from the memory, realizing Diego was watching him with that damn knowing smirk.

He scowled. "You gonna talk or drink?"

Diego laughed but let it drop.

They drank in silence for a moment, listening to the jazz band play a slow, smoky tune. The world outside the speakeasy felt far away—until the radio crackled to life behind the bar.

"*—and in other news, another act of violence in the Manhattan Restriction Zone as a child of Fey blood was found murdered along the docks. This raises the question: How long must decent, non-magical Americans endure this rampant crime? When will the city take action? Are we allowing these magical elements too much freedom?*"

The lazy warmth of the moment shattered, and Chase felt his jaw tighten—another one. The world had no room for peace, not even in a place like this. He reached for his glass, but the taste of whiskey had lost its charm.

Across from him, Diego sighed, setting his drink down. The two men exchanged a look, one of understanding, frustration, and the quiet, simmering anger of men who had heard it all before.

Diego shook his head, reaching for the bottle. "Another round?"

Chase nodded. "Yeah. And make it a strong one."

———

As Chase and Diego stepped out of Midnight Martini, the cold night air greeted them like a slap. Diego adjusted his coat, rolling his shoulders.

"Hell of a night, hermano."

Before Chase could respond, a voice cut through the street.

"Ain't done yet."

The man Diego had hustled earlier had returned with two friends. Their expressions were tight with anger, their fists clenched.

"Told you he'd bring backup," Chase muttered. Diego sighed. "Man can't take a loss."

The first thug lunged at Diego, but a flick of his wrist sent three enchanted dice, the Bones of Fate tumbling through the air, a shimmer of arcane energy rolling with them. Fortune Favors was the roll; the larger runic die landed on a palm icon while the two smaller traditional pip dice landed on a 6.

A standard effect roll that caused the thug to stagger, his footing suddenly unsteady as his own momentum turned against him, sending him face-first into the pavement.

Another thug swung at Chase. He dodged, driving a fist into the man's gut before sending him sprawling with a sharp elbow to the jaw. Diego sidestepped the last attacker, grinning as he delivered a quick kick to the back of the man's knee, driving him to the ground.

"Not much of a fight," Diego quipped.

One of the downed men snarled, pulling a Colt 1911 from his coat. Chase reacted instantly, grabbing the barrel with his bare hand. The sigils on his skin flared, heat surging through the metal. The thug screamed as the gun glowed red-hot, forcing him to drop it.

He turned and bolted into the night, his friends scrambling after him. Chase picked up the discarded Colt as it cooled, tucking it into his coat. Diego let out a short laugh.

"Never gets old watching you do that."

He turned to the fleeing men. "Come back anytime, putos! We'll be here!"

Chase smirked, shaking Diego's hand.

"Try not to get yourself killed, Salazar."

Diego grinned. "No promises."

With that, they went their separate ways into the night.

———

The biting evening wind howled through the narrow streets, rattling loose shutters and gnawing at exposed skin like a hungry beast. Bobby Franks sat hunched against the damp brick wall of an old bakery, the smell of yeast and smoke clinging to him like memory. His tattered overcoat offered little protection from the cold, and a thin frost gathered in his beard as he tilted his face toward the passing crowd.

His eyes—clouded, milky, and forever turned inward—saw nothing. But he heard everything.

Boots clicking on cobblestone. The flutter of newspapers in a gutter. The bark of a vendor hawking roasted chestnuts. The rhythm of the city was his sight now, and he read it like scripture. A tin cup rested between his gloved fingers, shaking slightly with each breath.

"Spare a coin for the blind?" he rasped, voice worn thin by age and too many winters.

"God bless you, kind souls."

Most ignored him. Some muttered that he should "get a job" — as if blindness were a choice. A few tossed coins without looking.

He had once worked, back before the world went dark. Back before the chain gang. Back before the false accusation that had stolen ten years of his life and both his eyes.

Bobby could still smell the iron of the fields, hear the overseer's whip crack, remember the sound of his own bones breaking under the guards 'batons.

They'd said he stole from the mill.

He'd said he hadn't.

The truth hadn't mattered.

When they finally let him go, he came north chasing the promise of a fairer world and found only more hunger. The bakery took him in, let him sweep floors until his back gave out. When he couldn't even do that anymore, the owner let him sit outside the shop with his cup.

Still, Bobby never complained. This block had become his world. The kids were his choir, the street his congregation.

And then—like bells through fog—came laughter.

He straightened, the years melting from his shoulders. "That you, Miss Grace?" he called out, a smile tugging at his cracked lips.

Two familiar voices answered, lilting and young.

"Evenin', Mr. Bobby!" Grace Parker and her friend Alison—their joy bright enough to light an alley. They were carrying a small basket, running some errand for their mamas, voices full of the music only children and fools dared still make in Red Row.

"Come now, let an old man earn his supper," Bobby said, tapping the cobblestones with his cane. The rhythm echoed soft and quick, a makeshift shuffle-tap he'd once learned on a prison yard to pass the time. He tapped a beat, and the girls giggled.

Grace clapped along, imitating him, her boots scuffing in time.

"Look, Alison, I'm dancin 'like Mr. Bobby!"

He laughed—a deep, raspy sound that warmed the frozen air. "You're gettin 'good at it too. Keep at it, and you'll be playin 'the Apollo by spring."

Alison giggled. "Mama says you could've been famous."

"Nah," he said, tapping again for rhythm, "I just make the street feel less lonely."

Grace reached into her coat pocket and dropped a coin into his cup. "Here ya go, Mr. Bobby."

He bowed his head. "Then may your kindness come back double, young miss. World needs more hearts like yours."

The girls tittered and started off, their laughter fading up the street —bright, innocent notes swallowed by the city's dark hum.

Bobby leaned back, humming a low blues line under his breath, the tap of his cane joining in rhythm. Then the wind shifted.

Something wrong crept into the soundscape—a stutter, a hush, a tension in the footsteps he could no longer see.

A sharp cry split the air.

"Let her go!" Alison's voice, high and terrified, from the alley just beyond the bakery.

Bobby froze, the smile dying on his lips.

The cup slipped from his trembling hand and clattered to the stones.

"Grace?" he called out, turning his head toward the sound. "What's happening there? Someone speak to me!"

No reply—just the city's heartbeat, muffled and distant.

He pushed himself up against the wall, reaching out blindly, one hand scraping the brick.

"Is someone in need? Please, talk to me!" he shouted, stumbling forward, cane sweeping the ground.

Silence.

Then—the sound of whistling.

A tune he hadn't heard in years.

Low. Taunting.

In the Hall of the Mountain King.

Bobby's blood turned to ice. He knew that melody.

The prisoners had used to hum it when the guards dragged a man off for a beating. The notes slithered through the dark like snakes, curling around him, drawing closer.

"Who's there?" he demanded. "What have you done?"

A muffled scream cut through the night—Grace's voice—and then nothing.

The whistling stopped.

Something brushed past him—cold air and the smell of leather and grave soil.

A whisper coiled into his ear.

"Nothing you can do, old man."

Then it was gone. The presence, the sound, the smell—all gone, leaving only the echo of that cursed tune fading into the wind.

Bobby sank back against the wall, shaking. His fingers fumbled for the fallen cup, clutching it like a talisman. Tears welled in sightless eyes that could no longer witness the world's cruelty but could still feel it pressing close.

Somewhere in the dark, a child had been taken.

And Bobby Franks could do nothing but listen to the city move on—indifferent, relentless, alive. He lifted his blind eyes toward the frozen sky.

"Lord," he whispered, "don't let her be another ghost."

The wind gave no answer.

CHAPTER 2

Murder, My Sweet

Senator Wilder's Broadcast on WBC Radio...

"Ladies and gentlemen of this great nation, I come to you today with a warning—no, a call to action. Arcanists are everywhere."

The papers won't say it outright. The so-called 'respectable 'news outlets dance around the truth. But I won't. The danger is here. It walks among us, hiding in plain sight.

"These... creatures have infiltrated our streets, our businesses, our homes. They practice their dark arts in secret, whispering incantations while decent folk sleep. They corrupt our children, twisting young minds to accept their unnatural ways. And what does our government do?"

A pause, the sound of papers rustling, a deliberate intake of breath.

"They hesitate."

"They wring their hands and speak of fairness, of rights, as if these monsters deserve the same privileges as hard-working Americans! As if they aren't the very reason our world is teetering on the edge of ruin!"

"The so-called 'Restriction zones 'are a step in the right direction, but they do not go far enough. We cannot coexist with a people whose very existence defies natural law! How many more good men and women must suffer before we act? How many children must go missing before we open our eyes?"

A slight distortion in the signal. A cough, the scrape of a chair shifting.

"I have introduced new legislation—The Arcane Containment Act. If passed, it will ensure stricter regulations, tighter restrictions, and harsher penalties for any Arcanist found outside of designated Restriction areas. No more loopholes. No more leniency. The time for mercy is long past."

"We will root them out. We will expose them. And we will reclaim our nation before it's too late."

The radio hums, a brief silence before the next segment begins—some lively jazz number, completely at odds with the vitriol that just spewed through the airwaves.

The morning came slow and unforgiving, the pale sunlight barely piercing through the smog hanging over Madhatten. It was always like this —the city waking up sluggish, like a boxer on the wrong side of a twelve-round beating. Chase Cassidy sat on the edge of his small bed, the weight of the previous night's events settling into his bones like an old wound.

His spacious railroad-style apartment in Harlem was spartanly furnished—barely more than a bed, a dresser, a rickety table, and a chair —but it was his. A small reprieve from the chaos beyond his door. A place where he could breathe, if only for a little while.

On the windowsill sat the one object that didn't quite belong with the austerity: a trumpet, brass dulled from years of use, the mouthpiece wrapped in worn cloth tape. Chase didn't play for anyone. He didn't even play well. But on nights when the job carved too deeply into him, when the silence in his head grew too sharp, he would lift the horn to his lips and breathe a little sorrow out into the dark. It wasn't music—not really.

But it was his.

He let his gaze drift across the room to the wall and the lone framed photograph hanging there.

Elijah Cassidy stood in the center of it, tall and unyielding, sharp eyes staring straight through the lens as if challenging the world to stare back. His mouth was set in that way Chase always remembered—tight, unsmiling, carved from stone. Elijah Cassidy had always looked angry at the world. He'd been a proud man, a dangerous man, and a brilliant man. Too damn brilliant. And he was the meanest bastard Chase had ever known.

Chase lingered on the image a moment longer, feeling that familiar mix of resentment and legacy coil somewhere behind his ribs.

Then he looked away.

His father's mind had been a labyrinth of spells and sigils, his hands crafting magic into steel like a sculptor working marble. Chase had spent years trying to outrun his shadow, but it still followed him. It always did.

His gaze drifted back, to the large revolver in his father's grip. Charon's Call. A work of arcane genius, a gun bound in arcane sigils, its bullets inscribed with hexes strong enough to pierce through anything that breathed—or didn't.

Chase had never held it, never even fired it. Elijah had kept it close, whispering to it like it was something more than a weapon, something alive. Chase let out a slow breath. What the hell ever happened to that gun? But beside Elijah, half-tucked beneath the edge of the frame, was the other photo.

The one Chase rarely looked at.

A woman — tall, elegant, striking in a way that made the old camera struggle to capture her. Her skin held warm gold undertones, her curls dark and wild around her face. High cheekbones suggested Mediterranean roots; her eyes, almond-shaped and storm-dark, hinted at something older, something Northern African or maybe not entirely human at all.

His mother.

Chase studied her for a moment, brow furrowing. There was a familiarity in her face he could never place — something in the eyes, the set of the jaw — but when he tried to dig for the memory, nothing came. Just fog. Funny, he thought. How he remembered every scar from the war, but almost nothing about her.

He rubbed a hand over his face, feeling the roughness of stubble and the faint heat of the sigils burned into his arms. They still pulsed from last night's fight outside the Midnight Martini. Diego had laughed, even as blood smeared his knuckles.

Chase could still feel the sting of his own fists against bone, the sharp crack of a jaw giving way under pressure. Another night, another fight. The work never stopped.

And what was the work, really? A paycheck? A duty? A slow way of drowning in someone else's problems? Chase exhaled, shaking the thought away.

He stood, rolling his shoulders before shrugging into his spare uniform, adjusting the badge at his belt. The weight of it felt heavier than usual today. The city outside called to him, like it always did. He could hear it—the street vendors hawking their enchanted wares, the soft hum of spells being whispered under breath, the steady rhythm of life fighting to survive in a place meant to kill it.

A girl barely ten levitated a marble between her fingers, her mother snapping at her to keep her magic hidden.

Down the block, a fruit vendor ran his hand over a batch of apples, their color deepening into something unnatural, turning them fresher than they had any right to be.

Magic was life here, even as the government sought to stamp it out. Harlem had a pulse unlike any other part of the Restriction Zone. It thrived under oppression, refused to be crushed. But beneath all that energy, beneath the music, the voices, the stubborn defiance, lurked something darker. Something that smelled like dispair.

Chase squared his shoulders and kept walking. The smell of fresh coffee, sizzling bacon, and buttered grits filled the air as Chase Cassidy stepped into Lucy's Diner.

The small, red-bricked establishment had been standing long before the Restriction Zone was even a thought, and despite the city's best efforts to grind it into the dirt, it endured.

A few heads turned when Chase entered, the soft jingle of the door chime momentarily pausing conversation. It wasn't fear or even hostility—just the natural wariness that came with wearing a uniform in Madhatten. He adjusted his shirt, nodding to the few familiar faces as he made his way to the counter.

"Morning, Lucy," he muttered as he slid onto one of the worn, red leather stools.

Lucy West, a tall, heavy-set woman with dark brown skin, gray-streaked hair, and a face like she'd seen everything and lived through worse, gave him a once-over. "You look like you been up all night."

"Something like that."

"You eating, or just here to make my place look ugly?"

Chase smirked. "Two eggs, sunny-side up. Bacon, extra crispy. And toast."

"Hash browns? You know it comes with hash browns."

Chase exhaled through his nose. "Yeah. Give me the damn hash browns."

Lucy grinned and walked off, slapping the order onto the grill as Chase took in the crowd.

The diner was full, as usual. The tables were a mix of humans and fey-blooded patrons, each of them trying to carve out some normalcy in a city that refused to let them forget what they were. A Rune-Forged Automaton sat motionless in the corner booth, its brass-plated fingers delicately tapping against the wood. Its face—sharp, thin, and fitted with three camera-lensed eyes—tilted toward the steaming cup of rune-grease set in front of it. Small lights flickered along its jawline, humming softly like the purr of a contented machine.

A newspaper lay open on the table beside it, the ink still wet from the morning press. One headline caught Chase's eye as he passed:

DISTURBANCE AT BLACKWELL ISLAND — AUTHORITIES CLAIM "MINOR ARCANE FAULT"

A grainy photo beneath it showed smoke curling over the asylum's seawall, ward-lamps flickering in the mist. Chase slowed a half-step, brow tightening. Blackwell Island didn't make the papers unless something had gone sideways. And arcane faults didn't cause explosions.

A man with pointed ears flipped through the morning paper by the window, steam curling from his untouched coffee. His wife's twitching brows marked Aziza blood; their son's golden eyes hinted at the Fae somewhere down the line. A few tables over, a Jengu mother murmured to her daughter, the girl's skin catching the light with a faint pearlescent shimmer.

Chase moved past them, nodding once before sliding into an empty seat.

Madhatten's mornings always looked like this—bloodlines and burdens eating breakfast side by side.

Near the counter, an Astomi perched on a stool, cradling a bouquet of flowers and sipping at the scent like it was a full meal. The little creature blinked as Chase passed, then returned to inhaling daffodils.

Chase saw more than a few patrons side-eyeing it, but no one said anything. Lucy slid his plate in front of him a few minutes later with a soft clatter. "Eat up, Cassidy. You're startin 'to look like one of them ghosts you keep chasin'."

Chase smirked, but it didn't quite reach his eyes. He picked up his fork, but his mind was elsewhere—back at the docks. Back to the lifeless body of the Fey child, crumpled like discarded waste. He ate in silence, finishing quickly before dropping a few bills on the counter.

"See you later, Lucy."

"You better," she called over her shoulder. "And try not to get shot before lunch."

Chase pushed open the door, stepping out into the already humid morning air. It was time to get back to the precinct. Time to figure out who left a child dead in the river.

Arriving at the precinct, Chase barely had time to step through the door before O'Leary intercepted him, his cigarette dangling from his lips. "Hold up, Cassidy. You got company."

Chase frowned. "Company?"

O'Leary smirked. "The mayor's office sent a man over. Not just them—the Governor General of New York is here too. And Weldon."

Chase exhaled slowly. "Hell of a lineup."

"Yeah, well, looks like you got their attention. Whitman's waiting for you in his office. Let's not keep them waiting."

Whitman's door swung open before Chase could knock. The captain stood there, his expression grim, and motioned him inside. Beside

Whitman's desk stood a man who seemed to draw the light toward him, all clean lines and cold authority—Governor General Malcolm Travers.

He was a shade taller than Chase Cassidy, though where Chase carried the weight of war in his shoulders, Travers bore the discipline of it. His frame was built from habit, not vanity: square-shouldered, broad through the chest, posture straight enough to shame a rifle barrel. The uniform he wore—dark navy wool trimmed in silver braid—looked as though it had been pressed with a straightedge and ironed by angels. Every crease belonged exactly where he'd ordered it to be.

His hair, once black, had turned the color of gunmetal, clipped with military precision. Skin pale as parchment stretched tight over the hard architecture of his face. But it was the eyes that froze a man—stark, piercing blue, the kind that looked through your words before you'd even spoken them. They didn't glint with cruelty or arrogance, only an intensity that came from carrying too much and setting it down nowhere.

Chase had seen that look before—the expression of a man who'd spent years standing between two impossible worlds, trying not to be crushed by either.

Travers nodded once in greeting, motion sharp, deliberate. "Officer Cassidy."

"Governor General." Chase returned the nod, resisting the instinct to straighten his overcoat. Those eyes made you want to stand at attention even when you weren't under his command.

Beside him, a younger man, clearly a bureaucrat from the mayor's office, looked out of place and uncomfortable. And at the far side of the room, arms crossed, stood Luis Weldon.

"Cassidy," Whitman said, motioning to a chair. "Sit. We got a situation."

Chase took the seat, his gaze flicking to Travers, then back to Whitman. "What's going on Captain?"

Whitman leaned forward, resting his forearms on the desk. His voice was low, weighted. "Another kid's gone missing. Fey-blood. Taken right off the street last night."

O'Leary stiffened, his jaw tightening. "That makes five this month."

Chase's eyes narrowed. "Five?" His tone was sharp, disbelieving. "When the hell did this start?"

Whitman and O'Leary exchanged a glance. The silence that followed made Chase's stomach turn. "No one's said a damn thing about missing kids," Chase pressed, his voice rising. "You're telling me five children have vanished, on top of the two that were found dead and nobody's been talking about it?"

Whitman exhaled through his nose, rubbing his temple. "It's been buried. Reports got lost, cases shuffled, misfiled—convenient mistakes." He met Chase's gaze. "But not anymore." "Which is why we're making this official,"

Travers cut in, his voice clipped, authoritative. "We want this solved, and we want it solved now."

Weldon nodded, his eyes never leaving Chase. "And I want an arcanist on the case. Someone who understands what's really going on here."

Whitman sighed and pulled out a small badge, sliding it across the desk toward Chase. "Effective immediately, Cassidy, you're being assigned as a temporary acting detective on this case. The Governor General wants results, and Weldon here isn't wrong. You know the Restriction Zone better than anyone, and you understand magic better than any of these other bastards."

Chase picked up the badge, turning it over in his palm. "So I do this, and then what?"

Travers folded his arms. "Then we'll see where you stand. You solve this, Cassidy, and you might just earn yourself a permanent spot."

Weldon smirked. "Or at least prove that the department needs more people like you."

Chase pocketed the badge. "Alright. Where do I start?"

Whitman leaned back. "Bobby Franks. He was the last to see Grace Parker before she vanished. Go talk to him."

Chase nodded and stood. "Then I've got work to do."

As he stepped out of the office, the weight of his new badge weighted heavy in his hand. The case had just gotten bigger, and now, the stakes were even higher. He headed to change.

Chase stood in front of the cracked mirror in his sectioned off changing area, peeling off his uniform piece by piece. He tossed the uniform jacket onto the chair, unbuttoning his shirt with slow, methodical movements.

Beneath the fabric, the sigils inked into his skin still pulsed faintly, a lingering reminder of last night's fight. With a sigh, he reached for clothes - a simple vest over a button-down, dark slacks, and a long coat to ward off the morning chill. Less official, less conspicuous.

He wasn't a beat cop anymore, wasn't just another cog in the city's rotting machine. He was an acting detective now. The title still felt strange in his head. It meant something different here, in Madhatten.

Outside the zone, a badge meant authority.

In the zone, it was just another reason to get shot in the back. Detective or not, nothing changed. The streets didn't care. The dead didn't care.

Sliding the badge into his pocket, he adjusted the holster beneath his coat, feeling the familiar weight of his revolver settle against his hip. Chase stepped out from behind the curtain, to see Governor General Malcolm Travers standing there, his gaze fixed on Chase.

"Cassidy," Travers said, his voice low but firm. "A word."

Chase glancing at the older man. Travers wasn't the type to make small talk. Chase tucked his hands into his coat pockets, his expression carefully neutral.

"Didn't think we were on speaking terms, Governor."

"I served in the war too, you know," Governor General Arthur Travers continued, his voice steady, but edged with something old— something bitter. His eyes scanned the precinct as they walked, taking in the officers who scrambled to look busy in his presence.

The weight of his title carried in the way men straightened as he passed, even if they weren't directly in his sights.

"Never much cared for your kind back then," he admitted, his gaze flickering toward Chase. "Still don't, if I'm being honest. But I've heard things about you from Whitman. What you did during the Red Mist Incident... that kind of thing sticks with a man."

Chase kept his steps even, his expression unreadable. He'd been on the force for two years now—long enough to know when someone was setting the stage for a proposition.

"My kind?" he echoed, keeping his voice measured.

Travers scoffed. "Hell, Cassidy, I couldn't care less about the color of your skin, you're spellbound, one of the magically enhanced. The ones they burned out or locked up after the war. The ones they still whisper about when they think no one's listening."

He clasped his hands behind his back as they turned down a quieter corridor. "The public thinks it's all over and done with. That magic in the military was a failed experiment, and that's why the Arcane Restraint Act was necessary. But the smart ones? The ones who've seen the battlefield?" He glanced at Chase. "We know better."

Chase said nothing. He'd seen what spellbinding did to soldiers. Hell, he'd lived it. He still felt the weight of the incantations burned into his skin, still heard the screams of men who hadn't been strong enough to handle the process. Project Infernus had turned men into weapons, but no one had ever thought about what happened after the war was won.

Some days, he felt like the only reason he'd survived was because they had wanted him to. And that thought was worse than dying.

Travers studied him with that same calculating gaze. "I hear you don't like using your abilities much. That right?"

Chase clenched his jaw. "They come with a cost."

Travers nodded, as if that answer didn't surprise him. "And yet, despite that, you've still used them. Your record on the force speaks for itself. The way I see it, there are only two types of men with power—the ones who abuse it for their own self-gratification, and the ones who use it to help those weaker than themselves."

He paused, letting the words settle before adding, "Whitman seems to think you're the latter."

Chase met his gaze, waiting for the part where Travers finally got to the point. And then, Travers stopped walking.

"I need someone who understands what's coming," he said, lowering his voice. "Someone who knows that what happened in the war isn't as dead as people think."

His eyes flicked to the faded edges of Chase's wards, the lingering hum of spellbound enhancements still visible beneath his skin.

"You were enhanced for war, Cassidy," Travers said. "And I feel a war is coming again."

Chase exhaled through his nose, his shoulders stiffening. He had no love for men like Travers—politicians who acted like the war had been a game they had played from the comfort of a leather chair. But the truth in his words was undeniable.

"I work for Whitman," Chase said carefully. "I already have a job."   Travers smirked. "And yet, you keep getting pulled into things bigger than petty criminals and smuggled booze."

Chase didn't argue.

"Things are changing, Cassidy. This city, this country—it's shifting under our feet. Some people, like me, we're trying to hold things together. Others, like Senator Wilder, want tighter restrictions, more oversight. They see magic as a threat that needs to be put down. And a lot of careers—mine included—are riding on what happens next."

Chase scoffed. "So what, you putting pressure on me?"

Travers shook his head. "I'm saying do your job, Cassidy. Find out who's behind this, solve it clean, and maybe you'll prove that people like you have a place in this city. But screw it up?"

He let the words hang for a moment before finishing, "Then Wilder gets exactly what he wants. More laws, more restrictions, more reasons to lock up anyone with magic, and that means anyone, including my daughter!"

There it was. The words hit harder than Chase wanted to admit. This wasn't just a case. It was a personal battleground.

Travers stepped back, adjusting his coat. "Think about it," he said, turning toward the exit. "Men like you don't get to retire quietly. You can either choose a side or wait until someone chooses it for you."

Without another word, the Governor General strode away, leaving Chase standing at the edge of the precinct, his new badge heavier than before. The case had just gotten bigger, and now, the stakes were even higher.

―――――

The morning chill bit through Chase's coat as he made his way toward the alley off Lexington and 124th, where Bobby Franks was known to set up.

The blind beggar had been a fixture in the neighborhood for years, always stationed in the same spot with his tin cup and his quiet observations. If anyone had "seen" what happened to Grace Parker, it was him.

Chase found Bobby where he always was, hunched against a brick wall, his tattered coat wrapped tightly around him. His milky white eyes were turned toward the street, as if he could still see the world passing him by.

"Mornin', Bobby," Chase said, stepping closer.

The old man's head tilted slightly. "That you, Cassidy? Heard you got a new badge. Guess congratulations are in order."

"Not sure if it's worth celebrating yet. Need to ask you about the girl. Grace Parker. Last person to...uh see her."

Bobby let out a dry chuckle, shaking his head. "I wish I could have seen her." He turned his fogged-over eyes toward Chase, the milky white orbs a haunting reminder of what he'd lost. "I didn't see anything."

He tapped the side of his head. "I heard it though."" Bobby exhaled, rubbing his gloved hands together. "I heard her voice. She and her friend were walking past, same as they always do. Dropped a coin in my cup. Then, not a minute later, I heard a scream. I turned toward the sound, but..." He shook his head. "All I got was the feelin 'of something bad. And the whistling."

Chase frowned. "Whistling?"

Bobby nodded. "A tune. I recognized it the second I heard it. 'In the Hall of the Mountain King. 'Always gave me the creeps, even when I could see."

Chase's stomach knotted. "You get any details? Anything useful?" The old man sighed. "Whoever it was moved fast. Brushed right past me. Cold as the grave, they were. And the way that girl screamed? That wasn't no simple kidnapping."

Chase crouched next to him. "Did you hear anything else? Smell anything? Magic leaves traces." Bobby hesitated. "Sulfur. Like something dragged up from below. And there was something... off about the air. Like it had been drained of life. I've felt that before, Cassidy, and it never means anything good."

Chase's jaw tightened. That confirmed what he already suspected—this wasn't just some desperate thug grabbing kids for ransom. Something darker was at play. Bobby's voice lowered. "You're walking into something deep, son. You best be ready for it."

Chase stood and adjusted his coat. "Noted," before dropping a few bills into Bobby's cup Chase walked off into wind.

———

Chase made his way back to the precinct, his mind already piecing together the pattern. Five children, all Fey-blood, all taken from the streets. If Grace Parker followed the same fate as the others, then her body would turn up soon—drained like the rest.

The precinct buzzed with the usual low-grade chaos: phones ringing, officers trading coffee for case files, typewriters clacking in rhythm like a tired orchestra. But as Chase stepped inside, a subtle hush moved with him. Not silence exactly—just a collective tightening of posture. A few uniforms glanced up, then back down, eyes sliding off him like oil on water.

No jeers. No words. Just that same quiet judgment that came with his badge—the one he hadn't earned through academy drills or precinct politics. The one they gave him because no one else could stomach the kind of cases he took.

Captain Whitman stood off to the side, arms crossed as two patrolmen wheeled a scratched-up desk down the hallway. "Got you a space," he muttered. "Don't ask for a nameplate."

The desk rattled on uneven wheels, turning a corner toward the back of the building—past the main bullpen, past the interview rooms, and finally into what used to be the officers 'changing room. The air still smelled faintly of sweat and stale soap. A single window, cracked at the corner, let in a sliver of gray light.

The patrolmen didn't say a word as they set the desk down. One of them, a thick-jawed man with a jaw that had probably broken more than once, gave Chase a look halfway between pity and contempt. Then they left without a nod.

Whitman followed him in, gaze hard but not unkind.

"This isn't charity," he said. "You saved my life in the Argonne, Cassidy. I remember who climbed that trench and dragged me back when the bombs blew sideways and the gas started eating bone."

Chase didn't say anything.

Whitman glanced at the cracked window, then back.

"The department didn't want you. Arcane, half-blood, wrong color. You scared them—and they hate being scared. But being spellbound? That made them think twice."

He leaned in a little, voice lowering. "Not always enough though. You'll have to remind them who the hell you are. Maybe more than once. Solving this won't be easy."

Chase looked at the desk. Then at Whitman.
"I'll do my best."

Whitman grunted, turning toward the door.

"You already have. Keep me informed." And with that, he left. Staring back at the room, Chase took it all in. The lockers were still bolted to one wall. A forgotten bar of soap sat in the corner of the sink like some sad relic. This was where they wanted him—out of the way, but not quite gone.

Footsteps approached. Heavy, deliberate.

Corporal O'Leary stepped through the doorway, balancing something under one arm. It was a brass desk lamp—an old one, scratched, the kind with a green glass shade. He set it down gently on Chase's desk and plugged it in. The soft glow spread across the paperwork like the first warmth in a long winter.

"I had a spare," O'Leary said. His voice was low, a little hoarse. "Figured you might want it."

Chase didn't answer right away. O'Leary met his eyes for a moment —really met them—and in that brief, silent moment, something passed between them. Not camaraderie. Not even trust. Just recognition. Of loss. Of duty. Of being a man built to carry things no one else wanted.

O'Leary gave a slow nod, then stepped back without another word.

Chase sat down. The chair creaked under him. For a few heartbeats, he just stared at the lamp's glow.

Then he pulled out the case files.

He spread them out over the desk, flipping through the grim details. Names. Ages. Locations. The bodies had all been found in abandoned buildings, tucked away like afterthoughts. Peter Calloway, age 9, found behind an old textile mill on 117th. Beatrice Rhodes, age 11, discovered in a collapsed tenement near the river. Daniel Tran, age 8, found in a drainage tunnel beneath the train yard.

Each one missing for days before they were dumped, their bodies eerily preserved—no decomposition, no blood, only empty, husk-like remains.

Chase's fingers tapped against the desk. The locations weren't random. Someone had a pattern.

He grabbed a precinct map from his bag, smoothing it out over the desk. One by one, he marked the sites. A slow realization settled in as he traced the points with his finger. They formed a rough circle around central Harlem, tightening like a noose with each abduction.

Whatever was doing this wasn't just hunting—it was closing in. And whatever lay at the center... it was waiting.

And now he had a desk. A map. And the lamp of a man who supported him, even if it was behind closed doors. It would be enough. For now.

Chase made his way to the Parker residence, a modest apartment tucked into the upper floors of an aging brownstone.

The door was answered by Helen Parker, Grace's mother, a woman whose grief had hollowed out her face. Dark circles shadowed her eyes, and her hands trembled as she clutched the doorframe.

"Mrs. Parker," Chase said gently, removing his hat. "I'm Detective Cassidy. I'd like to ask you a few questions about Grace."

She swallowed hard, nodding. "Come in."

The apartment was small but tidy, though the air felt heavy with sorrow. A framed picture of Grace sat on a nearby table, her bright smile

CHARLES DRAEVYN

frozen in time. Helen gestured toward the couch, sinking into the armchair across from him.

"You're looking for my daughter?" she asked, voice barely above a whisper.

"Yes, ma'am. Anything you can tell me—her routine, if she mentioned anything unusual, any people she might have feared or avoided?"

Helen wrung her hands. "She was a good girl. Smart. She loved books, always reading. She never had enemies, Detective, she was just a child." Her voice cracked.

"But... she did say something strange a few days ago. She said she felt like someone was watching her. That she kept hearing a tune."

Chase's pulse quickened. "A tune?"

Helen nodded, gripping the arms of the chair. "She hummed it to me once. It gave me chills. I told her it was nothing, that she was imagining it." Tears welled in her eyes.

"But she wasn't, was she?"

Chase sat back, jaw tight. "Mrs. Parker, do you know if Grace had any connection to the other children who went missing?"

Helen wiped her tears away. "She played with Peter Calloway sometimes. They'd run through the alleys behind the grocer. But the others? No." That was enough to confirm Chase's suspicions.

The victims weren't random. Before he could press further, the front door swung open with force, and James Parker, Grace's father, stepped in. A tall, slender man with the hardened look of a factory worker, he froze when he saw Chase sitting in his living room. His eyes narrowed, scanning Chase from head to toe before his expression twisted into something cold.

"Who the hell are you?" James demanded.

Helen quickly stood, her voice wavering. "James, this is Detective Cassidy. He's investigating Grace's disappearance."

James scoffed, stepping further into the room, his glare locked on Chase.

"Is that so? Funny, didn't see the police care much before. Now they send a damn rookie?"

Chase met his gaze evenly. "I was assigned to the case this morning."

James crossed his arms. "How long you been a detective?"

Chase hesitated, knowing where this was going. "This is my first case."

James barked out a bitter laugh, shaking his head. "Of course it is. My daughter goes missing, and they send a first-timer to make it look like they give a damn."

Helen reached for her husband's arm, but James pulled away, his voice growing sharper.

"You got any kids, Detective? Any family?"

Chase's jaw tightened.

"No."

"Then you don't understand," James snapped. "You don't know what it's like to feel this helpless. To know she's out there, alone, scared—if she's even still—" His voice caught, his face twisting with emotion before he turned sharply away, pacing toward the kitchen.

"This is a joke," he muttered. "They send a man who can barely hold a badge."

Helen's eyes shone with tears. "James, please—"

"I'm done talking," he said, his voice tight. "I got work to do."

As he disappeared down the hall, Helen hesitated a moment, then looked toward Chase, her voice soft and quivering.

"Alison... the Negro girl. Grace's friend. The one she used to play with after school. Was she taken too?"

Chase gave a solemn nod.
"So far, we believe so."

Helen brought a trembling hand to her lips. "Dear God."

Chase glanced at the hallway where James had vanished, then back to Helen. "It's tragic. Two girls missing. But only one name ever comes up." He adjusted his hat, voice low and steady. "Alison deserves to come home too."

Without another word, he stepped toward the door.

Helen's whisper followed him like a ghost.
"Grace called her her sister. Said they'd always be together."

Chase paused at the threshold, jaw clenched.
"Let's make sure that promise still has a chance."

He tipped his hat, then stepped out into the rain, the weight of silence heavier than the storm.

———

Julius Washington ran. His lungs burned, his legs ached, and the cobblestone streets of Madhatten blurred beneath him as he ducked between rusted fire escapes and crumbling brick alleys.

His breath came in short, sharp gasps, his heart hammering against his ribs. Behind him, they followed.

The Mourned.

Two of them, their long, emaciated forms moving in unnatural jerks, their faces twisted into hollow, hungry grins. The ragged remnants of old clothes clung to their frames—patches of military coats, tattered uniforms from wars long forgotten. Men who had died and risen again, but not as men.

Julius didn't know what they were, only that they never stopped. He leaped over an overturned trash bin, skidding into a narrow alleyway. A dead end. Panic.

The Mourned would be on him any moment. He steadied his mind. The arcane energy in his blood flared—green fey light coursed through him. His gift. His curse. His hands sparked with energy, and with a whispered incantation, he stepped between places.

The world lurched—for a split second, he was somewhere else. A place between this world and the next, where time bent, where air felt like thick, suffocating water. He had done it before, but never while running. He stumbled out of the fold, appearing on the rooftop above.

His stomach lurched, but he kept moving.

The Mourned shrieked from below, their long fingers scrabbling against the brick. Julius risked a glance back. Too slow, bastards. He grinned despite himself, the rush of survival flooding his limbs.

He was gonna make it. He was gonna—

A man in the red robe stepped from the shadows. Julius skidded to a halt so abruptly his boot scraped across the wet cobblestone. His lungs burned. His ribs ached with each ragged breath. But none of that pain compared to the cold that knifed through him the moment he saw the figure waiting at the end of the roof.

The stranger stood completely still, as if carved from darkness itself. Crimson robes draped over his frame, the fabric pooling like blood around his boots. Beneath the robe, Julius caught the faint outline of a red-and-black military-style uniform—precise lines, austere tailoring, and polished metal clasps that glinted even in the half-light. It was the kind of uniform that belonged on a parade ground… or a battlefield steeped in nightmares.

A hood concealed most of his face, shadows swallowing everything above the line of a sharp jaw. His hands—gloved in black leather stitched with threads Julius couldn't quite make out—hung at his sides with unnatural stillness.

But it was the feeling that struck Julius like a blow to the chest. A pressure in the air, wrong and heavy. Like a wound in the world. As if the very atmosphere recoiled from the man's presence.

Julius tried to take a step back, but the stranger tilted his head—just slightly—and something in that motion froze Julius in place. His heartbeat stuttered. His vision blurred at the edges. His legs refused to listen.Julius gasped as his body locked in place. His muscles seized, his breath caught in his throat. He tried to push against the spell, tried to bend space again—but nothing happened.

The magic held firm, stronger than his own. The Mourned climbed onto the rooftop behind him, their lips peeling back in something like hunger, something like joy.

"Please—" Julius rasped.

The red-robed figure said nothing. He only watched. The first Mourned struck first, its gaunt fingers ripping into Julius's shoulder. The boy screamed. Then the second joined in. They tore into him, claws and teeth sinking into flesh, rending it from bone.

Julius thrashed, his body convulsing, the sigil beneath him flickering as his own blood pooled across it.

And the man in red watched and whistled. A haunting tune...the Hall of the Mountain King. The last thing Julius saw before the world turned black was that deep hooded gaze, as cold and empty as the grave. And then, there was nothing.

———

The dump site was still cordoned off when Chase arrived. The stench of rot clung to the damp air, mixing with the briny stink of the nearby river. The alley was narrow, boxed in by looming brick buildings that cast long shadows even in the daylight.

Trash and debris littered the ground, but Chase's focus was on the dark stain where the last body had been found. A uniformed officer stood nearby, arms crossed, jaw tight. When Chase approached, the man barely acknowledged him.

"What do we got?" Chase asked, scanning the scene.

Silence.

Chase glanced up. "I asked you a question."

Still nothing. The officer's lip curled slightly, but he didn't speak. Chase inhaled sharply, stepping forward until there were only inches between them. "You deaf, or you just don't feel like answering to a detective?"

The officer's jaw twitched, but he remained silent. Chase held his gaze for a beat longer before shaking his head and muttering, "Figures." Ignoring him, Chase turned back to the alley. His eyes swept over the scene, looking for something—anything—that the initial investigation might have missed.

The ground was uneven, muddy in some spots, but a small object caught his eye near the bloodstain. He crouched, plucking it up between his gloved fingers.

A toothpick. Still damp, one end chewed down. More importantly, there was a red stain near the tip. Blood? Chase turned it over in his hand, narrowing his eyes. If it was blood, then whose? One of the missing kids wouldn't have been casually chewing on a toothpick.

As he stood, a soft voice reached him from behind. "You're really gonna find out who's doing this, aren't you?"

He turned to see a woman standing at the alley's mouth, her hands clasped in front of her. She was older, her face lined with exhaustion, her eyes heavy with something deeper than grief.

She wasn't crying, but there was an expectation in her gaze—a desperate kind of hope. Chase held up the toothpick, studying it. "I'm sure as hell gonna try."

Before Chase could leave the scene, another uniformed officer approached him, his face drawn and pale. "Cassidy, you're needed."

Chase turned. "Where?"

The officer hesitated, then exhaled sharply. "They found her. Grace Parker." Chase felt his stomach drop. The other children had taken days to turn up. Grace had only been missing for hours.

He made his way to the location of the murdered girl. The body lay on a stretcher, covered in a thin sheet, its small frame eerily still. The alley was silent, save for the occasional rustle of shifting fabric as the wind tugged at the edges of the cloth.

Chase crouched beside it, steeling himself before peeling back the sheet.
Grace Parker's face was frozen in a state of unsettling calm, but the telltale signs were there—her skin pale, her veins darkened and sunken, her body completely drained just like the others.

The eerie preservation of her corpse sent an unnatural chill through him. Something had stolen her life force, leaving behind only a hollow shell. Chase's eyes roamed over her small hands.

Mud beneath the fingernails. That wasn't uncommon, not for a kid who played outside. But her clothes were wet. He leaned down, bringing the fabric to his nose, and inhaled.

The distinct briny scent hit him instantly.
Sea water.

That didn't make sense. The Hudson was fresh water.

Chase straightened, his mind racing. That meant her body hadn't been drained here. It had been done somewhere near the East River.

A voice called from further down the alley.
"Detective Cassidy?"

Chase glanced up, jaw tightening.
I'm going to have to get used to that.

A uniformed officer motioned him over.
"We found the colored girl," the officer said, grim and hesitant.

Chase followed, his boots crunching over broken glass and damp grit, until they reached another stretcher—this one positioned in the shadows, a few yards away from where Grace had been discovered.

He knelt beside it and pulled back the sheet.

Allison. Grace's friend. Her dark eyes stared sightlessly into the gray sky, mouth partially open in a frozen gasp.

But something was different. Her veins weren't dark. Her skin hadn't lost its color. Chase touched her wrist. Cold... but not drained.

He shifted her collar and paused.

Bite marks.

Two small punctures, jagged and deep, just above the clavicle. Blood had clotted around them, thick and rust-colored. Unlike Grace, she hadn't been drained completely. She had been fed on—but only partially.

"No bloodline," Chase muttered, his thoughts darkening. "Whatever did this... it took what it wanted from Grace. But it left Allison behind."

He stood slowly, his eyes scanning the alley, then the skyline above. Now thats six. Each one marked. Each one deliberate. And the bastard was getting bolder.

The wind shifted again—cold, briny, wrong.

"You're not hiding," he murmured. "You're circling."

He took one last look at the broken girl beneath the sheet, then flicked the spent cigarette into the gutter.

"I don't know what you are yet," he said, voice low, steady.

"But I'm going to find you..." He stepped into the night, the shadows swallowing his silhouette. "...and I'm going to stop you."

———

The East River was quiet at this hour, save for the occasional creak of a docked boat swaying in the current. The mist rolling off the water carried the faint scent of salt and decay, a reminder of the filth the city dumped into its veins.

Chase walked the edge of the pier, his boots scuffing against damp wood, his senses sharp. The river was where Grace Parker had been drained. If he was going to find anything, it would be here.

As he moved through the dimly lit streets near the waterfront, he became aware of a presence behind him. The kind that sent a tingling sensation up his spine. Someone was following him.

Chase kept his pace even, his posture relaxed, but his hand drifted closer to the revolver at his hip. He slowed as he passed beneath a flickering streetlamp, glancing at the reflection in a nearby puddle.

A man, wearing a dark overcoat and a fedora, followed at a measured distance. Chase abruptly stopped and turned, his gray eyes locking onto the stranger. The man hesitated but then, as if nothing had happened, casually adjusted his hat and stepped into a side street, vanishing into the shadows.

A coincidence? Maybe. But Chase didn't believe in coincidences.

———

The morgue smelled of formaldehyde, damp stone, and grief. The cold air settled heavy in the room, making every breath feel thick, every movement slow. Grace Parker lay beneath a white sheet, her small form still, fragile.

Her parents, James and Helen Parker, stood beside the table, their eyes fixed on their daughter's lifeless body. James Parker was trembling, his hands balled into fists. His face was red, a mixture of sorrow and fury twisting his features into something sharp, something barely human.

Captain Whitman stood near the wall, arms crossed, his jaw tight. He'd been through enough of these to know how this would go. No one ever leaves a room like this the same.

Dr. Buzzard, the morgue's physician, stood at the foot of the table, his expression unreadable behind his small gold wrought wire-rimmed glasses. He adjusted his gloves, but he wasn't the focus of the room.

Chase Cassidy was. James Parker's eyes locked onto him like a bullet finding its mark. "This is what you call justice?" James spat, his voice trembling with rage. "My little girl—my baby—is dead, and you send me a goddamn negro detective to tell me you got it under control?!"

The room stilled. Chase stood silent, hands at his sides, his face unreadable. He'd heard worse, seen worse, but it never changed the weight of it.

"James," Helen Parker said softly, placing a trembling hand on her husband's arm. "Please, not now—"

James shook her off. "No! No, I won't—won't be told to shut up in my own damn city while my daughter gets dumped in the river like she was nothing!" His voice cracked, raw with grief. "And this copper is supposed to find who did it? This—this arcane darkie?"

Chase's jaw tightened. Captain Whitman shifted, stepping forward, but Helen spoke first.

"James, stop it," she said, her voice firm, her back straight. "Detective Cassidy is doing his job. And he's the only one willing to do it, considering the rest of your friends wouldn't lift a damn finger for our daughter."

James's breath hitched, his grief-swollen eyes darting toward his wife. "What the hell did you just say?"

Helen didn't flinch. "I said Chase Cassidy is the only one willing to get his hands dirty in this city. And I don't give a damn what color he is—if he's the one finding out what happened to Grace, then let him do his job."

James shook with anger. "You disloyal—"

He raised his hand.

The moment it moved, Chase caught it. The room flickered. Chase's grip tightened, his fingers locking around James Parker's wrist with the strength of something inhuman. The sigils on Chase's arms—normally dormant—flared with sudden, unnatural heat. Their glow bled through the fabric of his coat, pulsing like embers in the dark. James's breath hitched.

The world around Chase tilted. The morgue was gone. The air reeked of burning flesh, gunpowder, and blood. Screams echoed from the trenches, the sound of men being torn apart, their bodies reanimated before they could hit the ground. The Red Mist hung thick in the air.

"They're coming, Hellfighters!" He saw them. The undead. Hundreds of them. Hands clawing, jaws snapping, the hollow moans of the dead closing in.

"Cassidy." A hand on his shoulder. The war ripped away in an instant.

The morgue came back. The pale walls, the smell of formaldehyde, the cold steel table beneath the girl's body. Captain Whitman's hand was gripping Chase's shoulder, firm but steady. "Let go, Cassidy."

Chase blinked. His breath came in ragged pulls, heart hammering against his ribs like a war drum. His hand was still clamped around James Parker's wrist.

But something was wrong. James didn't yank away or curse. He just stared—frozen, pale as bone ash, his mouth trembling as if the words got lost on the way up. Then the smell hit. Like burnt hair and seared meat.

Chase let go.

James stumbled back with a gasp, clutching his wrist. Blisters already bubbled along his skin, the veins beneath swollen and blackened. The flesh had scorched beneath Chase's grip, sigils branded into his skin like angry welts before fading. The man dropped to one knee with a strangled groan.

"James!" Helene shrieked, rushing to his side.

Chase staggered back, his own hands shaking. The sigils beneath his skin glowed faintly still, pulsing like coals cooling in ash. He hadn't meant to hurt him—not like that. Not ever.

Helene hovered over her husband, torn between fear and fury, but when she looked at Chase, her eyes didn't carry the blame he expected. Just something sharper. Sadder.

"You're spellbound," she said softly. "I—I should've known. My brother... he came back from the war with those same marks. Same fire behind the eyes. Only lasted two months before it killed him."

Chase's throat tightened. He said nothing.

From the far side of the room, the rustling of linen and the sharp clack of shoes broke the silence.

Dr. Buzzard stepped forward, calm as a Sunday preacher. The mortician was always a strange presence— his eyes too knowing. "Let me see" he said, crouching beside James with a slow, almost reverent motion.

Helene looked up at him warily, but stepped aside.

James was panting now, his wrist a ruin of charred skin and open welts. The burn had gone deep—muscle, tendon, even bone in places. A third-degree brand, and it wasn't slowing down. Whatever energy Chase had channeled had left a mark more infernal than human.

Dr. Buzzard placed one skeletal hand just above the wound. "This'll hurt," he murmured—not to James, but to Helene. "But it'll work."

He closed his eyes, muttering something low and old in the First Tongue. A subtle glow pulsed from his palm—dull red, like banked embers. The skin around the burn twitched, then blackened further... before beginning to slough away.

James screamed. Not out of surprise, but from raw, primal agony.

The necromantic healing had begun.

The dead, charred skin curled and cracked, sloughing off like old bark. The flesh beneath boiled and bubbled, contorting as healthy tissue slowly grew inward from the edges. But it wasn't seamless. The process left rough, pink welts like melted wax, twisted and uneven. New skin knitted around the bone, but it was patchy, gnarled—like something grown in soil instead of flesh.

Chase stood frozen, jaw clenched.

"I stopped the bleeding. Purged the damaged flesh. But its not Fey healing," Dr. Buzzard said as the glow dimmed. "He'll have use of the hand, but it'll never look the same."

James collapsed into Helene's arms, sweat pouring from his face, body trembling from shock and pain.

She cradled him tightly, eyes locking once more with Chase. And this time, the sadness had turned to something else. Resolve.

"I know you didn't mean it," she said. "But people are gonna start asking what else you can do."

Chase nodded slowly, the amberlight in his veins dimming. "Let 'em."

Dr. Buzzard cleared his throat. "Well," he muttered. "That was a moment."

Whitman sighed, rubbing his temple. "Cassidy. Walk it off." Chase didn't argue. He turned, pushing past the swinging doors, letting the cold air outside bite at his skin. His hands were still shaking.

———

The Midnight Martini was buzzing with energy when Chase walked in, the rich scent of whiskey and cigar smoke clinging to the air. A jazz band played softly in the corner, filling the room with a lazy rhythm that drowned out the low murmur of conversation.

Diego Salazar was already there, seated at the bar, a drink in hand. His sharp eyes flicked across the room, scanning for an opportunity-or trouble, whichever came first.

As Chase approached, Diego smirked. "You look like hell, hermano." Chase grunted, ordering a whiskey before settling beside him. "Long day."

Diego swirled his glass. "Ain't they all?"

He nudged his chin toward a pair of young women seated at a nearby table. "That one's been eyeing me all night. Her friend doesn't look too bad either. What do you say? We go make their night?"

Chase exhaled, rubbing his temple. "Not in the mood." Diego gave him a sideways glance. "Must've been real bad if you're passing up a chance to charm the ladies." Chase didn't answer right away. Instead, he took a slow sip of whiskey, letting the burn settle deep in his chest before speaking.

"Had to meet with a family today."

Diego's smirk faded. "Shit." Chase nodded, setting his glass down with a little too much force. "Father's a bastard. Called me every name he could think of. Didn't bother me much." He paused, rolling the glass between his fingers.

"Then he raised a hand to his wife. I caught his wrist without thinking." Diego studied him, waiting. Chase flexed his hand, staring at the faint glow of his sigils beneath his skin. "I felt it. The heat. The power just… ready to burn. If I hadn't let go…" He trailed off, shaking his head.

Diego was quiet for a moment before saying, "But you did let go."

"That ain't the point," Chase muttered. He exhaled, rubbing his face. "Some days, it feels like the war never ended. Like I'm still out there, fighting ghosts."

Diego's expression darkened, his usual easygoing demeanor

slipping just a fraction. He swirled the last of his drink before downing it in one motion. "I try to forget," Diego finally said.

His voice was lighter than it should've been, but Chase could hear the weight underneath. Chase studied him. "Does it work?"

Diego tapped his empty glass on the bar, signaling for another. He didn't look at Chase when he answered. "Some nights."

The bartender poured another round, the ice clinking softly. The jazz band played on, a slow, mournful tune weaving through the smoky air. Chase nodded, staring into his drink.

"Yeah," he murmured. "Some nights."

Diego patted him on the back. "A distraction is in order, come," Chase snorted. "You make their night. I'll drink."

Before Diego could protest, the door swung open, and the man from earlier—the one who had followed Chase near the East River—walked in.

Chase tensed, watching as the man made his way toward them with deliberate steps. He was tall and lean, dressed in a well-pressed overcoat, a private investigator's badge tucked neatly into his breast pocket. He stopped just short of Chase and gave a small, professional nod.

"Detective Cassidy," he said smoothly. "Name's Tommy Dixon. I work for Anderson and Anderson. Mr. Thomas Anderson would like a word with you. Tomorrow. Noon."

Chase took a slow sip of his drink. "And if I say no?"

Dixon gave a dry smile. "Then I'd have to track you down again, and I doubt either of us wants that." He slipped a card onto the bar and turned to leave. "Midtown offices. Don't be late."

Chase watched him go, then sighed, rubbing his temples. Diego let out a low whistle. "Looks like someone's in demand, but when exactly did you get promoted to detective?" Chase pocketed the card and threw back the rest of his drink.

"This morning and I am an acting detective." He corrected.

Diego grinned and motioned toward the young women again. "That's great news! Come on. Just one drink, hermano. We gotta celebrate."

Chase exhaled, shaking his head as he stood. "Alright. One drink. Then I go home."

Diego laughed, slapping him on the back. "Now that's the spirit." As they made their way toward the table, Chase couldn't shake the feeling that things were moving too fast.

A private investigator following him, Anderson and Anderson getting involved, and bodies turning up everywhere. Something wasn't right. And he was running out of time to figure out what.

Diego led the way to the table where the two women sat, drinks in hand and eyes full of curiosity. The one who had been eyeing Diego all night was Lark Meadows, a striking woman with caramel skin, wavy dark hair, and eyes sharp enough to see through any man's lies. She was dressed in a red cocktail dress that clung to her frame, confidence radiating from every movement.

Her friend, Evelyn Nyx, was softer in demeanor but no less alluring —her golden-brown curls framed a face that carried just the right mix of mischief and charm. She wore a dark blue dress with a feathered trim, her smile playful as she regarded Chase.

Diego grinned as he slid into the seat beside Lark. "Ladies, allow me to introduce my good friend, Chase Cassidy. A man of mystery, danger, and —unfortunately—too much brooding." Rosa smirked. "That right?"

Chase chuckled, tipping his hat slightly as he sat next to Evelyn. "Don't believe everything he tells you. Diego's been known to stretch the truth."

Evelyn leaned in, resting her chin on her hand. "Oh? And what's the truth then, Mr. Cassidy?"

Chase swirled his whiskey, meeting her gaze with a smirk of his own. "That depends. You want the real story, or the one that sounds good over drinks?"

She laughed, the sound light and easy. "How about a bit of both?"

The conversation flowed smoothly from there, light flirtation mixed with laughter. Diego, ever the charmer, was already whispering in Rosa's ear, making her giggle as she playfully smacked his arm.

Chase, meanwhile, found himself pleasantly entertained by Evelyn's wit. She was sharp, perceptive, and clearly enjoying the game of words they played. As the night deepened and the drinks continued to flow, Chase finally set his empty glass down, stretching slightly. "Well, it's been a pleasure, ladies, but I should be heading out. Got an early morning ahead."

Evelyn tilted her head, her fingers tracing the rim of her glass. "Shame. I was just starting to enjoy your company."

Chase smirked. "That so?"

She nodded, leaning in slightly. "Maybe I don't want the night to end just yet. Maybe I'd like to see where a man like you calls home."

Chase studied her for a moment, then gave a slow, knowing nod. "Alright. Let's go." Diego winked at him as Chase stood, Evelyn taking his arm as they left the speakeasy.

The cold Harlem air hit them as they stepped outside, but neither seemed to notice. As they walked toward Chase's apartment, Evelyn's fingers lightly traced over the inside of his wrist, a touch that sent warmth through his skin.

They made it back to his place, stepping inside as he closed the door behind them. In the dim light, Evelyn turned to face him, her lips curling into a slow smile before pulling him into a kiss. The tension of the night, the chase, the hunt—all melted away in that moment.

Chase wasn't thinking about the case, the missing children, or the dangers lurking in the dark. For just a little while, he let himself get lost in something else.

———

The morning sunlight streamed through the blinds, painting golden lines across the tangled sheets. The faint scent of jasmine and whiskey lingered in the air, soft and bittersweet.

Evelyn stirred first, stretching with a satisfied sigh before rolling onto her side. She propped herself on one elbow, letting her fingers trace lazy patterns across Chase's bare shoulder. Her golden-brown curls framed a face that still carried the glow of laughter and exhaustion.

"I've never been bedded by a spellbound before," she murmured, voice still rough with sleep.

Chase's brows lifted. He turned his head slightly, the corner of his mouth tugging upward.

"How do you know I'm spellbound?"

Evelyn's smile deepened.

"Darling, it was all over the papers during the war. The army doesn't brand ordinary men with runes that shine under sunlight."

He huffed a quiet laugh, sitting up and rolling his sore shoulders. His undershirt lay forgotten at his feet, the carved sigils along his back catching the morning light. The markings shimmered faintly—ink and scar woven together like a map of everything he'd survived.

Evelyn's gaze followed the patterns. She reached out, fingertips grazing one of the raised wards.

"They hum," she whispered, almost in awe.

"That a problem?"

"Not at all."

Her fingers lingered over a complex spiral near his spine.

"What's it feel like?"

"Like carrying a storm under your skin," he said after a beat. "Some days it's quiet. Other days... it crackles."

"Mmm. I like storms."

Evelyn's fingertip drifted upward, following the curl of a spiral before settling over the largest sigil inked into his body—the one burned into the center of his chest. A circular pattern of interlocking lines, layered like armor plates and radiating outward in sharp, geometric branches.

"This one," she murmured. "What's it do?"

Chase's breath hitched—not from the touch, but from the question.

Of all of them, this was the one he spoke of least. He let his hand slide up behind his head, leaning back against the pillow. "That's the Great Seal," he said casually. "It keeps the others in line. Think of it like... a captain. Regulates everything, so I don't burn out or blow apart."

Her eyes widened slightly. "Sounds important."

"It is." More than she'd ever know.

Her fingers drifted lower, tracing the thick lines that branched from the Seal and wrapped around his ribs. Then her hand slid down to his forearm, where three circular sigils sat like coins pressed into his skin—raised, etched, humming faintly beneath her touch.

"And these?" she whispered, brushing one with her thumb. "The patterns match on both sides."

"Offensive runes," he said, giving her a half-smirk. "This one's for force projection. This is for heat release. And that's... well, that one's the messy one."

"What kind of messy?"

"The kind I try not to use in bed," he said with a grin.

She laughed, soft and throaty, and let her hand drift down—across his abdomen, lower. She paused there, playful, eyes glinting with mischief. "And the ones on your legs?" she asked, voice dipping.

He cleared his throat. "Glyphs. Enhancements. Make me faster., jump farther, react quicker. "

She nodded, though her gaze lingered longer than her hand did. Her delicate finger traced the runic lettering along his groin line. She smiled wickedly biting her lower lip teasingly "This one doesn't need any enhancement."

Chase shook his head as she shifted behind him, leaning in to ghost a kiss along the back of his neck. Her lips brushed a faintly glowing sigil etched just below his hairline. "And this one? Back here?"

Chase exhaled slowly. "Truesight."

"Meaning?"

"Lets me see what people don't want seen," he said quietly. "Illusions. Glamour. Hidden doors. Intentions."

She smirked against his skin. "Is that how you spotted me at the bar?"

"Exactly."

She hummed again, pleased with herself, and circled back around to face him. Her fingers danced lightly over his chest. "Show me one," she whispered. "The heat one. Or the force projection. Just a little."

Chase hesitated. A one-night stand wasn't supposed to get demonstrations. But she was looking at him like a girl watching fireworks at the county fair—bright-eyed, unafraid, hungry for something she didn't understand. He raised his hand, two fingers extended.

The rune on his forearm flared—subtle, controlled—and a small sphere of crackling light shot from his fingertips, rising like a spark from a struck match before dissolving harmlessly near the ceiling fan.

Evelyn's smile spread slow and wicked. "Well damn," she whispered. "You really are dangerous."

Chase only smirked. You have no idea, he thought. He leaned in, pulled her back to the sheets, and the moment dissolved into heat.

Her lips brushed his shoulder, light as breath. Chase closed his eyes for half a second, letting himself feel the warmth of her skin against his. The sheets were cool now, the night already slipping into memory. He knew this was supposed to be just that—a memory—but some foolish part of him held onto the way her laughter had filled the room, the way she'd looked at him as if he weren't made of scars and sigils.

She rose and crossed the room, the pale light tracing the curve of her back before she pulled her dress from the chair. He watched her dress, the quiet rustle of fabric a small reminder of how easily the world moved on without him.

"You can call me anytime, you know," she said, glancing back with that easy, dangerous smile.

"That so?"

"Yeah. That's so."

She closed the distance between them again, pressed a quick kiss to his lips, and whispered,

"Don't get yourself killed, Cassidy. You're too good-looking for that."

Chase chuckled low. "I'll do my best." Evelyn lingered a second longer, her fingers brushing the edge of his jaw before she pulled away. She was out the door before he could say anything else, leaving nothing but the scent of jasmine in her wake. He sat there a moment longer, rubbing the tension from his neck. He told himself it was a one-time thing. But as the sunlight crept across the empty side of the bed and the scent of her perfume refused to fade, he realized he was hoping it wouldn't be.

Chase exhaled, rubbing his face before pushing himself to his feet. His eyes drifted to the small table by the window, where the Colt 1911 he had taken from the goon a few nights prior rested beside his trusted revolver.

He picked it up, checking the magazine. Eight shots for the pistol.

Six for the revolver. He needed a new holster if he was to carry both properly. Dressed in a sharp, dark suit, Chase pocketed his badge and strapped on his sidearm. A new holster would be pricy as well as arcane ammo. He still had another week before payday. It would have to wait.

With one last look in the mirror, he grabbed his hat and stepped out into the city streets. It was time to see what Thomas Anderson wanted.

———

The offices of Anderson and Anderson sat in the heart of Midtown, an elegant building with dark wood paneling and polished brass fixtures. It smelled of aged paper, cigar smoke, and old money. Chase stepped inside, adjusting his collar as he scanned the front office.

Behind the reception desk, a woman sat with the faintest smile tugging at the corner of her lips, idly twirling a pen between her fingers. Her golden-brown skin glowed beneath the soft light slanting through the high windows, casting gentle halos across her cheekbones. Long lashes framed sharp, brown eyes that glinted with a knowing amusement. Her short, jet-black hair was parted to the side and styled in sleek finger waves —a classic bob that caught the sunlight at its edges, lending her an almost ethereal presence.

Chase stood frozen in the doorway longer than he meant to. It wasn't her face that held him—though it could've. It was her arm. Bared beneath the rolled-up sleeve of a loose blouse, the ink curled up from her wrist and along her forearm in bold, spiraling glyphs. Protective wards of a tribal design, if Chase was any judge.

The tattoo was alive, the shifting patterns undulating across her skin—spirals blooming into geometric angles before settling again in a dazzling, living mosaic. High-society women didn't wear tattoos, and if they did, they damn sure didn't wear them like this. Bold. Brazen. Breath-taking.

"Well," she murmured, resting the pen against her lower lip, "I expected someone older."

Chase cocked an eyebrow and slid his hat off, hanging it on the nearby rack. "Should I come back in twenty years?"

Her smile widened, eyes glinting with mischief. "No need. I'll break you in just fine."

Chase raised an eyebrow to that. Crossing the room, he leaned casually against the edge of her desk. "Detective Cassidy. I'm here to see

Thomas Anderson." He placed the card Tommy Dixon had slipped him the night before on the polished wood surface.

She didn't move. Her gaze drifted lazily over him, pausing just long enough on the faint scars across his face to make him feel it. "Skye Anderson-Pierce," she said, locking eyes with him. "Pleased to meet you, Detective."

Then—suddenly—she extended her hand. Chase took it. Her grip was firm, strong, despite her hand being smaller than his. There was a comforting heat to her touch, something that lingered longer than it should have.

Neither of them let go right away.

The door to the back office creaked open, cutting through the moment. Thomas Anderson entered, broad-shouldered as ever, graying at the temples, a cigar clamped between his teeth. His eyes were sharp, his presence still commanding. He gave Chase a quick once-over before stepping forward and extending a calloused hand.

"Cassidy," he greeted, southern drawl thick, his grip like stone. "Your reputation precedes you."

Chase returned the shake with a firm nod. "Hope it's not all bad."

Anderson chuckled. "No on the contrary I have heard nothing but good things about you. Skye did a thorough look into your background. She was very impressed and if she find you impressive, so do I." He gestured toward the back. "Come. We've got things to discuss."

Chase nodded at the revelation. The opinion of woman seated before him held a lot of weight and she seemed so comfortable using it . As he moved to follow, Anderson paused at the door, glancing over his shoulder at Skye.

"Behaving?"

Skye grinned. "I'm the picture of professionalism."

Anderson snorted. "Don't let her fool you. She bites."

Chase chuckled. "I think I can handle a few teeth."

Skye arched a brow, watching him with that same lingering gaze. "Brave of you to assume I'm the one you need to watch." Her words lingered in the air as Chase followed Anderson into the rear office, the weight of her stare following him long after the door closed behind them.

Thomas Anderson's office was the definition of old-money power —dark mahogany furniture, thick leather-bound law books stacked neatly on the shelves, and the faint lingering scent of cigar smoke and expensive bourbon. Behind his heavy desk, Anderson sat with the composure of a man who knew how the world worked and how to bend it in his favor.

Chase settled into the chair across from him, crossing one leg over the other. "You wanted to see me."

Anderson nodded, tapping the ash from his cigar into a crystal tray. "Straight to the point. Good. Let's talk about the missing kids."

Chase's expression didn't change. "Already on it."

Anderson leaned back, considering him. "I know. That's why I want to work with you."

Chase smirked. "That's so? And why would a high-powered law firm be interested in a back-alley case like this?"

Anderson didn't blink. "Because I represent people who don't trust the police to do the job right. The parents of Daniel Tran put me on retainer to find out who killed their boy. They don't want excuses—they want results."

Chase studied him. "And you think I can give them that?"

Anderson took a slow drag of his cigar. "I think you're the best shot we've got."

Chase exhaled, tilting his head. "And the part where I'm still working for the police? That doesn't bother you?"

Anderson smiled, a wolfish thing. "Plenty of coppers work both sides. It's a win-win. You follow the case through official channels, but you answer to me when needed. Get paid twice. No conflicts, just business."

Chase leaned forward, resting his elbows on his knees. "And if I say no?"

Anderson stubbed out his cigar, his voice even. "Then we both lose a valuable opportunity. And a lot more kids might end up dead." The silence stretched between them.

Chase could feel Skye's eyes on him from outside the room, watching, waiting. Finally, he sighed, adjusting his cuffs. "Alright, Anderson. I'm in."

Anderson grinned. "Smart man. Let's get to work."

Chase stepped out of Thomas Anderson's office, adjusting his cuffs as the door clicked shut behind him. The meeting had gone as expected—businesslike, calculated. Anderson wanted results, and he wanted them yesterday.

Waiting just outside, Skye Anderson leaned against her desk—only she wasn't behind it this time. She was on it—poised. One hip rested lightly against the edge, her weight balanced with the kind of ease only dancers and predators mastered. A stack of folders dangled in one hand, forgotten, her fingers draped loose, as if even paperwork knew to wait its turn.

She looked different. Chase could have sworn she wore a different shirt when he arrived. This one was a crisp white blouse that hugged her chest tightly, to tightly. Her sleeves were now down covering the tattoo he saw earlier. A charcoal vest cinched her waist in sharp feminine lines, but it was the trousers that truly defied the times—cut high, tailored close. Made to move. Made to provoke.

Skye didn't borrow power. She tailored it. Refit it. Wore it like skin.

Her heel tapped against the edge of the desk drawer in a slow, steady rhythm. Not nerves—never nerves. Just her way of measuring time. Of waiting. Of daring the moment to shift.

Chase stepped into the hall and faltered—just a second, but long enough.

He'd remembered her face. How could he not? Those sharp brown eyes, that smirk like a blade behind soft lips. But this—this wasn't the woman he'd just met outside her father's office. Then, it was her presence that had struck him.

Now, it was her body.

Not soft. Not dainty. Fit. Strong. Built like a dancer still in training —muscle fluid under golden-brown skin. But it was her hips and thighs that stopped him. The way those tailored slacks clung and shaped and sharpened every angle, every shift. It wasn't just confidence—it was command.

That familiar glint flickered in her eyes. She'd caught the look—and made no effort to hide that she had.

"Well, well, Cassidy," she said, voice dipped in honey and edged in flint. "Enjoying the view?"

"More or less," he muttered, adjusting his blazer as he crossed the room.

She held out a folder—his contract—her fingers brushing his as he took it. But before he could reply, the pen slipped from her hand and hit the floor with a quiet metallic clink.

"Oops," she said, with mock innocence.

Chase bent without thinking. And just as his hand reached the pen, she stepped in—slow, deliberate. One foot, then the other. The wool of her slacks brushed his cheek. Heat radiated through fine tailoring. His face was inches from the seam of tension and intention.

"Careful," she murmured. "We wouldn't want you to strain anything."

He rose slow, steady, pen in hand, his gaze catching hers with the same fire she'd kindled. Amused. Aroused. And absolutely aware of the game she was playing.

She smiled—sharp, unapologetic. The kind of smile that didn't beg permission.

"Your official retainer and an advance," she said, as if nothing had passed between them.

He flipped open the folder, brows arching. "That's generous."

"You're a private contractor now," she said smoothly, "and a proper one at that. Just understand that all reports, updates, and progress on this case—or any case going forward—come through me."

He tilted his head, mouth curving. "Not Mr. Anderson?"

She leaned in, just enough for her voice to drop to velvet over steel. "No, Cassidy. I'm your handler. Try to keep up."

Chase's gaze flicked down to the top page, noting an address printed in bold ink near the bottom.
"What's this?"

"A place of interest," she said vaguely, tucking the pen behind her ear. "Consider it a lead. Thought I'd make myself useful."

He studied her for a beat before nodding. "I'm guessing this also means you'll be keeping tabs on me."

"Naturally," she replied, tilting her head. "We need to check in at least once a week. More, if you're feeling sociable."

Chase smirked. "And if I don't?"

Skye leaned in slightly, lowering her voice just enough that the space between them suddenly felt smaller. "Then I'll hunt you down, Mr. Cassidy."

A flicker of something passed between them, unspoken but electric. Then, just as casually, she straightened, smoothing the front of her blouse like nothing had happened.

"Be careful out there, detective," she added, her tone playful yet carrying a thread of sincerity.

Chase tucked the papers under his arm, tipping his hat. "Are you always this charming?"

Skye flashed a knowing smile. "Only for you."

He turned toward the exit, but before he could take another step, she called after him.

"One moment."

Chase paused, glancing back over his shoulder. Her eyes lingered on him for a beat longer than necessary before she spoke. "Have we met before?" Chase frowned slightly, considering. "No. Don't think so."

Skye's lips curled at the corners, almost as if she didn't quite believe him. She twirled the pen between her fingers again.

"Of course. I'm sure you would have remembered me."

Chase chuckled under his breath but didn't argue. As he stepped through the doorway, he could feel her eyes still on him. Chase Cassidy wasn't sure what game she was playing.

But damn if she wasn't good at it.

CHAPTER 3

Detective Blues

Radio Broadcast from the Grim Truth for WBC Radio

"Folks, I ain't gonna sugarcoat it. We got ourselves a problem—a big problem—and it's walking our streets, taking our jobs, and corrupting our city from the inside out. It ain't just the Arcanists anymore. No, sir, we got another infestation."

"The so-called Restriction Zones? They were supposed to keep the magic filth locked away, but tell me—why am I still seeing Hexers and charm-peddlers running businesses in our neighborhoods? Why do I still see them lurking in alleyways, whispering spells, and selling their little trinkets to good, honest folk? The Arcane Act was meant to protect us, but it ain't doing the job."

"And it ain't just them—oh no, we got another problem creeping in. The Orientals. The Chinamen, setting up shop, bringing their so-called 'medicines,' their 'mysticism,' their foreign ways. We just fought a war to protect this country, and now we're letting them waltz right in?"

"How long before they start working with the naturally born arcanists? How long before this city ain't ours anymore?"

"You ask me, we need 'em gone. Both of 'em. The magic, the foreigners —hell, all the damn undesirables. We need them gone like yesterday."

"You listening, Senator Wilder? You listening, City Hall? The people are sick of it, and it's about damn time somebody did something."

"This is Walter Grimsby, giving you the Grim Truth no one else will."

The smell of formaldehyde and old incense clung to the air in Dr. Buzzard's mortuary, blending with the ever-present undertone of decay. Dim oil lamps flickered along the walls, their light casting long shadows over polished steel tables and wooden cabinets stacked with neatly labeled jars of preservation powders.

Dr. Buzzard himself sat hunched over a workbench, his gnarled, thin fingers carefully stitching up a body laid out in front of him. He barely looked up as Chase entered, but the air in the room shifted.

"Officer Cassidy." His voice was low, gravelly, aged like whiskey left too long in the barrel. "That temper of yours, cool down?"

Chase tipped his hat, stepping further inside. "It's Detective...active detective. And yes."

Buzzard finally glanced up, and the moment he did, his gaze latched onto Chase like a hook. He didn't speak right away—just studied him. Long. Hard. The silence stretched, and Chase felt the weight of it press against his skin.

"Excuse me, are you still here?" he finally asked, irritation creeping into his tone.

Dr. Buzzard didn't answer immediately. He just squinted, his yellowed eyes scanning Chase's face like he was seeing something deeper than skin and bone. Then, finally, he muttered, "You got your mother's eyes."

Chase went still.

Buzzard smirked, leaning back in his chair, his hands folding over his stomach. "She was a looker, your mama." He let out a wheezing chuckle, the sound rattling in his throat like old machinery in need of oil. "Had a way about her, that one. Made a man forget himself."   Chase's jaw tightened. "You knew her?"

Buzzard exhaled, like he was weighing how much to say. His eyes, dark and glinting with something too knowing, flicked to Chase's face. "Very well," he said before continuing, "But not like that. Her name was always whispered in the right—or wrong—circles. And your old man?"

Another chuckle, dry as dust. "Had that same damn look on his face you got now. Right before he blew my hand off with that arcane hand cannon of his."

Chase felt something tighten in his chest, but he pushed past it. His father had never talked much about his mother, not really. And now wasn't the time to pry.

Buzzard shifted, rolling back the sleeve of his coat. The glove on his right hand was old leather, stiff from years of use. He flexed his fingers, making the material creak, before hooking a clawed nail under the cuff. With a slow, deliberate pull, he peeled the glove away.

Chase's breath stilled. The hand beneath wasn't human. Not anymore. It was a fusion of cadaver and machine, flesh and metal intertwined in some grotesque mockery of life.

The skin—if it could even be called that—was mottled gray, sutured together from multiple sources, patches of decay fused with surgical precision. The fingers were long and skeletal, their joints reinforced with gleaming brass pistons and tiny, whirring gears. An automaton's precision, a corpse's grip. And at the center of the palm, a sigil burned faintly, pulsing like a dying ember. Fire-and-brimstone.

Chase had seen war-wrought magic, necrotech monstrosities, and things that clawed out of the Veil itself. But this? This was something else.

Buzzard flexed his fingers, the motion jerky but disturbingly fluid. A faint clicking sound accompanied each movement, like a clock counting down to something unseen. "Ugly, ain't it?" He grinned, gold-capped teeth flashing.

"Elijah Cassidy made sure I'd never forget him."

Chase forced his expression into something neutral. "That's why you're still breathing? Out of spite?"

Buzzard cackled, shaking his head. "Spite's a helluva fuel, boy. But nah. Some men find God. Me?" He lifted his grotesque hand, admiring the way the metal caught the dim light. "I found something better. A second chance. Ain't nothing in this world that can't be stitched back together if you got the right thread."

His dark eyes flicked to Chase's arms, where the faint glow of his own sigils pulsed beneath his skin. "Even men like you."

Chase didn't react. Didn't let himself react.

Buzzard reached for his whiskey and downed it in one slow, steady motion. Some wounds healed. Some didn't. And some—some just festered. He forced his voice to stay even. "Tell me about the kids."

Buzzard watched him for another moment before grunting, shifting in his chair.

"Bodies came in from the docks. Drained, hollowed out. Whatever did it took more than just blood. It took essence—Fey essence."

Chase frowned. "Necromancy?"

"Not just that," Buzzard said, shaking his head. "Something deeper. Older. I ran every test I could—tried to pull some kind of signature from the magic left behind."

He reached for a thick glass vial on his desk, lifting it so Chase could see. Inside, a thin wisp of something dark swirled sluggishly, like smoke trapped in water.

"This ain't normal necromantic residue. This is soul-rendering magic."

Chase's stomach turned. "The kind that binds."

"The kind that don't just take from the dead—it's tryin 'to build somethin 'new." Buzzard leaned back, letting the words hang in the air. Then, quietly:

"You have field experience, Cassidy. What's your call?"

Chase rubbed at the edge of his jaw, eyes narrowing on the vial.

"Definitely not a vampire. Fought one outside Verdun. Punctures from the Nosferatu breed are clean—two marks, even spacing, deep and straight through. These wounds?" He tapped the folder Skye had given him. "Multiple rows of teeth. More like something chewed its way in and drank as it tore."

Buzzard's brow rose. "Then we can rule out the sanguine families— Strigoi, Lamia, Dhamphir lines. None of 'em feed that sloppy."

"Could be a ghoul variant," Chase offered. "Or one of those corpse-feeders from the Catacombs—what did the French call 'em?"

"Les suceurs," Buzzard muttered. "Yeah, maybe. But ghouls don't drain essence. They eat flesh. And these shells still had skin left."

Chase exhaled through his nose. "So not a vampire. Not a ghoul. Not any of the usual blood-drainers. There's the Mourned, but there's not much known about them "

Buzzard nodded, grim. "The Mourned?. Possible. The Mourned craved sensation, longing for the remnants of life they had lost. Some sought it through pleasure, others through pain. Whatever it is, it's something that feeds on what's inside the inside." The mortician set the vial down, the black wisp twisting inside like smoke caught in a jar.

"You're walkin 'into bad business, Cassidy."

Chase scoffed, tucking his hands into his coat pockets.

"Well, it ain't the first time."

"Yeah, well," Buzzard rasped, pouring himself another finger of whiskey, "don't get yourself dead before you figure out what the hell this really is."

Chase stilled, but the old mortician just grinned. He didn't take the bait. Instead, he opened the folder Skye had given him and flipped through it. The address inside was scrawled in a precise, looping handwriting style.

Another lead. Another stop before this day was over.

He turned toward the door. "Appreciate the insight, Doc."

Buzzard chuckled darkly. "You don't appreciate nothin 'yet, Cassidy."

Chase didn't look back as he stepped out into the night. But damn if he didn't feel those old eyes still on him.

Back at the precinct Chase sat on the edge of his desk, one boot propped against the chair in front of him, rolling a cigarette between his fingers. The conversation with Dr. Buzzard gnawed at him like an old wound, something he hadn't expected to feel. "You have your mother's eyes."

He didn't remember his mother. Not really.

There were no warm recollections, no faded memories of lullabies or bedtime stories. No scent of perfume, no lingering impression of a soft touch. His earliest memories were of his father, Elijah Cassidy, always knee-deep in arcane projects, his hands stained with ink and gunpowder, his temper like a fire waiting for fuel.

But his mother? Nothing. A void.

Buzzard had called her a fire-and-brimstone looker. What the hell did that even mean? Chase exhaled slowly, lighting the cigarette and taking a drag. He had never given much thought to where he came from—what blood ran through his veins.

The war had stripped away those kinds of luxuries. He had been a soldier. Then a survivor. Then a cop. And now, he was whatever the hell this was—a man chasing ghosts, hunting monsters, and apparently carrying the eyes of a woman he had never known.

And then there was his father. "Had the same look right before he blew his hand off with that arcane hand cannon of his." Elijah had always been reckless, obsessed with his work. That much Chase knew. But there were gaps—things his old man had never talked about, things that had never added up.

Had his father's obsession with magic been about more than just power? Had it been about her?

Chase took another pull from his cigarette, watching the smoke curl toward the ceiling. He didn't have time for this. His mother was a ghost, and ghosts weren't going to help him solve this case.

Still… something about it lingered. Pushing the thought of the past away, he looked over the address Skye had given him. His mind suddenly drifted to the daughter of Thomas Anderson.

He'd only just met, but it was enough to leave a mark.

Skye Anderson-Pierce had that kind of presence—the kind that didn't just walk into a room, it *changed the air*. She read him like a lawyer reads a weak witness: sharp, deliberate, and just amused enough to let him know she wasn't impressed by the armor he wore. She flirted the way people lied under oath—carefully, convincingly, and with just enough truth to make it dangerous.

The pull was instant. Unwanted. Strong.

She wasn't just attractive—she was *alluring*. Confident, composed, and smart enough to keep things on the edge of professionalism. But there'd been something in her voice, in the curve of her mouth when she smirked—like she knew damn well the effect she had and wasn't afraid to let the leash out just enough to see if he'd follow.

Getting caught up in anything with a woman like that—especially one tied to his new employers—was asking for trouble. The kind that didn't come with second chances. But the feeling clung to him like smoke on his coat. Warm. Familiar. A little dangerous.

With a sigh, he crushed the cigarette into the ashtray, watching the ember die.

He grabbed his coat. Then the address she'd given him.

The Tran Family.

Time to lock it down.

There was work to do.

———

The offices of Anderson & Anderson had long since emptied for the evening. Filing cabinets stood like sentinels, the scent of lemon oil and old parchment thick in the air. Most of the legal clerks and junior partners had gone home, but the conference room still glowed warm beneath amber glass sconces. Jazz hummed from a worn phonograph in the corner— Bessie Smith low and velvet-smooth, more background than music.

Skye sat on the edge of the long conference table, legs crossed, sleeves rolled up on her white blouse, charcoal slacks creased from the day's work. Her expression was composed, but her fingers drummed in quiet rhythm. She wasn't here for a case review. Not exactly.

Across from her, Thomas Anderson stood near the window, silver at his temples and bourbon in hand, the light glinting off his vest buttons. Near the table, Donald Pierce moved with habitual care, reading glasses slipping down his nose as he set a case file onto the polished wood. His manner was gentler, more open, but there was steel under his soft tone— the kind that had seen war, law, and loss alike.

They were opposites in many ways, but forged from the same flame: the battlefields of San Juan Hill and El Caney, where they'd fought side by side during the Spanish-American War. One was a young Black artilleryman from Syracuse, New York, the other a white volunteer from Savannah, Georgia with a hidden knack for field medicine. The war had stripped them both bare—of country lines, of polite lies—and what was left had been honest. Real.

They hadn't gone home after the war. Not right away. They stayed in

Cuba for a few years, helping rebuild what the bullets hadn't claimed. And somewhere in the sun-struck outskirts of Havana, they found her—barely four, wild curls, golden-brown skin, and a voice that already questioned the world.

They named her Skye.

Skye Anderson-Pierce. Daughter of two men who had no place in polite society, and who made a place anyway. Raised between legal books and whispered protection wards, sharpened by truth, and loved harder than the world would allow.

Now she looked at them both, jaw set, fire in her blood.

"According to this he's spellbound," Donald said, finally breaking the silence. He tapped the folder beside him. "Cassidy."

"So say the rumors" Skye said evenly.

Thomas's brow lifted. "And that doesn't concern you?"

"It interests me," she replied. "He's dangerous, sure. But not reckless. Wounded, but not weak. He fights like a man who's already decided the world doesn't get to win. That tells me more than any case file."

Donald looked up from the papers. "It tells you something. But not always the right thing."

Skye's mouth quirked into a half-smile. "You think I'm being impulsive."

"I think," Donald said, gently now, "you've got a brilliant mind and a softer heart than you let on. And men like Cassidy... they tend to burn through both."

Thomas chuckled into his glass. "She gets that from you."

Donald smirked. "And you gave her the stubborn."

Still, Skye's voice shifted, laced with something sly.

"The fact he looked at my face more than my hips says a lot," she said, then added with a knowing smile, "And the fact he *did* look at my hips also says a lot."

Donald groaned. "Oh, stars help us."

"Hips and thighs" she continued unashamed smirking.

Thomas chuckled into his drink. "She definitely gets that part from your side of the family."

The two men exchanged a look. Not disapproval—just that slow, heavy pause that came from love and worry dancing together.

Then Thomas lifted his glass and said, "If you're going to court trouble, at least pick someone who can hold your coat while you argue."

Donald leaned in, tone a little drier. "Or at least make sure he can *dance*."

Skye blinked. "Excuse me?"

Thomas gestured with the glass. "You're a force, kiddo. If he can't move with you—if he trips when you pivot, or stiffens when it matters—you'll outpace him before the second number's done."

Donald nodded. "We're not saying no. Just… you've only just met the man, Skye. And already you're talking like you want to *pursue* him."

Skye straightened, voice cool and clear. "I should have a say in who I court. Unless you'd rather I settle down quietly now that my 'adventurous days 'are behind me?"

Thomas didn't miss a beat. "You mean like this past summer?"

Skye groaned and slid off the table. "That doesn't count. He was a painter with a cursed arm, and I was doing research."

Donald lifted a brow. "Research?"

"Extensive research," she muttered.

Thomas laughed into his bourbon. "Well, if Cassidy can survive *you*, he might just be worth keeping around."

Skye shook her head, but a smile pulled at the corner of her lips.

Then Donald slid another folder across the table.

"Then let's talk about someone who doesn't have that luxury."

ENZO RIVERA
Age: 17
Heritage: Half-Fey
Charge: Arcane breach, resulting in death of a Bureau agent
Status: Judicial Hold – Pending Execution

Skye's grin vanished.

"Public defender filed a stay," Thomas said. "It won't hold. The Bureau's already arranging transfer to Morwood Holding. Once he's in their custody..."

Donald didn't need to finish.

Skye picked up the file, flipping through the contents—photos, transcriptions, the smudged arcane sigil scorched into concrete.

Her pulse quickened. Seventeen. No training. No guidance. No chance.

"You want me to take this?" she asked.

"We're not assigning," Donald said. "We're offering."

"You've earned the name on the door," Thomas added. "Now it's time to decide how you want to carry it."

Skye looked at them both—two men who'd built something no one thought possible. Who gave her a name, a future, and a choice. "I'll think on it."

Donald kissed her temple. "Just don't think too long, mija."

Thomas squeezed her shoulder. "The world doesn't wait for great women to get ready. It wants you to set into the fire."

Skye nodded, rising slowly, the file still in her hands. Outside, the city burned with smoke and silence. And somewhere in its shadow, a boy named Enzo Rivera waited for someone to believe he was worth saving.

———

The Tran family's restaurant was small but well-kept, tucked between two larger buildings in Chinatown. Red lanterns swayed gently in the breeze, their warm glow muted by the harsh daylight. The scent of sizzling garlic, soy sauce, and fresh-baked buns filled the air as Chase stepped inside, removing his hat.

A woman, thin and weary, looked up from where she was stacking plates behind the counter. Her hands trembled slightly as she set them down, her gaze searching Chase's face. She already knew why he was here.

"Mr. and Mrs. Tran?" Chase asked gently.

A man emerged from the kitchen, his sleeves rolled up, his face worn from years of labor. His eyes, however, held something harder—

something unyielding.

"You're the detective?" Mr. Tran asked, wiping his hands on a worn dishcloth, the scent of sesame oil and burnt ginger still clinging to his sleeves.

Chase gave a slow nod. "I am. Detective Cassidy, 1st Arcane. Also working this case for Anderson & Anderson." He held up his badge, then tucked it away. "I need to know everything you can tell me about the night Daniel disappeared."

"You see!" Mr. Tran barked, gesturing to his wife with a mix of bitterness and pride. "How quickly they respond when you put money on the table."

He motioned for Chase to sit, but his eyes didn't soften.

Mrs. Tran said nothing at first. Her fingers worked the corner of her apron like she was trying to wring water from memory. Her voice came out low, worn at the edges.

"We fled China with nothing. Barely slipped in before the Immigration Block. We were ghosts... until someone saw us." She looked directly at Chase. "A kind family—The Hendersons. One of your people."

She didn't mean it with malice. If anything, there was a quiet respect there.

"Good people," she continued. "*Shùshì*, arcanists, like us. They helped us find our feet. Gave us a room, a prayer, and a name to use at the checkpoint. But now..."

Her voice cracked. The words dried in her throat like dust.

Mr. Tran took over, jaw clenched, voice firm. "Daniel was our future. Bright. Sharp. Always working, always smiling. Stayed late every night to help clean up the restaurant. Did his schoolwork between tables when business slowed. That night, he stepped out back to take out the trash." He stopped, swallowing hard. "That was it," he said flatly. "The last time anyone saw him."

Chase leaned in. "Nobody saw anything? No one followed him out?"

Mr. Tran's lips pressed into a thin line. "One of the kitchen boys heard a yelp. Said it sounded like a child getting surprised. Not hurt—just caught off guard. When they checked, Daniel was gone. No scream. No struggle. No footprints. Just... *gone.*"

Chase frowned, the crease between his brows deepening. "And you're sure he didn't run off? A fight at home? School trouble?"

Mrs. Tran looked up sharply. Her hands balled into fists against her apron.

"No," she snapped. "Daniel wouldn't do that. He *knows* what it took to get here. He wouldn't throw it away. Not without a word. Not without..."

She trailed off, eyes glassing.

Chase didn't look away. He let the silence settle for a moment before he leaned forward, voice low but solid. "I'm going to find out what happened."

Mr. Tran studied him. The weight of a father holding onto hope by its fraying threads. After a long pause, he gave a reluctant nod.

"You'll need to talk to the staff. The ones who were here that night. They're nervous. Some of them undocumented. But I'll come with you. Help translate."

Chase stood and offered his hand.

Mr. Tran took it.

"Let's get to work," Chase said.

He walked through the narrow dining area, following Mr. Tran—the muted clatter of dishes and the rhythmic chopping of knives filling the air. The restaurant was lively yet controlled, waiters weaving between tables with practiced ease, balancing steaming plates of roast duck, dumplings, and fragrant rice bowls.

The scent of five-spice and sizzling pork mingled in the air, a sharp contrast to the tension that followed Daniel Tran's disappearance. A few patrons glanced at Chase, a man in a well-cut suit, standing out in a place where familiarity was currency.

Mr. Tran led him through a beaded curtain into the kitchen, where the heat of stoves and the hiss of boiling water wrapped around them like a heavy fog. Woks flared with blue-orange flames as cooks tossed ingredients with precision, their faces slick with sweat.

Despite the constant motion, Chase caught the glances. The quiet side-eyes from the kitchen staff, the way their shoulders tightened as he passed. Something was off.

At the back of the kitchen, near a narrow break area, Mr. Tran gestured toward two older men standing near a prep station.

"Detective, this is Jin and Wei," he said in Mandarin before switching to English for Chase.

"They have been with me for many years. Hard workers. Good men." The two workers nodded stiffly, their eyes flicking toward each other before settling on Chase. "And where is Liu Feng?" Mr. Tran asked, frowning as if only now realizing the absence. "He was scheduled to work today." Jin and Wei hesitated.

"He's been acting strange lately," Jin muttered, rubbing his hands together.

"More nervous than usual. Jumpy." Wei nodded. "The day after Daniel disappeared, he barely spoke a word. Looked like he hadn't slept. When we asked him what was wrong, he just shook his head and kept his mouth shut."

Mr. Tran's frown deepened. "That does not sound like Liu Feng. He is always reliable."

Chase narrowed his eyes. "Where is he now?"

Jin hesitated, glancing toward Wei, who suddenly looked even more uncomfortable. "He was supposed to work today… but he's been coming in late, leaving early. Sometimes he doesn't show up at all."

Chase exhaled through his nose. "Where does he live?" Before they could answer, the kitchen door swung open with a sudden creak, cutting through the steady clatter of knives and the sizzle of hot oil.

A figure stepped in, tense, cautious. Liu Feng. His face was pale, drawn tight, his dark eyes flicking over the room like a man walking into his own execution. He didn't see Chase at first—his gaze moved to Mr. Tran, then to Jin and Wei, his co-worker, whose silence spoke louder than any words ever could. Then, finally, his eyes landed on Chase Cassidy.

For a single heartbeat, neither of them moved. The air between them felt thick, charged, as if the world had paused just long enough for reality to settle in. Liu knew. Knew who Chase was.

Knew why he was here. Knew that running was his only option.

His breath hitched. Then—he turned on his heel and ran. "Liu Feng!" Mr. Tran gasped, his face twisting in shock. But the young man was already shoving past the swinging kitchen doors, knocking over a stack of steaming bamboo baskets as he tore through the back exit.

Chase didn't hesitate. He shoved past the doorway and took off after him. Feng was fast—unnaturally fast. His robes billowed behind him as he weaved through the chaos of the evening crowd. Pedestrians shouted as he shoved past, knocking over baskets and tipping street carts in his frantic escape.

Chase could already tell he wouldn't catch him in time. Not like this. His breath steadied. Focus. The arcane Glyphs tattooed across his skin flared to life, burning with golden energy as he called upon the spell-work etched into his very flesh.

A surge of raw speed shot through his limbs, his muscles tightening, his vision sharpening. The world slowed. Chase pushed forward, his boots barely touching the ground as he blurred through the street, weaving past startled vendors and shocked bystanders.

His surroundings warped slightly at the edges—spellbound augmentation pushing his body beyond human limits. He was gaining on Feng. Fast.

Then—a crackle of arcane energy. Chase barely had time to react before a bolt of dark violet light shot toward him. He twisted mid-stride, his enhanced reflexes barely letting him dodge as the spell seared past, scorching a hole in a brick wall behind him.

"Son of a—" Chase snarled.

Feng skidded around a corner, his right hand sparking with magical energy as he turned to fire again. Chase was already moving—faster than Feng could track. The second bolt fizzled through the air where Chase had been just a fraction of a second earlier. Chase had enough.

His arm moved on instinct. He raised his revolver and fired twice.

The first round grazed Feng's shoulder, sending him spinning slightly. The second tore through his thigh. Feng staggered, his sprint turning into a stumble as his legs faltered beneath him.

He sucked in a sharp breath, his hand still sparking as he tried to summon another spell— A car horn blared.

The headlights illuminated his panicked face for a split second before the sickening crunch of metal against flesh echoed through the street. Feng's body hit the hood hard, the impact sending him rolling over the windshield before crashing onto the pavement with a brutal finality. The car screeched to a halt, its tires burning against the asphalt. The driver stumbled out, his face pale and shaking, eyes darting between the crumpled form on the road and Chase.

Chase skidded to a stop, the glow of his wards fading as he slowed his breathing. The surge of energy left his limbs, his muscles aching from the exertion. He approached cautiously, gun still in hand, his pulse still steady. Feng lay on his back, his limbs twisted at odd angles, his breath coming in short, wet gasps. But something was wrong.

Even with his injuries, his skin looked too pale—almost waxen. His lips were tinged blue. His body twitched, but not like a man in pain—more like a puppet with cut strings. Chase narrowed his eyes. Not natural. Chase reached out and pressed two fingers against the side of Feng's neck.

Cold. Ice cold. His stomach twisted. A Mourned.

Liu Feng had been one of the sentient dead, walking among the living, pretending to be one of them.

He knelt beside him, watching as Feng's body began to stiffen unnaturally fast. Rigor mortis didn't set in this quickly. His hand shot out, grabbing Feng by the collar. "Who sent you?" Chase growled.

Feng's lips moved, his breath rattling, but no words came. Then— a faint, whistling sound. Chase recognized it instantly. In the Hall of the Mountain King. His grip tightened.

"No, no—don't you die on me yet—"

Feng's eyes rolled back, his mouth twitching into something between a sneer and a grin. Then his body locked up completely. Chase let him go with a frustrated exhale, standing up, his mind already racing. Feng shuddered, his fingers twitching weakly.

Chase saw a key clutched in his palm, barely hanging on between his fingers. He plucked it free just as Feng exhaled one final breath and went still. Chase turned the key over in his palm.

It had an address engraved on it. His boarding house. Pocketing the key, Chase stood. Whatever Liu Feng had been hiding... It was waiting for him at that address.

Chase scanned the street for the nearest police call box, spotting one near the corner. The gathered crowd was still murmuring about the accident, but Chase ignored them as he strode over, lifting the receiver and waiting for the crackle of connection. "Operator," came the clipped response.

"Detective Cassidy. Get me Captain Whitman."

There was a brief pause before Whitman's voice came on, rough and irritated. "Cassidy, this better be good."

"Pursued a man named Liu Feng, who just got himself killed trying to run," Chase said flatly, watching as a couple of bystanders covered the corpse with a cloth.

"Turns out, he was one of the Mourned. I found a key on him. Address is engraved. I'm heading there now." A heavy sigh crackled over the line.

"The Mourned? Hell Cassidy. This just got worse. You going in alone?"

"No choice," Chase replied. "If I wait, we lose the trail. I'll check in after."

Whitman was silent for a beat before muttering, "Just don't get yourself killed." Chase smirked. "Don't plan too".

He hung up the receiver, adjusted his coat, and turned in the direction of Liu Feng's boarding house. Whatever he was hiding... Chase was about to find out. It was waiting for him at that address.

The boarding house was a run-down tenement, a looming brick structure with peeling paint and grime-streaked windows, its facade a testament to years of neglect.

The flickering hallway lights cast sickly yellow glows over the cracked walls, where layers of old notices and eviction warnings curled at the edges. The air was thick with the mingling scents of stale tobacco, cheap liquor, and the unmistakable bite of decay.

As Chase stepped inside, his boots creaked against the warped wooden floorboards. A low murmur of voices drifted from behind closed doors, occasional bursts of laughter or arguments bleeding through the thin walls.

Somewhere, a radio played faint jazz, the tinny sound distorted by distance. A resident near the stairwell glanced at him suspiciously, hunched over with a cigarette hanging loosely from cracked lips. His bloodshot eyes lingered on Chase's badge for a beat before he exhaled a stream of smoke.

"You a cop?" the man asked, voice rasping from years of cheap cigars and misery. Chase nodded once.

"Good," the man muttered.

"Because it smells like death up on the third floor." The stairwell groaned under Chase's weight as he ascended, the air turning heavier with each step. The scent of rot thickened, clinging to the walls like something alive.

The door to Liu Feng's room was ajar. Chase nudged it open, revealing a cramped space strewn with discarded clothes, broken furniture, and candle stubs melted into the floor. The air was thick with the sickly-sweet scent of something unnatural.

And in the center of it all— two mourned crouched over a body, their thin, pale hands gripping the lifeless form as they siphoned its essence. Their lips were parted, the faintest glow of stolen energy pulsing between their teeth.

The corpse at their feet was the boy Daniel Tran. Their heads snapped toward Chase as he kicked the door wide open, his coat flaring as he reached for his weapon. The Mourned let out a guttural hiss before bolting for the window, shattering glass as they leapt into the alley below.

They looked up from below, grinning, exposing rotting teeth through cracked lips assured that the man above would not follow. Their confidence shattered when Chase leaped, landing right after them, the impact absorbed by his wards as he straightened to his full height.

The mourned, stunned for only a fraction of a second, exchanged a glance before taking off at full speed. Chase pursued, his boots pounding against the pavement as they wove through a maze of narrow alleys, vaulting over crates, garbage bins, and the occasional sleeping homeless man.

They moved with unnatural speed, limbs flailing yet coordinated, their gaunt faces flickering in and out of the shadows. They burst onto a busy street, darting between oncoming cars as horns blared in protest. Chase didn't hesitate, weaving through the chaos, narrowly avoiding a near-collision as one of the Mourned turned and hurled a spell.

A sickly green bolt of energy streaked through the air, but Chase's spellbound wards flared, repelling it with a crackle of defensive magic. The Mourned didn't stop, skidding into another alley, this one narrower and descending down a long flight of stairs built into the hill.

The sudden downward slope forced Chase to adjust his footing, leaping down three, four steps at a time to keep up. The stench of rot and stagnant water intensified as the pursuit led them deeper into the city's underbelly, where fewer eyes would witness what was about to unfold, his coat flaring as he reached for his weapon.

The two split up, with one of the mourned turning sharply, its bony limbs propelling it toward an abandoned cathedral, its towering silhouette barely visible through the fog-choked skyline. Chase's stomach tightened. He knew this place.

St. Augustine's Cathedral had been left to rot for over a decade. Once a grand bastion of faith, its towering spires now loomed like skeletal fingers against the night sky. The stained glass windows, once vibrant with depictions of saints and martyrs, were shattered, leaving behind jagged edges like rows of broken teeth.

The wooden double doors hung crooked on rusted hinges, one yawning open as if beckoning him inside. The mourned didn't hesitate—it slithered through the doorway, vanishing into the darkness beyond. Chase cursed under his breath and followed.

The air inside was thick with decay. Every breath carried the scent of damp wood, old wax, and something far worse—the unmistakable tang of death. The rows of pews were warped and covered in dust, their surfaces scratched and scarred by time.

Thick cobwebs clung to the vaulted ceiling, dangling like forgotten nooses in the moonlight filtering through the broken windows. A gust of wind rattled through the hollow structure, carrying with it the whispers of forgotten prayers. Chase's boots echoed against the cracked marble floor as he moved cautiously down the nave, past the ruined altar where candles once burned for the lost souls of the city.

Now, the only thing that remained was a blackened sigil scorched into the stone—a necromantic rune still faintly pulsing with residual energy. This wasn't just a place of ruin. Someone had used this cathedral for dark magic. Recently.

A sharp growl snapped him back to the moment. At the far end of the cathedral, the mourned hunched near a gaping hole in the floor, where the stone had collapsed into an old subterranean passage. The tunnels.

Chase steadied his breath and raised his revolver. "No more running, you bastard."

The Mourned twitched, its gaunt body contorting as its jagged teeth gleamed in the low light. Its eyes, once human, now burned with an unnatural green glow, its pupils dilated with an insatiable hunger.

The stench of rot clung to its skin—a mix of decayed flesh and grave-dirt. It lunged. Chase barely had time to react before clawed hands shot toward his throat. He twisted, rolling onto the cold stone as its jagged nails sliced the air where his neck had been moments before.

The creature snarled, its skeletal limbs convulsing, its movements both feral and eerily precise. Chase kicked upward, driving his boot into its ribcage. The impact sent the Mourned staggering, but not down.

It was too light, too unnatural—more shadow than flesh. "Damn thing won't go down easy," Chase growled. The creature's jaw snapped open, revealing rows of blackened, decayed teeth. It was smiling. Then, without warning, it turned and threw itself down into the tunnels.

Chase clenched his jaw. No choice now. Gun drawn, he jumped in after it. Chase fired his revolver as he landed, but the bullets passed through the creature's decaying flesh, punching holes that reformed almost instantly.

The Mourned let out a shrieking laugh, as if amused by the futile effort, before slamming into Chase with inhuman strength. The impact sent Chase sprawling into the damp, fetid muck of the underground tunnel. His revolver skidded across the floor, disappearing into the dark, stagnant water pooling along the tunnel's edges.

The creature pounced on him immediately, its skeletal fingers digging into Chase's shoulders, forcing him down. Its teeth snapped as it lunged for his throat, strands of saliva hanging from its lips, eyes rolling back in near ecstasy at the prospect of a fresh kill.

Chase gritted his teeth, his arms straining as he pushed against the creature's strength. He could feel the heat of its rancid breath against his neck, the cold of its flesh seeping into his skin. He twisted violently, managing to roll to the side just as the Mourned's teeth clamped down, biting into the empty air where his throat had been.

The creature let out a furious snarl, slashing at him with jagged, claw-like nails. Chase barely dodged the swipe, rolling onto his knees and thrusting his spellbound hand forward. The sigils etched into his flesh ignited with a sudden, searing light.

A rush of fire erupted from his palm, engulfing the Mourned in an infernal blaze. The creature let out a shriek unlike anything Chase had ever heard—a sound of a thousand screams.

 Its flesh bubbled and blackened, limbs spasming violently as the enchanted flames devoured it from the inside out. It flailed, its body contorting unnaturally, before it collapsed into a heap of smoldering, twitching remains.

Chase exhaled sharply, his breath ragged. The flames died down, leaving only the charred husk of the creature and the lingering scent of burnt decay. He flexed his fingers, his sigils still glowing with residual heat, before shaking off the tension in his arms.

He looked quickly for his revolver, realizing quickly that he would never find it. If this Mourned had led him here, there was a reason. Something else was waiting for him in the dark. The tunnel stretched on into the black, a claustrophobic passage of crumbling brick and stagnant air. Chase pressed forward, the only sound the quiet splash of his boots against damp stone.

His spellbound sigils still faintly glowed, casting eerie shadows along the tunnel walls. Then he saw her.

A Mourned child stood in the center of the tunnel, her form hunched, her head tilted slightly as she observed him. Her breath came out in low, guttural growls, the remnants of language long lost to her undead existence.

Chase halted, every instinct warning him of the presence before him. A moment later, more figures emerged from the darkness behind her, drifting like specters. A pack of mourned, their gaunt, hungry faces barely visible in the dim light, their sunken eyes locked onto Chase.

They stood still, almost hesitant, their sharp fingers twitching with restrained impulse. Chase knew what this was. A warning. This was their domain. He had followed too far, and now he was outnumbered. His fists clenched as he considered his options, but there was only one real choice.

Live to fight another day. He turned and ran. A snarl rang out behind him, followed by the rapid pounding of feet. The pack had given chase, their inhuman speed carrying them across the tunnel floor with terrifying grace.

Chase sprinted, dodging low-hanging pipes and crumbling debris, his lungs burning as he pushed forward. The tunnel sloped upward, and in the distance, a faint glow of daylight seeped in.

Dawn was breaking. With a final burst of energy, Chase leapt forward, bursting through the tunnel exit just as the first rays of sunlight crested over the horizon. Behind him, the Mourned skidded to a halt, hissing as they recoiled from the approaching daylight. They lingered just within the tunnel's entrance, their blackened forms writhing in agitation, unwilling to step beyond their sanctuary of shadow. Chase stood there for a moment, catching his breath as he looked back at them.

For now, he was safe. But the hunt was far from over.

―――――

The tunnels beneath the cathedral stank of rot and old stone. The air was thick with the lingering scent of blood, sweat, and something older —something wrong. Baron Hermann von Epp stood in the shadows, ice-blue eyes glinting beneath the low lantern glow, his red coat brushed clean where the stone dust dared cling to it. The detective's fleeing footsteps faded down the corridor like a heartbeat receding into the dark.

Von Epp didn't pursue. He simply watched—chewing a toothpick with quiet irritation, calculation already moving behind his eyes. The little detective was quick. Quicker than any outsider who had wandered these halls in years.

His lips curled into something almost like a smile.

Impressive. No man has ever escaped these catacombs. Even the workers who built this place rest permanently within. "Who are you, little detective?"

Beside him, a Mourned knelt—his favorite. Her undead flesh wrapped in tattered lace, dark hair still strangely soft beneath the pallor of death. She shivered under his touch as he cupped her cheek, a guttural purr rattling in her ruined throat.

Even she had sensed it—the disturbance, the intrusion, the trespass into his sanctum of research. Von Epp spared the detective's escape route a final glance. He exhaled, a pale ghost of breath in the cold air, and began to whistle—In the Hall of the Mountain King.

The melody echoed down the stone corridors, a playful taunt curling through darkness like a whispered threat.

If only the Imperial German High Command had listened...

Trained. Intelligent. Obedient.

The undead could have changed the war.

But they had called him mad.

Von Epp chuckled softly. Then, with a final stroke of his favorite Mourned's hair, he turned toward the sigil-etched archway leading deeper into the heart of his sanctum. He placed his palm against the sigil-etched archway. The bone markings awakened—glowing sickly green—curling outward across the stone like veins filling with fresh blood. The tunnel shuddered, reacting to the command of the Second Seat.

Runes flared across the ceiling like serpents of green lightning. Stone groaned. Three outer tunnels collapsed inward, sealed forever. He wove a glamour over the last passage—a curtain of warped light that made the very concept of the tunnel slippery to the mind. No one without purpose would ever see it again.

A circle of runes ignited beneath his boots—writhing, spiraling, adjusting to his weight.

The air bent. Gravity folded in on itself. Stone peeled away like skin. With a single, surgeon-steady breath, Hermann von Epp stepped forward —and slipped out of the physical tunnel, vanishing between the seams of reality.

The space sealed behind him with a whisper.

He reappeared in darkness lit by pale green glow.

His inner sanctum.

Everything was in motion now—the docks prepared, the Fey children scouted, the "package" already inbound. The host, groomed long before he ever learned to walk, was nearly ready. All according to plan. Except for one trench-scarred detective meddling in affairs he could not possibly understand. This intrusion had come dangerously close.

Von Epp slid a fresh toothpick between his teeth.

He stepped deeper into the catacomb—the necromantic wards pulsing like a second heart. Shackled Mourned twitched in their rune-circles as if they sensed his displeasure.

"This chamber is secure," von Epp murmured. "But Blackwell Island... that is the true concern." The proving ground. Where the corpses first sang for him. Where the tether between soul and body had finally broken open under his scalpel. Where theory had become breakthrough. Blackwell Island was where it began. And now—His tone hardened. "It requires cleaning."

Two obsidian mirrors hovered above the central dais, veined with pale-gold script.

Von Epp waived a hand. The mirrors awakened. Dorian Blackwell flickered into view in the left mirror—sharp-featured, immaculate, irritation in every well-controlled breath. In the right mirror, Lildan Blackwell appeared—silent, unreadable, veiled in shadow silk.

Von Epp wasted no time. "The island needs to be cleansed."

Dorian frowned. "Why? It was abandoned after your experiments concluded—"

"Precautions Dorian " von Epp cut in. "It's birthplace of my breakthrough. I will not allow loose ends."

Dorian bowed—short, resentful.

"You will return to Blackwell Island. Sanitize itt. Quietly. Remove evidence. Collect viable samples. Dispose of the failures."

Dorian's jaw twitched. "You used my family's property for your work. Now you ask us too clean up your after your mess? We are on the other side of the country and were not to arrive until the ceremony"

"And you will change your plans. You are Fifth Seat," von Epp said coldly. "Your sister is Sixth. Remember your place."

Dorian nodded his head in deference. Lildan remained motionless His eyes lingered on her disrespect—just long enough to make a point.

"Do not fail me." The mirrors dimmed—snuffed out like candle flames.

———

Captain Whitman paced the length of the street, his coat pulled tightly around him as the early morning mist clung to the pavement. He had been searching for Chase ever since the Liu Fang incident, his gut telling him something had gone sideways.

The city wasn't just restless—it was on the edge of something worse. Missing children, murdered children, and now the Mourned prowling in the depths. Whatever was happening, it was spiraling fast.

He spotted Chase emerging from the alleyway, disheveled, dirty, and out of breath. His expression darkened as he strode toward him.

"Hell, Cassidy. You look like you've crawled through the gutter."

"Close enough."

Whitman folded his arms, eyeing him. "Tell me what happened."

Chase recounted the night—the chase, the tunnels, the Mourned child, and the pack that had nearly torn him apart. When he finished, Whitman swore under his breath.

"We got problems. Big ones. If we have a Mourned infestation, things are worse than I thought."

"Lost my revolver in the muck down there," Chase said. "It's gone."

Whitman grunted.

"That's the least of my concerns right now. You need to take a few days off, Cassidy. Clean yourself up. We're not solving this mess if you drop dead from exhaustion."

Chase shook his head.

"Can't do that, Cap. You don't understand—if they were Mourned, real Mourned, then this isn't just another nest. When they're full of essence, they can pass for normal. Skin warm, eyes clear, pulse steady. You wouldn't know one from a living man until it was too late."

Whitman frowned.

"You telling me they can walk topside without drawin 'suspicion?"

"If they've fed enough," Chase said. "They can even think straight—keep their urges buried for weeks. They're not like vampires; vamps can't hide their hunger. But a Mourned at the higher stages of preservation? They can blend in. Hell, they use the arcane gifts that they were born with. That's what scares me."

Whitman's jaw tightened. He glanced down the fog-choked street before lowering his voice.

"That's exactly why you need the time. No one else in the First Arcane can handle this quiet, but if you burn yourself out, the Bureau of Arcane Enforcement will step in—and they'll turn this city inside out lookin 'for monsters."

Chase's gaze hardened. "Maybe that's what we need."

Whitman cut him off with a glare.

"No. What we need is control. The Mourned, regardless of their unbeating hearts...have rights. Their own advocates, protection orders, sanctuary charters. We start callin 'them an infestation and we'll have every Inquisitor, Witch Hunter, and Purifier stormin 'these streets before sundown. You think the BAE won't love that? They'd lock down half of Madhatten and call it mercy."

Chase exhaled, shoulders sinking but eyes still sharp. "So we do nothing?"

"We move quiet," Whitman said. "We find proof. And until then, you rest. You come apart on me, and this whole case goes with you."

Chase looked past him at the waking city—the fog, the faint light, the silhouettes of people who had no idea what was stirring beneath their feet.

"Yeah," he said finally. "Rest. Right."

Whitman clapped him on the shoulder. "Get your report in, then vanish for forty-eight hours. That's an order."

Chase turned toward the station, his mind still running through the horrors of the night. The city was waking up, but he knew the darkness was still there, lurking beneath the surface, waiting for its moment to strike again.

He pushed through the precinct doors, the stale hallway lights buzzing overhead. O'Leary stood at the records counter, sorting through reports with the slow, practiced resignation of a man who had seen too much and expected even less. Technically, Chase outranked him now—an acting detective outranking patrol—but it was a title balanced on a thread. One misstep and he'd be back in uniform, taking orders from O'Leary again.

And O'Leary had always treated him square.

"Corporal O'Leary," Chase said, keeping his tone even, respectful without being meek. "You got anything in the archives on the undead? Case files, dusty binders… whatever we've got buried in the back."

O'Leary squinted at him.

"Undead? Christ, Cassidy…" He blew out a breath. "Yeah, there's a cabinet no one touches anymore. Locked, mislabeled, probably cursed. I'll pull what I can."

In his makeshift office, Chase sat at his desk. The lamp O'leary gave him cast long shadows over the files spread before him. The air was thick with the scent of old paper, whiskey, and the faint metallic tang of gun oil.

The city outside was settling into its usual nighttime rhythm—cars rumbling over uneven streets, distant sirens cutting through the humid air. But inside this room, the only sound was the soft scratch of his pen against paper.

He picked up the small evidence bag, holding it between two fingers. Inside was the toothpick—the same kind he'd found at multiple crime scenes. At first, he'd written it off as a quirk, some absentminded habit of one of the killers. But something about it wouldn't let go of him.

He flipped open the forensics report, his eyes skimming over the initial findings—wooden, cheap, splintered at one end. Nothing unusual. Then he reached the blood analysis. His stomach tightened. Human blood.

Chase leaned back, rubbing a hand down his face. That didn't track. He'd assumed—hell, he'd known—that the murders of the Fey children had been carried out by the Mourned. The way the bodies were torn apart, the way their life essence had been drained—that was all classic undead work. But if this toothpick had human blood on it... That meant at least one of the killers wasn't a Mourned.

Someone had been breathing at the scene. Chase exhaled, setting the report aside. He reached into his desk drawer and pulled out a small, battered case. The leather was cracked, the brass clasps dulled with time.

He flipped it open. Inside was the Witch's Eye—an arcane detection kit designed to analyze magical residue. The kit itself was a relic, something he had inherited from his father: a compact brass-and-iron contraption roughly the size of a microscope, its frame laced with delicate runic etchings that glimmered faintly when touched by light. A stack of triple-faceted prisms turned within a clockwork housing powered by a hand-crank, drawing ambient Aether into its focusing chamber. Small glass vials of powdered reagents—silver nitrate, monkshood tincture, crushed silverleaf—fit snugly into a padded tray beside a narrow glass monocle infused with etched runes.

In trained hands, it could read the echoes left behind on objects— traces of magic, of essence, of the unseen. When the crank was wound and a reagent applied, the prisms refracted invisible Aether into faint color flares: blue-white for arcane residue of Dragon-kind, and green-gold for Fey essence, yellowish green for Necromantic. It was fragile, temperamental, and half a century out of date—but it still worked.

Chase placed the toothpick on the table and donned the monocle. The runes flickered to life, faint at first, then brighter, casting thin veins of blue-green light across his vision. He sprinkled a pinch of witchroot dust over the toothpick and watched.

For a long moment, nothing happened. Then—a faint glow. Not just any glow. Bloodline energy. Chase's pulse ticked up. He adjusted the lens, fine-tuning it until the residual essence revealed itself.

The glow pulsed softly, muted, diluted. It wasn't strong, but it was there. That meant the person who had handled this wasn't just human. They had magic in their blood. His jaw tightened.

There were only two confirmed magical bloodlines. Draconic – Those with dragon ancestry, marked by physical resilience, elemental magic, and enhanced endurance. Fey – Descendants of the old spirits, their blood laced with natural magic, agility, and sensory gifts and the most common. The Fey were a promiscuous bunch.

Infernal and Empyrean? Chase dismissed them outright. Those were myths. Or, at least, he thought they were. His father, Elijah Cassidy, had never spoken much about their lineage.

He'd assumed—hoped—that he was Draconic, that whatever made him different had been passed down from something old and powerful. He could breathe fire. He could withstand magic that should have burned him to ash. What else could it be? And yet, there was a part of him that had always wondered.

His hands curled into fists. This wasn't about him. He turned his attention back to the glowing toothpick. This was proof. Whoever had dropped it at the scene was magical—but alive.

The office door banged open without a knock.

One of the patrolmen from earlier—the same one who'd muttered slurs about "spellbound freaks" until Chase warned him he was welcome to try it to his face—stood in the doorway with a sour expression and an armful of dusty folders.

He dumped them onto Chase's desk hard enough to scatter ash and loose pages.

"Records," he said flatly. "From the little shop of horrors downstairs."

Chase ignored the tone as the patrolman left. What caught his eye wasn't the files—it was the battered, leather-bound tome sitting on top of them. He lifted it carefully.

Codex Sanguinus: A Field Guide to the Profane
by Solomon Drake, Witch-Hunter of the
Inquisitors of the Divine Flame.

The cover creaked as he opened it. Ancient vellum pages whispered under his thumb. He flipped through diagrams of ghasts, revenants, corpse-walkers... until a heading snagged his attention.

"The Mourned Ones."

Beneath it, a sketch—gaunt, veiled figures with hollow eyes and carved runes weeping down their cheeks.

Chase exhaled slow. "Alright," he muttered to himself. "Let's see what the hell you are."

(Chapter VII — "On the Mourned and Their Lamentations")

The Mourned were not born. They were left behind. In the age scholars now call the Great Sundering, when the Seelie and Unseelie Courts—long rivals—joined their banners to drive humankind from the Waking Realm, the Fae suffered a defeat so absolute it cleaved their world from ours. The Courts sealed themselves behind the Veil, retreating into their pocket-realms of dream and twilight, abandoning many of their kin who could not flee in time.

Those forsaken souls struggled to follow their brethren, but the Veil had already hardened. Their spirits were torn—one thread anchored in the mortal world, the rest stretched thin across an unreachable horizon. So they wandered, bodiless, grief-stricken, unable to pass on, unable to return.

These were the first Mourned.

Unlike the shambling dead of lesser necromancies, the first Mourned bled. They had been Fae—creatures of flesh and magic—and when their lost spirits clawed their way back into discarded bodies, the magic that knit them into their hollow shells imprinted echoes of life, a memory of living, not life itself.

Later Mourned—those raised by mortal spellcraft or born through profane rites are puppets; their spirits are shackled, not severed.

But the old ones... the Fae-born Mourned...

They remember what it was to feel.

And that is what makes them perilous.

The Mourned hunger not for meat nor for blood, but for sensation— the warmth of a hearth, the brush of silk, the communion of touch, taste, breath. Denied these, they draw sustenance from the nearest likeness: the essence of the living. That spark mortals call vitality.

A Mourned deprived too long becomes a predator of yearning, its grief sharpening into cruelty.

Pity them, but do not hesitate.

For a creature that aches to live again will kill without malice... simply to remember what it was like to feel.

Closing the book, Chase understood now why the Fey-blooded made the perfect prey. Their blood was ripe with magic, their essence stronger than most humans. A single Mourned could live for weeks off a Fey child's soul.

And yet, there was something... off about this case. Mourned didn't drink blood. They siphoned life through their touch like a man drinking from a well in the desert. They wouldn't touch the blood. So what the hell was a toothpick, slick with human blood, doing at the scene?

Chase ran his tongue over his teeth, his mind working through the angles. Someone had been there. Someone living. Someone working alongside the Mourned. The thought made his stomach turn.

He pulled his notebook from his coat pocket, flipping to a fresh page. Find out who the toothpick belongs to. A simple task on paper.

But something in his gut told him this was about to make things even more complicated. Somethings were beginning to come together, but all this would have to wait. Orders from Whitman. 48 hours. He had to keep himself off the case for 48 hours. A distraction is what he needed.

Chase pulled his collar up against the cold drizzle, stepping off the curb and heading toward The Midnight Martini. The neon glow of the sign flickered in the damp air, the steady hum of jazz music spilling out from within. He wasn't sure why he stopped—maybe he hoped to find Diego, or maybe he just didn't want to go home yet.

The weight of everything he had uncovered sat heavy on his shoulders, and a drink seemed like the simplest way to quiet his mind. The warmth of the club was a stark contrast to the dreary night outside. Smoke curled lazily through the air, mingling with the scent of whiskey and cheap perfume.

Chase moved through the crowd, scanning for Diego. Nothing. No familiar grin, no dice rolling between nimble fingers. Then he saw. Evelyn. She was at a corner booth, perched on the lap of some well-dressed fella, her fingers tracing lazy patterns over his collar. She laughed—soft, sultry, effortless—the same laugh she had used on Chase the night before.

Her lips, still painted that deep shade of red, pressed against the man's neck as she whispered something that made him grin like a fool. Chase didn't flinch. Didn't slow his step. He wasn't surprised. That's just how things were.

He had never expected anything else from her—hell, he hadn't expected much at all. Still, something about seeing her so easily wrapped around someone else sat like a bitter note on his tongue. Not jealousy. Not anger. Just another reminder of what things were, of how fleeting they always seemed to be.

He turned and left without a word.

Outside, the rain had picked up, soaking into his coat and chilling his skin, but he didn't rush. He let the city swallow him, boots hitting the pavement in a steady rhythm.

The night stretched ahead, empty and quiet save for the occasional hiss of tires on wet streets and the distant wail of a siren. By the time he reached his apartment, his clothes were damp, and his bones ached from more than just exhaustion.

The familiar creak of the wooden floor greeted him as he stepped inside, shutting the door behind him with a weary sigh. He tossed his coat onto the nearest chair, his muscles aching from the long walk.

The city outside was already humming with the late-night bustle, but inside, the walls muffled the chaos, giving him a brief moment of quiet. He sat on the edge of his bed, rubbing his temples.

The last two days had been a whirlwind of blood, death, and shadows. Missing children. Dead children. The Mourned were crawling through the underground like rats. And now, he had lost his revolver—the one thing that had been with him since the war.

His eyes drifted to the Colt 1911 resting on his nightstand—the one he had taken from the goon back at the speakeasy with Diego. His fingers traced the metal, the weight of it solid and reliable. His revolver had done nothing against the Mourned, but this… this could be something different.

He needed to buy a proper holster for it. Chase exhaled and ran a hand down his face. He had relied on his guns for years, but last night, it hadn't been enough. He had been forced to use the full range of his spellbound abilities as of late. Something he had been avoiding since the war. Since the Red Morning.

The fire, the power—it had surged back to him with terrifying ease, burning through his veins like it had never left. He clenched his fist, feeling the phantom heat beneath his skin. Shaking the thoughts away, he stripped off his shirt and stepped into the small bathroom.

The water from the shower was lukewarm at best, but it washed away the grime and blood, leaving only the scars—old and new—as reminders of everything he had survived.

When he finally collapsed onto the bed, his body felt heavy, but his mind refused to quiet. He stared at the ceiling, the faint hum of the city outside filling the silence.

Sleep took him slowly, but the nightmares were waiting. The city was waking up, but he knew the darkness was still there, lurking beneath the surface, waiting for its moment to strike again.

CHAPTER 4

The Cuban Link

Journal Excerpt of Jannick Varrick – Project Infernus
December 7, 1917 – Classified Entry

The more I observe our subjects, the clearer it becomes—Project Infernus is a doomed endeavor. We have played at gods, binding raw Infernal energy to mortal frames that were never meant to wield such power.

The spellbound were intended to be weapons—soldiers reforged in fire and steel, wielding magic as easily as they breathe. But the truth is far more damning. Burnout.

The very force that strengthens them destroys them. We pour magic into their bodies, graft sigils into their flesh, etch runes into their bones —turning them into living conduits for power no man should hold. But no matter how precise the inscriptions, no matter how many wards we layer, one by one, they combust.

Thermal Meltdowns.

A term that barely captures the horror of what occurs. Their bodies cannot regulate the energy surging through them. At first, the symptoms are mild—heightened aggression, spikes in body temperature, arcane surges that discharge unpredictably. Then comes the sweating, the shaking, the fever that no spell or medicine can abate.

The body rejects the binding. Magic floods their veins, igniting from within. Their blood boils. Their flesh blackens. They burn alive, reduced to nothing but charred husks of what once were men.

Out of thirty subjects, twenty-eight have suffered this fate. Yet... two remain. Chase Cassidy and...

J. Varrick

The battlefield was a haze of smoke and fire, the air thick with the metallic tang of blood and cordite. Gunfire rattled in the distance, muffled beneath the screams of dying men and the heavy pounding of artillery.

Chase moved through the chaos, his breath ragged, his rifle long discarded. His trench knife gleamed red, clutched tight in his fist. He surged forward with the Harlem Hellfighters, storming the German line.

Trenches filled with enemy soldiers loomed ahead, and he leapt down, boots splashing into the muck of war. A German soldier turned, wide-eyed—too slow. Chase drove the knife into his throat, twisting before yanking it free.

Another enemy charged, rifle raised. Chase ducked low, slashing across his belly, spilling him into the mud. The trench was a maw of death, but Chase had long since stopped hesitating. Adrenaline and survival drove him forward. He reached a bunker, its dark entrance yawning like a grave. His breath came heavy, and he gripped his knife tighter.

Something moved inside. Then it came.

A Patchman.

A grotesque stitched-together abomination, its massive frame blocking the light behind it. Rotten flesh, jagged scars, metal bolts jutting from sinew. The thing lurched forward, its stitched lips peeling into something resembling a grin.

Chase staggered back, his knife feeling pitifully small in his grasp. The Patchman raised its monstrous, hammer-like fists, a deep, inhuman growl ripping from its throat.

Then it charged.

Chase awoke with a start, drenched in sweat. His chest rose and fell in sharp, staggered breaths, the phantom scent of blood still clinging to the back of his throat. He coughed once, scrubbing a hand down his face to steady his pulse.

It was the Red Morning, visiting him again. The room was dim, cast in long gray shadows from the city's early morning light slipping between half-closed blinds. Familiar. Grounded. Real.

The room was quiet but for the steady tick of the radiator. Chase Cassidy stirred awake, the remnants of the dream still clinging to him— blood, tunnels, and the cold echo of something that refused to die. He rubbed the grit from his eyes and sat up. For a second, he thought he was alone.

Then a cigar flared to life in the corner. The ember burned hot, briefly revealing the outline of a woman framed in smoke. The air shifted; expensive perfume cut through the stale night air.

She rose from the chair with unhurried grace, velvet shadows sliding off her like a cloak. Bare feet whispered against the floorboards. Every movement was deliberate, confident—like someone who knew how power sounded in silence.

Skye Anderson-Pierce.

She wore a black-and-white day dress, simple but sharp, the kind that spoke louder than sequins ever could. It fit her too well to be an accident. The neckline was low enough to make a statement, and ink coiled down one arm—tribal spirals and angled glyphs that shimmered faintly as she moved.

"Nightmares, Mr. Cassidy?" she said, stopping just short of him.

Her lower torso hovered dangerously close to his face, close enough that the fabric of her dress brushed against his face when she shifted her weight. The scent that came with her wasn't the heavy, perfumed kind he'd grown used to in speakeasies—it was subtle, deliberate. Vanilla, with a trace of lavender underneath—soft, expensive, and almost clean enough to make him forget where he was.

He blinked, focus narrowing to the faint glint of the cigar in her hand, the lazy spiral of smoke drifting between them. It wrapped her scent around the room, a strange mix of warmth and danger. His heartbeat found an irregular rhythm he didn't care to acknowledge.

She held his gaze, one brow lifting. The corner of her mouth curved like she already knew the answer.

He exhaled, dragging a hand down his face. "Hell of a way to wake up. What are you doing in my room?"

Skye took a long pull from her cigar, eyes half-lidded as she exhaled smoke toward the ceiling. "Checking in. You've been making waves. Word on the PI circuit is, our new detective made quite the mess last night."

Chase narrowed his gaze. "You got in how, exactly?"

Without answering, she lifted the hem of her dress. The motion was calm, practiced. Her leg was toned, the smooth line of muscle visible beneath warm golden-brown skin. A garter hugged her upper thigh—sleek black leather with silver fastenings, elegant and functional. From a garter holster she drew... a wand.

Not some parlor trick prop. Its handle was silver chased with blue runic filigree, each glyph etched with the precision of a master spellwright. The obsidian shaft drank the light around it, and the sapphire at its tip glowed with a quiet, living pulse.

A real wand. Bonded. Expensive. Elite. One didn't carry something like that unless the wielder was the real thing—a trained practitioner of the Arcane, someone with discipline, lineage, and the kind of raw talent that couldn't be faked.

It told him everything he needed to know about her: Skye Anderson-Pierce was dangerous, and she knew it.

"Locks," she murmured, turning the wand once between elegant fingers, "are easily bypassed by those with the right tools, Mr. Cassidy."

Chase's mouth twitched, half-smirk, half-warning. He'd heard that tone before from people who underestimated how fast he could draw. But the way she held the wand told him she'd survive the mistake if she ever made it.

Skye tapped the wand gently against the coffee cup sitting on his nightstand. The liquid inside steamed instantly. She lifted the cup, took a sip—unbothered, unhurried—then offered it to him.

"Like you, Mr. Cassidy."

He took it, cautious. The heat was perfect; the scent of cinnamon and smoke lingered from her lips. He drank, watching as she re-holstered the wand beneath her dress with the same easy precision. Every movement said she was testing him—and enjoying it.

"I heard you had the day off," she said. "Funny thing—so do I."
Chase raised a brow. "That so?"

She stepped closer, picking up an envelope that rested at the foot of the bed—sealed, stamped, heavy.

"I thought I'd come by and square up the remainder of the Tran retainer."

Chase breath froze. "I just found the boy's body yesterday."

Skye's expression softened, the tease briefly fading. "And the family is grateful," she said. "We alerted them as soon as the First Arcane sent confirmation of recovery. They insisted the payout be delivered immediately." She hesitated—just a heartbeat. "I do wish," she added, more quietly, "that you had called me personally when you found him. But... given the circumstances—fleeing from a hoard of Mourned from what I was told—I understand why you didn't."

Chase set the mug down. "You're keeping really detailed tabs on me, counselor."

Her smile curved slow and bold. "As I mentioned at the office, my eyes are only for you, Mr. Cassidy." She pressed the envelope into his hand. It was weighty—too weighty. Thick with cash.

He gave it a small bounce in his palm. "Cash?"

"Always cash." she said, eyes glinting. "Some families prefer not to leave paper trails. Especially grieving ones."

"It's heavy."

"They're appreciative of your swift closure to their suffering," she replied. "They added a bonus. A... substantial one. I'm sure you'll find it satisfactory."

He slid the envelope into his jacket, still feeling its mass even after he released it.

Skye folded her arms lightly, leaning a hip against the bed post. "Plans for the day?"

"I've got errands." He started counting them off in his head: ammo, cleaner's, new holster. He tossed the envelope onto the bed. "Don't have time to shop for makeup or whatever it is you want."

Skye clicked her tongue. "Why do men always assume we just want to shop?" Her eyes flicked over him, calculating. Chase could feel the weight of it. She was dissecting him, same way he'd been doing since she lit that cigar. Two hunters circling the same fire.

"I already know what I want," she said. "Get dressed, Cassidy. Let's get to know each other."

He sighed, the sound halfway between annoyance and curiosity. "Turn around."

She arched a brow. "Why? You got something I haven't seen before?"

He ignored the jab. She stayed where she was, perched on the edge of his bed like she owned the place, smoke curling around her in lazy ribbons. He stood, the sheet sliding away. He knew she was watching—hell, she wanted him to know it. He didn't give her the satisfaction of a reaction.

The morning light cut across his skin, bronze and scarred. The runes etched along his ribs and forearms glowed faintly, pulsing in time with his heartbeat. He felt them stir under her gaze, a low thrum like static before a storm.

He reached for his trousers, keeping his focus on the rhythm of simple things—belt, shirt, holster, calm. Still, he could feel her eyes tracing the sigils across his skin, the way people look at something they half understand and can't quite leave alone.

Her attention drifted past him, toward the window.

A small smile touched her lips.

"Is that a trumpet?" she asked, voice warm and teasing. "I'd love to blow it one day."

Chase froze for half a heartbeat, boot in one hand, heat crawling up the back of his neck as the double meaning landed squarely between them. Skye's grin widened—slow, wicked, knowing.

He cleared his throat, reaching for his shirt like it could shield him from her amusement. He slid it on, buttoning it slowly just to buy himself a breath.

"I thought dames smoked cigarettes," he said, reaching for his tie. "Isn't a cigar a bit much?"

She grinned around the cigar. "Why would I smoke a small, flaccid thing? Cigars are long, thick, and brown—which is what I like."

Chase felt the corner of his mouth tighten—half amusement, half defense. She was playing him, testing how easily she could get under his skin. He'd dealt with worse, but not often this pretty.

She sank back into the chair with a dancer's grace, one leg crossing over the other. The hem of her dress rose an inch—just enough to reveal toned calves and the elegant line of her ankle. Her heels waited beside the chair, neatly aligned, like she'd prepared this moment long before he woke up.

She didn't ask.

Just extended a foot toward him, calm and expectant.

Chase raised a brow. "Really?"

Her smirk was answer enough.

He knelt, more out of curiosity than obedience, and picked up the first shoe. The leather was warm from her skin. As he guided her foot forward, his gaze dropped—out of habit, out of instinct, out of something he didn't want to name too loudly.

Her foot was surprisingly graceful. Strong arch. Firm but smooth skin. A dancer's balance in the way she held it steady. And a tattoo—small, inked along the side of her foot near the arch. Two sharp lines crossing under a sweeping curve. He tilted slightly to read it.

LIFE.

Stylized, almost like a mantra. Of course she'd have something like that.

He eased the shoe over her heel, fingers brushing the warm skin at her ankle. She didn't pull away. Didn't even blink. Just watched him with that same unnerving calm, as though she were studying him just as carefully.

He fastened the tiny buckle, slow enough to take in the detail but quick enough to pretend he wasn't.

The second shoe waited.

So did she—quiet, unwavering, leg shifting just enough to show she was in complete control of the moment.

Part of him appreciated her confidence. Another part recognized the danger in it.

But he couldn't deny this: she had a way of taking ordinary things and making them feel deliberate, electric—charged with meaning he couldn't quite pin down.

"Next one?" he asked, voice lower than he intended.

She lifted her other foot without a word.

She offered the other without a word.

Once both shoes were fastened, she rose and smoothed her dress. Chase straightened, adjusting his coat, matching her calm with his own. "Let's go," he muttered.

Skye linked her arm through his, smiling like she'd just won something.

"Now," she said, "was that so hard?"

Grabbing his coat he didn't answer, but the faintest grin tugged at his mouth as they stepped into the hall.

————

Imperio Imports was a den of illicit magic masked behind the guise of a legitimate trade shop. The storefront was modest: a polished oak sign, neatly arranged displays of exotic incense, rare books, and minor trinkets meant to fool the uninitiated. But the real business happened behind a heavy iron-reinforced door, past a velvet curtain only the trusted crossed.

Inside, the scent of gun oil and alchemical smoke mixed with the tang of old magic. Glass display cases lined the room, filled with enchanted firearms, wands, spell-etched knives, and charms promising everything from protection to destruction.

Behind the main counter stood Nate Mercer—a burly man with a silver-streaked beard and an easy confidence. He glanced up from inspecting a rune-carved rifle, eyes narrowing with amusement.

Chase and Skye entered with their arms interlaced, their movements fluid, almost natural, like they'd been doing it for years. Nate raised a brow, giving Chase a knowing smirk.

"Well, well," Nate said, setting the rifle down. "Looks like Cassidy's got himself a new lady. About time."

Chase rolled his eyes. "It ain't like that."

"But it will be," Skye said, sweetness sharpened by certainty.

Chase shook his head and gestured between them with a nod of respect. "Nate, this is Skye Anderson-Pierce. She's a sharp one."

Skye extended her hand, clearly pleased by the introduction. "Pleasure to meet you."

Nate took it with a firm shake, eyebrows lifting. "Anderson-Pierce? As In…the Anderson, Anderson & Pierce?"

"One of the Andersons," she replied, coolly amused. "The junior one that's not as grumpy."

Nate chuckled. "Didn't think the firm let their own walk into places like this."

Chase smirked. "She insisted."

"Oh," Skye added smoothly, linking her arm tightly through Chase's. "He just thinks he brought me along. I was already coming."

Nate laughed. "I like her."

"Yeah. I noticed," Chase muttered, shaking his head. He couldn't ignore the way Skye fit so easily at his side. There was something about her—dangerous and intriguing—that made him uneasy in a way he wasn't sure he disliked.

Nate folded his arms. "So, what are you looking for today, Cassidy?"

"Need a shoulder rig for a Colt 1911. Extra ammo. Arcane inscribe if you have." Chase glanced around at the inventory.

Skye tilted her head. "After what happened to you, I'd think you'd want something better suited for putting down the Mourned—or anything else that crawls about at night."

Nate paused mid-reach. "Wait. What do you know about the Mourned?"

Skye met his gaze calmly. "Revenant-class entities. Semi-corporeal, soul-bound, drawn to trauma, pain, and emotional suffering. Vulnerable to holy wards, fire-based magic, and dark iron fused with lunar elements." She nodded toward the case near Nate's elbow. "That silver-braided wardstock might slow them down, but it won't kill them. Not unless it's been hex-tempered. At least thats the theory"

Nate blinked. "Damn. And here I was thinking you were just a smartly dressed dame hanging off Cassidy's arm."

Skye smiled. "I carry the name of Anderson & Pierce because of my academic prowess not because of my good looks, Nate."

Chase gave a low chuckle. "Told you she was sharp."

Nate narrowed his eyes, now genuinely intrigued. "You studied that kind of thing? The Mourned aren't exactly common knowledge."

"Hudson Academy of Thaumaturgy & Arcane Sciences," she said as she paced slowly down the counter.

Nate let out a low whistle. "Hot damn. What're you doing slumming it in the Zone?"

Skye winked at Chase. "I love the company."

"I see," Nate said with a grin. "They swarm. When they do, normal bullets don't always cut it." He grabbed a black leather holster from behind the counter. "You might wanna consider something with a bit more punch."

Skye nudged Chase. "I concur. A little more firepower wouldn't hurt."

Chase sighed, picking up the Colt 1911 he'd taken off a goon the night before, checking its weight. Solid. Reliable. But something about the way Mercer smirked made him pause.

"That piece?" Nate said. "That's a muddy pistol, Cassidy."

"Muddy?"

"Means mundane," Nate explained, tapping the gun's frame. "It'll kill a man. Might even sting a low-ranked mage. But anything higher? You're just poking shadows with a stick."

Chase glanced down at the Colt, suddenly aware of its limits. "What's the fix?"

"Needs to be inscribed. Arcane disruption sigils, runic-steel reinforced barrel, spell-wrought munitions. Otherwise, you're just making noise."

Chase exhaled. "How long?"

"Couple days for basic. A week if you want it done right."

Skye smirked. "Considering his luck? Go for the week-long special."

Nate chuckled. "Figured as much."

He set the Colt aside and reached beneath the counter.

"That said... I might have something better."

He unlatched a black case. Inside sat two gleaming revolvers, long-barreled and heavy, with faint sigils burned into the steel and grips inlaid with bone-white ivory. Silver-flecked runes pulsed faintly with latent energy.

"Twin Arcane Duelers," Nate said, almost reverent. "Custom-built. Arcane ammo ready. Spell-wrought steel. Meant to end a fight fast."

Chase picked one up. The weight was perfect. The metal thrummed beneath his fingers, the sigils flaring softly to his touch.

"Client never came back for 'em," Nate added. "Figured they'd gather dust unless someone with sense came along."

Chase turned the revolver in his hand. "Nice build. But they're not really my style anymore. Six shots ain't enough these days."

Nate raised a brow. "No? Most folks fall in love with 'em."

"They're clean," Chase said, handing it back. "But they feel dated. I need something meaner. Louder."

"Fair enough."

Skye was watching him—soft smile, eyes thoughtful.

"What?" Chase asked.

"Oh, nothing," she said, clearly amused. "Just enjoying the view."

Chase scoffed but smirked anyway.

As Nate packed up the case, Skye's gaze drifted towards a pair of Colts in a suitcase set further back in the glass display." What's that?"

Nate followed her eyes to a worn leather suitcase with brass corners and a faint blue magical glow. "That? That's trouble wrapped in craftsmanship."

He set it on the counter, and rotated the case around to give Skye a better look.

Inside: two long-slide Colt pistols, sleek and deadly, their frames humming with old power. Sigils burned into the steel, grips inlaid with dark ivory. Their presence filled the room.

"The Reaper Twins," Nate began, lifting the pair of long slides with a kind of reverence. "Crafted by…

"Malik Virelli" Skye interrupted matter of factly " back when he worked for Sigilworks. Arcane Duelers—built for killing shamblers at ten paces. Virelli stopped crafting after the Spire Massacre."

Both men looked at her.

Nate blinked—impressed, caught off guard.

"Uh… yeah. That's right."

Most folks didn't know that.

Hell, most mages didn't know that.

Chase wasn't easily impressed, but the way she said it—matter-of-fact, no bragging, no hesitation—hit a nerve he didn't expect.

He'd met plenty of people who pretended to know things.

Skye wasn't pretending.

Nate rolled with the surprise, fingers adjusting his grip on the pistols.

"You're right," Nate said, warming to it now. "These in particular were used in the Canteno–Lyon duel. Lyon won… then vanished. No idea why. Long story, and they ended up here."

She gave a knowing nod, like she could fill in the gaps herself if she wanted to.

Chase leaned closer to the weapons, noting the etched names inside each barrel. "They have names."

"Damn right they do," Nate said—still eyeing Skye like she'd just solved a riddle nobody asked her to solve. "Most folks don't know the Twins 'history. Especially not—"

He managed not to finish the sentence, but Chase heard it anyway.

Especially not a woman.

Skye noticed.

Of course she did. She just smiled—sharp, almost teasing—and let Nate wonder where the hell she'd gotten her education.

Chase hid a small smirk of his own.

Every minute he spent with her, the list of things she knew grew longer.

And stranger.

And more impressive.

He hadn't expected to like that quite as much as he did.

"Effie and Pearl," Nate confirmed. "Virelli always named his guns. Said they'd treat you better if you treated them like people."

Skye nodded, voice soft. "They're beautiful. And dangerous."

Nate shut the case slowly. "And they're not for sale. Not yet. Some weapons pick their owner."

"Then they've been waiting," Skye said.

He raised an eyebrow.

"And how many walked in here thinking they were the right ones?" she asked.

"Plenty."

"But Chase isn't plenty," Skye said. "He's the one who'll need them."

Chase blinked. "Skye—"

She held up a hand. "You heard what he's up against. The Mourned. Ghost-bound killers walking the streets in borrowed skin. And you're going to let those girls," she nodded at the pistols, "to continue to gather dust while the city goes to hell?"

Nate folded his arms. "Anderson, I like your style, but those guns come with a price."

"Then don't trade them for coin," Skye said. "Trade them for purpose."

Nate narrowed his eyes. "Go on."

"How about Chase owes you for the Reapers. Keep that on the table. Add one favor from me—Anderson, Anderson & Pierce. We don't usually work in your world, but I've got access, information, and strings most people can't pull."

Nate studied her. "You'd cash that in for him?"

Skye didn't look away. "He's worth it."

The room fell quiet.

Then Nate sighed and grinned. "Damn. Didn't think I'd get lawyered inside my own shop."

He carefully placed the Reaper Twins—Effie and Pearl—next to Chase's hands. "These are yours now. Don't lose them. Don't waste them."

Chase stepped forward, gaze steady. He reached for Effie first. The moment his fingers curled around the grip, the etched hexagram flared with golden light, pulsing once—twice—then settling into a warm, rhythmic glow beneath his palm. A whisper of air brushed his ear, though no one else moved.

Then he lifted Pearl.

The instant his skin touched her frame, a harmonic chime rang out, faint but clear, like a tuning fork struck against the bones of the world. The twin pistols trembled—not with resistance, but revelation.

Suddenly, the sigils on both grips began to shift—the lines folding inward, curling like ancient locks disengaging.

New runes appeared, burned into the metal just below the surface —marks only visible now that someone *worthy* had claimed them. They weren't just decorative. They were alive.

Unlocking. Listening. Accepting.

His heart skipped once. Then both weapons matched his pulse. A heartbeat in metal. One in each hand.

The glow from the sigils cascaded up his arms, tracing faint lines across the spellbound marks already inscribed on his skin. His forearm wards reacted, burning gently beneath the surface like iron left in sun.

"They've never done that for anyone else," Nate whispered, backing away. "Not even their maker."

Chase held them both. No weight. No hesitation. They felt like extensions of his hands.   They *belonged*. "Then I guess they were just waiting," Chase muttered. "For me."

"They have," Skye said, watching him cool and steady. "They were just waiting for someone who could carry the weight."

Nate nodded. "You two are somethin 'else. I'll draw up the favor contracts later. Now get outta here before I start regrettin 'this. Oh and here take this ammo". Nate handed two boxes of arcane enhanced cartridges to Chase. "Ward piercers, and incendiaries and yes I know their illegal. Better in your hands than mine."

Chase gave him a scolding look before pocketing the boxes. As they stepped into the street, Chase glanced at her. This time, he didn't see just courtroom polish.

He saw the spine. The edge. The strategist.

"You didn't have to do that," he said quietly.

"Sure I did," she replied. "You've got a bad habit of underarming yourself for a battle."

Chase chuckled. "You might not know the streets, but damn, Anderson... you sure as hell know how to move through them."

She winked. "Stick around, Cassidy. I've got a few more surprises."

And for the first time since they met, he believed it. As they stepped outside Imperio Imports, the cold afternoon air wrapped around them, carrying the scent of grilled meat from a nearby street vendor and the faint tang of rain on concrete.

Skye turned to Chase with a playful smile, her raven black hair catching the glow of a nearby streetlamp. "So, what's next?"

Chase adjusted his coat, rolling his shoulders. "The cleaners."

Skye scoffed, grabbing his bundled clothes from his arm with a graceful flick of her wrist. "No, you're going to entertain me."

Before Chase could protest, she tossed his clothes to the waiting driver—a mountain of a man leaning casually against a sleek, dark sedan.

Luther "Lute" Holloway caught the bundle one-handed, his thick fingers wrapping around the fabric like a vice. Lute was mid-50s, dark-skinned, built like a freight train that had derailed and decided to keep going. Broad shoulders strained the seams of his tailored vest, and his bare forearms—thick as tree trunks—were corded with muscle and a lifetime of work.

Despite his sheer mass, he moved with the careful ease of a man who knew his own strength. His sharp eyes, hidden beneath the brim of a well-worn newsboy cap, flicked to Chase for a moment—assessing, measuring—but his expression remained unreadable.

Lute gave a knowing nod, his deep, gravel-and-velvet voice rolling out like distant thunder. "Lady Kim's Dry Cleaning, 125th. I'll have 'em pressed and ready by the evening."

Chase watched as Lute tipped his hat, then climbed into the car with the kind of deliberate, unhurried movement of someone who had never once in his life been rushed. The sedan's engine rumbled like a caged beast before it glided off into the Harlem afternoon light.

Chase exhaled sharply, brow furrowed. "You really don't take no for an answer, do you?" Skye linked her arm through his once again, flashing him a devilish grin.

"Not when I see something I want."

Chase snorted but let her pull him down the sidewalk. They walked at a leisurely pace, the late afternoon buzzing with life around them—kids playing, the occasional honk of a cab, distant jazz drifting from a smoky bar.

Skye reached into her clutch and pulled out a cigar. She held it between two fingers, gripping it with her lips as she patted her pockets.

"You got a light?"

Chase, still half-distracted by whatever game she was playing, snapped his fingers. A small spark flared to life at the tip of his thumb, catching the cigar's end with a controlled flicker.

Skye's playful smirk faltered. Her sharp eyes narrowed slightly, watching as the flame glowed yellow—warm, golden, unnatural.

Not arcane blue. Arcane magic—real magic—always burned a cool, electric blue, the color of raw aether. Even fire magic cast by Magi or elemental arcanists carried hints of that otherworldly hue.

This? This was different. Something about it felt wrong.

She inhaled deeply, letting the cigar smolder for a moment before exhaling a slow, measured stream of smoke. Her gaze flicked to Chase's hand, then back to his face.

"Huh," she muttered.

Chase caught the shift in her tone. "What?"

She shrugged, her easy smile sliding back into place like a mask. "Nothing. Just didn't peg you for the parlor trick type."

Chase let the comment slide, but he noticed something—she was watching him now, just a little closer. Meanwhile, a few passersby had stopped mid-step, their eyes darting toward the flame.

A man across the street paused near a lamppost, his gaze lingering a second too long before quickly moving along. A woman with pointed ears—Fey-blooded—muttered something to her companion before they hurried past.

Even in a place like Madhatten, magic drew attention. And whatever Chase had just done? It wasn't the kind of magic they were used to seeing.

Skye took another slow drag from her cigar, then gave Chase a knowing look. "So, ready for a night out?"

Chase sighed. It was going to be a long day.

They arrived at The Velvet Fork, a quiet, upscale restaurant tucked between brownstones, the kind of place that prided itself on discretion. As they stepped inside, a few heads turned—some out of curiosity, others with thinly veiled disdain.

Two colored people, proud and confident as well as being arcanists —was bound to draw attention. Skye, however, ate up the stares, leaning into Chase with a coy smirk, resting her hand on his forearm, and letting her fingers trace slow, absentminded circles against his sleeve.

She laughed at things he hadn't said, brushed her knee against his under the table—making a show of it. Chase exhaled through his nose, half amused, half exasperated. "You enjoy making people uncomfortable, don't you?"

Skye took a sip of her wine, eyes glinting. "Let them be uncomfortable, how often is it us that are ones feeling out of place or not wanted. I don't care, don't tell me you don't?"

"Not usually my aim," he muttered.

She leaned in slightly, voice lowering just enough for only him to hear. "I like the way they look at you, Cassidy. Like they don't know whether to be afraid or impressed."

He arched a brow. "And what about you?"

Skye's smirk widened. "Oh, I know exactly how I feel."

Their food arrived, and as they ate, the conversation shifted. Skye tilted her head, watching him with a curious expression.

"Alright, tell me something real, Chase Cassidy. I know you fought in the war. I know you were in the Army. But what about before? Where'd you come from?"

Chase chewed thoughtfully, wiping his mouth before answering. "Orphanage. St. Emilani's. Me and Diego, my best friend ran off when we were sixteen, hopped a ship to England. From there we found our way eventually to France and into the Foreign Legion."

Skye rested her chin on her hand, eyes studying him. "So, no family?"

"My father," Chase said, measuring his words. "Elijah Cassidy. He was an artificer. A damn good one. Taught me a few things before he passed."

She caught the way his tone changed, the subtle shift in his posture. "And your mother?"

His jaw tightened just slightly. "Not much to say."

Skye let the silence settle before steering the conversation elsewhere.

"You know," Skye said, her voice softer now, eyes fixed on something distant, "we're not so different, you and I."

Chase tilted his head, curious.

"I wasn't born in Havana like most people assume. It was a little place—*San Diego de Núñez,* east of the city. My mother came from the Ganga, descended from the Taino and African maroon communities who fought to stay free long after the chains were broken. She was a *Caracaracol,* a kind of shaman. Her roots ran deep—Taino spirits, African fire. And all of it came through her like music."

She paused, just long enough for the weight of it to settle.

"My father was from Madrid, Spain. A sorcerer in service to the Spanish navy—old world magic, strict and exacting. He was drawn to my mother's power...but power like hers doesn't bend easily."

She hesitated, eyes dimming a little. "When I was still small, he tried to take me from her. Said he could give me a better life—his version of one. Papers, money, access to the European academies. He tried to claim me like a prize. That's when everything went south."

Her jaw tightened slightly. "My mother didn't fight him with fists. She fought him with spirits, with will, with every ancestor standing behind her. And she won. But the cost was exile. Silence. She raised me on her own after that, and we never spoke his name again."

Skye turned to him, voice steady now, the steel beneath the silk shining through. "So when people try to box me in—tell me I'm too much of this or not enough of that—I just smile. Because I know exactly who I come from."

"Sounds like an interesting mix."

"It was," she said with a small laugh. "Magic and the sea—both in my blood. My father eventually got caught up in something, got himself killed, and my mother... well, she soon was very ill. Died shortly afterward."

Chase set his fork down. "That's why you work for Anderson?"

Skye shrugged. "Thomas and Donald took me in when I was four—raised me as their own. I lived a good life with them. They even gave me an education, a job, and taught me how to work the system. But I never forgot where I came from."

She watched his reaction for a moment before continuing. "They sent me to Gallowglass Academy first—proper finishing academy for the magically inclined. Good on paper, but mostly pedigree and manners.

After that, I pushed for Hudson. Hudson Academy wasn't a school, it was a crucible. Hard. Brutal sometimes. It taught me to control what I had. Enough to pass the Arcane Aptitude exam and then off to Cornell Law."

Chase arched a brow. "Hudson? You mentioned that at Imperio. That place had a hell of a reputation."

Skye leaned back in her chair, casually crossing one leg over the other. "It did. I was First Duelist in my final year. Top of my class."

Chase let out a low whistle. "Damn. That's no small feat."

"No , its not especially for women, who are not allowed to participate".

"So, how did you…" Chase started to ask before she touched his lips with her finger.

"Thats a mystery you can unravel later." She smirked, then without breaking eye contact, reached beneath the table and pulled the hem of her dress up— perhaps to high. Toned legs revealed the gleam of steel nestled in a black garter holster.

Chase's brows climbed a little higher.

From a table across the room, an older woman let out a sharp gasp, her pearl necklace trembling as she clutched at her companion's arm. A few nearby patrons turned. Skye turned toward the source of the outrage, smile slow and deliberate. She winked. The older woman nearly dropped her teacup.

Unbothered, Skye returned to Chase and drew the weapon free—the sleek, midnight-black arcalam. She set it on the table between them.

"Family heirloom," she said, running her fingers along the etched grooves. "My grandfather's. Paternal side. He was a duelist back in Spain— before the crackdown."

Chase reached for it slowly, reverently. "Not your father's?"

"He wanted nothing to do with it. Too much history. Too many ghosts." She shrugged, resting her chin in her palm again. "So it passed to me."

Chase turned the arcalam in his hand, studying its weight. "Heavy legacy."

"Only if you can't carry it," she murmured.

He set it back down with care. "You always like showing off in public?"

Skye's smile returned, lazy and unapologetic. "Only when the right people are watching."

Chase didn't answer right away.

He watched her—the way she held her gaze, unblinking and unbothered, like she was always two moves ahead. The candlelight played along the edge of her jaw, glinting off the curl of her hair and the dark ink spiraling down her arm. Everything about her said control—and yet, somehow, she never seemed to need to assert it.

It hit him then, with the weight of a trigger pull: Skye wasn't afraid of power. She wore it. Wielded it. Played with it like smoke in her hands. Not to intimidate—to test who could keep up. And gods help him—that did something to him.

A flicker of heat sparked under his collarbone. Not imagined—felt. His shirt tightened subtly as the sigil beneath it pulsed, a faint shimmer of dull red light crawling beneath the fabric for half a second, barely perceptible. But it was there. So was she.

Skye's eyes dropped ever so slightly to the faint glow, a slow grin curving her lips like a fuse catching flame.

"So its not a rumor. You are spellbound. Those sigils and wards. The runes etched on your body."

Chase didn't flinch. He didn't confirm or deny it either. Just met her gaze—steady, unreadable—as the last ember of light faded beneath his collar.

"I don't usually glow for just anyone," he said quietly.

Skye lifted her glass, amusement dancing in her eyes. "No. I suppose not."

"And?"

She tilted her head, her dark eyes searching his face. "Did it hurt?"

There was no teasing in her voice, no playfulness—just quiet curiosity.

Chase was silent for a beat before he answered, voice low. "Yeah."

Skye's brows furrowed slightly. "How bad?"

"Bad enough," he said dismissively, picking up his drink.

She watched him for a moment before exhaling. "I have magical tattoos too, I'm sure you noticed. Early spellwork—nothing like yours, but…" She turned her wrist, where faint, shimmering inscriptions trailed along her skin, shifting subtly as if responding to her mood. "They were meant to help me focus my magic faster. My professors called it an early precursor to spellbinding."

Chase frowned, tilting his head. "They don't burn?"

She gave him a small smile. "No."

"Then they are nothing like spellbinding," he stated flatly.

The words landed harder than he intended. Chase saw it immediately—the way Skye's breath shortened, barely a hitch. The way her eyes fluttered, once. The faint flush rising beneath her cheekbones.

It wasn't pride. It was something softer.

A quiet need for connection that he had cut a little too sharply.

Her smile faltered—just for a heartbeat—but it was enough.

She looked away, collecting herself, and when she spoke again, her voice was even, but thinner at the edges.

"They shift, but they don't hold power like yours. They're amplifications. But they still had to be tapped in."

Chase let his gaze linger on the glowing marks along her arm—the spirals and angled lines that pulsed like tiny heartbeats.

"…Amplifications?"

She nodded once, eyes still lowered.

"I… didn't have a natural well to draw from. They thought I was a sparker."

Chase knew what that meant. Weak arcane throughput. Unreliable spellcasting. Flickers instead of flames.

She took a slow breath. "My magic worked. Then it didn't. Then it did again. These—" she brushed a fingertip along a shifting glyph, "—were designed to help me connect to the Aether. They provide a bridge to what's blocked. They're not spellbound markings. Just… aids."

He realized he'd hurt her. Not intentionally, but enough. The realization settled in his chest with a quiet weight. Chase softened his voice.

"That must've taken a hell of a lot of guts."

Her eyes flicked up—surprised, almost relieved—as if she wasn't expecting him to meet her halfway. He saw the slight easing of her shoulders, the way her breath finally leveled out.

He cleared his throat and nodded toward her arm. "That hurt?"

"A little," she murmured—still softer than before. "Nothing like spellbinding, I'm sure."

Something in his jaw tightened. He tried to shrug it off. "Pain was the least of it."

She frowned at his detachment. "Is that why you do not like to talk about it?"

Chase took a slow sip of bourbon, eyes fixed on the middle distance. "What's there to talk about?"

The silence stretched—not cold, but careful.   Purposeful. Then, gently, Skye reached out.   Her fingertips brushed the thin scar across the bridge of his nose, then the one beneath his right cheekbone. Her touch was featherlight, tracing old battles like reading Braille.

"May I?" she asked, voice barely above a whisper.

Chase didn't move. Didn't flinch. Just nodded.

 "How did you get these?"

He paused. A memory passed behind his eyes like smoke. "Artillery strike."

"Before the spellbinding?"

"Yeah. France. I was already wounded… bleeding out when the brass decided I'd make a good candidate."

"And they carved the magic into you while you were still healing from that?"

"They didn't wait." His voice was quiet. "Didn't care. Figured if I died, I wasn't meant to carry it."

As her fingers lingered, a faint flicker passed—his sigils responding to hers, a brief glow like heat lightning under their skin. Not pain. Not power. Recognition.

She blinked in surprise. So did he.

Her hand slowly fell to her lap.

Chase drew in a steady breath. "You always like digging through people's pasts?" The edge of his voice had softened, no longer sharp—more like a shield lowered halfway.

"Only the interesting ones," she replied, managing a small grin. "And you, Chase Cassidy... you're fascinating."

He let out a dry chuckle, shaking his head. A smirk ghosted across his lips. "You're trouble."

"And yet," she said, leaning back with that emboldened gleam returning to her eyes, "here you are." Their conversation drifted on after that—light, easy, unforced. Not the shallow nonsense people used to fill silence with, not What's your favorite color? or Do you like jazz? Nothing rehearsed or delicate.

Just small truths. Bits of life. Pieces of themselves offered without ceremony. He found himself... surprised. Skye wasn't timid—far from it. She was bold, sharp, and fearless in ways that sometimes made his pulse jump. But beneath the polish, beneath the arrogance and the witty comebacks, she had a kind of raw honesty he wasn't used to. No pretense. No games. Just saying what she felt when she felt it. There was an openness there—almost naïve at times, but not in a foolish way. More like she simply refused to armor herself the way everyone else did in this city. Like she didn't know she was supposed to. It was... refreshing. A relief he didn't know he'd been missing.

He caught himself watching her a little too long during one of those pauses, and the quiet smile she gave him in return was soft, almost shy —another surprise. Then the moment passed, subtle and warm, and they stepped out into the cooling night.

Evening settled over Harlem, warm and restless. The lamplight gleamed on wet cobblestones as the city exhaled the tension of another day. Jazz drifted from open doorways, winding through the air like smoke. Chase and Skye walked side by side along Lenox Avenue—close enough to feel each other's presence without touching. Their conversation carried on from earlier, light but honest, the kind that didn't strain to exist.

"So," Skye asked, tilting her head at him, "what did you do before all this? Before being a detective. Before the spellbinding."

"Odd jobs," Chase said. "B-Patrols. Arcane disturbances. Breaking up alley fights before some idiot set themselves on fire with stolen glyph-chalk. Nothing glamorous."

She smiled at that—soft, genuine. He wasn't used to that kind of listening.

"My turn," he said. "Tell me more about you. Did you ever go back to Cuba?"

She nodded, tucking her hands deeper into her coat pockets. "Yes," she said. "After law school."

Chase slowed his pace to match hers.

"I didn't go with family. Didn't stay in any hotels." Her gaze drifted somewhere far beyond Harlem. "I went back to San Diego de Núñez. Where my mother's people came from. Where the Maroon blood still runs thick."

He remained silent. She wasn't finished.

"I waited tables. Slept on borrowed mattresses. Performed in cabarets. And when money got tight..." She threw him a sly sideways glance. "I posed for painters," she said, then hesitated—just long enough for him to catch it. "Mostly with... very little clothing."

Chase raised a brow.

"So nude?"

She nodded once, unflinching. Her eyes searched his face, quietly gauging whether he'd judge her. "Nude," she confirmed. "Some of those paintings ended up in galleries. One of them..." She allowed herself a small, wry smile. "One of them hangs over my bed. Full figure. No illusions, no magical retouching"

A warm tension curled in the air between them. "Too scandalous?" she teased. "Do you think that makes me loose?"

Chase didn't look away. "No. I've seen things. Done things. That doesn't bother me." And it didn't. Hell, he'd slept with a woman he'd known for barely an hour at the Midnight Martini. Judging Skye for posing in a painting would've been damned hypocritical. He wasn't that kind of man—and whatever Skye had done to survive or express herself? That was her business. Nothing in him found fault in it.

Something subtle eased in her shoulders—relief she didn't try to hide. "I wanted to reconnect without pretense," she said softly. "No last name. No firm behind me. Just… living. Just the drumbeat and the heat. You ever just live, Cassidy?"

"Not in the cards for me," he stated bluntly. There was a moment of uncomfortable silence—not awkward, just vulnerable. Skye noticed, as she always did, but didn't press.

Instead, she shifted gears. "So… any leads on the Fey children investigation?"

Chase's jaw tightened. "Yeah," he said quietly. "Some."

They continued walking, the street noise dimming around them. "Tran," he said. "Eight-year-old boy. His body torn apart. A shame."

Skye's face fell, horror flickering behind her eyes. "I heard from the reports.

Exactly how did it happen?"

"Hollowed out," Chase said. "Not just blood. Essence. His Fey essence."

"That sounds like necromancy."

"Maybe."

He shook his head. "It's the Mourned."

Her breath hitched. "The Mourned don't… I've never heard of them attacking people, let alone a child. They feed off the emotional essence, usually from animals. Sometimes insects."

"They do now, apparently." Chase said grimly. "And they're organized. I tracked them through the cathedral tunnels. They were feral but controlled as someone's directing them."

She stopped. "You went down there alone?"

"It wasn't the plan," he muttered. "It just happened."

Skye's gaze softened—grief and resolve in equal measure. "How bad is it?" she asked.

Chase looked down Lenox Avenue, into Harlem's dark arterial lines. "Bad," he murmured. "Worse than anyone realizes. And this is just the start." Across the street, a group of men had gathered, waving signs and shouting slogans:

"No more witches in our schools!"

"Cleanse the bloodline!"

"Hexes kill!"

A larger cluster blocked the sidewalk up ahead—voices rising, anger swelling like a coming storm.

Skye followed his gaze. "Well," she murmured, "there goes our peaceful evening."

Chase exhaled, rolling his shoulders back. "Stay close."

She slid her hand subtly near her dress hem—close to the Arcalam. "I wasn't planning on wandering off." Then she stepped closer and laced her arm through his, drawing herself flush against his side with quiet, unwavering certainty. The gesture wasn't fear. It wasn't posturing. It was deliberate.

Chase felt the shift immediately. A silent message: I'm with you. Suddenly, a car engine roared. A black Ford came speeding through the crowd. The driver swerved to avoid a thrown rock, lost control, and the car jumped the curb with a screech, smashing into a lamppost just ten feet in front of them. Glass exploded. Sparks hissed from the busted vehicle.

Skye froze, but Chase was already moving—grabbing her and spinning her behind him. The doors burst open. Three kids—no older than fourteen—scrambled out, coughing and wide-eyed. One of them had a faint magical sigil glowing at his wrist. A shift-drifter, a arcane street rider, someone gifted with an arcane talent focused on driving.

An agitator pointed. "Witch-bloods! They caused it!"

Chase stepped forward, his coat flaring as his hand dipped inside. The agitator—a squat, red-faced man in a porkpie hat—snarled and took a step closer.

"Maybe you're one of 'em too," he spat eyeing Chase and Skye. "We don't need your kind bringing more danger—"

Effie cleared her holster. The black grip of Chase's new custom 1911 gleamed in his hand, aimed right at the man's head. The agitator froze mid-step, color draining from his face.

One of the others grabbed his arm. "Let's go. Ain't worth it."

But the first man just stood there—locked, breath held, staring into the cold barrel of Chase's long slide. Until Skye's hand came down gently on Chase's wrist.

No panic. No tremor. No hesitation.

Just calm pressure, enough to lower the weapon without breaking eye contact with the agitator. "You're done here," she said, her voice smooth as glass.

The agitator swallowed hard, stepped back, and the group retreated —muttering curses but keeping a wide berth as they melted back into the crowd. Chase exhaled slowly and slid Effie back into the shoulder rig beneath his coat.

But what held him wasn't the fading tension or the dispersing crowd.

It was her. Skye's composure—unshaken, steady, sharp—hit him harder than the adrenaline did. Most people flinched when a gun came out. Most people froze. Most people panicked. Not her.

She moved with the same cool certainty he'd only ever seen in Isabelle—the only other woman he'd known who could stand firm in a moment that could've turned bloody in a heartbeat. Isabelle had that same steel, that same sharp focus that didn't crack under pressure.

He hadn't thought he'd ever see that again. But here Skye was —breathing easy, collected, her presence pulling the heat out of the confrontation like a cooling spell. She looked up at him then, reading the last trace of tension in his shoulders, and let a smirk tug at the corner of her lips.

"You ever dance?" she asked trying to break the tension.

He blinked. "What?"

"Dance," she repeated. "Drums. Rhythm. Jazz. You do any of that? Or are you just all brooding and bullets?"

He let out a low chuckle—almost reluctant, but real. "I can manage."

"Good." She lifted one hand high, turning toward the curb, her voice bright again.

"Taxi!"

———

The elevator hummed softly as it ascended toward the upper floors of the Heights District, once Columbia University, now repurposed into elite housing and administrative offices. The proud halls of academia had long been gutted. Lecture halls became luxury flats, libraries were emptied of knowledge deemed "dangerous," and stone archways now bore the insignia of federal authority.

Skye's duplex apartment occupied the upper west corner of what had once been the main law building, now a sleek six-level residence steeped in legacy and quiet rebellion. Her adopted family had owned it for years. It was a rare sanctuary in a city that had learned to fear magic and envy the few who still walked with power.

When the elevator doors slid open, Chase and Skye stepped onto the polished floor of the old-world building hallway. The lighting was low, the sconces casting long golden streaks across marble and mahogany.

Waiting to board, with all the subtlety of a loaded musket, stood Mrs. Weatherby — fur-draped, pearl-armored, and radiating disapproval like it paid rent. At her feet: Ms. Prudence, her famously mean-spirited Boston Terrier, snorting like a steaming teapot.

Weatherby's eyes snapped to Skye instantly, scanning the tailored silhouette, the neckline that dared to breathe, the above-knee cut dress that suggested confidence rather than apology.

Her voice cracked like old bone.

"Miss Anderson," she sniffed. "One might think a proper lady would show a touch more modesty."

Skye smiled sweetly — the kind of smile that made sugar feel bland — and laced her arm through Chase's like he was her favorite co-conspirator. "Oh Mrs. Weatherby you should know by now there is nothing proper about me."

Then, as she leaned in like whispering a secret meant to be overheard, she lifted one leg, slow and elegant, just enough to reveal the garter strap clinging to her thigh.

Mrs. Weatherby recoiled as if slapped. Her cheeks bloomed crimson;

Ms. Prudence barked once in horror.

But Skye wasn't done.

As she and Chase continued down the hallway, just before the elevator doors began to close, Skye glanced over her shoulder with a final grin—and lifted the back of her dress, ever so briefly, flashing the curve of her bare backside like it was a punctuation mark.

A bold, deliberate full slap.

Mrs. Weatherby let out a choking gasp so sharp Chase thought she might actually combust on the spot. Her fingers fumbled at the elevator buttons as she disappeared into the car, clutching her dog and handbag like twin holy relics.

Chase blinked, then exhaled through a crooked smile. "Well, she won't forget that sight."

Skye tugged her dress back into place with the air of someone perfectly aware of her wickedness. "Sometimes," she said, tossing her hair over one shoulder, "words just don't get the point across."

Chase coughed back a laugh. "Apologies Mrs. Weatherby—"

Skye spun and blocked him just outside her door.

"If we're to be friends, Chase Cassidy," she said, voice low and edged in steel, "don't ever apologize for me. I know exactly what I'm doing."

He opened his mouth to explain—to soften the moment—but she didn't wait. She grabbed his lapels and kissed him.

Not a flirtation. Not a test. A kiss that demanded to be felt—slow, deep, and unyielding. A kiss that said: this is real.

When she pulled away, Chase was left reeling, his breath uneven, his hands still resting at her hips. He looked down almost shocked that he was touching her so familiarly "Well, I am sorry."

"Don't apologize to me either" she murmured, lips barely brushing his.

Then she turned, unlocked the door, and slipped inside.

Skye's apartment was a living portrait—art from Cuba, Paris, and forgotten islands, books stacked like altars, and soft jazz playing low in the background. The air was thick with the scent of jasmine, tobacco, and old paper — the perfume of memory and rebellion.

Chase stood just inside the doorway, caught somewhere between awe and instinct, watching her move through the space like she owned it— and everything in it.

She stepped onto the plush carpet and sighed, kicking off her heels with a groan of relief. "Finally," she muttered, flexing her toes and rolling her shoulders like she'd just dropped a hundred pounds of courtroom tension.

From the hallway, a voice called out dryly.

"You shedding your dignity already, Skye?"

Nadine Holloway—tall, dark, and no-nonsense—appeared in the doorway, a laundry basket hooked effortlessly on one hip and a fresh silk robe draped over her arm. Her uniform was crisp, but her posture was relaxed. Too relaxed for someone speaking to her employer.

Chase straightened slightly, studying her.

Nadine wasn't the kind of pretty that announced itself; hers was quieter, composed, the kind of beauty that knew exactly what it was worth and didn't need to prove a damn thing. Where Skye had wild, untamed edges—heat and motion and reckless light—Nadine carried herself like a pillar carved from calm stone.

A contrast. But not a lesser one.

And more than that…

She'd called her Skye. Not "Miss Anderson." No hesitation. No caution in her tone. That told Chase plenty. This wasn't a maid speaking to her mistress. This was someone who knew Skye's storms and had weathered enough of them to stop flinching.

Someone close. Trusted. Deeply familiar.

He filed that away.

"Don't mind her," she added, sweeping her eyes over Chase with a raised brow. "You will get used to her free-spirit, Mr. Cassidy."

Skye just grinned as she began unfastening the buttons of her dress, letting it slink from her frame in one fluid motion. She kicked it away without looking. "You know I hate armor at home, Nadine."

Nadine sighed, picking up he discarded fabric. "I know you hate hangers too."

Chase's eyes drifted away and then back again — helpless, really — drawn like a moth to a woman surrounded in flame. Damn.

Her body was a dancer's paradox — lithe but powerful, soft in the right places, forged in others. Her skin, that golden brown shade, like honeyed wood warmed by the sunrise, caught the lamplight like a spell. The inkwork along her left arm shimmered with subtle pulses — tribal spirals, fierce and sacred, alive across the surface.

Skye's fingers found the bandeau and unhooked it in a single, fluid motion, like she was unbuckling a weapon. She peeled it away with a soft breath, and her breasts fell free, high and heavy, round and full, as if relieved to finally breathe. Chase's eyes moved instinctively—then locked.

She wasn't shy about it. Wasn't performing. Just shedding something that didn't belong to her anymore. She tossed the offending garment over her shoulder without looking.

"I'm done with those."

Nadine caught it midair, barely flinching. "And I'm done pretending I don't live in a shrine to chaos."

Skye smirked at that, then turned—just slightly—toward Chase. The glow from the floor lamp danced along her skin, that rich shade of bronze kissed with fire, like a tree catching sunrise in its grain, alive with depth and warmth. And the tattoos across her chest and collarbone shifted subtly, weaving along the outer curve of each breast, sacred marks that moved as she breathed, as if they had their own pulse.

Chase's mouth was dry. He tried not to stare. Failed.

"Burn that monstrous thing, Nadine," Skye added. "I'll never wear it again. My girls are too big to be strangled like that."

She cupped her breasts lightly as she said it, half-joking, but her voice was absolute.

And then his gaze slipped lower—unapologetically this time. Her stomach, flat and firm, tightened slightly as she shifted her weight. Her hips, generous and defined, curved outward in a way that drew his eyes like gravity.

Her thighs, smooth and sculpted, parted just enough for his breath to hitch as her fingers slid to her hips.

And just like that, her knickers slipped down.

No fanfare. No hesitation. No shame.

And when the thin fabric passed over her thighs, Chase caught a glimpse of black curls nestled between her legs—untamed, natural, the kind of detail that made his pulse thrum with heat. She stepped out of them casually, like she was stepping into the earth itself. And then, with a playful flick of her foot, she kicked the panties straight at him.

They hit him square in the face.

He blinked, stunned, the scent of her still clinging to the air between them.
He peeled them off slowly, like they might burn through his fingers, and stared at the wisp of fabric in his hand. He didn't know what to do with them. Hold them? Drop them? Frame them?

Hell.

Skye turned again, just for herself—a slow, ballerina-like pivot, arms rising overhead as she stretched, long and fluid. The motion pulled her body taut, revealing the sculpted lines of her back, the power in her calves, the smooth glide of muscle under skin.

She wasn't putting on a show. She was simply *being*. And she was radiant.

Every inch of her bore strength and softness in equal measure—a woman built by will, not whim, by fire and grace and something Chase couldn't name. She turned and walked toward him, bare feet silent on carpet, hips swaying in that measured, queenly way a regent would direct her court.

"I don't dress for the world when I'm here," she said softly, eyes fixed on his. "Only for myself."

And Chase—scarred, spellbound and too used to silence—stood there, still holding her underwear in his hands like a man who'd just been stripped of reason.

She stopped a breath away from him. Naked. Beautiful. Unbothered. Chase took it all in enraptured. The swell of her breasts rose and fell with calm confidence. The black waves between her thighs caught the light. Her tattoos shimmered like starlight inked into flesh.

And then she smiled. Not to seduce, but to declare. Like she'd just offered him a truth too big for words and dared him to look away.

"Do you like what you see?" she said softly.

He drew in a slow breath, grounding himself. Letting the moment stretch. His voice was low, unreadable. He drew in a slow breath, grounding himself as the moment stretched between them. His voice came out low, unreadable.

"I do. But Skye... you barely know me. Do you really think—"

But even as the words left him, he knew the truth. He was already hers. He felt it in the tightening of his chest, in the dryness at the back of his throat, in the way his thoughts scattered behind his eyes like smoke caught in a draft.

Chase Cassidy had faced fire, war, death, demons—things that clawed at the body and scraped at the soul. None of them made him hesitate. None of them unsteadied him the way she did, standing there with nothing to hide.

Because Skye wasn't seductive. She wasn't performing. She wasn't teasing. She was simply being—utterly herself, stripped of every layer of pretense and expectation. A woman who lived with that same raw honesty she fought with. A woman who didn't armor herself the way the rest of the world did. Her boldness hit him harder than any arcane blow.

Not because she was uncovered—he'd seen plenty of bodies, been with women he barely remembered the names of. But Skye? This was different. This wasn't impulse or heat. This was her standing in the open, offering truth instead of seduction. Presenting herself without apology. Without shame. Without games.

Almost as if she were saying: This is me. Decide. And he understood that it wasn't recklessness. It was trust. It was bravery. It was her way of meeting the world head-on, demanding honesty in return. Maybe it was moving too fast. Maybe they should've taken more time. Maybe he should've stepped back. But Chase Cassidy knew exactly what this was. Knew exactly what she was offering. And what scared him wasn't the pace —It was that he didn't want to step back. Not even a little.

Skye tilted her head, cutting him off. "If I could pose nude for a painter I barely knew and never really liked, I can stand bare before a man I admire. This is me." She stepped forward, her tone softening but never losing its edge. "Besides, I saw yours. You can see mine. Fair is fair, Mr. Cassidy."

Her fingers brushed a loose curl behind her ear. "And besides people forget—freedom is natural. Shame isn't. It's something we're taught. Something pushed on us by a world too afraid to face its own reflection."

She let the silence linger, then turned around slowly and added as shew circled him, "The body isn't lewd, Chase. It's honest. The naturalist movement taught me that. No lies, no masks, no corsets to keep the truth tucked away. Just breath and skin, and the way sunlight feels on both. You strip away judgment with the clothes."

Her gaze held his. "And I'd rather be honest than decent by someone else's standards." He stared at her a moment longer in awe before glancing away, the faintest smirk tugging at his mouth.

"Come." she beckoned. Grabbing his hand. Chase followed her into her bedroom. There he spotted the nude painting she mentioned on their evening walk. It was Skye, a year or two younger, hair longer, flowing past her waist standing gracefully near a waterfall. He could have stared at that painting for hours, but the real thing demanded his attention. On they pressed into her private bathroom to find that Nadine already had the bath water running. Hot steam rose from the large basin, welcoming and inviting.

Letting go, Skye sank into the bath with a sigh of satisfaction, the water lapping around her collarbones, steam curling up past the mirror like incense. Chase leaned on the doorway, arms crossed.

"Hand me that soap, will you?" she asked casually.

Before Chase could move, a towel snapped through the air and landed perfectly beside the tub.

"Here's the soap," came Nadine's voice from the hallway. She stepped in without looking, slightly flustered, holding a small wicker basket with folded robes and fresh towels. Her eyes locked on Chase like a hawk tracking a mouse in the middle of an open field. She placed the bar of soap in his hand.

"And while you're at it, Mr. Cassidy," she added, setting down the bundle with a *thump*, "you can explain what exactly your intentions are with my young lady."

Chase blinked. "We're just talking." He said with a slight stammer.

"Mm-hmm. And I suppose you just talk with anyone in steam-filled rooms while they're stark naked."

Skye let out a laugh from the tub. "Nadine, leave the man alone."

"Just making sure he knows," Nadine said, turning toward the door, "if he steps out of line, you know where I keep the cast iron."

Chase gave a small, tight nod. "Understood."

Nadine vanished down the hall with a muttered, "I raised better wolves in my kitchen."

"I dont think your maid like me" Chase said when Nadine was out of ear shot.

Skye's eyes sparkled as she leaned her head back against the rim of the tub."She likes you, and Nadine is not my maid, she is my life crisis manager." Skye said, smiling lazily as she dipped the sponge into the water. Her voice was casual, but her eyes tracked him.

Chase started to apologize but remembering her early warning, he simply muttered "She's got a funny way of showing it," keeping his gaze fixed somewhere between the tiled floor and the cracked window.

"You stay over there much longer," she said, the water sloshing gently as she lifted one bare arm to lather her shoulder, "I might think you like watching."

"I do," Chase said simply—no shame, no grin, just the truth, steady as a heartbeat. That answer made her pause. Not because it surprised her, but because it didn't. He had the discipline to look away—but not the desire. And that told her more about him than anything he'd said.

" Here," she said standing, offering him the bar of soap without covering herself. "Wash my back, please."

Chase stepped forward and took the bar from her fingers. He wet it in the bathwater and slowly ran it across her back. Her skin was warm, smooth, soft in some places, firm in others. He felt the dancer's muscles beneath the surface as his hands drifted lower, tracing the contours of her waist. Then he stopped himself.

"Don't stop," she said softly.

She reached back, her hands covering his. Gently, she guided them down to her hips, then wrapped his arms around her. They stood there in silence—Skye inside the warm bath, Chase outside, arms encircling her.

"I could get used to this," she murmured.

"I think we'd better stop before…"

"Before you fall in love?" she whispered, finishing for him, teasingly.

"What?" he asked, caught off guard.

She chuckled, then dipped beneath the water. A moment later, she surfaced, curls slicked back, her skin glistening like warm bronze. "Dry me off," she said, standing and stepping out.

"You're serious."

"I don't play games unless I intend to win."

She tossed him the towel that Nadine had expertly thrown to the floor. He caught it, stepped forward, and began drying her—slowly, almost reverently. Her skin was warm beneath his hands, her scent soft and intoxicating in the quiet room.

"You act like we've known each other for years," he murmured.

Skye tilted her head, eyes bright with mischief and something deeper."Maybe we have. Perhaps in a past life." She paused, studying his face. "You do believe in reincarnation, don't you, Cassidy? I mean—where do you think all that energy goes when you die?"

Chase kept drying her shoulders, hands steady even as her words tugged at something unguarded inside him.

Reincarnation.

Maybe some people found comfort in that idea—souls looping back around, lives bleeding into one another like pages reused. Maybe energy did recycle, maybe it burned out, maybe it scattered like ash in the wind. He'd seen too much death to romanticize it. Too many bodies emptied of magic, of warmth, of anything that resembled a soul. Whatever came after… he wasn't sure anyone truly knew. He wasn't sure he wanted to.

Still, a part of him—some small stubborn spark—liked the thought that souls could meet again. Liked the thought that maybe he had known her before. Liked it more than he cared to admit. But he didn't say any of that. Instead, he gave a small, bemused shake of his head.

Skye smiled at his reaction—soft, knowing—and turned away. She walked toward the vanity, drying her hair as she went, curls catching the low lamplight as they darkened from damp to velvet.

"Tell me something, Cassidy. Have you ever been in love?"

He unfastened his holster, then paused. "Yeah. Or... I thought so."

"If you have to think about it," she said," it wasn't love. You'd know."

"And you?"

"I love many things—art, rhythm, women's laughter, a good cigar. But love like the poets write about?" She met his gaze in the mirror. "Not yet, but I think I'm close"

A beat passed.

"Tell me about Diego," she asked, softly now, like she'd just peeled another layer back.

Chase glanced away, eyes narrowing slightly—not guarded, just... remembering. "What about him?"

She shrugged gently, pulling her legs up beneath her. "You two are close. Yo mentioned St. Emilani's?"

He nodded once. The name alone stirred something beneath his ribs. "Yeah. That place was brutal. Diego made it bearable." He leaned against the bathroom wall the shadows hugging his profile as the memory unfolded—his voice low, not sentimental, but not cold either.

"You know the kind of place where kids disappear and no one asks why? That was Emilani's. Wards on the doors, prayers on the walls... but none of it was for us. It was for show. For control. For keeping the monsters *in*, not out."

"Diego showed up two days after I did. Thin, loud, too pretty for a place like that. A transfer from another orphanage he had run away from. He got beaten up on his first night for talking back to one of the older kids. I broke the guy's nose the next morning with a tray from the cafeteria. After that, no one messed with him—except me."

He smiled faintly, more shadow than warmth.

"We used to sneak out at night, climb onto the roof and lie there just watching the sky. Talked about running away. Talked about seeing the world. Diego wanted Spain. Said it had better food and worse people. I just wanted *out*."

He glanced at her, a flicker of something unreadable in his eyes.

"We left together. Didn't tell anyone. Just waited until the guards changed and slipped through the kitchen gate. Fifteen and free. Thought we were kings."

Skye studied him in silence, absorbing the weight behind every word. He didn't offer details about what happened between then and now. He didn't need to.

She could feel the truth in his voice.

"He saved me from a lot back then. And when I couldn't be saved... he stayed anyway." Chase looked down for a beat, jaw tightening slightly. "He's my brother. Not by blood. But where it counts."

Skye watched him as he spoke, letting the silence stretch before she finally said,

"I see he's important to you." Her voice was gentle, not probing, but deliberate. "I would love to meet him. Your brother. Anyone who's important to you would naturally be important to me."

Chase glanced at her, eyes unreadable but softening. He gave a small shrug, but his tone carried more weight than his posture.

"We left because this country never wanted us. Brown, tan, loud, magical — it didn't matter what we were. Just that we weren't what it wanted." His voice dropped a little lower, gaze drifting.

"Paris didn't ask questions. You could breathe there. Talk how you wanted. Dress how you felt. Be... something. Anything."

Skye tilted her head, just slightly.

"And yet, here you are."

Chase huffed out something between a breath and a laugh.

"Seems that way."

A knock at the door broke the moment.

Nadine stepped in, holding a tuxedo draped over her arms like it might start hissing. "Look what the cat dragged in," she said dryly. "Your carriage to high society."

Chase eyed the tux like it was a bomb. "I've never worn one," he muttered.

Skye didn't respond right away. She'd moved to the vanity, uncapping a small vial of oil and pouring a few drops into her palm. She rubbed it slowly into her skin, the scent of sandalwood and jasmine curling into the room like smoke. Her hands swept across her arms, over her collarbones, down the curves of her shoulders — slow, deliberate, not for show, but definitely not unaware.

"Then tonight's your debut," she said smoothly. "I want you sharp."

She nodded toward the hall.

"Spare room's down the corridor. There's a bath if you want to freshen up."

Then, glancing at him in the mirror with a teasing tilt to her mouth, she added: "I'll get ready alone. A girl's gotta keep a little mystery."

Chase leaned in the doorway, arms crossed.

"You giving orders now?"

She turned to face him full, her body glowing from the oil, hair falling in dark waves across one shoulder. "I've been giving orders since the day we met," she said, sly smile cutting through the quiet.
"You just haven't realized it yet."

Chase chuckled, shaking his head as she vanished into her private quarters. He stepped into the spare room adjacent to hers, the weight of the tuxedo still hanging in his hand.

The door clicked shut behind him. Quiet now. The room smelled faintly of vanilla and old wood. A single lamp cast an amber glow over the clawfoot tub and porcelain basin. He set the tuxedo down on the bed and moved into the bathroom.

In the mirror, he caught his reflection— a man suspended halfway between something broken and something dangerous.

He peeled off his shirt and unbuckled his belt, letting the clothes fall to the floor with a dull whisper. The air was cool against his skin, but it wasn't the chill that made him pause.

Skye Anderson-Pierce

He didn't know what to make of her.

Not the woman on paper. Not the sharp lawyer, the cool resolve, or even the magic that curled just beneath her skin.

Her.

The way she walked bare through her home like it was a temple. The way she spoke truth without dressing it up. The way she looked at him like she already knew how the story ended. He turned on the tap and let the water run hot. Steam curled in the air.

In Paris, he'd slept with poets, singers, and more than a few ghosts.

But love? No. Not really. He'd thought he'd found it once—with Isabelle. Beautiful, aching Isabelle.

`But that had been something else—survival dressed up as romance. Need mistaken for truth. And then Skye's words drifted back, smooth and simple:

"If you have to think about it, it's not love."

He stepped into the tub, sinking into the heat. Water washed over his arms, over the infernal sigils etched in flesh. The spellbinding didn't burn today—just pulsed quietly under the skin like a second heartbeat. He closed his eyes and let the silence breathe.

She was unsettling.

Not in the way danger unsettled—he understood danger. This was quieter.

More intimate. She peeled him without trying, layer by layer, like she already knew what lay beneath the armor and didn't mind the scars. Or the fire. And this was only day two since meeting.

He'd seen beauty before. He'd seen courage.

But Skye carried both like burdens, not badges. And that did something to him. Chase ran wet fingers through his hair, letting water drip off his brow before finally standing and reaching for a towel.

Minutes later, he stood in front of the mirror, steam still clinging to the edges of the glass as he fastened the final button of the crisp white shirt. The tuxedo hung just right—sharp lines against dark skin and muscle. He looked like someone else. Someone the world hadn't chewed up. Almost.

Effie and Pearl sat on the counter beside him, gleaming under the amber light. His fingers hovered over them. For a moment, the room seemed to shrink around him. A pang of dismay tightened his chest. He shouldn't be dressing up. Shouldn't be going out into neon lights and clinking glasses. Not when children were being hollowed out like carcasses and dumped in the river. Not when Tran's tiny body still haunted the inside of his eyelids. Not when the air in Madhatten reeked of something old and hungry. But Whitman had been clear. Forty-eight hours. Mandatory.

And if he didn't take them, someone else would start asking questions the BAE had no business asking. He let out a slow breath.

The guns remained beneath his fingertips—familiar weight, familiar promise. But tonight? Tonight wasn't a battle. Not yet. He picked up the twin pistols, weighed them, then slowly, deliberately set them inside the drawer beneath the vanity and closed it.

"I'm spellbound," he muttered to himself. "And she is a mage carrying an arcalam." A smirk touched his lips. Maybe he could finally learn to trust someone else with the fire. For once, that someone wouldn't be a soldier. Or the ghost. Of a romance from long ago. It would be her.

Chase returned from the guest room, adjusting his cufflinks, only to stop cold at the sight in front of him.

Skye sat at her vanity, bathed in the warm amber glow of a single lamp. She was in her undergarments—silk and lace hugging her petite, curved frame with unapologetic elegance. Her skin glowed like bronze under candlelight, and her hair was swept up in soft waves pinned with deliberate artistry. Her eyes, dark and thoughtful, studied her reflection—but shifted the moment he entered.

She didn't speak. Not at first.

Then, with a smirk tugging at the corner of her mouth, she picked up her arcalam wand—a sleek, rune-inscribed rod no longer than a stiletto dagger—and held it out toward him.

"Make yourself useful, Cassidy," she said, lifting one leg.

The motion was fluid, deliberate. Her thigh extended toward him, revealing the slim garter holster strapped in black satin just above her knee.

Chase raised an eyebrow, but stepped forward. He took the wand, felt its quiet hum against his fingers, and slid it carefully into place. It nestled against her skin like it belonged there—dangerous and discreet.

"Doesn't that ruin the lines of the dress?" he asked, more out of curiosity than objection.

She gave a faint, knowing grin. "Not if you know how to wear it."

He shook his head with a chuckle.

Skye stood then, reaching for the sheath dress—midnight blue silk that seemed to drink in the low light—and held her arms aloft. Chase helped guide it over her head and shoulders, the fabric whispering into place like water sliding over stone. He slowly looped each clasp, carefully, watching the dress mold to her frame.

When she turned, fully dressed, she was devastating.

"You're beautiful," he said, voice lower than he meant it to be. And this time, he didn't look away.

Skye stilled for a beat, caught off guard. Then something softened behind her eyes. "That's the first genuine compliment you've given me," she said quietly. "I'll remember it."

She turned, stepping into her sapphire-black heels, the delicate silver straps catching the light. Without a word, she held onto his shoulder for balance and extended her leg again.

Chase knelt, his fingers fastening the anklet clasps with surprising gentleness. Each link chimed faintly, a sound meant for intimacy, not audiences.

As he rose, she ran her hand down his chest, smoothing his lapel, then met his gaze with that ever-unreadable smile.

"Well, now we match," she said. "Sharp and ready for trouble."

He offered a crooked smile in return. "Trouble finds us either way."

"But at least we'll look good when it does."

And with that, she slipped her arm through his, and together, they stepped into the night.

CHAPTER 5

The Royal Rose

Excerpt from Police Report Entry 227-1923 First Arcane Police Department
Date: November 21, 1922
Report Filed By: Captain James Whitman
Subject: The Royal Rose – Unlawful Establishment Investigation Overview:

The Royal Rose remains an untraceable entity, one of the few establishments in Madhatten that continues to elude police scrutiny. While the First Arcane Department maintains intelligence on nearly every speakeasy, gambling den, and house of vice within the Restriction Zone, this particular club has remained an enigma—a place we know exists, yet one that refuses to be found.

Unlike other illegal operations—where greased palms and unspoken understandings ensure a semblance of law and order—the Royal Rose operates on a level of secrecy beyond any normal racket. We know that many of the city's most dangerous individuals, including known Arcanists, criminals, and underground figures, frequent its halls, but despite numerous attempts, no officer has been able to locate its exact address, thus we are unable to secure a warrant to raid it.

Despite our knowledge of countless illicit establishments, the reality is that law enforcement in Madhatten operates under an unofficial policy of 'out of sight, out of mind.' With the Restriction zones overwhelmed and understaffed, it is simply impossible to shut down every illegal operation. Instead, we allow certain establishments to operate in exchange for order, ensuring they keep their activities contained and do not spill into the streets.

The Royal Rose, however, has never played by these rules. It does not function like the other clubs. It is not a known quantity we can monitor, shake down, or control.

We do not know who runs it.

We do not know how it operates.

And more importantly, we do not know why it has remained untouchable. Until an officer locates its entrance, we have no means of enforcement, making it one of the single greatest gaps in the department's knowledge of Madhatten's criminal underworld.

End of Report.

Captain James Whitman
First Arcane Police Department

The faint hum of jazz filled the air, mingling with the low murmur of voices. Chandeliers crafted from enchanted crystal cast a warm glow, refracting light in shimmering fragments across the room. The Royal Rose Club—Madhatten's most jumping hot spot—was more than a jazz venue. It was a sanctuary.

Not just from Prohibition's dry laws, but from the chokehold of the Arcane Restraint Act—laws born of fear, designed to cage the gifted. Hidden deep within the city's labyrinthine streets, the club's location was a closely guarded secret. Its true purpose was unspoken but well understood: to shelter the spellborn. Arcanists, changelings, hedge witches, mages, and more—beings hunted or shunned—found protection here.

At the Royal Rose, magic flowed as freely as bootlegged liquor. Here, spells were cast without fear of reprisal. Humans, Fey, and those of mixed bloodlines mingled without shame. Unlike the infamous Cotton Club, the Royal Rose did not segregate by race, origin, or magical lineage.

The main floor was a kaleidoscope of color and motion. Showgirls in feathered fans and sequined gowns sashayed between velvet-draped tables, their movements dazzling under the glow. Some were human, others unmistakably otherworldly—eyes too bright, skin that shimmered like moonlight on water. Their beauty was not of this world, and they made no attempt to hide it.

A waiter weaved through the tables with a tray bearing a sizzling roast. With a casual flick of his fingers, he sent it gliding through the air on a current of magic. It hovered before a smiling patron—her scales catching the light beneath a silk shawl—before settling gracefully onto the table. She nodded in approval.

Near one of the club's discreet side entrances stood an automaton. Designated George CMA-A12, his bronze-plated frame gleamed under the low light. His features were sharp and angular, his glowing blue eyes quietly scanning every guest. A relic from the last war, George had traded trench lines for velvet ropes. Tonight, he was a sentinel of peace.

At the coat check, winter jackets came off one by one, revealing glamour beneath. A petite sorceress eyed another woman wearing an identical crimson dress. Her lips curled. One whispered spell later, and her gown shimmered into a deep sapphire. She strode away, smug and radiant.

The stage was lit in gold, bathed in soft lamplight. Smoke curled toward the ceiling in lazy tendrils, blending with conversation and the clink of crystal. The Royal Rose pulsed at its peak—alive with outcasts, thrill-seekers, power players, and whispered magic. A place where sorcery and vice danced in perfect harmony.

At the center of it all stood Veronica Garland.

She was a vision—burnished copper skin, perfect finger waves, lips the color of wine. Her dress was midnight blue, clinging like a lover, slit high along the thigh. Rings adorned her fingers, each one faintly glowing with enchantment. She held the microphone like it was a secret she intended to seduce from the room.

The band struck a slow, sultry chord—low bass, smoke-wrapped saxophone, the hush before a spell is cast. And Veronica began to sing.

Veronica closed her eyes and began to sing.

"Midnight Haze"
(Verse 1 – slow and smooth, dripping with allure)
In the smoky glow of midnight's haze,
She walks in slow, sets hearts ablaze.
A whisper soft, a deadly charm,
She'll steal your breath right from your arms.

The upright bass slides low as the piano shimmers beneath her voice—languid, seductive, like honey poured over velvet.

(Verse 2 – she trails her fingers over the mic, teasing the crowd with a knowing smirk)
Her lipstick's red like blood on lace,
A wicked smile, a poisoned grace.
A cigarette in fingertips so fine,
She sips your soul just like red wine.

The brass section swells—a sultry, lazy sax riff winding through the air like a lover's sigh.

(Chorus – soft, almost whispered, like a secret meant only for the doomed)
Oh, the magic she weaves, a perilous delight,
A siren's song in the dead of night.
Beware the charm, the sweet enchant—
For "Murder Magic" is her chant.

(Bridge – Instrumental. The saxophone wails in a slow, moaning solo. The drums roll with hypnotic rhythm, like footsteps in a dream.)

(Verse 3 – Veronica steps forward, voice deepening, rich and dark like aged bourbon)
With a snap of fingers, men kneel low,
They beg for love she'll never show.
Her laugh's a spell, her touch a curse,
You'll find your fate inside a hearse.

She lifts a single gloved hand and snaps her fingers—magic ripples from her fingertips. A shimmer of illusion—red smoke curling into the shape of a heart —then vanishes. The crowd holds its breath.

(Final Chorus – haunting, sultry, winding down like the last sip of forbidden liquor)
Oh, the magic she weaves, a perilous delight,
A siren's call in the dead of night.
Beware the charm, the sweet enchant—
For "Murder Magic" is her chant...

She holds the last note—breathy, lingering—then lets it fade into a whisper. The piano releases one final chord, low and ghostly. The room sits still in silence, like a spell has been cast and no one dares to break it.

Then, a spell—subtle but deliberate—rolled from her lips as Veronica blew a shimmering kiss into the crowd.

A soft glow spread over them, wrapping every guest in an intoxicating warmth. Smiles curled on lips. Sighs of pleasure slipped through parted mouths. For a fleeting moment, every soul in the Royal Rose felt kissed in truth.

A moment of pure magic.

The applause was thunderous.

Men whistled. Women fanned themselves. Even the hardest, coldest bastards in the room found themselves breathless—Chase Cassidy included.

Veronica chuckled and stepped back from the microphone, her dark, knowing eyes flickering across the room.
"Now, now," she purred, "don't fall in love just yet."

The band kicked into something lively, breaking the spell—but the night had already changed.

Chase and Skye entered the Royal Rose together, drawing more than a few curious glances.

Skye, radiant in her evening dress, was impossible to ignore. Her silhouette moved like music—soft and sinuous-each step accompanied by the chime of the diamond anklets.

She didn't just walk in. She *arrived*.

Men—married or not—turned openly in their seats. A pair of waiters collided in the aisle. Conversations faded, glasses paused mid-sip, and somewhere near the piano, a trumpet player missed his cue.

One particularly bold admirer, nursing a bourbon, leaned to whisper something to his friend, his eyes locked on the sway of Skye's hips.

His wife noticed.
SMACK.

The sharp crack of palm against cheek echoed across the lounge, followed by stunned silence—and then laughter from a nearby table.

Chase smirked to himself. "Should've known better."

As they moved toward the back, a sharp-dressed man in a pinstriped vest—Julius Jump-one of the Rose's more polished underworld regulars—raised his glass in salute.

"Damn, girl," he grinned. "Josephine Baker would be jealous of you tonight."

Skye didn't break stride. She gave a sly smile over her shoulder. "Why, she taught me everything I know." At the bar, a flapper with a short bob and a cigarette holder nudged her friend, gasping in awe.

"That's the bee's knees," she whispered. "Just *look* at her. She's walking magic."

Skye let her fingers trail over the edge of the bar as she passed, moonstone choker catching the light like a star slipping between shadows.

Chase followed a step behind, more amused than surprised. He knew walking in with her would cause a stir.
He just didn't expect her to drown the whole damn room.

At a nearby corner, Benjamin Bright, wiry and wide-eyed at eleven years old, spotted Skye first, awestruck. But soon his attention shifted upward—to Veronica on stage. His expression softened. To him, she wasn't just a singer. She was *magic made real*.

A firm hand landed on his shoulder. Miles Smith, a rugged spell-man and enforcer for the club, gave him a nudge. "C'mon, kid. Snap out of it."

Benjamin flushed and hurried after him, stealing one last glance at Veronica as he went.

———

Velvet drapes. The scent of lavender and pipe smoke. Function disguised as opulence. Behind a grand desk sat Isabelle Monceau. Enigmatic. Elegant. Dangerous. Her black-and-silver gown gleamed like moonlight. A cigarette holder balanced between two fingers as she watched the club floor through a one-way glass panel. Then she saw him.

Chase Cassidy.

Her breath hitched—barely—but it was there. A tremor beneath her practiced composure. It had been years, and yet... here he was. Moving through her club like fate had circled back for one more dance. Her fingers tightened on the holder. A slow exhale steadied her, the flicker in her eyes extinguished before it could betray her.

Renald Desmarais lounged on the couch nearby. French. Fey-blooded. Androgynous. Beautiful. His skin shimmered faintly in the light. His features shifted subtly—never quite the same in every glance. No one had seen his true face, and Renald liked it that way. He filed his nails with lazy precision, a sly smile curving his lips.

"Beautiful, isn't she?" Isabelle said, nodding toward Veronica on the floor below.

"She's okay," Renald chimed in, amused.

Isabelle gave him a sharp glance, then turned back to her guest. "How can I help you, Angelo?"

Angelo Sykes—broad, sleek in a charcoal tailored suit, fingers heavy with jewel-weighted rings—sat beside him, silent as stone. The smoke curling around him seemed to avoid touching his clothes, as if even the air knew better than to trespass.

Sykes wasn't just any mob boss.

He was the man in Madhatten's underworld—one of the premier controllers of vice, with blood-deep ties to the mundane Mafia families and darker dealings whispered among arcanists. The Italians respected him, feared him, and—where necessary—paid him. Angelo himself was a sparker: barely a flicker of arcane talent by formal standards, but what he lacked in magic, he more than compensated for in raw intelligence, ruthless pragmatism, and an appetite for violence that carved him a throne no wand could have conjured.

He controlled most of the import lanes that still functioned inside the city, every crate and barrel that crossed those docks moving under his watchful eyes. Only a few piers along the Hudson remained outside his grasp—territory belonging to the city's senior Mafia don—but everything else flowed through Sykes 'hands. Even rival families, brimming with ego and guns, had to pay him tribute just to bring their product ashore.

Slim Wilson was the compromise in all of that.

A freelancer. A neutral bookkeeper. A necessary buffer that kept the port from exploding into a three-way turf war. Slim wasn't tied to any single family; instead, he kept the shipments sorted. What belonged to Sykes went to Sykes. What belonged to the other bosses got sent along without tampering. Everyone stayed paid. Everyone stayed armed. And everyone stayed out of a bloodbath.

But when the shipments stopped? The whole machine jammed.

And Sykes didn't like jammed machines.

He leaned forward, voice grinding like gravel on steel."We got a problem. Slim says the shipments are getting held up at the docks. Which means product can't get through. Which means the families can't pay me what they owe. Already two months behind—and I'm done waiting."

Slim Wilson shifted in his chair, the overhead bulb catching the slick sheen on his brow. He was a slender man with dark brown skin, jaundiced eyes, and hands too long and wiry for anyone's comfort—soft hands, the kind that never worked a day on the docks. Sweat darkened the pits of his jacket in two clear circles, and Isabelle wondered—not for the first time—if the man ever stopped sweating.

Slim swallowed hard, voice trembling at the edges. "Look... we all know the G-Men are crackin 'down on magical contraband. Senator Wilder's out for blood. The BAE's got boys crawlin 'everywhere." His hands fluttered in a helpless gesture. "I sent my crew down to check it out, and none of 'em came back."

His jaundiced eyes darted nervously between Isabelle and Sykes.

"It's weird. Ever since those Europeans came in and rented out the top level, the whole place has been... wacky. Off. Like somethin 'up there's chewin 'up men and spittin 'out ghosts."

Isabelle's fingers drummed lightly on the desk. "Angelo, did you investigate?"

"No," Sykes said, flat as Miles entered with Benjamin in tow. No one regarded them other than Isabelle with a nod to Miles and faint smile to Benjamin.

"Then I'll send Miles" She said pointing to her spell-man. " If Slim's telling the truth, you'll work out a solution. If not... we'll resolve it accordingly."

Slim looked grateful. "I swear, Miss Monceau. I wouldn't lie."

"I know, Slim," she said gently. "But Angelo's patience isn't infinite."

Sykes stood, adjusting his cuffs. "Miles I know. Solid shooter. But who's the kid?" He nodded toward the door, where Benjamin was peeking in.

"My new...driver" Isabelle said, smiling. "Renald caught him swiping the grease caps off my Mercedes. Took a shine to him. Good kid."

Sykes scoffed. "You two and your bleeding hearts."

Renald didn't look up. "Compassion is strength. Not that you'd know."

Sykes glared, but let it pass. Everyone knew Renald was more than Isabelle's second, he was a button man, a dangerous one with a well earned reputation. Somethings had to be let go.

"Miles. Benjamin. Go with Slim," Isabelle said, smoothing her gloves as though this were the most mundane of errands.

She flashed a reassuring smile—one that never reached her eyes. "I'm sure there's nothing to worry about down at the docks. But..." Her gaze lingered on Benjamin just long enough to feel like approval instead of appraisal. "...I think it's time the boy saw a bit more of how our larger operation works."

Miles nodded. Slim twitched. Benjamin brightened.

Isabelle let out a light, musical laugh. "Provided he doesn't fall asleep on the drive over. He does that, you know." She waved them off with a gentle, practiced affection.

Miles nodded. "Yes, Miss Monceau."
Benjamin fumbled. "Y-yes, ma'am."

As the door closed, Isabelle turned to Renald. "Keep an eye on things. Let me know if anything unusual happens."

Renald saluted lazily. "Always." As he exited the office.

Benjamin trailed Miles as they pushed deeper into the club, his gaze lingering on Veronica, who now glided through the crowd. Her laughter rang like wind chimes, and patrons—male and female alike—reached for just a touch, a glance, a smile.

Meanwhile Chase and Skye took a seat at the bar. Skye slid smoothly onto the barstool, crossing her shapely legs as she sat. "Old Fashioned," Skye told the bartender.
"Bourbon, neat," Chase added.

Within seconds the an automation bartenders placed to drinks in front of them.

They raised their glasses.

"A toast?" Skye offered.

Chase quirked an eyebrow. "To what?"

She leaned in close, smile mischievous. "To new friendships. New partnerships. And whatever parts connects before the night ends." They toasted.
The whiskey burned warm, smooth.

But before Chase could get comfortable, a man approached. Well dressed, but nervous the type that was unsure of himself and walked uncomfortably in his surroundings.

"Skye," he greeted, trying to sound confident—but faltering under Chase's unreadable stare.

Skye's smile curled. She rested her hand on Chase's thigh, brushing her fingers just enough to make the message clear.
"Evening, Lance. Something on your mind?"

Lance glanced between them. "Didn't realize you had company."

"I always have company, darling," she said sweetly.

He muttered something and slinked off. Skye chuckled. "Men are so fragile."

Chase smirked. "And you enjoy breaking them."

She lifted her glass in silent agreement, then another presence entered the space. Smooth, radiant. Veronica Garland.

She approached with the effortless poise of someone who knew all eyes were always halfway on her. The hem of her silver gown shimmered like liquid light as she stopped beside the bar, her perfume already mingling with the scent of citrus and bourbon.

She nodded politely at Skye. "Skye. Its been so long."

"Veronica. Beautiful song, as always," Skye returned, just as smooth. Just as distant.

"Why, thank you." Veronica's voice was honeyed velvet. "You know I sing better when the right people are listening. Her eyes slid—casually, deliberately—to Chase.

He met her gaze without flinching, bourbon in hand, expression unreadable.

Before anything more could pass between them, Angelo Sykes strolled over and placed a hand on Veronica's back.

She turned with a smile that didn't quite reach her eyes, and just like that, the moment was gone.

Chase exhaled, took another sip. The night had just begun, and already the air was charged with tension, history, and the promise of things yet to come.

Benjamin halted in his tracks, transfixed, as Angelo Sykes approached Veronica. The men fawning over her scattered like leaves under the gangster's looming presence. Sykes leaned in, presenting her with a velvet box. A string of luminous pearls nestled inside.

Veronica's face lit up. Her delight was genuine.

"Beautiful pearls for a beautiful woman," Sykes murmured, low and velvet-smooth.

He stepped closer, brushing her hair aside to press a kiss against her neck. Veronica shivered, smiling playfully as she tilted her head to give him better access.

"You spoil me, Angelo," she purred, tracing a single finger down the front of his tailored suit. "What's the occasion?"

Sykes grinned, his gold tooth flashing. "Do I need a reason to appreciate the finest gem in the club?" His hand settled lightly on her waist, pulling her just a breath closer.

Veronica laughed softly, eyes glittering with mischief. "Careful, Angelo. You keep talking like that, I might start believing you."

"You should," he said, tone a mix of tease and possession. "Every word of it." The exchange drew a few curious glances, but no one dared interrupt. Not with Sykes standing there.

Benjamin stood wide-eyed and blushing until a loud throat-clear beside him broke the spell. Miles had caught him staring. Again.

With a sigh, he grabbed the boy's arm. "Listen, kid. That dame? Taboo. Keep your eyes straight and your head lower. You don't want to end up on the wrong side of Sykes 'temper. Man's got no problem hurting a boy your age. Trust me."

Benjamin swallowed. "Sorry."

They moved quickly to catch up with Renald and Slim, who were posted near the rear corridor alongside three thick-necked enforcers. Renald waited patently as Miles drug Benjamin behind him. He liked the kid, spirited and proud. He reminded him of himself at that age. He wished...the sight of a familiar face jolted Renald out of his thoughts.

Past Benjamin—to Chase.

Recognition flickered. The stance. The posture. The way he carried himself. Even in formalwear, somethings didn't change. Renald said nothing at first. Instead, he reached into a hidden pocket and pulled out a brass key, holding it out between two fingers.

"This," he said evenly, "is a rip key. Gets you to the garage. Benji drives. Miles checks the perimeter. If anything's off, you come right back. Got it?"

Miles lifted an eyebrow. "Wait—he's driving? Kid's barely tall enough to see over the wheel."

Benjamin crossed his arms. "I'm tall enough. I the best shift-drifter in the zone, I can out-drive anyone."

"Oh yeah?" Miles smirked. "Go-carts don't count!"

"Better than that," Benjamin shot back. "Been behind the wheel since I could reach the pedals. I've outrun G-Men, dodged Wardens, and parked in spots so tight you'd think I bent space to do it. You name it—I've done it."

Renald chuckled under his breath amused at the exchange but offered no comment.

Miles gave the boy a long, skeptical look—then relented with a grin. "Alright, hotshot. But if we die, I'm haunting you."

"You'll be eating my dust," Benjamin muttered, snatching the key from Renald's hand.

"Let's go," Miles said, jerking his thumb toward the broom closet up the hall.

Renald touched Miles's arm. "Give us a minute." Miles nodded and slipped into the closet, the faint scuff of his boots echoing before the door clicked shut. Renald turned to Benjamin, his expression shifting—less stern guardian, more worried uncle. He lowered his voice to a whisper.

"Here." From inside his coat, he produced a plain obsidian wand—unmarked, unadorned, its wooden handle worn smooth by use. He held it out carefully.

"I showed you how this works. You remember?"

Benjamin swallowed and nodded, fingers closing around the cool stone.

Renald crouched a bit, bringing himself eye-level with the boy. "If anything goes wrong—anything—you use it. Don't hesitate. Don't try to be brave. Just use it. Understand?"

"Yes, Mr. Renald," Benjamin whispered.

A small smile broke through Renald's sternness. He ruffled Benjamin's hair with a rough, affectionate swipe. "Good. Go on."

Benjamin turned. The closet door closed behind him with a soft, final click. And Renald stood alone in the hallway, listening to it latch, his jaw tight with a fear he didn't dare show.

He remained where he was for a beat. Then turned—not toward the bar as he'd planned—but toward Chase.

Deliberately.

Their eyes met across the floor. Not by accident. Not by surprise.

A beat of silence passed between them.

Two men.
A history written in blood.

France, The Withering Veil 1919

Screams carried on the wind, shrill and distant, like the war itself was howling in grief. Trenches had collapsed. Barbed wire curled like broken ribs across the mud. Shells no longer fell—not because the war was over, but because nothing alive remained to aim them.

This was the Veil. The place they didn't map. A no-man's-land so cursed the very ground rejected the dead. French, German, British—none of it mattered anymore. All that remained were bones that crawled and soldiers too stubborn to lie down.

Chase Cassidy moved through the corpse-choked trench like a revenant. Blood matted his sleeve, but the glow from the glyph on his chest—the Seal— still burned faintly beneath his torn tunic. Sigils scrawled along his forearms shimmered like embers in the gloom. He carried a trench knife in one hand, and a six-shot revolver scorched black with overuse in the other. The spellbound were built to endure. But even he was nearing his limit.

A shape dropped beside him from the rim of the trench, landing with the soft crunch of bone beneath boots. Renald straightened, his features still shifting, the last remnants of his transformation flickering across his face— wolfish ears retracting, teeth receding, pupils shrinking to human shape. He grinned, the blood of something long-dead still drying on his jaw.

"You're late," Chase muttered.

"I brought friends," Renald said, nodding behind him.

Chase peeked over the ledge. Two reanimated French officers were staggering forward in jerky, bone-snapping steps, but their heads had been torn clean off—presumably by Renald's claws.

"You always this dramatic?" Chase asked, flicking his knife to clear the gore.

"Only when the stakes are biblical," Renald replied.

A hollow moan echoed through the trench, and a mass of silhouettes appeared through the mist—dozens of them. Some still wore helmets, others carried rusted bayonets or gashed flags like banners. One wore the remnants of a British officer's coat, but his chest cavity had been split open, ribs splayed like wings as something black writhed inside.

Chase raised his revolver. "Looks like we found Black Dagger's objective."

Renald shifted beside him, his hands elongating into claws again. "You take the left. I'll make them regret the right."

They moved together like dancers in a violent waltz—Chase firing precise, rune-charged shots that exploded skulls in bursts of light and heat, while Renald tore through limbs and armor, shifting mid-leap into something faster, more feral, before returning to human shape with each breath. They fought back-to-back, blood and magic spilling into the mud.

For a moment, the world was nothing but motion, fury, and firelight.

And then—quiet.

The final body slumped. The mist recoiled, as if driven back by what they had become.

Back in the present, Renald and Chase stare across the polished floor of the Royal Rose. Suits and jazz have replaced mud and steel—but something in their gaze still hummed with battlefield memory, the aftermath of Operation Black Dagger. A mission that should've never happened. One that sealed the Veil—and buried everyone inside. Good men. Bad men. Men who refused to stay dead.

Renald walked to the bar first and ordered a drink.

Chase didn't move. Didn't blink. But his posture shifted. Subtle. Guarded.

"Well. If it isn't the Hellfighter himself. Never thought I'd see you outside a war zone." Renald said taking his drink.

Chase watched him evenly. "Didn't think you'd survived. Figured one of your many enemies would've found you by now."

"They tried," Renald replied, tapping his temple. "But I'm hard to hold onto."

Chase nodded once. "That you are."

They stood there, two shadows of the same ghost. Then Renald let out a short laugh. "Never thought I'd see you in a tux."

Chase smirked. "Don't get used to it."

Renald glanced toward Skye. "And I see your taste in company hasn't dulled."

Chase said nothing, his expression unreadable.

"Well," Renald said, finishing his drink, "try not to make a scene. My club and all."

Skye watched him disappear into the crowd before turning to Chase. "No introduction?"

Chase downed the last of his bourbon.
"Trust me," he said, eyes still on the doorway. "You'll never see the same face twice."

Upstairs, Renald paused as applause broke out. Veronica was taking the stage again.

He felt Isabelle before he saw her—like a pressure change in the air.

She moved with quiet authority. Perfume, whiskey, and something ancient swirled around her like perfume and power.

"I told Ricky to watch her," Renald said softly, nodding toward the stage. Isabelle's gaze lingered on Veronica.
"She's captivating."

Renald swirled the whiskey in his glass.
"Too many admirers for my taste. If I had to guess, she's part Siren."

Isabelle's expression didn't change.
"That, or she's simply very good at survival."

Renald's eyes narrowed, tone wry. "Tricks or not, she's got this place wrapped around her little finger."

Isabelle didn't respond immediately. Her gaze drifted to the music, to the crowd—gauging the room like she always did.

After a moment, Renald cut through her reverie.
"You see who just walked in?"

Isabelle arched a brow and took a slow sip from her glass. "Should I be concerned?"

Renald smirked. "Depends. How do you feel about Carmillo Del Gato breathing the same air as Sykes?"

Her lips pursed ever so slightly as she turned her head, just enough to glimpse the ganglord striding across the floor. His white suit shimmered under the lights, every step punctuated by the tap of his cane.

"Two of the biggest arcane gangsters in the Zone under the same roof," Isabelle murmured. She set her drink down. "You'd think they'd have the sense to avoid each other."

"Neutral ground or not, you can feel it, can't you?" Renald tilted his head toward the floor, where the noise had dipped a few notches. Conversations turned cautious. The storm was circling, and everyone could feel it.

Isabelle's fingers tapped the railing. Her eyes shifted to the stage, where Veronica Garland basked in the lingering admiration of her last song. She smiled gently.

"She's everything she said she was," Isabelle said, thinking back to the night she'd lured the singer away from Boozie Bonfire, a rival Harlem club. "And worth every coin."

"Have you heard from Lucian?"

The smile faded. "No," she said quietly. "Still no word."

Renald watched her, the usual teasing edge gone from his voice. But she didn't see him. Her eyes were fixed on the stage, lost in thought. He leaned on the railing beside her, swirling his drink. "You're never gonna believe who I just ran into."

Isabelle took a slow drag from her cigarette. Didn't even glance his way. "Chase Cassidy."

Renald's grin widened. "You know?"

"Cassidy," she repeated, as if tasting the name after too many years.

"Didn't say much," Renald said. "But you should've seen his face. Poor bastard still looks like he's carrying the war on his back."

Isabelle exhaled, the memory heavy behind her eyes.

The last time she'd seen Chase was in 1920, before she left for France. He'd chosen to stay behind. She couldn't. Not with the country tightening its grip around people like them. Chase had chosen the badge, the law, the idea of America. She had chosen freedom.

Her hand drifted—briefly—to her stomach. A gesture so quick even

Renald missed it. She scanned the club until she found him. At the bar. Beside a woman she didn't know.

Honey-brown skin. Sharp eyes. Confidence. The kind of presence that didn't just command attention—it bent the room around her.

"Who's the woman?" Isabelle asked, cool and even.

Renald followed her gaze. "Skye Anderson. Lawyer. Runs with her father's old firm. Smart, dangerous... from what I hear, she likes a good hunt. Courtroom or bedroom—makes no difference."

Isabelle's brow ticked up. "Meaning?"

Renald sipped. "She doesn't discriminate. Men, women... just as long as they can keep up."

They both watched as Skye leaned closer to Chase and said something into his ear. Her hand brushed his sleeve. He didn't move.

"He looks like hes keeping up just fine," Isabelle murmured. Smooth as silk. Edged like a blade.

"You going to talk to him?" Renald asked, half-teasing.

She didn't answer. Just kept watching Skye. "He hasn't come looking for me," she said finally.

"Would you?" Renald's voice softened. "You left without looking back."

Her lips pressed together. "Did he ask about me?"

Renald hesitated. "No."

Something flickered. Not quite pain. Not relief, either. A wound pressed but not opened.

"He's changed," she said.

"So have you."

Her eyes lingered on Chase—his posture, the set of his jaw, the way he held himself like someone who didn't trust solid ground. She'd imagined him dead once. In an alley. A trench. Somewhere too quiet for a man like him.

But he was here. Alive. Older. And not alone.

She stubbed out her cigarette. Then turned toward her private quarters.

Renald raised a brow. "Where are you going?"

"To change."

She reached for crimson—bold, unforgiving. The color of fire. The color of memory. As she slipped into the dress, the room seemed to bend with her confidence.

"If Chase Cassidy is going to walk into my club," she said, reaching for her glass, "he's going to remember who I am."

Renald chuckled. "Now this—I've gotta see."

CHAPTER 6

Out of the Past

Journal of Renald Desmarais

They say time buries things. I know better. It doesn't bury—just layers. Guilt, regret, longing—like ash on a fire that never truly dies. Tonight I watched a man keep his distance from the one thing he wanted most in this cursed world. Chase Cassidy. Soldier. Mercenary. Fool.

I've known a dozen men who wanted Isabelle Moriceau. I've killed three of them myself. And none of them lasted—not because she's cruel, but because she's unreachable. Like staring at the moon and thinking you could keep it in your hands. She is beauty sharpened to a blade, always half in shadow, and the rest of her dancing just out of reach.

But Chase...
Chase didn't try to trap her. He loved her and walked away. That takes a kind of strength most men don't possess. Especially when it comes to her.

Their romance was wildfire—brilliant, consuming, impossible to sustain. I saw it firsthand. The way they looked at each other like they were both starving. Like the world might end between breaths. Arguments that left the walls shaking. Nights that silenced entire floors.

And yet... he never tried to take her. Not really. Even after everything. Because Chase knew the one truth most men ignored:

Isabelle was always married.

Lucian Moriceau.
A ghost of a man, but never far. He haunts her, breathes beside her, bleeds for her. And for all her lovers—for all the men who came and went— Lucian is the one she keeps close. He's broken, maybe dying, but he's hers. And that matters more than any vow.

So when I look at Cassidy, I don't see just another lost soul pining after a queen he can't touch. I see a man who chose restraint over ruin. And gods help me, I respect him for that.

Still... I wonder if there's a corner of him that regrets not burning the whole world down just to keep her.

—Renald

The lights dimmed. Shadows lengthened across the Royal Rose. Veronica Garland's final note dissolved into smoke. A single spotlight bloomed. From the wings, a flurry of white doves took flight, ghostly silhouettes circling the ceiling before vanishing into the rafters. Then, a piano. A low, lingering note. Every conversation in the club died. And she appeared.

Isabelle Moriceau.

She stepped into the golden light like she owned it—because she did. The crimson gown hugged her frame like a secret, the fabric catching the light like flame. Every step was a memory. Every gaze, a reckoning.

Chase Cassidy turned at the bar.

And everything else disappeared.

She held no microphone—she didn't need one. Instead, her voice— smooth, sultry, and laced with just the right amount of sadness—poured into the air like aged whiskey.

 "La vie est une danse, mon amour, Chaque pas, une promesse, un jour... Dans l'ombre, dans la lumière, Nous tournons jusqu'à l'éternité." **(Translation: "Life is a dance, my love, / Each step, a promise, a day... / In shadow, in light, / We turn until eternity.")**

The room exhaled as one. A few patrons whispered in hushed tones, recognizing the song—an old French ballad of lost love and fleeting time.

Others simply watched, transfixed, unable to look away from the woman who owned not just the club, but the moment itself. Angelino Sykes, seated with Veronica, smirked knowingly but applauded all the same. Even he wasn't foolish enough to ignore the power of the woman before him.

At the bar, Chase Cassidy's fingers tightened around his glass. His expression didn't change—but inside, something twisted. That voice. Skye, ever perceptive, noticed.

She traced the rim of her glass with her finger, watching him from the corner of her eye. "Something wrong, Cassidy?" she murmured.

Chase exhaled slowly, keeping his eyes on the stage. "No."

Skye smirked. She didn't believe him for a second.

Back on stage, Isabelle's song reached its final verse. She let the last note linger in the air, then exhaled, slow and measured, as applause erupted. She smiled—a soft, knowing thing. Then, with effortless grace, she raised her hand, gesturing to the crowd as if greeting old friends and new admirers alike.

"Bienvenue, mes chers invités," she purred, her voice still dripping with the remnants of the song. "Welcome, my dear guests, to the Royal Rose." She paused, letting the applause settle, before continuing.

"You are here to forget your troubles. To dance. To drink. To dream." Her dark gaze swept the room, knowing and searching all at once. "And as always," she added, her lips curving slightly, "you are safe here."

She raised her glass in a toast, and the club followed. Across the room, Chase finally forced himself to breathe. He took a slow sip of his bourbon, his gaze steady on the stage as Isabelle's final note hung in the air like a lingering promise. The applause erupted like rolling thunder, an ovation fit for royalty.

Around them, the club came alive—waiters weaving through the crowd, trays laden with crystal flutes of champagne, the atmosphere shifting with her presence. The moment Isabelle stepped off the stage, the crowd parted for her, drawn to her the way moths circled a flame. She moved with the effortless grace of a queen accustomed to command, her every step deliberate, her dark silk gown trailing like liquid night.

A waiter approached swiftly, presenting her with a crystal goblet filled with deep Bordeaux wine. She accepted it with a knowing smile, her fingers delicate against the stem. Then, with a practiced ease that spoke of years navigating high society, she turned toward the bar—toward him.

But Chase wasn't the only one watching. Across the room, two of Madhatten's most dangerous men raised their glasses in silent acknowledgment.

Angelo Sykes, with his arm slung possessively around Veronica Garland, the club's reigning songbird. She perched beside him, radiating charm as she playfully twirled a lock of hair around her finger. But despite her flirtatious demeanor, she bowed her head slightly in deference as Isabelle approached—a silent nod of respect between women who knew the weight of power.

On the opposite end of the lounge, Camillo del Gato, the elusive leader of the Magic Circus Gang, lifted his glass in an almost theatrical salute. His smile was slow, unreadable, the gold rings on his fingers glinting under the chandelier's glow. Del Gato rarely showed his face in neutral zones, but tonight, even he acknowledged Isabelle Moriceau's dominion.

Chase took it all in—the silent exchanges, the careful maneuvering of power wrapped in silk and champagne. This wasn't just a club. It was a battlefield. And at its center—as always—was Isabelle Moriceau.

He felt her before he saw her.

The scent of rose and amber curled into the air, stirring something deep in his chest. A perfume he hadn't forgotten.

Then she was there.

"Chase Cassidy," Isabelle greeted smoothly, voice rich and knowing. "What a surprise."

Chase set his drink down deliberately before turning. "Isabelle," he said evenly. Controlled.

She held his gaze, letting the silence stretch. Then, as if only just noticing Skye at his side, she tilted her head, amused.

"You look... well," she murmured, lips barely curving. "Better than the last time I saw you in Paris."

Before he could answer, Skye's hand slid lightly over his forearm, grounding, firm.

Isabelle's eyes flicked to her, finally acknowledging her. Nothing changed on her face, but something sharp sparked behind her eyes.

"Skye Anderson-Pierce," Skye said with a warm, unbothered smile. "And you must be the famous Isabelle Moriceau."

"Famous? How flattering." Isabelle took a slow sip of her wine, gaze sweeping Skye like a ledger. "But I don't believe we've had the pleasure."

Skye's smile didn't waver. "Surprising. I imagine you like to keep tabs on the important women in Chase's life."

Chase exhaled quietly through his nose. Skye wasn't backing down.

Isabelle tilted her head, amusement dancing in her eyes. "Oh? And would you consider yourself... important?"

"I'd say so," Skye replied, arching a brow. Skye wasn't backing down.

A slow, knowing smile touched Isabelle's lips. "How charming."

Chase took a long drink. He'd survived gunfights, trench raids, and necromancers. But this? This was a different kind of fight. Then another presence swept in like smoke and perfume.

Camillo del Gato. He moved with the confidence of a man who believed the room belonged to him. His suit—crisp white linen, immaculate and bold—was paired with a blood-red shirt open just enough to suggest sin. Gold-thread embroidery traced the lapels like fire. His jet-black hair was slicked back, his manicured beard wrapping a mouth caught between smirk and snarl. Camillo del Gato didn't walk—he prowled.

He stopped before Isabelle, offering a slight bow.

"Señora Moriceau," he purred, accent thick with old-world Spanish. "A vision, as always."

Isabelle accepted the compliment with a polite smile, but didn't return it.

Then his gaze slid to Skye.

"You, however," he murmured, his eyes raking over her, "are something new."

Skye met his gaze coolly. Said nothing.

Camillo reached for her hand, pressing a lingering kiss to her knuckles. His lips barely grazed her skin, but his intent was clear. "Te ves maravillosa," he added in Spanish, voice low and predatory. "Me gustaría probar tu menú." (You look marvelous. I'd like to try your menu.)

Chase stiffened. His hand tightened around his glass, shoulders squaring. He didn't speak much Spanish, but he knew enough to recognize a line being crossed. The words, the tone—it wasn't flattery. It was a challenge.

Skye didn't flinch. She withdrew her hand immediatly, fingers grazing Chase's forearm like a silent tether. Then she turned to face Camillo, her smile serene and blade-sharp.

"Veo que tú no tienes nada en tu menú que me satisfaga."

(I can tell there's nothing on your menu that would satisfy me.)

Camillo's smirk twitched—just for a heartbeat—before settling into something thinner. Harder. He stepped forward. And that was a mistake. Chase moved like a shadow breaking loose. One solid step put him directly in front of Camillo—and his shoulder clipped the man hard enough to knock him slightly off balance. A deliberate body check. No apology. No hesitation.

Camillo stumbled half a step back, regaining his footing with a flash of embarrassment and growing fury. He blinked in shock. No one did that to him. Not ever. Not without consequence. Even Angelo Sykes, mouthy bastard that he was, knew where the lines were drawn. The older gangster might trade barbs, but he never crossed into this. He never physically stood in Camillo's way. Never like this.

But this man? This nobody with storm-dark eyes and a soldier's stillness? He didn't blink. Didn't boast. Just stood there like stone—coiled, calm, deadly. Camillo's grin stayed on his lips, but it no longer reached his eyes. Behind it, something twisted.

"Problem?" Chase said, jaw set. Eyes cold. His voice dropped, low and lethal.

Camillo straightened, his golden-toothed smile flickering like a faulty light. "None at all," he said tightly. "Just admiring the view."

But Isabelle had already seen the shift in Chase's eyes. And she knew that look. She'd seen it in the war. In the alleys of Paris. In the blood-slick streets of the European Containment Zones. Chase Cassidy didn't bluff. He didn't posture. He killed. And Camillo del Gato—smiling, flattered, dangerous Camillo—had no idea the kind of storm he was circling. No idea that the man he was toying with would tear through him and his entourage without hesitation. If she didn't intervene now, someone was going to die on her floor.

So Isabelle moved, smooth and controlled, lifting one manicured hand toward the bandleader with practiced elegance. She knew how to defuse this. Recognized the light accent that marked Skye as Cuban.

The music changed.

Not frantic or wild—no Charleston, no Lindy Hop. Son Cubano rising like a balm. Before the sparks could turn into flame. A slow, sultry sway of tres guitars, the pulse of double bass, the breath of percussion. Son Cubano.

Skye's head turned toward the stage. Recognition flashed across her face, followed by a slow, wicked smile. She turned back to Camillo—dismissive now. Then she took Chase's hand without breaking eye contact with the gangster. "Come on, Cassidy," she purred.

And she led him onto the floor.

Camillo's fists clenched, golden rings glinting under the lights as his jaw flexed. Isabelle took notice, took a slow sip of her wine, then, without looking at him, she murmured—low, precise, and cold enough to cut glass.

"You're an intelligent man, Camillo. I'd hate to see that change."

He said nothing. Just watched. But Isabelle continued, her voice like velvet drawn across a blade.

"I know him very well, Camillo. Intimately." She turned her head slightly, letting her words settle like a storm on the horizon. "Chase will kill you. No hesitation. And if you ever tried to touch that woman again?" She exhaled lightly through her nose. "He'd carve her name into your face before you hit the floor."

A beat.

"I know this... because he used to do that for me." Camillo didn't respond—couldn't. The smirk was gone now, replaced with something unreadable. Anger. Uncertainty. Fear. Whatever it was, it held him in check. And Isabelle—ever the strategist—just smiled. "Be smart, cariño," she whispered. "The man standing between you and your pride isn't like the others. He's already been to hell. And worse... he liked it there."

On the floor, Skye began to move. Not with showy flair or practiced performance, but with purpose—each sway and pivot a declaration. Not of ownership, but of choice. She chose who she danced with. She chose who touched her. And tonight, she was dancing with Chase Cassidy.

At first, he followed with careful steps—shoulders loose, brow furrowed slightly as he listened to the rhythm. Then something shifted. He caught it—the heartbeat of the Son, the breath and sway of it. Not just the timing, but the feeling. The music wasn't just in his ears; it rolled through his bones. He adapted. He always did.

When she pivoted close, he matched her. When she spun, he caught her. He let her lead, then met her step for step, never rushing, never forcing. There was strength in his hold, yes—but also restraint. Respect. Skye felt it in every turn. It wasn't just chemistry—it was trust.

"You've done this before," she murmured, genuinely surprised. Chase smirked, spinning her smoothly, confident now. "Picked up a few things traveling with Diego. Madrid. Havana. Buenos Aires. Man was a menace in dance halls. Dragged me along half the time."

Skye laughed—light and breathless. "I'd like to meet him."

"You'd like him," Chase replied, voice low, warm. The way he said it made her stomach flutter.

She dipped low and rose in a snap, hips rolling in time with the clave beat. He followed—perfectly. The crowd watched in stunned silence. Even those who'd never heard it before felt it in their marrow, drawn in by the pulse.

At the bar, Isabelle watched. Her nails tapped the wine glass. Her expression remained composed, perfectly still—but Renald, standing close, caught the crack beneath the surface.

"Careful, chère," he murmured, lips tilted in a teasing smirk.

"I'm not concerned," she replied evenly. But her voice dipped at the end. Even she didn't believe it.

Across the room, Camillo looked like he was chewing glass. His golden rings dug into the meat of his palm, knuckles white. He stared at them—at her. His mind burned. Who was this nobody who thought he could shove Camillo del Gato aside like some club drunk? This Black bastard with his quiet strength and haunted eyes?

He didn't just stand his ground. He didn't care who Camillo was. He stepped through him. Camillo's ego howled. His pride raged. And somewhere behind his grin, something darker formed. He would repay this. Not tomorrow. Tonight.

Then—

Sykes laughed. Loud. Delighted. "What's the matter, Gato?" he called, raising his drink like a toast. "Thought you were the cat who always caught the bird?"

Camillo twitched.

Veronica, lounging at Sykes's side, twirled her cocktail lazily with a long, scarlet nail. "Looks like she prefers a different partner, love."

Camillo tried to smile. "One dance means nothing," he muttered. But he was already watching Skye throw her head back, laughing as Chase spun her into a dramatic flourish. Her dress shimmered under the lights; her hand pressed firmly against Chase's chest. The way they moved together...

The way she looked at him...

It meant everything.

As the final notes of the song faded, Skye landed softly against

Chase, her hand resting over his heart. Their breathing slowed in tandem, their bodies still tuned to the rhythm they'd shared. Applause broke out—scattered at first, then swelling, honest and full-throated. They didn't bow. They didn't need to.

Chase glanced down at her, brow arched, half a smirk tugging at his mouth. "You always dance like that when you're trying to start a fight?" he murmured.

Skye looked up at him, eyes still gleaming from the rush. "Only when I want to make sure everyone knows who I'm with."

His quiet laugh was a private thing. Rough and low. She laced her fingers with his, and together they stepped off the floor as the next number began. A softer tune. A slower beat. The moment lingered—smoke and sweat and memory curling in their wake. As they passed the bar, Chase didn't even glance Camillo's way.

But Skye did. She met his gaze head-on without flinching. Her chin high. Her stare flat. And in that silence, she made something clear: You will never claim me. Camillo's lips parted, then pressed thin again. The smirk was gone.

Chase and Skye slipped through a side corridor near the rear of the club, away from the main floor—the narrow passage lined with velvet drapes, leading toward the back lounge and service doors.

They didn't get far.

Camillo del Gato stepped from the shadows of the hallway like a knife unsheathed, his white jacket now off, crimson silk shirt catching the lamplight. Two of his men blocked the way behind him; two more cut off the retreat ahead. The muffled thrum of music from the main room was the only witness.

His smile was sharp, but his eyes burned with humiliation and hate.

"Chase," he purred. "The dumb palooka who thought he could get between me and my next squeeze."

Chase shifted, stepping slightly in front of Skye without thinking about it. His shoulders rolled back, sigils under his sleeves prickling awake.

"I'm not your anything," Skye said, voice sharp, unmoved.

Camillo's grin twisted into something feral. He spat onto the hallway floor, contempt staining his every motion.

"Shut your hole. You'll be exactly what I tell you to be—my moll, my fuck toy—hell, when I'm done with you, maybe I'll pass you around to the boys."

That word hit like a match to oil.

Chase stopped moving. For half a second, everything blurred except her—Skye, standing there under the dim sconce light, jaw tight but spine straight, not flinching. He saw it: the fire behind her calm, the restraint coiled in her muscles. She didn't need anyone to defend her.

But Chase wanted to. He didn't even know where it came from. There was being honorable. And then there was... this.

This feeling—the one curling in his chest like a storm caught behind bone—wasn't about being a gentleman. It wasn't about justice. It was the deep, primal fury that bloomed when someone disrespected something precious. Something he hadn't realized he already wanted to protect.

Skye smiled—cool, dangerous. She noticed. "Careful, Camillo. Keep talking like that, and my man will show you exactly how fragile your ego is when your teeth are on the floor."

Camillo's eyes flared.

"Bitch."

Chase's voice cut through the tight corridor like steel drawn slow.

"I'm going to break your jaw for saying that."

Camillo's grin faltered. "You should be on your knees beggin', puto," he snarled, pulling a curved blade from his coat. The edge glowed with burning red sigils, angry and volatile. "You embarrassed me. In front of my enemy's." His voice dipped, slithering cold. "And in my world, that ain't somethin 'I let slide."

Chase rolled his shoulders, heat building under his skin. The spellbound sigils along his forearms began to smolder, responding to the rising threat with a soft, molten gleam. His hands flexed once, fingers curling with slow certainty. He calmly removed his jacket not wanting to ruin the first tuxedo jacker he had ever worn, a jacket Skye gave him.

"I just want those white horses clattering on the ground, Camillo."

That was all it took.

Camillo snapped his fingers.

The goons surged.

Luther moved first exploding from behind. The big man, never far behind had been shadowing Skye from the main floor, and when the shouting started, he shouldered his way down the side corridor in time to see the first thug lunge. Luther hit him like a train—arcane brass knuckles flashing blue, runes lighting up like struck iron. The man dropped instantly, dead weight crashing to the carpet runner with a dull, final thud.

Skye was already in motion, slipping sideways with liquid grace as the second goon drew a wand. Too slow. Her Arcalam wand shifted form, shell guard and quillon forming to protect her casting hand. With a twist of her wrist, a burst of kinetic force slammed into him. He flew backward, crashing into a stack of crates by the service door. Bottles shattered, glass exploding in a glittering spray. Before he could recover, Skye was already there, heel poised. She brought it down without hesitation, shattering his wrist and the wand in a single, brutal strike.

Chase met the third man head-on. The thug lunged with a knife; Chase rolled under a wild haymaker and slammed a fist into his ribs—sigil-charged and punishing. The man wheezed, ribs breaking in a sickening crunch. Chase grabbed his arm, twisted, and flung him sideways into the paneled wall so hard the wood splintered. A second later, his nose and jaw exploded under Chase's arcane-enhanced fist.

The last goon saw his odds evaporate and bolted back toward the main room. Luther took one step, cocked back, and hurled a thrown punch of raw force—ether knuckles discharging in a compressed blast. It caught the man square between the shoulders, launching him forward to sprawl across a table near the side doorway in a spray of glasses and startled screams.

And then, only Camillo remained. The gangster moved quick—blade slashing, red arcane energy sizzling through the air. Chase stepped into the blow, slipped it, and drove an elbow into Camillo's jaw.

Bone met bone.

Camillo staggered.

Chase didn't stop.

He drove Camillo back with a series of brutal, rapid-fire punches—to the gut, the ribs, the face—forcing him down the corridor, slamming him into the wall, then into a service cart stacked with crystal and silver.

WANDS AND TOMMY GUNS

Camillo spat blood, swinging at places Chase was no longer at. The man was outmatched, but Chase didn't let up. A sharp left hook sent him spinning. His back slammed against the wall beside a framed painting; the frame cracked, tilting askew.

Chase stepped in close, grabbed the gangster by the collar, and yanked him forward—then slammed him against the opposite wall, denting the plaster with a sick crunch of bone and wood.

Camillo fumbled, trying to reach for the gun tucked at the small of his back. Big mistake. Chase caught his wrist mid-motion and twisted. Camillo screamed, the joint snapping like dry wood. Then Chase let go— only to launch a devastating left cross into Camillo's cheekbone.

Blood sprayed, painting the wall. Camillo sagged, but Chase yanked him up again and drove another fist into his face. Teeth flew. Another blow. And another. It wasn't just a fight anymore. It was something else. It was punishment. Every blow landed with purpose—too much purpose. Not just to win, but to hurt. To break the spirit of the gangster. And he wanted everyone to see. A kick to the chest sent Camilo flying past the hallway curtin and onto the the Rose's main dance floor. Patrons gasped, the band scattered. Isabelle eyes flared in controlled anger. Fights did not occur at the Rose.

Camillo's face was pulp. Barely recognizable. But Chase's eyes had gone cold, distant—haunted by something deeper than the moment. His fists moved like they had a mind of their own, driven by memories and rage and the things he'd never been allowed to forget.

"Chase—¡cálmate! Lo vas a matar!" Skye shouted, voice sharp over the ringing in his ears.

Luther moved. The big man tackled Chase from behind, arms wrapping around his chest like a steel trap. "Enough!" he barked. It took everything he had to hold him back.

Chase jerked once—twice—muscles coiled with murder. Then he stopped. Completely. His breath tore in and out of him, ragged, hot. His fists hung limp at his sides, slick with Camillo's blood.

Camillo lay in a broken heap on the carpet runner, twitching, whining through shattered teeth. The floor beneath him was already darkening. Luther kept a hand on Chase's shoulder another beat before easing off. "That was too much, Cassidy," he said quietly.

Chase didn't answer.

Slowly, he lifted his gaze—and found Isabelle standing next to Renald. Her expression was unreadable. No shock. No anger. No judgment. Just cool, composed calculation. Chase felt a flicker of shame twist in his gut.

Isabelle held his eyes for a heartbeat... then offered the smallest nod. A curt, silent acknowledgment of what had happened—and what could no longer be undone. She turned away. With a flick of her fingers, the warded music system thrummed back to life. Jazz flooded the Royal Rose again, smooth and unbothered, swallowing the violence whole.

Two of her men appeared instantly from the shadows, moving toward Camillo's limp form. Professionals. Silent. Efficient. They began to lift him without a word. Chase exhaled slowly, trying to breathe through the heat still boiling under his skin. He rolled his shoulders once, shaking off the last tremors.

"Let's go," he muttered.

Luther didn't say another word. He turned, shouldering past the wreckage on the main floor. Skye followed, sparing one final glance at Camillo's crumpled body, her arcalam still glowing from her last spell.

They pushed through the velvet curtains and back into the narrow hallway where the ambush had started. The music was muffled here, distant, as though the Rose itself was trying to swallow what had happened. Chase stopped. The sigils on his arms glowed faintly beneath his sleeves—embers dancing along his skin, restless and agitated. The fury had sunk its claws in. And no matter how deep he breathed... It wasn't letting go.

Skye noticed. Without a word, she stepped in close, pulling a silk red handkerchief from her bosom. The fabric was soft, delicate, but her movements were firm, precise. She took his hands before he could pull away and wiped the blood from his fingers, his knuckles, the spaces between. He was still hot.

She could feel it—the heat of something not entirely human, not entirely safe. Chase kept his eyes down, but his hands trembled slightly. Skye didn't let go. Instead, she reached up and cupped his face gently. Her fingers were cool, her touch steady.

"Mírame."

The single word was soft, but commanding. Look at me. Chase's jaw was tight, locked, but after a moment, his gaze shifted to hers. Skye searched his face, her brown eyes filled with something deeper than concern. There was a pull there—silent, magnetic—but more than anything, she needed him to snap out of it. Her touch was enough. With a gentle pull they fled the dance floor.

"I shouldn't have done that," he muttered under his breath—to himself, not anyone else. He'd been in enough scrapes to know when a message was sent and received. Camillo had been broken three punches ago. Everything after that had been for something else. For the war still living under his ribs. For ghosts that refused to stay buried.

He expected to feel proud. Satisfied. He didn't. He felt... exposed. It hit him then—how it must have looked. The second day of knowing Skye Anderson, and he'd nearly bludgeoned a man to death in a hallway over a word and a threat. The kind of thing sane people ran from. He dragged in a slow breath, willing the sigils to quiet, forcing his heartbeat to level out.

Chase glanced sideways at her. Her arcalam wand was holstered again, but her fingers still hovered near it out of habit. He braced himself for the look he was used to seeing after moments like that—fear, revulsion, the careful distance people put between themselves and dangerous things.

But it wasn't there.

Skye's eyes were bright, wide with lingering adrenaline, yes—but not afraid of him. There was concern there, sharp and focused, tracking the tension in his shoulders, the way his jaw clenched. Underneath that, something else glowed.

Pleased wasn't the right word. Pride came closer.

Approval... maybe. Something deep and hot in her chest that she didn't bother trying to name.

Then—

Skye grabbed him.

A kiss—fierce, hungry, full of fire and adrenaline—crashed into him before he could take another breath. Her hands slid up the sides of his face, then around the back of his head, fingers threading into his curls as she pushed him backward until his shoulders hit the hallway wall with a dull thud.

Chase reacted on instinct.

His hands dropped to her waist, gripping tight, then sliding lower —fingers curling into the curve of her hips, then her backside, pulling her flush against him. Heat rolled off him in waves, the sigils beneath his skin still pulsing like banked embers trying to flare.

She kissed him harder. Then she broke the kiss slowly, lips dragging off his, breath warm against his mouth. She stayed close, their noses nearly touching, her eyes locked into his like she was daring him to look away.

"Chase," she murmured, voice low and steady. "He earned every hit." A long beat of silence lingered between them, charged, intimate, electric. Her hand slid down, fingers tracing the line of his jaw, then down his arm until she found his hand. Cool, deliberate, grounding. She didn't flinch at the bruised knuckles, the blood, the tremor still in his fingers.

She held on.

And Chase—still breathing hard, still half on fire—held back.

Without a word, she laced her fingers through his and tugged gently.

He let her lead.

They stepped out of the alley and back toward the thrum of Harlem's streets, Skye's hand still laced with his, Chase understood something he wasn't ready to say out loud: He'd already drawn a line in blood around her. And if men like Camillo del Gato wanted to cross it? He'd do it again.

The service door sighed shut behind them, cutting off the muffled jazz and clinking glasses. Out here, the night felt colder. They slipped out the back of the Royal Rose the way wounded men left battlefields—quietly, using the exits nobody talked about. The alley was slick with old rain and city grime, a single streetlamp throwing a weak circle of light over busted crates and stacked milk crates.

Luther moved ahead, scanning the mouth of the alley, shoulders squared and jaw set. He was on edge, but controlled. Professional. Skye walked a half-step at Chase's side, arms pulled tight around her chest, curls a little mussed from the chaos. The alley light caught the ink on her arm where it slipped from her sleeve—glyphs faintly pulsing as they settled.

The Royal Rose carried on beyond them—music, laughter, clinking glasses—as if nothing had happened at all.

CHAPTER 7

Kiss Me Deadly

Radio Broadcast from the Grim Truth on WBC Radio

"Good evening, New York. This is Walter Grimsby, bringing you the Grim Truth they don't want you to hear."

"Once again, the so-called 'authorities 'have failed us. Illegal arcane contraband floods our streets—smuggled in from every dark corner of the world. Cursed relics, unlicensed spellcraft, mind-rotting elixirs—foul, corrupting magic slipping through our ports like rats in the night. And what do the police do?"

"Nothing."

"They tell us they're 'doing their best. 'They tell us their hands are tied. But let me ask you this—who's tying them? Who's really pulling the strings in this city? Because I'll tell you one thing: it sure as hell isn't the good, law-abiding folks of New York."

"Mark my words, ladies and gentlemen. If we don't act—if we don't take a stand—this city will drown in the filth of arcane corruption. And when that happens? Don't say I didn't warn you."

(The broadcast crackles as the radio static swallows his voice, fading into the hum of the city...)

The docks were unnervingly still, the night air thick with the briny stench of the East River. Moonlight pooled in silver patches across the weathered planks and steel shipping containers stacked like rusted tombstones.

Benjamin's grip tightened on the steering wheel as their car rolled to a slow stop. The headlights washed over another vehicle parked at an angle—abandoned, door cracked open like a warning.

"That ain't one of ours," Charlie said, leaning forward between the seats.

Charlie was a brick of a man—square shoulders, thick neck, broken nose permanently set crooked from too many fistfights. A gold tooth glinted when he spoke, the only thing that ever made his scowl shine.

"Looks dead as my ex-wife," he muttered.

Beside him, Clyde squinted toward the warehouse. Shorter, wiry, his frame almost boyish—until you saw the hands. Big, knuckled things, too large for his thin wrists, hands made for choking or snapping necks. Men joked Clyde was born with a grip before he grew the rest of himself.

"Lights are off," Clyde said. "Building's too damn quiet."

Miles said nothing. He stared at the squat black mass of Warehouse 24, jaw clenched. The structure hunched in the dark like something asleep with one eye open.

He looked at Benjamin. The boy swallowed hard.

Miles swung the car door open and jabbed a finger toward the front seat.

"You stay with the car, kid. Engine running. No wandering. Got it?"

Benjamin swallowed hard and nodded, sliding behind the wheel. For an eleven-year-old, he sat with a kind of shaky pride—as if the seat belonged to him after all.

Miles grunted approval and turned toward the only other man in the vehicle.

Frank.

Frank snored softly, slumped against the window, mouth open, hat tipped low. He hadn't even noticed the car stop.

Miles slapped the door frame. "Frank. Frank, wake up."

Nothing.

He jerked his thumb at Benjamin. "Benji. Wake him up."

Benjamin leaned over and shook the man's shoulder. "Frank? Hey—hey, wake up."

Frank mumbled something unintelligible but didn't sit up.

Miles clicked his tongue in irritation. "Fine. Let him sleep. Listen up, kid." He crouched to eye level with Benjamin, voice dropping to a low, razor-tight growl. "If anyone comes running—anyone—screaming, shouting, bleeding, doesn't matter… you hit the gas. Understand?"

Benjamin nodded again, quick, pale, small hands tightening on the steering wheel.

Miles stared at him a moment longer, then straightened his coat. "Good. Keep your eyes open. Frank sure as hell won't."

He shut the door and headed off with Slim and the rest, boots crunching on dock gravel, leaving the boy alone with the sleeping man and the cold hum of the idling engine.

The night swallowed them.

Benjamin watched through the windshield, heart pounding. He didn't follow. Didn't dare. He kept the car idling exactly as Miles had told him, fingers drumming nervously against the wheel.

Ahead, the men approached the yawning doors of Warehouse 24.

Slim, jittery and sweating through his shirt, pointed with a shaking hand. "Door was open when I got here. I swear I didn't touch nothin'."

Miles ignored him. He nudged the cracked door with the barrel of his wand.

It creaked open on a stale exhale of mildew and rust.

The stink hit them immediately—mold, dust, and something metallic and rotten underneath it all.

Inside, a single bulb swung overhead, flickering weakly and casting warped shadows that crawled along the rows of crates. The silence wasn't just silence—it listened.

Charlie muttered, "This feels wrong."

Then they saw it.

Blood.

A thick smear dragged across the stairwell wall—dark, halfway dry, streaked like someone had clawed upward in terror.

Miles crouched, letting his hand hover just above the smear. The tang of iron hit the back of his throat.

"That ain't animal," he said flatly. "Something went real bad in here."

Slim, voice shaking, whispered, "I—I told you those European renters upstairs were weird…"

Miles 'expression darkened. "We're not here to debate it. We're here to find out what the hell happened."

He jerked his head toward the floor. "Charlie, Clyde—fan out. Look for survivors. Or bodies."

They moved.

Clyde melted into the rows of crates, wand raised. Charlie tromped toward the opposite corner, his heavy boots echoing like muffled gunshots.

Slim stayed near Miles, trembling.

"Should we… call the cops?" Slim asked.

Miles snorted. "Yeah? Tell the BAE we got blood on the walls of a warehouse filled with unregistered arcane contraband? They'd string us all up before askin 'a damn question."

Slim swallowed. Then—

"Hey! Miles!"

Charlie's voice cracked through the silence—sharp, terrified.

Miles spun and sprinted toward the sound, Slim stumbling behind him. Clyde appeared from between two crates at the same moment, wand raised. They found Charlie frozen in place, eyes wide, finger trembling as he pointed upwards.

Slowly—unnervingly slowly—a shape turned in the shadows near the ceiling, suspended in midair as if gravity had forgotten her. Wings—thin, torn, insectile—beat with a faint whirring sound, keeping her aloft. She rotated with the dreamy, mechanical grace of a figurine trapped inside a music box or a snow globe, spinning in place, head tilted slightly as if listening to a song only she could hear.

Then she descended.

Her arms drifted outward, fingers splayed, ballet-like but wrong—all wrong—as she spiraled downward in a smooth, floating glide. Dust motes swirled around her like ash caught in a draft. Her pointed toes brushed the floor with the delicate silence of a dancer returning to the stage after a long, haunted absence.

She touched down. And turned.

CoCo le Fey

She was a nightmare stitched into the remnants of a ballerina's dream. Her tutu hung in filthy tatters—torn lace and wilted ribbons clinging like the memory of a grace that had died long before she had. Once-iridescent wings shuddered behind her in sharp, insectile spasms, twitching in the shadows.

Her skin was corpse-pale, streaked with cracked stage makeup like porcelain left to rot in an attic. Long, oily black hair veiled most of her face —but behind those tangled curtains, two red eyes glowed faintly, fractured sparks of madness staring out.

Unblinking. Hungry. And she hummed.

A child's lullaby—off-key, drifting through the air like claws dragged down glass. She twirled once. She bowed.

Her eyes snapped open—and locked onto Clyd. He swallowed, voice cracking in a whisper. "She's got some gams on her…"

"Zip it," Miles snarled, stepping forward with his wand raised. "Hey there, sister. You wanna tell us what's going on?"

CoCo tilted her head like a marionette whose strings had been yanked too hard. Her lips stretched into a smile far too wide to be human.

"What's going on?" she echoed sweetly. "Why, it's a performance, silly!"

And then she moved. She dropped into a flawless leap—silent, fluid —landing so softly her ballet shoes barely whispered against the floor. She glided toward Clyd, closing the distance in a heartbeat.

Clyd froze.

Her breath brushed his cheek. "In delay there lies no plenty," she crooned, voice sugared and venomous. "Then come and kiss me, sweet and twenty."

Clyd's eyes widened. Then softened. Then glazed over entirely. He leaned toward her—helpless.

"No—!" Miles 'shout cracked through the warehouse—

But it was far, far too late. She kissed him.

A deep, ravenous kiss—her hands gripping his face tenderly, almost lovingly, as her tongue slid past his teeth with a wet, obscene sound. She inhaled as if his very soul were breath she'd been starving for.

Clyd's body jerked violently.

His eyes flew wide, then rolled back until only white remained. Foam bubbled at the corners of his mouth as his limbs convulsed— marionette spasms, wrong angles, sinew snapping under its own strain. His heels scraped against the concrete, spine arcing unnaturally.

Still she kissed him. Still she drank.

Only when his breath rattled into a final, wet choke... did she release him.

Clyd collapsed like an empty skin.

CoCo le Fey twirled away, wiping her mouth with a dainty, blood-smeared hand. Then she sang, voice tinged with rot: "I kissed thee, I killed thee..."

She vanished, but her laughter followed, cracked porcelain joy echoing into madness as she skipped backward on pointed toes.

Miles spat, yanked his wand up, and roared:

"FAN OUT! FIND HER!"

He didn't get the chance. The air buckled. A pressure wave of warped magic blasted across the warehouse. Miles was lifted off his feet and hurled across the room, smashing into a crate stack hard enough to crack wood.

Charlie skidded backward but managed to stay upright.

Slim stumbled, nearly falling, eyes wild.

Then the warehouse doors blew open.

Four Mourned charged in. Feral. Half-rotted. Eyes glowing with hollow hunger. Charlie didn't run. He planted his feet and loosed a barrage of spells, blue sparks tearing through the dark. One Mourned dropped instantly, chest blown open.

Miles staggered up, wand raised, teeth clenched. "Give 'em hell!"

Slim dove a hand into his jacket, ripping out two dusty regent components—powdered iron and a strip of salt-paper. His hands shook, but his voice steadied as he slammed them together.

"IGNIS LACERA!"

A ripping arc of jagged flame shot across the room, slamming into a Mourned's shoulder and detonating it in a plume of burning rot. Charlie barked a laugh. "That's it, Slim! Hit 'em again—"

A Mourned lunged from behind a crate, claws slicing across Slim's ribs and sending him spinning. His remaining components scattered across the floor.

"Shit!" Slim scrambled backward, trying to grab another mixture. Another Mourned tackled Charlie, jaws sinking into his shoulder. He screamed—short, sharp—before the creature ripped him off his feet.

Miles struck, firing a heavy bolt of fiery light into the Mourned's spine. It screwed as it was engulfed in flames.

"SLIM, MOVE!"

Slim tried to cast again, fingers fumbling over a shard of quartz— The Mourned's swipe knocked it from his hand. He bolted. He ran for the office, kicking the door shut behind him and slamming the deadbolt. Miles heard glass shatter as Slim tried the window—

Then a strangled scream.

A heavy thud. Silence. Miles, panting, bleeding, stood alone among the dead.

Outside, Benjamin sat stiff in the driver's seat, staring at the warehouse doors like they might breathe. Behind him, Frank groaned awake—slow, sluggish, like a man clawing his way up from the bottom of a bad dream. As if something had knocked him out and still clung to his voice.

"Wh… what the hell…?" Frank rubbed his face, blinking hard. "Kid… why'm I in the back seat? What happened?"

Benjamin didn't look away from the warehouse. "You fell asleep, snoring like a rhino. Miles and Slim went inside to check the shipment. They told us to stay put."

Frank snorted, easing upright with a wince. "Miles told you to stay put, not me."

"They've been gone a long time," Benjamin murmured.

Frank frowned at him. "So why're we sittin 'here like bumps on a log? We should go in. Check on 'em."

Benjamin shook his head sharply. "No. Miles said stay. He was serious."

Frank stared at him, eyes narrowing. "You're the one who usually conks out in the back seat, kid. Not me. Something ain't right. And I ain't sittin 'on my hands waitin 'for—"

A scream tore through the warehouse—high, sharp, human. Then a crash. Something heavy hitting the floor. And then Miles 'voice, ragged with terror:

"FRANK! BENJAMIN—GET IN HERE! NOW!"

Benjamin froze.

Frank smirked grimly. "Told ya." He yanked Benjamin from the car. They ran inside. The warehouse was a slaughterhouse. Frank stepped forward first, wand raised. "Stay behind me," he muttered—He never saw the Mourned drop from the rafters.

The creature landed on him with a wet crunch, claws tearing into his chest. Frank screamed once before blood bubbled up into his throat. Benjamin stumbled back—

And she descended.

CoCo le Fey drifted from the rafters in a slow, perfect pirouette, landing on pointed toes. Tattered tutu fluttering. Red eyes glowing like embers. Her smile widened unnaturally. "There you are…" she whispered.

"Come to me, sweet thing. Let Coo-Coo make you dance."

She glided forward, hips swaying with hypnotic rhythm. A shimmer of glamour misted from her wings—Benjamin blinked. It slid off him. The glamour failed. Her doll-like face cracked in fascination. "Oooh," she cooed, leaning close. "That's new."

Benjamin's hand shook as he drew Renald's wand. He fired. A crackling blue bolt shot straight at her.

CoCoo flicked her wrist. The hex shattered like glass. Her smile returned."Feisty."

Benjamin didn't wait. He turned and ran, boots hammering against concrete. He tore through the doorway, across the dock, lungs burning—

And skidded to a stop.

A massive figure crouched beside the car. Broad shoulders. Scarred hands. Thick neck. The smell of tobacco and blood. Slowly, the man lifted his head.

Domingo.

His grin revealed teeth filed to points.

"Hola, niño," he rumbled, stepping forward. "Been lookin 'for you."

The assassin stood slowly, massive, deliberate, a man carved from slabs of meat and menace. He was built like a bodybuilder: thick through the chest and shoulders, arms like battering rams, neck swallowed by muscle. He moved with the slow confidence of someone who had never lost a fight—and didn't plan to start now.

There wasn't a patch of skin left unmarked. His entire body was a tapestry of ink, layered in ancient glyphs and brutal iconography—symbols of bloodletting, sacrifice, and death etched into every inch of flesh like a living altar. Coiling lines ran over his face and scalp, down his arms, across his throat, each tattoo whispering of rituals no child should know the names of.

He wore a sleeveless black vest, the fabric stretched tight across his hulking torso. Two long knives hung at his hips—curved, bone-handled, and lovingly maintained. Their sheaths bore tally marks. Hundreds of them.

Loose harem pants billowed around his legs, cinched at the knees with crisscrossed wrappings. His feet were bare—thick, calloused, silent on the wood like the pads of a hunting cat.

Domingo cracked his neck, slow and deliberate, as he loomed over the boy like a butcher over a lamb.

Benjamin moved first. He snatched up his wand, raised it with shaking hands, and fired. The spell was wild—but fast. A column of pale-blue light hit Domingo square in the chest. A ring on the brute's left hand flared bright.

Absorption ward. The spell sank into it and vanished. Benjamin fired again—panicked, louder. The ring on Domingo's other hand flared. The second spell died just as easily. Domingo smirked. "Cute."

He clapped his hands together with a thunderous crack. A shockwave of shadow-magic rolled outward like a rippling sheet of black water. It slammed toward Benjamin—Instinct—pure, feral, terrified—took over.

Benjamin spun, slashed his wand through the air, and shouted—

"REFLECTUS!" A shimmering arc shielded him, caught the wave, and hurled it back. The shadow-force distorted midair, twisting like a serpent—and disintegrated. Benjamin stared at his own wand, breath trembling.

"I—I did that...?"

Domingo's expression shifted. Not impressed. Irritated. He inhaled sharply—then roared. A sound that shook the planks, a primal challenge that rattled Benjamin's bones. He reached for the bone-handled blade at his sash—

Before he could draw—A voice sliced through the mist.

"I would reconsider killing that one."

Domingo stiffened. He turned—and scowled.

Out of the fog walked a tall, wiry man in a deep plum coat. A silver-tipped cane tapped the dock at a measured pace. His pale hair was slicked back, spectacles perched perfectly on the bridge of his nose.

Sirus Magnus.

A man whose power didn't shout. It whispered. And things listened. Behind him drifted two shuffling figures—Mourned. Their bodies jerked in unnatural spasms, sniffing the air for mana-scent. And behind them stepped something worse.

A Gravecaller. Necromanic priests of the old world. Its robes flowed like drowned funeral cloth, black and clinging. A bone-white skull mask hid its face—smooth, featureless, carved with angles that hurt the eye. Its fingers were elongated, blackened, moving like jointed spiders.

Domingo didn't move. Didn't breathe. Even he knew better than to stare too long at that mask. Sirus approached Domingo without fear.

"The boy," he said calmly, "is worth significantly more alive."

Domingo spat to the side. "Don't tell me how to do my job, Magnus."

Sirus tilted his head. "If you prefer Makalith to remind you again—publicly—of your last… failure, I can summon him."

Domingo's tattooed arms flexed. Rage swelled—then cooled, forced down. He didn't answer.

Sirus stepped closer until the point of his cane gently touched Domingo's vest. "You will hunt him," Sirus murmured. "But not carelessly. Not loudly. He bruises easily—and the Court has plans for him."

Domingo growled. Sirus ignored him completely. He turned toward the warehouse. "I will secure the sarcophagus. The Seated arrive soon. You: bring back the boy."

Domingo's nostrils flared—but he obeyed. Behind him, the Gravecaller bowed its head in eerie acknowledgment, shadow tendrils swirling at its feet like hungry wolves. Sirus continued walking toward the warehouse, the Gravecaller stepping aside with a stiff, reverent motion. The Mourned shuffled after him, whispering death.

Domingo leaned back, cracked his knuckles—and hissed a command. His tattoos ignited. Black ink flared red-hot. From the darkness beneath his feet, shadows peeled away, taking shape—distorted wolf-like silhouettes with dripping jaws made of ink and malice.

Shadow-hounds.

Domingo pointed toward the alley Benjamin fled down. "Fetch." They sprinted into the dark.

Benjamin, far down the dock now, heard them before he saw them—hungry, distorted growls chasing him into the night. He ran harder.

———

Deep beneath Warehouse 24, past rune-sealed gates and tunnels etched in dead languages, lay a space untouched by time. No sunlight reached here—only the flicker of arcane torches burning with sickly green flame. At its heart stood a sarcophagus of obsidian and bone, massive and ancient.

Silver veins pulsed along its surface like the slow, steady beat of something not quite dead. Incantations weren't written but carved— etched by blood, memory, and madness. Magic so old it vibrated just below hearing.

Two of the Emerged-Mourned flanked the sarcophagus. Not the wild, screeching kind that haunted alleys and old train yards—these were curated. Perfect. Suited. Their skin drawn tight across elegant skulls, lips sewn shut in reverent silence. They didn't breathe. They didn't blink. They simply waited.

A figure stepped through the glyph-etched threshold.

Makalith Ravenwind.

He moved like a blade sliding from velvet—deliberate, quiet, deadly. His skin, black as polished stone, caught the torchlight in gleaming ridges. No robe, no veil of mysticism—just a tailored charcoal-gray suit threaded with arcane silk, a green pocket square curved like a dagger, and at his hip, a wand with an obsidian shaft and a handle carved from a dragon's broken jawbone.

Behind him lingered members of the Twilight Collective— mercenaries, dangerous and coin-loyal—but none followed him inside. Even killers knew better. This room smelled of resurrection.

Sirus Magnus was already waiting.

He inclined his head in greeting, tapping his cane once against the stone. "The vate is ready," he murmured. "She'll wake soon."

Makalith said nothing at first. He stepped forward, brushing a gloved hand across the sarcophagus. The runes rippled faintly beneath his touch, like skin reacting to a familiar hand.

"Then we stay on schedule," he said. "Ensure the bindings hold. If they falter for even a breath, this chamber will become our tomb."

Sirus tensed but didn't respond. His silence was its own protest. He hated this. Hated her.

Adriana Mortem Ruthven. The First Seat of the Court of Bones.

Reborn through necromancy and something older. A soul not native to this world. A vampire and a necromancer, melded into one perfect abomination. Even dead, her presence filled the air like the echo of a scream you'd never forget.

The air in the ritual chamber was suffocating—thick with grave-dust, alchemical fumes, and the pulse of the runes crawling beneath Adriana Mortem's sarcophagus. The coffin shivered, silver veins writhing beneath its stone surface like arteries under pallid skin.

A giggle broke the silence. High. Off-key. Wrong.

Coo Coo Le Fay drifted into the chamber like a fever-dream. Her movements were half-step, half-hover, wings flickering in blurred bursts that lifted her across the floor as though she skimmed over water. Bells chimed at her hips. Torn ribbons trailed like ghosts.

She spun once, then folded into Makalith's arms, kissing him fiercely, possessively. He accepted the kiss without yielding to it.

"You're late," Makalith murmured.

"I'm always late, did you miss me Makie?" Coco said brightly, twirling away. She drifted toward the sarcophagus, her hair curtain-soft, her red eyes glowing behind it.

She bowed deeply. "Hello again, Adriana."

The mercenaries near the walls retreated instinctively. Even hardened killers had limits.

Sirus Magnus adjusted his spectacles, lowering his voice so only Makalith heard—keeping it outside the Gravecaller's awareness.

"You know I trust your judgment," Sirus said quietly, "but the Court of Bones does not forgive loose ends. We deliver their First Seat... then we become liabilities."

Makalith traced a glyph with one fingertip, veins of silver light flaring beneath the stone.

"Calm yourself, Sirus. Our arrangement stands. With Adriana here and the boy secured, the Court gains their resurrection. We gain power. Afterward, we sever ties."

Sirus did not look reassured. He glanced toward the stairwell.

"About the boy…"

"What of the boy?"

"He escaped."

Makalith slowly turned his head, the motion deliberate, predatory. "Exactly how?"

Sirus exhaled through his nose In frustration "Domingo engaged him. The boy had a wand. He fought back. I sent Domingo in pursuit."

"A wand?" Makalith's voice thinned to a razor's edge. "Where would a gutter-born child get a wand? That was not the arrangement. He was simply supposed to be glamoured—"

He turned slowly toward Coo Coo.

Coco raised both hands cheerfully, fingers curled inward in a mock-innocent gesture—almost girlish. "Oh, oh! My glamour didn't work," she chirped. She paused suddenly, noticing a loose thread on her torn leotard. With a delicate flick of her fingers, she plucked it away, then examined her nails with exaggerated disinterest—careful not to meet Makalith's eyes.

"Little Benjamin just shrugged it off, very rude of him," she said lightly, almost sing-song.

Makalith's irritation sharpened into menace. "This complicates everything. Every motion of the ritual depends on the vessel being secured."

Sirus nodded. "Domingo is pursuing him now."

Makalith shook his head coldly. "Domingo is a sledgehammer. If he rages, he'll break the boy's spine just by breathing too hard." He turned sharply. "Send Utilis."

Sirus stiffened. "Utilis is guarding the vats. The essence pool is fragile. If corrupted—"

Makalith faced the Gravecaller. The bone-white mask tilted, unreadable, spirals etched across its surface shifting subtly in the candlelight. "You there," Makalith commanded. "We find ourselves short-handed. Leave this chamber. Go below. Guard the vats so they are not tainted. The First Seat must rise whole."

The Gravecaller bowed once—slow, reverent. Shadows pooled beneath its robe as it glided silently toward the stairwell. As soon as the creature vanished down the steps, Makalith turned back to Sirus.

"Now," he said with finality, "send Utilis."

Sirus nodded at once. "At once."

Coo Coo clapped, delighted. "Ohh, the hound is coming out to play."

Makalith returned to the sarcophagus, placing both hands atop its cold surface. The runes brightened. The air vibrated with a slow, ancient hum—like a heartbeat buried in stone.

Sirus kept his distance. "She's... waking."

"No," Makalith whispered. "She listens."

The runes pulsed again.

Coo Coo shivered with pleasure. "She's excited."

Makalith's expression hardened into something like reverence twisted with ambition. "Let necromancers cling to death," he said softly. "Let vampires fear it."He lowered his voice, awed. "Adriana Mortem was both... fused into a single perfect abomination. A creature who conquered the grave and then bent it to her will. The world forgot her because it had to."

Sirus swallowed hard. "And when she rises? When she turns on us?"

Makalith didn't look away from the sarcophagus. A faint smile curved the corner of his mouth. "You worry to much old friend. Have faith in the plan Sirus."

Sirus fell silent. The runes pulsed again—brighter this time. And somewhere beneath the stone lid...something stirred.

———

The dim gaslights of Madhatten flickered weakly, barely pushing back the darkness that choked the alleyways. The streets weren't streets here—they were veins, twisting endlessly, meant to confuse anyone who didn't belong.

Benjamin Bright ran.

His heart hammered in his chest, each breath sharp as a knife. Behind him came the sounds—the guttural rumble of something not fully alive, claws scraping across wet stone, bodies slithering in and out of shadow.

Shadow hounds.

He cut through a narrow passage between buildings, boots splashing through stagnant water, pressing himself against the damp brick as he tried to steady his breath.

A low growl rolled through the alley. Then—a flicker.

A shimmer of sickly purple-green light rippled across the darkness ahead, warping the air until reality folded inward like a turning page.

A doorway formed.

Not a real door. A sarcophagus—gothic, ribbed with bone-like ridges —materializing upright from nothing, splitting open along a glowing seam. Benjamin's blood turned to ice.

Domingo stepped out. Flanked by two spectral hounds emerging from the ink swirling along his arms. The brute smiled, teeth glinting like filed knives.

"You can't run forever, little fox. We have plans for you."

Benjamin's grip tightened on his wand. His pulse roared in his ears.

Domingo spread his arms lazily, as if pleased with the drama. "Whatever my beasts see..." His tattoos crawled like living snakes. "Whatever they smell..." The hounds growled, eyes burning red-orange. "I see, I smell." He grinned. "And wherever they stand—" The sarcophagus doorway snapped shut behind him. "I can join them."

With a sharp gesture, Domingo sent the hounds. They lunged forward—black shapes ripping out of the dark. Benjamin didn't think. He thrust his wand toward the closest hound.

"¡Ráfaga!"

A burst of force rocketed from the tip, slamming into the beast mid-charge. The shadowy creature imploded inward, dissolving into a mist of distorted ink. The second hound was already airborne. Claws raked across Benjamin's jacket—tearing through fabric and grazing his ribs. He rolled, skidded across gravel, came up on one knee, wand raised, eyes wide.

Domingo laughed—a deep, delighted rumble. "That's cute, niño. Try again."

One hound re-formed behind him. The others circled to the side. Benjamin's mind raced. Renald's lessons. They were useless here. Nothing the shapechanger had taught him had prepared him for beasts made of shadow and ink. Benjamin tightened his grip. There was nowhere left to run.

Then—A rumble.

Headlights swung wildly around the corner. A delivery truck barreled down the intersecting alley, brakes screeching. Domingo snarled and flicked two fingers. A hound leapt—silent and furious—straight at the oncoming truck.

"NO!" Benjamin gasped.

Too late. The hound hit the windshield. The truck fishtailed into the wall with a deafening crash. The driver barely crawled out before the other hounds descended on him—tearing and rending in a frenzy of shadow.

Domingo turned back toward the boy, irritation simmering. Benjamin was already running. He sprinted down the alley, past a pile of debris and spotted the ladder of a fire escape above him. He leapt—fingers snagging cold iron—and scrambled up three rungs before Domingo barked: "AFTER HIM."

The hounds turned at their masters call. The dying driver nothing more than an afterthought.

Benjamin yanking it upward with both hands. The metal rungs clanged as the ladder ripped out of Domingo's reach. He climbed—hard—arms burning, feet slipping. He reached the landing, threw himself onto the roof—

A shadowbird slammed into him. Talons of darkness raked his shoulder, knocking him flat. The bird shrieked, circling high above—a huge, tattered condor-shaped thing, made of smoke and teeth.

Benjamin crawled backward, wand raised—

A pulse of violet light cut the air behind him.

A sarcophagus-shaped tear in reality unfurled on the rooftop. Domingo stepped through it, cool, calm, like stepping off a train. Two hounds phased in behind him, their bodies knitting back together from smoke.

Benjamin's stomach dropped.

"Nowhere left to go," Domingo rumbled, drawing the wicked bone-handled blade at his sash.

Benjamin backed up until his heels hit the roof's ledge. Domingo advanced. Benjamin's mind raced. His spells were not strong strong enough. No tricks left. Only one insane option. He flicked his wand toward the roof beneath the hounds.

"¡Fractura!"

The tile and gravel exploded. The rooftop collapsed, opening like a jagged mouth. The two hounds dropped instantly—yowling into the darkness below. Domingo snarled as the ground gave way under him. He lunged, grabbing the edge with both hands—muscle bulging, tattoos flaring.

Benjamin scrambled back, panting, staring down at the brute hanging from his fingertips. Domingo looked up at him, eyes full of fury and promise. "This isn't over," he growled as he pulled himself up.

Benjamin didn't stay to watch. He turned—took three running steps —

and jumped off the roof.

Domingo's shout tore the night: "¡Hijo de puta!"

Mid-air, the ground rushing up to swallow him— Benjamin snapped his wand downward.

"¡Levitar!" His fall slowed—body drifting like a feather, legs dangling as he floated down the side of the building. His boots touched the cobblestones with a light thud.

He didn't breathe. Didn't think. He ran. Through the alleys. Past the whispering walls. Toward the only place left in Madhatten where someone might protect him.

The Royal Rose.

———

Makalith stood in the shadows, arms crossed, observing the ritual chamber with a carefully neutral expression. The air reeked of rot masked by incense—too sweet, too thick, clinging to the stone like regret. Even the best perfumes couldn't hide decay for long. He had walked in darkness, commanded it, shaped it to profit. But this—the way Adriana Mortem Ruthven's servants conducted their rites—unsettled him in a way he would never say aloud.

This is power.

He watched the sarcophagus's silver veins pulse with faint, rhythmic light. But also excess. Crude. Indulgent.

Sirus Magnus approached at a measured pace, cane tapping against the stone. Three Gravecallers glided behind him—robed in whispering black, their bone-white masks etched with spiraling runes that pulled at the eye. Beneath their shadowed robes, Makalith glimpsed skeletal plate, rib-like armor shifting with unnatural grace.

The largest Gravecaller bowed stiffly. "Lady Ruthven stirs."

Before Makalith or Sirus could answer, Coco Le Fay burst into the chamber in a whirl of torn silk and wild delight.

"Boooring, booooRING!" she sang, spinning, wings twitching in frantic half-beats. "All this waiting! All this dust! Is she dead or just being a lazy bones?"

She stopped sharply, head tilting at a grotesque angle, pupils dilating with childlike curiosity and predatory hunger. One Gravecaller turned precisely toward her. Their mask betrayed nothing. "She slumbers. She wakes when she chooses."

Coco pouted dramatically. "Oh good. I was this close to kissing her awake."

Sirus shot her a glare edged with panic. Coco only giggled.

Then—

A tremor.

A low groan.

The sarcophagus shifted. Silver veins brightened. The stone lid slid aside with a hiss of cold mist curling outward like a dead breath loosed. Inside lay Adriana Mortem Ruthven, First Seat of the Court of Bones. Her porcelain skin was threaded with blue-black veins. Rot marred her arms and chest in patches that looked half-decayed, half-frozen in time. Her lips were corpse-blue.

And her eyes—

Twin crimson fires—ancient, hungry, alive.

She sat up with unsettling grace.

Sirus blanched. Makalith went rigid.

"She wakes—now?" Sirus whispered. "The Court has not yet arrived."

Adriana stepped out of her coffin, bare feet touching the stone with soundless poise. Her voice was soft. Regal. "Where is Von Epp?"

Makalith snapped to action. A rare crack in his composure. "Summon him. Immediately." To the nearest Gravecaller: "Go. Fetch him from the lower halls."

The Gravecaller bowed and faded into the shadows.

Coco Coo clasped her hands in glee. "She couldn't wait! Oh, she couldn't wait!"

A second Gravecaller approached Adriana with reverent precision, gesturing toward the massive stone basin at the center of the chamber— already filled to the brim with congealed, thrumming blood.

Adriana drifted toward it, her long black gown trailing behind her in tatters of silk and shadow. "My bath," she murmured. She stepped in without hesitation.

Blood swallowed her. And the glow began.It pulsed.

Once...

Twice...

Then surged like a heartbeat. Rot vanished. Veins cleared. Her flesh smoothed, perfect once more. Her lips turned rich crimson, full of life that was not hers. She rose from the basin—reborn.

Coo Coo squealed with joy.

Sirus swallowed hard.

Makalith's distaste sharpened. Even now she is ruled by hunger. Dependent. A queen chained to blood.

One Gravecaller returned—this time pulling a child with him. A boy. Maybe nine. Golden hair matted. Wrists bound in iron links etched with runes. Fey blooded from a strong lineage.

Makalith stiffened. The sight hit him like a knife to the ribs. He stepped forward instinctively. "What is this?" he demanded. "We agreed their would be a feeding but our agreement was no Fey. The Court agreed my lady—"

"Silence." The command struck the room like a hammer. Cold. Absolute. Sovereign. Adriana was suddenly before the child, her presence overwhelming, her aura cold as winter steel.

"Come," she whispered.

The boy stepped toward her. Not by choice. By command.

Adriana cupped the boy's chin and drew him closer.

Makalith stepped forward on instinct—hand half-raised in protest.

"Lady Ruthven, please let us reconsider—"

Adriana did not even turn her head.

Makalith froze. His jaw clenched hard. Slowly, painfully, he lowered his hand.

Footsteps. Heavy, urgent, echoing down the corridor. A tall figure strode into the chamber, fastening the last clasp of his black military-style greatcoat. His uniform—trim, precise, adorned with bone-white stitching and the sigils of the Second Seat—gleamed faintly under the torchlight.

Herman Von Epp.

He stopped the moment he saw her. Adriana Mortem Ruthven— First Seat of the Court. Recovered. Restored. Alive. Von Epp dropped to one knee so fast it echoed. Head bowed. Fist pressed to his chest. "My First Seat," he breathed.

Adriana acknowledged him with only the faintest tilt of her chin. She turned her attention back to the child. Her cold fingers slid along the boy's cheek—gentle, almost tender. She inhaled deeply, the way one might savor the scent of a rare bloom. The boy trembled. But under her touch, he could not look away.

Adriana smiled. Soft. Warm.

Motherly.

Then she lifted his chin—and sank her fangs into his throat.

The child's gasp was tiny—a bird crushed in a closing fist. Blood spilled in thin red ribbons.

And Coo-Coo Le Fey screamed. A shriek ripped from her lungs—raw, primal, piercing. Not madness. Not theatrics. Fae. Pure Fae. Responding to the slaughter of her own kind. Her wings spasmed violently. Her nails elongated. Her pupils split like a feral animal's. She lunged—

"NO—NO—NO—NO!"

Adriana did not pause. Did not flinch. Did not even acknowledge the shriek.

Makalith moved instantly—faster than any human seer could track. He seized Coo-Coo by the shoulders, pinning her to the wall just as she thrashed, spitting tears, her entire body sparking with fractured glamour. Her nails scraped against the stone. Her ghost-light wings beat furiously, scattering motes of silver dust.

"LET ME GO—SHE'S KILLING HIM—SHE'S KILLING—"

Makalith's voice cut through her hysteria—low, strained, urgent.

"Coco—Coco, look at me. Look at me." She fought him wildly, sobbing. Her forehead pressed against his chest, wings trembling with grief and rage. Makalith wrapped his arms around her, physically holding her together as Adriana finished her feast behind them.

The boy's body hit the stone with a soft, sickening thump. Coo-Coo choked on a broken sob. Makalith held her tighter. Behind them—

Von Epp rose at Adriana's command, still trembling with reverence. Sirus swallowed hard, gaze darting away. The Gravecallers stood perfectly still—silent sentinels of the macabre.

Adriana wiped a single bead of blood from her lips with an elegant finger.

Then she lifted her crimson eyes to the assembled court.

"Now," she murmured, voice smooth as polished marble,   "tell me…"

Her gaze swept over Von Epp, then Sirus, then Makalith holding Coo-Coo tight against his chest—

"…what has transpired in my absence?"

CHAPTER 8

Stand Your Ground

From the Annotated Lectures of Magister Orwin Hale, "Principles of Aetheric Conduct" (3rd Ed.)

Magic is not a single discipline, but a hierarchy of hungers.

Arcane magic is the most common—what scholars call The Shaped Art. It bends willingly to the trained mind. Where there is logic, structure, and focus, the Arcane follows. Its sigils obey geometry; its spells thrive under discipline. But Arcane power is merely one way to manipulate the Aether. There is also Necromancy, which answers not to will, but to memory. The necro-arts are fueled by the lineage of loss; they demand a price in echoes, blood, or bone. Most who practice them do not understand them. Few survive their own learning.

Rarer still is Void magic—the Silent Longing. It has no shape, no tether. It is absence pretending to be power, a hunger so profound that other forms of magic recoil from it. Those who wield the Void do not cast spells. They open doors. And what steps through is never entirely theirs to command.

And somewhere between these forces—between the disciplined, the dead, and the devouring—stand the beings touched by ancient bloodlines. Dragon and Fey-born. Their magic is neither learned nor stolen. It is.

And that makes them the most hunted of all.

The alley behind the Royal Rose smelled of rain, blood, and the last fading notes of Son Cubano. Luther stood beside the Hispano-Suiza like a silent sentinel, arms crossed, jaw tight, eyes flicking from Chase to the service door they'd just come through. The tension carved across his frame said everything. He didn't rush them. Didn't speak. Just watched.

Chase blinked away the last sparks of fury still buzzing under his skin and pulled open the back door, motioning Skye inside first. She slid into the car, curls wild, arms bare, dress clinging to her like the heat of the fight hadn't quite left her. She hadn't bothered retrieving their coats from the Royal Rose coatroom. Neither had he. Chase followed, sinking into the seat beside her and exhaling hard as he shut the door.

Inside the car, everything was quiet. Too quiet. The only sound was the ticking of the Hispano's engine cooling in the night air. After a beat, Luther's voice drifted back through the open front partition. Low. Rough. Not judgment — worry.

"Christ, Cassidy."

Chase stared at his hands, at the split knuckles, the dried blood. He didn't answer. Luther shifted in the driver's seat, glancing back once as he started the engine. "You damned near put that man through a wall." Still nothing.

Because Chase didn't have an answer that didn't make him sound worse. The Royal Rose fight replayed behind his eyes — the bone-deep impact of fist against flesh, the way Camillo sagged like a broken puppet, the cold, distant place Chase had gone inside himself.

He braced for Skye to pull away. To shrink from him. To see him the way others always eventually did — as something dangerous, unstable, too raw inside to be trusted. Instead, her hand slid gently onto his forearm. He looked up.

Her eyes held no fear. Concern, yes. Intensity. And beneath that... something he wasn't used to seeing aimed his way. Pride. Excitement. Desire threaded through all of it. "You protected me," she said softly. The words landed deep — deeper than any blow he'd taken tonight.

"You shouldn't've had to see that," he murmured, voice rough. "I wasn't— I didn't—"

"Chase." She leaned closer. "You're not a monster."

That hit him harder than Camillo's blade ever could. Her thumb brushed across his cheek, slow, deliberate. She studied him the way a spellwright studies runes — all attention, no judgment. Her breath warmed his skin.

"You can kiss me," she whispered.

He didn't know who moved first. Maybe they both did. Their faces were inches apart, the world narrowing down to breath, heat, the trembling closeness of almost...

The Hispano-Suiza lurched violently. Skye's hand flew to Chase's chest as the car skidded sideways on the slick cobblestones. Luther slammed both feet on the brake, cursing under his breath. The headlights cut across the soaked street and illuminated—

A boy.

Small.

Terrified.

Running.

He staggered through the beam of the headlights, coat torn, eyes wide with panic. And behind him—two shadow-beasts burst from the darkness, their bodies flickering with arcane tattoos, jaws stretching open into impossible shapes.

Chase was out of the car before the door could fully swing open.

Rain splashed under his shoes as he hit the street. The sigils on his arms ignited like struck matches — heat rushing through his veins, strength coiling beneath the skin.

"Chase!" Skye called behind him, scrambling out after, wand already in hand. He didn't answer. Benjamin veered into a narrow alley, breath hitching, a raw spell bursting from his fingertips in a desperate flash of blue-white energy.

The beasts kept coming.

Chase sprinted after them — a streak of amber-lit force and barely contained fury. The sigils inked into Chase's arms lit up with a low hum, flickering like wildfire beneath his skin. His spellbound abilities surged— speed sharpening, strength coiling, senses widening like a lens snapping into focus. And then he was gone—blurring forward into the alley in a burst of kinetic force.

The narrow passage was choked with trash bins, rusted fire escapes, dripping pipes, and old posters flapping in the damp air. Benjamin scrambled up a stack of crates, trying to reach the fire escape ladder. One of the Shadow Beasts lunged.

Chase intercepted mid-air—shoulder-checking the creature into the brick wall hard enough to split mortar. Its body burst into writhing smoke for a heartbeat, the creature howling as the energy radiating from Chase's body disrupted its form—then it vanished.

Straight out of existence.

A cold spark crawled down Chase's spine.

"CHASE!" Skye screamed behind him. He spun, but too slowly. The beast reappeared at his back in a burst of warped shadow, jaws stretching wide toward the base of his skull—

A column of blue arcane fire ripped past Chase's cheek, scorching the air as it hammered into the creature. The blast didn't kill it, but it staggered violently, its form stuttering in and out of coherence as if reality couldn't decide whether it deserved to exist.

Skye came tearing into the alley behind him—barefoot, her heels clattering across the cobblestones where she'd shed them without hesitation. Her movements weren't the brute, grounded motions of a street fighter. They were sharp, elegant, controlled—the refined footwork of a trained duelist, a woman who understood rhythm, distance, and lethal timing.

Her wand was changing.

The silver-and-obsidian foci shifted in her grip, plates sliding apart with a whispering hiss of arcane metal. The transformation unfurled with the elegant, unmistakably Spanish lineage of a duelist's weapon. A flared shell guard blossomed around her hand like wrought iron coming to life. A cross-guard swept into place with crisp mechanical finality. A curved knuckle guard arced around her fingers in a protective loop. The obsidian shaft extended to the length of a small sword

In her hand was no longer a simple wand, but a fully awakened Arcalam, an arcane duelist's blade of focused will and lethal intent.

"Cassidy—MOVE!" she shouted as she took her stance, weight forward, sapphire tip glowing like a star about to detonate.

Another beast flickered into existence at Chase's left. He twisted, ducking as it snapped at his ear, its cry like tearing parchment. Chase's fist lashed out but the creature dissolved into shadow a split-second before the blow connected, reappearing next to him.

Chase spun, dropping low as claws raked the air above his head. These things weren't mindless. They were coordinated. Predatory.

Benjamin fired a wild bolt of blue-white magic from the crates, missing by inches. The creature pivoted toward the boy—

"NO—!"

Chase lunged, grabbing the beast by the back leg mid-flicker.

Shadow rippled under his grip like liquid smoke. He swung it hard into the alley wall—half of its form splattering, reforming, snarling. Another flicker—

It appeared above him. Claws arced toward Chase's face.

"¡Atrás!" Skye shouted.

She traced a series of spirals in the air, her movements sharp, precise, beautiful in their deadliness. Glowing runes erupted from her wand, binding fragments of shadow mid-shift, locking the beast into the material plane just long enough—

Chase drove his fist upward, sigils blazing.

Bone-shaking impact.

The beast slammed into the fire escape above, the ladder shaking violently as it shrieked, form rippling with instability. It tried to teleport again but the spell Skye had cast anchored it for a moment too long.

"Tir-Anatu!" Her voice rang hard and commanding in the First Tongue. A spear of radiant light erupted from her wand, ripping through the creature's chest. It detonated outward—shadow ripping apart into drifting smoke. The second beast shrieked and reappeared behind Skye—

Chase hit it mid-flicker. His heel connected squarely with its skull —a pulse of spellbound force firing through his leg. The creature's head imploded into shadow-smoke, body dispersing in a sudden inward collapse.

The alley crackled with leftover magic. Smoke coiled where the last Shadow Beast had been—but another ripple shuddered through the air. A third one.

Chase felt it before he saw it—the temperature drop, the shadow bending unnaturally, the faint hiss of something coalescing behind him.

Skye's breath hitched.

"Chase—behind you!"

He spun. The final Shadow Beast erupted out of the brickwork like living ink, its form barely stabilizing as it lunged—jaws wide, claws elongated, hunger palpable in its flickering outline.

Chase didn't have time to close distance. Instinct—and training— took over. He raised his right hand. Two fingers extended. The circular sigil burned into the back of his hand flared— a molten ring igniting across his skin, lines of gold rushing like hot oil through his veins.

The world around him dimmed for a split second. He felt the Infernal Lance sigil awaken. Heat surged up his arm, coiled in his palm, and then—a lance of concentrated Infernal fire erupted from his fingertips— narrow, blistering, precise. Pure killing heat.

It speared the Shadow Beast through the center of its chest.The creature combusted mid-pounce.The fire bored straight through it with a howling shriek that tore at the walls of the alley. Its form destabilized violently—shuddering, breaking apart from the inside out. Then— It blew outward in a cyclone of smoke and ash, collapsing into nothing.

Silence crashed down.

Chase lowered his hand, breathing hard. His fingers still glowed faintly, the Inferno sigil throbbing like a living coal beneath the skin. A faint curl of steam rose from the tips of his fingers.

Behind him, Skye stared. Not afraid. Not quite. But shaken. Alert. He felt her eyes on his back, the way her breath caught, the shift in her magic as her wand lowered—but did not retract.

"That…" she whispered, voice hushed. "Cassidy… that was Infernal."

Chase didn't turn immediately. He flexed his hand, jaw clenching as the sigil cooled, fading back to its normal color. The echo of the fire still throbbed in his bones. "It's just a binding," he muttered.

But even he heard the lie.

Skye stepped beside him now, her bare feet quiet on the damp cobblestones. She kept her wand down but angled protectively toward him anyway. "No," she said, eyes still on the fading embers drifting through the air. "That wasn't a arcane spellbound energy. That was… demonic energy. Pure and unfiltered."

He met her eyes. Her face wasn't twisted in disgust. Or fear. It was something far more complicated—awe mixed with concern, sharpened by recognition. For a moment, neither of them spoke. Her arcalam shifted to it its wand form, the sapphire tip

Then Benjamin collapsed behind them, and the moment broke. Skye blinked, snapping back into motion. "Help him," she said quickly.

"Chase—he's crashing."

Chase moved instantly, kneeling beside the boy. "Easy, kid," he murmured. "I've got you." But he felt Skye's gaze linger on his hand. And he knew she was replaying that blast in her mind. So was he.

Benjamin's head fell against his chest, utterly spent. Skye approached, wand lowering, breath sharp but controlled. Her jaw was tight, fury mixing with shock "This just got a hell of a lot more complicated," she said.

Chase exhaled through his nose, adjusting his grip on Benjamin. "Yeah. And something tells me it's about to get worse." They headed back toward the waiting Hispano-Suiza.

Lute stood beside the car like a carved statue of dark stone, arms crossed, brass knuckles glowing faintly as the enchantments settled. His face shifted—from concern, to calculation, to a quiet, simmering readiness. He cracked his knuckles as they approached.

"Trouble?" he asked calmly. His eyes already knew the answer. "Just the usual," Chase muttered, shifting Benjamin's weight. The kid was breathing—shallow, shaky, but alive.

Lute gave Chase a slow once-over. "We pickin 'up strays now?"

Chase smirked, faint and grim. "Didn't have much choice."

Lute grunted and opened the back door. "Well, get in. Before somethin 'nastier comes sniffin 'around." Chase slid into the car with the boy, Skye following close behind. Her wand was still in hand. Her eyes still burning. And the night was far from over.

The drive to the Heights was quiet. Not comfortable quiet— the heavy kind, thick with things nobody wanted to say first. Luther handled the Hispano-Suiza like it was made of glass, guiding it through the wet streets with steady hands. Streetlights slid across the windshield in long, gold smears. The city outside was all neon and shadow and December breath.

In the backseat, the boy lay half-curled between Chase and Skye, his head resting against Chase's thigh. His coat was still damp. His small hand was clamped around the wand like a lifeline, knuckles white even in unconsciousness.

Chase couldn't stop looking at it. A real wand. A proper foci. In the hand of a kid who could barely be shaving. That wasn't right. Wasn't normal. Most adults of the bloodlines couldn't channel through a wand without blowing their fingers off.

"His grip hasn't relaxed once," Skye murmured beside him.

He glanced at her.

She was watching the boy too, her features tight and intent. Bare arms goose-pimpled in the chill, bare feet tucked under her on the leather seat thoughts racing from the aftermath of the night and the weight of what they'd just survived.

"He's not just some stray," she added quietly. "Whoever gave him that wand knew exactly what they were doing."

Chase exhaled. "And whoever sent those shadow mutts knew exactly where he was."

Luther's voice drifted back from the front. "We picked up anyone's heat tonight who's gonna come callin 'later?"

"Camillo will," Chase muttered. That name soured the air for a beat. Chase could almost feel the memory of Camillo's broken face under his fists, blood on his knuckles, Luther's arms dragging him off before he finished the job.

Skye's tone was flat. "If Camillo can still stand."

"He'll heal," Chase said. "Men like him always do."

"And men like him always want payback," Luther added. "Especially when you beat 'em in front of half of Manhattans underworld."

Chase rolled his jaw. "Let him try. He knows where to find me now."

"Yeah, and that's the part I don't like," Luther said. "I'll talk to Mr. Pierce. Get a couple of the firm's boys sweeping the building for a few nights."

Skye nodded. "He'll agree. Camillo del Gato is bad for everyone's business. Legal and illegal."

"Fine," Chase said. "But that's a side problem. The real mess is still the kids." The car fell quiet again. The missing children. The drained bodies. The Mourned in the tunnels. Now a boy with a wand and tattooed shadow hounds hunting him through Harlem. That wasn't a string of coincidences. It was a pattern.

"Pulling in," Luther said. The Hispano-Suiza turned off the main avenue and onto a narrower street lined with older buildings pressed shoulder to shoulder. Lute eased the car to the curb under a flickering streetlamp and killed the engine. The night felt too quiet.

"I'll carry him up," Luther said, opening his door.

"I've got him," Chase said, already sliding an arm under the boy's back and knees. The kid was lighter than he looked. Too light.

They moved together—Luther leading the way, Chase cradling the boy in his arms, Skye walking defensively by his side. Her keys jingled softly. The doorman was not there so they entered on their own accord. The foyer inside smelled like old wood, polish, and faint incense.

Passing on the elevator they took the stairs. Landing on her floor, Skye pointed her wand down the hall and cast a illusion displacement spell in either direction. Anyone or anything hiding would have been revealed.

"It appears clear" she said opening the door.

"Upstairs, guest room's ready."

They carried the boy up, feet thudding softly on the wood. The guest room was small but comfortable—single bed, clean linens, a small writing desk, and a window overlooking the street. Lute and Chase eased the kid onto the mattress. Chase slid the wand carefully out of his fingers and set it on the nightstand within reach.

The boy made a faint, hoarse sound but didn't wake.

"He's burned out," Skye said from the doorway. "His aura's all over the place."

"Yeah, I noticed," Chase replied. "He was throwing bolts in the alley on instinct and still staying ahead of those things."

"And he's lucky we were there," Luther added. "Or he'd be meat."

Skye stepped in, expression shifting into something clinical. "Let me get a read on him before he wakes. I don't want to guess at what he is."

Chase stepped back, giving her space.

She moved to the bedside and knelt, resting her palm lightly against the boy's sternum.

Chase felt the shift.

Her tattoos—those Taino spirals and sharp-edged glyphs curling down her arm—glowed faintly as she whispered words in the First Tongue. Not loud, not dramatic—just a low, steady hum, like a song she already knew by heart.

A faint shimmer rose over the boy's body, like heat over a road.

"Diagnostic?" Chase asked quietly.

"Basic resonance test," she murmured. "No reagents, just aura echo. Think of it as a… stethoscope for the soul."

Luther snorted softly. "That's not creepy at all."

Skye ignored him. Her brows pulled together.

The glow intensified, swirling now in muted colors Chase could just barely see—gold, then blue, a shimmer of green before finally stabilizing. Then something else. A soft, translucent flicker around the boy's shoulders. He'd seen it before. In the tunnels. Around dead kids.

Fey green.

Skye pulled her hand back, eyes narrowing.

"Well?" Chase asked.

She took a breath. "He's human. Mostly. But he's carrying Fey ancestry. Strong. Not the usual diluted stuff you see in containment kids."

"How strong?" Chase pressed.

"Enough that his aura carries a tertiary layer," she said, voice tightening. "That's how he's casting like this at his age. His channels are wider. His capacity's higher. It's why he didn't burn out sooner. Possibly his parents were half-bloods."

Chase's jaw clenched.

Fey ancestry.

Missing Fey children.

Bodies drained of Fey essence.

His gut had been right.

"This isn't random," he muttered. "They're hunting specific blood."

"And using constructs to do it," Skye added. "Those weren't

natural spirits. Those hounds were summoned and bound through arcane channels."

"A warlock maybe," Chase said quietly. "A witch could do that also."

Luther folded his arms. "You think whom ever summoned them could have spotted us?"

Chase remembered the way the hounds moved—how they'd reacted to his spellbinding, how they'd adjusted mid-fight. Summons that sharp didn't act blind.

"Those things weren't just tracking scent," he said. "They were keyed to intent. They felt me the second I lit up my sigils."

"And I hit them with high-grade fire," Skye added. "We both lit up the night. If their summoner had any kind of sympathetic tether, he got an eyeful."

Luther grunted. "So he watched his pets die. Through them."

"And now he knows who killed them," Skye finished.

Chase glanced at the window.

The streetlights outside looked suddenly weaker.

"So we assume he knows the boy's still alive," Chase said. "We assume he knows we took him. And we assume he's not done."

Skye nodded once. "Then we treat him like an active target under protection."

Luther cracked his knuckles. "I'll post on the landing. Nobody gets up here without going through me first."

"Ward the apartment," Chase said to Skye. "Nothing flashy. I don't want to broadcast to half the neighborhood that we're scared."

"We're not scared," Skye said, already moving. "We're prepared."

She touched the guest room doorframe, murmuring a short, tight weave—a simple alarm glyph. The wood drank in the symbols, invisible once they sank in. She did the same to her front door and the window near the boy's bed—small tripwire spells, just enough to bite and shout if someone tried to force their way in.

Chase watched her hands move—precise, efficient. No unnecessary flourish.

"Temporary wards only," she said. "These will fade in twelve hours unless I reinforce them. But that's enough for tonight."

Luther nodded and stepped out to the hall. "I'll be right outside. Holler if he starts doin 'anything weird."

Skye snorted softly. "Define weird."

"Anything worse than what we already saw," Lute called back. His footsteps faded down the hall. Skye lingered at the doorway, looking in at the boy. The edges of her earlier fire softened a fraction.

"He can't be more than eleven," she murmured.

"Old enough to kill. Old enough to carry more weight than he's built for." Chase said quietly.

She looked back at him.

"That supposed to make me feel better?" she asked.

"No," he said. "Just honest." They both fell silent.

The boy shifted.

It was small at first—a twitch in his fingers, a small sound in his throat. Then his breathing changed, sped up, hitching like someone fighting their way out of a nightmare.

Chase stepped closer to the bed.

"Easy," he said quietly. "You're alright, kid. You're safe." The boy flinched at the sound of his voice, eyes scrunching tighter—then snapping open all at once. They were a sharp, startled hazel, wild with terror.

"Don't touch me!" he yelped, scrambling back, hand fumbling for the wand on the nightstand.

Chase's hand shot out first. He caught the wand, held it loosely but firmly. "Hey," he said, keeping his voice low and even. "You try to fry me, it's gonna bounce off and cook your eyebrows instead. Let's not go there."

The kid froze, chest heaving, eyes flicking between Chase, Skye, and the unfamiliar room. "Where am I?" he demanded. "Where—where'd they go? The dogs, the—the—"

"Gone," Chase said. "We handled them. You're in a safe place. That's all you need to know for now."

Skye stepped into view, hands visible, palms open. "You ran in front of our car," she said gently. "We saw those things chasing you. We weren't about to leave you in the street."

The boy's gaze locked onto her for a second, confusion flickering through the fear. "You were at the club," he breathed. "The lady with the wand."

"Good memory," she said. "What's your name?"

He hesitated, eyes narrowing with suspicion.

Chase recognized that look. He'd worn it once. "You don't have to trust us," Chase said. "But those hounds are gone. And whoever sent them is gonna come looking again. We're the only reason you're not smeared across some alley right now."

The boy's throat worked as he swallowed. "Benjamin," he said finally. "Benjamin Bright." The name landed like a stone in Chase's gut.

Bright.

He'd seen that last name before. An old file. Connected to other things. Other kids. Other bodies. "Alright, Benjamin," Chase said. "I'm Chase. That's Skye. Big man outside is Luther. We're going to ask you some questions. You can lie if you want. But incorrect answers might get you killed. So I don't recommend it."

Benjamin stiffened, nodding once.

Skye moved closer, crouching beside the bed. "Tell us what happened. Anything you remember."

Benjamin licked his lips. "I—I only did what she told me to do."

Chase leaned in. "Who?"

His voice was barely a whisper. "...Miss Isabelle."

Chase and Skye exchanged a sharp glance.

Isabelle Moriceau. Of course it was her.

Skye's tone shifted—quieter, controlled. "What did she ask you to do, Benjamin?"

The boy's small fingers twisted into the blanket. "She... she told me to help. I was just supposed to drive. I'm a good driver." His voice wavered. "She said I was their best shift-drifter. Better than the older boys."

Chase exchanged a quick look with Skye. A kid shift-drifting? That alone said plenty—and none of it good.

Benjamin swallowed hard. "Miles and Slim—they were with me. We were supposed to look into some missing stuff for Angelo. I didn't know what it was."

Chase's jaw tightened. Angelo Sykes. Contraband. Smuggling. Kids running errands.

Classic. Ugly. Predictable.

But then Benjamin's face drained of all color. "And then... the lady came."

Chase's spine stiffened. "What lady?"

Benjamin's eyes filled with tears. "She wasn't human."

Skye froze beside the bed—breath caught, body going still. Benjamin lifted a trembling hand and fluttered his fingers weakly, mimicking wings. "They were real," he whispered. "Not cloth. Not fake. They... they moved."

The room seemed to shrink around them. Chase felt it—like the pressure drop before a storm. A pure-blooded faerie. Or close enough to be lethal.

"We ran," Benjamin continued. "Miles pushed me ahead. Slim tried to fight her—he had a wand too, and he tried—but she... she grabbed him." His voice cracked. "Then everything was screaming. And then those dogs came."

His small hand lifted, shaking. "From the tattoos... on the big man's body."

"A tattooed summoner," Chase muttered. "Not a warlock. Someone trained."

Benjamin's head bobbed in a weak nod. "Then the man came after me. He said his name was Domingo." Both Chase and Skye went still.

Domingo. The butcher. The summoner who'd nearly torn Benjamin apart minutes ago.

Skye reached out, touching the boy's hair gently. "It's alright. You're safe now."

Benjamin's eyelids drooped again—the weight of exhaustion

smothering him like a heavy blanket. Chase watched the kid fight to stay awake, breath fluttering like a candle in wind.

"Benjamin," Chase said quietly, leaning closer, "we're going to protect you. You hear me?"

The boy managed the faintest nod then collapsed sideways into the pillows, wand still clutched in his small hand even in sleep. Skye pulled the blanket over him, smoothing it over his small shoulders. Chase stood there a moment, arms folded, staring at the sleeping boy like he was a live grenade someone had just placed in their laps.

"Bright," he muttered. "Damn it."

Skye rose slowly beside him. "He's out," Skye murmured.

Chase nodded. "Burned through everything he had."

They eased out of the room. Chase didn't latch the door—just let it rest in the frame. He didn't like the idea of anything separating him from the boy if trouble came calling. Stepping into the hall, Chase leaned a shoulder against the wall, rubbing a hand along his jaw.

"Skye," he said quietly, "listen… I know you can handle yourself in a fight. You proved that tonight. But this—" he gestured toward the bedroom "—this is different."

Her eyes narrowed slightly. Not offended—alert. "What are you saying?" she asked.

"I'm saying," Chase replied, exhaling hard, "I can take the boy and disappear for the night. Whitman will put him under protective custody. He's a good man. He'd take this seriously."

Skye crossed her arms slowly. "And you think that's wise?"

"It's safer than having him here," Chase said.

"For who?" she countered. "For him? Or for you? Or for me."

Chase didn't rise to the bait. He just shook his head.

"I know the First Arcane has… issues," he said. "They're not exactly known for sympathetic responses to Arcanists. Half the city's brass believes kids like him should be tagged and restrained before they even learn to cast."

"And Whitman?" Skye asked.

"Whitman's different," Chase said. "He'd do what he could."

"But what he can't do, is the problem," Skye replied, voice even. "They'd put Benjamin in holding. Maybe observation. And after that?"

Chase didn't answer.

He didn't have to. Because they both knew.

He scrubbed a hand over his face, jaw tightening. "They'd funnel him into foster care."

"And he'd run," Skye said softly. "Or be thrown back on the street. And whoever is hunting him will just pick up the trail again."

Chase stared at the floorboards for a long moment.

He knew she was right.

Hell, he'd seen enough kids slip through the cracks to know exactly how that story ended. Magic or not, nobody in the system would look twice at a skinny street kid with a wand. He'd disappear. Permanently.

"We hold out for the night," Skye said, stepping closer. "In the morning, I can have my fathers send their men. Trained, armed, discrete. Private agents—not rent-a-cops."

Chase lifted an eyebrow. "Anderson & Pierce muscle?"

"Better than anything First Arcane would do," she said. "And they'll actually protect him."

Chase took several slow breaths. He was a detective. He was supposed to hand things over. Follow the proper channels. But this wasn't a proper case. This was a kid being hunted by a summoner powerful enough to send constructs across the city.

He pictured Benjamin curled around that wand.

Terrified. Trembling.

And Chase felt the answer settle in his gut like a stone. "He stays here," Chase said finally. "At least until morning."

Skye exhaled, relief mixing with resolve. "Good."

Chase nodded. "We'll keep him alive until your fathers can get extra hands here."

"And until then," Skye said, turning toward the stairs, "we fortify this place. And we prepare."

Chase looked at her then, really looked at this enigma of a woman. Her resolve, the quickness on how she precessed information and made a descision. From following him down a alley in pursuit of Benjamin to kicking off her heels and fighting in bare feet. And something in him tightened—not with worry, but with a sharp, unexpected flicker of admiration.

She wasn't rattled. Not really. Not the way most people would be after fighting shadow constructs in an alley and hauling an unconscious kid to safety. Plenty of mages talked a big game about discipline and training. Skye lived it.

Look at her, he thought, following her up the steps.   Focused. Resolute. Moving like someone who'd already mapped out the next five steps while he was still breathing through the last fight.

There was fire in her—steady, contained, but unmistakably there. A strength that didn't come from spells, or schooling, or the fancy wand she carried. This was something else. Something deeper.

Most young mages folded under pressure. She sharpened. And Chase felt that—felt the truth of it—settle under his ribs like a quiet, dangerous comfort. She's stronger than she looks. Stronger than she lets people think. Stronger than he gave her credit for.

And even now—with her hair sticking to her neck, dress torn and stained, adrenaline still humming—Skye Anderson was poised like a woman who refused to be prey to anything. Not to shadow beasts. Not to summoners. Not to fate. Not even to fear.

"Come on," she said softly" I need to get out of this." Chase followed after her, feeling the first, real edges of trust click into place. And, just a little—

Pride.

Entering her bedroom without ceremony, Skye gripped the torn shoulder strap of her dress and pulled. The whole thing slid off her body and puddled to the floor. No modesty. No pause. Just swift, deliberate motion.

And Chase didn't look away.

She crossed to the closet, bare and unbothered and pulled out a white shirt and brown slacks. The shirt went on first, swallowed over her shoulders in one smooth motion. Then the slacks, tugged up efficiently, buttoned and set. She didn't bother with shoes. She walked back to him, close enough that he felt her warmth. Her fingers found his belt buckle. He arched a brow.

"You," she said, calm and matter-of-fact, "need to get out of that tux and back into something you can actually fight in. Your clothes are in there." She stepped aside as she pulled the belt loose.

In the closet, Chase saw his street clothes—clean, pressed, folded neatly. She must've had Nadine handle them earlier. He stripped out of the tux, muscles tense from the adrenaline still running under his skin, and changed quickly. Shirt, slacks, vest. Comfortable. Familiar. Grounding.

While he dressed, they kept talking.

"He said 'faerie dancer,'" Skye murmured. "With wings."

Chase folded his arms. "Not costume wings."

"No," she said, buttoning her cuffs. "He meant blood."

"A full-blooded Fey?" Chase asked.

Skye shook her head. "None confirmed in the city for decades. Maybe longer. But whatever he saw—it stuck. Kids don't invent traits that precise."

Chase leaned against the wall, shoulder muscles still tight. "Could be a hybrid with strong lineage."

"Strong enough to draw attention," Skye corrected. "And strong enough to get a kid hunted by shadow constructs."

Chase's jaw flexed. "Those hounds were summoned. Bound to tattoos. They weren't operating blind."

She turned to him. "Which means the summoner knows they died."

"Yeah," Chase said. "And he knows who killed them."

She nodded once. "Then we assume he's coming."

Chase let that truth settle. Heavy. Cold.

"Tonight."

"Tonight," she echoed.

Skye crossed to a shelf, opened a brass container etched with Taino spirals, and lit a stick of palo santo. Smoke curled up, softening the edges of the room.

Chase watched her move—focused, steady, unflinching.

"We need answers," he said. "That kid isn't random. He's tied to the murders, to the drained bodies. To the tunnels."

Skye nodded in agreement. "And someone out there wants children with Fey blood." She set the palo santo down. "We protect him. And we find out why."

Chase studied her profile—the certainty in it. The strength. She'd seen him nearly lose control in the alley. Seen the Inferno Lance burn through his veins.

And she hadn't stepped away.

She turned, eyes searching his. "You okay?"

He hesitated. "Fine."

"That a lie?"

He smirked faintly. "Probably."

She stepped closer. Close enough he felt her breath. "I was..." she swallowed once, rare vulnerability flickering through her voice, "...hoping you'd stay the night."

Chase blinked.

She didn't look away. Didn't turn it into a joke. Didn't armor it with bravado. "Not because of the fight," she added softly. "Not because I need protecting." Her voice steadied. "I just... didn't want to be alone. Not tonight."

Chase inhaled slow. "I would love too" he said quietly.

A faint, relieved smile touched her lips—gone almost as soon as it formed.

She straightened. "Domingo won't wait for morning."

"No," Chase agreed. "He'll come when he thinks we're tired."

"Which is why I'll reinforced the ward at the stairwell."

"Good," Chase said. "That will slow anything down."

"I like how we are working."

He stepped closer, holstering Effie and Pearl.

"We'll be ready."

They both glanced toward the hall—where Benjamin lay unconscious again, breathing soft and shallow. A summoner had sent killing constructs. A child with Fey blood was the target. And the summoner now knew exactly where to find them. The night pressed in—tight and electric.

Skye's voice was almost a whisper. "Tonight... we fight together."

Chase nodded, steel settling behind his ribs he placed his hands at her waist.

"Together."

Outside, the city muttered to itself. Somewhere in that mutter, a butcher with dead glyphs on his arms felt the echo of his dead hounds.

CHAPTER 9

Night of the Hunter

(Excerpt from the Journal of Professor Reginald F. Halverson):

"The greatest mistake modern mages and spellwrights make is assuming magic obeys language alone.

"Magic is not a thing one simply casts, but a current one surrenders to. While it is true that one must be of the magical bloodlines even to feel the most subtle speck of arcane energy, the ability to speak in the First Tongue or one of the few arcane linguistic offshoots greatly enhances one's ability to bend magic to one's will.

True magic predates words—it pulses in the First Tongue, in rhythm and sensation, in hunger and heat. One does not simple speak the First Tongue. One remembers it."
—*Professor Reginald F. Halverson, On the Primordial Origins of Arcane*

The moon hung high behind a veil of clouds, casting long skeletal shadows across the rooftops of the Heights. Down below, Harlem slept under winter's breath. From this vantage, rooftops felt like watchtowers—silent, knowing, watching over the restless streets.

On a rooftop across from Skye Anderson's brownstone, a shadow-door formed. Not opened—formed. A tall, coffin-shaped slit ripped itself upright out of the night. Wisps of living darkness curled along its edges. No sound escaped it. No light survived it. It was a wound in the world.

Domingo stepped through.

Sandals hit gravel. Tattoos under his skin writhed, disturbed by the magic he'd invoked. He pressed two fingers against the boxed sigil carved over his ribs. The doorway reacted instantly—shuddering, folding in on itself, collapsing into a smear of darkness before sinking back into the ink on his skin.

Domingo inhaled the night—wet iron, brick dust, and coming violence. Perfect. He crept to the roof's edge, lowering himself into a crouch. His gaze fell on the brownstone below.

Warm arcane light glowed from its windows. Inside, he saw the spellbound and his mate—conversing, tightening wards, moving with quiet urgency. But when his eyes landed on woman. Domingo went still. Absolutely still. Her presence struck him like a blow—sharp, electric, primal.

She wasn't just beautiful. She was magnetic—fire wrapped in silk, strength balanced with grace. A woman carved from confidence and danger. Something ancient and animal rose inside him.

Desire. Claiming. Possession.

And in an instant, the boy he'd been chasing—Benjamin—fell out of his mind completely. Domingo's jaw tightened, teeth grinding. He felt the old wound flare—humiliation, loss, fury—born from another woman who once danced in moonlight.

Coco Le Fey.

Not his lover—never that. He had tried to take her. Tried to force a bond she never wanted. And Makalith—Fae-blooded, elegant, effortless Makalith—had shattered him for it.

Now here was another woman. Another spark. Another chance to take what fate had denied him. A rival man beside her. A spellbound. Strong. Confident. A threat. Domingo's lips peeled into a slow, savage grin. He would not be humiliated twice. He'd break what the spellbound loved. He'd make her scream his name. Make the man watch. Make them both remember what real fear tasted like.

The ink across his ribs stirred—serpent coils tightening, eyes glowing a faint red as the dragon tattoo yawned awake. Movement behind him.

A shape materialized from the shadows like a nightmare dragged into moonlight.

Utilis the Rover.

Spindly limbs jerked unnaturally, his body folding and unfolding like broken scaffolding. A Victorian coat hung from his skeletal frame, stiff with gore and alley grime. Tufts of patchy blond hair clung to his skull. A cracked gas mask covered his mouth, the snout connected to a ribbed tube that pulsed with each rattling breath. Behind his tinted goggles, neon-green necro-fluid sloshed like lightning trapped in jars. A harness of rusted metal extended from his back—mechanical forearms ending in razor-tipped claws. A massive bone-handled cleaver lay strapped across his chest, etched with years of dried essence.

Domingo hated him.

Hated all the undead filth. But Utilis? Utilis enjoyed killing. And worse—he enjoyed talking. Utilis tilted his head. "Didn't realize you missed me," he rasped. His voice was wind scraping through bone. "Sirus said you'd be here."

"Took you long enough."

"Had to eat." A claw tapped against his goggles—ting, ting. "Can't hunt on an empty tank."

Domingo growled low.

Utilis chuckled, gravel in a tin can.

"So," Utilis rasped, "You grab the kid? I slit their throats?"

"No," Domingo said. "We take them all alive"

Utilis snorted. "Since when are you careful?"

Domingo didn't answer. He was still staring at Skye. Utilis noticed. Of course he did. "Ohhhh," he whispered, grin widening behind the mask. "That's it."

Domingo's tattoos flared.

Utilis leaned closer, voice dripping venom. "You think she's his? Or you think the man is just keeping her warm for someone... stronger?"

Domingo turned—very slowly.

"You ever get tired of breathing through holes someone else put in you?"

Utilis lifted both metal-clawed hands. "Feisty."

Domingo stepped forward, shadowed ink rising. "She's mine."

Utilis barked a laugh. "She was never yours. Not this one. Not the last one either."

Domingo froze. A muscle twitched under his eye. Utilis continued, cruel and delighted: "You tried to take Coco. You tried to force yourself on her. And Makalith broke your bones for it. Or did you forget?"

Domingo's roar was low, rumbling, barely contained.

Utilis only shrugged. "Maybe try not repeating history, hmm?"

"Get out of my sight."

Utilis bowed grandly. "As the King of Ink commands." He melted away into the shadows, laughter rattling in his mask.

Domingo turned back to the brownstone. Movement—She stepped outside onto the patio.

Alone.

A faint spark of fire flared as she lit a cigarette. The glow painted her in warm red-gold, outlining her curves, her cheekbones, the soft fall of her pixie-cut hair. Domingo's breath caught. The dragon tattoo on his ribs stirred—eyes opening, lips peeling back in a silent snarl. Time to hunt.

———

Skye padded down the stairs, quiet and barefoot, each step sending soft creaks through the bones of the old duplex. Through the front door she could hear Chase's low voice talking to Luther in the building's foyer—steady, clipped, all business. She needed a moment before the storm hit.

Skye slipped onto the balcony and let the cold night wrap around her. The Heights stretched below—cobblestone streets, iron lamps, and the faint hum of a city holding its breath. Smoke, river salt, and winter air curled together in the dark.

She braced both hands against the railing and exhaled.

Her body was still trembling—not from fear, but from the echo of power. Her wand had sung tonight, the First Tongue rolling off her lips with a clarity she hadn't felt since Hudson Academy. Not practice. Not a duel. Real danger. Real stakes. Real harm.

And she hadn't hesitated.

That truth sat heavy in her chest. So did another truth: Chase Cassidy fought like violence was part of his breathing. No wasted motion. No flourish. Just precision and weight. A man who didn't start fights, but ended them with the same inevitability as gravity. She didn't know if that scared her...or made her feel safer than she had in years.

Skye shook the thought off and dug a half-rolled cigar from her pocket. Her wand was upstairs—a fact she felt sharply—and her tattoos were restless under her skin, shifting with her mood.

Foci-casters didn't summon sparks freely. A focus mattered. Tonight, she was unarmed. She found a small brass lighter—Thomas's old one, still carrying a faint scent of engine oil—and coaxed a flame to life. She leaned in, drew from the cigar, and let the smoke warm her lungs.

She needed a minute.

Just one.

Then a soft shape wandered into the amber glow of the streetlamp below.

Mrs. Weatherby. Her faded green walking coat, her tiny wiry frame, and the ever-useless menace, Prudence—the little white terrier with far more bark than sense.

Skye almost smiled... until she noticed the dog freeze. Prudence went rigid. Ears pricked. Body trembling. A low whine rattled out of her —fear, not noise. Then she bolted. The leash snapped clean out of Mrs. Weatherby's frail hand as the dog tore across the street, yelping like something had clawed at her soul. Mrs. Weatherby cried out, stumbling after her, but the sound seemed distant—muted by the heavy press of the night.

Skye straightened slowly. Her tattoos rippled along her forearms. Not shifting—they were warning her.

Something was out there. Something the dog sensed before she did. Something hunting.

Skye's fingers tightened on the balcony rail. "Not good," she whispered. A pressure settled under her ribs—cold, sharp, metallic. The same wrongness she'd felt in the alley. The same arcane signature she'd felt when Benjamin collapsed in Chase's arms.

An attack wasn't coming someday. It was coming now. Her breath hitched just slightly.

"...Chase?" she said.

He was still inside, she heard chase and Luther muffled tones by the front door She wondered if he even heard her. Skye never got the chance to call again.

A shadow dropped from above—ink-black wings outstretched, eyes glowing like molten metal. It swept past her face, claws carving the air where her cheek had been. Another struck her shoulder and drove her backward through the patio doors, glass shattering around her as she hit the wooden floor.

Her breath knocked out of her, she blinked hard, vision swimming. And then she looked up.

Domingo stood on the balcony rail, balanced easily despite the narrow footing. Ink writhed across his bare chest like living things eager for release, each tattoo pulsing in time with his shallow breaths. His gaze fixed on her with feral intent, lips curling into a slow, hungry smile. He jumped down from the railing as though descending into his rightful dominion.

———

The foyer of Skye's duplex carried the muted scent of cleaning solution and old varnish—the perfume of buildings too stubborn to die. Nadine was passionate about her bleach. A flickering fluorescent bulb buzzed overhead, stuttering in a tired rhythm. Chase leaned against the wall, arms folded, the last embers of his cigarette glowing between two fingers.

Luther stood a few feet away, posture loose, gaze alert. Brass knuckles hung from his belt like a quiet warning.

"She doesn't bring people here," Luther said suddenly.

Chase lifted a brow. "That so?"

"Means something." Luther's eyes flicked toward the door. "This place is her quiet. Takes a lot for her to let someone inside." He gave Chase a sidelong look. "Means you got a fighting chance."

Chase huffed a short breath. "Not sure I'm lookin 'to fight."

Luther's chuckle rumbled low. "Looks to me like the battle already started."

Before Chase could answer, something thudded inside the duplex— dull, heavy, wrong.

He froze.

Another impact followed, sharper, the sound of objects skittering across the floor. Chase didn't hesitate, Luther right on his heels.

The living room had become a warzone. Shadow-shapes dropped from the rafters—vultures wrought of ink and smoke, wings whipping the air in jagged, unnatural arcs. Their eyes burned gold as they descended, bodies twisting with impossible geometry.

Chase drew Effie in one fluid motion. With his free hand, sigils flared along his forearm, molten gold rushing into shape as a warding buckler formed from elbow to wrist—the Searing Aegis snapping into existence.

A shadow vulture struck the shield and recoiled, its form rippling like smoke against sunlit glass. Luther was already in motion, blue-lit brass knuckles cracking into another beast and scattering it into dark embers.

"They're ink constructs," he barked, bracing for the next. "Like the ones in the alley." Chase didn't reply—his gaze had zeroed in on the devastation near the patio.

Skye lay in a scatter of broken glass, struggling to rise. Blood streaked her cheek, curls matted with shards. And above her—

Domingo stood by the balcony railing like something the night itself had spat out. Ink writhed beneath his skin—wolves, serpents, ravens shifting restlessly across his torso, each tattoo pulsing with hungry life. His grin was feral, triumphant.

Something hot and sharp twisted inside Chase's chest. More creatures erupted from the shadows—panthers streaking along the walls, serpents uncoiling from the ceiling, vultures swooping low at his flanks. Chase fired, bullets of arcane light cleaving through shadowflesh.

He pushed forward, shield raised, carving into the swarm. A panther lunged—he met it head-on, driving the ward into its throat and scattering it in a burst of embers. Another dove at his shoulder—he turned, Effie barking once, twice, dispersing it mid-air.

Luther slammed one beast into the wall with brute force, splintering wood as it dissolved. A second leapt onto his back; he seized it by the throat, crushed it against the plaster, and tore through its smoky body with a steel-hard punch.

Chase didn't slow.

Sigils across his chest glowed brighter, heat rising beneath his skin in response to the threat. He drove himself forward, using the weight of his own momentum to clear space, shield cutting a path through claw and fang. He forced the last creature aside and broke through the swarm—

And saw Skye.

Still on the floor. Still trying to rise. Domingo stepping toward her.

"Skye!" Chase roared.

The constructs surged again, bursting from beams and shadows. Malformed silhouettes—too many, too fast. Chase spun, firing in tight, efficient bursts. Effie spat streaks of gold that tore through beasts and splattered their forms across the walls like ink thrown against stone. Still they regrouped, snarling in silent waves.

Luther cursed as one clamped onto his back. He hammered it off, ramming his shoulder into the wall before smashing the creature apart with a broken table leg. Another shadow-beast lunged at Chase's flank.

The ward buckler slammed into its jaws. It recoiled with a shrill sound, dissolving at the edges. Chase fired point-blank, tearing it into a cloud of dying embers.

The protective charm Skye had placed on Luther earlier flickered dangerously, strain showing as a larger construct hurled itself against it.

"Move!" Chase shouted. "I have to get to her!"

"I'm tryin', dammit!" Luther bellowed, swinging again.

Chase lowered his shoulder and plowed through the chaos, glyphs blazing along his arms, each step cracking through glass and broken furniture.

He moved with purpose. With fury. With fear he refused to name. He would reach her. He would reach her or drown the room in fire trying.

———

The hallway had gone eerily still. Only the trembling sconces along the walls dared to move, their yellow flames bending and stretching with every distant crash from inside Skye Anderson's apartment. Shadows swayed like nervous spectators bracing for the next blow.

Behind the door, something heavy smashed into a wall. Then came the roar—deep, guttural, inhuman.

Utilis the Rover paused near the stairwell, half-hidden by the darkness pooling there. His long, gloved fingers drummed idly along the cold wrought-iron railing as he tilted his head, listening.

Inside, Domingo was fighting like a starved animal unleashed from chains.

A savage. A brute. A creature of ink and appetite. But an effective one.

Utilis smirked, the pale stretch of his cheeks just visible beneath the straps of his breathing mask. The green alchemical fluid sloshing behind his goggle lenses cast a ghost-sick glow across the hallway.

"Listen to him go," he murmured. "Like a dog tearing into bone." Another crash echoed—furniture splintering, glass breaking, the grunt of a man taking a heavy hit. The spellbound's voice followed—strained, but steady.

Utilis blinked once.

"Still alive," he mused, genuinely surprised. "More than alive... still fighting." His eyes narrowed behind the goggles. Domingo had gone in confident. Too confident. Arrogance was practically tattooed across his knuckles. And despite all his snarling and posturing, everyone in the Hollow knew one simple truth:

Domingo hated Utilis. Hated the way Utilis watched things. Hated the way he moved without sound. Hated that Makalith had sent him here tonight—not as a partner, but as insurance. A fail-safe. A leash. Utilis's grin stretched wider.

Domingo would rather eat glass than admit he needed backup. But Makalith didn't care for pride. He cared for results. And the boy—the feyblood boy—was too important to trust to a single rabid dog, no matter how decorated his ink.

A new ripple of sound reached Utilis. Domingo snarled. Cassidy responded with steel and spell. A barrier cracked. A body struck the floor. Something heavy tumbled across the room.

Utilis's smirk softened into something contemplative.

"Spellbound," he whispered. "A trained soldier. Holding his own against Domingo." That... was interesting.

Utilis reached into his coat and flipped open a tarnished silver case. Inside lay a neat row of thin cheroots—blood-brown paper, hand-rolled, each one dipped in a mild embalming tincture so he could taste them without dulling his senses.

He selected one, tapped it twice against his palm, and rolled it between his fingers. From further down the hallway came the rapid patter of footsteps. The building's janitor barreled into view—eyes wild, mop still dripping onto the tiles. He bolted past Utilis without even seeing him, mumbling frantic prayers in his mother tongue.

Utilis tilted his head as the man disappeared around the corner. "Mortals always know when death is in the house," he murmured. He brought the cheroot to his lips—unlit, just for the comfort of motion. Old habit from when he still had lungs that needed warmth. Before the Mourned curse rewrote him into something leaner, hungrier. A final crash thudded inside the apartment.

Cassidy roared. Domingo answered with a snarl that rattled the light fixtures. Utilis leaned back into the shadows, letting the darkness swallow his gangly silhouette.

"Domingo," he whispered with amusement, "looks like you might've bitten off more than you can chew." A hollow laugh—his own—echoed softly under the stairwell. "A disturbance like this..." he murmured, eyes glinting behind the goggles, "opens all sorts of doors."

He let the cheroot fall from his lips, caught it between two skeletal fingers, and tucked it behind his ear. "Let's see Domingo," he said, voice a rasping purr, "how far you willing to bleed."

And with that, Utilis let the shadows fold around him, dissolving into the darkness of the stairwell— Watching. Calculating. Waiting for the perfect moment to enter the fray if he was going to enter at all.

———

Skye was on the floor, struggling to rise, blood trailing from a cut above her brow. Domingo loomed over her like a storm about to break— his tattoos shimmering, coiling with life. From the ink across his chest, a massive lion peeled free, formed from shadow and raw intent, its paws thudding as it leapt toward Luther. A shadow panther followed.

The beast collided with him mid-step, sending both crashing through a side table. Luther shouted, fighting to keep its jaws from closing around his throat.

Skye scrambled to her feet—disoriented—but Domingo was already on her. He caught her ankle, yanked her hard. She hit the floor with a cry, dragged toward him.

"Pretty little thing," Domingo rasped, sliding his knife into his belt.

He pulled her close with one arm, his strength crushing her, grinning as he pressed his mouth to hers in a mockery of affection.

She froze, her mind spiraling in panic as Domingo's tongue lashed about inside her mouth. The brute swelled with satisfaction, mistaking her stillness for submission. He pulled back, grinning, reveling in the look of shock and disgust on her face.

Skye blinked. Then bit down on his nose.

Domingo howled.

She didn't stop. Her thumbs slammed into his eyes, driving deep. He shrieked, voice raw, and hurled her with a roar. Skye flew across the room, crashing across the far side of the sofa. Her body crumpled to the floor with a dull, breathless thud.

"Skye!" Chase shouted.

Effie bucked in his hand. The shot tore into the lion, arcane flame ripping through shadow. The beast recoiled, its form unraveling—but Chase was already reloading.

Domingo turned, blood streaming from his face, one eye half-blinded. His knife came free again.

Too slow.

Chase charged.

With his shield-arm, he grabbed a high-backed chair and hurled it across the room. It shattered against Domingo's back just as Chase tackled him into the bookshelf. Wood splintered. Tomes collapsed like rain.

They went down hard.

Domingo came up swinging.

The knife whistled past Chase's head, missing by inches. Another swing—closer this time. The knife hissed through the air and caught Chase clean across the forehead.

Blood welled instantly—but it wasn't alone. The slash triggered the wards etched across Chase's skin, and his spellbound defenses flared to life in a burst of amber light. Sparks erupted where steel met magic, and the force of the backlash sent Domingo stumbling a step.

"What the hell—?" Domingo snarled, blinking past the flare.

"Spellbound bastard."

He didn't wait for an answer. He lunged again, blade aimed for the throat this time.

Chase deflected with his left, the shimmering buckler of arcane energy locking with the knife. The two clashed, grunting, muscles straining. Chase twisted, trying to use his body weight to knock Domingo off balance, but the man held firm— his strength impressive, fueled by bloodlust and something darker.

"You lot just don't die easy," Domingo spat. "Thought your kind got culled with the rest."

Chase bared his teeth. "You talk too much."

He drove a knee into Domingo's gut. The air whooshed from the man's lungs, but he twisted on instinct, slicing a gash across Chase's ribs before the buckler knocked the blade wide.

They broke apart—breathing hard, circling again.

In the background, Luther was at Skye's side, one hand pressed to her shoulder, the other still gripping the broken table leg. A shadow panther stirred near the fireplace, trailing smoke.

"You good, girl?" Luther whispered, eyes flicking from her to the fight beyond.

Skye grimaced, nodding weakly. "I have…to get my wand."

Domingo's laughter echoed off the walls, sharp and taunting. "You spellbound bastards always think it's a fair fight," he snarled, his voice thick with venom. With a guttural word in a dead tongue, he slapped his palm to his chest, and the remaining tattoos erupted from his skin like smoke igniting into flame.

A pair of ink-streaked hounds burst forth, their bodies rippling between muscle and mist, eyes glowing with emberlight. They lunged— fast and silent.

Chase pivoted, raising Effie. Two quick shots, glowing arcane tracers, punched clean through the first hound, dissipating it mid-air. The second veered—too late. Chase slammed a boot into its skull, firing at point blank range, the beast dissolving into tendrils of smoke that clung to the air like burnt ozone.

Then he saw her.

Skye—clutching her side, blood streaked at the corner of her mouth —moving with Luther toward the stairwell. Her eyes locked with Chase's for a single heartbeat. *Go*, she mouthed, then shouted to Luther, "Protect the boy!"

Domingo roared. *"You're not running from me!"*

He bolted after her.

Chase moved to intercept—but Domingo was already summoning the beast stitched across his back: the dragon.

The ink uncoiled like a wound unraveling, scales of shadow pulling away from his flesh in long strands of darkness. The creature tore free with a thunderclap of shrieking wind, its wings vast, skeletal, and rimmed in black fire. The shadow dragon landed between Chase and the stairwell, jaws yawning wide.

Chase skidded to a stop. "Of course you'd cheat."

He clenched his jaw, raised Effie, and activated the sigils across his arm. Amber light surged—his ward flared, forming a curved, glowing buckler in the air before him.

The dragon struck.

Chase met it head-on.

Skye tore up the stairs, her breath ragged, bare feet pounding wood and dust. Behind her came the sound of claws—then a *snarl* and a *crash*. She glanced back just in time to see Luther slam into the shadow panther, tackling it away from the landing.

"*Go!*" he shouted, even as the creature's jaws clamped into his shoulder. His ward flared one last time—then fizzled to nothing. Blood sprayed the wall as Luther went down in a heap with the beast on top of him.

Skye didn't look back again.

She hit the top of the stairs and sprinted down the hallway. Domingo's footfalls thundered behind her—closer, closer. She didn't cry out. Didn't scream. Her room was just ahead. A few more steps.

She sprinted upward—and as she hit the top landing, her ward flared. The protective sigil she'd woven hours earlier—stitched across the stairwell threshold—crackled awake. It shimmered with lines of burning gold, geometric patterns glowing like hammered sunlight.

Domingo reached the base of the stairs and charged after her. When he crossed the midpoint—The ward hit him like a hammer.

A blast of arcane force erupted across the landing, the sigil blazing so bright it painted the walls in molten light. Domingo snarled, staggering, one hand flying to his face as the shockwave struck his senses.

Behind him, the shadow-panther that had shaken free of Luther barreled upward—and ran headfirst into the collapsing ward. The beast detonated into black mist instantly, its form shredded by the ward's backlash. Domingo threw an arm up against the glare, teeth bared in fury. The ward buckled—strained—then cracked like glass flexing under pressure.

Skye reached her room, slid inside, and slammed the door. The lock clicked.

She braced both palms against it, chest heaving. Then—the compromised ward gave way. The explosion ripped down the hallway. The door blew inward, the force hurling Skye off her feet. She hit the floor hard, shards of wood and sigil-light scattering across the room like dying stars.

The shadow-beast was gone—reduced to smoke. Silence pulsed once.

Then—

Domingo stepped through the torn frame, hulking and shirtless, tattoos crawling like serpents beneath his skin. "Not bad," he grunted, cracking his neck. "Didn't think you had that kind of fire in you."

Skye kept her wand up, breath sharp, chest rising and falling. "You've got no idea what I've got in me."

Her eyes darted to the vanity— her arcalam wand. Sapphire tip gleaming.

"Udayate"

It flew into her hand. She fired a blast of arcane energy.

Too late. He moved with terrifying speed, catching her bolt mid-cast with a shimmering ward. The arcane bolt fizzled against his barrier as he surged forward and slammed her into the bed. She grunted, the air knocked from her lungs.

Domingo laughed—low, brutal. "I'll see your insides soon enough."

He slammed her wrist down, pinning it beneath his grip. His full weight bore down on her, crushing, suffocating. Skye gasped, her slender frame straining under the pressure, every breath a struggle.

With no other choice, she reversed her grip on the wand—held it like a blade—and drove it upward, stabbing hard.

Domingo howled, clutching his right eye. "You little bitch!"

Blood streamed down his face, but rage drowned out the pain. He barely hesitated—fist curling tight before driving it down like a hammer.

Skye's head snapped back against the bed. Her eyes rolled, dazed—barely conscious. Domingo ripped open her shirt.

"I will breed you raw over and over as I claim you for my own." The sash around his pants opened. His intent was clear.

"No," she mumbled, almost incoherently. Her fingers still gripped the arcalam. Through trembling lips, she whispered,

"Agni-Kalumtu."

A gout of fire erupted from her wand, engulfing the brute in a surge of arcane flame. The force was enough to stagger him—his wards flickered violently, barely repelling the blast.

Domingo spat, staggering. "All your fancy tricks won't matter."

But it had been enough. Skye rolled off the bed and hit the floor hard, sliding backward on her rear. She raised the wand with both hands, defiance burning in her eyes.

"Jahna kree!"

Three arcs of slicing light shot from her wand. Domingo spun through them, tattoos igniting as his skin hardened to iron. One beam sliced across his side, drawing a hiss of pain—but the others skittered off harmlessly.

He kept coming. With a surge of speed, he grabbed her by the throat, lifting her off the ground.

Then—a flash of green light exploded behind him.

Domingo's body seized—spine arched, mouth frozen mid-sentence—as a binding hex struck him square in the back. He twisted in fury, releasing Skye just in time to see Benjamin Bright standing wide-eyed in the doorway. Both of the boy's hands shook—one clutching his wand.

"Get away from her!" Benjamin shouted.

He turned toward the boy—

Too late.

"Suthar'ael," Skye said, her voice sharp with finality.

The room dimmed. The air turned thick—oppressive, heavy with death.

Domingo's eyes widened. "Wait—" But the word never finished.

A spear of obsidian light ripped from Skye's wand, shrieking through the air like a curse made flesh. It struck him dead center—piercing his chest, deep, final, absolute. His body convulsed. Tattoos cracked and flickered. His mouth opened in a silent scream as the spell tore through him, unraveling wards, shredding his arcane core, shredding him from the inside out.

He collapsed. Eyes wide. Blood spilling from his nose, ears, and chest. The light drained from him slowly. Her wand lowered. Her voice broke.

"He... he was going to..."

Benjamin nodded. "I know. I saw."

———

The shadow dragon reared back, its serpentine body coiling with smoke and malice. Chase ducked a swiping claw, then fired three times —each enchanted round from Effie slamming into the beast's form, splintering arcs of golden energy across its chest. The creature shrieked, the sound like tearing metal and distant thunder.

One more step forward and Chase, raised his arm—activating the buckler ward on his forearm. The arcane shield blazed to life, absorbing a blast of shadowflame from the dragon's gaping maw. He gritted his teeth, surged forward—and just as he prepared to deliver a final blow...

The dragon *vanished*.

Snuffed out like smoke in wind.

Chase didn't wait to question it.

He turned and ran.

Luther was slumped against the banister, a nasty gash along his side and scorch marks along his chest where one of the panthers had raked him. His shirt was torn, blood soaking through his undershirt, but he was alive —breathing, swearing under his breath.

"Luther!" Chase dropped to one knee.

Luther groaned. "Go. She's upstairs. I saw her—the tatted man—*go!*"

Chase didn't hesitate. He sprinted up the stairs, shoes echoing on hardwood, heart pounding with a single thought thudding louder than all the rest.

Please let her be alright.

He reached the top landing. The hallway was scorched. Smoke drifted from blackened plaster. A wall had been half-collapsed near the guest room. The door to Skye's bedroom hung open, broken on its hinges.

Chase stepped inside.

Skye lay near the foot of her bed—clothing shredded, shoulders trembling, her wand still clutched tight in one hand. Her hair was wild, tangled. Blood stained her lip. Her chest rose and fell in rapid, uneven gasps, tears streaking down her cheeks. But she was alive.

Next to her stood Benjamin, stiff with fear and concern, eyes flicking between her and Domingo's broken and bleeding corpse still crumpled on the floor.

Skye looked up as Chase entered. She tried to stand. Their eyes met —something in her broke.

Her knees gave slightly—not in weakness, but in grief. In the crashing weight of what she had just survived. Of what she'd had to become.

Chase crossed the room in seconds. Effie clattered to the floor from his hand. He wrapped his arms around her, cradling her tightly against his chest.

She didn't speak. She just sobbed.

Not loudly. Not wailing. But the kind of silent, shaking cry that only came when the danger had passed, when the mask could finally fall. Chase held her, strong and steady, resting his cheek against her temple.

"I got you," he whispered, over and over, like a prayer. "I got you."

He didn't speak for some time—just holding her, trying to gauge how deep the damage went. Blood streaked her collarbone. A bruise was already blooming on her left hip. And her eyes—sharp, calculating eyes that usually met his without flinching—were distant.

Chase turned to Benjamin, looking up to meet the boy's gaze.

"Listen to me, Benjmain" His voice was firm but not unkind. "I don't know what this is yet, or who's behind it—but they're after *you*. And they're hurting people to get to you."

Benjamin swallowed hard, his eyes darting toward Domingo's body.

Chase continued. "I need you to be strong. Take that wand and if anyone tries to hurt you or the people with you... you stun them. No hesitation."

Benjamin hesitated, but then nodded. "I can do it," he said quietly. "I *will*." Chase gave his shoulder a quick squeeze, then turned back to Skye.

She blinked hard, her focus catching on his face. Her lips parted. "I... I killed someone."

Chase said nothing for a beat, then helped her gently to sit up on the bed. His voice was steady. "It was either him or you."

Her gaze fell to her hands, fingers still twitching, skin stained with blood and arcane residue. She looked haunted. Guilty. Human.

She looked down—and realized.

Her shirt hung open completely, exposing her bare chest.

She blinked once. Then looked at him.

"I... I need to change."

"I'll get something."

He crossed to the closet, grabbed a clean blouse—soft white cotton with mother-of-pearl buttons—and returned. He knelt again, helping her ease out of the shredded remains. Skye let him, she didn't flinch, didn't protest. Her body moved, but her mind was still catching up.

"Benjamin," Chase said over his shoulder.

The boy turned away instantly, face red. "Not looking."

Chase helped Skye into the shirt and buttoned it carefully, hands steady despite the tightness in his jaw. Then he knelt lower, pulling her Oxfords from beneath the dresser.

"Foot up."

Skye lifted one, then the other. He laced them quickly, efficiently, like muscle memory from a thousand wartime mornings.

When he looked up again, she was watching him—present, but subdued.

"You good?"

Her breath caught, but she nodded. "Yeah."

She reached for her arcalam, fingers tightening around its smooth shaft like a lifeline.

"We move now.

Chase supported her as she rose, quickly picking up Effie and for good measure, put two rounds in Domingo's skull.

Skye didn't flinch at the sounds of gunfire, so distant were her thoughts. Chase looked at Benjamin.

"Gotta make sure"

Together, they descended the stairs, Benjamin bringing up the rear. At the landing, they found Luther slumped halfway against the wall, blood leaking from a tear in his side. His brass knuckles were still on, stained dark.

"On your feet, soldier," Chase said, grabbing one of his arms.

Luther grunted as they lifted him. "Two good legs," he growled. "Ain't dead yet."

Down the steps they went. Effie leading the way, clearing every corner until they reached the lobby. It was full of residents, most wary from sleep. Mrs. Weatherby walked in cradled the stiff, lifeless body of Prudence to her chest. Her sobs echoed in the night, her husband Clarence hovered nearby, helpless before the storm of her grief.

"She was just barkin'..." she wept. "Didn't deserve this... not like this..."

Then, with a sudden twitch, Prudence's tail gave a weak thump.

Mrs. Weatherby blinked. "Prudence?" The little dog gave a weak yawn, then sneezed—and promptly sat up.

"You were playing possum?" Mrs. Weatherby gasped. "Oh, you smart girl!"

Prudence locked eyes with Skye, ears folding back in instant recognition. Despite her bruises, the tiny beast let out a determined bark, hoarse but righteous.

Skye blinked at her. "I do wish the tattooed man had gotten that one."

Chase stifled a laugh. "We can't stop now."

The Hispano-Suiza gleamed under the gaslight, waiting like a getaway car in a heist. Chase opened the rear door and helped Luther in, Benjamin sliding in beside him.

Skye paused a beat longer before slipping into the passenger seat, her arm across her lap like a drawn line in the sand.

Chase slid behind the wheel, checked the rearview, and pulled away from the curb.

The night wasn't over.

But for now—they had survived. But deep inside, he already felt it— that gnawing crawl beneath his skin like they were being watched.

And someone was about to make their next move.

CHAPTER 10

The Hexbreaker Clause

"A Hexbreaker is not simply a profession—it is a sentence.

Many wear the title. Few survive the work.

The best Hexbreakers are the Spellbound. Men fused with living magic on their skin.

And among the Spellbound, those made through infernal rites...

rival the power of magic cast in the First tongue

Of those, none walks the line between man and monster more dangerously than Chase Cassidy."

—Excerpt from The Arcane Containment Unit Field Primer (BAE Restricted)

The clock on the nightstand ticked softly, steady as a heartbeat in the dim glow of Captain James Whitman's bedroom. His wife, Nora, lay curled under the blankets beside him, breathing deeply—snoring with the kind of unapologetic volume only twenty years of marriage could make endearing.

Whitman smiled faintly into the darkness.

They'd married at eighteen, two kids playing at adulthood. Somehow it stuck—through boot camp, the Great War, and the endless grind of the First Arcane. Nora had carried the weight of every long shift, every missed anniversary, every night he came home smelling of cigarette smoke and crime scenes. And she never complained—not once.

She snored like a freight train, though.

The shrill ring of the telephone cut through the room like a blade. Whitman tensed. Calls at this hour were never good. He reached across Nora, careful not to wake her—though honestly, God Himself could descend trumpets blazing and she'd sleep right through it. He lifted the receiver.

"...Whitman," he whispered, already sliding his legs out of bed.

A clipped voice crackled over the line. "Captain, this is Colonel Robert Langley, adjutant to the Governor-General."

Whitman froze halfway to standing.

Langley. Politics.

Which meant trouble.

"One minute, Colonel let me take this on the other line," he murmured, already tiptoeing out of the bedroom. He eased the door shut, muffling Nora's rumbling snores behind the wood. He crossed the small living room—past family photos, past his service medals gathering dust—and slipped into his cramped home office. He closed the door and sat at the desk.

"Situation in the Restriction Zone has escalated," Langley said. "The confirmed presence of feral Mourned within Manhattan's borders."

Whitman's hand tightened around the receiver.

"Military?" he asked quietly.

"Senator Wilder is pushing for the Bureau of Arcane Enforcement to assume full authority. He wants federal troops on the ground. His proposal includes removing the Magistrate and placing the Zone under direct B.A.E. control."

Whitman swore under his breath.

He'd known Wilder was ambitious—hungry as a shark with blood in the water—but this wasn't ambition anymore. This was a power grab.

"And the Governor-General?" Whitman asked. A pause. Too long.

"He's… considering options," Langley said finally.

Whitman leaned back in his chair, the wood creaking under him. If Wilder pulled this off, the Zone wouldn't just be under federal control—it would be a staging ground. A pretext for martial law. Manhattan wouldn't survive the kind of sweep the B.A.E. authorized.

Langley cleared his throat. "Governor-General Travers wants alternatives. Viable ones."

Whitman rubbed his temple, thinking hard. Military takeover. Federal authority. Everything he'd spent years trying to prevent was about to collapse on his head.

And then—

A memory surfaced. A legal footnote buried deep in the Arcane Enforcement Acts. Obscure. Controversial. But still binding. "The Hex-Breaker Clause," Whitman said slowly.

Silence stretched over the line.

"You're suggesting deputizing a Hex-Breaker?" Langley finally asked.

Whitman opened his desk drawer and pulled out an old case file—the one stamped with the faded sigil of the Hex-Breaker Office, struck from use decades ago.

"It's still on the books," he said. "Extreme circumstances only. A certified Hex-Breaker can be granted temporary federal authority. Independent jurisdiction. Mandate to neutralize supernatural threats without B.A.E. interference."

Langley exhaled, long and low. "That is... dangerous."

"Less dangerous than Wilder getting an army," Whitman snapped.

Another pause. A deeper one this time.

"The Governor-General will consider it," Langley said.

"Tell him not to take too long," Whitman murmured. "Because if Wilder's plan goes through, we won't have a Restriction Zone left to govern. Just a battlefield."

"Understood," Langley replied. "We'll be in touch." The line clicked dead. Whitman set the phone down and stared at it for a long moment. He knew exactly who the Hex-Breaker had to be. And he knew Chase Cassidy was about to get a call he wasn't going to like.

⬜

The hospital doors swung open, the fluorescent lights inside casting a stark glow over the battered trio. Skye and Chase hurried in, supporting Luther between them. The older man gritted his teeth, his face pale with blood loss, but he refused to stumble.

"I'm fine," he muttered.

"You're bleeding all over the damn floor," Chase shot back.

Skye tightened her grip on Luther's arm. Her own body ached—

bruises across her ribs, cuts at her lip, dried blood trailing down her collar —but she held steady. "You've been with me for too long to play the tough old soldier, Luther." Her voice was softer now, her usual bravado tempered by exhaustion. This wasn't just a bodyguard—this was her family.

The nurses at the front desk jumped to attention at the sight of them, eyes widening at Luther's bloodied shoulder, Skye's bruised face, and the crimson smear along Chase's shirt. One of them grabbed a stretcher, motioning for them to lie Luther down.

A uniformed officer standing at the nurse's station stiffened as they approached. His sharp blue eyes locked onto Chase, suspicion flickering behind them. His hand drifted to his nightstick.

"Alright, hold it." He stepped in front of them, eyeing the damage. "What the hell happened here?" Before Skye could answer, his gaze flickered to her cuts and bruises. His posture shifted immediately.

"Miss, are you alright?" His grip tightened on the baton. "Did he do this to you?"

Chase let out a slow breath, shoulders stiffening. He saw the officer's hand twitching, ready to reach for his gun if he got the wrong answer.

Skye's eyes narrowed. Despite the throb in her jaw and the fire in her ribs, her voice was steel. "Are you serious?" she snapped. "This man saved my life."

The cop didn't look convinced. "That right?" he asked, sizing up Chase like a suspect already guilty.

Chase slowly reached into his coat, pulling out his battered badge. "Chase Cassidy. First Arcane Police Department. Badge number 367."

The officer's brows furrowed as he inspected it. Then, reluctantly, he stepped back. "Shit."

Chase shoved the badge back into his pocket. "Yeah. Shit."

The tension didn't fully leave the officer's face, but he waved them through, nodding to the nurses. "Get them looked at."

They wheeled Luther away, a nurse hurrying after them while Skye and Chase remained in the waiting area. Chase slumped into a chair, exhaling heavily.

Skye sat beside him, one arm braced against her ribs. Her hair was a mess of sweat and blood. Her blouse—now buttoned—clung to her with drying red streaks, but her eyes remained alert. Bruised but unbowed.

A doctor approached, glancing over Chase's file before crouching beside him. "Let's take a look at that wound."

Chase motioned to his forhead. The spot where Domingo had cut him was still smeared with dried blood—but the gash was gone. The skin beneath was unmarked, smooth, untouched.

The doctor blinked. "I… thought you said you were injured?"

Chase smirked. "Guess I heal fast."

The doctor didn't press further, muttering something about needing a drink before walking off.

Skye was staring. "You didn't tell me that was part of being Spellbound."

Chase stretched, rolling his shoulder. "I don't exactly advertise it."

Another nurse came over with a clipboard. "Ma'am, you need to be examined. We've already prepped a room."

Skye raised an eyebrow, but nodded. "My law firm pays top shelf premiums," she said, easing herself to her feet with a wince. "Make sure Luther and I get the best."

The nurse frowned. "We treat everyone as best we can."

Another muttered behind her breath, "Even Bloodborn?"

A doctor passing by snapped in a low voice, "Do your job."

Skye gave them all a withering look before limping down the hallway with the nurse.

Meanwhile, Chase turned to Benjamin.

The kid sat curled up in one of the waiting room chairs, small fingers gripping the edges of his too-large coat. His eyes flickered toward the hospital doors, his expression wary, exhausted.

"Benjamin."

He didn't respond at first. Chase crouched beside him, wincing as her ribs protested. "I know you've been through a lot tonight. But I need to know what happened at the docks. Tell me everything."

Benjamin swallowed hard, finally looking up. "Miles," he murmured. "Slim. Sykes. The Fey dancer."

Chase surprising even himself, took Benjamin's hand gently. "Start from the beginning." And as the night wore on, Benjamin Bright told his story.

————

At the 1st Arcane Precinct, the phone rang with a shrill buzz. Desk Sergeant Juno reached for it without looking, pen still scribbling across his nightly logs. "1st Arcane Precinct."

A voice came through, tight and direct. "I need two uniforms, and someone to take custody of a protected witness. Name's Benjamin Bright. We're at Mercy General."

Juno froze mid-sentence.

Then his mouth twisted into a dry smirk. "Cassidy?"

"Hey, Juno."

"Haven't heard from you since that mess with the mourned," Juno said, sitting back in his creaky chair. "You got another body on your hands?"

"Got another one.. And if your people don't show up fast, there'll be more. Get a meat wagon over to this address"

Juno clicked his tongue and copied the address before weighing a response. "Look, Cassidy, I don't know if we've got the manpower tonight. Half the squad's still sweeping the Narrows."

A pause. Then Chase's voice sharpened. "Then maybe I should call Whitman. You want me to wake the Captain for this?"

Juno stopped writing. He blinked, then let out a slow breath like a leaking valve. "You serious?"

"You know I don't bluff."

Juno muttered something under his breath that made the rookie on night duty look up. "Alright. Two officers. Twenty minutes. I'll send someone with clearance for the boy."

"Tell them to be polite. The kid's been through hell."

"They screw up, you'll make noise."

"Damn right I will."

Juno hung up the phone, muttering, "Hell of a night."

———

Chase pushed open the door to Skye's hospital room. The overhead lights hummed gently. The walls were sterile white, lined with muted green tile, and a faint antiseptic smell hung in the air. A nurse stood nearby and immediately stepped forward.

" Only family allowed past this point."

Chase didn't blink. "I'm her husband."

The nurse frowned. "You're not wearing a ring."

Skye stirred in the bed, face swollen, lip split, one eye half-shut. Benjamin was curled in a chair beside her, his small body covered in a hospital blanket.

Continuing his lie, Chase said, "That's our boy."

The nurse glanced at the boy, then back at Chase, suspicious. But she said nothing and walked away.

Chase approached quietly. Skye cracked her good eye open and offered a faint smirk. "Husband?"

"Was the quickest lie I could come up with."

She chuckled, then winced. "Don't make me laugh. Everything hurts."

Chase sat at the edge of the bed, his expression hardening. "I shouldn't have let this happen. After what Benjamin told me... I need to move fast. It's too dangerous. I'll wait for the uniforms to arrive, and then I'm gone."

Skye shifted, wincing again. "You mean to leave me behind?"

"I mean to keep you safe."

"I've known you three days, Chase. And somehow that's been enough to flip my whole life upside down."

Chase looked away. "That's why I can't stay."

Skye reached out, taking his hand. "I need to tell you something. Before all this... before you... I'd never even taken a case of my own. All that bravado, the sharp tongue… it was just armor. I was terrified."

He met her eyes.

"I'm one of three women lawyers in New York City. But I never dared to make my own stand. Not until tonight."

Chase said nothing. Just squeezed her hand.

She smiled through the pain. "I had a friend. Sybil Menendez. She used to read cards. Said I'd meet a man who carried hell in his blood and purpose in his shadow. Told me I'd have to choose whether to follow him or let him go."

Chase started to speak, but she cut him off. "I've already chosen."

Benjamin, barely awake, rolled to his side in the chair, clutching the blanket tighter. Chase rose. "Once the uniforms arrive, they'll guard the room. Then I'll head out. It's best we don't see each other again."

Skye's voice sharpened. "You don't get to tell me when I'm done, Chase. That's my call."

He paused.

Skye's eyes welled, but she held steady. "When I said I thought I was close to knowing what love is—I was wrong. I know exactly what it feels like. It's standing by your man and facing the fire."

She reached out her hand.

Chase looked at it for a long moment… then took it.

This time it was her who squeezed Chase's hand.

"Besides, what kind of wife would I be if I let you face danger alone?"

———

Across the street, atop a rooftop drowned in fog and moonlight, Utilis crouched in perfect stillness.

The mourned assassin's silhouette looked wrong—too long in places, too thin in others. Patchy blond hair fluttered in the icy wind. The gas mask affixed to the lower half of his face exhaled slow plumes of necrotic vapor, the breathing tube slithering down into the ribbed plating grafted onto his collapsed chest. Green necromantic fluid pulsed faintly through the goggles strapped over his ruined eyes.

His left arm—replaced from elbow to wrist with grafted bone and brass—clicked as the clawed phalanges flexed.

Radiant wards flickered on the hospital entrance below. Chase Cassidy stood visible through the glass doors beyond them—watchful, coiled, impossibly stubborn.

Utilis tilted his head, studying him.

"So the spellbound mutt lives," he rasped, voice hollow through the filters. "And stands guard." He paused. That was more than Domingo had managed. A faint, thin smile touched his lips beneath the mask.

Domingo.

Poor, stupid Domingo. The big brute had overplayed his hand—fixating on the woman, underestimating her completely. Utilis could still picture her in the doorway of that apartment, wand blazing, will unbroken. The little mage had cut Domingo down like she'd been waiting for him. And Domingo, drunk on old grudges and old losses, had been too fixated on Cassidy to see it coming.

"He watched the battlefield instead of the woman" Utilis murmured. "The first mistake of every dying man."

His claw drummed once against the stone parapet.

"The spellbound is dangerous. Yes." Another tap. "But she? …She is something else." He still didn't know her name, but he knew this much: she had fire. The kind that didn't flicker. The kind that survived.

Domingo never understood that kind of fire. Makalith never will. Utilis did. And the boy—Benjamin Bright. Utilis shifted, eyes narrowing behind green-glowing goggles. Bright had power in him. Fey blood, unmistakably potent. And more importantly—

"He survived," Utilis whispered. "Survived the dancer. Survived the brute. And lived."

That made the boy valuable.

That made the boy a liability.

That made the boy worth killing—or capturing.

Sirus wanted him alive, though. Fine.

Alive it is.

Domingo's failure was also convenient for Utilis. No one would question his tale when he returned with the boy. No one would think twice about how Domingo died. "Tattooed fool," Utilis hissed softly.

He rose slowly to his full height—ungainly, spindly, cadaverous. His coat rippled around him like a long shroud, stitched from several different eras and several different people. A broad executioner's blade hung across his chest, strapped tight with cracked leather.

Below him, the hospital lights flickered. Utilis tasted the necromantic static in the air. Yes. The boy was inside. The spellbound was too. The big man with the brass knuckles. The woman, wounded but alive. An overextended little unit—the perfect place to strike.

"Three defenders," Utilis counted. "One spellbound, one injured fighter, one mage who cant cast without a foci"

His claw tapped twice. "And one asset."

The shamblers he would raise were not tools so much as storms —unthinking, ravenous, unbound once made. The corpses in the morgue downstairs would rise swiftly, hungry and directionless. They'd ignore him, as all his dead did. They would not answer to him.

But they would answer to instinct. Chaos. Noise. Movement. Vulnerability. He did not need to control a storm to use it. "Let the dog guard his humans," Utilis whispered. "Let him divide himself to protect them."

A corpse, recently expired, lay near the far end of the rooftop —an overdose, unattended, unclaimed. Utilis approached, crouched, and pressed his clawed hand atop the still chest.

The corpse convulsed. Bones snapped. Skin split. Something inside shuddered awake. A shambler's empty eyes rolled open. "Good," Utilis murmured. "Wake them. Wake all of them." The shambler rose and soon was seen shuffling across the street.

His goggles pulsed. It would enter the hospital, and make another. And another. And another.

Lights inside the building began to flicker—one by one, from the morgue, stairwell by stairwell, floor by floor—like someone was dragging a cold finger along the spine of the structure.

Utilis stood at the roof's edge. Domingo had weakened them.

Domingo had softened the circle. Domingo had bled on the doorstep. But Utilis...? Utilis would break it.

"With the boy in hand," he whispered, "I return the victor." He stepped backward, dissolving into the deeper shadow behind him. At the hospital entrance something old, cruel, and mechanical crossed the threshold.

———

In Room 312, Skye lay asleep, her face still bruised and puffy, though her breathing had evened out. Beside her, Benjamin Bright slept curled under a blanket in the chair, his small body twitching faintly with dreams. The hum of the heart monitor and the soft hiss of the oxygen machine were the only sounds.

Chase, however, remained awake.

He sat in a chair near the window, coat draped over his lap, Effie and Pearl resting in their holsters. His eyes never strayed far from the door.

A knock came, followed by the creak of hinges.

Two uniformed officers stepped into the room. One was older, his stance steady and eyes cautious—clearly a veteran. The other, younger and wide-eyed, looked fresh out of academy. He nodded awkwardly toward Chase.

"You the guy who called this in?" the vet asked.

Chase stood. "You're late."

"Had to detour through the Narrows," the vet muttered. "Whole squad's stretched thin tonight."

The younger cop gave a quick salute. "Officer Robert Daniels, sir."

Chase studied him a moment, then nodded. "First time walking a post like this?"

Robert hesitated, then admitted, "First time watching over a protected witness, yeah."

The vet, already pulling out his sidearm to check the cylinder, added, "Kid's green, but solid. Patrick McFinny, by the way. Everyone calls me Patty"

"Fine Patty it is. Keep your eyes open. If anything—and I mean anything—feels off, you don't hesitate."

"Yes, sir."

Chase gave Skye and Robert one last glance before slipping past the officers and into the corridor.

The nurse's station was empty.

Chase frowned. He walked around the desk—no clipboard, no sign-in sheets, not even the usual stale coffee cup. The chair was turned at a strange angle.

Across the hall, at the far end of the corridor, a man in janitor's coveralls stood silently, slowly mopping the floor. The overhead lights flickered above him.

"Hey," Chase called. "You see the nurse?"

No answer.

He took a step closer. "Hey! You deaf or something?"

The man continued his repetitive swaying motion, mop dragging through the same dark smear. Chase squinted.

Blood.

The smear wasn't water—it was deep red. The mop handle creaked with each pass.

Chase's breath caught. The face came into focus.

It was the maintenance man. The same one he and Luther had seen at Skye's apartment building. The one who'd disappeared.

Then came the hiss of steam.

A shadow moved.

Chase turned just in time to catch a blur of motion.

Utilis exploded from the ceiling duct behind him, mechanical limbs unfolding with sick precision. His clawed hand slashed toward Chase's back.

Chase rolled forward, Effie already drawn—but too late.

The janitor let out a low moan, eyes lifeless, and lurched toward him, swinging the blood-slick mop like a weapon.

Chase aimed and fired.

The round hit center mass—but the thing didn't stop.

Down the corridor, lights began to flicker violently.

From behind doors and curtained partitions, more shapes began to emerge.

Nurses. Doctors. Every single one of them turned.

Utilis, rising to full height behind the janitor-zombie, let out a hollow laugh.

"Welcome to triage, Spellbound."

And the hospital became a killing floor.

————

Back in Room 312, Patty and Robert kept watch over Skye and the boy. "You been hearing all the weird chatter lately?" Robert whispered.

Patty grunted. "If you mean the dead Fey kids, yeah. And the disappearances—thirty people missing citywide. Feels like we're under siege."

Robert hesitated. "There's a rumor going around. That Captain Whitman's about to deputize a Hex-Breaker."

Patty scoffed. "That's bunk. No one's used the Hex-Breaker Clause in decades." The door creaked open.

A nurse entered, standing motionless just inside.

Patty straightened. "Everything alright, ma'am?"

No response.

Robert started toward her, concern etched on his face.

Patty's eyes narrowed. Something was off. "Robert, hold up."

Robert paused mid-step.

Patty drew his arcane revolver. "Back up. Now."

The nurse twitched. A low moan escaped her lips.

Robert froze as she lunged for a bite—

Bang!

The nurse collapsed to the ground. A smoking hole in her head.

Behind them, Benjamin stirred, blinking groggily.

"Where's Chase?" he shouted in a paniced cry.

Patty's voice was firm. "Find the detective. Now."

Robert nodded and moved toward the door, pulling it open.

He turned and thne backed up quiclkly.

"Uh… Patty?" he called.

From down the corridor, the sound of gunfire erupted—followed by a low, mechanical growl and the wet thump of something hitting the wall.

Robert looked back, pale. "I think the detective's busy."

———

The shamblers surged. Chase backpedaled fast, alternating fire between Effie and Pearl—left, right, left—staggering the recoil so he never stopped moving. Brass casings pinged off the walls, spun across wet tiles, skittered through puddles of blood.

From his left, a nurse dragged a patient into the hallway, eyes wide at the sight of him retreating under fire.

"Get inside!" Chase barked, firing past her shoulder.

She shoved the patient back through the doorway—but two shamblers barreled in before she could slam it shut. Her scream tore through the corridor. Then the patient's. Then nothing but wet tearing.

Chase gritted his teeth and kept moving. He couldn't save them— not with the horde at his heels. A more-intact figure burst through the swarm—a doctor, white coat trailing, mask melted half into his cheek. He sprinted with unnatural speed.

Chase double-tapped his throat with Effie, severing spine and spell. Then, using Pearl, he backhand him, then fired into the doctor's skull, blasting him sideways to clear the line.

Another shambler lunged over the body. Chase fired point-blank, bone and mist sprayed across his coat. Effie's slide locked empty.

He moved without thinking. But a shambler came up from behind. Chase dropped back, drove a kick into the chest of an incoming shambler, the spellbound strength in his legs sending the corpse crashing through a rolling supply cart.

At the same time, he dropped Effie's mag, and slapped a fresh one home. He used Effie's frame to rack the slide against his belt, chambering the next round while already drawing the pistol back up.

The hallway flashed red as emergency lights strobed. A shape descended from above—an infected nursee dropping out of the ceiling tiles, IV tubing trailing like veins. Chase jumped over a blood-streaked cart and fired upward, the shot punching through her jaw and out the top of her skull. She collapsed over him twitching. He shoved her off with a grunt.

A howl echoed down the corridor. A Mourned assassin.

He stood at the far end like a conductor in a broken opera, arms spread, clawed fingers angled like wings, moving as if plucking invisible strings. His mechanical grafts shone with necrotic light. Every corpse in the hallway jerked in time with his gestures.

"Run, Spellbound," Utilis crooned, voice metallic and hollow. "I want your blood hot when I tear it out."

A shambler swung an mope like a club. Chase ducked, pivoted, and put a round through the orderly's temple, spraying the wall with arterial haze. Another tackled him through a glass crash door. They hit the floor hard, shards cutting into Chase's arms.

The creature snapped inches from his face. Chase slammed both pistols under its chin and fired, its head disappeared in a spray of gore. Before he could rise, a second shambler pounced. Chase forearm-blocked, felt its teeth scrape the leather of his coat, then shot it twice—chest, head— and tossed it aside.

He staggered to his feet. Pearl clicked empty. He ejected the mag, swearing under his breath. A glance at his arm—his coat sleeve torn, skin grazed just enough that necrotic ichor smeared the surface.

Too close.

Even a spellbound's body couldn't purge necrotic infection. One bite he could heal. Two or three, and he'd turn. He wasn't ready to test the limits. He raised Effie and fired at Utilis 'silhouette—

The shot missed as Utilis slipped behind a corner like a mocking shadow. Chase didn't stop to chase him. He turned.

Ran. Leading the swarm away from Room 312. He didn't intend to die.

Not yet.

———

The two coppers knew they were in a fix. Robert stood by the door, revolver already drawn. It had been minutes since they'd heard Cassidy's gunfire. Now it was silent.

Too silent.

He peeked out the window and jerked back just as a shambler lurched past—its jaw slack, nostrils flaring as it sniffed the air. The thing paused, sensing something... then staggered on.

Patty exhaled through his nose frustrated. "From the Narrows to this. Lord I hate this town"

Behind them, Skye stirred. Her eyelids fluttered, breath catching as consciousness clawed its way back.

Patty was already at her side, a hand on her shoulder—firm, but careful. "Ms. Anderson," he whispered urgently. "You need to get up."

Her brows pinched. She shifted, ribs flaring with pain that drew a sharp hiss through her teeth. Still, she didn't complain. She forced herself upright, one arm braced against the bed rail.

Benjamin hovered next to her, trying to hide the trembling in his hands.

"What... what's happening?" Skye rasped.

"Hospital's gone to hell," Patty said. "Cassidy drew 'em off, but we gotta move. Now."

Skye swallowed hard, steadying herself. "My robe."

"I got it," Benjamin said quickly. He grabbed the folded hospital robe from the chair and passed it to her. Skye slid her arms into it, grimacing as the fabric brushed her ribs. Patty turned away politely while she tied it closed over the open-backed gown.

"My wand," she said next.

Benjamin was already reaching for her personal-effects box. He held it out with both hands. Inside lay the arcolam—its metal faintly luminescent even in the dim room.

Skye gripped it. The wand hummed in recognition.

"All right," she breathed, bracing herself. "We have to get to Luther. I believe he is in the west wing."

Robert cracked the door again. The hallway was chaos—shamblers streaming toward the emergency wing like a river of meat and hunger.

"Clear enough to move," he said. "For now."

They stepped into the corridor.

A horde of the dead surged down the far end—limbs jerking, jaws snapping, flesh hanging loose from bone. Every one of them moving away from them.

Chasing something.

Chasing someone.

"Cassidy," Patty muttered. "He must be drawing 'em off."

"Then we go the opposite way," Skye said through clenched teeth.

They slipped into the nearest room to avoid a straggler. A patient lay strapped to the bed—alive no longer. His skin gray, eyes vacant, teeth gnashing as he strained against the leather restraints. Benjamin recoiled.

Skye didn't.

She raised the arcalam, breath unsteady. "Ashtu–Ginash."

The true tongue ripped from her lips like a blade. A spectral bolt fired from the wand's tip, spearing the creature clean through the skull. It went still immediately. Skye sagged against the wall, the spell tearing strength from her already-injured body.

Patty steadied her. "Easy."

"I'm fine," she lied. "Keep going."

Room by room, the group pressed on—twice doubling back to avoid shamblers, once slipping through a lounge streaked with claw marks and overturned chairs. Something twitched in a corner, but none dared look.

Skye forced herself forward. Benjamin clung to Robert's shoulder until his eyes widened suddenly. "Stop," the boy whispered. "They're getting closer."

He dropped down, rummaging in his coat, pulling out a chalk stub wrapped in butcher paper. "I can try something."

Patty glanced back. "Kid—what?"

"A minor sign, a sound glyph" Benjamin said. "My mom taught me." He sketched a tight spiral on the wall, jagged corners crackling faintly. He pressed his palm to it— A loud crash erupted far down another hallway. As if a steel gurney had collapsed. Several shamblers instantly turned and sprinted toward the phantom noise.

Robert blinked. "Kid… damn good work."

"Don't thank me yet," Benjamin whispered.

A door creaked at the far end. Two more shamblers emerged. Patty fired once—clean through the skull. The second charged only to drop as Robert places a well aimed shot between the eyes.

"Move!" he barked.

They crossed into another ward—probably a convalescent wing. The overhead lamps flickered weakly, powered by a backup generator struggling somewhere below. A cracked glass globe swung from its fixture, casting long, jerking shadows across the walls.

A tipped crash cart lay overturned near the door. Beneath it, a half-eaten orderly sprawled on the tiles, organs spilling like wet rope across the floor.

Patty didn't blink—he fired once. The corpse stilled.

A mechanical alarm bell trilled faintly down the hall, its rhythm erratic, half-choked by damaged wiring. The smell of ether and burnt fabric hung thick in the air. Steam hissed from a ruptured radiator along the wall, filling the corridor with a wavering haze that distorted their silhouettes.

Every hallway was a snare. Every doorway a gamble. But they pushed forward anyway. Because behind them was death— and ahead, was the only path left that might save them.

.——

Chase vaulted a collapsed gurney and skidded through a smear of blood, breath ripping through his lungs. Effie and Pearl both ran low—he could feel the rhythm of their recoil weakening, the arcane cores cooling with each shot.

Too many.

He ducked behind an overturned medicine cart, wiping sweat from his brow. The dead swarmed the hall—jerking, hungry, deaf to pain. Meat puppets. But their puppeteer?

That bastard was was the cause of this. What was he? A Mourned? Possibly but from the sight of him he looked like a construct. A flesh golem perhaps. Regardless of what it was Chase was certain about one thing. If wanted this to end, he had to cut the strings.

"No more running," he muttered. "Time to end this."

A crash thundered through the distant corridor—sharp, metallic, deliberate. The pack of shamblers froze... then veered toward the sound, shuffling mindlessly after the phantom noise.

A sound-glyph trick.

"Benjamin," Chase whispered. "Smart kid."

He moved quickly, ducking into a maintenance hallway behind the emergency wing. Darkness swallowed him. Steam hissed from fractured pipes overhead, and condensation dripped like rain on stone.

Halfway down the corridor, he stopped. A gated door opened into the emergency wing. Chase eased forward and peered through. There he was.

At the far end of the corridor, puppeteer stood perfectly still, spine arched, mechanical tendons twitching like exposed nerves. His gas mask gleamed under the flickering red lights. It stood still as a corpse, head tilted like he was listening through the walls. Most of the shamblers had wandered off, chasing Benjamin's decoy.

Perfect.

Chase holstered Effie and Pearl. This needed his fists. His boots struck the tile in measured steps, the leftover blood on the floor reflecting the flicker of failing emergency lights.

The Mourned spoke without turning. "At last," Utilis rasped, "the Spellbound shows himself."

Chase squared his shoulders. "Yeah. Spellbound. Name's Cassidy."

Utilis swiveled his head in a grotesque half-bow. "Utilis The Rover. And I... will be the last living thing you look upon." His eye glowed brighter.

"Living?" Chase fired back. "There is nothing living about you."

Utilis nodded his head "Excuse my poor metaphor then. We can agree that I am not what you call living, yet I still think, still move. Is that life"

Chase stepped forward, fists balled in tight fists. "I'm not here to discuss philosophy. What do you want?"

"The boy? Give him to me, and this ends."

"Can't do that." Chase ignited Infernal Surge—heat roaring under his skin, sigils flaring like molten gold. He sprinted forward in a blitz meant to shatter ribcage and skull in one strike.

With a screech of metal pistons, the Mourned vaulted over him, body whipping upward in a predatory arc. His claws scissored downward, aiming cleanly to decapitate Chase mid-charge, timing the strike for the exact moment Chase's momentum locked him into his path.

Too fast. Too precise. Chase realized instantly he wouldn't be able to stop or dodge, not at this speed. He was dead.

Instinct took over. His mind raced and fired the only thing that might save him, the Glyph of Infernal Pulse. It was not supposed to be fired at the same instant as Surge. To much of a strain on his body but this was life or death.

A Stutter Step hit him like a fist through his chest. A wrenching, impossible displacement of time and space. Chase blinked out of the kill zone and reappeared crashing into the wall ten feet away.

Dust rained down. His head spun. "...what the hell—"

Utilis landed in a crouch where Chase should have died, claws embedded in the floor. He jerked his head toward Chase, eye narrowing. "...odd," the Mourned murmured. "That blow should have landed."

Chase pushed off the wall, dazed. "Yeah. Tell me about it."

Utilis's eye flickered with hungry calculation. "That was no spellbound trick. Spellbound do not bend space."

Chase stood. "Guess I'm full of surprises."

Utilis spread his arms, inviting the conflict.

Chase took a single step forward and Utilis was already there, claws carving downward in a brutal arc, followed immediately by a second strike meant to split skull and spine.

Chase ignited a Ward of the Searing Aegis just in time. A golden shield flared across his forearm. necrotic residue sizzling as it skidded across the ward's surface.

Chase countered hard. A Spellbound haymaker burning with infernal weight, crashed into the side of Utilis's mask. Plating dented. Glass split. Dark necro-fluid hissed from a ruptured seam.

Utilis screamed, a metallic howl of static and rage, and kicked Chase square in the chest. Chase hit the ground, rolled backward, boots skidding, and came up fast. The Mourned assassin was already charging.

Chase snapped his left hand up and unleashed the Infernal Lance—a spear of searing fire cutting the air between them. Utilis twisted sideways with inhuman grace, the lance streaking past his ribs, leaving burn-warped metal. He retaliated instantly, claws slicing toward Chase's head.

Chase dropped low, rolling beneath the strike. He came up inside Utilis's reach and hammered a fist into the construct's ribs—metal buckling under the blow. Utilis absorbed it, snarling, and elbowed Chase in the face. The hit snapped Chase's head sideways, sending him stumbling, vision blurring.

Claws came again. Chase blocked with the other Searing Aegis. The ward flaring, then flickering as necrotic magic hissed across its surface, trying to eat through it. Too close.

Chase activated the Sigil of Infernal Strife—a brutal, furnace-hot channel of raw force. His next punch detonated like a cannon. It struck Utilis dead-center in the chest. The Mourned assassin lifted off his feet—flew backward—skidding across the floor, arms flared wide.

He wasn't down long. Utilis bounced up, ran, leapt, planted both feet on the ceiling, and shot downward like a falling blade.

Chase rolled forward, just barely, feeling the claws shred the back of his jacket as the assassin landed where his spine had been a second earlier. Chase slid on the slick floor, boots carving a line through smeared blood.

As he slid, he turned and drew Effie and Pearl and unloaded. Muzzle flashes strobed the hall. Rounds punched through Utilis's torso, tearing open quarter holes. Utilis barely reacted. The holes didn't bleed. They healed. Closing before Chase's eyes.

"Oh hell," Chase muttered.

He dropped both pistols—empty—and surged back to his feet. Utilis rushed him. They collided at close quarters— a whirlwind of claws, fists, wards, and infernal sparks.

Chase moved fast— faster than any human— but Utilis's claws were relentless. Every strike aimed to maim, sever, or kill. Chase parried with he Aegis, ducked, rolled, smashed elbows into steel ribs, shoulder-checked the creature into a wall, anything to stay ahead of those scissoring blades. The hall shook with the violence of it.

Two shamblers lurched into view behind Utilis. Chase didn't hesitate. He flung the Searing Aegis free from his forearm—its golden edge blazing—and hurled it like a discus. The shield bisected both shamblers cleanly, dropping them in a spray of necrotic ichor.

He lost that shield. Only one remained.

Utilis came at him again.

Chase grabbed a toppled IV pole, swung it like a quarterstaff. Utilis bent backward at an impossible angle, the pole whistling over his face, claws digging into the tile as he arced back upright. Letting go of the pole, Chase stepped in and punched down with the remaining Searing Aegis at point-blank range.

The shield carved through Utilis's shoulder joint, tearing the entire mechanical arm free in a storm of sparks and black fluid. Utilis stumbled, shrieking.

Chase ignited Infernal Torrent, fire spiraling up his arm but pain exploded down his side. The severed arm, still twitching with necro-commands, stabbed itself into his thigh, claws puncturing clean through muscle.

Chase roared, dropping to one knee. Metal fluid sprayed across the tiles. Utilis scrambled forward, lunging. Chase whipped a backhand across his face with all the strength he had left.

The blow shattered the mask and the jaw beneath it. Utilis spun and crashed to the floor, gurgling sparks. Chase sagged, teeth clenched, and ripped the embedded claw from his thigh, blood streaming down his leg.

He stepped forward, ready to finish it but Utilis flinched, twisted, and fled. Half-crawling, half-running, his body contorting into something spider-like against the wall, he left a trail of black ichor and sparks.

He vanished into the shadows, gone before Chase could raise an arm. Chase exhaled hard, breath ragged, vision tunneling. Lights flickered. Steam hissed. His blood dripped onto the tile. He didn't follow. He couldn't.

The corridor doors slammed open, bursting inward with a shock of blue ward-light. The 1st Arcane Police surged through—armor gleaming, rifles crackling with restrained spellcharge. Sigils rippled across the ceiling as their entry wards snapped into place like shattering glass.

At the front, baton drawn and eyes sharp, strode Sergeant Juno.

Behind him, coat whipping around his boots, came Captain Whitman. His gaze swept the destruction—blood, scorch marks, bodies—and then locked on the only detail that mattered: Whitman's eyes swept the carnage. Then he saw Chase.

Chase took one shaky step toward him—and the world buckled. His vision tunneled. His skin burned like forge metal, the signature agony of overclocked spellbound healing battling necrochemical rot still crawling under his skin.

His knees buckled.

"CHASE—!" Skye's scream cracked through the static.

He collapsed hard, the tile rattling under his weight.Chase tried to push himself upright, but the necrochemical venom and spellbound overburn tore through him like wildfire. His veins glowed faintly red. Steam rose from his skin. He sagged sideways—and Skye burst from a nearby ward room, barefoot, wearing nothing but a tattered medical gown.

"CHASE!"

She slid across the tile and caught him before he hit the floor again, cradling his burning face in both hands. "He's boiling—somebody help him! NOW!"

Medics from the 1st Arcane moved to respond—and then another voice cut through everything.

"EVERYONE HERE IS NOW UNDER BUREAU OF ARCANE ENFORCEMENT AUTHORITY."

Agent Gerald Froud was the kind of man who made silence feel like a verdict. Tall, narrow-shouldered, and razor-straight in his Bureau blacks, he carried himself with the precise stiffness of someone who believed in rules more than people. His hair—iron gray, clipped close—matched the cold glint of the augmentation nodes embedded along his jawline, faint runes pulsing like dim stars beneath the skin.

His expression rarely shifted from its default setting: clinical disdain. Not anger. Not even impatience. Just the steady, suffocating disappointment of a man convinced everyone in the room was already guilty.

The glowing gauntlet at his wrist hummed softly, calibrated for containment rather than combat—tools he wielded with the same detached efficiency as a surgeon handling scalpels.

Froud did not shout.

He did not threaten.

He simply arrived with paperwork, protocols, and Bureau authority at his back—and somehow that was always more frightening than a gun. Where Whitman had presence, and Juno had grit, Froud had inevitability. To him, the law was a machine, and he was merely its voice.

A cold, meticulous voice that never forgot a clause, never forgave a breach, and never hesitated to put anyone—mage or mundane—into a containment cell if the forms were in his favor.

Skye whipped her head toward him, fury blazing.

"He's dying—move aside and let the medics triage him!"

Froud didn't even look at her. "Spellbound overburn combined with necrochemical exposure constitutes a Class-Red anomaly. The suspect will be detained for federal arcane quarantine."

Skye surged to her feet. "He's not a suspect! He's the reason half this hospital isn't dead!"

Whitman stormed forward, planting himself between Froud and the medics. "Back the hell off, Froud. Cassidy is under my protection."

Froud raised a brow, unimpressed. "The Bureau outranks local authority in all matters involving—"

"Oh, shut up with the handbook," Whitman snapped. "We're not playing your jurisdiction pissing contest tonight."

Behind them, their arguments rose—sharp, heated, overlapping, echoing down the ruined corridor.

But Skye heard none of it.

She knelt back down beside Chase, gripping his shoulders. "Stay with me, baby... come on... look at me." Chase's skin radiated heat like a furnace. His runes pulsed under the surface of his forearms, glowing angrily through the grime and dried blood. His breath came in ragged bursts, each one hotter than the last.

A medic tried to edge past the BAE gauntlets. "Ma'am, his temperature is spiking—his spellbound regeneration's going berserk—"

Froud stepped forward again.

"No treatment. Not until containment protocols are complete."

"YOU TOUCH HIM AND I SWEAR TO GOD—" Skye snarled, half rising.

Whitman barked at both sides: "Juno! Get these people pushed back! Get me space around Cassidy!"

Sergeant Juno raised his voice above the chaos: "1st ARCANE—SHIELDS UP! FORM A LINE!"

The armored officers moved instantly, creating a protective semicircle around Chase and the medics—blocking Froud and his containment team.

Skye pulled Chase's head into her lap as his body trembled violently. "Please," she whispered, forehead pressed to his. "Please don't burn out on me."

Faintly, Chase exhaled her name. More shouting erupted behind her —Whitman and Froud nearly chest-to-chest—but Skye didn't care. The only thing that mattered was the man melting in her arms. And the faint, rapid thrum of his heart fighting not to stop.

The standoff between Whitman's Arcane officers and Froud's containment team was seconds from boiling over when the crash doors burst open again.

This time, it wasn't soldiers. It was lawyers.

Donald Pierce strode in first—wiry, sharply dressed, glasses catching the wardlight, his tailored mustache immaculate even in the chaos. His boutique-cut jacket hugged his frame like it was stitched for war, not courtrooms. Behind him thundered Thomas Anderson—a burly wall of a man, thick-necked and broad-shouldered, reddish-gray hair swept back and still somehow dignified despite the sprint that brought him here. He moved like a linebacker, but there was panic in his eyes.

"ENOUGH!" Donald shouted, voice cracking like a whip.

Froud froze mid-sentence.

Donald lifted a thick sheaf of stamped, rune-sealed documents high over his head. "This," he said, "is an emergency order signed by Federal Judge Nigel Keller. Effective immediately, Chase Cassidy falls under the protective custody of Anderson & Pierce, operating as deputized private security under federal authority."

He jabbed the paperwork toward Froud like a dagger. "This supersedes the Bureau's claim. Step aside."

Froud's nostrils flared. "You are interfering with a federal—"

Thomas Anderson stepped forward, looming over him like a brick wall with opinions. "Interfering?" Thomas rumbled. "Son, I am federal interference."

Skye let out a shuddering breath of relief—but she never let go of Chase's face. Whitman allowed himself a satisfied nod. "You heard the man, Froud. Court order beats your handbook. Stand down."

The BAE containment officers hesitated, looked at their commander. Froud's jaw clenched... then he stepped back an inch. He'd remember this slight.

Whitman barked at the medics. "MOVE HIM!"

Four medics surged in, lifting Chase gently but urgently. His body radiated heat like a forge. His limbs trembled with overburn and necrochemical backlash. Skye ran beside the gurney, one hand never leaving his chest.

A nurse tried to stop her. "Ma'am you can't."

"I'm his wife." Skye lied brushing past the started woman. "Chase—

look at me. Stay with me. Don't fade now."

His vision was smoke and fragments—Skye's silhouette trembling above him, tears streaking through ash on her cheeks... Whitman arguing with Froud in the distance... the blinding blue sigils of the Arcane wards...

Then something soft touched his wrist. A small hand. Chase turned his head—barely—and saw Benjamin, eyes wide, face blotched red from crying, held tightly by Luther, who shook with fear but stood firm.

"Mr. Cassidy... don't go..." Benjamin whispered. The world pulsed. Heat. Darkness. Skye's voice fading, distant: "CHASE—STAY WITH ME!"

His eyes slipped shut. And everything went black.

CHAPTER 11

Regrouping

Journal of Makalith Ravenwind — Entry Fragment

The scholars of the Arcane Society still write of the Fae as though we were myths—creatures of moonlight and mischief, bound to Courts that no longer exist. They do not understand. They never have.

At first, all Fae were shapeshifters. We became whatever the moment demanded—light, shadow, claw, breeze, dream. But time has a way of settling even the wildest things. Our forms solidified. Wings for some, none for others. And the shapes we kept are the ones humans now confuse as our "true" selves.

The females bear wings and can fold themselves small as candle-flames. Humans call them sprites. Incorrect, of course, but mortals are enthusiastic in their ignorance. The males—my kind—remain wingless. Our magic turns inward, rooted in the soil and sorrow that bind us.

Long ago, we had Courts to anchor us—Seelie for the bright-hearted, Unseelie for the fierce and cruel. But when the Courts destroyed each other in the Fae Wars and sealed themselves away, they left behind those who did not fit cleanly into either world. The Dusk-Born. My kin. Children of twilight, of endings, of the quiet places between choices.

Nearly a third of the Fae left on this plane descend from us. There are no purebloods anymore. Even little Coco—brilliant, fragile, chaotic—carries threads of humanity in her veins. She insists it makes her stronger. I suppose she might be right.

Mortals think of us as tricksters, pests, woodland fancies. They do not understand that we are the remnants of a people abandoned by their own gods. Exiles from a home that no longer remembers our names.

Still… we endure. Twilight is all the world left us. Twilight is where we remain.

The lamps in Makalith's private quarters burned low, their pale violet flames licking shadows across the stone walls. Down here beneath the docks, the air always carried the scent of cold brine and embalming salts—a reminder of who truly claimed these tunnels.

Makalith sat on the edge of the bed, bare torso etched with runes that glowed faintly like sleeping embers. He inhaled, slow and precise, then reached for his trousers—silver-threaded, tailored, impeccable even in the darkness.

He slid them on, hooked his suspenders over each shoulder, then buckled the strap with a final, decisive tug.

Behind him, Coco Le Fay lay sprawled across the silk sheets—naked, wings half-folded around her glowing form. One wing draped over her hips in something resembling modesty, though Coco had never been burdened by such things. She slept deeply, breath soft and feline, wings fluttering faintly as she dreamed. She had to be restrained after she witnesses the draining of the Fey child, it took all his power and patience. When she calmed she said she wanted a baby. The things one does—Makalith sighed.

Calming her had been more than necessity—it had been survival. Fey did not abide kin-harm. Even diluted, even distant. The moment those bright, predatory teeth of Adriana Morton dripped crimson, Coco erupted—screaming as if she herself had been bitten, wings slicing the air, lashing to kill. She would've tried to tear Morton apart, Court or no Court, hierarchy or no hierarchy.

And Makalith—gods help him—was the only thing standing between her and an execution sentence. It had taken everything he had to keep her from ripping free. Binding sigils. Soft words. Hard grip. Fey dominance. A half-breed's instinct pulling at a three-quarters 'fury.

He felt her emotions like wildfire under his skin—rage, grief, ancient instinct screaming for vengeance. He had taken the blows she meant for Morton. Taken the screams meant for the room. Held her until the storm stopped shaking her bones.

Only once she had collapsed into exhausted trembling had he taken her to bed—not for lust, but for stabilization. Because Fey did not calm through reason; they calmed through connection, through skin, through shared breath and shared pulse.

And because he could not let the Court see Coco as a feral threat. She was too important. Too rare. Too easily destroyed for the convenience of politics. Besides—she was his payment. Not coin. Not favor. Not rank.

The deal had been simple: He would serve the Court of Bones, clean their messes, fix the catastrophes their arrogance created...and in return, they would turn over Coco Le Fay, prisoner held in isolation for the murder of her sister. Letting her out had been an act of hubris on their part. Keeping her alive would be an act of devotion on his.

Makalith watched her now, peaceful and glowing under the lamplight—utterly unlike the shrieking storm he held earlier. Her madness, her beauty, her volatility—they were his responsibility. His burden. His reward.

When she whispered she wanted a baby, he had only sighed. Because Fey desires were never simple wants. They were instinct. Prophecy. Blood-truth. And a child of Coco Le Fay—gods. The Court had no idea what they had traded away.

A knock cracked against the door—sharp, urgent. Makalith didn't turn.

"Enter."

The door opened and Sirus Magnus stepped in, tall and severe, rainwater dripping from his black coat onto the stone floor. His scarred jaw seemed tighter tonight. His eyes were hollowed with worry.

Makalith smoothed a wrinkle from his vest. "Well? What news? Did Domingo retrieve the child?"

Sirus hesitated. "No, Makalith."

Makalith's hand paused mid-motion.

Sirus continued, voice rough: "Domingo is dead."

A soft laugh came from Coco—her wing twitched, curling tighter around her body. Makalith exhaled slowly through his nose, not angry, just calculating. "And Utilis?"

"Alive," Sirus said. "But burnt to the damn bone. A man—Cassidy is his name— and a female mage, stopped them both from what I gleamed from Utilis. The Rover is crippled for now. Possibly for days. Posssibly for months."

Makalith turned fully, eyes narrowing like drawn blades. "And the child?"

"Our tracker... broke," Sirus said. "Something severed it. Spell backlash or a counter-ward we weren't prepared for."

A muscle ticked in Makalith's jaw. The Court of Bones would

demand progress. Proof that the prize was at hand. And he had corpses and excuses. He stood, crossing the room with smooth, gliding steps, tapping his fingertips lightly along his suspenders—a quiet rhythm of decisions forming in the dark.

"Domingo dead. Utilis wounded. The boon severed. And the Court will arrive in three nights..." His voice was soft. Too soft.

Sirus waited, still as stone.

Makalith stared at the ceiling as though weighing which sin would cost him least. "Not a word to the Court," he said at last. "Not yet. They smell weakness like blood. I will decide how they hear this... and when."

A lazy purr drifted from the bed. "Mmm..." Coco murmured, stretching beneath her wings. "Sounds like someone's evening didn't go well."

Makalith didn't look back. "Dress yourself, Coco," he said quietly, death settling into his tone like frost. "We're not done tonight."

———

Chase floated in a warm dark fog, distant voices brushing against the edges of his mind. "...highly unusual to place a man and a woman in the same recovery suite—"

A second voice, exasperated: "She told us they were married. And she refused to be moved. What did you want me to do? Stand up to an angry mage with a wand?"

A muffled chuckle. "She will hex you for sure"

"Look, doctor, I just let them have the room."

Chase's eyes fluttered. Light. Sterile. Too bright. He groaned. A soft hand touched his cheek. "Chase... hey... you with me?"

Skye lay in the bed beside him—hospital gown, hair pulled back, face still pale but no longer bloodless. Her brown eyes shimmered with the kind of relief that stripped a person bare.

"You've been out for two days," she whispered. "Scared the hell out of me."Chase blinked, trying to sit up. Pain flared down his leg—bandaged thick, stitched neat. The rest of his body looked as if nothing had happened. Spellbound regeneration had done its job everywhere except the necrochemical burn in his thigh.

He sucked in a breath. "...damn. That one stings."

"Doctor said you're lucky you didn't lose the leg." Skye smirked weakly. "I told him luck had nothing to do with it. You're too stubborn."

He opened his mouth to answer—but stopped when he noticed the guard inside the room. A tall Anderson & Pierce private security officer leaned against the wall, a Thompson submachine gun slung casually across his chest. His eyes never left Chase. Raising a hand he knocked on the door.

As if on cue, another guard outside knocked.

"He's awake," the guard called through the crack.

Bootsteps. Low conversation. Then the door swung open.

Captain Whitman, Donald Pierce, and Dr. Halvorsen entered with the nurse in tow. The doctor stood stiff, irritated; the nurse simply nodded to Skye with quiet respect.

Donald was the first to speak. "Doctor, nurse—thank you. We'll take it from here." The medical staff hesitated but stepped out. The guard shut the door. Whitman approached the bed. Chase tried to stand.

Skye immediately grabbed his arm. "You idiot—lie down!"

"Orders say I'm supposed to rest," Chase muttered, grimacing as he swung one foot to the floor. "Never been good at that." He stood, swaying slightly, but straightened when Whitman folded his arms.

"Cassidy," Whitman said, "we've reassigned the case. Detective Paul Rourke from Homicide is taking lead until you're back on your feet."

Chase frowned. "Rourke? Isn't he—"

"—the only detective we could pull who wasn't terrified of the BAE," Whitman muttered. "And don't get attached. Odds are he'll be eaten alive."

Nobody disagreed.

Whitman reached into his coat. "I'm joking. Rouke's good enough for now. But that's not why I'm here." He pulled out a small leather-bound case—heavy, embossed, unmistakable. Chase's breath stilled. Skye straightened beside him.

Whitman placed the case on Chase's chest. "Governor General Travers is initiating the Hexbreaker Clause." His voice dropped to a formal, somber register. "Once you're cleared, if Rourke can't get ahead of this—and between us, he won't—Travers wants you reinstated with full authority."

Chase stared at the case. "This is... judge, jury, and executioner."

Skye whispered, "That's exactly what it is."

Whitman nodded once. "A Hexbreaker's badge. Not ceremonial. Not probationary. Active status. You'll be empowered to bring this whole nightmare to an end."

Chase didn't move. Skye slid her hand into his. He looked at her, voice low. "How long have we known each other?"

She held his gaze without flinching. "...four days."

He huffed out a breath—half disbelief, half awe. "This path... you don't have to follow me. You can always walk away."

Skye stepped closer, placing her free hand over his heart. "I'm all in, Chase. Whatever comes next."

He nodded, jaw tightening with something fierce and grateful. He handed the badge back to Whitman. "When its time I'll be ready."

Whitman picked up the case and stepped back toward the door. "Get your strength back. The city's circling the drain... and it's waiting for someone to pull the plug."

He left them there—Chase standing unsteadily, Skye at his side or a sentence.

———

Makalith stepped through the broken front door, coat brushing against shattered molding. Coco Le Fay floated in behind him, wings half-furled, moving with the ghostlike ease of a creature who left no sound on wood or tile. Her eyes widened, taking in the destruction as though it were a twisted art gallery.

Makalith raised a hand. "Reviathe."

The Aether vibrated. Pale, spectral shapes flared into being—etheric fingerprints burned into space by violence and spellcraft.

Coco gasped softly. "Oh! A picture show." She hugged her wings lightly around herself. "But everyone forgot to speak."

Makalith smiled faintly. Of course she would say that—Coco could only see the images. But he heard everything. The echoes of shouted names, the residual sound imprints burned into the room. The reconstruction unfolded:

Luther Holloway crashing through the dining table. Chase Cassidy firing his Colt, arcs of sigil-flare blooming with each shot. Shadowbeasts surging from corners like living smoke. Skye—hair wild, face cut—running for the stairs as the monstrous silhouettes multiplied.

Coco pointed. "Look. She's running." Her voice was soft. "Smart girl."

Domingo's etheric form materialized—huge, hulking—barreling after Skye. Glass shattered. Furniture toppled. The beasts lunged for Cassidy and Holloway as the two men fought side by side, their signatures bright and volatile.

Makalith narrated quietly, almost to himself. "Utilis was here..." He paused, leaning closer to the faint after-image lingering near the stairwell—distant, unfocused, detached from the central chaos. "...watching from the distance." A slow smirk crept across his face.

"The rover simply watched." He straightened, eyes narrowing with cold amusement as the reconstructed Skye fled upward and Domingo thundered after her.

"Domingo chased her up the stairs," he continued. "And Utilis didn't lift a finger." The line carried all the meaning Makalith needed: Utilis had not been assisting Domingo. He had been observing. Letting Domingo fail.

Coco drifted forward, transfixed, as Skye's glowing after-image sprinted up the staircase.

They followed the etheric trail to the second floor. The bedroom door hung crookedly from a single hinge, splinters littering the floor. Inside, bloodstains and ruptured sigils still scarred the walls. Makalith stepped across the threshold and and waved his hand.

The room came alive in silent spectral motion. Domingo slamming Skye onto the mattress. Her struggling beneath him. His weight pinning her wrists. The Shadow Beast curling behind him like a vulture made of ink.

Coco looked once—and tore her gaze away, wings clamping shut around her body like a cocoon. "No," she whispered. "No more of that." Her voice trembled—not with madness, but memory.

Makalith watched the reconstructed Skye being thrown across the room. Watched her hands shake as she pointed her dueling wand. Watched her cast a arcane spear of dark light into Domingo's throat. "She killed him here," Makalith said quietly.

The reconstruction faded into drifting sparks. Coco's wings slowly opened. "He tried that to me once," she said. Her voice clear. Sharp. Perfectly focused. "When they first released me."

Makalith's jaw clenched. Coco turned to him fully, her pupils narrowing to thin vertical slits—pure Fey, pure truth. "You should have killed him then."

For the first time in years, Makalith felt something jolt in his chest. Fear?

No. Respect—for how perfectly lucid she was in this moment. He took her hand gently. "I should have."

Coco exhaled, long and controlled. "Domingo is dead." She looked around the ruined bedroom. " But I don't... I don't want to kill this one." A soft smile. "I like her."

Makalith studied her. "The Court will demand punishment," he murmured. "Von Epp will want a name."

Coco tilted her head, wings fluttering faintly.   "Not her."

"No?" Makalith questioned. He exhaled slow and stepped back, letting his gaze rise toward the wall. The nude portrait of the woman stared back at him—fearless, elegant, painted with the self-assurance of a woman who refused to hide. The signature at the bottom matched the monogram on the journal lying half-open on the nightstand.

He reached for it, brushing away broken glass and dried blood. He flipped it open. The handwriting was sharp, precise. The first page read: Personal Writings of Skye Anderson-Pierce. Maklith carefully flipped to the most recent page, amid legal notes and case sketches, one line was written casually in the margin:

"Meeting with Chase Cassidy today." Makalith stared at it, then let the journal fall shut. "Agreed," he said quietly. "Not her."

Coco's fingers tightened gently around his. "So... the other one. The man?"

Makalith nodded once, definitive. "We give Von Epp the name... Chase Cassidy."

———

Later that night. Diego slipped in through the back window of Chase's apartment, landing quietly on the wooden floor. Dust drifted where he stepped. The place was still. Too still. Diego frowned. Chase wasn't the type to go this long without sending a note or a smart remark.

Something was wrong.

He flicked on a small arcane lighter, illuminating the living room. Furniture untouched. No coffee cup. No coat. The quiet had weight to it.

"Chase?" he called softly. "You here, hermano?"

No answer.

He moved deeper inside, instincts sharpening. His boots made soft thuds on the floorboards—one toe poking out through a hole in his sock. "Tch. Need a new pair," he muttered, half-heartedly trying to keep things light.

Then he saw it.

The old war-locker sat propped open beside the bedroom doorway, the metal lid dented, scorched, and pitted from two wars 'worth of ghosts. Diego knelt beside it, one hand resting on the rim as if afraid the thing might bite. The faint lamplight caught the contents inside—a jumble of history neither of them had touched in years.

Diego's own Legionnaire gear lay folded with surprising care: the dark blue greatcoat that had carried him through the Argonne, his cracked leather bracers, the deck of bone dice he swore had saved his life more than any officer ever had.

Beside it waited Chase's past.

The Model 8 Hellfighter helmet sat on its side, runic lining faintly visible beneath soot-stains that refused to clean away. His Legionnaire coat —stitched, patched, and burned at the sleeves—was tucked beneath the heavy U.S. Army trench jacket he'd worn when the world turned red. A field journal warped with rain and blood lay against a bundle of dog tags, the metal bent where shrapnel had caught him years ago. And under it all, wrapped in oiled canvas, the old bayonet with infernal scorch marks etched along the fuller, a relic from the night everything changed.

Diego lifted the helmet, studying the polished curve. "Man... you really kept all this?" A chill traveled his spine. Chase only opened this box when demons—old or new—were stirring.

Diego set the helmet down and stood. His expression hardened.

"Alright, Cass." He kicked off his boots, flexing that torn sock with annoyance. "Wherever you are... I'm gonna find you. Dead gods or no."

He cracked his knuckles. "And if someone hurt you?"

His eyes narrowed.

"They're gonna wish they hadn't."

BOOK 2

CHAPTER 1

Where Heat Meets the Coming Cold

Journal of Skye Espe Anderson-Pierce
Date: Unknown, but etched in me all the same
They say some battles leave scars no blade can mark. Mine wasn't a war fought with artillery or magic. It was older. Uglier. The kind where a man decides he owns you—your body, your breath, your very right to say no.
The Tatted man came for me with that look. That twisted conviction that I was something owed to him. Something he could take.

But I fought. Gods, I fought. Not just for myself—though I'd be lying if I said that didn't matter. I fought because if I didn't stop him, he would do it again. To someone else. Someone who might not get back up.

People talk about survival like it's luck. They don't talk about the decision to refuse fear, to drag yourself off the floor and bite back. I bled. I screamed. And I burned with the will to make him understand I was not prey.

He understood that right before I killed him.
I passed through fire. And I didn't just survive—I endured.

That night changed me. Not into something broken—but forged. Hardened. I don't flinch when someone reaches for me now. I watch. I calculate. I move.

And when I look at Chase... he sees it. He doesn't pity me. He doesn't coddle or tiptoe. He respects the fire in me. Maybe because he's walked through his own. Maybe because we both carry the weight of violence that tried to make us something small—and we refused.

He doesn't look at me and see just a woman. He sees a warrior.

And I will never be anything less.

—Skye

Eagles Nest Safe House - November 1923

Morning spilled through the blinds, slanting gold across a modest apartment. The warmth settled on two bodies tangled beneath a white sheet—bare skin, long limbs, and the quiet breath of sleep shared in close quarters.

Three weeks had passed since the hospital infestation, the ambush at Skye's apartment, and the bloodbath at the docks. Days blurred into nights filled with rest, slow healing, and an endless rotation of rearranged furniture to stave off boredom.

The six-room apartment had become their momentary refuge from the chaos they'd narrowly escaped. With Benjamin under constant police protection and the agents of Anderson, Anderson and Pierce securing their location, Chase and Skye were finally granted the rarest luxury—peace. However temporary.

The two double mattresses had been shoved together on the floor sometime last week. Neither of them remembered who suggested it first. It just made more sense than the twin beds bolted to opposite walls. More honest. More intimate. An unspoken agreement that neither had questioned.

Skye stirred first. Her hair, a halo of knots and sleep-mussed waves, clung to her cheek. Her mouth was dry. She blinked into the morning light, rays painting her bare shoulder, collarbone, and the soft curve of her hip in warm, honeyed hues.

She shifted, the sheet rustling with the motion. Chase lay beside her, one arm flung over the pillow, his chest rising and falling with the slow, steady rhythm of deep sleep. She smiled faintly and reached out to gently shake him.

"Chase," she murmured. "The light." She gestured weakly at the window.

He grunted, not fully conscious. "Huh?"

"The damn light," she repeated with a groan, flopping back onto the mattress.

Chase blinked awake, squinting at the window. Still not quite fully aware, he swung his legs off the mattress and stood, naked and unbothered, scratching absently at his ribs as he yanked the window shade down with a thwack.

Behind him, Skye peeked with one eye open, her gaze trailing lower.

"I see the magic soldier is at full attention," she said dryly.

Chase glanced down, eyes widening. "Oh. That—uh. Yeah." He cleared his throat and dove back under the sheet. "Morning formation."

Skye rolled onto her side, laughing softly. "That what they taught you in the Legion?"

"That, and how to keep a straight face under fire." He teased in return.

She leaned in slowly, brushing her lips against his shoulder, then his chest—soft, unhurried.
"You're not under fire now."

He turned his head, eyes meeting hers. For the first time in weeks, she wasn't trembling. The fear that had gripped her in the dark had quieted into something else—something steadier.

Skye climbed on top of him with a gentle grace, her breasts brushing softly against his chest. "I've been waiting," she whispered, pressing her forehead to his. "I didn't want the first time to be when I was still afraid."

Chase cupped her waist, his hands reverent. "You're not afraid now?"

"No," she breathed. "Not of this."

She kissed him—slow, tender, sure.

They moved together, gently at first, then with the hunger of two people who'd faced death too many times to keep waiting. She arched her hips and reached down, sliding him inside her. Chase felt her warmth, her wetness, the tightness of her inner love. Her hips found a rhythm, and he matched it, his hands gripping her thighs, his breath catching every time she moved.

She placed her head in the crook of his neck and wove her fingers into his. She pushed down harder, gasping as she slid up and down. Time seemed to slow down as they breathed the same air. There was a release. A surge of joy she had never felt with anyone else.

Chase held her as she rested on his chest. She breathed slowly taking in the feeling pulsing through her. Then slowly she began to wind her hips. Skye was not done. She wasn't a selfish lover; she continued to ride him, clenching her inner wall muscles as he thrusted deeply inside her. He flipped her over, his weight now pressing down on her. He reached under her, grabbing her backside firmly and pressed her upwards. She gasped, her heart beat slowed and then she felt it.

Just for a heartbeat. Just at the edge of climax. She'd felt something ancient. Something watching.

Something wrong.

Not spellbinding—she knew the texture of that magic.
No glyph or ward hummed like this.

As he released inside her, she'd felt more than heat.

A presence.
A shape. A shadow.

A woman.

Marrowynn

Not physical. Not quit a memory either. More like a brand that pulsed beneath his skin—one that hadn't been made by war or ritual. It wasn't pain.
It was possession.

And now, lying here, fingers brushing the sigils carved into his side, Skye stared at the ceiling and whispered a thought she didn't dare say aloud:

That wasn't just Chase inside me.

She turned her head and studied his face.

His features were still, peaceful even. Vulnerable in a way she hadn't expected. But beneath that bronze skin, behind those scars, something coiled. Something inherited. Or worse—bound.

She swallowed hard.
She didn't regret it.
Didn't want to take it back.
But there was something she needed to understand. And soon.
Before whatever that was inside him decided it wanted more than just a moment.

The room was still. There was a long silence. Chase lay beside her now—warm, silent, breath slowing. She was still trembling. Not from the pain. Not even from the aftershock. Just... the magnitude of it.

They had crossed a line. No turning back now.

There had been no lies in the way he touched her.

No distance in how he held her.

It had been raw. Real.

Like he was trying to etch her into his memory before the world came crashing again. And just like that the feeling passed. She kissed him, lips curling into a smile. "Thank you," she whispered. He chuckled low in his throat, brushing a lock of hair behind her ear. "That good, huh?"

She grinned, nuzzling his jaw. "You're lucky I'm not grading you."

He leaned back, smirking. "What was that lady in your building? The one with the tiny dog that barked at us?"

"Mrs. Weatherby?"

"Yeah, her. She'd faint dead away if she saw us like this."

"She'd call for a priest," Skye said, laughing.

"And that dog of hers—what's her name? Prudence?"

Skye arched a brow. "Oh, she'd call me a hussy."

"You kinda are," he teased.

She swatted his chest, but she was smiling—eyes bright, laughter soft, the heat between them still simmering beneath the surface. "Shut up. That was my first time... in a not so long time..."

Chase raised an eyebrow as he laughed. "Well, Miss Anderson... I'm honored."

She nuzzled against him, then slid on top of him again. "You should be, my pussy is one of a kind and yes it was good. I don't regret it."

He stroked her back, slow and absent. "So the' magic soldier'?"

She snorted. "What, you want me to get clinical?"

"No, no. I like it. It's got... charm."

"Well then," she purred, "The fortress gate is open whenever the magic soldier is ready to report for duty."

Chase burst out laughing. "You're ridiculous."

"I'm serious. That's what we'll call it. 'The fortress.' Because its locked up tight and you want what's inside. So if I say it's time for the magic soldier to visit the fortress gates, you'll know."

He grinned. "Then those gates had better be ready for daily breaching." Now it was Skye's turn to laugh, and she belted out a snorting boisterous scream.

"I snorted," she said, eyes wide with mock horror as they both cracked up like 10-year-olds.

They settled into a quiet after that, Skye's fingers tracing the arcane patterns etched on his skin. But even as her body relaxed against his, something caught in her chest. When he released inside her... she'd felt something.

Not just the rush of sensation. Not just the thrill of skin and heat. An *impression*—a shadow, feminine and old, threaded through the marrow of him. Cold silk and fire. Eyes behind eyes. A name she didn't know but felt.

Marrowynn

She said nothing.

Didn't pull away. Didn't move. Didn't even blink. Just lay there with her head on his chest and let the silence wrap around them like a sheet. There were questions. But not for tonight.

Tonight, she told herself, was for softness. For choosing to feel something beautiful after so much ruin. Then, softly: "We should've done that a dozen times by now," Skye murmured. "Every day since the hospital."

Chase looked down at her. "You needed space."

Skye chuckled, half-lidded and lazy. "No argument here."

They didn't talk much after that. Didn't need to. The kind of silence that followed wasn't hollow—it was full, deep, content. And somewhere beneath all that softness, Skye Anderson closed her eyes...and pretended she didn't feel haunted. They drifted off, bodies still touching. The world outside could wait.

Late afternoon had settled into the room like a secret, warm and hushed. The shadows on the floor stretched long and soft, like fingers reaching for something just out of reach. Skye sat at the edge of the mattress now, legs folded beneath her, a cup of tea cooling in her hands. Her skin still held the glow of sleep and sweat and something more tender. Her freshly healed scars stood out in the dusky light—unhidden, unapologetic.

Chase sat a few feet away, bare-chested, lacing his boots with slow, deliberate movements.

"Twice in one day," Skye said quietly, lips curving into a small, smug smile.

He glanced over his shoulder, grinning. "Maybe thirds—once I get back with the wine." She laughed, soft and throaty, but her gaze drifted to the window, watching the light turn gold at the edges. Then, without meaning to, her eyes found him again.

And lingered.

Something ached in her chest. Not sharp. Just... constant. *Goddamn it,* she thought, *I want more.* It was his body, the thrill of being intertwined with him. It was the way he looked at her like she wasn't broken. The way he touched her like she was real.

As much as she was afraid of what *he* might be—of what pressed beneath his skin, that strange and silent presence she refused to name—it didn't change the pull she felt. The danger. The hope.

Again, she thought, and her pulse quickened at the word.

"Careful, Mr. Cassidy," she said, trying to sound flippant, though her voice dipped low. "I might start thinking you actually like me."

He looked up, meeting her gaze. And for a moment, the air between them thickened—not with lust, but with the kind of weight that only comes when you know you're standing too close to something that could wreck you.

"I do," he said simply.

Her heart stuttered in her chest.

Her breath caught.

She stared at him, the truth of his words wrapping around something raw inside her. Her throat worked once, then again, trying to swallow it down. But it wouldn't go. Setting the tea aside, she rose slowly—bare, unashamed—and crossed the floor to him.

She stepped between his legs, her hands unbuckling his trousers, her forehead brushing his. "Then maybe," she murmured, "you shouldn't keep me waiting."

He didn't speak. He just leaned into her touch like it mattered.

She guided him back toward the mattress, her voice low and sure. "No more pretending it's just comfort."

"No more pretending," he echoed, his voice barely audible.

And when their bodies came together again, it wasn't just urgency. It was a surrender.

———

Fog crawled thick along the docks, clinging to the ship's hull like damp shrouds. A freighter—its paint blackened and its lanterns shuttered to thin amber slits—slid into berth with predatory silence. Makalith watched from the pier, coat snapping in the cold harbor wind. Coco Le Fay huddled close to him, wings twitching, eyes flicking from shadow to shadow.

A line of figures descended the gangplank. The Mourned. Not the degenerate, half-feral things that prowled the lower tunnels These were tall, silent, controlled.

Faces masked in lacquered bone, movements precise as clockwork. These were Von Epp's elite auxiliaries—each one twice as aware as the shambling beasts used for patrol duty. They carried iron-bound ceremonial crates, each one thrumming with muffled heat and the scent of embalming salts.

The dock foreman stood nearby, swaying slightly, eyes glazed and unfocused. His voice drifted out in dull monotone as he directed workers forward—entranced, trapped in Von Epp's invisible leash.

Coco wrinkled her nose. "He's dreaming-awake," she whispered. "They scooped all his thoughts out."

Makalith made a noncommittal sound. "Von Epp's handiwork. Heavy, crude, but necessary."

As The Mourned lifted the lid from one of the crates, a wave of fetid air rolled out—vomit-soaked earth, rotting leaves, the musk of a drowned forest. The ritual components inside shifted faintly, as though something living had just exhaled.

Makalith's eyes narrowed. And as that stench hit him—familiar, ritualistic, unmistakable—his mind slipped backward, unbidden.

Back to the chamber below the docks.Back to earlier that month. Back to the moment he had spoken to Von Epp. The present bled into memory like ink.

⬚

The chamber trembled with the low hum of necrotic energy. Green torches guttered. Coco scuttled in uneasy spirals behind Makalith. Sirus Magnus waited with crossed arms. A Gravecaller stood motionless, mask glowing faintly in the gloom.

Then the footsteps came—measured, superior, heavy with authority.

Herman Von Epp emerged from the corridor like a long shadow deciding to walk. Gaunt. Severe. His officer's coat embroidered with bone-thread sigils that pulsed with slow, malignant light. Eyes like frozen amethyst.

Makalith inclined his head—respectfully, not subordinately. "Herr Von Epp," he began. "We have—"

Two fingers lifted. An invisible force snapped closed around Makalith's throat and hurled him upward. His boots left the stones. His breath strangled off. Runes flickered on his arms.

Von Epp's voice was quiet. Deadly. "Spare me the preamble."

Coco whimpered. Sirus stepped forward instinctively. Makalith managed to snap his fingers—stand down—even as black spots formed in his vision.

Then Von Epp released him. Makalith collapsed, palms slamming to the stone.

"That child," Von Epp said, pacing with glacial calm, "was prepared by prophecy and design. And yet he fled."

Makalith growled back, wiping blood from his lips. "Because the delivery plan was sabotaged. We were told he would be asleep—drugged, contained. Instead, your agent left us a warehouse full of mercenaries and scavengers. We had to improvise."

Von Epp's eye twitched. A fracture in the mask.

"We recovered names," Makalith continued, voice steady. "The ones who opposed us."

Coco clutched his coat sleeve and whispered, "Not her, not her," as he produced the torn page from Skye's journal.

"Skye Anderson-Pierce," Makalith stated. "She was central. But not our

target for... removal."

Von Epp's gaze slid toward Coco, assessing the trembling Fey. Makalith continued without hesitation. "The other one. The detective. Chase Cassidy. He is formidable, a spellbound"

At that, Von Epp's lips curled faintly.

"Cassidy. Yes. That will suffice." The chamber dimmed. The torches guttered. The memory began to dissolve.

PRESENT

The stench from the open crate pulled Makalith fully back into the night air. Coco tugged at his sleeve, staring at The Mourned as they marched past, each one flawless in their synchronization.

"They're getting ready," she whispered. "Everything smells like ending."

Makalith scanned the dock—entranced workers, the exposed pier, the city skyline in the distance. Sirens murmured somewhere far off. "Law enforcement's tightening patrols," he said quietly. "The BAE especially. And still Von Epp insists on using this dock as if no one is watching."

Coco's eyes widened. "Bad secret place?"

"Terrible secret place," Makalith muttered. "But Von Epp's arrogance blinds him. Just because the family running this waterfront works for him doesn't mean we're invisible."

He watched The Mourned vanish deeper into the warehouse, ceremonial crates in tow.

The ritual was coming. The preparations accelerating. And Von Epp's expectations—impossible as ever. Makalith felt the tension coil in his spine. "We should not linger," he said. "Too many eyes. Even dead ones."

Coco nodded, wings fluttering. They disappeared into the fog, the faint pulse of ritual sigils echoing behind them like a heartbeat under the docks.

———

Herman Von Epp stood before the twin black mirrors of his sanctum, watching the rippling images within as if observing two tiny worlds trying—and failing—to matter.

In the left mirror, Makalith and Coco Le Fay moved through the dock fog, directing the unloading of ceremonial crates. Coco twitched and paced, her wings fluttering like torn vellum in a storm. Von Epp's expression barely shifted, but his thoughts sharpened. How much longer must he entertain this charade? The Twilight Collective—once useful—were now nothing but frayed rope. He had enough Gravecallers to wage a private war. Enough Mourned to swarm a district. Enough other creations lurking in the tunnels to shatter half the Outer Boroughs. And still Adriana insisted on using the Collective.

He understood her logic: deniable assets, expendable mercenaries, easy scapegoats. But their reliability had evaporated. Their luck thinning. Their effectiveness diminishing. They were becoming liabilities. His gaze settled on Coco Le Fay—no longer pacing, now staring blankly into the harbor.

Three-quarters Fae. Blood perfect. Arcane retention higher than any vessel candidate they'd ever seen. She had once been intended to hold the Benefactor itself. But her mind—her fractured, shattered mind—had been beyond repair. Still mourning the death of her sister, who's death had been nothing but a wonderfully convenient turn of fate for the Court.

They locked her in Blackwell Island trying to piece back her mind only to remain stumped by her infliction. To prevent waste of her bloodline they locked her up until Makalith invited that she be his payment. A deal easily agreed to as Le fey could not be considered viable.

The mirror rippled and the image shifted. Benjamin Bright. Their next perfect candidate. Male. Correct alignment. Correct blood. And now shielded. Hidden. Unscryable. A boy that should have been asleep on a stone slab was instead loose in the city—untouchable behind a veil of arcane interference.

Which meant: Aspen Willowbark. The final viable host. Von Epp watched the boy's reflection appear in the second mirror—standing on a rural train platform, violin case in hand, coat too large at the shoulders. Three-quarters like Le Fey Stable. Male. Perfect. Arriving in two days. The ritual could still be saved. But loose threads threatened everything.

Chase Cassidy.

Von Epp's jaw tightened. A spellbound, Makalith claimed. Von Epp doubted the claim, few spellbound survived the war. He assumed the half-fey made it up to cover his failures. But then the reports came: Cassidy had defeated Utilis and a hospital full of shamblers. Cassidy had fought Domingo and survived. And though this Skye Anderson-Pierce, delivered the finishing blow, Cassidy's involvement had prevented Domingo's success.

Then came the worst realization. A conclusion Von Epp reached on his own: Cassidy was indeed spellbound. And spellbound men did not simply appear in New York City without pedigree. Spellbound men had been made. Forged. Through agony, alchemy, and war.

Von Epp remembered the Great War's occult arms race, each nation clawing for supremacy by sculpting monsters out of men. Imperial Germany had its Moonglades, alchemical werewolves bred for trench raids. Britain deployed Project Blackthorn, gear-grafted soldiers fueled by arcane engines. And America—late, panicked, reckless—countered with two desperate initiatives: Project Draconus, attempting to fuse pure draconic blood into dragon blooded human hosts and Project Infernus, injecting infernal fire directly into mortal vessels.

Only Tesla's infernal containment arrays kept the Infernus trials from reducing Long Island to a crater. Only Varrick the Unbound's soul-matrices stabilized the subjects long enough for a handful to survive.

Von Epp's eyes narrowed. If Cassidy bore Infernus augmentation, the probabilities shifted drastically. It meant— He must have survived the Red Mist, that infernal detonation that liquefied the Western Front. He must have endured Project Black Dagger, where American soldiers sealed the breach in reality.   He must have walked through the Western Front Veil—The Scar— a place where most men went insane and or simply disintegrated.

If Cassidy had truly walked away from that...then he was not a nuisance. He was something far worse. A survivor of the war's darkest experiments. A remnant of a battlefield that consumed ordinary soldiers whole. A war-forged anomaly— stubborn, dangerous, and now shielded by a blind spot Von Epp's magic could not penetrate.

A threat. A true one. And worse—Cassidy's unscryable nature matched Benjamin Bright's. Von Epp's lips thinned. Were they together? Was Cassidy shielding Benjamin— or was Benjamin shielding Cassidy?

Either way—Unacceptable.

Their connection within the zone had failed the Court completely, she who was supposed to deliver Benjamin Bright, and use her influence within the BAE to keep law enforcement away. She had gone silent and now become an additional liability.

A faint scraping drew his attention. Wört, his most senior Gravecaller, stepped into the sanctum, skull mask polished, bone-plated robes clattering softly.

"Herr Von Epp," Wört rasped. "The Mourned have secured the crates. The ritual chamber is nearly—"

Von Epp raised a finger."Watch." He pointed to the left mirror. A motorcar rolled into view through the fog. A detective stepped onto the docks, lantern raised, uniformed officers behind him.

Wört stiffened. "The police? Again? But the dockworkers—"

"Are enthralled," Von Epp said. "And the BAE's assurances were worthless. Frightened men make unreliable allies."

Wört swallowed. "Herr Von Epp... shall I summon Makalith? Have him remove the intruder? The Collective—"

Von Epp never let him finish.

"No." Soft, but absolute. "I will deal with this myself."

A verdict, not a command.

Wört bowed instantly. "As you command."

Von Epp stepped back from the mirrors. "Coco and Makalith remain useful until Aspen Willowbark arrives," he murmured. "After that... their fates are negotiable." His eyes lingered on officers reflections— the detective stepping deeper into the fog, oblivious to the doom drawing near.

Von Epp smiled. "Yes, I will handle this myself." The torches dimmed. The mirrors rippled shut like twin eyes closing over an execution already decided.

———

Detective Paul Rourke tugged his coat tighter as he stepped off the motorcar and into the mist that always clung to the sea port. He was an unremarkable man by most measures—average height, average build, brown hair cropped neat, a spray of freckles across his cheeks that made him look younger than he felt. But there was sincerity in his posture, a kind of earnest focus that marked a man still new enough to believe the job could be done right.

Two uniformed patrolmen followed behind him: Officer Walden, broad and heavy-footed, and Officer Griggs, thin as a rail with nervous eyes.

Rourke took in the rotting planks, the black water lapping beneath, and the thin lines of fog curling like fingers around the pylons.

"This the place?" Griggs asked, voice small.

"Yep. Foreman said he said he movement in one of the storage spaces. This is the same place Benjamin said he attacked by that tattooed man," Rourke replied. "We swept this area a month ago, with the BAE, found residue strong enough to choke a horse but that was it Whatever was here wasn't small."

Walden shifted uneasily. "You really think the kid saw somethin'?"

Rourke lit a cigarette. "After what happened at that hospital? I believe anything."

He stepped forward, the dock groaning under his weight.

The night was too quiet. As they advanced, the lamps flickered—once, twice—then steadied.

Rourke raised his lantern, casting long orange shadows across the boards."Spread out," he said. "Two-yard distance. Eyes sharp."

They walked further onto the dock, boots thudding in a rhythm that was swallowed by the fog. Somewhere beneath them, the Hudson slapped against the pilings like something breathing.

Walden exhaled. "I hate this place."

Griggs swallowed hard. "Feels like... something's watchin'."

Rourke slowed. A shiver crawled along his spine. "...You're not wrong," he murmured. A whisper moved through the fog. Not carried by wind. Carried by breath.

Griggs spun around. "Who's there?!"

The whisper came again — low, drawn-out, wet:

"...fresh clay... warm bones..."

They stepped inward, shoulders touching, lanterns raised. Fog coiled close around their legs. And from the water beneath the dock came a sound like wet rope sliding free—slow, deliberate, wrong.

Something rose between the planks.

Long fingers—living fingers—pale as drowned skin but unmistakably human, gripped the wood. They were adorned with bone rings and carved talon-like extensions, each piece inscribed with faint necromantic sigils.

Officer Walden screamed, stumbling back. The figure climbed upward with ritualistic grace. A Gravecaller—a living necromancer of the Court of Bones. His body wrapped in layered black-and-grey robes stiffened with bone plates and stitched charms, each one rattling softly like teeth in a cup.

An armored skull mask covered his face, carved from bleached bone and warded with rune-etchings that pulsed faintly with sickly green light. The masks empty eye-sockets glowed from within, with undeath.

Its boots dripped sea muck. Its fingers flexed with quiet hunger. The air around it dropped ten degrees.

Officer Griggs choked out a whisper: "Saints preserve us..." He fired. The bullet cracked the mask but didn't stop the dark mage.

It lunged. One swing crushed Walden's jaw. He hit the planks and didn't get back up.

"WALDEN!" Rourke roared.

Footsteps approached—slow, confident. Herman Von Epp stepped out of the fog, coat drifting behind him. His expression was carved from marble, neither amused nor angry—simply inevitable. Griggs bolted.

"GRIGGS—DON'T—!!" Rourke yelled.

Von Epp raised a hand. Wört the Gravecaller obeyed instantly. His robe snapped around its legs as it straightened, one hand rising from beneath the layers of bone-studded cloth. A bone-handled wand slid into its grip—ivory white, etched with runes that crawled like insects under the surface.

It aimed. A low, vibrating hum built in the air— an arcane necromagnetic charge gathering at the wand's tip. Griggs reached the lamp post—fingers brushing metal—the spell struck him square between the shoulders.

A wave of force and death-current folded his spine like wet cloth. His lantern flew from his hand. His scream barely formed before it dissolved into a bloody choke. Griggs collapsed mid-stride, dead before he hit the boards.

Rourke's pulse hammered. He grabbed his revolver and with his other hand seized the arcane flasher clipped to his belt. A last-ditch police tool. Barely field-tested. He thumbed the striker.

A sphere of blinding white-blue light erupted across the pier. Fog blasted back. Von Epp shielded his eyes. Wört recoiled, mask steaming. Rourke didn't waste the second.

He fired, the bullet smashed into Gravecaller's face, fracturing the mask from crown to jaw. The mage staggered.

Paul Rourke ran. He tore across the dock toward the callbox, boots echoing like gunshots. He slammed inside, grabbed the receiver, and cranked the line with shaking hands.

"Come on—come on—"

A click.

"Froud speaking."

Rourke gasped: "Trouble at the docks—The Benjamin boy was right. Send a full response team, undead…"

A hand punched through the metal wall behind him. Bone fingers wrapped around his neck. The receiver fell from his grip.

Von Epp's voice drifted in with absolute calm. "End him." Wört obeyed. A single twist—A wet snap— Paul Rourke collapsed, eyes wide but unseeing. The fog closed over the callbox like a closing grave.

The dangling receiver crackled. "Rourke? …Detective Rourke? … Answer me—!" Only the tide answered.

———

The floor creaked beneath her bare feet as Skye padded into the kitchen, the hem of her robe swaying against her thighs. She tightened the sash absently, though there was no one to see but him.

Chase was already there, leaning against the counter, shirtless, his dog tags resting against the glow of sigils still faintly pulsing on his chest. He'd never made it out to fetch the wine. Judging by the half-empty glass of water near his hand and the absent stare out the window, he hadn't planned to.

The scent of them clung to the room—salt and sweat and skin. Lust, spent and still lingering.

Skye said nothing at first. Just stepped past him, opened the small cupboard, and pulled down two chipped mugs. She filled them with hot water from the kettle he must have put on without thinking. A spell flickered softly in the steam—barely more than a heat-sustaining cantrip.

"I know how you take it," she murmured, pouring in a splash of honey and nothing else.

"You pay attention," he said, voice low. Gravel-thick.

She passed him his mug, their fingers brushing. They didn't pull away.

They stood like that for a while. No small talk. Just the hush between them and the press of something unsaid.

Skye finally broke it, voice husky but measured. "We never made it to the wine."

Chase's lips twitched into a crooked smile. "You didn't seem to mind."

A soft chuckle escaped her as she took a sip, then leaned her hip against the counter beside him. "Don't get cocky."

"You love it when I'm cocky."

Her eyes slid to him, slow and amused. "Only in certain contexts."

A minute passed. Then another.

"You gonna ask what I'm thinking?" she asked, not looking at him this time.

"No," he said. "But I got a feeling you're gonna tell me anyway."

She nodded faintly. "Might."

Then she looked at him—really looked. Her eyes swept over the lines of his body, the ones she'd traced earlier with her mouth, her hands. He looked whole here, calm even, but it was a lie. There was something wrong.

Something more than war or magic or time could explain.

She hadn't said a word then. She wouldn't now. But it clung to her thoughts like smoke. Still, as she watched him sip his tea, hair messy, muscles relaxed, eyes just a little softer than usual—she wanted more.

More of this. More of *him.*

Her pulse betrayed her. Her thighs tightened just slightly under the robe and she loosed the belt letting it fall open.

Chase raised an eyebrow without looking up. "You're staring."

Skye smiled around the rim of her mug. "So?"

He grinned, teeth flashing. "You thinking what I'm thinking?"

She took a breath. Slow. Deep. Then nodded.

"Oh, definitely. We're not done."

Chase set his mug down gently. "So what do we call it when the magic soldier returns for his *fourth* tour?"

She laughed, low and sinful. "We call that a veteran."

And then she set her cup down and reached for him again.

———

1st Arcane Precinct Headquarters

Conference Room B

8:42 p.m.

Captain James Whitman sat alone in his cramped office, surrounded by the soft clatter of typewriters and the distant murmur of the late-night desk sergeant. The precinct smelled of old coffee, metal filing cabinets, and a lingering hint of cigarette smoke trapped in the ceiling tiles. Midnight had arrived without ceremony, leaving him hunched over a growing stack of case files he didn't have the manpower or the patience to handle. He rubbed his eyes and flipped open the next report.

A sealed warehouse near Canal Street—three bodies found inside, no signs of forced entry, no footprints leading in or out. A line of wet handprints along the concrete floor. Another case detailed disappearances rising in the Lower Underwalk, people vanishing without struggle or ransom notes. Then the strangest of them: five British nationals arrested in the restricted subway tunnels beneath Midtown. No identification. No visas. No explanations.

Whitman frowned and reached for the next folder.

Reports of an influx of foreign visitors, all from the same obscure English village—Winterset, a quiet place on the outskirts of the infamous Porton Down. Too many arrivals in too short a span..

A folded newspaper sat on the corner of his desk. He tapped it with a knuckle, lips thinning. The Madhatten Meridian. Walter Grimsley's column blared across the front page, accusing the BAE of wasting resources on foreign arrivals. His tone was as caustic as ever, but this time Whitman couldn't dismiss the unease he felt reading it.

He set the folder down, leaned back, and exhaled slowly. The night felt wrong. Footsteps approached. Officer O'Leary stopped in the doorway, hat in hand, worry creasing his brow.

"Captain?"

Whitman looked up. "What is it?"

"Patrols checked in from East Pier, Red Hook, the ferry lanes… but Detective Rourke and his two men still haven't called in from the south docks. We've radioed him twice. Nothing."

Whitman's eyebrows drew together.   "Nothing at all?"

"No sir."

A beat of silence stretched between them. Whitman drummed his fingers on the desk, processing the possibilities. "Alright," he said finally. "Try them again in ten minutes. If they still don't answer, I want a car sent down there."

"Yes sir."

O'Leary disappeared down the hall.

Whitman pulled a pen from behind his ear, made a quick note across the duty roster, and was reaching for another file when the desk phone rang—sharp and decisive, a sound that cut through the quiet like a blade.

He answered. "Whitman speaking."

A familiar voice, firm and clipped, filled the line.

"Captain. Travers."

Whitman straightened. "Governor-General."

"No time for formality tonight," Travers said, each word heavy. "We have confirmed arcane interference at the docks. Patrol silence. Rourke's unit is unresponsive."

Whitman felt the knot in his stomach tighten. "What do you need from us?"

"We're escalating. I'm activating one of your operatives."

Whitman knew before the name left Travers's lips.

"Cassidy."

The word landed like a hammer.

"Effective immediately," Travers continued. "Get him moving. Whatever's happening down there—we can't afford to lose control of that port."

"Yes sir," Whitman replied quietly.

Travers hung up.

Whitman lowered the receiver, staring at the roster again. Rourke's name lingered near the bottom, neatly typed, now echoing in the silence like an accusation.

Somewhere out in the fog, a detective had gone missing. And Chase Cassidy—activated once more—was about to walk straight into the dark

———

The sheets were tangled, soaked in sweat and scent. The air in the apartment was heavy—warm with magic, sex, and something ancient that still pulsed faintly beneath Chase's skin. The windows were cracked, but the breeze did nothing to dispel the heat.

Skye lay on her side, her robe askew across one arm, chest rising and falling slowly. Her legs still trembled. Chase lay beside her, one hand resting lightly on her hip, fingers absently tracing the edge of a fading bruise he hadn't meant to leave.

They'd lost count after the fourth time. Five, maybe six. It didn't matter.

She turned her face toward him and gave a small, breathless laugh. "We've been rutting like animals all damn day."

Chase didn't argue. His body hummed with satisfaction, but even now, beneath the contentment, there was that pull—that low, dangerous hunger in his blood. One he was learning to suppress, but never fully deny.

Skye slid her hand down his chest, nails grazing the wards etched across his skin. "And the worst part?" she murmured. "I still want more."

Chase's eyes darkened just slightly, and she saw the shift—the flicker of gold in the black. She leaned closer, nipping his lower lip. "Whatever you are, Cassidy... it's addictive."

He caught her wrist gently, kissed her palm, then stilled. "I try to keep it in check. I don't want to take too much."

"You don't," she said. "I give. Willingly. That's the difference."

For a while they lay quiet, letting the haze of magic and exhaustion settle between them. Then, Skye shifted back, propped on one elbow, and studied his face.

"You always talk about your father," she said softly. "Elijah. But you never mention your mother."

Chase blinked, then shrugged, as if the thought had never fully formed. "I don't remember much."

"What was her name?"

He frowned. "That's the thing. I... can't recall. Isn't that strange?"

Skye didn't move, watching his expression carefully. "It was Marrowynn."

He turned his head, brows raised. "Yeah. That's it. Marrowynn. How did you know?"

She smiled faintly and lied. "You said it once. Right before you dozed off."

He let the name roll through his mind, mouth tasting it like a foreign word. "Marrowynn..." he murmured. "Huh."

Skye's voice lowered. "Chase... do you know what that name means? What it implies?"

He shook his head.

CHARLES DRAEVYN

"I studied infernal nomenclature back in university. It was part of magical law and origin rites. Marrowynn isn't a human name—it's demon-born.'"

Chase didn't speak. He shook his head.

She slid off the bed in one fluid movement—still naked, still shining with the warm sheen of candlelight on skin—and padded across the room to her bookshelf. Her hips rolled with a dancer's grace, the faint curve of her waist catching the glow. Chase watched her—mesmerized.

She scanned the shelf, fingers gliding over leather spines until she found a thick, ancient volume bound in cracked black hide.

Daemonologie, by King James VI, published 1597.

She brought it back, settling on the bed beside him, the old paper whispering as she flipped through pages inked with archaic demonography and origin rites "Marrowynn," she said softly, tapping a passage. "Old Tongue. Infernal. It translates to 'Mother of Bone and Fire.'"

Chase stared at her, confusion giving way to the slow crawl of dread.

Skye touched his cheek gently, grounding him. "Your eyes shift when you're worked up. Your scent changes when your magic flares. And the way you… pull from people—emotion, heat, essence—it isn't human. It isn't even spellbinding."

Her voice lowered to a whisper. "Chase… I think your mother was a demon. Maybe a succubus. Maybe something older."

His throat tightened. "My father never talked about her. All I know is… he died. And she—he said she killed him."

Skye's fingers combed slowly through his hair, calming the tremor in his breathing. "Maybe she didn't belong in this world. Maybe she was summoned. Bound. Controlled. And maybe Elijah Cassidy… tried to keep her caged."

Her eyes searched his. "And she broke her leash."

He looked away.

"Hey." Skye guided his face back to hers with both hands. "You aren't a monster. Whatever is inside you—it doesn't define you. But it's real. And it's older than your spellbinding. Older than the war. Primeval."

Chase swallowed hard. "How do you know?"

Skye hesitated only a second. "Do you trust me?"

"Of course."

She reached for the arcalame wand on her nightstand and held his hand gently in both of hers.

"This won't hurt."

She nicked his fingertip with the sapphire tip. A crimson bead welled up. They both watched it gather... gather...and then begin to bubble, tiny flickers of ember-red heat crawling across its surface.

Skye turned her hand palm-up. "Let it fall."

The blood drop slid off his skin—and the moment it touched her palm, it boiled.

Not evaporated. Not sizzled. Boiled upward, like it wanted to return to him. A single molten bead rolled against gravity, climbing her skin until Chase snatched his hand back instinctively.

Skye exhaled. "That's infernal regeneration," she whispered. "Your blood wants to go back to its source. It wants to heal you. Protect you. Repair you." Her eyes lifted, soft and terrified and awed all at once.

"Chase... that's not spellbound magic. That's heritage."

He sat very still, pulse pounding loud enough he wondered if she could hear it. For the first time in his life... he wasn't afraid of the truth. He was afraid it might explain too much.   He nodded slowly. "I always wondered why I survived Project Infernus when the others didn't. Why the markings didn't burn me out. Maybe now I know."

Skye curled against his chest, laying her head just above the pulse in his neck.

"Does it scare you?" he asked quietly.

She looked up. "A little."

He tensed.

"But not because I'm afraid of you," she said. "Because I know what it means. To carry something inside that the world would destroy if it saw it. You hide yours under fire and tattoos. I hide mine under law books and dance. But it's the same."

He touched her hair, tangled and damp. "You think we could ever be… normal?"

Skye smiled. "Not a chance."

And then, after a few precious seconds:

"But we could be honest. That's better."

She kissed his shoulder, then pulled away and stood, wrapping her robe loosely around her body. She walked toward the small kitchenette and turned the dial on the radio.

"*Another day, another silence,*" he announced through the crackling speaker. "*Still no official statement from the Bureau. No answers from the hospital. And the Governor General's office refuses to comment on the sudden deployment of Arcane Enforcement agents in the Containment Zone. But we all saw the flames, didn't we? We heard the screams. We felt the ground shake.*"

"I hate that man with a passion," Chase said.

She switched off the radio with a flick of her wrist, the silence that followed heavier than before. Skye drifted back to bed, letting the sunlight catch her again as she curled into the warmth they'd made earlier.

Skye pulled back slightly, just enough to look at him, her robe half-open, the curve of her thigh pressed to his. Her hair was a wild halo around her face. Her mouth, still kiss-bruised, moved slowly as the words fought their way out.

"What are we, Chase?"

He blinked at the ceiling, then turned to meet her eyes. "We're us," he said, trying to smile. "I'm your guy. You're my gal."

Her brow furrowed. "You know that's not enough."

He didn't answer right away.

"I'm twenty-four," she went on, voice steady. "All the women I knew in college? They're married. Some with children. One's on her second already. I'm not saying I want that—hell, I don't even know if I believe in that—but I can't pretend this is just a good time."

Chase exhaled, slowly.

She shifted again, sitting up slightly, letting the robe fall from one shoulder. Her skin shimmered with heat and candlelight, and Chase saw it for the first time, the faint glimmer of scales dancing just beneath her collarbone—an echo of the draconic blood in her lineage. Old magic hummed in her veins, just like his did. Just not the same kind.

"I'm Cuban, Chase. A brown woman in a country that barely tolerates me, much less loves me. I have shamanistic roots and a draconic bloodline no one taught me to understand. I was called wild, fast, untameable. And you—" Her gaze pierced him. "You're a spellbound man. Brown like me, labeled colored by the government that branded you and your people. Forged by war, body carved by magic. They called you Hellfighter, but they never knew what that meant. And now?"

She touched his chest, just above the Great Seal burned into his skin.

"Now we know you're something else, too. Something more."

Chase didn't speak. He didn't need to. The silence between them pulsed with truth.

"I feel it every time you're inside me," she whispered. "That hunger. That… draw. It's more than pleasure. It's like being devoured. It's infernal. There is a name for that".

He nodded once. Barely.

"Cambion. I'm not mad. I'm not afraid of you, Chase. But I need to know the truth. I need to know everything, because…"

She took a long, trembling breath.

"…because we didn't use anything. Not a cap. Not even a prayer. And I don't know what that means for me. Or for what could come from me."

His hand tightened on hers.

"I'd never let anything happen to you," he said, voice low, raw. "You know that. If something's growing in you, it's part of me. And I'll stand by you. By it Skye."

"It?" she asked.

Silence again. Heavy. Real. Then she spoke, softer this time, like admitting something to herself.

"I love you, Chase. I do. The minute I saw you. All that pain in your eyes, all that fire underneath. I wanted to touch it. Tame it. But not change it. I love you as you are."

She leaned in, kissed him slow, deep.

"But what are we going to do?" she asked, when they parted. "You and me. In a world that would hunt us both if it truely knew what we were?"

He pulled her into his lap, arms wrapping around her bare waist.

"We burn," he said.

Her brow lifted.

"We burn bright. Burn hot. And maybe we burn fast… but we burn together." Skye smiled then, something fierce and aching in it. "Then don't stop, Chase Cassidy. Don't you dare stop."

He kissed her again—and this time, when the fire rose between them, neither of them tried to smother it.

Then—knocking. Sharp. Firm. Authoritative. Both of them stilled.

Chase didn't hesitate. He rolled out of bed, grabbing the nearest pair of trousers and hauling them on, the muscles in his back tensing like he expected trouble even half-naked.

"That won't be Bureau," he muttered. "Guard would've warned us first."

Skye groaned, dragging the sheet over herself as she sat up. "Whoever it is, they're about to get an eyeful."

Another knock.

From the hall, a muffled voice: "Mr. Cassidy? Miss Anderson? Mr. Pierce is here to see you." One of Anderson & Pierce's security detail. The man with the Thompson. Good. Not BAE.

Skye snagged her robe off the chair, shrugging into it and yanking the sash tight around her waist. She padded across the floor, bare feet whispering on the boards.

She cracked the door open. The guard stood there, Thompson at low ready, eyes politely averted. Beside him, in a sharp dark coat and perfectly knotted tie, stood Donald Pierce, glasses fogged slightly from the cold outside.

"Dad" Skye said. "You're up indecently early."

Donald's gaze flicked over her—rumpled hair, flushed skin, robe hastily tied—then drifted past her shoulder to catch a glimpse of the demolished sheets, the tangle of blankets on the floor, and Chase in half-buttoned trousers, bare-chested, dog tags resting against faintly glowing sigils.

His nostrils flared once. The room smelled like sweat, sex, and faint ozone.

"I can see I'm interrupting... recovery," Donald said dryly.

Skye rolled her eyes. "You're the one who set us up in a safe house with no distractions."

The guard stepped aside. "I'll be right down the hall, sir."

"Thank you," Donald murmured, stepping into the apartment. The guard closed the door behind him.

Donald carried a folded newspaper under one arm. He set it on the small table by the window and smoothed it out with precise fingers.

The headline stared up at them in bold ink:

ASPEN WILLEBARK TO GRACE METROPOLITAN OPERA — EUROPEAN NIGHTINGALE ARRIVES IN NEW YORK

Beneath it, a photograph of a poised young woman in a high-collared coat and hat, eyes dark and unreadable even through cheap newsprint. Skye moved closer, frowning. "Opera gossip? That why you came all the way uptown?"

Donald shook his head. "Front page is fluff. It's the back half that matters."

He flipped the paper, revealing a smaller article near the fold:

THREE BODY's DEAD IN CHINA TOWN— POLICE TIGHT-LIPPED

Chase's expression sharpened instantly. "No details?" he asked.

"None they'll share with the public," Donald replied. "Bodies pulled from the lower docks. First Arcane locked the area down, and the Bureau went quiet. Thats all I know"

Skye's mouth tightened. "Its the them."

Donald didn't confirm, but he didn't have to. For a moment the only sound was the radiator ticking in the corner. He turned back to them, adjusting his glasses. "Before we get to that... there's something else."

Skye crossed her arms under her robe, chin lifting slightly. "If this is about the smell—"

"It's about intentions," Donald cut in, not unkindly.

Chase straightened, shoulders squaring out of habit—the stance of a soldier awaiting a superior's verdict.

Donald looked between them, and for the first time since he'd walked in, the cool lawyer's mask slipped. Just a little. Enough to show the man underneath: older cousin, guardian, man who'd taken Skye in when the world wanted to chew her up.

"You're sharing a bed," he said plainly. "Not just a room. You're living like a couple. That's your choice. I won't moralize."

Skye arched a brow. "Could've fooled me."

"But," Donald continued, "Skye is my family. And whether you acknowledge it or not, Chase, that makes you my concern."

Chase didn't flinch. "Then ask what you need to ask."

Donald studied him for a long moment. "What is this? Between you two. Is it just comfort while the world burns, or are you building something that has to survive the fire?"

Skye glanced at Chase, then back to Donald. "You don't have to—"

"Yes, I do," Donald said quietly. "Because whatever you two are becoming, the world outside that door will use it against you. Colored war hero. Cuban woman with arcane blood. You think Wilder and his kind won't jump at the chance to mark you as deviant, dangerous, obscene?"

Chase's jaw ticked. "I'm not using her."

"I know," Donald said. "I've seen men who do. You're not one of them. But intent isn't enough. Do you understand what staying means? Really staying? Through scandal. Through Bureau scrutiny. Through a city that'll happily put a bullet in both your heads if you step out of line?"

Chase didn't answer with words at first.

He stepped closer to Skye, fingers brushing her knuckles, then lacing with hers. He looked Donald square in the eye.

"I'm not going anywhere," he said. "She knows what I am. More than I do, sometimes. And she's still here."

Skye's grip tightened. "I'm all in, Donald. No half measures."

Donald's shoulders loosened, tension bleeding out on a quiet exhale. "Then that's the only answer I needed."

He looked at Chase. "Understand this, then: by choosing her, you've chosen us. Thomas and I. Anderson & Pierce. Our secrets. Our enemies. Our expectations. You are in this family. We protect our own. But that means you don't get to disappear when things get hard."

Chase nodded. "I disappeared once. It cost me more than I can ever get back. I won't make that mistake again."

Donald held his gaze a moment longer, then gave a small, rare nod. "Good."

Another knock sounded at the door—short, official, nothing like the guard's deferential tap.

Donald glanced at Skye. "That'll be for him."

Skye opened the door.

Captain Whitman stood in the hall, trench coat on, hat in hand, rain still beading on the shoulders. Behind him, the Anderson & Pierce guard watched the corridor, jaw tight.

"Morning," Whitman said. His eyes swept the room in a quick catalog: the rumpled mattresses, the robe, Chase's bare chest, the faint linger of heat and arcane scent.

He didn't comment.

"Captain," Skye said slowly. "This a social call?"

"Wish it were," Whitman replied. He stepped inside, closing the door gently behind him, though the tension in his shoulders made the quiet gesture feel out of place. "We've got problems."

Chase straightened. "What kind?"

Whitman exhaled through his nose. "There's suspicion the containment around Dock Twenty-Four was breached. Night patrol swept the area after BAE cleared it, and… we've lost contact with a unit."

Chase's brow furrowed. "Who was on it?"

"Rourke," Whitman said, jaw tightening. "He took two patrolmen with him. They went down there last night to follow up on Benjamin's statement. Haven't reported in since."

Chase shook his head. "Rourkes solid. A veteran. He doesn't miss check-ins."

"That's why I'm here," Whitman said. His voice had a low, uneasy edge. "O'Leary's been calling for two hours. Nothing. Radio silence. No visual confirmation at the docks. No return call from the patrol car. It feels wrong."

Skye moved a little closer to Chase. "What do you think happened?"

Whitman shook his head. "Don't know yet. But whatever it is… after the hospital fiasco? I'm not ruling out anything."

A heaviness settled over the room. Whitman reached into his coat. He pulled out the leather case with the Hexbreaker badge and set it on the table beside the morning newspaper—Aspen Willowbark's smiling photograph staring up from the front page.

"We tried it their way," Whitman said. "You resting. Rourke taking lead. The Bureau tying off the crime scenes. It's not working. And with patrol units going dark—" He tapped the badge. "We're doing it my way now."

Chase looked from Whitman to the badge, his jaw tightening.

Skye's shoulder brushed his. "Travers activated the clause," she said quietly. Chase stared at the badge. She moved to his side, her shoulder brushing his.

Whitman nodded. "Travers signed the order this morning. Hexbreaker authority, full and official. Once you step back onto the board, Cassidy, you won't just be a acting detective with a chip on his shoulder. You'll be judge, jury, and very likely the last thing these bastards see."

Chase gripped the badge in his hand, the metal cool against his skin.

Donald cleared his throat. "Before you two start planning to run into burning buildings again," he said, gaze locking onto Skye, "I need to make something very clear."

Skye folded her arms. "Donald—"

"No. Listen." His voice was firm, but not unkind.

"You nearly died. The firm is stretched thin protecting you. The city is unstable. And this?" He gestured to the room, the papers, the badge.

"This is Cassidy's case. Cassidy's jurisdiction. Cassidy's fight."

She went still. "You're telling me to sit out."

"I'm telling you," Donald said, "that if something happens to you, Thomas and I will never forgive ourselves. And Chase will tear this damn city apart."

Whitman nodded in agreement.

"He's right. No civilians on this investigation. Not after what happened at the hospital. We don't know what we are dealing with, it's too dangerous."

Chase looked at her immediately.

"Skye—"

She held up a hand to stop him, and for a moment her expression was unreadable. Then she exhaled, slow and steady. "Fine," she said quietly. "No fieldwork."

Donald let out a breath he'd clearly been holding.

"But let's be clear," Skye continued, stepping beside Chase and linking her arm with his. "I'm still part of this. Just not with a badge or a gun. You need background, you need legal patterns, historical precedent, occult research, old texts, building permits, property records — you come to me. That's where I shine."

Chase nodded, relieved. "That sounds perfect."

Whitman pointed at her.

"That? That I can live with. But you step foot on a crime scene or try to follow him into danger, I'm hauling you out myself."

Skye smirked, lifting her chin.

"You try hauling me anywhere, Captain, and I'll see you in court."

Donald pinched the bridge of his nose. "God, she's your problem now, Cassidy."

Chase grinned despite the tension. "I wouldn't have it any other way."

Skye's eyes softened, but she didn't look away from Whitman. "So long as the rules are clear. Chase leads. I support."

Whitman sighed.

"That's all I needed to hear."

He reached for the doorknob.

"There's a car waiting downstairs. Get dressed and meet me outside. Whatever took those officers—whoever they were working for—we need to know."

Chase nodded. "I'm right behind you."

Whitman stepped out, boots echoing down the hall.

Donald paused at the threshold, looking between them once more.

"You two want to build something together?" he said quietly. "Then survive this. Both of you."

Then he left them alone.

Skye turned back to Chase, fingers brushing the new badge on his chest.

"You sure about this?" she whispered.

He covered her hand with his own. "I have to be."

A moment passed — heavy, warm, intimate. Then she nodded, kissed him softly, and stepped back.   "Go," she said. "I'll start digging."

Chase grabbed his coat and holsters, the weight familiar, the metal badge colder than before.

"Be safe," he murmured handing her a key. " Bring your things too my apartment. We can live and work out of there."

"I will, and umm take care of my magic soldier." She teased.

He smirked and left the room — and Skye watched him go, already turning toward the papers on the table, the gears of her brilliant mind shifting into motion. The gears in her mind were already turning, faster than her breath could steady. Case files. Statements. Maps. The names Benjamin whispered in fear. And the shadow that had moved through Chase—Marrowynn—still clung to her thoughts like smoke she couldn't exhale. But Chase needed space to work. To do what he did best.

She murmured to the empty room, "Time to clear out, Anderson." She stood and crossed to the small table, fingers brushing over the scattered papers. She straightened them out, sliding a few into her satchel —the ones she knew she could study later without setting off Whitman's alarms.

Then she paused, resting her palm on the handle of the bag.

Benjamin.

She hadn't seen him since the hospital incident—aside from a rushed check-in the day after. She missed the boy. Missed his wary smile and too-grown eyes. He was with Luther and Nadine. A visit was long overdue.

Her voice softened. "It's been too long." She tucked a stray curl behind her ear and went to the bathroom doorway, turning on the shower. Steam curled out almost instantly. A real bath. A long one. The kind she hadn't had in weeks.

CHAPTER 2

Where Paths Cross

The First Arcane Police Department vs. the BAE

A Conflict of Jurisdiction, Pride, and Power The First Arcane Police Department was born out of necessity—an urban answer to an urban problem. Its officers lived in the boroughs they patrolled, understood the slums and the sigiled back-alleys, and knew the difference between a frightened arcanist and a real threat. Their mandate was simple: protect the city from arcane danger without turning it into a battlefield.

The Bureau of Arcane Enforcement never cared for simplicity.

Formed by federal decree and empowered by sweeping emergency statutes, the BAE marched into Manhattan with military posture and political backing. They called themselves regulators, guardians, and national defenders of the arcane order. But to the men and women of the First Arcane, they were something else entirely—outsiders with guns, badges, and permission to break anything they didn't understand.

The tension was inevitable.

The First Arcane believed the city was theirs—its alleys, its enclaves, its hidden warrens and clandestine spell-markets. They'd bled for those streets, earned the right to police them, and they resented every BAE suit that swaggered into their precincts like landlords coming to inspect the property. And while the First Arcane liked to paint themselves as protectors, too many among their ranks carried the same prejudices they accused the Bureau of wielding. They distrusted arcanists who lived too deep in the shadows, despised practitioners who refused registration, and viewed the Madhatten district as a place that needed firm hands more than fair ones.

But the BAE operated under a different faith altogether.

Fueled by men like Senator Wilder—zealots who saw magic as a plague and arcanists as carriers—the Bureau enforced law with military zeal. They swept blocks, raided wards, tore through neighborhoods under the banner of federal authority, and called the wreckage "compliance." Every action came stamped with orders from Washington, every operation justified in the name of "national arcane security."

To the First Arcane, the BAE were invaders.

To the BAE, the First Arcane were amateurs.

And caught between their territorial pissing contest was an entire city —one slipping further into containment, corruption, and the slow, choking fear that both agencies claimed they were trying to stop.

Captain James Whitman -1st Arcane

The wind off the East River carried the stink of salt, rust, and something older—like metal left too long in a grave. Madhatten never truly slept, but the docks had a way of pretending it did. Lamps flickered weakly across the pier, their dull golden halos barely cutting through the creeping fog. Chase Cassidy stepped out of the Ford and shut the door quietly behind him.

Captain Whitman swung his own door shut, the motion practiced, weary. "Hate this place," he muttered, adjusting the brim of his hat against the mist. "Every time we clear it, something slithers back in."

Chase didn't answer. He was staring at the Bureau of Arcane Enforcement cruiser parked at an awkward angle near Warehouse Row. The engine was cold. Both doors stood open "Where's their team?" Chase asked.

Whitman shook his head. "Should be two agents minimum."

"Looks like they left in a hurry."

"Or didn't leave at all."

Whitman drew the revolver from his waist holster. Chase reached under his coat and loosened the strap of Pearl.

Fog coiled around their ankles as they approached the silent cruiser. A torn BA dispatch sheet fluttered against the windshield like a warning no one had read.

Whitman grunted. "Seasoned agents don't abandon their post." He flicked his hand toward the open door. "Let's move."

They crossed the pier, boots crunching on broken seashells, the tide slapping against the pylons beneath them. A faint light glimmered somewhere deeper on the docks—toward the old warehouses. Chase didn't like the way it pulsed.

The door to the foreman's shack hung open, one hinge struggling to stay attached. Chase stepped inside first, sweeping the room with practiced ease.

Empty. Ransacked.

The small lamp on the desk was overturned, wires exposed like torn veins. A ledger lay open, pages wrinkled from damp air. Whitman stepped in beside and scanned the room. "Feels wrong."

Chase didn't disagree. He picked up the ledger, eyes flicking across the neat ink entries.

The same shipping company. The same handwriting. Dozens of crates. All incoming from Europe. All arriving within the same three-week span. All routed to Warehouse 24. He thumbed backward several pages. When the children were taken.

"Whitman," Chase said quietly, "look at the dates."

Whitman leaned closer. "Son of a bitch. That lines up with the Tran boy. And the Gail twins. And…" He stopped himself.

No need to say the rest.

Chase pushed the ledger aside and pulled another book from under a stack of papers—a personal journal. The foreman had scrawled entries in a heavy, aggressive hand: Fae workers not showing up again. Parents asking questions. Another family missing. BAE won't respond. Something's hunting here… something's taking them.

Whitman swore under his breath.

Chase flipped to the last page. Names. Dates. All matching the dead children they'd already found. Whitman rubbed the back of his neck. "We cleared this place twice. Me. The BAE. Thought it was just smugglers. Christ, we were blind."

A sudden flicker of light caught his eye through the broken window.

Warehouse 24.

Whitman stiffened. "Why's there a lamp on in there? That place should be sealed."

Chase holstered the ledger. "Stay here."

Whitman bristled. "Like hell—"

"Captain," Chase snapped, "if that warehouse is crawling with Mourned, I need to move fast. You're a damn good cop, but you're not arcane."

A tense beat.

Whitman's jaw flexed. "But I'm a former soldier, a Hellfighter like you. You take the bruising, but I'm two steps behind you. That's the deal."

Chase nodded once admiring Whitmans resolve. "Two steps."

The massive iron door to Warehouse 24 sat crooked on its track. A faint purple glow leaked from the gaps, barely perceptible in the fog. Chase breathed in once. Twice. Then he kicked the door open.

The hinges screamed. The warehouse swallowed them whole. Rows of crates sat overturned, smashed apart. Blood clung to the concrete in long, dragged streaks. Something heavy had been scraped across the floor, leaving deep gouges.

Whitman crouched beside one of them. "Whatever sat here... weighed a damn ton."

Chase moved toward the staircase. "Upstairs." They climbed. The second floor was worse—abandoned crates, broken chains, and dust patterns showing clearly where something enormous had once been. A rectangular imprint. Perfectly coffin-shaped. Large enough to hold a giant.

Chase moved toward the staircase. "Upstairs." They climbed. The second floor was worse. Several shattered crates of imported soil lay scattered, dark loam spilling across the floorboards. Broken chains dangled from above, and dust patterns showing clearly where something enormous had once been. A rectangular imprint. Perfectly coffin-shaped. Large enough to hold a giant.

Chase knelt, touching the indentation. "A sarcophagus."

Whitman swallowed. "Who the hell ships a sarcophagus the size of a car?"

Chase crouched beside the imprint, brushing fingers across a handful of soil. It was cold. Too cold. He recognized the scent—iron, crushed herbs, a faint trace of nightshade. He wasn't an academic like Skye. But he knew enough.

His eyes narrowed. "Vampire"

Whitman swallowed. "So someone brought... what? A noble? A lord?" "Or something higher?"

"Who knows." Chase answered. "Let's check below."

Chase led the way, Effie angled low, Whitman close behind him. As they approached the torn floor panel, both men paused. Beads of water clung to the ceiling above—hundreds of them—trembling, then sliding in thin rivulets upward, gathering along the joists before trailing down the far wall like a swarm of liquid insects. Condensation should not move like that. Not unless something deeper was pulling at the environment.

Whitman stared. "What in God's name causes that?"

Chase glanced at him, expression unreadable. "...No idea," he lied.

He dropped into the darkness first.

The sublevel was colder than the river itself. Narrow stone tunnels stretched away in both directions like veins carved under the docks. Oil lamps flickered weakly on hooks, each one wrapped with talismans and bone charms.

Whitman landed awkwardly and grunted. Chase looked back.

"You good, Captain?"

Whitman waved him on. "Lead. I'll keep up."

They moved in. A soft wet scutter echoed from the dark.

Then a figure turned the corner ahead, carrying a crate of alchemical jars. A Necrotech. Human—barely. Hooded. Bone-thread robes. A bandolier of syringes, powders, and glyph-stamped tools. He froze.

Chase lunged before the man could scream. One enhanced strike—combustion-charged—cracked across the Necrotech's jaw. The man flew sideways, jars and vials shattering across the stone. Glass scattered, chemicals hissing.

Whitman whispered, "Christ—Cassidy—what if he—"

A sound answered him. A low, hungry rasp.

From the shadows ahead, a Mourned stepped into view—hunched, twitching, its ruined nostrils flaring as it sniffed the air. The runes stitched into its chest pulsed.

Whitman's voice barely rose above a whisper. "That... thing... that's what you've been fighting?"

"Back up," Chase said quietly.

Whitman stepped—onto broken glass. Crack.

The Mourned's head snapped toward them. More wet claws scraped. More glowing eyes opened. Shapes crawled from adjoining tunnels... Chase drew Effie and Pearl in one smooth motion.

"MOVE!"

The Mourned surged.

Gunfire filled the tunnel—thunder in metal lungs. Muzzle flashes strobed the dark as Chase put down the first wave, bullets punching through ruined flesh and carved bone.

Whitman fired at a second Mourned. "These things are worse than shamblers!"

"They're controlled!" Chase shouted. "Somebody—" A deeper shadow shifted behind the pack. Chase's breath hitched. A Gravecaller stepped forward—tall as a lamppost, draped in bone-plated robes, a skull-mask carved with spirals that seemed to twist the air itself.

Whitman whispered, "What—What is that?"

"A Gravecaller," Chase said grimly. "Stay behind me." The necromancer raised a hand. Black energy flared. Chase slammed his forearm forward, invoking the Sigil of Searing Aegis. Infernal light erupted in front of him. The spell struck the shield with a sound like stone cracking underwater.

Whitman staggered back. Chase fired—three shots. The first round detonated against the Gravecaller's protective ward in a burst of sparks. The next two punched through the mask's side and into its chest.

The Gravecaller collapsed. But the shadows behind it moved.

Two more Gravecallers advanced, flanked by a fresh surge of Mourned. Whitman fired wildly—dropped one. Effie's slide kicked back, spitting .45 ACP rounds etched with ward-piercing runes. Each impact blew through Mourned like wet paper—chests exploding, limbs ripped clear. Pearl answered in kind, faster, tighter, two shots to the chest, one to the skull. Perfect rhythm.

The Gravecaller raised both hands. A wave of necrotic force

slammed into them. Chase's shield shattered. Whitman hit the wall. A Mourned grabbed his arm—sending Pearl skidding on the floor. Two finger pointed at the creatures skull, the sigil of the infernal lance burst to life and a spear of fire shot forwards severing and burning the head at the same time. Chase scrambled to his feet as another Mourned took the place of the other. Chase shot it point-blank, with Effie sending it spinning backward.

"CAPTAIN—MOVE!" He yelled as he scooped up his fallen 1911.

They sprinted only to see more Mourned boiling up from a second tunnel, cutting off escape. Chase grabbed Whitman's vest and yanked him toward a rusted maintenance crosswalk overhead. A sudden ripple of violet light swept the tunnel.

A laugh. High. Musical. Beautiful. Insane.

Coco Le Fay unfurled into existence—wings like shredded opal, hair floating, eyes burning ruby-red.

"Well helloooo, boys." Her glamour washed over Whitman like warm honey. His eyes glazed.   Chase's wards flared—burning her influence away instantly.

Coco blinked once—slow, feline—then her grin blossomed, wicked and delighted.

"Ohhh... so you're the spellbound everyone's whispering about. You took little Benji bad bad boy" Coco giggled.

She moved—hips, shoulders, wrists—like a dancer slipping into the opening steps of a choreography only she could hear. A shimmer rippled off her skin, and the air bent with her.

Then the spell hit.

A fan of cascading lights burst from her hands, unfurling like a peacock's tail—shards of gold, violet, rose—sweeping across the room in a wide, blinding arc. Chase dove aside, boots skidding on the warehouse planks as the lights scorched past where his head had been. He came up in a crouch, Effie and Pearl up, eyes locked onto the fey.

He fired.

Coco twirled—literally twirled—her body collapsing in mid-spin into a hand-sized pixie form, wings flaring in a burst of shimmering light. Effie thundered again and again, each round slicing through the air in perfect deadly lines.

But Coco was faster. She whipped past the first bullet, spiraling around it like a leaf in a storm. The second and third shots followed—Chase tracking, adjusting, firing with trained precision—yet she wove between them, darting in tight, impossible corkscrews that left the rounds hissing harmlessly by.

A sharp, delighted giggle chimed through the rafters as she shot upward, a tiny blur of wings and glittering motion.

"Try to keep up," she teased, voice tinkling from somewhere above. Behind her, the Mourned shattered the sub-level door. Claws and teeth poured through.

Whitman snapped open his revolver, cursed, and slammed it shut again—empty.

"Cassidy—"

"I know." Chase's eyes tracked the rafters. "Run."

A Gravecaller stepped over the threshold, hands raised.

Chase didn't hesitate. Violet fire streaked toward them—and both of Chase's forearms flared, sigils igniting like molten script crawling up from elbow to wrist.

He brought his right arm up— The Searing Aegis erupted across his forearm, catching the Gravecaller's first spell in a violent crack of sparking energy. A second blast slammed against his left Aegis— Chase gritted his teeth, the force driving him back half a step as the ward drank the worst of it. A third spell—denser, coiling with necrotic mass—smashed both Aegis wards at once. The shields shuddered, runes strobing with strain.

"Damn it... burning too hot," he growled. The sigils and wards along his arms pulsed erratically—he was *overheating*.

Whitman spun toward the way they'd come, the door they'd entered slammed shut on its own, iron bolts hammering into place with a clang that echoed like a coffin lid. Whitman shouted, "Door's still sealed! We're boxed in!"

Chase lowered his stance. "Not for long." He crossed both forearms over his chest—glowing amber Aegis shields fusing together for a heartbeat—then swung them outward in a brutal arc. The stored energy of the wards discharged simultaneously, erupting in an explosion soft light and force, ripping through the outer warehouse wall, opening a way to the docks outside.

Cold river air howled in through the breach.

"Move!"

They sprinted, boots hammering across the warped planks. The Gravecaller shrieked behind them. Chase didn't look back. He grabbed Whitman by the collar, dragged him the last yards AND LEAPT.

They plunged straight into the East River. The shock of the water tore the breath from their lungs. The mourned followed, leaping into the river like hounds chasing a fox. They were not prepared for the cold depths. Whatever skills they retained from their former life, swimming did not transition over. The Mourned sunk, vanishing into the mirky darkness.

Whitman surfaced first, sputtering and cursing. "Cassidy—hell's bells—warn somebody next time—!" Chase surfaced beside him, hauling them toward the shadowed pier supports.

"Cassidy Whitman said hoarsely, "that wasn't a smuggling operation"

Steam rolled over his body as Chase stood slowly. He met Whitman's gaze, tired and edged with something darker. "No it wasn't. It was a nest."

———

Skye Anderson climbed the stairs two at a time, the winter air still clinging to her damp curls. She smelled faintly of Chase's cologne—smoke, cedar, warmth—and the bathhouse steam that hadn't yet faded from her skin. Her blouse and slacks were crisp, but her pulse still carried the echo of the morning: Chase's revelations, his mother's name, the infernal truth simmering beneath his flesh.

Marrowynn. Mother of Bone and Fire. A demon. And Chase—something more than human. She pushed the spinning thoughts aside as she reached the familiar door. Benjamin Bright mattered now. She knocked lightly.

Nadine Holloway opened the door with one hand and immediately pulled Skye into a hug with the other—tight, warm, and a little chaotic, like every embrace between sisters who hadn't seen each other in too long.

"Girl, finally," Nadine said, swatting Skye's shoulder as she pulled back. "You disappear for a month and expect me not to march down to that fancy safe house and drag you out by your hair?"

Skye snorted. "If anyone could do it, it'd be you."

"Damn right." Nadine smirked, flicking Skye's curls. "Still too skinny, still too sleepless, still too stubborn. Same old Skye."

Skye rolled her eyes but hugged her again, longer this time. "I missed you."

"I know," Nadine said, softer. "Come inside."

The Holloway apartment was alive—warm lamplight, laundry hanging to dry, the smell of fried plantains and brown sugar. And on the wall near the coat rack—

Skye paused.

"Are those... sticks?"

Two polished rattan batons hung neatly crossed on pegs. Skye stepped closer. "They look like—"

"Arnis sticks," Nadine said proudly, hands on her hips. "My mama made sure I learned. You wanna see? I can show you a sinawali drill later."

Skye blinked. "Nadine... since when do you—"

"Girl," Nadine laughed, "did you think I was just 'Nadine from the Holloways'? I from the Philippines."

Skye smiled. "I like it."

"Oh, you'll love it when I teach you to crack someone's skull with them."

They moved to the kitchen, cups clinking as Nadine poured tea that tasted like ginger, cinnamon, and chaos. They talked fast, catching up in quickly—Skye's recovery, the safe house routine, the investigation.

Eventually, Nadine raised a brow. "So. You and Chase working together now?"

Skye hesitated. "...Yes."

"And how's that going?" Nadine said, leaning forward like a gossip-hungry cougar. "Professionally? Emotionally? Sexually?"

"Nadine—!"

"Oh please. Spare me the lawyer innocence." Nadine twirled her hand. "Spill."

Skye's cheeks heated instantly.

Nadine's grin sharpened. "Uh-huh. I knew it."

Skye gave in. The blush deepened. "Fine. Yes. We did."

"And?" Nadine said, eyes sparkling like a cat who'd found someone's secret stash of treats.

Skye looked around, made sure no one was walking in—then extended her hand. She held it out in front of her. Straight. Measuring. Like she was indicating the length of a damn sword.

Nadine's jaw dropped. "SKYE. ANDERSON. YOU LET HIM PUT THAT IN YOU—!"

Skye's face was already buried in her hands. "Oh my God, Nadine, shut up—"

"NO. No, ma'am. You cannot come into my home after vanishing off the map and show me that mans —" Nadine mimed the same measurement, eyes huge. "—and expect me to act normal!"

Skye groaned into her palms. "Please stop talking."

"I will NOT." Nadine walked in a circle, fanning herself. "Good heavens, that man is PACKIN 'like a calvary horse. My God, Skye—no wonder you've been scarce."

Skye muttered, voice strangled, "It was... good."

Nadine cackled, pointing a finger. "Uh-huh! I knew it! I knew that quiet brooding thing meant he had demon dick—"

A sudden sniff. Nadine froze. "Oh hell—the pancakes!" She sprinted to the stove as smoke curled from the pan. And that was when the front door rattled. Heavy footsteps thudded through the hall.

"That's them," Nadine said, flipping pancakes with the speed of a professional brawler. The door burst open. Benjamin Bright flew into the room like a comet. "SKYE!" Before she could brace, he crashed into her, arms wrapping around her waist.

She held him tight, laughing. "There's my favorite boy."

Luther stepped in behind him—broad, warm, stylish mustache

making him look like a 1900's prizefighter. He scooped Skye into a bear hug that squeezed a tiny squeak out of her.

"Good to see you up, Miss Anderson," he rumbled.

"You too, Luther." She eyed the mustache. "New look?"

"Benjamin said it makes me look distinguished." Luther puffed his chest.

"He really does," Benjamin said proudly. "He looks like a detective!"

Luther's grin softened. They sat, they ate brown-sugar pancakes, they laughed, they listened to Benjamin talk about climbing trees and having his own room for the first time.

Once dinner was done, Benjamin tugged Skye's sleeve. "Come see my room! I decorated it myself!"

Skye stood, smiling. "Lead the way." He beamed, grabbed her hand, and pulled her down the hallway. And as she disappeared down the corridor, Nadine watched her go—hands on hips, smirking like the older sister she had always been.

The room was small but bright—posters on the wall, a worn copy of The Mark of Zorro open on the bed, and neatly folded blankets that did nothing to hide the nervous pacing lines on the carpet.

Benjamin sat cross-legged on the bed, turning the granite wand in his small hands. The polished wooden handle—crafted carefully by Juan Reynald—glowed softly in the afternoon light. Skye stepped into the room, her heart loosening a little at the sight of him.

"You still use it?" she asked.

Benjamin hesitated. "I think about it," he said quietly. "But... I don't think I want to."

Skye sat beside him, voice gentle. "Because of what happened?"

His fingers tightened around the wand. "The tattooed man" he whispered.

The mention of her nameless attacker made Skye's stomach tighten.

Benjamin swallowed hard. "He grabbed you. I stunned him. I didn't mean to—I just… he scared me." His voice cracked. "And then you… you."

Skye placed a steady hand on his back. "You saved my life, Benjamin. You did exactly what you were supposed to."

He took a shaky breath. "Miss Sk—Skye… do you think… do you think they wanted to hurt me too?"

Skye didn't sugarcoat it. He deserved the truth. "Yes," she said softly. "They were hunting you, Benjamin."

His eyes widened slightly, trembling. "But… why?"

"We don't know yet," she said. "But we will find out. I promise you that."

Benjamin looked down again. "The winged lady… she tried to glamour me. Everything went shiny, like frost. Like my head was full of someone else's voice. I didn't want to listen, so I threw a spell. Zorro would have done that."

A faint, broken smile tugged at Skye's mouth. "Is that why you like him?"

Benjamin nodded. "He protects people. Even when he's scared. Even when he's outnumbered."

He hopped off the bed and flicked the wand in the air in an overly dramatic flourish.

"En garde!" He slashed the air like a tiny swordsman, then pointed the wand like a duelist invoking justice.

Skye laughed softly. "Very heroic."

She reached for his shoulder. "Before Miss Isabel… you lived where?"

He thought, brow furrowing. "Saint Agatha's Orphanage. Lots of kids like me. Some had ears like mine. Some with eyes like cats. Some with hair that glowed."

Skye froze. A Fae orphanage. Burned down. Erased. "I'm going to look into that," she murmured softly.

Benjamin brightened. "Miss Isabel was the best. She bought me books. She smelled like roses. She said I should read about brave men."

"She was right," Skye said. Before Benjamin could answer, Nadine's voice floated down the hall:

"Pancakes are ready!"

Benjamin lit up. "Come on!"

He grabbed Skye's hand and pulled her toward the kitchen.

Luther sat with Benjamin at the table, cutting another stack of pancakes. His new mustache suited him; he looked like a man trying very hard to appear stern and failing because of the soft spot he had for the boy.

Nadine slid a plate toward Skye and gave her a look that blended affection and exasperation in equal measure.

"Girl, you need more rest," she said, shaking her head. "And more food. You still look like someone folded you up wrong."

Skye laughed, hugging her. "It's good to see you, Skye."

"You too," Nadine murmured, squeezing her tighter.

They caught up quickly—Skye's injuries, the chaos at the safe house, the investigation she couldn't say much about. Nadine listened like the older sister she'd always been.

After a few minutes, Skye stood.

"Listen, I love you both—more than I can say—but I have to go. Keep him safe."

Nadine nodded. "Always."

"Anderson & Pierce will send more money for his upkeep—"

"Skye," Nadine interrupted with a warm but firm smile, "he's no burden."

Luther grunted his agreement. "Not one bit."

Skye exhaled, the relief visible. "I know. But I don't want everything falling on you two."

"Well, stop worrying," Nadine said. "Family's family."

Benjamin looked up from his syrup-coated plate. "Come back soon, okay? And bring Chase next time!"

Skye bent to kiss the top of his head. "I will." She turned to Nadine and Luther.

"When this is over, I want to talk to both of you about being more...

involved. Nadine—you're not just my maid. You're truly my life crisis manager. My right hand."

Nadine blinked, the words hitting deeper than she expected.

"And Luther," Skye added, "you've been my protector for years. I'd like you to stay on… as a bonded agent."

Luther straightened, pride swelling in his broad shoulders. "You got it, Skye."

Skye smiled at all of them—her second family. Then she stepped into the hallway, coat over her arm. The warmth of the Holloway home slipped away behind her. And now the truth was stark and cold: Benjamin wasn't just a witness. He was a target.

————

The First Arcane Apothecary looked nothing like a hospital, though half the patients who came through its doors left with more stitches than pride. The brick storefront sat wedged between two shuttered speakeasies, marked only by a sigil-lit lantern that flickered a muted violet—visible to arcanists, ignored by everyone else.

Chase Cassidy shoved through the front door, dripping river water, boots leaving a grim trail across the tiled floor. Whitman stumbled in behind him, coughing hard, eyes watering from the stench of salt and rot.

"Saints preserve me," Whitman wheezed, gripping the side of a table as another sneeze ripped through him. "That river's got more disease in it than the damn plague quarter."

Chase smirked. "Sorry I couldn't find a cleaner place to jump."

"You could've warned me, Cassidy."

"You would've said no."

Whitman sneezed again. "Damn right."

Chase dropped his coat onto a chair and leaned against the nearest exam table, muscles still burning from the fight. Violet sigils along his forearms pulsed low under his soaked sleeves.

Across the counter, Old Man Fenwick—the crotchety arcanist who'd been patching up mages since the Spanish-American War—narrowed his eyes.

"You two look like river corpses somebody forgot to finish burying," he rasped. "What hit you?"

Chase exhaled. "A Gravecaller. Maybe two. And a Fae witch wearing a tutu."

Fenwick blinked once. "I'm too old for this nonsense."

He shuffled off to fetch supplies, muttering curses against every magical bloodline known to man. Whitman slumped onto a bench, blotting his nose with a handkerchief.

"You alright?" Chase asked.

"I'm gonna die of pneumonia before any necromancer gets me," Whitman groaned. "But yeah. I'm fine."

He reached into his sodden coat and pulled out something wrapped in oilskin.

The ledger.

Chase raised a brow. "You grabbed it."

"Damn right I did." Whitman coughed. "Wasn't gonna let all that bloodshed be for nothing."

He unwrapped it, revealing the shipping ledger they'd found in the foreman's office—pages inked with the comings and goings of cargo ships from Europe. Names, dates, freight codes.

Chase flipped through it, jaw tightening.

"Every murder we've connected to the Fae kids? Same window as these shipments." He tapped a line. "And every one marked for Warehouse 24."

Whitman rubbed his eyes. "The damn place is cursed."

Chase shook his head. "Not cursed. Used."

Whitman's voice dropped. "We have to keep this quiet. At least until we know what we're dealing with. If BAE gets wind of this... Wilder'll run straight to the Oversight Board, Travers will get sacked and then we'll have a citywide panic on our hands."

"And ever archaist lives under martial law or worse" Chase finished.

They looked at each other.

"We keep this between us," Whitman said. "No BAE. No precinct. No Wilder."

Chase nodded. "Agreed."

Fenwick returned and dropped a medical kit onto the table with the enthusiasm of a man slapping down a tax bill.

"You gonna stand there broodin', Cassidy, or you gonna let me check your damn ribs?"

"I'm fine," Chase said.

Fenwick pointed at him. "If you die in my shop, I'm charging your ghost rent."

Chase lifted his hands in surrender and let the old man prod him. His body healed faster than most, but Fenwick didn't need to know why. Or how.

Whitman cleared his throat.

"So," he said, "What's your next move?"

Chase pulled his shirt back on, eyes hardening.

"We identify the witch."

Whitman frowned. "The dancer?"

"Yes" Chase said quietly. "She knew Benjamin's name."

Whitman went still.

"How?"

"I don't know," Chase admitted. "But she wasn't working alone. Gravecallers don't show up for petty crimes. Something bigger is happening at those docks."

Whitman scrubbed a hand through his wet hair. "You think they were after the boy specifically?"

"I know they were."

Whitman whistled low. "Then we're in deeper than we thought."

Chase moved toward the weapons locker in the back room. Fenwick grunted but didn't stop him.

"You taking something?" Whitman asked.

"Insurance."

The locker hissed open.

Chase pulled out a sleek, oil-blued Thompson submachine gun—ruined along the receiver, sigil-etched drum magazine sitting beside it like a promise.

Whitman gave a low whistle. "You planning for war?"

"I'm planning for whatever comes next."

Fenwick tossed him a small wooden box. "Special rounds," he muttered. "Ward piercing flashers. They penetrate and burn. So aim careful. They punch through damn near anything."

Chase nodded gratefully.

Whitman crossed his arms. "Alright. I'll keep my men off the docks. Quiet-like. No alarms. No chatter up the chain. Avoid the BAE"

Chase slung the Thompson's strap over his shoulder and looked toward the door.

"I need to find this witch. And figure out why she wants the boy."

Whitman studied him.

"You going alone?"

Chase glanced toward the night.

"Yes ," he said quietly. "But I'll consult with someone I know who knows almost everything about magic. And she's already looking after the kid."

Whitman smirked. "Skye?"

Chase ignored the smirk. "She's the best we've got."

Whitman pushed himself to his feet.

"Then go. I'll lock things down here."

Chase nodded once, gripping the Thompson and the ledger.

"Stay safe, Whitman."

"Don't tell me what to do," Whitman muttered, grabbing his handkerchief just in time for another thunderous sneeze.

Chase was already out the door, the cold wind hitting his face like the opening bell of a fight he hadn't yet seen—but could feel coming.

Necromancers were brewing something in Madhatten.

And he was walking straight into it.

———

Skye Anderson climbed the narrow stairwell leading to Chase Cassidy's railroad apartment, a leather suitcase bumping her leg every few steps. The hallway smelled of boiled cabbage, cheap cigars, and the permanent damp of an old building that had learned to endure winters through resignation rather than insulation.

A small blur shot past her. A little girl—barely five—darted down the hall clutching a wooden soldier missing an arm. "Anna! Get back here!" her mother called from a doorway. Anna skidded to a stop in front of Skye and blinked up at her with wide hazel eyes. "You're really pretty," she declared.

Skye softened. "Thank you, sweetheart."

The mother grabbed Anna gently by the shoulders and ushered her back inside, giving Skye a mortified smile before shutting the door. Skye adjusted her suitcase, inhaled deeply, and stepped toward Chase's apartment. The door was unlocked—a detail that immediately tightened her grip on her wand.

She nudged the door open with her foot. Warm light spilled across the hardwood floor. The air carried the scent of strong black coffee—and something else.

A voice.

A man's voice.

Not Chase's.

She drew her wand in a smooth, practiced motion.

A towel-wrapped figure stepped out of the bathroom, steam billowing behind him. His hair was damp, toothbrush wedged in his mouth, one hand holding the towel at his hip. He froze mid-stride when he saw her—Skye in the doorway, wand raised, eyes narrow.

He blinked once.

She blinked back.

"Mrrf—hmmphhh—mrrgah?" he attempted around a mouthful of toothpaste.

It sounded alarmingly like a spell.

Skye reacted instantly. " Jahna Kree".

Three streaks of arcane light screamed from her wand.

"WHOA—HEY—WHAT—!"

He dove sideways, barely avoiding the hex as it blasted the plaster behind him. He stumbled, one hand gripping the towel desperately, the other still clutching the toothbrush now foaming aggressively.

He spat out his toothbrush to yell properly.

"WAIT—WAIT—WAIT—!"

Skye flicked her wrist, sending another bolt. He vaulted over the arm of Chase's sofa, towel flapping dangerously. The bolt singed past him and shattered a ceramic mug on the table.

"STOP TRYING TO KILL ME!" he shouted.

"STOP CASTING AT ME!" Skye shot back.

"I WAS BRUSHING MY TEETH!"

"LIAR!"

He popped up behind the couch, eyes wild, towel barely holding on. His fingers snapped once—dice flew from his discarded trousers, skittered across the air like they had minds of their own, landing perfectly into his waiting palm.

Probability magic.

Great.

He rolled.

A pulse of shimmering distortion warped the air as a defensive shield snapped into place around him. Her next spell curved mid-flight and detonated against the wall instead—shattering a picture frame.

"HEY! THAT WAS A GOOD ONE OF CHASE!" he yelled.

Skye advanced, wand glowing brighter, curls frizzing with heat. "Drop the shield!"

"Lady—I don't even have pants on!"

"Then die with dignity!"

He yelped, stumbled backward, slipped on a puddle of water from his shower—went down hard, towel flying loose—

And at that exact moment, the front door banged open.

"What the—"

Chase froze on the threshold, Thompson slung across his back, eyes darting from a half-naked Diego sprawled on the floor to Skye standing over him like an executioner.

"What the hell is going on here?!"

Both Skye and Diego pointed accusingly at each other.

"You know her?"

"You know him?"

Chase dragged a hand down his face. "Unbelievable." He stepped inside, kicked the towel toward Diego's ankle, and pointed between them.

"Diego, meet Skye. Skye… meet my best friend, Diego Salazar."

Diego scrambled to his feet, snatching up the towel and fleeing back into the bathroom with as much dignity as a bare-assed man could muster.

Skye lowered her wand, cheeks heated—not from embarrassment, but from ongoing irritation. "You didn't tell me anyone else lived here."

"No one lives here," Chase said. "Diego crashes when he needs to. Which is more often than I'd like."

A door slammed in the back. Muffled grumbling followed. Skye raised a brow. Chase sighed. A minute later Diego emerged, properly dressed, hair slicked back, smelling faintly of lavender soap and mint.

He pointed at Chase immediately.

"You disappeared for for over a month," Diego snapped. "A month! I thought you were dead, hermano."

Chase lifted both hands in apology. "I know. I'm sorry."

"You owe me a drink. A big drink. And possibly your firstborn as emotional compensation—"

"I don't have a firstborn."

"Then make one with her and give it to me!"

"Diego," Chase growled.

Diego huffed and crossed over and hugged his friend. Skye found herself suppressing a smile.

"So," she said, stepping forward, "now that introductions are mostly done… can we talk about the docks? Did anything happen there?"

Chase didn't answer right away. Only then did she notice the water dripping from the ends of his hair, the damp collar of his shirt, the way his boots squelched faintly when he moved.

Her face paled.

Chase," she breathed, "why are you soaked?"

He exhaled through his nose—slow, controlled.

"We found the warehouse," he said. "Me and Whitman."

"Oh my God—Chase." She rushed over, hands already tugging at the collar of his soaked coat. "Get out of those clothes before you get sick."

"I'm fine," he grumbled.

"You smell like the East River. Bathroom. Now." Before he could argue, Diego strolled out of the kitchen in a loose shirt and rolled-up sleeves, raising a brow at the puddle forming under Chase's boots.

"I'll make more coffee," Diego said. "Strong. You look like something dragged you halfway to Jersey." Chase shot him a look but headed for the bathroom.

Chase emerged ten minutes later, towel-dried hair and warm loungewear clinging to him—gray henley shirt, loose drawstring pants. The steam still clung to him. He looked alive again, if only barely. Skye and Diego were chatting up like old friends, they already had one thing in common, they both like walking barefoot in the house. All he could do was shake his head.

Skye handed him a mug the moment he entered the kitchen. He took it gratefully.

Diego leaned against the counter, coffee in hand. "Alright, hermano," he said. "What the hell happened?"

Chase set the mug down, braced his hands against the table, and exhaled.

"Warehouse 24," he said. "It wasn't abandoned. Someone was clearing it out—professionally. But they didn't get everything, we interrupted them before they could finish."

Skye sat. Diego didn't move.

"There were mercs," Chase continued. "Necrostechs and Gravecallers."

Diego's smile died instantly. "You're joking."

"I wish. Three of them."

Diego folded his arms. "Gravecallers don't take jobs unless someone is paying obscene money."

"Exactly," Chase said. "And they weren't alone. There were Mourned. Same glyphs as the one that killed David Tran."

Skye's brows lifted. "So they really were being controlled."

"You doubted it?" Diego asked.

"I doubted the idea they would willingly work with necromancers," Skye said. "But if they're branded? That explains everything."

Diego nodded slowly. "I've heard of feral Mourned before. It's always bad news. But being controlled, thats new."

Chase's jaw tightened. "And we found something else. The woman with wings. The one Benjamin saw. Full Fey or pretty close to it. But most importantly she was wearing a straightjacket"

"If she has wings thats as close as you cam get " Skye said. "And a straight jacket means she was held somewhere."

Chase nodded. "Also means she escaped from somewhere."

Skye didn't hesitate. "Blackwell Island?"

Diego grimaced. "That tracks."

Chase continued. "She was strong. Glamour tried to hit me—wards burned it off. But the Gravecallers... they forced us into the river. Whitman and I barely got out."

Skye's hands tightened around her mug. "You could've died."

"Wouldn't be the first time."

Skye shot him a concerned look "And it shouldn't be that often that you casually shrug it off." Chase nodded and squeezed her hand. It was a new feeling being with someone who cared for him so deeply. Skye was the real thing.

Diego stepped forward. "Alright. What about the kid? We connecting anything yet?"

Skye inhaled sharply. "I saw him today," she said. "Benjamin is trying hard to be brave. But he's carrying survivor's guilt. He only saw one man die—but the way he describes everything around that warehouse..." She shook her head. "Someone was hunting him."

Chase's eyes narrowed. "Domingo. Was one. The Mourned with the scissor hands was another. But their just muscle. We still don't know who is pulling the strings"

Diego stiffened.

Skye continued, voice settling into professional cadence. "I traced Benjamin's history. It's thin. Too thin. His entire life is the orphanage, a few years running the streets, and then Isabel. That's it."

Diego clicked his tongue. "Convenient."

Skye glared. "I'm not assuming Isabel had anything to do with sending him into danger."

"I'm not saying she did," Diego replied quickly. "I'm saying the timing stinks."

Chase rubbed his forehead. "I'm not accusing her. Not yet. But she keeps secrets. Always has."

Diego snorted softly. "Chase, she's always been shady. Even when you two were—" He stopped himself when he saw Skye's look. "—uhh knew each other," he corrected, clearing his throat. "Point is, secrets are the Rose's main currency."

"Still," Chase said, "she's not not like that. She's not the type to put a child in danger."

Skye nodded. "You hope she wouldn't. When was the last time you "knew" each other.?"

"It was during the war..." Diego began almost excited to tell the story. But one shot from Chase silenced him. "Yeah lets table Isabell for now."

"For now," Chase confirmed.

Silence settled as all three absorbed the tangled mess before them.

Finally Skye said, "There's one more thing. If that woman escaped from Blackwell, then whatever happened there is tied to Benjamin. Maybe tied to the other missing kids too. We to establish a connection."

Chase stood straighter. "Then we split up."

Skye blinked. "How?"

Chase pointed to himself. "Blackwell Island. Alone. I can handle whatever's still there."

Skye nodded. But still gave him a concerned look.

"Then I'll hit the orphanage. I want records. Names. Anything that ties these kids together."

Both turned to Diego. Diego grinned. "Oh, I've got a source."

Skye raised a brow. "Another detective?"

"Nope," Diego said proudly. "A Mourned."

Skye nearly dropped her mug.

"A what—?"

"Narkiss, at the The Hollow." Chase supplied. "Deep under the subway. Diego's been dealing with her for years."

Diego shrugged. "Narkiss keeps tabs on Mourn movements. She'll know if someone's been buying them, branding them, or moving them around."

Skye stared. "How am I only learning about this now?"

Diego winked. "It's the Underwalk, counselor."

Chase finished his coffee, set the mug down, and holstered both Colts. "We move at dawn."

Skye stood. "We protect Benjamin."

Diego cracked his knuckles. "And we find out who the hell is pulling the strings."

Chase opened the door, checking the hallway. "Alright," he said, voice low and steady. "Let's get to work."

———

The street outside Chase Cassidy's apartment lay quiet beneath the early-morning haze, lamplight pooling in long golden streaks across the cobblestones. A man in an overcoat stepped from the shadows, collar raised, hat low. He crossed the street with practiced nonchalance—just another worker heading out before dawn.

He wasn't.

He reached a dented black Ford parked halfway down the block and slipped into the passenger seat. The other man inside—thin, sharp-eyed, chewing a toothpick like it owed him money—didn't look away from the windshield.

"Well?" the driver asked.

"It's confirmed," the scout murmured, wiping mist from his glasses. "That's Cassidy."

The driver let out a low whistle. "Damn. Boss has been waitin 'to settle up with that prick. About time the bastard surfaces."

The scout nodded, glancing back at the brownstone windows. One still glowed faintly.

"And he ain't alone," the scout added. "The dame's with him."

That got the driver's attention. A slow, nasty grin crept across his face.

"Oh-ho... think the boss'll throw in some extra chips for that little detail?"

"Bet your last tooth he will."

The driver rubbed his hands together—slow, delighted, predatory. "Then let's go tell him. No sense keepin 'good news waitin'."

The Ford growled to life, exhaust coughing a cloud of smoke as the tires rolled away from the curb. The car slipped down the street, swallowed by the thinning fog. Behind them, Chase's apartment stood quiet. Unaware he'd just been found.

CHAPTER 3

Into Blackwell's Madness

The Price of a Name —from the private journal of Chase Cassidy

Negro. Colored. Black. Every one of them a name given to us by someone else. Labels handed down by people who needed to sort the world into boxes they never planned to climb into themselves.

Same with the word Arcanist.

Am I not human?

Just because the blood of the ancients runs hot in my veins—blood I never asked for—does that make me less? More? Or simply different in a way the world feels justified in fearing? Humanity loves names. Loves categories. Loves carving people open and sorting them into neat piles— useful, dangerous, disposable.

And somewhere along the way, we learned to accept those names as truth.

Wear them. Carry them. Bleed under them.

But there are days I wonder what it would feel like to live without any of it.

To just be.

As the ferry cuts through the gray water, and Blackwell Island rises out of the fog like a rusted tooth, I feel the truth settle heavy in my chest.

No.

The world will never let me simply be.

Daybreak bled slow and gray over the East River, turning the water into a sheet of cold metal. Madhatten's jagged skyline hunched behind Chase's shoulder, a wall of stone and smoke receding as the ferry chugged away from the Containment Zone.

Blackwell Island lay ahead. A dark smudge in the fog.

He stood at the bow, coat collar turned up against the knife-edge wind, one hand resting on the plain black case at his feet. It looked like a musician's trunk, the kind of thing you'd haul a violin or clarinet in.

Inside was anything but music.

The Thompson sat in pieces within—receiver, barrel, drum magazine, all nested in velvet-cut grooves. Beside it: extra drums, each marked with a faint chalk sigil for arcane reinforcement. Over his shoulder, his twin Colts rode in their leather rigs, the weight of them familiar, grounding.

On the ride out, the naval guard hadn't been thrilled.

"Orders say Blackwell's closed to civilian traffic," the petty officer had said on the pier, hand held out like a stop sign. "You want a scenic tour, go look at Lady Liberty."

Chase had produced the badge. Brass. Scarred. Hexbreaker sigil etched deep enough to feel. "I'm not a tourist," he'd said.

The petty officer had scoffed—right up until Chase recited a a regulation it, flat and calm.

"Article Fifteen, of the Hexbreaker Clause. Willful obstruction of a Hexbreaker engaged in active pursuit of duty shall be considered an act of Arcane Interference, subject to summary execution as determined on-site by the Hexbreaker in question."

The man's face had gone pale. His hand dropped. "Permission granted," he'd muttered, stepping aside.

Chase hadn't enjoyed saying it. But he'd said it anyway. Some doors only opened if you reminded people what you were allowed to do.

Now, as the ferry cut through the gray chop, the petty officer kept a healthy distance, pretending to be busy with ropes and rigging while sneaking glances at Chase as if expecting him to start throwing lightning around for fun.

The pilot, an older man with a weathered face and cap pulled low, stuck close to the wheel. He cleared his throat once, then twice, as if arguing with himself before finally speaking.

"Been runnin 'this route fifteen years," he said. "Never seen the island this quiet."

Chase looked ahead. The asylum loomed out of the fog—brick

buildings crowding the shoreline like a cluster of rotten teeth. No smoke from chimneys. No movement at the docks. No patrol on the catwalk.

"Guardhouse should have a flag up by now," the pilot continued. "And there's usually orderlies out, takin 'a smoke before shift change."

"Today they're late," Chase said.

The pilot's fingers tightened on the wheel. "Yeah. Maybe."

They pulled up to the creaking dock. The ferry thudded against the pilings with a hollow, empty sound. No one came to meet them.

Chase slung the gun case in one hand, the other resting on the butt of Pearl beneath his coat, and stepped onto Blackwell Island. The wood felt wrong under his boots. Too still. Too empty.

The petty officer hovered at the rail. "How long you plan on being out there, Detective?"

"Hard to say," Chase answered. "Stay close."

The pilot snorted. "We don't dock here without orders, son. You want a ride back, you pop a flare. We'll see it from the river."

The petty officer added, "Assuming there's not a blizzard or fog thick enough to chew."

"Comforting," Chase said dryly.

The pilot dug into his coat and produced a red signal flare, brass-bodied and thick. "Pull the ring, point up, don't aim at my boat and we'll get along fine."

Chase took it, slid it into his coat pocket with a nod. "I'll call when I'm done." He turned away from the ferry. The engines revved. A moment later, the boat pulled back into the fog, leaving him alone with the hush of water and the low groan of the dock shifting against pilings.

The guardhouse sat at the top of a short set of steps, a squat stone building with barred windows and a half-rotted flagpole out front. The flag at its peak hung limp and torn. The outer gate—heavy iron, reinforced with thick crossbars—was ajar.

A shoe held it open.

Leather, cracked and scuffed. Laces snapped. A dried brown smear at the heel where it had been dragged. Chase's jaw clenched. He nudged the gate with his shoulder, gun case shifting in his grip, and slipped through.

The courtyard beyond was a rectangle of packed earth and broken stone. Benches overturned. A cigarette still smoldering in an ashtray on a barrel, ash long and unbroken as if abandoned mid-drag. A cap lay upside down near the steps, the Blackwell security patch torn.

No birds.

No voices.

Just wind.

The front doors of the main building were not ajar—they were bowed outward, the heavy oak panels warped at the hinges as if something inside had tried—hard—to break through them. The left door hung slightly crooked, its metal bracing bent in the center. Deep gouges scored the wood from the inside, long and uneven, dragging downward in frantic arcs.

Something had clawed its way out. Or died trying.

Chase stared at the damage, jaw tightening. The cold wind snuck through the cracks between the warped doors, carrying with it the stale reek of antiseptic... old paper... and beneath it— Blood.

His grip tightened on the gun case at his side. This wasn't neglect. This wasn't abandonment. Something had happened here. And it hadn't been quiet. Chase set the case down by the guardhouse, flicked both latches, and opened it.

The Thompson's parts glinted dully in the weak morning light. He assembled the weapon by touch more than sight—receiver sliding into stock, barrel twisting into place, foregrip snugged tight. The drum mag locked in with a solid, satisfying clack. He slung the strap over his shoulder, barrel down and close. With a gentle kick the gun case slide up against the guard house.

Then he rolled his right sleeve up past the elbow. The infernal sigils carved along his forearm pulsed faintly—dormant, coiled energy under the skin. They didn't need touch to awaken... but touch focused them. Directed them.

He placed his palm over the iron chain locking the front doors shut.

Heat flared instantly beneath his hand, racing along the sigil-lines like fire finding a fuse. The chain hissed, glowed red—then sagged and

CHARLES DRAEVYN

snapped with a wet metallic groan, molten ends dripping onto the stone. Chase shook the slag from his hand.

Darkness waited beyond the doorway. Absolute. Silent. Wrong. He reached up with two fingers and tapped the small, curved glyph etched just behind his right ear.

The sigil answered at once. Light bled beneath the skin in a soft amber glow, spreading like fine cracks of molten glass across the runic pattern. His vision stretched—sharpened—changed.

Edges cut cleanly through shadow. Residual magic clung to surfaces in faint glimmers, like frost catching dawn. Every scuff mark, every gouge in the warped doors, every disturbance in the dust became painfully clear.

True Sight.

Alright, he thought. Let's see what the dark's been hiding.

Inside, the foyer was a mausoleum. A receptionist's desk stood to the right, papers scattered across it like fallen leaves. A ledger lay open, pen dried in an inkwell beside it. A metal chair lay on its side. The wall clock above ticked with stubborn determination, still keeping time as if nothing had changed.

The smell hit him harder here.

Not just blood.

Fear.

It clung to the walls like smoke.

He moved down the central corridor, boots whispering against worn tile. Office doors stood open on both sides, some torn from their hinges. A file cart lay overturned, manila folders spilling across the floor in a paper tide.

His upgraded sight picked out details in the dim: gouge marks along the walls where something with claws had raked, streaks on the linoleum where bodies had been dragged.

At the first intersection, he stopped.

An orderly lay slumped against the wall, legs splayed, back leaving a dark smear where he'd slid down. His white uniform was soaked through, the fabric almost black around the shredded ruin of his throat.

The man's eyes were open.

Staring.

Chase crouched, quick but thorough. No pulse. Skin long cold. Bite marks, not tool cuts. Too wide for a normal human jaw. The flesh around the wounds bore faint blackening, veins spiderwebbed with deadened aether.

He'd seen similar marks before.

On David Tran.

On the bodies that had marked the beginning of this nightmare.

"Mourned," he murmured. He straightened, jaw tight, and moved on.

Two more dead orderlies turned up before he reached the main administration. One lay half under a desk, fingers still clutching a broken baton. The other hung from a stairwell rail, neck snapped, body limp and swaying slightly in the draft.

Whatever had torn through here hadn't bothered with subtlety.

The warden's office sat at the end of the corridor, door closed but splintered around the knob as if someone had tried to claw their way in. Chase touched the wood. Felt the faint hum of old wards, burned out and useless now—a faded hint of Aether hung in the air

He shoved the door open.

The warden's office still smelled like mildew and stale paper—Blackwell Island's last attempt at normalcy before the place had rotted into a mausoleum. The big oak desk was covered in stacked files, some toppled, papers fanned across the blotter. A chair lay overturned on the floor. The windows were cracked, one spiderwebbed from an impact. A portrait of the governor general hung crooked, glass shattered.

Chase sifted through a stack of old personnel logs, eyes drifting toward a crooked frame on the cluttered desk.

Names. Dates. Incident reports.

His eyes snagged on one file in particular, half-buried under a stack.

MIRELLE LE FEY

He drew it free.

The black-and-white intake photo paperclipped to the folder was grainy, but the bones were there—a young woman with high cheekbones, big eyes rimmed in smudged stage makeup, hair in tight curls. Her expression hovered between sullen and dazed. This was Benjamin's fey dancer, the one that Chase fought at the warehouse.

Below, in cramped handwriting:

Stage performer. Prior residency in midtown theater district. Exhibits delusional ideation centered on "the stage" and "the audience." Confirmed Fae ancestry. Episodes of uncontrolled glamour projection and violent outbursts...

He flipped through the pages. Notes from various doctors. "Subject speaks in nursery rhymes during stress events." "Extreme response to music—especially waltzes and lullabies." "Recommendation: long-term confinement."

Then, a later entry, underlined.

Increased agitation following visits from listed benefactor. Patient refers to him as "The General."

Chase's eyes narrowed. He read the name printed in neat, elegant ink.

Visitor: Morphan Veep

The letters shimmered faintly under True Sight. Not mundane ink at all—arcane. Someone wanted the name to look unremarkable to anyone without the Sight. A fake name. Had to be. He flipped another page. A loose memo had been tucked near the back.

Recommend transfer of subject to lower secure ward as per request of consultant Morphan Veep. All unusual activity in East Wing correlates with her presence. See disturbance reports, ref: "Veil Intrusions."

—Chief Medical Officer J. E. Wycombe

Chase's jaw clenched. He turned the page. Another note, scrawled later—hurried, almost angry.

Request denied. Subject displays deepening instability. I fear what she may become if exposed to outside magical stimuli. Recommend indefinite retention.

But below that, in heavier ink, a final addendum had been added by a different hand:

> **Overridden. Release approved by order of the Institute Board. Directive from Chairman D. Blackwell: subject Merilee Le Fey to be remanded to consultant's custody immediately.**

Chase cursed under his breath. Whoever this "Morphan Veep" was, he sure as hell wasn't hiding well enough. He skimmed the last lines again.

Blackwell.

Everyone in Madhatten knew that name. Old money. Old magic. Old rot. Chase felt something tighten in his chest as the pieces edged closer—still not forming a picture, but grinding toward one.

The Blackwells had always been… strange. Too clean on the surface. Too connected beneath it. And there'd been scandals—whispers of inbreeding, a daughter who vanished, a son rumored to have snapped and been sent away. He frowned, memory scraping forward.

Right. An asylum transfer.

Back in his rookie days someone mentioned a Blackwell heir—Dorian—stepping in after the old chairman died. Taking over operations on the island. Revamping everything.

Chase exhaled, slow. He should've read more damn newspapers.

Instead, he was standing in the gutted shell of an institution, reading glamoured guest logs and seeing the fingerprints of one of the most powerful arcane families in the city smeared across every page.

Whoever "Morphan Veep" really was, it wasn't some consultant. And whatever went wrong here…the Blackwells were right in the middle of it. He pulled another file toward him, this one thicker, stamped with a faded red marking.

DISTURBANCE LOG – EAST WING

He rifled through it. Reports of patients hearing voices. Lights flickering. Staff experiencing vertigo, missing time. Then:

Staff report "door made of shadow" appearing in Ward C. Door dissipates upon approach. No physical damage noted—but patients in vicinity suffer simultaneous panic attacks. Subject Le Fey found humming and twirling in her cell, eyes black, restraints strained.

Then another:

Security breach. Two orderlies missing. Basement access door warped from inside. Recommend lockdown until city representatives can review. At the last page: a rough map of the asylum layout. Wards marked. Stairs. Sub-levels. One section circled in pencil.

Ward C – Cell 313: Le Fey, M.

Chase folded and slid the Coco file inside his overcoat. Time to see where they'd kept her. As he was about to exit the office he noticed in the corner a photograph in a broken frame. A brass name plate dangled loosely on one screw. Dorian and Lilidan Blackwell. Stepping closer he saw two faces staring back at him.

Dorian Blackwell—clean-cut, severe, coat tailored to aristocratic precision. Brown hair combed back, eyes a cold, bright blue that seemed to follow Chase across the room.

Beside him stood a woman almost identical save for sharper cheekbones and a shadow in her expression—Lildan Blackwell. Fraternal twins but indistinguishable in posture, poise, and the faint aura of privilege captured in the still image.

He kicked the photo with his boot and moved on.

The wards lay deeper in, past another set of double doors that hung askew on their hinges. The air grew colder as Chase descended the hallway, the smell turning from antiseptic-and-blood to something more sour.

Whispering drifted from the open doorways. Not words at first— just jittering sound, like teeth clicking together in a dozen mouths.

He passed the first occupied cell and glanced in. A man crouched in the corner, arms wrapped tight around his knees, rocking. His hair was a matted halo, his hospital clothes stained. He murmured to himself, eyes fixed on some invisible point on the wall.

"...bone men, bone men, count your teeth, chew the light, chew the light..."

The man's gaze snapped to Chase as he passed. Pupils blown wide.

"They're coming," he hissed. "You hear 'em? Boots on the floor, bones in the walls. Deep, deep down. Coming for you, too, pretty man."

Chase kept moving.

Another cell. A woman pacing, bare feet slapping the tile in a manic, repetitive pattern. Her nails were raw, tips stained crimson where she'd clawed at something. Her eyes tracked him with animal suspicion. She smiled then urinated on the floor.

He moved on.

Ward C lay at the far end. The steel door had been bent outward, as if something had forced its way through. The lights here flickered steadily, a sickly yellow strobe that set his teeth on edge.

Cell 313's door was wide open.

Inside, the padded walls had been shredded. Long, ragged tears exposed the stuffing beneath. Chalk sigils scrawled across every surface—circles, spirals, jagged notes written in a child's looping hand.

On the far wall, someone had drawn a stage. Stick-figure audience. A ballerina in mid-twirl, skirt flared. Every face in the crowd was a skull. The restraining straps on the bed dangled, cut clean through.

Chase stepped inside, True Sight flaring. Residual glamour clung to the room like perfume—faint, fading, but distinct. The air tingled against his skin. He imagined her here: humming, twirling, planning. Waiting for a man named Morphan Veep to open doors that should've stayed closed.

"She was here," he said softly. Empty rooms still listened. Something thumped, faint but distinct, from the cell next door. Chase froze. Turned his head.

The door to 314 was closed, padlock snapped shut on the outside. Deep gouges scored the wood around the handle—as if someone had tried desperately to get in, not out.

Another thump. Followed by a weak, hoarse sound.

"...help..."

He stepped over, brushed his fingers over the ruined lock, and tapped another sigil on his arm through the fabric of his sleeve. Heat surged down to his fingertips. The metal hissed, glowed, then sagged and dripped. He kicked the slag free and shoved the door open.

The stench hit him first.

Stale sweat. Soured breath. Old fear.

Inside, in the far corner, a man sat lashed to a chair. Hands bound. Ankles tied. Dried blood streaked his face, his lips cracked and caked in it.

His eyes were cloudy, unfocused—but they turned toward the light.

"Please," he croaked. "Please... no more... no more tests..."

Chase moved in, quick, checking the restraints, the man's pulse. Weak but there. He wore a tattered white coat beneath the grime, the faint outline of a name stitched over his chest.

Dr. Wycombe

"Doctor," Chase said. "Dr. Graves. You're safe. The door's open. Who did this to you?"

The man flinched at his voice, then squinted, as if trying to peel him into focus. "Not... safe," Wycombe whispered. "They're still here. Down below... down... down..."

"Who?"

Wycombe head lolled. "The bone men. The masked ones. With their dead eyes and dead prayers. They came up from the floor..." His chest hitched. "We thought she was just... just another mad Fae. But she opened the cracks. He taught her."

Morphan Veep

Chase didn't say it aloud, but the name burned on his tongue.

"Who taught her, Doctor?" he pressed. "Who?"

Wycombe fingers twitched against the ropes. "The German consultant, He lied. He was not who he said he was—" His jaw clenched as if something seized it from within. His eyes rolled back. A shudder ran through his frame.

A whisper of cold slid along Chase's spine. He'd seen curses take hold before. "Easy," he said, reaching for the bindings. "I'm getting you out —"

The lights flickered.

Once.

Twice.

Then went out. The corridor outside erupted in screams. Not human. Not entirely. High, ululating howls that scraped the marrow.

Chase spun, he pulled the Thompson's stock tight against his shoulder. His eye sigils flared brighter, turning the pitch dark into a grainy, gray-toned vision.

Shadows moved in the hall.

Four-legged. Twisted and bent.

Something heavy slammed into the far wall, shaking plaster loose.

Wycombe sobbed. "They're awake—oh God, they're awake again—"
"Stay here," Chase said. "And don't make a sound."

He stepped back into the corridor. They came in a pack. Stitched bodies. Bolted joints. Jaws wired wide. Not Mourned—something crueler, cheaper, stitched in a hurry.

Howlers.

He faced them in the war. The Germans would unleash them as their vanguard during assaults. Lean, patchwork shapes—stitched limbs, mismatched flesh, seams puckered with crude surgical knots. Arms too long. Necks bolted. Fingers bristling with rusted nails. Skin mottled in slabs of pallid gray, swollen purple, and corpse-blue, like someone had assembled them using whatever pieces were within reach.

And their heads—

That was the worst part.

Jaws unhinged, wired open with metal staples. Teeth from different people jammed into black gums. Their lips long rotted away or intentionally carved off to expose the whole screaming mechanism. Their eyes burned with a dim, animal orange.

Unlike the Mourned who feed off of essence, Howlers hungered for flesh

Chase opened up with the Thompson. Rounds tore through the leading constructs—bursting seams, shredding limbs, spraying black tissue across the tile. But the damn things absorbed punishment like wet rope; even crawling halves kept dragging themselves forward by knuckles and exposed ulna.

More of them skittered along the walls, spider-fast, claws scraping tile. A howl detonated in the corridor. The sound hit like a pressure wave—vibrating his vision, stabbing behind his ears. Another joined it, then three more. The air became a weapon.

He staggered, teeth grinding. "Enough," he hissed. The sigils along his right forearm flared—ember-orange, spiking heat into his palm.

He snapped his wrist forward. The Searing Aegis. The buckle of molten-orange sigil-iron formed over his forearm—flat, circular, edges shimmering with burning script. The moment it stabilized, he hurled it.

It screamed through the corridor like a thrown comet. Three Howlers were cleaved mid-lunge—bisected torsos flopping apart, limbs spinning. A fourth was nearly cut in half before the Aegis flickered, destabilized, and burst apart in a spray of molten glyphs. Energy gone.

And the rest of the pack kept coming.

"Shit."

The Thompson clicked empty. He dropped the spent drum and didn't reach for another. No time. Too many. More howls. The floor tiles trembled under their synchronized shrieks. He turned and sprinted down the corridor. and nearly collided with Chief Medical Officer Wycombe.

The emaciated doctor staggered into the hall, robe torn, eyes fixed behind Chase. He saw the Howlers. Wycombe froze, let out one soft, hopeless breath—then bolted back into his room.

The pack tore after him. They flowed into the doorway like a nightmare tide—claws scraping walls, jaws clacking, their howl harmonics rising in a fever-pitch frenzy.

Wycombe screamed. It cut off fast. Chase didn't waste the sacrifice. He used the moment. Boots pounding, he tore down the next stretch of corridor before the pack refocused. True Sight pulsed through his pupils— every shadow sharp, every detail crisp.

He hit the stairwell door with his shoulder, shoved it open, and bounded down the steps two at a time as he reloaded the Thompson. Howls rose behind him again. Hopefully he had put enough distance between them. He burst through the bottom door onto the second floor and skidded to a stop.

It was tall. Too tall.

A gaunt figure in a tattered hospital smock, its arms bound behind its back in a reinforced straitjacket, straps criss-crossing over a ribcage that jutted like broken bones. Metal bands encircled its limbs, nailing sleeves and pant legs to its skin.

Over its head, bolted across its jaw and crown, sat a metal helm. Iron. Heavy. Seamless, except for the narrow horizontal slits where its eyes glowed a sick, swampy green.

Chains trailed behind it, dragged through the gore on the floor. Chase's stomach turned.

Experimental restraints ran up and down its spine, plates engraved with sigils he didn't recognize. Tubes fed into the helm from a harness on its back, where glass vials sloshed with neon fluid.

It cocked its head at him. The chains rattled.

"Of course," Chase breathed. "Your someones pet project"

The helmed Mourn lunged. It moved faster than its size suggested, closing the distance in a blur. Chase dove aside as the thing hit the wall, stone exploding in a shower of dust, then rebounded with terrifying momentum.

He fired as he rolled.

Bullets chewed into its side, ricocheting off the metal plates with showers of sparks. A few found soft tissue; black ichor spattered the floor. It barely seemed to notice.

Its helm snapped toward him. The slits narrowed. It charged again.

Chase dropped the Thompson, grabbed the edge of a doorframe, and yanked himself up and over as the monster barreled past. It hit the opposite wall, kept going, and smashed through into the next ward.

The floor shook.

Patients screamed.

A man's voice rose above them all, shrill and breaking.

"Bone men! Bone men! I told you so!"

No time.

Chase snatched up the Tommy gun, heart slamming. He needed a choke point. Needed space, sight lines, something he could use. The map from the disturbance log flashed in his mind.

Sub-level access at the far end. Experimental ward. Drainage to the river. He started moving.

The deeper he went, the more the asylum shifted from hospital to something else. Stairs led down into a concrete corridor lined with thick metal doors. Warning runes had once been painted over the archway—wards once meant to keep things in. They'd been deactivated. A powerful mages hand was all over them.

The air here hummed with stale power. His sigils tingled in response, like a low-grade static crawling over his skin. He passed a room whose door hung open. Inside, under flickering aether lamps, iron gurneys stood in neat rows. Leather restraints lay empty on their surfaces. A rack of bloodied tools: saws, clamps, knives with channels cut into their blades.

In another chamber, thick glass vats lined the walls, cables feeding from their bases into humming machines. One vat lay shattered on the floor, green fluid leaking out in a sluggish puddle. Inside, half-suspended, was something that had once been human.

Its mouth was locked open in a soundless scream. Its chest was carved with glyphs. Its eyes had been replaced with vials. Chase swallowed hard and moved on.

He found the records room by accident—a small annex with cabinets lining both sides. Papers littered the floor, some soaked in that same green fluid. He saw enough in a few quick glances.

Subject: Fae-Blood Resiliency Trials – Ruthven Protocol

Objective: Determine optimal blend of mortal and Fae lineage to sustain prolonged necromantic occupancy of host body.

Note: juvenile subjects show highest compatibility. Essence density increases with proximity to pure Fae.

Ruthven. Another name to figure out. Bile rose in his throat. He shoved as many files as he could into his overcoat, barely bothering to read more than headings. Take it. Sort it later. Get out alive first. A low, wet growl rolled down the hallway. Followed by the clink of dragging chains.

The helmed Mourn. Closer now.

The experimental ward opened into a long room that might once have been a hydrotherapy center. Now the central pit was dry, metal grates exposed, a tangle of pipes running along the bottom. Rusted catwalks crisscrossed above. If he could get it into the pit... maybe he could buy himself enough of a lead to reach the surface.

The Mourn stepped into the doorway behind him, hunched to fit beneath the frame. It straightened, chains snaking along the floor. Its gaze locked onto him. Chase didn't give it time to decide.

He grabbed the nearest rusted stretcher and hurled it at the creature. It bounced off its chest with a screech of metal, barely making it flinch—but it got its attention.

"Come on, you ugly bastard," Chase muttered. "Let's dance."

He fired a burst into the ceiling just above the Mourn. Cracked plaster and concrete rained down, dust choking the air. It roared—the sound muffled by the helm but no less chilling—and charged.

Chase ran.

He sprinted along the catwalk, the grating rattling under his boots. The Mourn followed, too heavy for the flimsy structure. Metal groaned beneath it with every step, bolts squealing in protest. Halfway across, Chase skidded to a halt, turned, and lifted his sleeve with his teeth, exposing more of his ink.

The infernal lines crawled brighter, heat lancing up his arm and into his chest. His heart stuttered, then pounded harder, sweat breaking out along his spine.

"Just enough," he whispered. "Not more. Not now." He slammed his palm against one of the catwalk supports and spat another word.

"Torrent"

Hellfire leapt from his hand into the rusted beam. Metal glowed white-hot in an instant, softening, warping. The heat bit his skin, but he held it, teeth gritted, until the sigil in his flesh screamed in protest.

The Mourn hit the weakened section at full tilt. The beam snapped. For one suspended heartbeat, the helmed figure hung in the center of the room, chains flailing. Then the catwalk collapsed. The stone, chain, and twisted metal crashed down into the empty hydro pit in a shriek of steel and bone.

The impact shook the room. Dust billowed. Aether lines sparked where cables ruptured. Chase threw himself flat on the remaining section of catwalk, arms wrapped around the rail as the structure rattled, then steadied.

Below, in the haze, the Mourned moved. Of course it did. It shoved the wreckage off its back, helm tilting up toward him. One of its legs bent wrong now, bone jutting, but it still dragged itself forward, hands clawing at the concrete wall of the pit with tireless, inhuman strength.

"Persistent son of a—" Chase pushed himself to his feet, lungs burning. A howl cut across his curse, high and keening. More Howlers. Coming from the corridor he'd entered by.

"And friends," he muttered. "Great."

The room's far wall featured another door, half rusted, half new steel. Above it, he saw the faint outline of an emergency exit sign, long dark. He bolted for it. The door was barred on his side with a heavy metal rod. He slapped the latch free, heaved the bar up, and threw his weight into the door.

It opened onto a narrow, damp stairwell. The air that rolled up from below was cooler. Fresher. He smelled water, salt, old brick. River access. He stumbled down, the sound of chains and claws echoing behind him, mixed with the approaching chorus of howls.

The stairs ended at a low tunnel that sloped gently down to a heavy grate. Beyond its bars, he could see river water lapping, dim light filtering in. And between him and the grate, hunched in the half-dark, something shivered.

It was small. At first.

Then it uncurled, rising on spindly legs, its body unfolding too far, too many joints, too many angles. Its skin shimmered like oil on water, surface shape warping as his gaze tried to settle on it.

A Boggart.

It wasn't supposed to be here. These things haunted closets and basements, feeding on childhood fears—not the drainage tunnels of an illegal lab.

Under True Sight, its glamour peeled back. He saw the raw thing beneath: a knot of shadow and hunger, claws that were more idea than flesh, its face a constantly shifting mask of whatever your mind least wanted to see.

It opened its mouth. His father's face spilled out. Elijah Cassidy, as he'd last seen him in flashes of nightmare—eyes accusing, skin burned, mouth black with infernal fire.

"Boy," it hissed, in a voice that wasn't quite right. "You know what she did. You know what you are."

The words hooked under old scar tissue in his mind, tried to rip.

His sigils snarled. Heat surged, this time without him calling it. The world edged red. For an instant, he tasted brimstone and the metallic tang of blood on his tongue in a way that wasn't memory.

He bared his teeth. "Wrong monster," Chase said. He emptied the last of the Thompson's drum into the Boggart.

Bullets weren't the right weapon for a thing that was mostly idea, but each round carried a lick of the infernal charge he'd stirred. The air around the creature ignited in lines, harsh and jagged, searing its shadow-flesh. It screamed with all the voices it had ever stolen.

Sound bounced off the tunnel walls, a feedback of agony. The shape convulsed, fracturing, until it collapsed inward—shrinking, shrinking, then vanishing into a smear of dark that seeped into the cracks and was gone.

His drum clicked empty.

Behind him, the stairwell shook as the helmed Mourn dragged itself closer, howls echoing down the chute like wolves baying in a well. Chase ejected the spent drum, let the Thompson hang from its strap, and strode for the grate. The lock was newer than the stone around it—thick, secure.

He didn't bother with finesse this time. He grabbed the bars with both hands, let the sigils have what they wanted. Hellfire roared through his veins, spilling from his palms in molten lines. The metal screamed, glowed, then sagged. He kicked the weakened section with both feet. It gave.

Freezing river water surged in, splashing around his boots. He sucked in a black, cold breath, then shoved himself through the gap and into the channel beyond. The current almost took his legs out from under him. He staggered, caught himself, then waded toward the faint circle of light where the tunnel opened onto the island's outer edge.

He could hear them behind him—chains clanking, claws skittering on wet stone, howls rising. He didn't look back. The drainage tunnel spat him out under a low arch near the riverline. He stumbled onto slick rocks, water soaking him to the thighs. Above, the asylum crouched over the shoreline like a mad king at the edge of his throne.

Chase dragged himself up onto the dock, lungs burning, muscles screaming. He could feel the infernal energy flickering inside him, restless and hungry, wanting more. Not now, he thought. Not like this. He forced it down with a growl, palms smoking where the sigils cooled, the remnants of hellfire dissipating into the winter air.

Something moved at the tunnel mouth behind him, shadows clustering but not quite crossing the threshold into open morning. Whatever whatever twisted monstrosity remained didn't like daylight. Or cold. Or the river.

Small mercies.

He quickly sprinted to the guardshack to retrieve the gun case and signal flare and then returns to the docks. After stuffing the case with the river soaked papers, Chase tore the flare ring free, and pointed it skyward. It ignited with a shriek, streaking into the gray clouds and bursting into red fire. He stood there on the dock, soaked to the bone, Thompson hanging empty at his side, gun case heavy with stolen files on his back, watching the signal burn.

After a long moment, far out on the water, an engine sputtered as if returning life. The ferry was close. Chase exhaled slowly, the taste of smoke and river salt thick in his mouth.

The ferry groaned as it pulled away from Blackwell Island, its rust-coated hull cutting a dark seam through the freezing river. Chase stood at the stern, soaked to the bone, watching the asylum recede into the fog like a wound being swallowed by the night.

The gaslamps along the shoreline flickered weakly, dying one by one as distance claimed them. Only one light remained. A single window on the second floor of the administration building—dim, cracked, barely holding onto its glow. Chase squinted, unsure why that one light bothered him more than the corpses, the empty cells, or the things he'd fought beneath the floors.

He stared a moment longer. Nothing moved. Nothing changed. Just a broken window with the light behind it trembling against the wind. He exhaled, turned away, and rested his hands on the ferry rail—already replaying the battle, the runes, the dead. Already thinking of Skye. Of Benjamin. Of everything waiting for him on the mainland.

High above the courtyard, behind a cracked observation window veiled by dust and shadow, two figures stood in silence. Dorian Blackwell watched Chase walk across the cracked concrete below—coat swinging, jaw set, eyes scanning every shadow as though expecting the island itself to bite.

"The detective" Dorian murmured. "Pity we did not arrive earlier." Beside him, Lildan tilted her head—her pale face unreadable, fingers brushing lightly against the glass. She said nothing, but her eyes narrowed faintly, as though assessing Chase the way one might study a specimen in a jar.

Dorian adjusted his cuffs.

"He'll be trouble later."

Lildan didn't look away.

"He's trouble now."

They stepped back from the window, shadows swallowing them as they retreated deeper into the asylum corridors—just as Chase, unaware, continued towards Manhattan.

CHAPTER 4

Crawl Space

—from the field notes of Diego Salazar, licensed hazard to polite society

Welcome to Manhattan—my tour guide voice starts here. City of murder, magic, mayhem...and that's just before breakfast.

Mundies—that's mundane folk—love to talk about how dangerous this place is, how cursed, how unpredictable. But the truth is they don't know the half of it. They don't know what it's like to feel power humming under your skin, or to step off a train platform and slide sideways into a reality stitched together by different rules.

We've got hollows—pocket dimensions older than the first brick laid on this island.

We've got Veil-rips that touch places no sane mind should map.

And then we've got the Underwalk, the city's grand experiment in urban recycling: turn abandoned rail tunnels into "low-income housing." Sounds noble. Looks like hell with track lighting.

And deeper still—the Hollow. A refuge for every being that ever wanted to escape the human gaze. A maze of hunger, secrets, and old grudges packed tight as subway heat. Thing is... whenever I wander down there, I always end up asking myself one question:

If the monsters fled underground to get away from humanity— then who's really the monster in this story?

Snow clung to the city like a shroud. Skye Anderson stepped off the streetcar and tightened her coat as a cold wind swept down Madison Avenue, knifing through the thin seams of her gloves. Ahead of her, framed by the skeletal branches of dead winter trees, stood The Maddison Street Home for Foundlings. Or what was left of it.

The orphanage had been shuttered for months—maybe longer. Boarded windows, padlocked gates, old protest flyers plastered like brittle skin along the fence. The once-bright mural of smiling children on the brick façade had faded into ghostly silhouettes, washed pale by rain and neglect.

Skye took a breath.

Benjamin Bright had lived here for years. Whatever answers they needed—whatever threat was hunting him—began in this place. She stepped through the broken iron gate.

A shape shifted behind the window at the entryway. A moment later, the front door cracked open, and a wiry older man peered out, spectacles perched crookedly on the bridge of his long nose.

"Can I help you, miss?" His voice was thin but steady.

Skye flashed her badge. "Skye Anderson. Private counsel. I'm looking into the records of children formerly housed here." Recognition flickered in his eyes. "Ah. Thought someone might come eventually. News about them murders…" He shook his head. "Awful business."

He opened the door fully and stepped aside. "Name's Calloway. Last watchman the state kept on. Records keeper too, I suppose. There's no one left but me and the dust."

Skye followed him inside.

The foyer smelled of paper rot and old floor polish. Desks sat overturned, filing cabinets gutted, spiderwebs clinging to corners like forgotten memories. The air was stale—as if no one had breathed here in years.

Calloway led her through the main hall. "You'll want the files," he said. "What's left of 'em." He pushed open the office door.

Stacks of papers, boxes, ledgers, and old adoption forms cluttered every surface. A single lantern burned on the desk, throwing long shadows across the chaos.

Skye turned slowly, absorbing the decay, the silence, the weight of abandonment.

"Is it true," she asked quietly, "that there was a lawsuit?"

Calloway nodded, rubbing his hands together as if the memory chilled him.

"Whole mess of it. Civil suit. Parents claimed the Home was funnelin 'Fae-blood kids into somethin 'called the underwalk—some underground settlement under the east tunnels. You know how it is. Poor families, immigrant families. Easy to strip rights from 'em."

Skye's pulse quickened.

She had heard the term, from Diego—the cities plan to provide more housing to the Arcane and arcane species prefer more darker accommodations.

"Funnelled how?" she pressed.

Calloway sighed.

"Placement programs. Adoption agreements. 'Special Opportunities for Arcane Youth, 'they called it. Most the kids never came back. Said they got adopted. But I saw the numbers." He tapped the ledger with a trembling finger. "Too many vanishings. Too many files with missing signatures."

Skye flipped open a ledger. Page after page listed children—dates, notes, remarks.

And beside half the names: ADOPTED. But the adoption fields were blank. No guardians listed. No addresses. No follow-ups. The murdered children's names sat among them like gravestones. Her stomach tightened.

"Calloway... this boy." She pointed at one name. Benjamin Bright.

The old man leaned in, squinting. "Bright? Oh, yes. I remember him. Clever kid. Fast on his feet. Always gettin 'into something."

"What happened to him?" Skye asked.

Calloway scratched his chin. "He ran off. Day before his scheduled placement. Funny thing—the placement order wasn't signed. Blank as a fresh tombstone. Figured he got spooked."

Skye's brows pinched. A thought surfaced—too obvious not to ask.

"What about his parents? Anything known?"

Calloway exhaled through his nose, almost a sigh. "Father turned up dead in an alley. Knife work. No witnesses. No real investigation—this city chews men like that and forgets their names before sunrise."

"And his mother?"

"That's the strange part." Calloway leaned back, lowering his voice as if afraid the walls were listening. "Rumor was she was some high and mighty socialite. Never stepped foot through our doors. But every few months a package would arrive—nice things, expensive. Toys, books, clothes that weren't department-store scraps. No return address. No note. Just… gifts."

Skye frowned. "So she cared enough to send things, but not enough to show her face?"

"Like I said," Calloway muttered, "the paperwork trail's cleaner than a priest's conscience. It's like someone pulled every page on purpose. No names. No signatures. Just a boy who shouldn't have fallen through the cracks… but somehow did."

Skye's brows furrowed. "Do you know who was supposed to adopt him?"

"No record." Calloway shrugged."

She closed the book slowly. This wasn't coincidence. This wasn't bureaucracy. Someone erased Benjamin on purpose.

Calloway continued, oblivious to the storm building behind her eyes. "Poor kids. They deserved better." He looked toward the empty hall. "Every last one of 'em."

Calloway held out the tarnished ring of keys, hand trembling faintly.

"Most of the files, logs, staff notes… they're all in the back archives," he murmured. "But listen—this place didn't shut down because of funding. It shut down because someone wanted it forgotten."

Skye extended her hand. The moment the cold metal touched her palm—

Calloway froze.

Not startled. Not hesitant. Frozen. As if someone had clamped a fist around his mind. His pupils dilated into inky pits.

"Calloway…?" she said cautiously.

His head snapped toward her with a snapping-twig motion. Before she could brace, his hand shot out and clamped around her throat, slamming her against the wall so hard dust rained from the ceiling.

Skye's breath vanished. Pain flashed white across her vision. Mesmerized, her mind supplied. Cursed. Triggered by touch. She still held the keys. She let them fall. Her right hand shot up—palm strike to the bridge of his nose, sharp and and true.

Calloway grunted, grip loosening by a hair. Skye stomped her heel down on his boot—bone or cartilage cracked—and he staggered just enough. Her left hand swept to her hip, fingers closing around the smooth, familiar shaft of her arcalam wand.

She flicked it up beneath his chin.

"Fracta!"

Blue-white sigils burst at the tip of the wand——then detonated against Calloway's chest. The stun spell hit like a mule kick. Calloway convulsed, limbs jerking in unnatural angles, then dropped heavily to the floor. His breathing stayed shallow, his eyes unfocused, the curse that had been puppeteering him snuffed out by the backlash.

Skye doubled over, hand on her bruised throat, dragging in air.

"Damn it..."

She kept the wand leveled at him—sigils still faintly glowing—while she retrieved the keys. Then she seized him by the coat collar and dragged the unconscious guard down the corridor, every scrape echoing like a threat in the hollow building. A rusted radiator waited against the wall. She knelt, took Calloway's own restraint cuffs, and shackled his wrists to the radiator bars—tight, locked, and double-checked.

Only then did she exhale.

"Sorry, Calloway," she whispered. "Whatever got into your head isn't getting into mine."

She stood. Ahead lay the long hallway to the archives—dark, boarded, silent. The kind of silence that listened. Skye tightened her grip on the wand. The shadows shifted. She moved toward them anyway.

———

Some tunnels ran deeper that others. A labyrinth of old abandoned subway tunnels lay beneath the city feet, tunnels were never meant to breathe. Diego Salazar climbed down the rust-choked maintenance ladder beneath 116th Street, a dim amber lantern-charm cupped in one hand. Each rung carried him deeper into cold air that smelled of wet stone, old magic, and the faint copper tang of things long buried.

At the bottom, the world widened.

Abandoned rail lines spider-webbed into blackness. Half-finished alcoves and forgotten utility corridors yawned like open graves. Pipes arced overhead like skeletal ribs, dripping condensation that echoed through the dark like whispers trying to remember their own names.

Far above him, the Restriction Zone groaned under curfews, riots, and political fire.

But down here—beneath the cracked crust of Madhatten, past the last BAE check points and the wards stitched into the upper tunnels—the real power breathed. The Underwalk pulsed with a quiet, unnatural rhythm, a snow globe of frozen twilight and drifting ash, a place the city had tried to bury but never could.

Diego adjusted his coat, exhaled slowly, and stepped forward. This was the Underwalk—

a forgotten dream of underground housing, arcane refuge, and municipal expansion…

turned graveyard of failed ambition.

And somewhere beyond the crooked maze of tunnels lay the Hollow. Diego reached a wide dead-end wall of soot-dark stone. Embedded in the center was a gargoyle head, mouth open in a jagged metal grin.

He winced. "Well," he muttered, rolling his shoulders, "let's hope you're still in a good mood, buddy."

He pressed his hand into the gargoyle's mouth. Its stone jaw snapped shut. Diego hissed through his teeth as fangs of cold iron bit into his palm, tasting his blood—tasting his essence.

The gargoyle's eyes flared fey green. It hummed. It swallowed the sample. Then—Click. The jaw opened, releasing him. Blood trickled down his wrist. Diego noticed the dried stains around the teeth—brown, fresh, and splattered like someone had pulled away too slowly.

"Yikes," he muttered. "Some poor schmuck got the appetizer special."

The wall shivered. A vertical seam of violet light appeared, splitting downward like a knife cut through fabric. A doorway opened. And Diego stepped through.

The world blurred—and then reformed.

The Hollow. A pocket haven for the old world. Buildings leaned crookedly as if drunken architects had pushed them into existence. Lanterns in mismatched colors floated overhead, glowing on their own whims. Narrow alleys twisted like veins. Smoke curled from chimneys, flavored with incense, alchemical fumes, and cooking meat.

A half-troll fishmonger shouted prices over the din of whispering customers. A cyclopean seamstress haggled with a goblin over thread. A trio of shifters played cards on overturned crates, tails flicking with every bluff.

Diego exhaled. "Home sweet middle-of-nowhere." He walked down Ashen Row, the main thoroughfare—a crooked stone street lined with shops, stalls, and more shadows than light. The wealthy mages lived high in magically stretched brownstones. The less fortunate crammed themselves into makeshift lean-tos and hanging shacks bolted into stone.

And then came the Market Macabre. The air chilled. Lanterns dimmed. The clientele grew stranger. Necromancers peddled bottled whispers. Bone-wrights hawked skeletal familiars. A hag stirred a cauldron of floating eyeballs, grinning with too many teeth. Diego ignored the stares. He turned down a narrow lane where a violet sigil pulsed over a carved wooden sign:

THE PAINTED ESSENCE

His heart jumped. He pushed the beaded curtain aside. Inside was dim, soft, and scented with jasmine and cold rain. Shelves lined the walls—each holding jars of shimmering essence: joy, grief, hope, sorrow, excitement. The colors shifted like liquid auroras trapped in glass.

And at the center, reclining on a velvet couch like a queen of shadows—

Narkiss.

Wings folded behind her like divine angelics, thin nearly see-through membranes laced with frost-silver veins. Her skin was pale as moon milk, almost translucent over bone. Her hair, long and black, drifted like underwater silk. The gauzy robe she wore was nearly transparent, clinging to curves sculpted with unnatural perfection.

Her eyes—luminous violet—lifted the moment he entered.

"Diego, my little gambler" she breathed. His name sounded like a caress.

He swallowed once. "Hey, Nessa."

She rose with a dancer's glide, bare feet silent on the floor. Cold lips brushed his his. His breath caught. "H-hi."

"You look exhausted." Her voice was smoke and velvet. "You only come to me when danger circles your shadow."

"Yeah, well... it's circling fast this time."

She tilted her head—birdlike, unnatural and hauntingly beautiful. "Tell me."

He did. He told her everything— the Mourned at the docks, the carved glyphs, the collars... the unnatural coordination. The way they fought like trained soldiers, not mindless feeders.

Narkiss listened without blinking. Her expression didn't shift, but Diego felt the weight of her attention settle on him like cold water. At last, she whispered, "What do you know of my kind?"

Diego scratched at his temple, trying to play casual and failing. "Well... the Mourned. I mean... from what I heard, each one's got a sad tale. Something holding them back. Their spirits hover above their bodies —kinda disconnected. Like grief keeps 'em from passing on."

He winced. "That's just what was in the books."

Narkiss's lips curved—sympathy, amusement, and something older. "So not much."

She lifted a hand. Glowing runes unfurled from her fingers in slow spirals, casting pale light across the chamber.

Her voice softened to a whisper of drifting ash. "Our souls do hover," she said. "Suspended above our bodies, tethered by a single vine of memory. A life unmade but never released." She turned her palm, and the rune fractured into three distinct sigils.

"There are three true castes of the Mourned," she said.

"The Roused. The lowest. Newly made. Wild. Their minds still exist, but only in shards. They think—but only enough to survive. Hunger rules everything."

A second sigil brightened. "The Emerged. Those who have begun the climb. They remember pieces of who they were. They can restrain themselves... sometimes. Emotion and instinct war inside them."

The final sigil flared brightest.

"The Ascended. They retain their minds fully. Their memories, their desires, their sorrows. They are bound to the living world by a single, powerful thread."

Her eyes shimmered faintly, catching light that wasn't there. "An Ascended may choose whether to hunt. Whether to love. Whether to feel. But few of the Mourned ever reach this level"

Diego frowned. "So... that's you then? Third caste?"

She gazed at him—tender, ancient, melancholy. "No, my dear." The sigils winked out. Her wings unfolded behind her with a soft, ghostly hum. "There is one more caste." No rune formed for this one. No symbol could. Her voice dropped to a tone that felt like winter wind brushing bone.

"The Exalted." "So rare that the books pretend we do not exist." "And of that caste..." She stepped closer. Her pale fingers lifted Diego's chin with featherlight touch. "...there is only one."Her violet eyes lifted to him.

"I remember my child. I remember the man who strangled me for daring to carry his seed."

Diego's throat tightened. "Nessa... I'm sorry."

She brushed his cheek with cold fingers. "The living always are."

He hesitated. "But these Mourned I saw—they were manufactured. Someone's creating them, shaping them. Any idea who?"

Her expression turned grave.

"I do not know. I have heard rumors of their existence. Whomever did this is playing with old sins. The Mourned are not meant to be made in numbers. Only born through the suffering of ones soul."

Diego cleared his throat, uneasy under the weight of her gaze. "I will...tell me something," he said. "How do the Mourned feed on essence? What is essence, exactly?"

A smile touched Narkiss's lips—soft, wistful, old. "Essence," she said, "is emotion made manifest. A kind of aether, but tinged with the resonance of a living mind. Happiness, sorrow, terror, longing... it all leaves a flavor."

She lifted a jar from the shelf, the violet liquid swirling as if stirred by invisible fingers.

"We do not crave flesh," she continued. "We crave the ability to feel. Essence grants us fleeting echoes of what we lost. A rush of grief. A flicker of joy. A memory of warmth that is no longer ours."

Diego blinked. "So you can—what? Sense emotional states?"

Her smile sharpened faintly.

"We smell them. Taste them. A living aura is a lantern in the dark. And the way we died… determines what we seek. Some chase sorrow. Some hunger for fear. Some little shadows yearn only for laughter." She replaced the jar with a reverent touch.

Diego exhaled slowly. "So these… manufactured Mourned—"

Narkiss tilted her head. "We called them the Shackled. Its fitting as their souls are chained to bodies that were pushed to the point of death"

He nodded. "Ok, so the Shackled Mourned… they're being trained. Conditioned. That's how they've been finding the fey children."

"It seems so," she murmured. "If you bind a creature's death to hunger alone, it will seek what it was shaped to devour."

Diego rubbed the bridge of his nose. "Damn. So that's what we're dealing with down here."

He looked up—at her. She watched him with ancient quiet, her dark hair drifting like silk in water. "I have to stop it," he said quietly. "A kid's life is on the line."

Narkiss studied him—really studied him—and for the first time, her expression flickered into something like… sorrow. "You feel peace with me," she said softly.

He swallowed. The truth stung because it was so disarming. He did feel peaceful with her. More than he should. More than made sense. Her fingertip brushed his cheek—cool as moonlight.

"No, You love me," she murmured, almost amused. "Or you lust. Humans blur those lines so easily."

Diego opened his mouth—closed it again. His thoughts tangled. Love? Hell, maybe. Lust? Definitely. But mostly… this calm. This strange, eerie calm she wrapped around him like a warm fog.

Diego flushed. "Narkiss—"

She lifted a single silver-white finger to his lips. "If you ever touched me," she whispered, "you would know a pleasure so profound it would stop your heart. Your soul would rip free just to stay with me."

He froze. She leaned forward and kissed his forehead once more—winter-cold, eternally lonely... and unbearably tender.

"Now go, little gambler."

Diego nodded slowly, still processing everything Narkiss had revealed.Then—the beads behind them rattled. A delicate chime. Gentle enough to seem accidental. Wrong enough to spike Diego's nerves.

Narkiss froze mid-breath. Her wings unfurled —darkening and terrifying.

Diego had not fully turned but his angled head caught just enough of the the reflection in a jar of glowing essence on the table. A silhouette. Tall. Dark. Menacing .

A Gravecaller.

It stepped into the lantern glow with the slow, deliberate weight of inevitability. Diego's stomach turned to ice. He had heard of them—in trenches, in smoke-choked backrooms, in the half-whispered boasts of rogues who fled them.

Chase had earlier claimed he killed one. And fought off three others. Diego had laughed inwardly then, but Chase was not known for embellishment. Now he wished Chase had been exaggerating.

The Gravecaller tilted its head. The spirals in its mask crawled like living ink. Pressure tightened around Diego's chest—cold fingers squeezing his heartbeat. Beside him, Narcissa hissed—low, ancient, feral.

"You dare step into my shop" she whispered. "Robber of the dead!"

The Gravecaller did not answer. It merely lifted one hand. Long fingers flexed once—like plucking a stem from a dying flower. Green necrotic light flared.

Everything slowed. Light curled behind the Gravecaller's raised hand. Narkiss's wings spread wide as she spoke a word in a language older than breath. Diego reached instinctively for his pouch—fingers catching the familiar weight of the Bone Trio.

His lifeline. His hope.

He felt them warm in his palm—each die humming its own frequency. The Gravecaller cast. So did Narckiss. And Diego—

Let. The. Bones. Fall.

The three dice spun from his fingers like sparks off steel. The master die ignited midair—azure light flaring across its carved sigils as it struck the stone. It rolled. Slowed. Landed.

BIG RED.

The number eight.

Heat welled under the Gravecaller's skin—an inner fire blooming outward. Smoke curled from his forearms. The necromancer staggered. Its knees buckled— not from injury, but from fever. The miscast hit it first— its necrotic spell collapsing in its own hand, energy imploding backward.

Then Narkiss's spell struck— a tornado of obsidian flame churning upward from her palm. It engulfed the Gravecaller in roaring black fire, swallowing its scream whole.

"GO!" Narkiss shrieked, her wings flaring wide.

Another silhouette darkened the doorway—then another—and a third. Three more Gravecallers entered, masks glowing with death-sigil light.

"I said GO!" she roared.

Diego ran.

———

Hermann Von Epp watched the Sanctum of Mirrors hum with shifting reflections—

each pane flickering with fractured glimpses of the Hollow beneath 59th Street.

At the forefront:

Dorian's "brilliant" plan unfolding in real time.

Von Epp clicked his tongue, the faintest smirk tugging at the corner of his mouth.

"Really, Dorian? Four Gravecallers? Almost half our necromancers?"

The first had already fallen— reduced to a steaming smear of bone ash as Narkiss's feyfire devoured him. Her silhouette flickered across the mirror's glass— pale wings now black, surrounded by faint green light, the air bending around her like she was the axis on which the Hollow turned.

Von Epp's jaw shifted in something like annoyance... but also admiration. "If I had captured her years ago..." he murmured, "...the Shackled would have become the dominant caste by now."

Yes. Shackled. Those half-made, soul-splintered versions the Court created in labs instead of sorrow from graves. They lacked the elegance of the true Mourned, but held potential. Controllable potential.

He leaned closer to the mirror. Narcissa—the Exalted—flared again. A second Gravecaller stepped forward. And just as quickly, he burned. Dark feyfire gnawed him down to nothing.

Von Epp sighed. "You could have been my masterpiece..." he whispered to the image of her. "Captured—not killed. The tether that makes you Exalted would have been... exquisite. A perfect catalyst. The ritual would have been accelerated."

The third mirror showed Dorian—still posturing, still believing he could impress Adriana with decisive action. Von Epp actually laughed— a low, dry sound like bones shifting in a crypt.

"You played your hand too early, boy." He watched the third Gravecaller enter the fray.

The mirror flared white— then cracked down the middle. Narcissa's power bucked through the Sanctum like a pulse. Von Epp didn't flinch.

Instead, he lifted one finger, brushing the mirror's jagged line. The image stabilized just long enough to see what he already predicted: The final Gravecaller convulsed, their life-force unraveling, and Narcissa's dark light swallowed them whole.

He exhaled. "They can't retreat now And you, Dorian... oh, you never understood restraint." He stepped back from the mirrors, coat swaying in the necrotic glow.

"I could have joined them," he said softly. "Lend my own power. Turn the tide."

Von Epp paused. Considered. But did not regret his decision He turned toward the sanctum's exit, boots echoing on the cold stone.

"Still this was... useful." He cast one last look at Narcissa's blazing outline, wings unfurled like a god made of grief.

"Now I've seen you up close," he whispered. "I'll know how to take you when the time comes." The mirrors dimmed behind him as he walked away. And beneath the city, the Hollow burned in feyfire.

————

Diego bolted through the door as a blast of necromantic force tore the frame apart above him. Wood and bone-etched plaster exploded into a storm of splinters. A second bolt followed—hot, hissing—charring the exterior wall inches from his head.

Diego didn't think. His hand flew up. The dice returned to his palm like loyal dogs.

He rolled on all three on instinct. Gambler's Grotto. A compressed shield of wind snapped into existence in front of him just as the next deathbolt hit.

The impact slammed Diego backward—skidding across the polished stone of the Hollow. He groaned, pushing himself onto an elbow —and froze.

Standing amid the scattering crowd of market-goers was a woman in wearing a black spider weave dress cloaked in black robes, a golden mask staring blankly ahead. Her hand arched forward—and behind her, the Shackled swarmed.

A whole cluster— twitching, half-rotted, their tethered souls flickering like ghost-lanterns overhead.

Diego swallowed. "Oh... that's not great."

He forced himself to his feet, staggered— and then sprinted deeper into the Hollow. Crooked lanterns swung wildly. Shopkeepers shouted. Cauldrons spilled spell-smoke across the cobblestones. Alleyways shifted like living mazes.

Behind him— Another deathbolt ripped through the street, disintegrating a bystander in a burst of pale light. Diego stumbled—but didn't stop. His hand fumbled for his dice. "Come on, baby...Daddy needs every favor you owe me."

Another blast detonated too close—shattering a clay urn beside him and splashing glowing black ichor across his boots. He vaulted over a stack of empty ley-essence jars, slipped between two startled vendors, and cast the dice across the cobblestones. It was a direct cast to the two pip dice.

Not as grand as the master die effects, more local, more focused on defense. Exactly what he needed.

The dice clattered. They glowed. BreakFold — 8 Space creased around him— a wrinkle in the air that folded him out of his own momentum. Diego vanished mid-stride, reappearing a heartbeat later around the next corner with a sharp snap of displaced wind.

Behind him, the Shackled rounded after him— hungry, twitching, their tethered souls flickering like dying halos above their heads. The first Shackled that turned the bend met its true death— body collapsing like a puppet with severed strings. Smoke rolled out the muzzle of Diego'r revolver. He turned and ran again.

But ahead—shadows moved. More Shackled. Approaching fast. They would cut him off. He juked right—but one lunged, slamming into him. Diego hit the ground—hard. The creature clawed at his coat, jaws snapping—until Diego drove an elbow into its jaw sharp enough to crack bone, then mule-kicked it off and scrambled to his feet.

That's when the ground beneath him cracked. A hiss—like a rupturing steam pipe—

A monstrous worm breached the surface—thick as a subway tunnel pipe plated in sewage-slick chitin glistening like wet obsidian.

Its mouth opened, ring of grinding razored teeth and tendrils snapping outward like living cables. It towered above him, turning its hungry maw toward the Shackled...and then toward him.

Diego backed up until his spine hit brick. "...Okay," he breathed, shaking. "We're gonna pretend I did NOT jinx myself."

The golden-masked Gravecaller rounded the corner behind him— hand raised, dark power building for the kill. Diego was cornered. Between death—and something that ate death.

The Gravecaller lifted its hand. The Mauler lunged first.

———

Lildan Blackwell slipped through the chaos like ink poured into water—quiet and seamless. She lived for the hunt. Her golden mask reflected the shattered lantern-light, smooth and cold as a funeral coin. She moved with the grace of a blade unsheathed.

Ahead, the gambler darted between collapsing stalls and scattering civilians, bouncing off crates and dodging bolts like a rabbit with too much luck and not enough sense. Her wand hummed in her palm. Kill the meddler, the thought whispered. End the disturbance. Silence the Hollow.

She raised her wand— A clay jug exploded inches from her face as something clipped the air beside her. A bottle? No— Too fast.

A dice-shaped shard of hardened probability magic screamed past her cheekbone, slicing a lock of her hair as it tore into a pillar behind her.

"Impossible," she hissed. He was rolling spells blindly, chaotically, and yet the dice obeyed him as if they had been born from his bones. He dodged left. She mirrored him instantly, cloak snapping behind her like a second shadow. He vaulted a stack of crates. She took two long gliding steps and cleared them without touching wood. He crashed into a fruit stall. She glided over the debris as if weightless. She lifted her wand again—

A violent pulse of raw probability blasted out of him, sending a lantern swinging wildly overhead. Its chain snapped. The lantern fell between them, flames licking upward. Lilidan snarled behind the mask. Enough games. She sliced her wand through the air.

Necrotic sigils ignited—cold, surgical— and she fired three bolts in rapid succession. —one—two—three— The gambler dove behind a toppled cart. Her spells hit the ground, detonating in plumes of green-black fire. He fled into a narrow alley.

She followed, steps silent, wand raised. A tremor shook the stone beneath her. Her eyes narrowed. "No..."

The street cracked. Heat—rot—pressure- The world split upward— And the Mauler erupted. A mountain of wormflesh, plated in glistening chitin, tendrils unfurling like the arms of a drowning corpse. Its maw opened, spiraling rings of teeth glistening with filth.

It reared between her and the gambler. Her words stuck in her throat. The Mauler turned toward her."No—"

She sprang back, cloak flaring. A tendril snapped around her waist. She was yanked into the air—spinning, feet kicking, wand falling from her fingers. The world blurred below her: stones, lanterns, bodies and then nothing but the THOUSANDS of razor teeth rising to meet her.

Her eyes went wide behind the mask. She twisted—desperate, fast— And vanished. A burst of violet smoke shredded in the Mauler's jaws as the tendril snapped down on empty air.

———

Diego saw her go flying. One moment the robed woman—gold mask gleaming under the false sky of the Hollow—was lifting her wand to kill him. The next—A Mauler tendril snapped around her waist and flung her upward like a broken puppet.

Her golden mask spun in the light. Her cloak fluttered like a torn shadow. She twisted mid-air, eyes wide behind the mask, seeing nothing below but a spiral of razored teeth rising to swallow her whole—

And then—She vanished in a burst of violet smoke. The Mauler's jaws snapped on empty air with a wet, bone-grinding clack. The beast reared back, enraged, tendrils whipping wildly, spattering gore across the broken street.

Then. Its attention swung, right to him. "Oh come on," Diego groaned. "Pick on someone your own—building." The Mauler lunged forward, smashing through lantern stands and trader stalls, sending fountains of flaming oil and sparks into the air.

Diego sprinted, dice already flicking between his fingers.

He cast mid-stride— ▢ Probability Break— 9. A rusted sign overhead snapped its chain and crashed down between him and the Mauler, slowing the worm just long enough for Diego to vault over a stack of crates and sprint across a wobbling plank bridge. The Mauler hit the fallen sign splintering it like matchwood, already slithering after him.

He sprinted, heart jackhammering, the world tilting slightly— Probability Blend humming through his bones, bending fate around him like a safety net made of chaos.

He didn't need to roll again. The universe was already cheating for him. The Shackled converged. One lunged from the left—claws like hooked bone. Another racked from the right—mouth stitched open in a perpetual scream. Behind them, the Mauler reared up, barbed tentacles unfurling like spears.

"Ah, hell—"

The Mauler strike descended. A barbed tendril whipping downward, powerful enough to cleave a man in half. Diego moved.

Probability Blend turning the world fluid beneath his feet— twisted in midair, spine arcing like a ribbon of spring steel— the one Shackled's claws swiped under him—missing his head by inches—The second Shackled's swipe grazed the air above his head—as Diego spread his legs mid-flight and let the strike hiss through the narrow gap between them. He hit the ground in a roll, boots skidding.

Behind him—The Mauler's tentacle impaled the street, carving a crater where he'd just been. Crushing both Shackled in its wake.

Diego pushed off the ground and ran. He dove headfirst through a shattered window into a narrow tailor's shop glass exploding around him as he crashed into a family of mannequins. They toppled like corpses in a puppet show. Behind him the Mauler rammed the building.

Stone burst outward. A tendril lanced through the wall and stabbed the floor where his head had been a heartbeat ago. Diego ducked low, scrambled over ruined shelves, and sprinted toward the back of the shop. He didn't even look when he smashed through the rear window— just tucked his knees and let momentum carry him into the alley behind it.

He hit the ground hard—rolled—looked up—and froze. Bare, pale feet stood just inches from him. Moonlit skin. Wings like frost-laced petals unfurling behind her. Narkiss.

Before her the Mauler smashed through the building, its massive head grinding through shattered beams and crushed stone, plates scraping, tendrils clawing for Diego's body.

Narkiss raised one delicate hand. Every tendril froze mid-snap. The Mauler's entire colossal body locked in place, plates tightening like seized metal. A spark of black fey-fire ignited deep in its chest. It grew. It roared. It imploded.

The Mauler collapsed inward, flesh folding like wet parchment, then detonated in a geyser of shadowflame and liquefied chitin. The shockwave shattered every window in the block.

When the echo died, the Shackled were nothing but ash drifting on cold air. Narkiss stepped past Diego, wings dimming.

"Until next time, Little gambler." she whispered. She dissolved into drifting motes of silver and shadow, leaving the ruined Hollow humming with fading magic. Diego closed his fist around his dice.

Burned. Exhausted. Alive.

"...Yeah," he breathed. "It's time to go." Diego clenched his dice in one shaking hand.

———

Lildan Blackwell materialized in a burst of violet smoke two alleys over, hitting the ground hard on her hands and knees. Her mask—cracked from the Mauler's tendril—clattered across the cobblestones. Her lungs burned. Her ribs ached. Her pride... hemorrhaged.

For several long, shuddering breaths, she didn't move. Not because she was injured. Because she was humiliated. She pushed herself upright, fingers trembling with fury, brushing ash and sewer grit from her bodice of black spider-silk. Her illusionary cloak flickered, Shredded from the Maulers attack.

"Damn him," she hissed.

The probability mage.

She didn't know his name, but she knew his power the impossible slips,

the near-misses that defied math, the way fate bent around him like a shield of cheating gods.

She spat blood to the side and seethed. A mere dice-slinger. And he had made a fool of her. But he hadn't been the true threat. The true threat had been her. Narkiss.

Lildan's hand unconsciously rose to her throat. The Exalted Mourned had turned the entire fight on its head in seconds. Even now, Lildan could still feel the weight of that presence—

cold, ancient, suffocating. " Two dozen Shackled and three Gravecallers," she whispered bitterly,

"and she swatted us aside like dust."

Her thoughts spiraled. Her brother would be furious. Not outwardly —Dorian never wasted emotion —but that quiet, disappointed silence that made her feel like a child again.

And Von Epp... Her stomach twisted. Von Epp probably watched the failed assault. He always watched. The thought of him observing her failure with amusement made her teeth grind. The idea of his smug anticipation — that they would fail —that Dorian was weak, that she was weaker —made bile rise in her throat.

"We should have killed her decades ago," she muttered. The Exalted Lady of the Mourned had always been an inconvenience —a ghost-queen of the Underwalk, too reclusive to bother hunting, too old to risk provoking. But tonight had proved the oldest nightmare of necromancers: The Mourned remember their killers.

Lildan stood, retrieving her cracked golden mask. She held it in the glow of a dying lantern— the fractures along the cheekbone looked like a spiderweb. A perfect metaphor. Her and Dorian's plan had collapsed. Their careful stalking of Narkiss had failed. Their attempt to clear the way for the Court had failed. And Dorian would blame her. He always did.

She slid the mask back over her face, the broken edges biting into her skin. "Next time," she whispered, voice low, venomous, shaking with restrained fury, "I will not underestimate either of you." She stepped into the shadows, robes swirling around her like living ink, determined that the next time she crossed paths with that dice mage, one of them wouldn't walk away.

———

Chase's boots hit the floor heavier than usual—wet, cold, still reeking faintly of Blackwell Island's rot and disinfectant. He'd changed into dry pants, but his shirt clung to him, dark and damp around the collar. He keyed the lock. "Skye? Diego?"

A voice floated in from the back room.

"Back here." Her voice was the first warm thing he'd heard all day.

Chase stepped inside. Papers, books, maps — everything was strewn across the room in a way Skye somehow made look organized. She sat cross-legged on his bed, wearing only one of his shirts, sleeves rolled up, hem brushing her thighs. A pencil was tucked behind her ear; a glass of wine perched beside her knee.

She didn't look up.

"You're soaked again," she said.

"And you're wearing my shirt," he replied.

"This is as clothed as you're getting me while we have an male house guest." Then, without looking away from the papers: "Your best friend doesn't get a Ziegfeld Follies show."

Chase smirked tiredly. "Fair."

But her humor faltered the second she saw his face. "What happened?"

He told her. Everything. The empty docks. The missing guards. The dead orderlies. The mad inmates whispering about "bone men." The chained Mourned. The doctor trapped in a closet. Coco Le Fay's destroyed cell. The Howlers. The Boggart.

By the time he finished, Skye's hand trembled around her wine glass. "That's..." she whispered. "That's horrific."

A sudden rap-rap-rap... rap-rap sounded at the window.

Skye didn't even flinch. "Diego."

Chase crossed the room, unlatched the sill—Diego Salazar climbed through the window like a man escaping a burning building — coat torn, hair wild, chest heaving as if he'd sprinted across the city.

He opened his mouth—Then saw Skye's bare legs.

"Okay, I swear, I was not looking—"

Skye didn't lift her eyes. "This is as clothed as I'm getting, Salazar. Shut up."

"I'm not complaining—"

"Also stop staring at my thighs."

Diego immediately stared at the ceiling. "Yes, ma'am."

Chase cleared his throat. "Diego."

"Right." Diego reached into his coat and dropped something onto the bed with a thunk.

A cracked, scorched bone-white mask.

Skye froze. "...Is that—?"

"A Gravecaller mask," Diego said. "One tried to evaporate me in the Hollow."

Chase stiffened. "You're sure?"

"Oh, very sure." Diego pointed to a blackened sigil burned into the fabric. "And look what was carved into his robes."

Chase's blood ran cold.

Skye leaned in. "What is that symbol?"

Chase exhaled through his teeth. "Its the symbol the Office of Death-Science, the Amt für Totenwissenschaft, lead by Herman von Epp."

Skye frowned. "What and Who?"

Diego looked at Chase. "You want to tell her, or should I?"

Chase rubbed a hand over his jaw. "Skye... Herman Von Epp was a German necromancer during the war. Not a battlefield caster — a mastermind. Verdun. The Ossuary Fields. He specialized in turning men into... things."

Diego nodded grimly. "Walking ossuaries. Bone choirs. The kind of horrors that don't stay buried."

Skye swallowed. "So you're saying... he's here? In New York?"

Chase shook his head. "We don't know. But someone loyal to him is definitely here."

Diego tapped the mask again. "That mark? Soldiers used to whisper about it. If you saw it on a trench wall, you turned around. If you saw it on a corpse... you ran."

Skye looked between them, troubled but focused. "Let me see the files," she whispered.

Chase handed her the damp ledger from Blackwell Island. She flipped pages slowly... then stopped at the visitor entry Chase mentioned earlier. Visitor: Morphan Veep. Skye stared. Brow furrowing. Her lips moved silently. "Morphan... Veep..."

She rearranged letters in the air with one fingertip. Chase watched her expression sharpen. Diego leaned in. Then Skye whispered:

"Oh my God. Chase... it's an anagram."

"For what?" he asked.

She swallowed.

"For Von Epp."

The room fell into a stunned silence. They gathered around the bed. Chase laid out everything from Blackwell Island. Skye arranged adoption records and missing-children files.

CHARLES DRAEVYN

Diego set the scorched Gravecaller mask between them like a cursed centerpiece.

"The Mourned we have been facing are not natural at all" Skye said as she traced a fingertip over the sketched collar sigils, voice low as she recognized intentional construction. "Someone had carved those markings, forced inmates past the Veil and bound them into walking husks."

"But, there hadn't been enough of them. Not enough bodies, not enough materials, not enough infrastructure. This wasn't mass-production," Chase said quietly. "Blackwell Island wasn't a factory. It was research. Testing. They were building something specific... not an army." Diego set down the scorched Gravecaller mask, jaw tightened. "And Gravecallers don't go shopping in broad daylight, if one was chasing me through the Hollow and the Market Macabre at that, someone high—very high—was sent them to kill or maybe capture Narkiss."

Skye flipped through adoption ledgers and orphanage logs, breath catching as she aligned names and dates. "All the murdered children came from the same orphanage. All except David Tran... and he had Fae blood too. A pattern. A harvest. A selection. "

Chase felt the realization settle like ice beneath his ribs: Domingo, the Mourned, Coco Le Fay—every one of them had converged on Benjamin. Coco had been experimented on and released by the same hand. Which meant Benjamin wasn't a casualty of circumstance. He was the objective. The target. The intended product of Von Epp's research. And Herman von Epp—Germany's butcher-mage of Verdun, the necromancer who stitched horrors out of dead men—wasn't dead at all. He was here, moving pieces across Manhattan like a general preparing for another war.

Silence settled over them. Then Skye stood, smoothing the hem of Chase's shirt.

"We need history," she said. "Documentation. Records the public never saw."

"The Arcane Historical Society," Chase agreed.

Diego nodded. "Good. Maybe they can tell us why a Gravecaller's wearing Von Epp's brand."

Skye began gathering papers into neat stacks. She picked up the envelope — the money from the Tran family — and tucked it into her briefcase. She snapped the latches shut. "Let me grab another bottle," she murmured, crossing toward the kitchen. "We'll need it."

Chase, exhausted down to the marrow, pulled the damp shirt from his shoulders and tossed it aside. The muscles in his back flexed, runes faintly visible beneath the skin like smoldering charcoal. He started unbuttoning his slacks, ready to finally breathe, finally shut out the world for a few hours.

Diego sat backward in one of Chase's chairs, elbows on the backrest, idly rolling a pair of dice across his knuckles. His dark eyes tracked Skye's movement with rueful amusement.

"Careful," he said lightly. "You start drinking that wine without me, I'll—"

The dice in his hands flared. A sudden pulse of pale, cold light.

Diego froze.

"...Chase," he whispered.

Chase's head lifted instantly, instincts snapping tight. Skye stopped at the edge of the kitchen, bare toes brushing the tile. "Diego?"

The dice glowed brighter.

Bright white. Then violet.

Then—

The world detonated.

A shockwave slammed through the apartment with a bone-rattling BOOM, blowing the kitchen windows inward in a shower of molten glass. She hit the far wall with a sickening thud and crumpled.

The flame roared across the ceiling like a living thing—racing along the beams, blooming into hungry orange claws that devoured the curtains and licked at the dividing walls.

Chase was already moving. "SKYE!"

Bookshelves ignited behind him. Papers caught fast. A thick carpet of heat rolled across the floorboards, smoke belching into the room in choking waves.

Skye didn't respond.

Chase lunged toward her, muscles coiling, dragging her limp body into his arms. Her head lolled against his chest, hair plastered to her cheek by ash and heat.

Outside the shattered window, voices rose in the alley: "Light another one! BURN THE BASTARD OUT!"

Another firebomb struck the outer brick with a wet whump, flames racing up the outside walls—hungry serpents climbing toward them.

Chase's eyes burned amber.

"Diego—BACK ROOM! Now!"

Diego didn't argue. He grabbed Chase by the shoulder, helping haul Skye's unconscious form toward the hallway. They half-carried, half-dragged her through the smoke, stumbling past the bookcase now roaring with flame. The door to the back room swung open window in sight—Diego's entrance route from earlier. Beyond it lay the fire-escape patio and a brief gap of cold night air.

Behind them, the apartment door splintered. Footsteps pounded in. Killers.

Half a dozens armed man. Boots. Metal striking wood. Scents of grease, cigarettes, and cordite.

"Make sure he's dead—check every damn corner!" a man snarled.

Diego shoved open the window to the fire escape, coughing hard, guiding Skye out into the freezing air. Her bare legs scraped against rusted metal, her breath shallow, unconscious but alive.

"You got her?" Chase growled.

"Yeah—yeah, go!"

Chase turned back.

And walked into hell.

The first thug burst into the burning kitchen and barely had time to register Chase's shadow before a fist hit him like a battering ram.

His jaw shattered. Teeth flew. He was dead before he hit the floor, spellbound strength fractured his skull across the kitchen. Gunfire erupted behind the doorway—wild, panicked. Chase moved through it like a storm.

Five left.

Another charged through the drifting smoke, firing wildly. Chase rolled across burning floorboards, heat licking his back. He came up under the man's guard, pointed tow fingers and drove it up beneath the jaw—an infernal lance punched through soft palate and into brain. The man's body seized, then sagged.

His eyes glowed—amber, sharp, predatory. Nothing human lived in that stare.

Four left.

Three men pushed forward in a wedge, guns out, shouting hoarsely through the roar of flame.

Chase's right forearm flared—the Sigil of the Searing Aegis ignited in a ring of ember-bright geometry. A hexagonal shield of molten orange light snapped into existence before him. A burst of gunfire slammed into the Aegis. The rounds hissed as the sigil drank the kinetic force. Chase flicked his wrist—and hurled the shield.

The Searing Aegis spun like a blazing discus, carving a burning arc through the smoke. It struck the first gunman at the waist. He came apart cleanly, the top half tumbling one direction, the legs collapsing in another. The shield cut through the wall behind him—wood sizzling—the exploded killing another goon, before dissipating in a burst of sparks.

Two left.

The next man raised his pistol—but Chase was already on him. His left forearm sigil erupted again: the Sigil of Infernal Lance. He thrust it into the attacker's midsection—the lance punched through ribs, lungs, and spine, then erupted from the man's back in a shower of smoking gore. Chase lifted, severing the man vertically.

One left.

The last hitman fired again. Chase dodged aside—firelight streaking across his face as he slid behind an overturned table. The gunman took a step forward— Chase surged up, Sigil of Infernal Strife glowing along his knuckles.

He punched the man in the chest. The blow landed like a grenade. Ribs detonated outward. The man flew backward into the burning wall, leaving a crater of splintered wood and soot.

"Wh-what the hell ARE you—?" He asked before death took him. Silence swallowed the room. Only the crackle of fire. Only the stink of gunpowder and burning bodies. Only Chase Cassidy—chest rising slowly, sigils dimming back to sleep—standing amid the dead.

The apartment was collapsing around him. He turned and sprinted toward the fire escape. Gunshots cracked from below. Chase vaulted through the window—feet skidding across the metal grating. Smoke trailed behind him in dark ribbons.

Diego stood at the edge of the landing, panting, revolver smoking in his shaking hand. At his feet lay a dead mafioso—his body twisted, skull leaking onto the alley stones.

Skye stirred beside him, blinking awake at last, eyes glassy and unfocused. "...Chase?" she murmured.

He dropped to his knees beside her, cupping the side of her soot-marked face. "I've got you," he breathed. "Sky—look at me. I've got you."

Diego looked up at the burning apartment behind them. Flames burst from the windows, climbing the brick like molten vines. "That," he said between harsh breaths, "was not random."

Skye's fingers tightened weakly around Chase's wrist.

The building continued to burn—a roaring inferno swallowing everything they owned. But they were alive. And someone wanted them dead badly enough to send an army. Chase looked up at the night sky, jaw clenched so tight it trembled. "They just made the biggest mistake of their lives."

CHAPTER 5

The Gathering of Graves

"Perhaps this will be the only thing I ever write."

A queen does not confess—she records. And so I set down this truth, if only to savor it:

The Court of Bones was never meant to be a council. It was a promise. A covenant for the forgotten, the cast-off, the dead who refused to remain dead. Others see only rot and ritual, but we are the memory of power—power stolen, reclaimed, reshaped in marrow and silence.

Each seat in the Court is a grave.

Each grave is a throne.

And every throne demands sacrifice.

And I have sacrificed much.

The living quake because they sense it—

the dead have begun to move with purpose again.

And soon, when the last light falters,

they will remember who taught them to fear the night. **A. M. Ruthven**

The chamber beneath the East River thrummed with necromantic pressure—stone sweating, torches flickering with violet flame, and the blood bath behind her still hot enough to steam. The scent of iron hung thick in the air.

Adriana Mortem Ruthven stood at the edge of the pool, reborn.

Her porcelain skin gleamed—flawless once more. No rot. No decay. Only the ageless beauty she had possessed before death first claimed her. Wisps of crimson steam curled from her; the lingering heat of the Fey child's blood still pulsed through her veins.

Two Gravecaller knelt before her, their bone-masked faces bowed as they wiped the last traces of coagulated blood from her legs with reverent care. Their skeletal gloves never trembled. Their devotion was absolute.

A third stepped forward, offering her a robe of midnight silk woven with argent sigils. Adriana lifted her arms with regal indifference as they dressed her in ritual layers—mantle, corset, gown, and finally the silver-chained cuffs that jingled faintly with fragments of bound souls.

She stepped onto the raised dais.

The Court of Bones had arrived.

Dorian Blackwell entered first—lean, pale, with the sort of slicked-back blond hair only an aristocrat could maintain in an underground crypt. His sister, Lilidan, followed with a serene smile that never touched her eyes.

They bowed shallowly.

"First Seat."

Adriana blinked once, unimpressed.

Next came six Gravecallers—hooded, masked, crimson-and-black robes whispering across stone as they moved their numbers dwindled after the Blackwells failed assault on the Pale Mother. They knelt in perfect synchronicity, heads bowed. They were living monoliths of death's authority.

Then the air fractured with a ripple of malignant power.

Hermann von Epp stepped into the chamber. Tall, skeletal, dressed in his old Imperial death-mage uniform—black coat with tarnished gold trim and epaulettes that whispered of toppled kingdoms. Frost followed him like a loyal dog.

He bowed deeper than the Blackwells, but not by much.

"First Seat."

Behind him, the Twilight Collective entered.

Makalith Ravenwind led them—viper-graceful, Fey-blood sharp, duelist's coat immaculate. His expression was one of studied boredom, but his green eyes flicked sharply from shadow to shadow.

Sirus Magnus followed, cane clicking as he walked, gaze calculating, loyal only to profit. And last came Coo-Coo Le Fay—still in her tattered ballerina rags, and dirty straight jacket humming to herself, twirling, then stopping abruptly to stare at Adriana with rapt adoration.

Lucien Monceau's seat remained empty. Von Epp noticed. He said nothing. Not yet.

Adriana lifted her chin, silver chains chiming softly.

"Faithful... we are nearly restored." Her voice was velvet stretched over knives. "The old world forgot us. But we did not forget the old world." A whisper of agreement slithered through the chamber.

Von Epp stepped forward, fists clasped behind his back.

"And the vessel? Is our benefactor pleased with the new body?"

"The host is agreeable," Adriana said. "Aspen Willowbark—three-quarters Fey. The Lord of Bones will walk again."

Lilidan's eyebrows lifted."A bold choice."

"Necessary," Adriana replied. "Benjamin Bright has escaped us, and the boy bears the taint of prophecy. We shall not wait for fate's whims."

Von Epp's nostrils flared with rare anger. "His escape should have been impossible."

Makalith's jaw twitched. Sirus's eyes narrowed. Coco giggled. "He wriggled away. Like a fox with tiny little paws."

Adriana silenced them with a glance. "Regardless, we move forward." She turned slightly, the jewels on her wrists glowing. "The sarcophagus is restored. My flesh renewed. But for the ritual to proceed, we must reclaim what was taken from us."

Von Epp stepped closer. "The Crown of Mortem."

Gasps fluttered through the Blackwells. Even the Gravecallers stirred. Adriana smiled—a slow unfurling of predatory delight. "Yes."

"That relic," Adriana continued, "rests in the vaults of the Arcane Historical Society. Guarded. Ward-bound. Watched over by fools who believe lineage grants dominion."

Her eyes drifted to Makalith. "You will retrieve it."

A muscle in Makalith's jaw ticked. "As you command, First Seat." He said bowing deeply. With a sharp spin on his heel he exited. Sirus followed.

Coco clapped lightly as she trailed behind "Ooooh, a heist! Can I dance with the crown on and be a faerie queen?"

No answer can from either mage. With the collective gone, the seated continued with darker business. Von Epp glanced at the empty chair to Adriana's left. "And the Fourth Seat? Still absent?"

Adriana's expression flickered. "Lucien Monceau is... misplaced."

"He fled, like the coward he is." von Epp muttered.

"He will return, they always return. And when he does, with his secrets and the Lord of Bones returned, nothing will stand before us. " she repeated, voice cold as a crypt. No one spoke after that. Adriana raised her hands. "The lord will rupture the veil and our dominion will be begin."

The Gravecallers bowed as one. "As you will it, First Seat." Adriana Mortem Ruthven's smile sharpened. The ritual chamber emptied. Adriana's voice—serene, cold, triumphant—still seemed to vibrate in the very bones of the stone.

———

In a deeper antechamber lit by guttering green lamps, the air felt different. Thicker. Meaner. A cold slab dominated the room. Upon it lay Utilis the Rover—long limbs splayed, spine bowed, the cracked gas mask fogging with each rasping inhale. His right arm was gone from the elbow down, the wound still ringed with necrotic stitching.

Makalith stood over him, sleeves rolled past the elbow, surgical gloves slick with embalming gel and essence-oil. Arcane tools floated in the air around him—needles, bone screws, clamps, and rune-tipped drivers —each guided by precise movements of his fingers.

A necro-mechanical arm rested on a tray beside him.

A marvel.

A horror.

Copper, bone, and soul-steel braided into one seamless limb, its runes still smoldering faintly from their final forging.

Coo-Coo Le Fey prowled the periphery of the room, bare feet whispering across stone as she muttered broken lullabies. Every so often, she cast a murderous glare toward the chamber they'd just left. Sirus Magnus leaned against the wall with his cane resting between both hands, watching Makalith work, jaw tight.

Makalith secured the last pin, then stepped back. "There," he said smoothly. "Try it."

Utilis flexed his new fingers. The metal tendons tightened with a hiss of steam and whispered soul-fire. The claws clicked together—beautifully articulated, horribly sharp.

The necrotic fluid in his goggles sloshed with hungry excitement. "Ohhh," he whispered through the mask. "She purrs."

Coco's laugh cracked like porcelain. "Better enjoy it, Utilis. You'll need both hands when I peel Adriana's skin off her bones."

Sirus stiffened. "Lower your voice. The walls have ears."

"They're welcome to hear me!" Coo-Coo snarled, wings flaring violently. "She drained that child. A child, Makalith! A songborn!" Her voice splintered into a sob, then a giggle, then a hiss.

"Enough," Makalith said sharply. The room fell quiet. He peeled off the surgical gloves, tossing them into a bin of burning green flame. The gloves disintegrated instantly, leaving only ash.

Sirus cleared his throat. "That arm," he said. "Where did you get the graft? That's not standard necro-chassis."

A thin smile curved Makalith's lips. "From a mortician. A local one. A specialist." He wiped his hands on a cloth. "Doctor Buzzard."

Sirus blinked. "The city coroner?"

"He prefers 'medical necro-mechanist,'" Makalith said dryly. "He does excellent work. He had no idea who the limb was intended for—and he was paid to ask no questions."

CoCo twirled once and stopped sharply—too sharply. "Buzzard... Buzzard... I like that name. Buzzards eat dead things."

Utilis flexed his new arm again, letting the claws click. "Dead things... like me."

Makalith ignored his theatrics. "I didn't bring you all here to admire my craftsmanship."

He stepped closer, lowering his voice. "We have a problem."

Sirus stared hard. "Von Epp."

"Von Epp," Makalith confirmed. "He wants a scapegoat for losing Benjamin Bright. The Court will not accept blame. They will not hold their confidant accountable. They are looking at us."

Sirus's grip on his cane tightened. "And if they decide we're no longer useful…"

Utilis hummed, mimicking the sound of a neck being snapped. Makalith's voice dropped lower, colder. "We will secure Willowbark as they asked, will get the Crown of Mortum, and afterward… when she and von Epp perform their ritual…"

Utilis 'head tilted. "We kill them." Sirus inhaled sharply—but did not disagree.

Coo-Coo's smile spread slowly, unnervingly, like blood in water. "I want her last breath," she whispered. "I want her eyes when she realizes the child she drank is why she dies."

Makalith didn't flinch. "You will get your wish." He leaned over the slab, tightening one of the soul-steel screws in Utilis's arm.

"Von Epp wants to be First Seat, he will strike after the ritual. when Adriana will be at her weakest, drained from the ritual." His voice softened to a razor's whisper. "If we kill him during the ritual, when Adriana and the Blackwells are distracted…"

Sirus nodded."…then Von Epp dies with no help."

Makalith looked up. "The Blackwells will not defend Adriana, we move on her after the ritual as Von Epp is planning. "

Utlis interjected" But first we must get Aspen and the Crown."

"Yes." Makalith said "We need those to get them to lower their guard. They will be flushed with success the will not suspect. We go tonight. We hit the Arcane Historical Society first. Then Willowbark. Then we gut the Court when they are most vulnerable."

Utilis flexed his new claws. Coo-Coo twirled, giggling. Sirus tapped his cane twice, sealing his approval. Makalith Ravenwind placed both palms on the slab.

"The Court thinks we serve them." His smile sharpened. "They are wrong."

———

Hermann Von Epp stood alone at the center of the room, coat folded neatly behind him, pale hands clasped behind his back. Behind him, a slanted table was covered in scrolls, old vellum maps, necrotic diagrams, and a rendered sketch of the Crown of Mortem.

He did not turn when the little homunculus scampered inside. He did not need to. "I heard you coming," Von Epp murmured. "Report."

The creature climbed his coat, scurried over his shoulder, and perched on his collarbone like a ghastly familiar. Its stitched mouth opened—and Makalith's voice emerged. Every word spoken in the antechamber. Every threat. Every whispered treachery. Von Epp listened with the stillness of a frozen lake. When the tiny creature finished, he plucked it from his shoulder and set it on the table beside the scrolls. Its beetle-eye blinked once, twice, awaiting orders.

Behind him, footsteps approached.

Dorian Blackwell entered first—tall, elegant, aristocratic, his movements smooth as oiled gears. Liidan followed, her smile thin and cruel, raven-dark hair falling in waves over cold blue eyes. Dorian inclined his head. "You summoned us."

Von Epp nodded once. "The Twilight Collective intends betrayal."

Lilidan laughed softly, her voice like cracking ice. "Oh Makalith, you arrogant little dove. I told you he would try something."

Dorian folded his hands behind his back. "Do they know we're aware?"

"Of course not." Von Epp touched the homunculus gently beneath the chin. "They believe themselves clever."

Lilithan arched a brow. "And are they? Clever enough to cause us inconvenience?"

Von Epp's lips curled faintly. "Not anymore." He stepped toward the central table where a map of Manhattan lay spread across black iron. "The Collective means to seize both the Crown of Mortem and the alternate vessel before delivering them here. They expect gratitude. They believe once we start the ritual, our eyes will be so focus on the rise of our Lord, that we will be susceptible to betrayal "

Dorian scoffed. "Makalith never understood power. He mistakes proximity for partnership."

Von Epp looked down at the homunculus—the dark little thing watching them with mismatched eyes. "Let them proceed."

Lilidan tilted her head, amused. "Let them?"

"Yes," Von Epp said plainly. "Makalith is efficient. He will retrieve the Crown. He will bring the Willowbark boy. He will do our work." His eyes hardened. "And once he arrives—once the Collective is within our walls, exhausted from battle, holding stolen relics—"

Dorian smiled slowly. "We kill them."

Von Epp nodded. "Every one of them."

Lilidan stepped closer, her gown whispering like dead leaves."And Adriana?"

Von Epp's face remained unreadable. "She will be grateful for the removal of complications. And when her ritual begins, no mercenary interference will threaten the ascension."

Lilidan purred, "There this something you should be made aware of. There was... a disturbance"

"Go on." Von Epp demanded.

Dorian stepped forward, jaw tight. "Blackwell Island has been breached."

Von Epp's quill paused just slightly. "How far?"

Dorian exhaled through his nose. "All the way. Down to your inner laboratories. All restraints and wards were compromised."

Von Epp lifted his head then. Very slowly.

Lilidan continued, "The intruder decimated the security rovers, neutralized the Bogarts, bypassed the inner seals, and discovered the altered Mourned." She leaned closer to the mirror, eyes gleaming. "Someone touched your work."

A pulse of necrotic energy flickered around von Epp's fingers. "Someone?" His voice was cold marble. "Or something?"

Dorian inclined his head. "The Spellbound. The same one from the docks. The one accompanied by the First Arcane officer."

Von Epp's gray eyes settled on him with a quiet, lethal amusement. "Everything is relevant," von Epp hissed. "Clear out what you can. Destroy the rest. "

Dorian cleared his throat, grateful for the shift in focus. "There is more. Four Gravecallers—ours—were slain in the Hollow. Their remains recovered, their marks destroyed. Except one."

Von Epp's lips twitched. "What were they doing in the Hollow?" Von Epp knew already having spied the twin's ill fated assault on the pocket veil.

Lilidan's smile widened. "We went after…Narkiss, Herr von Epp. A foolish decision, but one we felt necessary."

"Necessary?" von Epp repeated, "It was bold…and foolish. Narcissi has long been a thorn in my research but she is nota player on the board. She cares only for her shop and those who have the means to pay for her services."

He turned to face the twins. "And this Spellbound… does he have a name?"

Dorian answered quickly—too quickly. "Chase Cassidy."

Von Epp lowered his quill. "Cassidy," he murmured.

Dorian added, "We also believe he is aligned with a woman. A young attorney. Skye Anderson."

Von Epp frowned faintly. "Anderson 'means nothing to me."

Lilidan tapped her nails against the mirror's surface, amused. "It means something to us. Our family retained Anderson & Pierce once—years past. Their firm is… inconveniently competent. Thomas and Donald, an odd couple. A negro and white man in business."

Dorian added, "Their daughter is of age now. Likely the same Skye Anderson working alongside the Spellbound."

Von Epp leaned forward. "So Cassidy… and the Anderson girl… have interfered with my Gravecallers, my laboratories, my experiments… and my patience." Cold light flared in the chamber. "And retaliation is required. For my Gravecallers," he said, "I want two lives. Thomas Anderson. Donald Pierce."

Lilidan inhaled, delighted. Dorian bowed his head once. "They will die," he said.

"Quietly," von Epp added. "Cleanly. No spectacle. I want precision, not chaos."

The homunculus rattled its stitched jaw. Von Epp looked at it with cold affection. "Go. Continue watching the Collective. Report eveything " The creature bowed, scuttled down the table leg, and vanished into a crack in the stone. Silence settled.

Then Dorian spoke lazily, brushing dust from his cuff. "And if—just if—Makalith survives the encounter. He will be a dangerous enemy?"

Von Epp's smile was thin and final.

"He won't." Von Epp ordered" Prepare the Mourned to attack their quarters when they return."

The twins exchanged a glance. Dorian bowed. "As you wish." Lilidan echoed the gesture... but her eyes flickered with something else. Something hungry.

———

Once they left Von Epp, the twins did not descend into the barracks or the ritual halls. They slipped into the far northern wing of the underground lair into a chamber sealed with black resin and bone-lattice locks.

Only siblings could enter together. Their magic required synchronicity to open the door. The moment the seals clicked shut behind them, Lilidan spoke first. "Brother. He's grown arrogant."

Dorian nodded. "Von Epp always overreaches. Adriana trusts him... but the Court obeys legacy, not genius. Second Seat is hereditary by prestige, not merit."

"And we," Lilidan murmured, touching her brother's face with graceful fingertips, "are Blackwells. Our claim is older. Purer."

Dorian smiled faintly, adjusting his cuffs. "He used to frighten me. Now? He is sloppy. Emotional. Furious about losing the boy. A man like that makes mistakes."

Lilidan tilted her head. "And mistakes open doors."

Dorian crossed to the far wall where the orb hung suspended, its silver surface rippling as if disturbed from within. A twist of his fingers parted the mists, revealing the chamber of the Twilight Collective beyond.

Makalith and Sirus were deep in low conversation. Utilis sat on a stone slab, grunting as necro-mechanical grafts were bolted into the marrow of his arm—sparks jumping, flesh hissing. He endured it with the dull patience of something half-made for pain.

Lilithan tilted her head. "Shall we warn them?"

Dorian's smile sharpened. "No."

She blinked once, surprised. "If Von Epp means to purge them—"

"All the better," he murmured. His eyes never left the window of swirling light. "Let them flail. Let them scramble. Let them realize, far too late, that they were nothing but tools."

Lilithan stepped closer, voice soft. "But if they panic, they might interfere with Adriana's ritual."

"They might," Dorian agreed. "And if they do, we learn exactly how Von Epp responds when his perfect order begins to crack." His eyes glinted. "Weakness bleeds through cracks."

Lilithan considered that, then relaxed against the wall beside him. "So we watch."

"We watch," Dorian said, "and wait. If Von Epp falters—if someone reveals where his little... source is hidden—then we strike. Not before."

Below, the orb's image shifted: the Collective continued unaware, Makalith drawing sigils in the dust, Sirus checking runes, Utilis flexing his newly bolted claws with a hiss.

Dorian closed his hand, and the orb darkened.

"Let Von Epp clean his own house," he said. "If he destroys them, good. If they destroy him, better." A faint, pleased breath. "And if both are wounded in the struggle..."

Lilithan smiled. "Then Second Seat becomes vacant."

"And we," Dorian whispered, "ascend."

———

The bowels of The Bitter End stank of bile, sweat, and old executions. Smoke clung to the ceiling in greasy layers; rusted hooks swayed gently with every footfall above. Beneath a single drooping bulb, Camilo Delgado sat in his reinforced chair—the one scarred with tally marks, each scratch a grave no one talked about.

His face was still a disaster.

Chase Cassidy had broken him—literally. The bones healed crooked despite the potions and bone-knitting tinctures. One cheek sat higher than the other, his nose permanently offset, and one eye twitched in a constant spasm that made his rage look feral.

The humiliation festered.

Camilo drew on his cigarette long and slow. When he exhaled, the smoke came out warped through the ruined cartilage of his nose.

Three of his men sat before him. Heads down. Hands trembling. He let them sweat before speaking. "So," he rasped, voice ruined stone, "Cassidy survived a goddamn inferno."

None answered. The closest one licked his lips. "We—we planted the device right, boss. The firebomb lit the whole floor, shoulda cooked him good but—"

Camilo punched him. Hard enough to make teeth scatter across the concrete. The man collapsed, choking on blood.

"Cassidy is a curse in a suit," Camilo snarled. "I told you rats that fire wasn't enough."

He stood, moving slow, letting them feel the weight of him. He wasn't tall, but he radiated violence the way some men radiated heat.

"You bring me excuses after he walked out smiling." A second man tried speaking. "Boss... we got word from the docks."

Camilo paused. Turned. "The docks?"

"Yeah. From Sykes 'boys. Something's wrong with one of the inbound lanes. The big overseas crates—you know, the French whiskey and the Havana shipments they run through Warehouse 24—they didn't clear the way they were supposed to."

Camilo's good eye narrowed. "What do you mean didn't clear?"

"They say the shipments got delayed. Guards went missing. Foreman too. Some crazy talk about screams under the floorboards. And then the BAE rolled in and shut down the whole pier. No one gets near the place."

The third goon jumped in. "Even Luciano's men couldn't get product through last night. Everyone's grumbling. Sykes is locking everything down."

Camilo leaned back, absorbing that. Sykes—king of the docks. Sykes—who every bootlegger, thief, mage-runner, and blood-dealer in Madhatten had to pay just to move crates. Sykes—whose position Camilo hated almost as much as Cassidy.

Camilo's voice dropped to a chilling murmur"So my own shipments get held hostage... because Sykes lost control of his pier."

A muscle ticked in his jaw. "And Cassidy?" he whispered. "Wasn't he sniffing around Warehouse 24 two nights ago?" No one answered. They didn't have to. The connection was obvious.

Camilo flicked ash onto the unconscious goon's coat. "That ain't coincidence." He paced a slow circle, ruined face half in shadow. "If Sykes' house is shaking," he said, "then the king of the docks ain't as untouchable as he thinks."

Silence. Then:

"Send one of our boys down there," he ordered. "Quiet. Someone who knows how to keep their nose down and their eyes open. I want to know exactly what the BAE blocked off, why the guards disappeared, and what's crawling around under Sykes 'floorboards."

One goon scrambled to his feet.

"And tell the rest of you rats," Camilo continued, "to start sniffing out alternate routes. If Sykes 'pipeline is crackin'..." His good eye twitched. His smile was thin and sharp. "...then maybe it's time someone else puts a knife in the river king's ribs."

He crushed the cigarette under his heel. "And if Cassidy's at the center of this mess—" He exhaled once, a hot, ruined breath. "—then we gut him before he gets a chance to breathe."

CHAPTER 6

The Anatomy of a Court

*The Old World & the New —Atticus Grey, Curator
of the Arcane Historical Society*

The Old World of magic was built on lineage, ritual, and restraint. Power moved in measured circles—inheritance, tradition, consequence. In the East, a spell was a covenant, and every wand stroke bore the weight of centuries.

But the New World... the New World treats magic like machinery. Spellbinding grafts, infernal engines, arcane munitions—tools forged with no patience for the cost. America bends the supernatural the way it bends steel: quickly, violently, and with little regard for what breaks in the process.

Old magic remembers.

New magic forgets.

And between the two stands a generation—caught in the friction of forces neither side fully understands.

Dawn crept up on Madhatten like a bruised eye opening. The apartment building was a charred carcass, ribs of blackened wood jutting into the pale morning sky. Smoke drifted in thin ghosts from the shattered windows, hissing where it met the cold. Fire hoses sprawled across the street like shed serpents. Steam rolled in waves. Neighbors stood behind police tape—shivering, some crying, others staring in shock at what was left of their homes.

Chase Cassidy stood barefoot in the ruined doorway.

His soles ground against broken glass. The frame around him was half-collapsed, a skeleton of blistered wood and twisted metal. What remained of his living room was little more than cinders. But some things had survived.

Effie and Pearl lay on the floor near his scorched warlocker— their runes glowing faintly blue, undamaged by the blaze. The Thompson machine gun case beside them was blackened at the edges but intact.

Everything else was ash.

Captain Whitman stepped up beside him, breath fogging in the cold air. His overcoat was half-buttoned, his hat missing, and he looked like a man who hadn't slept in a week. "This was no gas leak," Whitman growled. "This was a damned execution." Behind them, flames sizzled as O'Leary directed the last of the fire crews, shouting at two rookies like they'd personally offended his ancestry.

A crunch sounded behind Chase.

Skye Anderson stepped through the debris, lifting her knees carefully over a fallen beam. She was still wearing one of Chase's shirts, oversized and barely long enough to count as clothing—its hem brushing the tops of her thighs. Ash streaked her bare legs. Her hair was yanked into a messy knot, face smudged with soot.

She spotted a pair of battered work boots half-buried under a collapsed shelf. Without ceremony, she toed them upright and pulled them on barefoot.

Whitman turned, eyes widening. "Jesus, Anderson—lucky you weren't in the kitchen when the bomb went off."

Skye fixed him with a flat stare. "I was in the kitchen."

Whitman froze. "...Hell."

"You should get checked out," he said reflexively.

"I'm fine."

"That's not a suggestion."

Skye bristled. "Captain Whitman, with all due respect, no one is calling a medic for them." Pointing to Chase and Diego " And no one is calling my parents. I'm a grown woman. So please—stop treating me like a child."

Her voice trembled—not with fear, but with raw anger.

Whitman swallowed hard. "Right. Fair point."

Chase stepped forward, voice low. "You sure you're okay?"

Skye's jaw tightened. "I'll live."

Diego approached from the window frame, brushing ash off his sleeves. He looked pale, shaky, still coming down from adrenaline and smoke.

Whitman's eyes caught him. He snorted. "I should've known trouble was coming the moment I saw you."

Diego grinned weakly and shook his hand. "Good to see you too, Captain."

"Still gambling with fate, Salazar?"

"Against all odds."

Whitman huffed. "I'll take what I can get."

Chase gestured to the charred walls. "This was Del Gato."

Whitman nodded grimly. "Matches his signature. Homemade accelerants. Improvised firebombs. Bastard used enough to bring down a stable."

Skye's gaze drifted to the apartment next door, where paramedics tended to a crying woman and her burned husband.

"People got hurt," she whispered. "Families. Kids."

Diego tightened his grip on his dice. "We can't live in places like this anymore. Not with maniacs throwing bombs through the windows."

Chase exhaled. "Yeah. There's your duplex duplex. How do you feel after... everything."

" I'm definitely not staying there," Skye muttered.

Whitman rubbed his brow. "You three need someplace discreet. Warded. Off-grid."

Skye nodded. "That leaves one option."

"The safe house?" Chase guessed.

She folded her arms. "I'll need Donald and Thomas's approval."

"After last night," Chase replied, "they'd be insane to say no."

A voice called from the street.

"Skye!" Nadine Holloway hurried up the steps, bundled in a heavy coat, face etched with worry. She carried a garment bag and a satchel.

"Oh my god," she breathed. "I came as soon as you called. I could believe it until I saw it with my own eyes. Lets get you sorted. " Without waiting for permission, Nadine dropped the bag at her feet and pulled out a large blanket" Here, let me hold this up and...Skye!"

Skye impatiently unbuttoned Chase's shirt without waiting for Nadine's modesty blanket—Whitman choked, Diego whipped his head away—and she stepped into clean trousers and a blouse. She slipped on a long coat Nadine had brought, tying it tight. Nadine rolled her eyes "Unbelievable."

"Ms. Anderson?"

Skye turned sharply. A young man in a rumpled suit jogged up the steps, clutching a leather satchel to his chest. He was pale, out of breath, and clearly terrified of interrupting anything involving fire, police, or Chase Cassidy. Skye gave Whitman a burning look.

Whitman raised both hands immediately. "Not me. I didn't call him."

The clerk swallowed. "Ms. Anderson—I'm from the office. Mr. Pierce sent me."

Skye's eyes narrowed. "This better be good."

"It's Enzo Rivera," the clerk said, breathless. "His case... it's been moved up."

Skye froze. "What?"

He nodded anxiously. "Moved up to today. His appointed counsel withdrew this morning."

"What reason?" she snapped.

"No reason listed, ma'am." The clerk offered the satchel with shaking hands. "Mr. Pierce said you'd want the updated files."

Nadine muttered under her breath, "Railroading that poor boy..."

Skye tore open the satchel, scanning the documents inside. Her jaw tightened, tension coiling through her posture like a drawn bowstring.

Chase watched her closely.

Duty was pulling her in two directions — hard. "Why, why is this happening now of all times, can a girl have a minute."

He stepped closer. "Skye... go."

She looked up at him, conflicted. "Chase, after last night—"

"After last night," he said quietly, "that kid needs you more. Diego and I can handle what's next."

Diego nodded firmly. "Yeah. Go defend the innocent. We'll go punch necromancers."

Whitman cleared his throat. "Preferably not in that order, Salazar."

Diego shrugged.

Skye exhaled, shutting the satchel. "Fine. But you two stay in touch. No running off without telling me."

Chase smirked. "Wouldn't dream of it."

She gave him a tired, warm kiss— then turned and strode toward the street with Nadine in tow, coat sweeping behind her, satchel clutched tight.

———

The Society of Arcane History sat like a forgotten mausoleum at the far edge of Midtown—once a grand marble institution, now half-swallowed by scaffolding and soot. It rose out of the mist like a cathedral carved from old secrets.

As the steps of the Society rose before them, weathered by rain and old magic. Chase slowed. Then stopped. Diego took two more steps before realizing he was suddenly alone.

He turned. "What? You forget how stairs work now?"

Chase didn't smile. He just looked at him—really looked at him—smoke still clinging to his coat, the firebombing fresh behind his eyes.

"Are you sure about this?" Chase asked quietly.

Diego blinked. "About what?"

"This." Chase gestured vaguely—toward the ruined city, toward the Society, toward everything. "The war was one thing. Hell, we didn't even expect to live through any of it. But this?" He shook his head. "This is my job, Diego. You don't owe it a damn thing. Skye shouldn't even be part of it. We're dealing with the Court of Bones... and now a mobster who can't take an ass-kicking with dignity."

Diego's jaw tightened. "Speaking of which—what exactly are we doing about that firebomb bullshit? Because, last I checked, I was in that house too."

Chase exhaled through his nose, something hard passing through his expression.

"Right now? We've got bigger problems than Camilo De Gato. I'll get him soon enough."

"Chase," Diego said firmly, "you're my brother. That means your enemies? They're mine. Doesn't matter if they're shamblers, necro-witches, mobsters, or ghosts wearing skin. I'm here. That's the beginning and the end of it."

Chase held his eyes a moment longer, then nodded once. They climbed the remaining steps together. Chase pushed open the heavy brass door, Diego following beside him, his usual swagger dimmed but intact. Inside, the air smelled of dust, candlewax, and old magic,

The foyer was quiet—eerily so. Rows of glass cases lined the walls, each holding artifacts older than the city itself: cracked grimoires, preserved runic bones, preserved foci, ancient spell staves.

A small desk sat beneath a sign:

INFORMATION – DR. ATTICUS GREY

Diego whispered, "This place gives me the creeps."

"Everything gives you the creeps," Chase muttered.

"No, Cassidy. This place feels like it's waiting for us."

Chase couldn't deny it. His sigils—still faintly inflamed from the firebombing fight—itched beneath his sleeves. Danger wasn't here, exactly... but something watching was.

Across the marble floor, a thin man drifted from behind a bookcase —long white hair, spectacles perched on the bridge of his nose. His velvet coat brushed the ground like fog.

"Good morning," he said, voice ghost-soft but sharp. "You look like men seeking answers. Or men seeking trouble."

"Usually both," Diego said.

Dr. Atticus Grey's eyes glinted with humor.

"And what brings the Spellbound Hexbreaker and his probability-warping companion to my humble archive?"

Chase stiffened. "How did you—"

Grey waved a dismissive hand. "Magic leaves footprints. Your partner leaves bootprints all over the metaphysical floor."

Diego blinked. "I... do?"

"Yes. It's a miracle you haven't been arrested by reality yet."

"I knew it," Diego whispered.

Chase stepped forward. "We're looking for information on a man named Herman von Epp. Ex-Imperial German necromancer. Likely operating on U.S. soil."

Dr. Grey stilled. It was the kind of stillness that meant a name had weight. A name carried by ghosts. He turned slowly toward a dark alcove. "Follow me."

The alcove led into a stairwell spiraling downward into a subterranean chamber lit only by floating witch-lights. Dust motes drifted like ghost fire in the air.

Grey stopped before a massive iron cabinet covered in bone sigils. "This," he said, "is the Archive of the Unburied. Records of things the government by way off the Bureau tried—and failed—to erase from history."

He unlocked the cabinet with three keys and a whispered charm. Metal hissed open. Inside lay a single leather-bound tome. Its cover was branded with a crowned skull.

Diego stepped back. "...yeah, no. Nope. I don't like that."

Chase's pulse quickened. "What is that?"

Grey exhaled, voice dropping to a reverent hush.

"The Codex Ossium. Chronicle of the Court of Bones."

Diego swore under his breath. "Court of what now?"

Grey removed the book with careful hands. "The Court of Bones," he repeated. "One of the oldest necromantic orders in Europe. Predates the

Inquisition. Von Epp name sits among their ranks."

Chase and Diego exchanged a look. Grey continued.

"They were believed extinct. Hunted down. Scattered. Their High Seat—Adriana Mortem—was thought to have died in the 1600s."

Chase's jaw clenched. "Mortem. I saw that name written in a ledger on Blackwell Island"

Grey paused mid-turn. "Its an old family blessed with questionably long lifespans. One known for the use of sacrificial rights among other perversions. There were rumors that their long life was due to... vampirism."

"That explains the soil at the docks." Chase's voice was flat. "She was... sleeping."

Diego added quietly, "And she's here now."

Dr. Grey paled. He opened the tome with shaking fingers and turned several pages. Script written in ink that looked suspiciously like dried blood detailed their hierarchy, their rituals, their relics. Then he found the page he was looking for.

"The Crown of Mortem," he whispered. "A tether between life and death. The Court's greatest relic."

"What exactly does it tether? " Chase asked as he leaned over to look closer to the tome.

"Souls. Mr. Cassidy. The crown is placed on the brow of a host. The poor victims own essence is ripped out to make way for another. " Grey explained.

Chase frowned at the thought. "That simple huh"

Grey shook his head. "Nothing is that simple. The crown is needed yes, in fact it is the most crucial part of such a complex ritual, however" he paused "the host must be prepared. The body tempered to withstand the great energies that must sustain. For that you will need a rampart, something to shield yet funnel the energy."

"Like a sarcophagus?"

"Good deduction." Grey applauded flipping a page. " There are rumors that the Mortems possessed such a sepulture. Capable of preserving the life-force of the one laid inside. An ancient like Adriana would have certainly acquired one to sustain her own life."

Diego squinted. "Suspended life, tethering, sound like the Mourned?"

Chase nodded. "Exactly. Von Epp probably used his experiments on the Mourned to build a host to tether what ever it is he is after."

Grey frowned, horrified. "What he is after is the Lord of Bones. And with Adriana's crypt, the crown, an appropriate host and enough arcane conductive fluid, he will walk again."

Diego tapped the page. "Define 'walks.'"

"Returns," Grey said. "Reborn. Not just undead. Not spirit. Incarnate. A necromantic sovereign."

"What exactly is this Lord of Bones." Chase asked, mind racing.

"A necromancer, a death mage who's reached the very pinnacle of power, or so the legends claim. One who could commune with entities beyond the veil. One as it is claimed, can open a veil and command the creatures on the other side,"

Diego shivered at the thought. Chase however understood the possibilities. "So perhaps Von Epp is looking to resurrect this Lord of Bones. He uses the Mourned, who better suited. They are walking examples of souls wanting true life. Those experiments fail to give him his results. A host body. So he needs another, the boy Benjmain. You said arcane conductive fluid. Well all the fey murderes. There's your fluid. So he uses this Adriana. her sarcophagus. And all he needs is the Crown."

Diego whistled. "Talk about a long term plan. But even if he has all that he still needs Benjamin. As long as we keep him protected, no Lord of Bones"

"Unless," Grey interrupted "There is another host, More than one body can suffice. Anyone borne of similar blood lines, similar astrological alignment could make a suitable vessel." He snapped the tome shut.

"What are we supposed to do, guard every person born of the summer equinox?" Diego complained. "Thats a tall order".

Chase agreed, but his thoughts drifted to something more practical. "The Court of Bones is here. The Gravecallers. The Shackled Mourned, the Fey murders. It all tracks. And no" he pointed to Diego "we cant guard every person. And we won't have to. We are going to find exactly where this ritual is being conducted, and we stop them."

Silence settled like falling ash. Diego whispered, "Cassidy... this is bad. Like... world-ending bad."

Chase stared at the skull emblem on the cover. Then looked to Diego. "We keep Benjamin safe," he said. "We find Von Epp. We kill him."

Chase exhaled, eyes tracing the display case where the Crown of Mortem sat beneath reinforced glass and a lattice active runes. "This isn't staying unguarded," he muttered. "We'll circle Whitman in—have him pull a couple of First Arcane boys to stand watch. Quiet, discreet, no reports up the chain. Just enough muscle to make sure no necro-lunatic walks out of here wearing that thing."

 Diego nodded, tension tightening his jaw. "Yeah," he said. "Because if the Court of Bones wants that crown... they're not sending amateurs."

Professor Grey closed the codex with a resounding thud. "Then we should prepare for an attack. I will alert the guards." The old curator placed the tome back and secured it under lock and ward. "Is that everything, Mr. Cassidy?"

Chase hesitated. His fingers drummed lightly on the edge of a display case—a nervous tic he hadn't realized still lived in him. "Actually..." he said quietly. "One more question."

Grey lifted a brow. "Yes?"

Chase kept his voice low. "The bloodlines. Fae. Draconic. We all learned the basics in academy. But there are... rumors. Empyrean. Infernal."

Grey lips twitched—half amusement, half caution. "Ah. Those rumors."

"They're not real?" Chase asked.

"Oh, quite real." The professor's chuckle was dry but not unkind. "Simply... inconvenient truths that most institutions prefer to downplay. Primordial bloodlines are not like the Fae or Draconics. They are not external species— they are forces."

Chase forced his breath to stay steady. "Hypothetically... could such a union produce a child?"

Grey folded his hands behind him, posture straightening into lecture mode.

"In most cases? No. Primordial energies—Empyrean or Infernal —burn through mortal vessels. The womb cannot contain them. The pregnancy collapses within weeks. Stillbirth is the general rule."

Chase's throat tightened.

"But on exceedingly rare occasions," Grey continued, "the child survives." He stepped closer, lowering his voice. "Such children are fragile at first. Sickly. Unstable. Many do not see adolescence. But those who do..."

A glimmer passed through his eyes—equal parts awe and fear. "By the teenage years their bodies... adapt. Strengthen. And by the age of twenty-one, the metamorphosis completes."

Chase looked away, jaw tense. "Into what?"

"Into a Nephilim—if Empyrean. Or a Cambion—if Infernal. Not simply touched by magic but rooted in it. Their physical beauty is... unsettling. Their intelligence preternatural. And their connection to their progenitor's power?"

A soft exhale. "Limitless. Terrifying."

Grey paused, studying Chase with a historian's eye. "You look troubled, Mr. Cassidy. Your interest—purely academic?"

Chase nodded once. "Hypothetically... what if one of these children never completed that metamorphosis? Say, their nature was... restricted."

Grey frowned. "Restricted how?"

"Spellbinding."

The professor actually laughed—a short, startled huff. "My dear boy... who in their right mind would spellbind a Cambion?" He shook his head. "That is like fitting shackles onto a lightning bolt."

Chase's pulse thudded in his ears.

"Well," Grey continued, "if someone were so profoundly foolish... the results would be paradoxical. The spellbinding would contain the primordial core but not extinguish it. You would have a spellbound with... unusual resilience. Resistance to burnout. Reservoirs of power that should not exist."

He leaned in. "And if such a person lived past twenty-one? Well..."

His gaze sharpened. "That would be a very dangerous man."

Silence curled between them. Grey eventually stepped back, smoothing his coat, tone returning to crisp professionalism. "Of course, all this remains theoretical. No confirmed Cambion or Nephilim has been documented in over two hundred years."

"Of course," Chase said.

"If you have further academic inquiries," Greymoor said, offering a cordial nod, "my door is always open... Mr. Cassidy."

Chase nodded back, expression unreadable. "Appreciate it, Professor."

Diego who remained uncharacteristically quiet during the entire conversation finally spoke up . "So you think you are part demon?" Diego asked" Brother I could have told you that. No way you survived the front like you did, always charging headlong into fire. "

Chase turned toward the exit. He was silent. "Lets get out of here. Mages have the strangest collections."

"Yeah," Diego murmured. "You got that right."

They stepped out into the thin sunlight of late morning, boots hitting the steps of the Arcane Historical Society with a muted thud. The world felt unnervingly normal — streetcars rattling past, vendors shouting over their carts, the city pretending its underbelly wasn't rotting out by the hour.

Diego shoved his hands into his coat pockets, dice clicking softly inside. Chase walked beside him, quiet. Too quiet. The curator's words still echoed in his skull, but that wasn't what hollowed him out. Not today.

Diego finally glanced sideways. "You're thinking so loud I can hear you over traffic."

Chase didn't answer at first. They reached the sidewalk. Chase stopped, leaning a shoulder against a lamppost, jaw tight, eyes distant. "Three attacks," he said finally. "Domingo. The warehouse. And now the firebombing."

A humorless breath left him. "That's more than most people face in a lifetime."

Diego nodded. "Yeah. Rough week."

Chase looked down at his hands — steady as stone in battle, but now faintly trembling. "This isn't her world. Skye didn't ask for any of this. She's should be doing pro bono work, wearing dresses and heels, showing up to courtrooms and charity galas. She didn't sign on for morgues, monsters, or bombs through the damn window."

Diego blinked. "You're... worried she'll break?"

Chase exhaled. "I'm worried this is too much for her. Too damn fast. She didn't grow up in alley brawls or trench raids. She didn't spend her twenties chasing ghosts through warzones. He stared off down the boulevard, eyes shadowed. "She might be strong, but strength isn't the same as choosing this life."

Diego scratched his cheek. "Huh."

"Huh?" Chase echoed, annoyed.

"I mean," Diego said, shrugging, "you're talking like you get to decide that for her."

Chase stiffened. "That's not what I—"

"No, it is." Diego stepped in front of him, for the first time fully serious. "Look, man... I barely know her. But here's what I have seen."

He held up a finger. "One: she's still here. If she wanted out, she'd have been gone the second Domingo kicked in that door."

Second finger.

"Two: she's the one who ran toward danger half the time. Using spells on the fly. Asking the right questions. Getting involved whether we like it or not."

Third.

"And three?" Diego let his hand drop. "Any woman who listens to your brooding ass talk for more than ten minutes without leaving? That's commitment."

Chase snorted despite himself.

Diego softened. "What I'm saying is... the only person who gets to say she's had enough?" He tapped Chase on the chest. "Is her. Not you."

Chase swallowed, throat tight. "You think I'm overthinking it?"

"Brother," Diego said dryly, "you overthink the way some people breathe."

A silence stretched between them. Warm. Heavy. Real. Then Chase straightened, rolling his shoulders. "Alright. Fine. You made your point."

Diego grinned. "Good. Because the Historical Society scared the hell out of me and I'd rather talk about your love life than necromancers any day."

Chase huffed a small laugh. They started walking again. Behind them, the Society doors closed with a soft metallic click — sealing away secrets that would soon tear their lives open.

———

The Municipal Courthouse of Upper Harlem buzzed like a disturbed anthill—clerks shouting, defendants muttering prayers, bailiffs pounding nightsticks against marble pillars. The winter sun slanted through tall windows, turning floating dust into golden static. Skye Anderson pushed through the doors with her briefcase, breath fogging in the cold air. She'd made it with less than five minutes to spare.

A junior clerk from Anderson & Pierce jogged at her side, red-faced.

"They moved Rivera's case up again, Miss Anderson. He is going in now. My apologies—I tried to notify you sooner—"

"It's fine."

She wasn't out of breath, but her pulse thumped hard. Her first case as lead counsel. Thrown straight into fire. She scanned the benches. There—at the far end.

The Rivera family looked out of place: poor, anxious, hunched against the courthouse chaos. Between them sat a teenage boy in an ill-fitting suit, trying to disappear into himself.

Enzo Rivera. Sixteen. Scared. And nearly railroaded. Skye approached with a controlled smile. "Mrs. Rivera? Mr. Rivera? I'm Skye Anderson- Pierce your son's attorney."

Mrs. Rivera blinked, frowned, and clutched her rosary.

"They sent us a woman?"

Skye's jaw tightened by a millimeter—but she kept smiling. "Yes, ma'am. Anderson & Pierce assigned me as lead counsel."

"How many cases you done?" The woman's eyes narrowed with suspicion. "You don't look old enough to try a parking ticket. Women faint. Women cry. What if you get—your—your—monthly—in the middle of court? You'll scream and throw a fit!"

"Mamá," Enzo hissed, face burning. "I don't have any lawyer right now."

Skye crouched to his level.

"You have me," she said softly. "And I'm not going anywhere."

Enzo swallowed hard. His parents exchanged a look—fear, pride, doubt. Skye opened her briefcase, pulling out the arrest record. "I've reviewed what happened. Officers Grant and Halpern claimed you were involved in a rum-runner ambush."

She tapped a specific line. "But their report is sloppy. And inconsistent."

Enzo leaned forward. "I didn't run. I—I froze. They shoved me in a truck."

"I believe you."

Mrs. Rivera's expression faltered. "You think they... set him up?"

"I think," Skye said, "those officers botched a sting. And they needed a quick arrest to cover their failure."

Mr. Rivera inhaled sharply.

Skye placed a hand over Enzo's. "Trust me. We're going to straighten this out."

A bailiff strode down the hall. "Case 2147—People v. Rivera. You're up."

Skye snapped her briefcase shut. "Stay close," she murmured. "We fight now."

Courtroom 3B was packed. The prosecutor, a long-nosed man named Mr. Avery—stood behind his stack of files, looking smugly confident.

Skye guided Enzo to the defense table. The judge, a tall man with silver hair and spectacles perched low on his nose, scanned the room. "This is the matter of the State versus Enzo Rivera. I see the defendant is present..."

His eyes shifted. "Where is counsel?"

Skye rose. "Right here, Your Honor."

The judge blinked behind his glasses.

"You're... counsel?"

A few chuckles rippled through the gallery. The Mr. Avery, adjusted his glasses, squinting at Skye like she was an exotic insect.

"Your Honor," Avery began before the judge had even settled, "before we begin, I must question whether defense counsel is... appropriately attired."

Judge Oswald's brows lifted. "Explain."

Avery gestured stiffly. "Miss Anderson is wearing pants. That is highly irregular for female representation. This is a court of law, not a—"

Skye spoke before he finished.

"With respect, Your Honor, U.S. Attorney General Harry M. Daugherty issued a formal statement earlier this year affirming that women attorneys are permitted to wear trousers in court if they deem it appropriate." Her tone sharpened. "Which I do."

A murmur of amusement rippled through the benches.

Judge Oswald cleared his throat. "Mr. Avery, kindly confine yourself to the case."

Avery reddened. He rapped his gavel sharply. "Order."

Skye didn't flinch.

"Yes, Your Honor. Skye Anderson for the defense."

The prosecutor smirked.

"Your Honor, given the nature of these charges and the inexperience of opposing counsel, I request—"

Skye spoke first.

"Objection."

The word cracked through the air. She slid the arrest record forward.

"Your Honor, the prosecution's evidence is compromised. The officers 'logs list seizure of five crates of contraband alcohol—yet the inventory tag here shows only three were logged into evidence."

A murmur swept the room.

"Furthermore," Skye continued, flipping pages with surgical precision, "the arrest time recorded by Officers Grant and Halpern conflicts with dispatch call records by exactly fourteen minutes." She tapped another page, eyes burning bright. "That discrepancy alone violates chain-of-custody protocol."

The prosecutor paled. The judge raised a brow. "You're saying the arrest was procedurally contaminated."

"Yes, Your Honor," Skye said, unwavering. "And any evidence gathered is inadmissible."

The gallery erupted again.

"ORDER!" the judge barked.

Silence.

He leaned forward, studying her with keen interest.

"Miss Anderson... that's an astute observation. Very astute." He glanced over the file again. "A procedural breach this severe cannot be ignored. The State's evidence is hereby invalid. Charges dismissed."

Mrs. Rivera gasped. Mr. Rivera grabbed his son in a crushing hug. Enzo blinked in disbelief. Skye exhaled quietly. She'd done it.

As the Riveras gathered their things, the judge cleared his throat. "Miss Anderson. Approach."

Skye did—calm, composed, though her stomach fluttered.

He lowered his voice. "Counselor... few attorneys could dissect a file that quickly. Even fewer in the hallway five minutes before trial." His eyes narrowed, curious. "Tell me—are you one of the bloodlines?"

She held his gaze. "Yes, Your Honor. Draconic."

His expression brightened with recognition and understanding. "As am I," he said. "Hoard memory runs strong in us. Consider it a gift. And a responsibility."

Skye inclined her head respectfully. "Thank you, Your Honor."

"You'll do great things," he said quietly. "Just don't burn out too fast."

Outside the courtroom, Enzo flung his arms around her in a sudden, grateful hug.

"Miss Anderson… thank you."

Skye returned it gently. "Don't thank me yet," she said. "We still need to file for dismissal with prejudice. Make sure they can't try this again."

Mrs. Rivera wiped her eyes. "I was wrong about you," she admitted.

Skye smiled faintly. "You were scared. That's allowed."

Enzo sniffed. "Do… do I still owe you anything?"

Skye shook her head. " You owe me one thing."

He blinked. "What?"

"Stay out of trouble."

Enzo managed a small grin. "I'll try."

She clasped his shoulder.

Skye's smile softened. "Good." She snapped her briefcase closed. "If either of you need anything, call the office. Truly." She glanced toward the courthouse doors. "I have to go."

And with that— mind already pivoting back to necromancers, and murdered children, Skye Anderson strode out of the courthouse and into the winter sun.

———

Winter wind scraped across the marble steps of the Arcane Historical Society, carrying the faint sting of snow and coal smoke. Midnight settled over the city like a held breath. Sergeant O'Leary pushed open the front doors with a grunt, stepping out with two uniformed officers—Denton and Hawkins.

"Alright, lads," O'Leary said, tightening his coat, "final check before I make my rounds. Denton stood stiff as a poker, pale with the kind of nerves only rookies had around arcane sites. Hawkins looked steadier, but not by much.

O'Leary pointed toward the double doors behind him. "Two officers in the lobby, aye?"

Hawkins nodded. "Yes, Sarge."

"And two more at the artifact vault," Denton added quickly. "Plus the automaton stationed in the corridor."

O'Leary exhaled smoke. "The brass bastard. Don't stand in its way unless you enjoy bein 'dented."

Both officers cracked uneasy smiles.

"Good," O'Leary said. "If the Society loses even a teaspoon in there, we'll all be kissin 'Travers 'boots for a month. Keep your eyes sharp. I'll do the circuit and check the vault myself."

The men nodded.

Satisfied, O'Leary stepped back inside, pulling the heavy door with him—and then he paused. Music. Faint. Off-kilter.

A warped carousel melody drifted through the winter dark. Slow. Lopsided. Like a child's lullaby wound backward. O'Leary's gut tightened. "Christ above..."

He pushed the door back open and stepped out again. At first, he saw nothing. Then she danced into the streetlamp's glow.

Coco Le Fay.

Black ballet slippers. A ragged tutu spattered with old paint. Hair streaming like ink in the wind. Eyes mismatched—one soft, one burning with fractured color. Beautiful the way a lightning strike was beautiful.

O'Leary's breath hitched. "Don't look at her—don't—" Too late. Both officers stiffened, eyes dilating as the glamour brushed their minds like velvet soaked in opium.

Hawkins swayed. Denton smiled dreamily.

"Sarge..." he whispered. "She's... beautiful..."

Coco giggled—a sound like chimes dropped down a well.

O'Leary fought the pull, fingernails digging into his own palm. "Lads —snap out of—"

Coco lifted one hand, graceful as a conductor.

"Dance for me."

The officers 'knees buckled. They collapsed at her feet like strings cut from marionettes.

Coco twirled once, snatched Hawkins 'key ring, and clapped her hands in delight.

"Such good dolls," she sang.

O'Leary staggered backward and ducked inside the Society, slamming the door—

—and froze.

Coco stood in front of him.

Inside.

As if she'd been waiting.

She leaned forward, eyes wide and glowing. "Boo."

Before O'Leary could cry out, she seized his collar, rose on her toes —and kissed him full on the mouth. The glamour hit like warm drowning. O'Leary dropped bonelessly to the marble floor.

Coco hummed, skipped to the front door, and swung it open wide. "Your turn," she chimed.

Sirus Magnus stepped inside, robes sweeping the marble. His hands moved in silent mudras. Behind him, the sewer grate across the street shuddered. Metal groaned. Then the first shackled Mourned crawled out— twisted limbs clicking, rune-collars glowing faintly as they emerged one by one, slinking toward the Society doors like starving dogs scenting fresh blood.

Coco placed a finger to her lips.

"Shhh… libraries need quiet."

And the Mourned slipped inside after her.

Atticus Grey, senior antiquarian and keeper of vault protocols, was shelving a silver-inlaid grimoire when the front doors creaked.

He frowned. No one should be here.

"Sergeant O'Leary?" He called.

No answer. Only faint music. His blood ran cold. A figure slid into view between the shelves, spinning slowly, arms lifted above her head in a dancer's fifth position. Coco Le Fay. Feet now tapping softly, her outline flickering like a candle flame trapped in motion.

Atticus gasped. "N-no... you can't be here—this is a sealed institution—!"

Coco dipped into a curtsy. "I'm here for storytime."

She twirled. Power rippled off her. Books trembled. Light dimmed. The chandeliers swayed as if caught in a breathless wind. Around the hall, librarians froze mid-step, their faces slackening as the glamour seeped into them. One apprentice rose off the ground as if pulled by invisible strings—

Snap. His body hit the floor as the music echoed. Coco placed a finger to her lips. "Shhh. Quiet."

Atticus stumbled backward—heart hammering—trying to summon a ward. But Coco flicked her wrist. A pulse of magic hit him like a wave slamming him into a bookshelf. She slumped, dazed but alive.

Coco stepped past him without a glance.

Deep in the corridor, gears engaged. The Arcane Enforcement Automaton rose from its charging cradle—eight feet tall, plates interlocking, runes burning to life along its chest and arms.

INTRUSION DETECTED.

ENGAGING HOSTILE ENTITIES.

It strode into the hall just as two masked Gravecallers slipped through the entrance behind Coco, drifting like shadows. They did not expect resistance. The automaton aimed its arc-lance.

HOSTILE IDENTIFIED. GRAVECALLER.

A bolt of azure lightning streaked across the hall and struck the first Gravecaller dead center. The necromancer convulsed violently as the charge overloaded the enchantments in her spine. Black smoke poured from the eyeholes of her bone mask. She crumpled, limbs twitching.

Coco gasped, delighted. "Ohhhh! It squished her!"

The second Gravecaller hissed in fury, summoning a coil of black death-magic. The automaton charged. Its metal fist smashed into the Gravecaller's jaw, sending him skidding across the stone. Before he could rise, the machine stomped down, shattering ribs and runes alike.

HOSTILE NEUTRALIZED.

Coco pouted. "You hurt my playmates."

The automaton turned toward her.

THREAT LEVEL: EXTREME.

DEPLOYING COUNTERMEASURES.

Coco giggled and twirled, utterly unfazed. "Big metal man can't be glamoured," she sang. "No eyes. No mind. How boring."

The automaton fired again—another lance of lightning cracking through the hall. Coco dodged with inhuman grace—pirouetting beneath the bolt, skirts flaring. She landed beside a decorative indoor tree—an enchanted ash sapling planted in a sculpted clay bed, roots thick with dormant magic.

She pressed her palm to the trunk. "Wake up."

The tree groaned. Its roots writhed free of the soil. With a dancer's flourish, Coco flicked her wrist and the animated tree lunged. A thick branch punched straight through the automaton's back plating, spearing its arcane reactor. Blue flame burst from the breach as the runes along its torso flickered violently.

CRITICAL DAMAGE.

SYSTEM FAILURE—

The automaton fell to one knee. Coco leaned in, patting its metal cheek."Shhh. Sleep."

The arc reactor collapsed inward. The machine went still. Coco skipped past the smoking wreckage.

The vault was a cathedral of forbidden relics—sarcophagi, bone scrolls, preserved organs of long-dead kings. But at the center, encased in a brass-and-glass housing, rested the Crown of Mortem. A circlet of obsidian and bone. Breathing. Faintly. Like a slumbering beast.

Sirus disabled the clockwork lock—gears turning backward under his fingers until the securing runes broke. "Open sesame," he said softly.

The case parted. Coco glided forward and lifted the crown with delicate reverence. The room shuddered. Wards cracked. Candles guttered.

Scrolls screamed in dead voices. The crown pulsed in her hand like a heartbeat.

A wave of necrotic power swept the hall—shattering glass, unraveling seals, rattling bones beneath the floor.

Sirus remained still. Only his coat fluttered. At the back of the vault, he spotted something else—the Iron Heart. Beating faintly in crystalline suspension. He palmed the relic. Cold seeped into his fingers, crawling up his arm like a promise. "Time to go," he murmured.

Coco skipped to the exit with the crown bobbing on her head. They left behind a wilted black rose—already rotting—as their calling card.

———

The aria of Die Feen soared through the opera house like a spun-glass spell, delicate and shimmering.

Aspen Willowbark stood under the grand chandelier, center stage, his voice a clear, bright thread unspooling into the dark. His pale green suit caught the glow of gaslights, and his golden eyes shone with the soft ache of the Fae ballad—love, sacrifice, the long road home.

High above, in the shadow of the private boxes, Makalith Ravenwind watched.

He leaned on the carved rail, gloves immaculate, duelist's coat smooth as poured ink. His sharp features were lit from below by the stage, making his Fae-blooded cheekbones look almost skeletal.

For a moment, the song touched something in him. A memory: his sister laughing, standing on a mossy stone under a midsummer sky, singing a woodland round in the Old Tongue.

He crushed the memory before it could bloom. Sentiment was a poison he could not afford. This wasn't personal.

Backstage, a stagehand hauling scenery caught a glimpse of something moving in the shadows and froze. A tall, emaciated shape glided between the hanging curtains—its frame encased in metal braces and leather straps, tubes snaking from a gas mask to the tank on its back. Fingers glinted—long, jointed blades instead of nails. Utilis the Rover.

The stagehand opened his mouth to shout.

Utilis raised one hand. One casual slash One wet sound. Blood sprayed across a rack of costumes. The body slid down the wall without a sound, leaving a red trail against painted backdrops. Utilis moved on.

The director, a stocky man with a thinning hairline and sweat shining under his collar, rounded the corner a few minutes later, eyes wide with frantic irritation. "Props!" he snapped. "That crash in the wings better not have dented the—"

He stopped. Makalith stood in the middle of the corridor. "Who the hell are—" the director began.

Makalith spoke a word older than borders. The director choked on the rest of his sentence. Veins stood out in cords along his neck. His eyes bulged, fingers clawing at his chest. He pitched forward onto his knees, gasping soundlessly, then fell facedown, still.

Onstage, Aspen faltered on a high note, something in his gut twisting. He turned his head slightly, as if he could see through curtain and brick and bone.

Makalith stepped into the wings. The boy turned toward the shade of the side curtains, breathing hard, sweat sheen on his brow.

Makalith lifted his hand. A thin strand of shimmering arcane force snapped out like a whip, coiling around Aspen's throat. His next note died in his mouth. He stumbled forward, hands clawing at invisible bindings. From the shadows behind him, Utilis slid closer, skeletal hands locking around Aspen's arms, holding him fast. The hiss of alchemic vapor leaked from the tanks on his back.

"Don't struggle," Makalith said mildly. "We need you alive. For now." High above, in two concealed alcoves flanking the chandelier, the Gravecallers stepped from the darkness.

Both wore bone-white masks carved with spirals; both robed in crimson and black. One—a woman, throat webbed with old scars—raised a hand over the audience. "Witnesses," she rasped. "Unacceptable."

Necrotic flame bloomed in her palm. It spilled outward in a wave—soundless, invisible to mortal eyes, rippling across the velvet seats. Dozens of men and women froze mid-cheer. Their skin blanched. Veins spidered black beneath the surface. One by one, they slumped where they sat, heads lolling, eyes filmed over. Aspen watched, horror tearing through his muted voice. Tears streaked his face.

Makalith's jaw clenched. "That was not part of the plan," he said.

The Gravecaller bared her teeth behind the mask. "You were hired to bring us the vessel. We were promised the dead." She started to lower her hand again, new sigils forming in the air—this time the kind that raised what they had just felled.

Makalith moved. He blurred. One heartbeat he was at Aspen's side; the next he was behind her, stiletto flashing out of his sleeve. The thin blade slid between her ribs and into her heart. She stiffened. Makalith leaned close, lips near the edge of her mask. "Learn restraint," he whispered. "Or die a dog's death."

He twisted. She crumpled, necrotic magic sputtering uselessly from her fingertips before guttering out. The second Gravecaller—a silent figure with an unblemished mask—stared, hand half-raised. Makalith turned his head, eyes cold green fire. "To think," he said flatly, "your kind once frightened me."

The second Gravecaller swallowed. "I— I will report—"

"You will die," Makalith said. He flicked his wrist.

A lash of shimmering power snapped across the distance, wrapping around the Gravecaller's masked head. There was a wet crack—too sharp to be bone alone. The body folded, tumbling from the balcony to crash among the dead below. Makalith didn't watch him fall. He snapped his fingers. The chandelier's chain shattered.

Crystal and steel plummeted, smashing onto the stage with a roar of shattering glass and splintering beams—burying the sightlines, obscuring the view of Aspen and his captors in a storm of glittering debris.

From below, security finally broke free of their stunned shock. Doors burst open. Men in tuxedos with concealed revolvers, ushers with wands, uniformed house guards—they rushed the aisles, shouting, coughing on dust.

Makalith stretched out his hand, voice as calm as a lullaby. "Sleep."

Enchantment rolled through the wings and orchestra pit like a narcotic wind. Six bodies dropped where they stood, weapons clattering from limp hands. The air filled with the shrieks of those few still alive and conscious in the boxes. "Time to go," Makalith said.

Utilis hoisted Aspen over his shoulder like a sack of grain, blade-fingers careful not to pierce the prize. The boy's muffled sobs were swallowed by the hiss of the mask and the distant panic of the wounded crowd. They slipped into a side corridor, footsteps vanishing into shadows. Behind them, the opera house became a mausoleum—chandelier shattered, gilded ceiling cracked, dead patrons slumped in their seats like discarded dolls.

By the time emergency response would arrive, the stage would be empty. Aspen Willowbark—Fae-blooded, gifted, chosen—was gone. And in the dark below the city, the Court of Bones tightened its grip on the pieces it had just torn from Madhatten's beating heart.

———

The restaurant was busy in that quiet, expensive way — voices low, glasses clinking softly, the smell of roasted lamb and saffron drifting through the air.

Donald Pierce and Thomas Anderson sat at a corner table, legal folders stacked between them, waiting for their client to arrive.

Donald checked his pocket watch. "He's late," he murmured.

Thomas shrugged. "Clients in this zone always are."

They didn't notice the couple enter. A man and woman — impeccably dressed, unremarkable, almost forgettable.

Except for the eyes. Lilidan Blackwell smiled faintly as she scanned the room, her gloved fingers trailing along the backs of chairs like she was testing wood grain. Beside her, Dorian Blackwell moved with the quiet confidence of a surgeon choosing where to cut. They sat at the bar. Didn't order drinks. Watched. Waited.

The chef yelled orders, pans clattered, steam rose in waves.

A waiter bustled through with a silver-covered dish — Donald Pierce's lunch — when Lilidan brushed past him, "accidentally" bumping his tray.

She whispered a word so soft it was almost breathless. "Cineris."

Her fingers flicked, nearly invisible. The food inside the covered dish twitched — just once — as if something beneath the lid woke up. The waiter blinked, oblivious, and carried the now-hexed meal toward the dining room. Lilidan watched him go without turning her head.

Their food arrived. Donald thanked the waiter, cut into the dish, and lifted a forkful to his mouth. Thomas Anderson took a quick sip of his wine and stood. "Back in a second, Don."

He pushed open the restroom door. The lights flickered once, then steadied. He stepped toward the sink and the door exploded inward. Dorian Blackwell moved like a shadow with bones. His hand shot out, grabbed Thomas by the back of the skull, and SLAMMED him into the porcelain sink hard enough to crack it.

Thomas gasped, bleeding from the temple. "W-who—?" Dorian's voice was calm. Gentle. Terrifying. "You represented my family once. Admirably, so I take no pleasure in this."

Thomas tried to fight, but Dorian was stronger than a man should be. A black-obsidian shafted wand slid from Dorian's sleeve. "Crucio Ossium."

Thomas eyes widened as his bones fractured within, blood spreading in a dark halo. Dorian closed the door. "One for two," he murmured. He stepped over the corpse, adjusted his cuffs, and walked out onto the restaurant floor

Donald sat there enjoying his food. A moment later, his face tightened. "Hot," he muttered, fanning his mouth. "Damn, that's—" Then the pain hit. His eyes bulged. The fork clattered to the table. Smoke began leaking from his nostrils. Lilidan watched him from the bar, her chin resting on her hand, smiling as if admiring a painting. Donald clutched his throat.

His skin flushed red. Then blistered. Then cracked. A faint, acrid smell rose — like burnt parchment. He tried to stand, but his legs failed. He thrashed once against the tablecloth, sending glasses shattering. People screamed.

Donald Pierce collapsed sideways out of his chair, his mouth opening in a silent, burning plea. Lilidan stood and walked past him as he writhed, the hem of her dress lifting elegantly off the floor as if the air itself stepped aside. She paused only long enough to whisper: "Payment rendered."

Then she joined Dorian by the door. They exited the restaurant calmly, their faces serene. Behind them, chaos erupted. Anderson & Pierce was now headless. Exactly as von Epp ordered.

———

Skye Anderson climbed the steps of Anderson, Anderson & Pierce with a paper bag pressed to her ribs and a false warmth trembling in her chest. A morning that had begun in fire and blood—in smoke, fear, and collapsing ceilings—somehow had ended in victory. A real courtroom win. Her first. Her body ached. Her ribs felt bruised from being blown across Chase's apartment. Her throat was sore from shouting over the blast. Her hands trembled if she let them. But she carried a fresh bagel still warm from the cart downstairs, steam escaping the paper bag like a tiny promise.

Donald will pretend he doesn't like it, she thought. Thomas will steal half. They'll both be proud. She'd replayed the judge's dismissal a dozen times on the walk over. How Enzo's mother cried. How the boy almost collapsed in relief. How she had stood her ground. For a moment, she'd felt… whole.

She pushed open the door. And froze. Tommy Dixon, Harold Jones, and Victor Hale—three senior partners—were standing in the lobby. Standing. Waiting. Not working. Not smiling. Not moving. Tommy's face was pale, eyes swollen. Harold's knuckles were white around his coffee cup. Victor's jaw worked like he was swallowing gravel.

Skye blinked slowly. "Um… hi?" she said, lifting the warm bag. "I brought breakfast. I figured you all might want—" "Skye," Harold said softly.

"Sit down."

Her heart thudded off-beat.

"Why? What's—"

"Sit," Victor repeated, voice cracking.

Something cold crept up Skye's spine. She sat on the edge of the reception chair. The bagel folded in her hands like damp paper. Tommy cleared his throat—once, twice—but the words wouldn't come. His lower lip trembled.

"Skye…" he whispered. Her pulse hammered. "Where are my dads?" she asked.

Silence.

Skye laughed. A small startled sound that came out sharp and wrong.

"No—really. What is going on?"

Harold stepped closer. "There was an incident," he said. "At Vittorio's. A... violent incident."

Skye stared blankly.

"Incident," she echoed. The word felt meaningless. "They're lawyers, Harold. Not bootleggers."

Harold swallowed. Victor looked away. Tommy finally forced the words out.   "They're gone."

The world did not tilt.   It simply stopped. Skye blinked once. Twice. The bagel slipped from her fingers. Steam curled into the air between them, thin and fragile.

"No," she said quietly. "Try again."

Tommy flinched as if slapped. "They were meeting a client. The client didn't show. Mr. Anderson went to the restroom. He never came out." His voice broke. "And Mr. Pierce—he collapsed. At the table. They said it looked... targeted."

Skye's mind refused to process it.She stood abruptly, too fast, too stiff. "No," she said again, voice rising. She shook her head violently. "No."

The door behind her chimed softly. Chase and Diego entered, mid-conversation—until they saw her face. "Skye?" Chase asked, stepping forward. "What—what happened?"

Skye opened her mouth. Nothing came out. She tried again. Her throat closed.

"Chase," Tommy whispered from behind her, "there was an attack."

Skye's knees didn't buckle. She didn't faint.   She didn't scream. She just... froze. Like a statue cracked at the center.

Chase rushed to her side. "Tommy. Tell me. Now."

Tommy wiped his face with the back of his hand. "It was coordinated. Someone hit both of them. They said Mr. Anderson was... was killed in the restroom. And Mr. Pierce—something in his food—"

"Poison," Diego said softly.

Skye's breath hitched on a sob she didn't seem to realize was hers.

Chase grabbed her arms gently. "Skye. Look at me."

She didn't.

Instead, she turned robotically, picked up the bagel from where it had fallen, and sat back down in the chair. She took one bite. Chewed once. Twice. Then her face crumpled. "My dads..." she whispered. The words broke. Then the sob rose from somewhere deep—raw, wounded, animal."My dads—my dads—my dads—"

She folded over the bagel in her hands and wept so hard her entire body shook. Chase stood over her, jaw clenched so tightly it shook. Because he knew. He knew exactly what this was. A message. A declaration of war. And the worst part was, it wasn't meant for him. They had struck her. Skye rocked forward, sobbing into Chase's jacket as he crouched and pulled her close, her cries breaking against his chest like shattered glass.

"My dads... my dads..."

Chase closed his eyes. "We'll get them," he whispered. "All of them."

But Skye didn't hear. She was somewhere deeper—somewhere hollow. Somewhere she would never come back from the same.

CHAPTER 7

Tough Decisions

"I have to say, the dead never trouble me; it's the half-rotted souls walking upright that keep me up at night."

Dr. Horatio Buzzard

The elevator rattled on the way down. It always did. Old cables, old city, old ghosts clinging to the brick and steel of Madhatten as if the place owed them one more breath. Chase Cassidy stood with one hand braced against the wall, watching the floor numbers flicker past in dull, jaundiced light. Diego leaned in the opposite corner, dice clicking softly in his palm. Skye stood between them, briefcase clamped in a white-knuckled grip. Her face was composed. Her eyes were not. The doors shuddered open on the basement level with a tired ding.

Cold rolled out to greet them—industrial chill, disinfectant, and the faint iron tang of blood. The city morgue sat at the end of the hall, a slab of frosted glass in a field of flaking green paint. A single overhead bulb buzzed fitfully.

Chase stepped out first. "Last chance," he said quietly, glancing back at Skye. "You don't need to be here for this."

She stared straight ahead.

"They were my fathers," she said. "Thomas signed my first acceptance letter. Donald taught me how to read a contract before I could ride a bicycle."

Her throat moved once. "I'm not waiting upstairs."

Diego opened his mouth, thought better of it, and just squeezed her shoulder once before letting his hand drop.

They walked. At the morgue door, Chase rapped his knuckles twice. A familiar rasp answered from inside. "If it's the press again, you can tell them to—"

"It's Cassidy," Chase called. "Anderson. Salazar." He announced

The lock scraped. Bolts slid. The door swung open.

Dr. Buzzard looked like he'd hadn't slept in days. Large bags hung under his eyes. His normally pristine , tailored appearance was replaced by fatigue. He blinked once. "Well," he said. "If it isn't my favorite trouble magnet." His gaze moved past Chase and landed on Skye.

The flippant tone dropped out of his voice. "Miss Anderson."

She nodded. "Doctor." He looked at her for a beat, taking in the set of her jaw, the tightness around her eyes, the way she held the briefcase like a shield.

"Come in," he said softly. "All three of you."

The metal door clanged shut behind them. The morgue was a long, tiled room lined with silver drawers and stainless-steel tables. Overhead lights painted everything in harsh white. A drain ran down the center of the floor, dark and harmless-looking until you thought about why it was there.

Two gurneys waited near the far wall. Two bodies on them, covered in sheets up to the chest. Skye drew in a breath that never made it all the way down. Buzzard noticed. "Do you want a minute?" he asked her. "Before I—"

"No," she said. The word came out too fast. She swallowed and tried again. "No. Please. Just… show me." Buzzard's expression tightened almost imperceptibly. He stepped to the nearer gurney and folded the sheet back with the care of a priest lifting a shroud.

Thomas Anderson lay pale and still, silver hair combed back neatly, jaw slack. There was a faint soot-stain at the corner of his mouth, as if he'd taken one long drag off a cigar just before the end.

Skye's hand went to her lips. "Papa…" she whispered.

The word was too small for the room. Chase moved a half-step closer, not touching her, just being there, a solid presence at her shoulder. Buzzard cleared his throat softly. "External trauma as severe. Arms and legs twisted at odd angles. I retired them to their normal positions." His voice slid into his professional cadence—a buffer for both him and them. "Internally, he was worse… I believe this was a Crucio Osmium curse"

He turned to Donald. He tapped a fingertip gently against his sternum.

"From his lungs down to his stomach, it's like someone set a coal stove inside him and shut the door."

Diego grimaced. "Poison?"

"Something worse." Buzzard's gaze flicked to Chase. "Ring any bells, Cassidy?"

Chase stared at the old lawyer's chest—at the unmarked skin covering what he knew must be horrors underneath. A memory rose, unbidden: a workshop lit by hellfire, Elijah Cassidy laughing like a madman as a blast of searing energy tore past Buzzard's hand, leaving it a ruin of charred flesh and bone.

"Looks like Charon's Call work," Chase said quietly remembering what he knew of his father's hand cannon.

Buzzard gave him a humorless smile. "Gold star, soldier. It's similar to your daddy's handiwork, but—" He held up his own hand, flexing the necromechanical fingers Elijah's bullet had once destroyed. "Elijah's burns were directional. Entry wound, exit wound, line of destruction in between. This?" He tapped Thomas's ribs again.

"This is omni-directional. Heat blooming outwards from the center of the chest cavity. Like someone lit a furnace inside him and turned it up."

Skye tore her eyes away from Thomas long enough to look at Buzzard. "You've… seen this before?"

Buzzard hesitated. "Yes," he said at last. "Once."

"Where?" Chase asked.

Buzzard's mouth twisted. "The war," he said. "Working with the French medical corps. We got a batch of corpses from the from the Legion. All of them with hearts cooked like holiday roasts while their skin stayed mostly intact."

"So not Delgado," Diego murmured.

Buzzard blinked. "Del Gato?"

"Camilo Del Gato," Chase said. "Gangster with more swagger than brains. He firebombed my apartment. This is… cleaner. Precise. He doesn't have this kind of finesse."

Buzzard nodded. "Street pyros don't do internal-only burns. This is controlled arcane combustion. Imperial-style. You know the name, Cassidy."

Chase's jaw clenched. He did. Amt für Totenwissenschaft. The German Office of Death Sciences. Whispered about in the trenches like a ghost story that bled into real casualty reports.

And one name above all. Hermann von Epp.

Skye made a strangled sound. Her knees buckled. Chase caught her before she hit the floor. "I've got you," he murmured, one arm around her shoulders. "Easy. Breathe." She pressed a hand over her mouth, eyes squeezed shut. A hot tear slipped out anyway, cutting a clean track through the ash-smudged skin at her cheek.

Buzzard stepped back respectfully.

Diego hovered nearby, helpless, looking exactly like a man who'd faced down monsters in tunnels and still had no idea what to do with a woman's grief. After a long moment, Skye straightened, pulling gently out of Chase's arms. She wiped her face with the back of her hand.

"I'm alright," she lied.

Buzzard studied her carefully. "The burn pattern is identical," he said. "Same internal burn, same locus. He ingested whatever killed them."

"At a meeting," Skye said hoarsely. "They went to lunch with a client downtown. Tommy Dixon said they never came back."

Diego frowned. "So whoever wanted them dead got to the kitchen, not the street." Chase's eyes narrowed. "Restaurant staff, maybe. Or someone with access to the food delivery."

Skye stared at the bodies. "This is because of us," she whispered. "Because of me. Because I wouldn't drop Benjamin's case. Because I got involved with you."

"Hey." Chase stepped in front of her, forcing her to meet his gaze. "No. This is because a bastard who should've stayed buried decided to start playing war games in our city."

She swallowed, jaw twitching.

Buzzard cleared his throat softly. "For what it's worth, Miss Anderson, the method here? This isn't a warning. It's retribution. Whoever did this wanted two specific men dead in a specific way. Like they were balancing a ledger."

"That tracks," Diego muttered. Gravecallers like body count math. So more than likely they are planning another hit."

Buzzards head snapped toward him. "Gravecallers?"

Chase nodded grimly. "Killed several at the docks. Diego killed a few in the Hollow. Somebody upstairs is keeping score."

Silence settled heavy for a moment, broken only by the distant drip of a pipe and the faint hum of the refrigeration units. Chase dragged a hand over his face. "Alright," he said. "We know the what. We need the who and where. You said you'd seen this pattern before, Doc. Von Epp. Could he be behind this?"

Buzzard's gaze sharpened. "The Death Mage of the Kaiser himself? I thought he was hanging from a rope in The Hague by now."

"So did a lot of people," Chase said. "They were wrong."

There was a beat of stillness as that sank in.

Diego whistled low. "You have very uncomplicated enemies, hermano. Totally normal." Buzzard snorted despite himself. "Well, if Von Epp's back in business, that explains the burns. Band it explains the restt."

Chase frowned. "The rest?"

Buzzard jerked his chin toward the far corner of the room. "Come take a look at this." Skye stayed by the gurneys, one hand resting lightly on Donald's cold forearm, as Chase and Diego followed Buzzard across the tiled floor.

The mortician's workbench was a chaos of tools—bone saws, clamps, tiny brushes, etched metal plates, vials of preserved tissue. Jars of preserved organs floated on shelves above, watching like disembodied witnesses.

On the center of the bench sat an arm. Or something that had once been one. It was a necromechanical construct from elbow to fingertip—metallic bones interlaced with pale, rune-etched slivers of actual bone, tendons replaced with braided wire and preserved sinew. The hand ended not in nails, but in hooked talons articulated with unnerving grace.

Chase felt the hair rise at the back of his neck. He knew that silhouette. He'd seen it tearing gouges through dockside stone. Raking furrows into steel. Reaching out for his throat in a shadow-tainted warehouse.

He wore softly. "No. No, no, no. Tell me that's not what I think it is."

Buzzard lifted his necromech hand in a mock toast. "Prototype," he said. "Doesn't move, doesn't respond. Just a model to work out the rune lattice and tendon tension."

Chase stepped closer, True Sight twitching behind his eyes. The sigils along the knuckles, the way the bones had been jointed, the anchor point at the wrist—it was all the same.

"You sold the finished version," he said flatly. Not a question. Buzzard didn't bother pretending otherwise.

"About a week ago," he said. "Customer paid extra for rush work."

Diego dragged a hand down his face. "Let me guess," he muttered. "Creepy bastard. Hood up. Smelled like grave dirt and arrogance."

Buzzard raised a brow. "You two do this job or you a fortune-teller, Salazar?"

"I'm a mentalist," Diego said. "We cheat."

Chase tore his gaze from the arm and looked at Buzzard. "You didn't ask who it was for?"

"I did," Buzzard said dryly. "He said—and I quote—'A valued asset.' Which is corpse-speak for 'not your business, doc. 'I don't love the ethical implications, mind you, but I'd like to keep the other hand."

Diego snorted.

Chase stared at the arm again, memory overlaying reality, the lunging through gloom, mechanical claws shrieking against his Aegis, Mourned eyes gleaming behind cracked goggles full of green fluid. "The Mourned at the hospital," he said quietly. "The one with the cleaver and the claw-arm. That's his arm."

Diego nodded, jaw tight. "He carved the wall open with something just like this."

Buzzard grimaced. "Fantastic. So my handiwork's ripping up my city. Again."

"Again?" Skye's voice carried from behind them.

She'd come up silently, grief shuttered behind a lawyer's composure. Her gaze flicked from the mechanical arm to Buzzard's necromech hand... and back again.

Buzzard wiggled his fingers. "Your friend's father blew this one to ash in '18," he said. "I rebuilt it. Learned a lot. Apparently someone's been paying attention."

Skye's eyes hardened. "Whoever commissioned that arm is connected to the people who killed my fathers."

"Yeah," Diego said. "And to the ones trying to carve up Fae kids and resurrect a necromantic demigod."

Skye exhaled shakily, then straightened. "Where," she asked Buzzard, "did you hand it over?"

Buzzard hesitated.

"I'll need the exact location," Chase added. "Drop point, access route, anything you remember. This could be our only trail."

Buzzard sighed like a man who'd spent too long breathing formaldehyde and bureaucracy. He shuffled to a drawer beneath the bench, rummaged through a stack of invoices and carbon copies, and pulled one out. He squinted at the scribbles, then passed it to Chase.

"Here," he said. "Delivery instructions. Client didn't want to come topside. Wanted the package left in an access-way near Henry Street."

"You have a map of the city?" Chase asked

Dr. Buzzard nodded, producing a folded map from one of his many binders. "Here."

Chase opened the map and spread it across the desk. Scanning, he pointed to downtown Manhattan. "Here,"he said, "This is where I pursued the two Mourned into tunnels after finding the Tran boys body. St. Augustine's Church. It's right nearby the drop point. "

Diego leaned in, glancing between the note ands the map.

"Sub-basement tunnels," he read. "Third maintenance door past the south platform. Coded knock, leave and walk away." He clicked his tongue. "Classic creepy cult logistics. This connects to the Underwalk, All of it. They're using every forgotten corner of this city like arteries."

Skye stood next to Chase, eyes scanning the notes—her mind already mapping out routes, lines of approach, jurisdiction nightmares. Chase folded the invoice carefully and slid it into his coat pocket.

"Then we cut into one," he said. "And see how far the blood runs."

Buzzard eyed him over steepled hands. "You planning to stroll into an access tunnel alone, Cassidy? That's suicide."

"Not alone," Diego said. "I'll be by his side"

Skye's expression tightened. "And me."

Chase opened his mouth. She lifted a hand before he could speak. "Do not say I've had enough," she warned. "Do not tell me to sit this out. I going to bury two men who tucked me in every night as a child and called me 'kiddo. 'The people responsible for that are Von Epp, the Gravecallers, the Mourned. They are responsible for what is happening to children in this city."

Her voice dipped, low and dangerous. "I am not sitting in an office while you two run off to play soldiers and martyrs."

Diego's lips twitched. "Told you," he murmured to Chase. "Women tell you when they've had enough. You don't get to decide for them."

Chase rubbed a hand over his jaw, studying her. She looked shattered. She looked furious. She looked exactly like someone who might burn the world down before letting it take anything else from her.

"Alright," he said finally. "We follow the trail from Buzzard's drop. Quiet. Careful. We see how deep this goes."

Buzzard snorted. "You don't do 'quiet 'or 'careful Cassidy. 'You do 'gunfire 'and 'property damage.'"

"Occupational hazard," Diego said.

Skye stepped back to the gurneys, fingers brushing Thomas Anderson's sleeve one last time. She leaned down and pressed her lips to Donald Pierce's cold forehead. When she straightened, her eyes were bright but dry. "Thank you, Doctor," she said softly. "For taking care of them."

Buzzard's shoulders slumped a fraction. "Wish I'd seen them sooner," he muttered. "Might've been able to make them more presentable" He pulled the sheets back up, covering the faces of Thomas Anderson and Donald Pierce. For a moment, there was nothing in the room but the soft whisper of linen settling.

Chase reached for Skye's hand. She let him take it. Three of them, facing the cold steel of the morgue drawers, the mechanical arm on the bench, the invoice in Chase's pocket that pointed toward the dark veins under the city.

"Alright," Skye said quietly, voice like a blade being sheathed. "We've mourned. Now we move."

Chase nodded once. "St. Augustines then, we enter the tunnels there. Sweep and clear."

Buzzard watched them go, rubbing absently at the joints of his necromech fingers. "Try not to bring me any more friends," he called after them.

Chase didn't look back. "No promises," he said.

The morgue door closed behind them with a heavy, echoing thud, leaving the dead to their silence. The cab ride to the Safe House was silent. Skye leaned against the window, eyes hollow, clutching her briefcase with both arms as if it were the only thing keeping her upright. The city blurred past in streaks of gray and winter ash. Chase sat beside her, broad shoulders rigid, glancing her way every few seconds. Diego rode in the front, chewing his lower lip, dice clicking anxiously in his hand.

When they pulled up to the brownstone, Skye's voice finally broke the silence.

"Chase..." Barely a whisper.

He turned to her immediately. "Yeah?"

Her breathing hitched once—quiet, almost hidden. "Take me inside," she murmured. "Please. I... I can't keep it together out here."

He opened the door without another word. The Safe House was exactly as the left it, a libraries worth of book and light on the furniture.It had been their home for a month as they lay on two mattresses thrown together on the floor. Two armed Anderson & Pierce security men stood inside, tense and alert. Another stepped out from the shadows—bald, tattooed, robes cut short for movement.

A batter caster. The street term for their kind was "spell-slinger." Hard-bitten, ward-savvy mages trained specifically to counter spellcasters in close quarters. The mage nodded to Chase. "Rooms are secured. Wards reinforced. No one gets in."

Skye barely acknowledged him. Her voice was thin and frayed. "Where's Nadine?"

"On her way," Chase said gently. "Luther too."

She closed her eyes, nodding once.

When Nadine arrived minutes later—coat half-buttoned, worry etched deep—Skye collapsed into her arms without a word. Nadine hugged her fiercely, smoothing her hair the way she used to when Skye pulled all-nighters at law school.

"Oh, honey," she whispered. "Come lie down. You don't have to talk. Just breathe." Skye let herself be led to the bedroom. She paused at the doorway, turning back toward Chase.

Her voice trembled. "Just... stay close. Don't leave with out me I don't want to wake up and find out you two are gone"

Chase stepped forward, kissed her forehead, and rested his palm against her cheek.

"I'm not going anywhere." He lied She held his hand for a beat—long, shaking—then released it and went inside with Nadine. The door shut softly.

Moments later Luther arrived, jaw tight, shotgun slung over one shoulder. He posted himself in the hallway like a silent sentinel.

The house settled. Low murmurs. The faint buzz of wards. Footsteps receding. And then, quiet. Skye Anderson-Pierce for the first time in forty-eight hours, slept.

Chase paused at the entryway.

Even in the dim lamplight, Skye looked impossibly young—fragile in a way she would have hated anyone to see. He braced a hand against the doorframe and exhaled once through his nose, steadying himself.

"Go," Nadine murmured without turning. "Just... bring her back something worth wakin 'up to."

He gave a small nod and stepped away before the weight of her words could settle.

Diego was already half-dressed in chaos. He yanked open the trunk they'd dragged from Chase's burnt out apartment —their unofficial "war box"—and pulled out gear with the energy of a man who had survived too many fronts by improvisation. He shrugged into his old French greatcoat, that dark blue relic of the Régiment Étranger patched at both shoulders.

An American surplus vest went under it, pockets bulging with dice bags, chalk sticks, short wards, an oilcloth-wrapped mystery, and the absolute confidence that he'd need every ounce of it.

The dice-loop bag hung from his bag. The bandolier followed across his chest.

"You look like somebody robbed three dead soldiers and wore all their clothes at once," Chase said.

Diego smirked. "Joke's on you. They weren't dead when I took them."

A heavy bootstep echoed behind them. Luther Holloway filled the hallway broad shoulders inches away from each wall. "This one's for you," Luther said, handing the shotgun to Diego. "Slugs and disruptors. 1897 Winchester, my old girl. Make me proud."

Diego held the weapon like he'd just been handed a holy relic. "Oh, sweetheart," he murmured, stroking the barrel, "take me on a date first."

Luther snorted. "I'll tell Nadine you said that."

Chase knelt beside the open trunk. Inside was the past he kept trying to outrun: the trench vest with burn marks from battles that no longer made the papers; three arcane grenades he hadn't seen since France; magazines, field tools, and the long, brutal lines of the Thompson from the APD armory leaning just to the side.

And at the bottom—wrapped in its oilskin shroud— The Model VIII helmet. Rune Steel . Heat and impact warded visor. Rune channels etched by hands he would never shake again.

He reached for it. His fingers froze inches above the metal. Verdun's fog rose in front of him. Black Dagger's tunnels. The Ossuary. Screams in German and French and English overlapping until none of them were words anymore. His hand curled slowly into a fist.

"Not tonight," he whispered. He shoved the helmet back into the trunk and slammed the lid.

Effie and Pearl went into their holsters, the weight familiar as ribs. The Thompson strap settled across his back. The grenades found pouches. He buckled the trench vest tight, settling into a skin the world had tried and failed to peel off him.

Diego watched him quietly, expression shifting from humor to something older.

"You're walking like the Hellfighter again," Diego murmured. "Like the trenches are callin 'your name."

Luther leaned against wall, arms crossed over his broad chest, the lines of age and old wars carved deep around his eyes. "She's gonna be furious when she wakes up," he said. "Skye don't take kindly to bein 'left behind. You know that."

Chase exhaled through his nose, thumb brushing the grip of Effie. "Trust me," he said, half grim, half weary. "I'm not lookin 'forward to hearin 'about it when this is over."

Luther huffed a soft laugh and stepped closer, heavy hand coming down on Chase's shoulder. "She's seen too much already," the older man said, voice low. "Too much fire, too much death. You boys ain't wrong to leave her be tonight. Me and Nadine'll... smooth things over best we can."

Chase nodded once, grateful but unable to say it. He lifted the Thompson again, testing its balance, the weapon settling against him like an old truth.

"Then let's hope we come back with something worth explainin'," he said.

Luther stepped back, letting him pass. "Go on, then. Bring the fight to the bastards."

Chase adjusted the sling, eyes sharpening to a predator's focus.

"Believe me," he said as he crossed into the cold, "they're about to get one."

Two veterans. Two broken men. A Hellfighter and the Legioneer walking into the night ready war, ready to tear the Underwalk apart until the Court of Bones had nothing left to hide behind.Together, Chase Cassidy and Diego Salazar disappeared into the winter dark—brothers beyond blood and battle

———

The chamber was ancient—built long before the rise of cities, carved into the bones of the world. Its walls bled whispers, and the low thrum of magic pulsed like a heartbeat through the stone. Shadows flickered across the high, vaulted ceiling, cast not by candlelight—but by something older. Hungrier. The air stank of burnt parchment, clotted incense, and embalming salts. A sarcophagus-shaped table, etched with ossified runes, stood at the room's center like an altar waiting for its god.

Two obsidian mirrors floated in the air above it.

Hermann von Epp stood between them—hands clasped neatly behind his back, silver cuffs gleaming like shackles made regal. His gaze was distant, calculating.

The first mirror shimmered. It showed Makalith Ravenwind striding through the carnage of the opera house. Aspen Willowbark lay unconscious in Utilis 'skeletal grasp. Behind them, the Crown of Mortem glowed faintly with its sickly power.

The second mirror danced with images of Coo-Coo Le Fay slicing through the halls of the Arcane Society, laughter trailing behind her like perfume. Another distraction. Another success.

Von Epp's lips curled into a slow, satisfied smile. "It is all falling into place," he murmured. But even as the mirrors showed victories won and chaos sown, his mind circled around only one name.

Adriana Mortem Ruthven. The First Seat of the Court of Bones. His supposed superior. His Matron. His leash. His final obstacle. He stepped toward a table beside the sarcophagus, fingers brushing a rolled scroll— an original diagram of the Binding Ritual, scrawled in blood-ink by the Reforger of Souls himself.

"She believes the Lord of Bones will share the throne," von Epp said softly. "That he'll honor her loyalty. Her centuries of service." His fingers tapped the bone-carved table. Once. Twice. "She is mistaken."

A third mirror—yet dark—quivered at the edges as if sensing the shift in thought. Von Epp flicked his hand. All three mirrors vanished into smoke.

Behind him, the iron door groaned open. Dorian Blackwell stepped through. Clad in black, neat as a mourner at a tasteful funeral, he moved with quiet precision. The scent of old spell-ink clung to him.

He halted just inside the threshold and inclined his head. "Second Seat," Dorian said. "Your summons?"

Von Epp didn't turn immediately. He let the silence hang a heartbeat too long—then spoke. "The host is secured," he said. "Aspen Willowbark is in Makalith's hands. The true Crown of Mortem is no longer under the

Society's glass."

Dorian's eyes flicked to the now-empty air where the mirrors had hovered. "And the First Seat?" he asked. "Adriana still believes this all serves her design?"

Von Epp's mouth curved, humorless. "She believes everything serves her design," he said. "That the Lord of Bones will rise and kneel to her like a penitent child." He finally turned to face Dorian, eyes cold. "She is wrong."

Dorian wet his lips. "Does she suspect your intentions?" "She suspects everyone," von Epp said. "But she underestimates me. She always has." He moved toward a sealed pedestal at the edge of the chamber. Thick glass encased a fragment of blackened, splintered bone. It twitched, almost imperceptibly, as if dreaming.

"The Lord's essence is restless," von Epp murmured. "He feels the crown moving. The vessel taken. The pieces aligned."

Dorian's gaze lingered on the bone. "Whispers say others inside the Court are uneasy," he ventured carefully. "That some fear your rise as much as they revere it. The Twilight Collective are formidable. Are you against simply paying them and having them depart? Isn't that the wisest choice?"

Von Epp snorted softly. "The Twilight Collective are mercenaries," he said. "Useful only so long as they carry the weight I assign them. After that… ballast to be cut away."

He turned fully, expression sharpening. "When Makalith delivers the bard and the crown—when theLord's new vessel reaches the sanctum —you will be ready."

Dorian stiffened slightly. "Ready for what, Second Seat?"

Von Epp stepped closer, voice dropping to a blade's edge. "To kill them," he said. "Makalith. Magnus. Le Fay. Every last member of the Twilight Collective. They have outlived their usefulness the moment they set foot in the inner chamber."

Dorian bowed his head. "As you will it."

Von Epp's smile deepened, thin and hungry. "And then," he continued, "we turn to the First Seat." He tapped the glass over the bone fragment with one gloved knuckle. "She has sat on hat seat far to long."

Dorian hesitated. "Poison?" he asked quietly. "Blade? A spell prepared in advance?"

"You will see in do time. She however, will not see it coming, I assure you" von Epp said. "And it will not be swift." He glanced back at Dorian. "When Adriana falls, the First Seat is vacant. The Court will need stability. Authority. A clear line of succession."

"And you," Dorian said, voice carefully neutral, "ascend."

Von Epp's eyes gleamed. "I ascend," he agreed. "And you, Fifth Seat, will be rewarded for your loyalty."

Dorian raised a brow. "With what, Second Seat?"

"Survival," von Epp said simply. "And a greater place at my table—if you prove capable of doing what must be done."

He turned away, gaze settling once more on the pulsing shard of bone.

"Prepare yourself, Blackwell," his voice lowered to a reverent whisper. "...we take the First Seat. And the Lord of Bones walks again."

The bone sliver pulsed once—twisting under the glass like something waking up.

Dorian bowed, the shadows swallowing most of his expression. "As you will it, Second Seat," he said. The chamber shuddered faintly around them, as if the world itself was listening.

————

The cavern breathed like something half alive. Runes glowed faintly along the ribbed stone walls, pulsing in sick crimson waves that made the very air feel swollen with hunger. Two Ascended Mourned glided around the sarcophagus—pale, graceful things in tattered silver robes, their movements smooth as drifting ash. They worked in silence, binding Aspen Willowbark's wrists and ankles with cold-iron shackles, each clasp sealing shut with a soft, cruel click.

Aspen's eyes were sewn shut, lips stitched the same. His chest trembled weakly, but he lived. Barely. Adriana Mortem Ruthven stood above him, black silk trailing like poured smoke. Her expression was one of quiet, terrible anticipation. Behind her, the Crown of Obsidian and Bone rested atop a stone pedestal, humming softly—as though excited.

Footsteps echoed from the stair. Makalith Ravenwind entered first, cloak slashed with blood not his own. Behind him came Coco Le Fay —her wings hidden, her steps light as a dancer's—and Sirus Magnus, cane tapping in short, worried beats. Utilis the Rover followed last, his movements too smooth, too quiet, blades tucked deceptively close to his sides.

They carried Aspen's limp, unmarked body to the sarcophagus. Makalith lowered him with ritual precision, offering Adriana a shallow bow of respect.

"It is done," Makalith said. "Despite... difficulties, the asset remains intact."

Adriana regarded Aspen as though inspecting a rare orchid. "Alive. And unspoiled. You've performed adequately." From the shadows beyond the stair, new footsteps sounded—measured, cold.

The six remaining Gravecallers emerged first, bone masks gleaming dully. Behind them came Dorian Blackwell, calm as winter, and Lilidan Blackwell, her faint smile sharp as a blade-edge.

Sirus stiffened, murmuring, "This... wasn't part of the meeting."

The Gravecallers fanned out. Makalith's hand edged toward his wand. Adriana never looked away from Aspen.

"You have fulfilled your half of the bargain, Makalith," she murmured. "But a ritual of this magnitude requires more aether filled blood banks. I will expend much energy and that must be replenished. "

Dorian's voice floated across the chamber, smooth and ceremonial. "A pure-blooded Fae, to feed the orchestrator of the resurrection."

Coco froze.

"Coco is not a pure blood. And that was never agreed to, her freedom was my payment First Seat. " Makalith said, stepping in front of her.

"She is close enough" Dorian replyed. He nodded once—almost lazily—toward his sister.

Lilidan struck first.

A violet shard of necromantic force snapped through the air, aimed straight for Coco's heart. Sirus Magnus reacted instantly, cane lashing upward. The wards along its length erupted in brilliant, spiraling light, intercepting the blast inches before it struck.

The impact cracked like thunder. The chamber erupted.

The six Gravecallers surged forward as one, robes snapping, bone masks leering. Their claws dripped black fire. Makalith's wand split into streaks of blue heat, severing a deathbolt in midair and rebounding another into the stone ceiling.

"Betrayers!" Sirus shouted. He never saw Utilis move.

The Mourned pivoted with impossible fluidity, one arm splitting open to reveal a serrated blade of alchemic steel. It punched clean through Sirus Magnus's back, erupting from his sternum in a gout of blood and ether-light.

Sirus gasped. His eyes dropped to the blade protruding from his chest. "...Uti...lis...?"

Utilis wrenched his arm free. Sirus collapsed in a boneless heap, cane clattering to the floor.

Coco screamed—a sound that shook the runes. "You bad, bad dead man!" she shrieked.

Utilis turned his furnace-bright eyes toward her. No remorse. No conflict. Only obedience—to someone else. Von Epp's voice drifted calmly from the stair as he appeared, hands clasped behind his back.

"Oh, my dear sprite. Did you truly think one of my creations would ever be loyal to you?"

Coco's face collapsed into horror. Makalith didn't hesitate. "MOVE!" he barked. He spun, intercepting a Gravecaller's claw strike with a burst of blue force that shattered its mask. A second Gravecaller lunged. Makalith slashed a sigil across the ground; the stone cracked open beneath it, swallowing the creature to the waist as the runes cinched shut around its limbs.

Coco vaulted upward in a burst of glamour, shrinking mid-leap into a palm-sized sprite of fractured light. She zipped above the melee, firing concentrated bolts of Sylvan energy that scorched two Gravecallers off-balance.

Lilidan fired again, her spell slicing upward in a crescent of shadow —but Coco dropped a glamour pulse in her face, knocking her backward into a pillar.

Makalith fought like a man who had survived a dozen wars and sworn never to flee another. He ducked beneath a Gravecaller swipe, severed its arm with a blade-sigil, then hurled its mask into another's face, shattering bone. But there were too many.

Von Epp stepped fully into the light, smiling like a serpent in a library. "You continue to impress me, Makalith," he said conversationally. "Truly. But you overestimate your place in this world."

Makalith snarled and hurled a bolt of spiraling blue fire straight at Von Epp's throat. The necromancer flicked two fingers. A sickly green ward snapped into existence, swallowing the spell whole. "Predictable," he sighed.

Makalith launched himself forward, closing the distance in a blur. His blade clashed with Von Epp's conjured ward, showering sparks.

That was when Dorian intervened. A razor-thin lance of white energy sliced across Makalith's footing, cracking the stone beneath him. He slipped—just an inch—but enough. Utilis appeared behind him like a falling guillotine. The first strike hammered Makalith's ribs, the second crushed his shoulder, the third clipped his jaw so hard his teeth loosened. The fourth sent him tumbling across the chamber.

He hit the stone and didn't rise.

Coco saw him fall. Saw Sirus dead. Saw Utilis standing over the broken bodies of the only people who had ever fought beside her. And as Von Epp's laughter filled the chamber—

She fled.

Her tiny form snapped into a streak of blinding light, slipping through a crack in the failing brick near the ceiling.

"Find her," Von Epp said mildly. "Alive."

The remaining Gravecallers hissed and scattered. Adriana finally looked away from Aspen, her eyes gleaming with triumph. "Enough theatrics," she murmured. "The bard is secured. The ascended are ready. The Crown stirs."

Her lips curled. "We begin." Aspen convulsed. The runes blazed crimson. And deep in the shadows of the cavern, something ancient inhaled for the first time.

CHAPTER 8

Into the Breech

Thoughts from the Fractured Mind of Coco Le Fay

I hate Adriana. I hate Adriana.

I really hate Adriana.

(And not the cute hate, either. The stab-a-neck-and-stomp-her-foot kind.)

She hurt Maky. She hurt the children. She hurt me.

Nobody hurts me unless I say they can, which is almost never unless Maky gives me a spanking. I like Maky's spankings—

Oh look! A cookie.

Mmm. Yum.

I forgot what I was saying.

Something awful, probably. Most awful things lead back to Adriana. She called me broken.

But that's fine. Broken things still fly.

And I am very good at flying.

The heavy wooden doors of St. Augustine's groaned as Chase shoved them open. Moonlight spilled across the nave, illuminating shattered pews, scorched hymnals, and a desecrated altar that looked as if something massive had crashed straight through it. The air reeked of incense, dust, and old blood.

Diego whistled low. "The Mourned came in here?"

"I followed them," Chase said, voice flat. "Chased them through an alley, then dove through that."

He pointed to the altar. Or rather, what remained of it—just a splintered slab and a yawning black cavity beneath.

Chase slung the Thompson off his back, checked the drum, and flicked the weapon to half-cock. Diego followed, sliding a warding charm up his wrist as he approached the ragged opening.

"After you," Diego said.

Chase dropped first.

The landing was quiet, practiced. Diego followed, boots clicking against stone. They stood in a narrow passage of old brickwork that ran beneath the church like the throat of something long buried. Rotted candles lined the wall in rusted cages. Smudges of soot suggested recent movement.

Chase scanned left, then right. "Tracks," he murmured. "Fresh ones."

Diego knelt to inspect the scuffs. "Shackled Mourned" he said. "Their gait's sloppy. Drag marks here… here…"

The two friends understood the truth. They would soon be facing overwhelming numbers of sentient undead and what other horrors Von Epp manufactured. There was no turning back. They moved.

The corridor widened into a low chamber where broken pew remnants and ossified bone shards lay scattered in unsettling patterns. At the center, scorched sigils spiderwebbed across the floor—fresh, layered over older markings.

Diego lifted his lantern charm. Its amber glow crawled across the runes. "Trap," he said. "A nasty one."

"What kind?" Chase asked.

Diego crouched, tracing a finger above—not touching—the nearest runes circle.

"These sigils are oscillating. Means they're reactive. You step wrong…" He drew an imaginary circle. "Skeletal limbs erupt from the ground. Bind you. Possibly tear you in half."

Chase exhaled through his nose. "Good. Something to look forward to."

Diego ignored him, digging in his vest for a chalk stick, two dice, and a fold of silk.

"Can you diffuse it?" Chase asked.

Diego smirked. "Of course I can diffuse it. My mother didn't raise an idiot."

A beat.

"She raised twelve idiots and me," he clarified.

He cast the dice gently across the sigils. They bounced, spun, and came to rest—one glowing faintly blue, the other red. The glyphs beneath them sputtered.

"Good," Diego whispered. He blew across the silk, letting powdered ash settle in a thin veil over the runes. They dimmed Then darkened entirely. The ward died like a snuffed candle.

Chase stepped forward. "You sure it's out?" Diego tapped the toe of his boot against the floor. Nothing happened. "I'm positive," he said then corrected himself. "I'm mostly positive."

"That's not—"

"Let's keep moving."

The next stretch of tunnel wound deeper beneath the city, narrowing and widening in strange intervals as though the architecture was less designed than grown. Small alcoves hollowed into the walls held remnants of bedding—filthy cloth, straw, half-chewed bones.

Chase swept his flashlight across one nook and froze.

A tiny handprint, burned into the stone. Blackened. Old.

"Ferals lived here," he said quietly.

"Not recently," Diego murmured. "These alcoves are abandoned. Long abandoned." Broken jars littered the floor—glass warped, stoppers missing. A faint residue sparkled inside one, like crystallized moonlight. Diego knelt, lifting the fragment gingerly.

"Essence jars," he murmured. "But these are... old. The stuff Narkiss sells is fresh, bright, fragrant. These look like they were bottled decades ago."

Chase looked up the corridor. "So they were feeding down here."

"Not feeding," Diego corrected softly. "Sleeping. Hiding. Dying." He let the glass fall. It shattered like frost. "This place is old, Chase. Older than the Dutch settlements perhaps.."

Chase didn't answer. His eyes were on the walls—studying cracks, shadows, shapes. Something felt wrong. The tunnel ended abruptly. A blank stone wall—smooth, unremarkable, unsuspicious.

Diego groaned. "Oh, come on. Don't tell me these monsters just… what? Teleported?"

Chase stepped forward, touching the stone with his palm. "Something's off," he muttered.

The glyph of True Sight flared across his eyes, burning bright amber. He scanned the wall. Nothing shifted. No illusion rippled. No glamours cracked.

"It's solid," Chase muttered. "No veil. No projected sigil. Nothing."

"So we came all this way for a very impressive pile of absolutely nothing?" Diego asked, throwing his hands up. "Perfect. Wonderful. All dressed up and no one to kill."

Chase stepped back, frowning deeper. "Not nothing," he said. "I can feel air. Barely. A draft. There's space behind it."

Diego stared at him. "…You can smell drafts now?"

"Years underground," Chase answered. "You learn things." He pressed his ear against the stone. A faint sound pulsed behind it.

Diego swallowed. "That's comforting."

They stood there in the half-dark, the cold draft the only proof the tunnel wasn't lying to them, both men cursing their luck in the same tired silence. This wasn't how an assault on the Court of Bones was supposed to begin—staring at a dead wall in the guts of a church, feeling the wrongness thick in the air, knowing in their bones that whatever waited ahead was already shaping up to end badly.

———

Coco shot through the crack in the ceiling like a firefly being chased by God's broom.

Her tiny four-inch body shimmered violently, glamour flickering in and out, wings buzzing so fast they whined like struck violin strings.

She ricocheted off a stalactite.

"OW—stupid rock—"

Then slapped a slimy wall for balance and launched herself forward again. Behind her, down the winding stone throat of the catacombs, came the hisses. Not breaths. Not voices. Not creatures.

Gravecallers.Hunting.

Her pulse fluttered, too fast, too small. They killed Sirus... they killed him... The memory hit like a slap. His eyes widening. The blood. The betrayal. Then Makalith—her Mak—hit by Utilis so many times and then cold laughter of Hermann von Epp.

Her wings faltered.

"Maky..." she whispered, voice thin as paper. "Maky, I'm sorry, I'm sorry, I should've...."

But she hadn't. She couldn't saved him. Nor Sirus. Couldn't even save herself without shrinking into useless sprite-size and fleeing like a scared lantern moth. She burst into a wider passage and hovered, clutching her own ribs as though sheer will might keep her heart from splitting open.

What do I do? What do I DO? Maky was captured—maybe alive, maybe not. Sirus was dead of that she was sure. Utilis—Her breath hitched into a shudder.

"I knew we should've never trusted that dead thing," she spat, voice trembling with rage and heartbreak tangled together. "Filthy corpse puppet. I told him, I told him—Mak said he was different, but NO, no he wasn't—"

She punched a pipe. It hurt. She punched it again anyway. Her thoughts spiraled. First my sister. Now Sirus. Now Maky... gone, maybe dead, maybe worse... Alone again. Always alone.

She curled inward midair, wings drooping like wilted petals.And then—Voices.

Close. Coco shot upright and darted behind a rusted pipe, peeking around the edge. Two men stood in the corridor ahead—lit faintly by fungus glow and leaking arcane light from Chase Cassidy's forearms. He held a machine gun at low-ready, scanning each shadow as if daring them to move.

Another man stood beside him, shotgun slung, dice loop rattling nervously. Coco's pupils expanded, filling her eyes. A whisper escaped her lips: "The Hexbreaker..."

She shrank back instinctively. *Oh stars, oh rotten stars, him. I tried to kill him and he punched me in the face.* She pressed both hands to her temples. She'd heard his name mentioned by Lby Von Epp.

Chase Cassidy. The Spellbound. The one who kills Gravecallers like they're made of wet bread.

The man next to him muttered something, irritated. "This is the third dead end, Chase—I'm telling you, these tunnels ain't right. They're shifting or something."

Coco trembled. *Should she fly away? Stay hidden? Approach him? No, no, no, he hates me, he hates me, he tried to shoot me.* She was small. Alone. Fracturing at the edges. *If she stayed alone—terrible things always happened.*

Always.

Her thoughts swirled: *Cassidy doesn't like von Epp. I don't like von Epp. He kills Gravecallers. I hate Gravecallers. He fights monsters. I need a monster killed. And Macky's plan has gone absolutely, perfectly, gloriously to poop—*

She slapped her cheeks with both hands. *Think, Coco. THINK. Von Epp needed her for something—she wasn't sure what—but the ceremony had never required her from what she remembered. Which meant he had lied.*

"He must've been trying to scare Mak," she whispered to herself. "Or bluff. Or he needed me for something he didn't say. Rotten bone-eater liar..."

Her wings buzzed wildly. And that left one option. Only one. Find the Spellbound.

Tell him what happened. And pray he doesn't shoot me on sight.

She peeked again. Chase stepped forward, eyes cutting the dark like twin golden knives. Coco swallowed hard. "Okay, Coco," she whispered. "No big deal. Just approach the men hexbreaker. Ask for help. He will see that you are just a bit crazy."

She fluttered out from behind the pipe—and froze. Because Chase Cassidy turned sharply toward her hiding spot. Eyes narrowing. Hand resting on the machine gun.

Coco exhaled the tiniest squeak. "...oh stars... please don't shoot the fairy..." And then she forced herself to drift closer because she had no choice. Alone was death.

Cassidy was danger...but maybe also salvation.

———

Solid stone. Not illusion. Not glamour. Not a trick. Just a wall of jagged rock that probably hand been there months, if Diego's grumbling was to be believed. Chase swept his hand along the rough surface anyway, eyes narrowed, Thompson balanced loosely in his grip. "It's here," he muttered. "There has to be a way forward."

Diego paced beside him with his Winchester 1897, pump already half-racked. "Yeah, well... unless the entrance decided to grow legs and—"

A giggle cut the air. High. Cracked. Too close. Both men snapped to ready positions—Chase bringing the Thompson up to his shoulder, Diego raising the shotgun smooth as a reflex forged in war.

"Who's there?" Chase barked. The giggle bounced again, ricocheting off the stone like a skipping coin on glass. A shimmer flashed. A sparkle—bright, frantic. Then a tiny, trembling head poked up from behind a rusted pipe.

"...Hi."

Chase almost squeezed the trigger. Diego nearly dropped the shotgun. A sprite, a fey who miniaturized for quick travel, floated fully into view— clearly resembling the manic killer who'd tried to glamour him at the docks.

She wore the same tattered insane-asylum straitjacket, sleeves cut free and hanging in strips like unraveling bandages. A torn tutu clung crookedly to her hips. Her wings jittered weakly. Makeup—thick stage paint—ran down her cheeks in smeared rivers of rose and black.

She looked like a broken doll someone had tried to throw away.

"Oh gods—don't kill me!" she squeaked, hands up, palms out. "Please don't kill me! I bruise EASY, like a peach—like a VERY PRETTY PEACH — a pretty peach with cute buttcheeks... Wow that rhymed."

Chase's eyes narrowed. "Coco Le Fay."

She gasped as though he'd recited poetry.

"You KNOW my name?! That is so SWEET! Nobodyremmebrs my name once m y show closed. Except Makie, and Sirus and stupid Von Epp and..."

"No, it's Miriam Le Fay," Chase corrected, voice harder.

Her true name.

Coco froze mid-flutter. "...okay," she whispered, eyes narrowing, "That is less sweet. That is VERY MUCH less sweet."

Diego edged forward, shotgun still leveled. "Back up. She's one of them."

"Noooo..." Coco whined, shaking her head so violently her tutu wobbled. "I'm one of me. The ONLY one left of me. And Maky's dying!"

Chase stiffened. "Maky?."

"Makalith!" she babbled. "Slender, tall, half fey, green eyes, silky black hair and the most perfect brown skin! My beau! My dark-and-stormy man! He saved me once, so I need to save him, but THEN THEY CAME—"

She spun in midair, pointing in all directions at once.

"—and they killed Sirus—SIRUS with an S, thank you—and Utilis betrayed us, the Mourned bastard, and Maky's bones are cracking and EVERYTHING IS TERRIBLE and you two are VERY VERY late!"

Coco zipped close—Chase recoiled on instinct. "And YOU!" she said, pointing at Chase's chest. "Hexy! You're supposed to be mean and scary. You look smaller up close."

Chase stared. "...what?"

Diego muttered, "Why is she like this?"

"I'm MENTAL AND TRAUMATIZED," Coco snapped. "Do not shame my coping skills." She fake cried into her elbow.

Chase steadied the Thompson. "Where's the entrance, Coco? We've been walking circles for ten minutes."

Coco giggled—soft, hollow, exhausted. "Oh, Hexbreaker... the doorway's been here the whole tiiiime." She floated to the stone wall and tapped it with one tiny finger. Nothing shimmered. Nothing flickered.

Instead the rock itself began to slide. Chasms split along invisible seams. Pebbles rained down. The stone peeled back like thick bark cracked open by fire. What revealed itself was no glamour. Not illusion. Not Fae mist. A fully summoned mass of earth magic—an elemental wall, grown into place by ritual shaping. The arch behind it pulsed faintly with bone-white runes.

Coco sniffed. "I told him this was overkill. But does von Epp listen? Nooo. He hates the Fae, but he LOVES using Fae magic. Hypocritical corpse-sniffer."

Chase stepped closer, awe and fury mixing.

"Pure elemental shaping... that's why True Sight couldn't see through it."

"YES," Coco said dramatically. "Because it's not fake rock—it's REAL ROCK THAT'S ONLY THERE BECAUSE THEY ARE TRYING TO HIDE THEIR SECRET LAIR. "

The arch finished unfurling. Cold air spilled out like the exhale of something old and starving. Diego racked his Winchester once, the sound sharp in the still air. "So... we go in, right? Into the murder hallway?"

Chase tightened his grip on the Thompson. "We go in. We stop the ritual. And we get Aspen Willowbark out alive."

Coco flinched at the name. "Ohhhh, you really are late. They started already" She drifted backward into the darkness. "Follow me," she whispered. "Before the hungry ones smell you."   Chase and Diego stepped across the threshold. The elemental doorway folded shut behind them and the Underwalk swallowed all three whole.

———

The ritual chamber throbbed with power—sickly, rhythmic, hungry. Red sigils crawled across the obsidian floor like veins pulsing under diseased skin. The Crown of Mortem hovered inches above Aspen Willowbark's chest, suspended by a lattice of bone-light.

Aspen lay in the center of the runic circle. His wrists were bound with cold-iron shackles. His ankles were fused to the stone with crystallized necrotic resin. His mouth and eyes were still sewn shut with black thread. He trembled. Not from fear. From the magic burning through him.

Three Gravecallers watched in silence—robes smelling of embalming salt and crypt-rot, their masks glinting like wet bone.

Adriana Mortem Ruthven stood over Aspen, a high priestess of the dead, her gown woven of shadows and bone-silk. Her fingers dripped with his blood—fresh sigils carved across his ribs, still glowing faintly.

She raised her hands. "The vessel is prepared." Her voice echoed, multiplied, as if the chamber itself spoke with her.

Behind her, Hermann von Epp stepped forward, wiping dried ash from his gloves. His eyes—cold, unblinking—swept across the room.

"Good," he said flatly. "Our Lord longs to return."

Dorian Blackwell and Lilithin approached from the side staircase, silent and poised like twin blades waiting to be drawn. Their expressions were unreadable. Their hunger was not.

A Gravecaller bowed stiffly. "Second Seat… the door ward fractured. The sprite escaped."

Von Epp's jaw twitched. "Le Fay."

He turned to Dorian and Lilithin, voice sharp as shrapnel.

"Take two of Gravecallers. Sweep the tunnels. I want the sprite found—and torn apart."

"Yes, Second Seat," Dorian said smoothly. His eyes flickered to Aspen. Then to Adriana. But he kept his expression perfectly placid.

Lilidan smirked. "Consider her clipped."

Von Epp raised a hand. "Dorian stay. Adriana will require assistance stabilizing the first phase."

Two of the masked Gravecallers stepped out of the circle standing behind the younger Blackwell twin. Their hands glowed with necrotic energy seeping from their fingers like black steam.

Aspen flinched—every muscle locking—with a muffled cry behind the stitches. Adriana ignored the sound. Von Epp turned, cloak snapping behind him.

"Begin without delay."

Liidan and the two Gravecallers strode toward the exit—shadows swallowing them as they vanished into the tunnels. The chamber dimmed. Only Adriana, Von Epp Dorian, Aspen, and the single Gravecallers remained.

Adriana placed both hands over the bard's heart. "Now," she breathed, "let the Reforger's work be remade."

She spoke the invocation—Old words, born in a dead god's throat.

"By crown of bone, by blood of song, By breath once pure and turned to wrong— Awaken, Lord of hollow form, Rise by vessel, death, and storm —"

The runic circle ignited. Aspen convulsed.

The iron chains rattled as his spine arched—hard enough to crack bone. His stitched mouth tore at the corners as heat surged through his chest, the sigils carved across him pulsing brighter, brighter, brighter until the Crown of Mortem slammed down onto his head with a sound like a tomb sealing.

His scream—silenced by the thread—rippled through the floor.

The Gravecaller leaned in, channeling necrotic force directly into the wounds carved across his ribs. Darkness seeped under his skin, spreading like ink through parchment.

Adriana smiled. "The transformation begins."

Aspen's body jerked violently— A second heartbeat emerged beneath the first. Louder. Deeper. His skin split along the sigils. From within, something moved. Something trying to claw its way out of the bard's chest.

Adriana closed her eyes, savoring the sound the wet snap of bones reshaping. the muffled, gagged scream behind sewn lips. The ancient power stirring like a beast waking from centuries of sleep.

Outside the chamber, faintly, deep in the tunnels— There was an echo. Footsteps. Two men. Armed. Coming closer. But inside the ritual chamber, none heard it. The Lord of Bones was opening his eyes.

———

They entered the tunnels. Narrow. Cracked. Runes carved into the stone at irregular intervals—some fresh, some old and leaking magic like wounds that refused to close.

"Still active wards," Diego muttered, tracing a claw-shaped glyph.

"Von Epp's work," Chase said. "Crude. Brutal. Effective." A wet dragging sound cut the air.

Chase raised a fist—halt. Something crawled in the dark. Breath rasping. Famished. Then it charged. A Mourned—half-rotted, eyes black and glassy—lunged from a side corridor.

Chase met it clean. An Infernal lance erupted from his two fingers straight through the eye. The living corpse crumpled mid-snarl.

"Damn," Diego whispered. "You still got it."

"Basics," Chase muttered. "Don't get sloppy. Some of these still think."

Diego's jaw tightened. "Yeah. They're not all gone."

They moved deeper. The air thickened with rot and spell residue. The floors shifted from cobble to scorched steel. Even here, long-dead wards pulsed faintly, like dying heartbeats.

Chase frowned. "Odd, the defenses are off," he muttered. "The Court left this path open."

Diego pointed right, a chamber bathed in sick green lantern-light.

A lone Gravecaller knelt beside a Fey man, palm pressed over the chest.Black tendrils siphoned essence in glowing ribbons. The Fey convulsed and went still. The necromancer turned toward the next cage—

A little girl, crying silently. Chase and Diego said nothing. They simply nodded once.

The Thompson roared. The Gravecaller exploded into rags and bone shards before he could stand. Everything shattered at once. But what came next set them on their heels.

Rotburn zombies and Shackled Mourned pouring from the tunnels like a ruptured vein.

"Right side!" Chase barked.

Diego's shotgun turned the first Mourned into mist. Another slammed into a wall, ribs popping like wet twigs. Followed by another shredded by twelve gauge buckshot

"Reloading!" Diego ducked behind piping.

"I've got you," Chase snapped—sweeping the Thompson across the choke point. Incendiaries ignited Rotburn from the inside out.

Chase swapped drums. "Moving!"

Diego cleared the flank. Two left. Chase surged forward—crushing one under his spellbound boot and shredding the other with a burst. Then — the cages. Dozens of them. Stacked three high across the cathedral-like walls.

Fey children. Bruised. Branded. Bleeding. Huddled like animals waiting their turn. A soft sob escaped one. Diego whispered, "They're batteries. They're using them as ritual batteries…"

"Break them out," Chase ordered, voice like a blade. Diego booted a latch. "Go—run—"

But the children didn't run. They stayed curled. Silent. Terrified.

Then—she appeared. The Mourned girl from the Church tunnels. Tattered dress. Sigil burnt into her neck. Movements eerily calm. Eyes dark but still aware.

She stepped forward. Raised a hand. Beckoned. Slowly—one child crawled out. Then another. And another. Soon they followed her, single file, toward the far hallway.

Diego exhaled. "I don't know what she is… but she's with us tonight."

Chase nodded. "Let her lead." Boot-steps echoed. A new figure stepped into the green light.

A senior Gravecaller, Wořm, Von Epp's most rusted—mask lacquered bone, inscribed with writhing sigils. Two Necroplague Technicians flanked him—leather aprons blood-soaked, one carrying a bone saw, the other a syringe the size of a dagger.

The children were nearly gone. Chase raised the Thompson. Diego loaded fresh shells. The Gravecaller lifted his hands and the lights died. A whisper fluttered through the dark.

A giggle. High. Musical. Coco Le Fay.

A spotlight fell from nowhere—faint fae glamour—and she pirouetted into view like a ballerina stepping onto her favorite stage. Ballet slippers. Ripped tutu. Hair wild. Smile sweet and deadly.

Both Necro-tech froze mid-movement—glazed eyes wide. He swayed. Sighed. Then collapsed face-first into the dirt, drooling quietly.

Coco wiggled her fingers. "Oops."

Chase didn't hesitate. The Thompson ripped through the glamoured Necro-tech's skull Bone and ichor splattered across the far wall. Coco was already skipping forward—wings fluttering in panic, dress swirling as she darted into a side tunnel like a startled cat.

"Sorrysorrysorry—Macky's in trouble—fix it fix it fix it BYE!" She vanished.

Diego hissed, "Damn it! I knew we couldn't trust her—"

He didn't finish. Because the cavern ceiling groaned—and collapsed. Stone cracked. Sigils burst. Dust and debris exploded downward, splitting the room in half.

Wořm howled an order. The remaining Necro-tech lunged. Chase raised the Thompson. Diego snapped the shotgun into place. And the ritual chamber ahead pulsed with a rising, impossible glow. The lights died. All at once.

A breathless blackout spread throughout the tunnels —no torchlight, no glyph-glow, not even a spark from the runes laced into the stone. Just breath. Dust. And the thick, cloying stench of rot, blooming in the void like a corpseflower.

For a heartbeat, nothing. Then—the whisper of shuffling feet. Not one pair. Not two. A chorus of them. Dragging. Dripping. Hungry.

"Flares. Now," Chase said, his voice a quiet gunshot in the dark. Diego cracked a flar and red fire hissed to life, casting a sickly glow across the necrotic walls.

The shadows didn't just leap. They twitched. Because the things making them were already moving.

Rotburned. Massive. Steam hissing between sutures like broken bellows. Their rune-stamped organs pulsed visibly through torn flesh. Feral Mourned. Snapping jaws, limbs jerking in spasmodic lunges, as if puppeteered by panic.

And the Gravecallers—two of them. Silent. Waiting. Each one a small apocalypse wrapped in robes.

Diego rolled his neck. "No fey kids this time."

"Just us," Chase said, locking a drum magazine in place with a metallic slam, "and the dead."

Wořm lifted his staff. The concussion spell hit like artillery. Chase flew back, smashing into a pillar—stone cracked in a spiderweb behind him. Diego tumbled across the floor, coughing blood, his shotgun skidding a few feet away. The Rotburned charged.

Chase rolled and came up firing. Ward-piercers shredded the first Rotburned's chest open, ripping through organ sacs and bile glands. It collapsed screaming like boiling water poured over bone.

The second didn't even flinch. It hit Chase like a battering ram, slamming him across the cracked tile. Diego dove, rolled, snatched the Remington, and fired from the hip. The Rotburned's head vaporized. The rest of the body stayed upright for a moment, twitch-running on instinct, before collapsing in wet chunks across Chase.

A Feral shrieked and launched off a pillar. It lost half its torso midair. The remaining half hit the floor twitching. "Reloading!" Diego barked, sliding behind a broken column.

"Covered!" Chase answered. He wasn't lying. He hit the floor in a skid, pivoted on his heel, and fired the Thompson in a sweeping arc so tight and clean that three Mourned dropped in the same breath—skulls rupturing like rotten pumpkins.

The flare sputtered, dimming. The dark gathered around them. And then—the second Gravecaller lifted a bone dagger. He carved a symbol in his own palm. Blood spilled. The glyph ignited. Chase turned—too late.

A Feral blindsided him, clawing, gnashing. He jammed two fingers upward as the infernal lance drove through the creature's jaw into the brainstem setting it on fire. It spasmed and collapsed.

"Left side!" Diego shouted.

The third Gravecaller unleashed a necrotic pulse that buckled the ceiling. A rain of shattered stone fell. A massive slab crashed between Chase and Diego, sending shockwaves through the hall. Dust. Ash. Screams. The floor trembled under them. Not from collapse.   From movement. The stone warped beneath their boots. The walls twisted like wax. Arches stretched. Pillars bent. The geometry turned abstract. A planial shift. Reality itself was folding.

"Chico!" Chase shouted—his voice echoing sideways, as if coming from the wrong direction.

"I see it!" Diego answered. "The whole hall's rewriting itself like a—" A corridor appeared between them, long and narrow, spiraling in on itself like a bone corkscrew. Impossible angles made the flarelight bend and run like melting paint.

The hallway swallowed Diego's echo. "Don't stop moving," Chase barked. "Push forward. Keep breathing. I'll find you."

"You better!" Diego called. "I hate walking alone in the dark!" And then—

A Rotburned lurched through the newly twisted corridor, dragging a cleaver the size of a small door. Steam vented from the glyphs hammered into its ribs. Chase fired, click. Empty. The beast hit him full-force, slamming him into the tilting wall.

Chase let it. He grinned a feral grin as the sigil carved into his palm flared, burning from amber to white. He jammed that burning hand into the Rotburned's chest. The creature detonated in a tower of hellfire and ash. Its remains painted the warped hall red and black.

"You good?" Diego's voice echoed through the distortion—distant but alive.

"I ain't pretty," Chase said, wiping blood and soot off his jaw, "but yeah."

"Glad you can admit the truth," Diego shot back. "See you on the other side, hermano."

A second flare ignited in the distance like a bleeding star.

Then Diego vanished.

Chase turned toward the depths of the tunnels.

The walls groaned. The sigils throbbed. The ritual ahead beat like a war drum calling them deeper. The veil was waiting.

———

The chamber was not of this world. It pulsed—flesh and stone fused in impossible geometry. Roots, not of any tree born on Earth, slithered through the walls like veins. A low, rhythmic thrum echoed with each beat of the sigil-burned heart suspended above the altar, pumping dark ichor into the channels carved across the ritual floor.

Adriana Morteum Ruthven stood at the center of it all, arms raised. Her gown of weeping silk swayed unnaturally, untouched by wind or breath. Her eyes had rolled back into white, and her voice—no longer entirely her own—poured forth in a chant that blistered the very air.

Fey children lay in concentric circles around her, sedated, surrounded by runes carved into the stone. Their bloodlines glowed in threads of blue, silver, and green—each strand drawn like a tributary into the great heart beating above them.

On the edge of the ritual's light, Dorian Blackwell watched in stiff silence. His fingers twitched at the hilt of his ceremonial dagger. He did not like the way Adriana changed when she chanted. The voice was hers, yes but something older, deeper, and infinitely colder echoed through it.

Adriana inhaled sharply, her voice layering on itself in broken harmonics. "It's all so closer" she whispered.

The ironbound doors burst open. A young acolyte stumbled in, one sleeve torn and slick with blood.

"My lady—my lord—the western sanctum—there's fighting—"

"Who?" Dorian snapped.

"Two intruders—one Spellbound, one dice mage—they're cutting through the lower sanctum, the cages—"

He never finished. Adriana flicked two fingers. His spine twisted in on itself like wet rope. He collapsed face-first, twitching against the floor stones. The ritual never faltered.

Dorian's rage sharpened. "He knew the breach point. We NEEDED him."

"He had fear in his blood," Adriana murmured, her voice echoing in a dozen cadences. "I will not let it poison the rite."

The runes flared in answer. The heart pulsed harder. The walls trembled. Dorian exhaled a slow, furious breath. "We're exposed now," he said. "We need to end this quickly." He wiped a fleck of the acolytes blood from his sleeve with silent irritation. The poor mans body still twitched on the stone, its warning hanging in the air like smoke:

"Spellbound... and a Dice Mage... in the lower tunnels—killing everything—"

Adriana didn't even look up from the sarcophagus. Her fingers traced glowing sigils across Aspen Willowbark's chest as if painting runes onto a canvas of living clay.

Dorian reached into his coat and withdrew a small black mirror, no larger than a man's palm, its obsidian surface shimmering like trapped night. He held it between his hands, palms facing inward.

A thin strand of shadow curled from his fingertips, twisting, binding, awakening the glass. The mirror pulsed once. Lillidan's face appeared within, framed by darkness and motion. She was moving, stalking, breath steady as a predator's.

"Brother," she whispered, her voice a silken blade. "Ihave almost cornered the sprite. Shall I—"

"No." Dorian's voice sliced across hers.

Lillidan stilled.

"There are intruders," he said. "A Spellbound and a Dice Mage. They're cutting through our forces in the lower tunnels."

Her eyes narrowed. "I know," Lilidan replied coolly. "I already sent my two callers to... tidy the interruption. Stop pestering me with trivialities."

Dorian's jaw tightened.

"You will stop what you are doing," he said, voice dropping into the tone that once ruled the Blackwell household. "Immediately."

Her expression hardened into something predatory. "The ritual," Dorian continued, "is reaching its apex. Nothing can disrupt it. Nothing. Deal with the intruders now."

Lilidan tilted her head, annoyed — but listening.

"And once they're dead," Dorian finished, "you may track down the Fey at your leisure."

A slow smile curled her lips. "As you command... Brother." The mirror rippled, her image shattering like ink in water. Dorian pocketed the shard, expression unreadable.

Dorian faced Adriana again.

The chamber thrummed with rising power—channels of liquid red light crawling up the walls like veins feeding a monstrous heart. Aspen convulsed against the chains, his sewn eyelids fluttering rapidly beneath black stitches. The two Ascended Mourned assisting Adriana leaned over the sarcophagus, their hollow eyes glowing with borrowed essence, hands moving in eerie synchronicity.

Adriana's chant deepened, her voice no longer entirely human.

Dorian stepped back into the shadows beside her, folding his hands behind him. Eyes narrowed. Mind sharpened. "Let them come," he whispered.

His sister would bleed the tunnels dry. And if somehow, the intruders reached this chamber they would face something far older than death.

———

The Sanctum of Mirrors is were Von Epp set up his command post. What was just two obsidian mirrors floating in the air, was now dozens, suspended by a lattice of whisper-thin runes that pulsed with sickly violet light. Each mirror showed a different corridor of the catacombs. A different battlefield. A different death.

Hermann von Epp moved between them with the precision of a surgeon and the silence of a corpse. His long coat—red and black billowed behind him like a funeral shroud. His gloved fingers brushed a mirror as he passed, bringing its image into sharper clarity.

Chase Cassidy appeared in the first mirror—blood on his face, fire in his eyes, Thompson raised as he advanced through the bone-warped corridor. Every step was violence held on a leash. Von Epp's lip twitched upward. "Spellbound... Infernus."

He turned to another mirror.

Diego Salazar flickered into view, flare in hand, shotgun blasting a Rotburned off its feet. He rolled under falling debris, muttering curses through smoke. Von Epp clicked his tongue "Probability mages... so unpredictable. Statistical chaos given flesh."

He moved again, stopping at a larger mirror rimmed in bone and brass. This one stitched images together—Chase and Diego in separate planes, but both moving inexorably toward the same convergence point.

His laboratory. His work. His legacy.

A Gravecaller shuffled into the chamber behind him, robes dragging, mask cracked from a blast of stray magic. The creature bowed low.

"Second Seat," it rasped, voice buzzing with the drone of a dozen hungry flies. "Should we redirect the remaining Mourned? Bring reinforcements to the western corridors? The intruders... they are advancing faster than expected."

Von Epp did not turn. He watched Chase's silhouette cutting down another Rotburn, watched the monstrous fire bloom against the mirrored glass.

"Advancing faster than you expected," he corrected quietly. "Not I."

The Gravecaller shifted uneasily. "But Second Seat—the ritual— Adriana commands we maintain defense. If the Spellbound reaches the ritual chamber..."

Von Epp finally turned. His pale eyes were colder than the stone underfoot. "Are you... absurd?"

The Gravecaller recoiled as though struck, bowing lower. Von Epp's voice remained soft—but razor-edged. "We do not 'divert 'forces. We do not panic because two pawns gnaw on the edges of our sanctum. We are the Court of Bones. These tunnels have bathed in blood long before their grandmothers birthed them." He leaned slightly toward the mirror, watching Chase reload with expert speed.

"And besides... It has been a while since I killed a spellbound. His death must ... add my legend."

The Gravecaller hesitated. "Second Seat... the probability of a breakthrough is rising. The dice mage—he breaches predictive paths."

Von Epp raised a gloved hand. The Gravecaller's jaw snapped shut with an audible click."Your lack of faith is noise. Silence." The masked wretch froze in terrified stillness.

Von Epp turned back to the mirrors, switching his attention from Diego to Chase. Something had changed. Chase was angling through a corridor that should have led nowhere. And yet, the walls had shifted.

Rearranged by the ritual bleed. The Spellbound had, by sheer instinct or fate, found the direct approach.

The path toward Von Epp's sanctum. Toward his laboratory. Von Epp's reflection caught in the mirror—his smile widening by a fraction, pupils dilating with predatory interest. He straightened his coat with a surgeon's grace, shaking dust from the crimson fabric. He adjusted his gloves, fingers flexing once, and thumbed the blade at his hip—its edge glinting under ritual light.

He didn't bother facing the Gravecaller behind him. "Prepare the sanctum for sealing," he said. "Any who follow me die."

"Yes, Second Seat," the Gravecaller rasped.

Von Epp stepped toward the mirror the obsidian surface rippling like disturbed water, parting for him alone.

"Yes I will stop Cassidy myself." Before crossing, he paused, tilted his head slightly and spoke into the shadows just beyond the runic arch.

"Utilis."

A shape unpeeled itself from the dark. Utilis the Rover stepped forward, gait uneven but deliberate. His breath came in faint, rattling growls, his grafted arm twitching with predatory instinct.

Furnace-orange light pulsed weakly beneath cracked rib grafts, the mechanical augmentations working to keep the revenant upright. He waited, head low, like a loyal hound built from the dead.

Von Epp still did not turn. "You will stay hidden," he murmured. "You will wait until I command it."

Utilis's jaw clenched, the metal pins along his cheekbone creaking.

"And when I give the word," Von Epp continued, "you will tear Cassidy apart."

A low, phlegm-thick growl answered him— obedience shaped by pain and necromancy, not loyalty. Von Epp stepped through the mirror. The surface sealed behind him with a whisper—leaving Utilis crouched in the cavern gloom, a Frankensteined revenant trembling with restrained violence, waiting for the moment his master would let him kill again.

CHAPTER 9

Take Out the Head

"God Damn, Let's Go!"

- Harlem Hellfighter Motto

The flicker of arcane wardlight danced along the chamber walls. Beneath Chase's boots, the stone was stained with old blood and the rust of forgotten chains. The air stank—rot, incense, and scorched bone. The hum of machinery filled the silence, pulsing with the low murmur of tortured things kept just below consciousness.

Chase stepped into the corridor's end chamber.

A laboratory.

Long tables covered in blood-soaked linen. Surgical instruments soaked in arcane resin. Mason jars with preserved eyes, tongues, and spinal cords suspended in glowing blue liquid. A chalk diagram on the floor was half-drawn, half-burnt, with bones forming glyphs around a shallow pit.

And cages. Cages full of things that used to be people.

Rotmourned.

Mourned in various stages of transformation. Some moaned softly, skin sloughing off in fungal chunks. Others sat wide-eyed and still, bound by sigils carved directly into their skin. A child's voice whimpered in the far corner.

Chase didn't hesitate.

He leveled the Thompson, thumbed the fire selector, and muttered, "Mercy is coming for you."

He pulled the trigger.

The first arcane flare rounds lit up the room like a festival fire. The bullets burned hot blue—incendiary sigils etched into the tips igniting the undead where they struck. The creatures thrashed, howled, disintegrated. Glass shattered. One Rotburned lunged, limbs jerking with unnatural speed.

It collapsed mid-air in a ball of fire and bone.

A warning rune on a wall lit up. Chase ducked. Two Mourned Acolytes stepped from a side chamber, arms raised, chanting.

Chase tossed a grenade. The blast ripped through the room, obliterating shelves, cages, the pit. The flames sucked back and then roared forward with a howl of vengeful air. The acolytes slammed into the wall—one broken, the other on fire.

Chase moved. He stepped through the smoke like a ghost in greatcoat and brimmed hat, barrel hot, smoke curling from the gun's vents. His face was grim. Focused.

He approached the cages.

The child was gone—just an empty collar and arcane restraints smoldering. Another survivor? Or another weapon now loose?

Didn't matter.

He brought the Tommy Gun back to ready, eyes narrowing as he saw the next set of double doors: iron-bound, freshly marked with necromantic sigils.

Whatever was beyond them was worse.

He exhaled. "What's next?"

And kicked the doors open.

———

The corridor twisted like the spine of a dead god—low ceilings, torchlight smothered by arcane haze. Diego crouched low, waiting. Breath steady. Shotgun heavy at his hip.

Footsteps.

A Gravecaller rounded the corner—robes of stitched vellum, wand carved from a child's femur. Diego fired first.

The buckshot tore through flesh and spell before a curse could leave the Gravecaller's lips. The body collapsed into bone dust.

He pumped the weapon, eyes sharp. That's when she came.

Lilidan.

Elegant, pale, a stitched smile on perfect lips. Her eyes glowed lavender.

"Well, well," she said smoothly, "You again. I underestimated you the first time dice mage, I won't make that mistake again."

Diego aimed the shotgun toward her face. "Neither will I and this time I bought buck shot."

He pulled the trigger—
Click.
The metal glowed red.

Lilidan smiled. "Guns are so... *uncivilized*."

It exploded as he tossed the ruined weapon.

From the dark behind her came a groan—a mountain of necrotic meat. A Patchman. Eight feet tall. Cleaver-arm. Stitched runes pulsing necrotic green.

With no weapon, Diego reached into his pocket and pulled his "ace in the hole", the Bone Trio: two pip-marked dice and the master die bearing one of six ancient runes. Diego whispered, "Let's dance."

He tossed.

Master Die: ⬚ Fortune Favors
Pips: 5 + 4 = 9

Effect: Hand of Fate (Buff) — His reflexes sharpened. Time slowed.

He dodged a swipe from the Patchman by inches, continuing past Lilidan's outstretched hand, and rolled against the dice returned to his hands.

Master Die: ⬚ Shattered Coin
Pips: 3 + 3 = 6 – DOUBLES

Effect: Popping Smoke (Combo Trigger) — His form blurred. An illusion double burst into existence beside him. Thick smokescreen exploded, cloaking his retreat.

Lilidan snarled and fired—her spell cracked stone, hitting nothing.

The Patchman charged through smoke blindly.

Diego flicked another trio.

Master Die: ⬚ Big Red

Pips: 6 + 6 = 12 – DOUBLES

Effect: Ashwake (Combo Trigger) — A spiral of fire howled from Diego's hand. It struck the Patchman square, igniting its skin, burning stitches apart. It screamed—a wet, guttural sound spasmed from three different voices.

Lilidan raised a shield of bone, deflecting the edge of the inferno. She was burning, furious. She shrieked, "Crush him!"

The Patchman surged. Slashing wildly. Diego dodged, a cork srcew roll midair as the Pathman missed badly, impaling its cleaver into a steam pipe. Hot gas erupted in the creature's face. It screamed again, flailing its other arm and connecting against the dice mage hard.

Diego took the hit full on. Slammed into the far wall. Blood in his mouth.

Still, he rolled. One hand. One breath.

Master Die: ☐ Counting the Odds
Pips: 2 + 5 = 7

Effect: Risk of Ruin (Jinx) — The Patchman faltered. Its runes glowed unstable flickering as the probability magic took its effect. It lurched, cleaver arm going limp as it stumbled about.

Diego scrambled back, drew his arcane pistol, and fired— Click. Nothing. The runes had failed.

He reached for one last throw.

Master Die: ☠ The Black Mark
Pips: 4 + 4 = 8 – DOUBLES

Combo Effect: Final Hand

A black sigil flared beneath the Patchman's feet. Its body seized— cursed and claimed. Diego knew this was the final hand.

He rose to his full height, blood trailing from the corner of his mouth.

"Pay your debt."

He hurled the Bone Trio, now pulsing with raw arcane energy, straight into the creature's chest. The rune on its feet ignited—detonating with cursed precision.

The Patchman convulsed violently as the dice phased in and out of its body, tearing through muscle and stitch with each pass. Arcane currents surged through its frame.

Then—with a sudden crack—the three dice collided mid-air, releasing a final pulse of energy that cleaved upward through its neck.

The creature's head spun free, rolling across the stone like a coin tossed by fate.

Lilidan screamed caught in the backlash of the arcane explosion, vanishing—sucked into a rift of shadow magic. Not dead. But retreating.

Smoke curled from Diego's hands.

He leaned on the wall. "House always wins bitch."

Skye woke with a sharp gasp. For one disorienting second she didn't know where she was—only that her head throbbed, her throat was raw, and her cheeks felt stiff with dried tears. The ceiling above her was carved timber, not plaster. The air smelled like cedar oil and old spell-ward dust. The safe house.

A quilt she didn't remember lying under was pulled up to her chin. Luther's. Someone had cleaned the soot from her face. The same someone had brushed the ash from her hair. Nadine. The Holloways had always taken care of her. And even now in this time of crisis they stood by her.

The soft murmur of voices filtered from just outside the bedroom doorway. Skye pushed herself upright—slowly at first, then faster as the memories hit: her fathers, the blood in Vittorio's restroom Chase carrying her to the safe house Diego's hand steadying her as she fell apart—and then darkness.

Her breath quickened. She swung her legs over the bed.The door opened a crack. "Skye?" Nadine's voice—gentle, careful. "Hey... you're awake."

Nadine slipped inside, her expression a knot of worry beneath her cropped curls. Behind her hovered Tommy Dixon, stiff-backed and pale, hands clasped like he was holding himself together. Luther stood in the hall behind them, arms folded, eyes stern and protective. And at his hip—

Benjamin Bright, clutching the strap of a small satchel, his face blotchy from crying, eyes huge and frightened.

All of them froze the moment Skye looked up. She cleared her throat. "What... what time is it?"

"After sundown," Nadine said quietly. "You were out for hours. You needed—"

"Where are they?" She asked noticing the distinct lack of a certain spellbound hexbreaker ands his dice throwing friend.

Nadine hesitated. "Chase and Diego—they left about an hour ago. They didn't want to wake you."

Skye's heart hammered in her ribs.

"Where," she demanded, "did they go?"

Luther stepped forward. "Skye, listen—"

"No." Her voice cracked. "Tell me where they went."

Tommy rubbed the back of his neck nervously. "They—uh—they went to follow up on what Dr. Buzzard told everyone at the morgue. About the prosthetic arm he built. And where it was delivered."

Benjamin's voice piped up, small and shaky: "Miss Skye... they went down there. To stop the bad people."

Her pulse roared in her ears. Of course he did. Of course he went charging straight into hell. Skye stood, legs trembling but determined.

Nadine put a hand out, instinctively. "Skye—sweetheart—stop. You need more time. You're grieving, you're exhausted, you're still—"

But Skye was already grabbing her oxfords. "No. No more waiting."

She shoved her feet into them, lacing them with shaking fingers.

Luther stepped in. "Chase said to stay here. You're safe here. Guards are outside. Anderson & Pierce sent a battle casters—"

"My fathers are dead," Skye said, voice raw and low. "And Chase is down there fighting the people who killed them." She crossed the room, snatched her arcalam wand from the bedside table, checking dueling wand with a meticulous eye. The runes flared a sharp electric blue.

She moved to the lockbox in the corner—a small black safe with arcane etching. She spun the dial, opened it, and pulled out her polished revolver. She checked the cylinder, snapped it shut with a flick of her wrist, and holstered it under her coat.

Benjamin stepped forward, grabbing her sleeve. "Please don't go," he whispered.

She paused. Knelt. Placed a trembling hand against his cheek. "Benjamin... I have to."

He swallowed and nodded, trying not to cry. Skye stood.

Nadine tried once more. "Skye, please—"

Skye's eyes lifted, fierce and focused in a way that left no room for argument.

"Chase and Diego are down there," she said.

"My fathers deserve justice."

"And I'm not letting other people fight my battles for me."

She stormed toward the door.

Luther moved to block it but Skye snapped her arcalam up in one hand. The wand buzzed with dangerous charge.

"Move, Luther. Now."

He stepped aside. And Skye Anderson—coat half-buttoned, wand crackling, revolver at her hip, eyes burning with grief and fury, threw open the safe house door and strode out into the night.

———

The steel storm of the Thompson roared again. Chase Cassidy let out a breath and squeezed the trigger, walking a line of ward-piercers into the ribcage of the Gravecaller lurching from the shadows. Runes lit up across its decaying form as the enchanted rounds punched through what was once a man, now just a puppet of death and spellcraft. Its torso shredded into pieces, it collapsed in a heap of gore and ash.

"Rot in pieces," Chase muttered, swapping mags with a practiced flick.

The corridor stank of incense, rotting blood, and alchemical potions. He pushed forward into a vaulted laboratory carved beneath the cathedral, metal walkways suspended above tanks of brine and bone. Runes pulsed along the walls. Vats hissed and boiled, housing partially formed Mourned—some still twitching in agony.

And then he felt him.

A cold presence slid in like a blade between his ribs.

Hermann von Epp.

The man stepped from the shadows in full formal regalia—black high-collared coat lined with Imperial German filigree, pale hair slicked back, and eyes that burned with arcane obsession. He stood atop the mezzanine, flanked by two figures who moved with eerie, unnatural grace.

Two Mourned assassins.

Not feral. Not rotten.

Refined.

Their flesh was pale and stretched taut, bone-plated limbs inscribed with sigils Chase didn't recognize. Their eyes glowed with a faint violet pulse. One carried a pair of bone daggers; the other had spined cords protruding from its wrists—like living garrotes.

"Mr. Cassidy," Von Epp called from the upper walkway, voice smooth as lacquered rot. "Of all the gnats buzzing about, I had hoped it would be you. Soldier to soldier. Remnants of the last war."

Chase stepped into the flickering half-light, Thompson gripped low in one hand, boots crunching over bone-dust. "You should've stayed buried, Herman."

Von Epp turned toward him with the slow poise of a man greeting an expected problem "A Spellbound," he mused aloud, voice smooth as cold marble. "I had hoped the reports were exaggerations. But here you are — living proof of America's most reckless experiment."

Chase's jaw flexed. "Save the lecture."

But Von Epp was already walking a slow circle, studying him like a specimen.

"You know, I always regarded American arcane research as... provincial. Impatient. You bind before you understand. You cut corners. You call it innovation." He tutted softly. "But Spellbinding — ah, that was bold. To fuse infernal fire into mortal flesh? To mix human soul with hell-touched sigils? A criminal act, really. Unethical. Wasteful."

His pale eyes glinted with surgical interest. "And yet... I must give your generals credit. And Tesla, of course — arrogant, erratic, but visionary when properly leashed. The ritual worked on so very few of you. Most...

burned from within. Others lost themselves. Many took their own lives before the corruption claimed them."

Chase said nothing, but the air around him warmed — faint sigils beginning to stir beneath his skin.

Von Epp smiled thinly. "But you, Herr Cassidy... you survived Verdun. You survived Ypres. You survived the Ossuary." He leaned closer. "And still the fire does not consume you."

Chase raised the Thompson an inch, eyes hard. "It consumes plenty. You're next."

Von Epp chuckled. "Still the blunt instrument. Fire, fists, and trauma stitched into a uniform."

A beat.

"But I confess, your resistance fascinates me. Why your soul does not tear. Why your mind has not collapsed." He lifted a gloved hand. "Something in you is... exceptional. Rare."

Then, with quiet hunger: "And when I peel you open, I intend to find out what."

Chase's answer came in a growl: "Come find out." The Thompson came up and opened fire.

Von Epp threw up a shimmering shield—translucent like fractured glass—and dove aside.

From the shadows, the Mourned attacked.

One dropped behind Chase like a guillotine, its corded limbs snaking toward his throat. He rolled under the strike, rose with brutal force, and cracked the butt of the Thompson across its skull before riddling it with flare rounds. Fire burst from its sockets—it shrieked but didn't fall.

The second came fast—blade flashing. Chase took a cut to the ribs, dropping the Tommy gun he grabbed the attacker's wrist, slamming it against the wall. Pulling his trench knife, he drove into its jaw. The creature bucked, headbutted him hard, and sent him staggering, blade pulling free as he went.

They circled like jackals.

Above, Von Epp watched, composed, arrogant. "I'm birthing a new species, Cassidy. Perfected. Bound by evolution and magic. Not even your spellbound tricks can stop what's coming."

Chase spat blood and activated his sigils.

The Seal across his chest flared, runes blazing beneath his skin. Pain bled into fury. Wards glimmered over his muscles like translucent armor. His voice, when he spoke, was pure grit.

"I'm going to kill you."

He surged forward.

The first Mourned lunged.

Chase dropped low, caught it mid-air by the ribs, and *drove* it through a rusted pressure tank. Brine and bone exploded outward in a wet blast. The thing twitched, screeching, but it wasn't dead.

The second Mourned came from the flank—cords snapping forward like spiked whips.

Chase activated the Ward of the Searing Aegis.

A sigil on his left forearm blazed to life, forming a flaring, gossemer buckler of infernal glass just as the cords struck. Sparks flew as the whips ricocheted off the burning shield. Chase rotated with the impact, caught the momentum, and *slashed* forward with his trench knife.

The Mourned twisted aside, barely avoiding the blade—its counter came fast. A kick to his leg, a cord aiming for his throat.

Chase checked low with his knee, *bashed* the incoming cord aside with the buckler, then drove his elbow up under the creature's chin. Bone cracked. He grabbed the opening.

The Sigil of the Infernal Lance erupted. With two fingers, a shearing blade of fire projected forth, slicing the mourned assassin's helmet. It stumbled back, oozing ichor from its face. Its movement assisted by a boot to the chest. Turning, Chase launched a much-needed distraction..

He hurled an arcane grenade toward Von Epp.

The blast shattered the upper railing in a flare of radiant fire. Von Epp screamed, stumbling back, his protective ward fracturing in a cascade of brittle light.

The second Mourned lunged again—this time more cautious, more deadly. Its cords feinted, one high, one low. Chase parried the top strike with the Aegis, ducked the lower cord, then twisted inside its guard. He *slammed* the trench knife between its shoulder blades, let go and activated the infernal lance sigil.

Infernal fire surged up the blade, devouring the creature from within. It shrieked—mouth wide, eyes melting—before collapsing in a convulsing heap.

Behind him, the first Mourned rose from the wreckage.

Its mask was cracked, face half-rotted and steaming. It charged, howling, eyes glowing with unnatural fury.

Chase turned—too slow.

The creature tackled him, slamming him to the ground. Clawed fingers wrapped around his throat. Pointed tips dug into his flesh

Chase growled, using Aegis again jamming the burning buckler between them. It scorched into the Mourned's chest—blackening flesh, cooking bone—but it kept pressing, screaming in his face.

Chase let it.

Then he pointed his two fingers again under the chin, igniting the infernal lance. The monster's body seized, fire pouring from its eyes and mouth.

Chase shoved it back, drew Effie with a smooth snap, and *emptied* the magazine into its skull at point-blank range.
Bone split. Flesh sizzled. The Mourned dropped—its skull cratered, its body still twitching with dying sparks of magic.

Above, Von Epp stood again—burned, bleeding, but smiling.

"You've grown into your spellbound abilties, Mr. Cassidy," he said, voice still silk.

Then his hand moved.

A blade of glowing arcane light flared to life in his palm—an arcane saber, forged of runes and blood-etched steel.

"Let's see if the Hellfighter reputation lives up to the fame."

The chamber filled with heat, blood, and the rising hum of sorcery.

———

The air was thick with rot and ozone. The stone corridors twisted like veins beneath the cathedral, every turn cloaked in whispers and stale magic.

Diego Salazar moved like a shadow—quiet, precise, controlled chaos. Dice clinked between his fingers, ready to cast. His other hand gripped his arcane pistol, but he hated using it. Too loud. Too crude.

He turned a corner—and froze.

Lildan emerged from the smoke—elegant, cold, terrifying.

Her robes shimmered like fluid ink. The twin sickles in her hands glowed violet, runes spiraling along their curved blades. Her eyes, twin lanterns of seething arcane light, locked on Diego.

"Well," she murmured, "the rat survives a third sweep of the trap."

Diego blew out a breath. "Lady, if I'm a rat, you're the cat that keeps missing."

Her smile sharpened. "Do you truly believe your luck will save you again?"

He flipped a die across his knuckles. He caught the die between two fingers, the pip-marks glowing faintly. "I am luck."

Diego tilted his head, cocked a smirk, and flicked his wrist.   They rolled forward—

⬚ Rune: ⬚ Fortune Favors

⚃ + ⚀ — **7 Total**

The air around him shifted.

Diego's pulse slowed, but the world around him sped up—every twitch of her fingers, every gleam of light on steel became crystal clear. Then she moved.

Twin arcane sickles at the ready. She struck fast.

Diego leaned back, the first arc of silvered metal missing his throat by a whisper. The second slash came low—he hopped over it, twisting mid-air, landing behind her in a crouch. Lildan whirled, her blades dancing in a figure-eight pattern. A storm of cuts. No wasted movement.

Diego ducked left, pivoted, let one blade slice the edge of his coat. He threw himself into a shoulder roll, came up low, and vaulted backward off the wall in a half-flip to avoid a rising vertical strike.

He landed upright, boot skidding across the floor. Breath steady.

She snarled and lunged again—horizontal slash.

He leaned into the motion, letting it pass an inch from his nose, then jammed the muzzle of his pistol against her side.

Her ward cracked. She recoiled, gasping, spun, and slashed again—this time in an overhead X-pattern.

Diego dived into a controlled fall, slid under the cross strike, and kicked upward as he passed beneath her, catching her in the ribs and sending her staggering back.

He kipped up fast, sweat flying from his brow, eyes narrowed.

"You done dancing?" he panted, smirking.

She didn't answer.

Her lips curled into a sneer—and her hands glowed again.

Volley incoming.

He rolled the dice again—
⬚ **Rune:** ☠ **The Black Mark**
⊡ + ⊡ — **7 Total**

A black sigil exploded beneath her feet. She staggered, one glyph on her shoulder flaring red-hot. "Debt collected," Diego spat.

Her spell cracked. The backlash flared through her chest—she screamed as her ward exploded inward like shattered glass.

She retaliated, hurling a sickle at his head.
Diego ducked just in time—his shoulder still burned.

He needed to end it now.

One more cast.

⬚ **Rune:** ⬚ **Big Red**
⊡ + ⊡ — **Double Fives**

Diego's arm lit up with ember-crimson light. His skin seared with pain—but his muscles surged, strength humming under his skin. He sprinted at her, pistol raised.

Lilidan tried to cast again—but her mark was still flaring.

He fired twice—center mass.

Both shots punched through.

She staggered.

Diego dove and drove a glowing coin-shaped ball into her chest—the final spark of Big Red igniting.

"Boom," he whispered.

The sigil detonated.

Lilidan was thrown backward into the altar wall—cracking it, then collapsing in a heap. She wasn't dead. But her aura flickered like a dying fire.

Diego stood over her, hand trembling as the final embers of Big Red faded from his arm. His breath came fast, chest rising with adrenaline and pain.

Then he heard it. A metallic groan. Heavy, rhythmic footfalls. Lumbering down the corridor, dragging a cleaver the size of a door—Another Patchman.

Its eyes glowed like furnace coals, steam hissing from the vents in its spine. Diego's shoulders sagged. "Curse my luck," he muttered. He turned and ran—boots hammering stone, dice clutched tight in one hand. He vanished into the corridor's curve. He wasn't retreating.

He was leading it away.

Diego's boots skidded across the slick stones as he dashed into the sacrificial chamber. The blood vat stood at the center. Wide as a carriage. Deep enough to drown a horse.

Behind him, the Patchman thundered closer—runes burning along its frame, dragging a cleaver forged from sewer iron. But it wasn't alone.

Lilidan limped into the chamber, face warped with rage. Her leg was twisted, dragging behind her like dead weight. One arm hung useless, charred black from shoulder to wrist. And still, she came. Her fury was keeping her alive now—pure, blind wrath.

Her good hand clutched the remaining sickle. Dark tendrils of corrupted magic snaked across her throat and jaw, writhing like worms beneath her skin.

She didn't speak. Her eyes said enough.

"Seriously?" Diego muttered. "You're held together with spit and spite." No time to banter. He vaulted over a collapsed brazier, dice already in motion.

⏿ Rune: Shattered Coin. Pips: 5 and 2.

A shimmer raced across his form. Illusion fractured around him—his outline flickering like broken light through smoke. His body distorted, harder to focus on. To strike.

The Gravecallers arrived next—two of them—emerging from the tunnel mouths with raised scythes and stitched robes. Their chants clawed the walls, vibrating bone-deep.

Diego moved fast.

He ducked beneath a cleaving swing from the Patchman, rolled under its arm, and popped up behind the blood vat. He fired twice—one round catching a Gravecaller in the throat. The other hissed through Lildan's tattered cloak, just missing.

Her sickle slashed.

Diego twisted, the illusion field absorbing the blow—but it staggered him. "Dice don't fail me now," he gasped, throwing again.

⏿ Rune: Fortune Favors. Pips: 6 and 3.

A shimmer of gold raced across his limbs. His eyes sharpened. Muscles surged with adrenaline and arcane charge. Time seemed to slow. Lilidan lunged, screaming—a sound half human, half banshee.

She slashed—he ducked.
Stabbed—he twisted.
She flipped the blade mid-swing—he backflipped over her.

Her movements were fierce but sloppy now. Pain dulled her grace. Her steps faltered. Rage flared hot, but her body was breaking beneath it. Diego countered—low jab to her ribs, twist, elbow to her temple. Her knees buckled. Still she fought, teeth bloodied, tears of fury in her eyes.

"I. Will. End—"

He kicked her back. She slammed into the base of the altar, wheezing. She tried to rise. Her legs said no. The sickle clattered to the floor beside her. Diego picked it up and slammed it into her shoulder pinned her to the alter. "Stay put".

The Patchman roared, charging, rapidly closing the distance.

Diego turned, grit in his voice. "One more roll."

⬜ Rune: The Black Mark. Pips: Double 4s.

Perfect.

He hurled the die at the Gravecallers as they finished their chant.

The curse flared.

The mark carved itself across their chests, glowing crimson. Chains of spectral bone erupted from the walls, slamming into their bodies—binding, branding, crushing. Their own spell rebounded, rupturing their mouths and eyes in twin bursts of black flame.

They dropped.

Only the Patchman remained still charging.

Diego grabbed his last die.

⬜ Rune: Big Red. Pips: Snake Eyes.

It pulsed in his hand, burning hot enough to sear skin. He threw it skyward. The blood vat ignited.

A shockwave ripped outward—cursed ichor and explosive magic detonating at once. The Patchman caught the full brunt of it mid-step. Its limbs flared white-hot, runes bursting like veins under pressure. It stumbled, screeched, and exploded—shrapnel and viscera splattering the stone walls.

Lilidan, pinned at the altar, tried to raise her hand one final time.

But the Black Mark had spread. Her heart stopped with a jerk. She didn't burn. She snapped—folding in on herself in a burst of crimson light and bone dust. Silence returned.

Diego knelt, coughing, shaking, scorched from the blast.

He wiped a streak of blood from his cheek, stared at the smoking dice.

"Snake eyes," he muttered shrugging. "Lucky me."

———

The corridor burned with the scent of scorched bone and ozone. Chase stepped through the breach, sigils faintly glowing beneath torn sleeves. The smoke parted just enough to reveal his enemy.

Von Epp. The necrosaber in his grip pulsed with sickly green flame—its edge serrated with fused bone, trailing death with every swing.

He didn't wait.

Von Epp struck first, driving the saber in a wide arc. Chase barely deflected with a summoned buckler—Searing Aegis flaring into place on his left forearm, a disc of infernal heat meeting the necrotic edge in a shriek of clashing magics.

Sparks. Fire. Screams—some not of this world.

Chase slid under the next strike, twisting up inside Von Epp's guard. The infernal lance came for ribs—but Von Epp turned, the saber parrying in a shower of ghostlight.

"You're better than the others," Von Epp hissed. "But they said that about the last one too. Before I carved his wards from his bones."

Chase didn't answer. He struck again, and again—each blow calculated. Fluid. Controlled.

But Von Epp adapted.

He swung wide and channeled through the blade. A necrotic arc tore across the floor, rupturing tiles and clawing for Chase's feet.

Chase vaulted back, landing in a low crouch, sigils burning brighter now—like veins of magma crawling beneath his skin.

Von Epp pressed. Thrust. Riposte. Overhead slash.

The saber screamed with every movement—each pass of its edge draining light from the air.

Chase caught one swing on his buckler, then ducked and drove his shoulder into Von Epp's chest. The necromancer stumbled—but barely gave ground.

"You're holding back," Von Epp taunted, circling. "I've killed your kind before. Spellbound or not—you bleed."

Chase's eyes narrowed.

The light in his sigils flared—*brighter*.

He surged forward, abandoning defense. His infernal lance trust low, then high, baiting Von Epp's guard. A feint—then a real cut to the thigh. The infernal energy of the lance kissed flesh. Von Epp grunted, but pivoted and countered—catching Chase across the ribs with the saber's backside. The blow sent Chase spinning, heat blooming in his side.

Chase rolled, came up hard, *angry.*

Infernal Surge activated—embers cracking along his jaw and hands as strength and speed multiplied. He blurred forward.

Von Epp was fast—but Chase was *faster.*

Fire met bone. Sparks flew. A grazing cut across Von Epp's neck opened, sizzling black.

The necromancer backpedaled—face pale, expression shifting.

"...What *are* you?"

Chase advanced without a word.

His buckler absorbed a blast of death magic—then he dispelled it, driving his heel into Von Epp's knee. The necromancer crumpled sideways—but twisted and slashed upward with the saber.

It grazed Chase's cheek—cold and biting.

The taste of rot hit the back of his throat.

Von Epp rose again, gasping. "You're not just spellbound. No... they wouldn't dare bind this kind of power."

Chase answered with the flat of his knife across Von Epp's mouth, splitting his lip.

"Guess you figured it out."

Von Epp staggered—then screamed. His saber flared, sucking energy from the room as he raised it in both hands, preparing a finishing blow.

Chase's arms lit *fully* now—**The Seal** pulsing on his chest, binding his sigils together. The floor beneath him cracked with heat.

The Searing Aegis flared across his forearm in a burst of molten gold—catching the blow, turning the necrotic edge aside with a hiss of clashing wards.

Von Epp snarled and swung again.

Chase pivoted under the blade, boots skidding across blood-slick stone. He slid behind the necromancer in one fluid step, planting his stance, fingers already alight with burning sigils.

Von Epp whirled—Too slow.

Chase pressed two fingers to the necromancer's spine.

"Infernus."

The Infernal Lance detonated point-blank. A spear of white-hot hellfire blasted through Von Epp's back and erupted from his chest—shearing through ribs, flesh, and enchantments alike. The chamber lit up with a violent, hungry glow, shadows stretching long across the bone pillars.

Von Epp spasmed, choking on smoke and his own disbelief. Chase leaned close, voice low and deadly steady in the old man's ear. "I'm not like the others."

The Lance flared again—harder this time, a final rupturing burst that carved a molten crater through Von Epp's torso and hurled his body forward in a charred, collapsing heap.

The flames guttered out. Chase lowered his hand, breath ragged, eyes burning ember-red in the dark.

Von Epp's body convulsed, the saber dropping from limp fingers. His flesh blackened and cracked, his body slumping forward—still, at last.

Chase let him fall.

Steam hissed from his sigils. The light in them faded to an ember's glow.

The silence after was total.

Then Chase spat blood, leaned against the wall, and muttered:

"Bet that wasn't in your report." Chase exhaled, chest heaving, the air around him thick with smoke and death. He turned toward the wall where he'd dropped it earlier the Tommy gun, arcane runes along the receiver flickering like dying coals. Chase picked it up and slammed a fresh drum into place.

He turned back toward Von Epp's corpse.

And stopped.

The body twitched.

Then *jerked*.

Bones snapped in unnatural angles. The blackened chest split open as something *beneath* the skin pushed out—spines, ridges, serrated bone erupting through charred muscle. A long, rattling breath filled the air. Not life—*unlife*.

———

Dorian Blackwell felt the moment his sister died. It wasn't a noise. It wasn't a scream.
It was a tear—a sudden ripping sensation deep in his chest, as if a string that had always been there, taut and silent, had just been severed.

His breath hitched. A tremor ran through his hands. Lildan. Gone.

For a moment the world tilted around him, blurred at the edges. He set a steadying hand against one of the bone pillars—felt its cold, slick surface anchor him as the chamber's heartbeat thundered in his ears.

But he did not fall. He did not scream. He did not mourn aloud. He simply exhaled, long and slow, and let the grief crystallize into something harder.

I am the last Blackwell now.

A flicker of pain twisted through him. Then he let it go. Around him, the ritual raged.

Aspen Willowbark lay inside the osarcophagus—body pale beneath the lattice of silver runes carved into his skin. Adriana Mortem stood above him, her blade of bone-ivory tracing slow, precise arcs as she cut fresh channels across the bard's limbs, chest, throat. The blood ran in steady streams, all guided toward the glyph-lined grooves that spiraled outward like a hungry maze.

Every drop was caught. Every ounce of suffering siphoned. The Gravecaller walked the ritual circle, his voices a grinding harmonization of old languages—words that had never been meant to pass mortal lips. His staffs thumped the ground in perfect precision , each pulse sending a ripple of necrotic power radiating through the floor.

A procession of Mourned shuffled in from the far corridor. Dozens of them.

Each one placed a trembling hand into the basin before the sarcophagus. As soon as they touched it, the runes flared—and their bodies withered instantly, collapsing into heaps of desiccated skin and brittle bone. Their stolen essence spiraled upward into the growing glyphs suspended above the chamber.

Purple light bled through the air like ink spilled through water. The wounds—those strange, star-shaped tears in reality—hung in the ceiling, pulsing to the rhythm of the ritual. With every Mourned drained, the wounds grew.

Dorian stared at them. Portals, he thought. Or cracks. Or veins. Or perhaps all three. He understood them only in the way one understands the shadow of a predator long before seeing the beast itself.

Adriana Mortem smiled faintly as she felt the resonance shift. She was close. So close.

Dorian's lips thinned. He glanced to the side. Makalith Ravenwind stood rigid, jaw tight, eyes burning with a fury held barely in check. His hands flexed at his sides; restless, reacting to the magnitude of power thickening in the air.

Dorian studied him for a long moment then considered his own fate. His sister—gone. His family line—broken. His future—suddenly unmoored. He needed leverage. He needed a new thread to weave.

His gaze lingered on Makalith. A fey man carved from vengeance and grief. A puppet—but one with sharp teeth. Adriana believed herself untouchable. Von Epp believed himself ascendant. Makalith thought himself damned.

But Dorian…Dorian had always been a survivor.

He stepped closer, voice barely above a whisper—meant only for himself. "Time for a new deal… Makalith."

The ritual thundered on. And the purple wounds above pulsed wider, hungrier, like eyes opening to witness the birth of something monstrous and old.

———

Gunfire tore through the darkness. Chase Cassidy moved like a man possessed, the barrel of his arcane-inscribed Tommy gun glowing red as he laid waste to the necromantic horror looming before him. Flare rounds lit the lab chamber like lightning strikes—each impact searing flesh, igniting runes, ripping chunks from the hulking Rotmourned that Von Epp had become.

What was once a man now towered in twisted form—seven feet of sinew and bone, patches of charred uniform clinging to swollen muscle. Pestilent tendrils coiled from his spine, twitching and burrowing through the floor. His face was stretched, rotted, burned, but his eyes still held the same cold, methodical hatred.

"You came all this way," Von Epp growled, voice now split between three layers—his own, a chorus of the dead, and something deeper. "And you still think bullets will save you."

Chase fired again. "If they keep you off me, I'll take it"

The Tommy gun roared, rounds punching into Von Epp's torso —burning runes flaring along the receiver. Necrotic blood splashed the stone, glowing with a sick green light. But Von Epp didn't fall.

He advanced. The ground ruptured.

Sharp spikes burst upward, barbed and writhing like vines of plague. Chase dove, rolled beneath their reach, came up firing again, rounds tearing through the air in a tight arc that clipped one of Von Epp's reaching limbs and set it ablaze.

Then—a bone spike erupted from the floor where Chase had just stood, skewering air. He kept moving.

The Rotmourned shrieked and extended his hand.

A pestilence swarm poured forth—flies, beetles, and ash-colored wasps, all buzzing with the screams of the dead. The swarm hit like a tidal wave of rot, chasing Chase back across scorched stone. He ducked low, twisting through the cloud, slapping away the ones that bit and chewed through his collar. His skin burned, welts rising along his neck and jaw as the first of them burrowed toward the heat of his blood.

He clenched his fists.

Sigils flared red-hot along his chest.

"No more."

With a guttural word in Infernal, Chase ignited the Sigils of the Infernal Torrent. The effect was immediate.

A roaring column of hellfire exploded outward from his body—a storm of flame and pressure that shredded the swarm midair, incinerating insects in mid-flight and blasting charred corpses across the lab. Wings sizzled. Shells burst. The storm caught the cloud like dry tinder and turned it into a shrieking bonfire.

The heat cracked the stone at his feet.

His greatcoat caught fire, hell-heat licking up the sleeves in hungry curls—

but Chase snapped his thumb against a tiny rune sewn beneath the cuff. A suppression glyph flared, quenching the flames in an instant and leaving the coat smoking but intact.

Heat still rolled off him in waves. Glyphwork blazed beneath the fabric like molten metal beneath thin steel—every line of infernal script pulsing with volcanic fury. Smoke curled from his collar, rising around him in twisting plumes. He stepped forward, fire trailing from his hands like sculpted ribbons of wrath. His silhouette burned at the heart of the infernal storm—and his eyes glowed like twin furnaces, alive with the promise of destruction.

Across the chamber, Von Epp recoiled, snarling, raising a warding bone-spike shield to deflect the wave of flame. But instead of retreating, he roared and charged straight through the fire, his necro-shield ablaze, skeletal plates blackening and cracking as he plowed through the infernal torrent.

He crashed into Chase like a juggernaut.

The impact hurled Chase backward, the Tommy gun spinning away across the floor in a clatter of metal. He barely caught his footing, his boots skidding, his lungs seizing from the impact.

But he didn't fall.

Chase surged forward and grabbed the twin horns of the burning necro-shield, locking up Von Epp's momentum. Their boots scraped and gouged the floor as they fought for ground, muscles straining—one living, one long dead.

Von Epp's jaw split into a smile of yellow teeth and rot. "You burn bright, Cassidy," he growled. "Let's see how long your flame lasts."

He let go of the shield—just dropped it—and swung his necro-saber in a deadly arc, a line of green-slick bone and plaguefire screaming for Chase's throat.

The Searing Aegis buckler ignited in Chase's off-hand, catching the blade in a blinding burst of heat and light. Sparks and ash scattered into the darkness.

With his other hand, Chase drew on the sigils carved deep into his flesh.

Infernal Lance.

A searing line of molten fire ripped from his fingers like a whip of helllight, cutting straight through the necro-blade's guard and slicing into Von Epp's arm, cleaving it at the elbow. The blackened limb flew, spinning end over end into the shadows.

Von Epp howled—but didn't slow.

He lunged, driving a heavy boot into Chase's chest.

Chase flew backward, slamming into a pillar hard enough to crack it. He coughed smoke and blood, blinking through fire and pain.

Across the room, Von Epp retrieved his severed arm, already crawling with rot-born tendrils.

"The dead heal faster than the living, Cassidy." He jammed the stump into place. Black veins pulsed. Bone knitted. Flesh crawled back into shape like worms rebuilding a corpse.

Chase stared, chest rising and falling, sweat and blood mixing with soot. He raised his arm again—

Infernal Lance—again.

He carved through Von Epp's thigh.

It grew back.

He burned away half his ribs.

They regrew.

Every attack bought seconds, not victory.

Chase's sigils began to smolder, white-hot beneath his skin. His breath came ragged now, the infernal pressure building. He remembered the warehouse—the pain, the searing pulse of unstable energy. He was close to burning too hot. One more push and he'd go full Infernus.

"I gotta end this," Chase muttered, dragging himself upright.

Von Epp was already on him—faster, more feral, bone plating knitting across his limbs as the necro-plague forced his body through another grotesque evolution. The necromancer seized Chase by the throat and hurled him across the chamber.

Chase hit the ground hard, the breath exploding from both lungs and Utilis crashed down on top of him like a guillotine with legs. The mourned assassin's scissor-claws stabbed downward.

Chase caught both blades in his hands. His armored gauntlets barely hold back the cutting edge of the blades. Metal screamed against metal. Sparks jumped across his gauntlets as the reinforced leather tore, steel plating buckled and the claws kept pushing.

Utilis 'bone-pistons throbbed beneath the grafted flesh, driving the claws inch by inch toward Chase's sternum. Chase's arms shook violently. The claws punctured the gauntlet plates. He felt a hot sting across his palms blood.

Utilis leaned closer, jaws clicking, breath reeking of embalming oils.

Chase growled between clenched teeth: "I should've killed you at the hospital."

Utilis hissed and drove down harder. The claws broke deeper through the gauntlets. Pain shot up Chase's arms. He didn't have the leverage to throw Utilis off—So he changed the leverage.

With a violent twist of his torso, Chase rolled sideways, pulling Utilis with him. The sudden rotation wrenched the assassin off balance. Chase drove his boot hard into the back of Utilis 'knee joint—The limb buckled.

Utilis pitched forward. Chase released the claws at the same instant and vaulted over the collapsing assassin, rolling to his feet in a single battered motion. But he had no time to breathe.

Von Epp struck him from the flank like a battering ram— a necrotic shockwave slamming into Chase's ribs and hurling him into a row of shattered lab consoles. Glass and metal detonated around him.

Chase gasped, vision swimming.

Von Epp and Utilis advanced together now. Predator and blade. Master and mutilated servant. "You are outmatched," Von Epp rasped. "Two against one. No mage survives those odds."

Chase spat blood. "Good thing," he said, "I'm not a mage."

Von Epp lunged—but Utilis reached him first, scuttling with inhuman speed. The claws snapped toward Chase's throat.

Chase didn't try to dodge. He stepped into the attack. Caught Utilis by the forearms. And pulled the assassin in close, chest-to-chest—so close Chase could smell embalming fluid steaming off the grafted flesh.

Utilis shrieked.

Chase raised his right hand, sigils blazing white-hot, heat distorting the air around his arm. "Burn."

He unleashed the Infernal Torrent directly into Utilis 'torso.

The hellfire didn't just blast through the mourned assassin, it filled him. His grafted organs ignited. His arc-tanks detonated. His ribcage burst outward in a molten spray as hellfire poured out of every wound and seam. Utilis 'scream cut off as his entire body collapsed in on itself, melting into a smoking heap of fused bone and metal slag.

Chase staggered back, arm trembling from the recoil. He was burning hot. The sigils are his arms started to flicker.

Von Epp screamed—a raw, animal howl of fury—and charged.

———

Rubble littered the nave, pews overturned and blackened with soot. The altar had collapsed inward, revealing the jagged mouth of a tunnel gouged into the stone floor—still warm with residual magic and scorched by fire.

Skye Anderson stood at the edge of it, boots crunching over ash and broken glass. Her coat fluttered in the cold draft rising from below, the stench of blood, oil, and rot thick in her lungs. She drew her **arcalam**— with a flick of her wrist and a whispered word, the blade hissed to life. An elegant shell guard formed with cross guards catching the stained light.

A slim beam of azure light extended from the core, shimmering like starlight through smoke. It cast flickering shadows along the ruins, illuminating her path.

She stepped forward. And jumped.

The descent into the tunnels jarred her knees, but she rolled smoothly into a crouch. The corridor before her was chaos—walls scorched, sigils half-melted, claw marks raked through old stone. This was Chase's trail. And Diego's. A reckless storm had passed through here.

Skye followed.

Her wand lit the way, revealing grim remnants: broken restraints, shattered glass, stains that hadn't yet dried. Her jaw tightened. She passed a ruined cell door, its iron bars bent outward like something had *escaped*.

Then she heard it.

A soft whimper.

Skye spun, arcalam ready—then froze.

A child stood in the shadow of a broken cage. Pale. Eyes too large for her sunken face. A shimmer of Fey lineage in her ears and glow-touched skin. Behind her, three more children emerged, huddled, frightened—but alive.

Skye lowered her wand and knelt.

"Hey," she said gently, voice steady. "You're safe now. I need you to be brave just a little longer."

The first child nodded mutely.

"This way." She gestured back up the tunnel toward the cathedral. "Follow the light. Head for the door at the end. You'll see the sky."

One of the children hesitated. "Will... will you come too?"

Skye's eyes softened. "Soon. I have friends to find."

They went. Quiet. Trusting. She watched until they vanished up the incline, swallowed by the distant light. Then she turned and went deeper. She exhaled and stood.

A rustle. A groan.

From the side tunnel, a Rotburned lurched out—skin peeling, limbs twitching, eyes hollow but locked on her. It staggered forward with a wet snarl.

Skye didn't flinch.

She raised her arcalam, pivoted, and cast.

"Agni-Kalumtu."

A radiant burst of arcane fire erupted from her wand, searing straight through the creature's chest. It convulsed—then dropped, smoldering.

She stepped over the corpse and pressed on, deeper into the dark, the weight of the moment pressing into her ribs.

Chase was ahead.

And something far worse awaited.

———

Von Epp struck like a freight train. Chase ducked just enough—the necromancer's bone spines tore a trench in the stone wall behind him. Chase slammed a palm into Von Epp's sternum and unleashed a short blast of infernal force, searing through mutated flesh, but the necro-plague knitted the wound almost instantly.

Von Epp laughed—a wet, bubbling sound. "You burn beautifully, Cassidy."

Chase's vision swam. Heat shimmered off him in waves. He could smell his own clothes scorching. The heat rolling off his own skin was becoming dangerous—sigils flickering, stuttering, warning him he was running out of time.

Von Epp lunged again.

Chase barely dodged—bone spines grazed past his cheek, carving sparks off stone. He hit the ground in a roll, skidding to a stop beside something half-buried beneath rubble.

A blade. Slick, curved, humming faintly with necrotic energy. Von Epp's Necro-Saber—dropped earlier when he still wore a human shape. Chase snatched it up.

The weapon vibrated in his grip like a starving beast sensing new prey.

Von Epp spun toward him, snarling, "You think you can use my own craft against me—?"

Chase didn't answer. He moved. He slashed the saber upward in a vicious arc. Necrotic steel met corrupted flesh with a sound like tearing wet parchment. The blade carved deep across Von Epp's chest, leaving a line of blackened bone exposed through the split ribs.

Von Epp screamed—more anger than pain. "That blade was forged in the Ossuary!" he howled. "It serves ME!"

"It serves whoever swings it," Chase growled. He swung again—this time taking Von Epp across the arm, severing a tendril of bone growth that writhed on the floor like a dying snake.

But Chase felt it—his sigils flickering, searing hotter, vision blurring at the edges. He was seconds away from burning himself alive. He needed something bigger. He needed something final.

Von Epp lunged, monstrous, limbs elongating in spasms. Chase ducked, rolled, and ripped free an arcane grenade from his belt.

He thumbed the rune, felt it activate—a sharp, rising whine.

Von Epp saw it too late. "No—NO—"

Chase slammed the grenade against Von Epp's sternum.

"Chew on this." As he activated both Sigils of the Searing Aegis on his forearms.

The explosion tore half the chamber open. The spellbound shields collapsed under the explosive pressure, absorbing enough to keep Chase unharmed. Von Epp flew backward in a shrieking arc of bone and torn flesh, crashing spine-first into the massive necro-vat. Reinforced glass spiderwebbed and shattered.

Black-green necro-serum poured over him in a violent flood. Von Epp writhed, screeching as the unstable serum soaked into his wounds, into his marrow, into the runes carved into his bones. He began to mutate again. Too fast. Too violently. His body couldn't stabilize.

Chase knew exactly what to do.

He sprinted to the vat's pump system—sparking, cracked, still half-alive—and slammed his fist onto the manual override lever. Pipes rattled. Pressure screamed through the lines.

He grabbed a hanging feed tube and shoved it directly into Von Epp's exposed ribcage.

The necro-pump detonated to life.

A geyser of raw serum blasted into Von Epp's chest cavity. "No—NO—STOP—" Von Epp shrieked, voice splitting into layered, overlapping tones.

His limbs ballooned, ruptured, reformed. His spine shot upward in a spiral. Bones cracked, multiplied, then shattered under their own growth. Chase backed away, stumbling, heat distorting the air around him.

"You wanted evolution?" Chase rasped. "Choke on it."

Von Epp swelled—ten feet, twelve, fifteen—his skin splitting like wet paper. Necro-serum boiled beneath his flesh, glowing brighter and brighter.

He reached for Chase—and detonated.

A shockwave ripped through the chamber, slamming Chase off his feet. Bone shards scythed through the air like shrapnel. Steam, ichor, and necrotic flame poured across the floor. Chase hit the ground hard, rolled behind a fallen support beam, and curled into a tight brace as the blast swallowed the room.

When the roar died, only silence remained. Smoke drifted. Molten ichor puddled across cracked stone. The spot where Von Epp stood was now a vast, glowing crater.

The Second Seat of the Court of Bones was gone. Destroyed by the very abomination he once mastered.

Chase rose slowly, wiping blood from his forearm. His greatcoat was scorched, sigils dimming but still burning faint beneath the fabric. He breathed out once, ragged and exhausted.   "Should've stayed buried," he muttered.

Then he turned toward the corridor. Aspen Willowbark was still alive. And Chase Cassidy was not done.

———

Diego Salazar climbed the final steps two at a time, lungs burning, sweat stinging his eyes. The air down here felt wrong—thick, metallic, tinged with the coppery taste of old blood and ruptured magic. Not quite like the trenches of Arras. Not quite like the Ossuary.

But close. Too damn close.

He paused at the landing, braced a shoulder against the cold stone wall, and cracked open the cylinder of his arcane revolver. Six spent rounds dropped out, clinking softly on the steps. He thumbed in fresh cartridges —silvered casings etched with faint runes he'd carved himself during long, sleepless nights.

Haven't seen shit this bad since Black Dagger... The thought crawled uninvited through his mind. Hope the big guy's holdin 'together.

He wiped his forehead with the back of his glove. Sweat smeared into grime, leaving a streak that felt too much like war paint. A distant roar trembled through the tunnel walls. Chase. Or something trying very hard to kill Chase.

Diego exhaled slowly. "Hang in there, hermano. I'm comin'."

He snapped the cylinder shut with a practiced flick, holstered the revolver at his hip, and rolled his dice once between his fingers—comfort, habit, a litany of survival whispered through bone.

Then he moved forward. The tunnel opened. Heat brushed his face. Whispers curled along the walls like diseased ivy. He stepped past the archway, through smoke and half-shadow—Chase Cassidy emerged, his coat singed, the *Tommy gun* low at his side.

They locked eyes. And then—they both saw them.

Six Mourned.

Different than the mindless husks from the lower levels. These stood silent, upright, armor-stitched with ritual leathers, mouths sewn shut in reverence. They held curved blades and bone-blessed polearms, their chests emblazoned with a crimson rose: the mark of Adriana Ruthven.

Her personal guard.

Diego pressed into the column, gesturing low.
"Six of them. I say we bait them into the pillars—break their formation. I've got a shadowbind die ready to go."

Chase, crouched behind a broken statue, shook his head.
"Too risky. They're armored. Won't fall for your usual show."

Diego whispered back, "That *usual show* kept us alive in France, hermano."

"Yeah, and this ain't France." Chase reached into his belt pouch, fingers wrapping around a jagged metal sphere. The last arcane grenade. Spell-welded. Infernal core.

He stood up.

"Hey, boneboys—catch this."

He lobbed it straight down the center aisle.

The grenade hit stone—bounced—then exploded.

Arcane fire lanced outward, turning the six elite Mourned into shrieking silhouettes. Their armor cracked. Flesh blistered. Magic screamed as they were reduced to ash and scorched bone.

Diego blinked.
"Well… guess subtlety's off the table."

Chase walked up beside him, reloading the *Tommy gun* with a smooth click. "Door's still on it."

They stood side by side, staring at the great double doors ahead—rusted iron rimmed with warded glyphs. Faint chanting echoed from within, a pulse of dark power trembling the air.

"You alright?" Chase asked, not looking over.

"Ran into a mage," Diego said, voice low, eyes still scanning the broken stonework around them. "Mean one. Pale, elegant, eyes like amethyst fire. She came at me with twin sickles like death on silk." He shook his head. "Don't know her name. But she's not breathing anymore."

Chase's jaw tightened. "One of the Blackwells," he said grimly. " You took down a monster."

Diego offered a crooked smirk, but it didn't last long. "The Blackwells that run the Asylum?."

Chase wiped a smear of black ichor from his cheek, breath still harsh from the fight. "Von Epp is gone," he said quietly. "Dead. For real this time."

Diego blinked. "You're sure?"

"I watched him come apart," Chase answered. "Burned him, cut him, and the unstable necro-serum did the rest. He won't be getting back up."

Diego let out a low whistle, half awe, half exhaustion. "Good. That butcher deserved worse than whatever you gave him." He nudged a chunk of charred bone with his boot. "Hell—maybe there is a bounty on him. Would've been nice to get paid for killing that lunatic."

Chase snorted, just a flicker of tired mirth. "Not a bad idea but don't hold your breath. Men like him don't stay dead in the paperwork."

"And the other one?" Diego asked. "The… mourned with the blades for hands?"

Chase's jaw tightened. "He's ash. Whatever he was."

"Good," Diego muttered. "Thing damn near tore you in half the first time you met. Glad you put him down."

Chase didn't answer. He shifted the Tommy gun to his shoulder and looked toward the ritual chamber, where the walls pulsed with sick red light.

Diego followed his gaze. "Von Epp's gone," he said. "So why do you still look ready to punch a god?"

Chase exhaled. "Because the real fight hasn't started. And Aspen's still in there."

Diego nodded once—solemn now, no jokes left.

"Then let's finish this."

They stood in silence for a beat, the sound of arcane chanting growing louder—a ritual nearing its apex. And then they moved. Toward the doors. Toward the end.

CHAPTER 10

The Mouth of Madness

On the Nature of the Withering Veil - by Aurelia Solenne Valtheris Nyxorian, Scholar of Planar Cartography and Former Adjunct to the Hudson Institute of Theorematic Arts

The Veil is not one thing—this is the first mistake most scholars make.

The Seelie and Unseelie Courts retreat behind curated boundaries, veils woven with intention: artistry, power, law. Their thresholds are crafted to separate realms without harming either side. But the Withering Veil is no such boundary.

It is a wound.

It is what forms when reality fractures under too much suffering—when emotion bends space, when terror saturates the air, when the living die so fast their souls do not know where to fall. The Withering Veil is shaped not by magic, but by pain.

The Great War birthed many horrors, but none so enduring as the scar carved between France and Germany. So much death in one place tore the world thin, like wet paper pulled too far. Behind that tear lies a realm without rule or mercy: a place where the lost drift, where the dead whisper, and where the living cannot linger long without losing themselves. Other veils open into elsewheres.

The Withering Veil opens into madness. And madness, once awakened, spreads...

The stairwell opened into smoke. A low, ashen haze clung to Skye's boots as she stepped lightly over broken stone and splintered bone—every breath stung with burnt alchemical residue. The glow from her arcalam wand cut a narrow column of pale blue through the thick dark, revealing a carnage she could barely comprehend.

Blood smeared the walls in wide, violent arcs.

Chunks of flesh—too large to be human—lay scattered like butcher's leavings. A ribcage fused with runic metal was half-melted into the cracked floor. A jawbone twitched once, then stilled.

Hermann Von Epp was dead. Thoroughly. Irrevocably. His legendary unkillability reduced to dripping anatomical ruin.

Skye lowered her wand.

"Chase...I wish I could have seen it," she whispered softly, but the chamber answered only with the hiss of settling steam.

Movement stirred at her right. The mourned girl.

The same child she'd seen in the tunnels—the one with the sigil burned down her throat like a broken halo. She stood over the remains of Von Epp's body, silent, barefoot, her tattered dress fluttering in the sour wind that seeped from the vents. Her dark eyes lifted to Skye's.

Skye felt her breath catch. Not in fear—in recognition. Pain. Suffering. A long road of torment suddenly, finally, ending. The girl gave a tiny nod.

A soft shuffle echoed behind Skye. She turned sharply—wand raised in both hands.

Dozens of Mourned stood in the shadows. All sizes. All ages. Some still bearing the carved sigils of control. Some half-rotted, others nearly whole but hollow-eyed. Every one of them staring at her.

The room chilled. Then—one by one—they vanished into the darkness behind her. No aggression. No pursuit. Just the silent dispersal of souls freed from the hand that had twisted them.

Only the mourned girl remained, her small frame outlined in the weak blue glow. She nodded toward the stairs leading upward—toward the ritual chamber.

Permission. And a warning. Skye exhaled shakily and stepped forward— A clatter broke the silence. A figure sprinted from behind a fallen steel cabinet—robes stained with necro-fluid. A Necrotech, one of Von Epp's lab surgeons, clutching a bundle of cracked notebooks. Notes. Research. Ritual primers.

He didn't even look at Skye—too desperate, too frantic. He just ran.

Skye raised her arcalam, voice cold and razor-steady: "Stop."

He ignored her.

She flicked her wrist A bolt of blue arcane energy shot from the wand, punching clean through his spine and out his chest. The Necrotech spasmed mid-stride, notes scattering like dying moths, and collapsed face-first onto the stone.

Smoke drifted from the hole in his torso. Skye stepped past him without slowing. The mourned girl watched her go, expression unreadable. At the base of the next staircase, Skye paused—tightened her grip around the wand and the revolver holstered at her hip—and glanced back once.

The girl was gone. Only the echo of soft bare feet remained. Skye swallowed, drew in a breath that tasted of fire and fear, and climbed. Up toward the pulsing violet glow bleeding through the ceiling stones. Up toward the ritual. Up toward Chase. Up toward hell.

———

The chamber pulsed with violet and green light—ritual wards dancing like fire across the floor's obsidian inlay. Adriana Mortem Ruthven stood tall at the center, arms raised, her voice laced with ancient syllables not spoken in the world of the living for centuries. Veins of rotlight spiraled from the altar, wrapping upward around a man suspended midair —Aspen Willowbark, limp, unconscious, glowing faintly as sigils burned beneath his skin.

Dorian Blackwell stood beside her—robes pristine, wand poised. His expression was a blend of awe and clinical detachment, eyes flicking over the rising energy.

And across from him, bound to a rune-etched pillar, Makalith Ravenwind watched in silence. He was wounded—badly.

His coat hung in ragged strips, charred black at the edges. Blood soaked one sleeve, dripping steadily from a deep wound in his abdomen. Shackles of necro-steel bit into his wrists, forcing his arms behind him, binding him at angles meant to break lesser men. Dorian had carved suppression sigils into the floor beneath him—runic chains glowing a dim, sickly red to keep his magic locked down.

Still, he stood upright. Silent. Eyes burning with quiet fury. The chamber quaked as Adriana chanted louder.

Then. A concussive blast rocked the far end of the room. The doors shattered inward in a blaze of light and shrapnel. Adriana shrieked, ducking low, yanking Aspen toward her with a gesture. Protective wards flared around them as the echo faded.

"Stop them!" Adriana screamed. "The host must not be harmed!"

Dorian didn't flinch. He stepped forward calmly, eyes narrowing. Out of the smoke strode two figures—burned, bloodied, and dragging ash behind their boots.

Chase Cassidy, infernal sigils still faintly aglow beneath his great coat. Diego Salazar, coat torn at the sleeve, eyes flitting over the room's geometry like a gambler reading his final hand.

Dorian descended the stairs toward them, wand in hand but lowered. He gave a cordial nod. "Well. You've made it farther than I expected."

Chase tilted his head. "You must be the welcoming committee."

Dorian's smile was tight, practiced. "And you must be Cassidy. Your reputation precede you."

Behind him, Makalith's chains rattled as he shifted—barely. His eyes never left Chase. Or Diego. Or the ritual swallowing the chamber.

Adriana rose behind them, brushing hair from her face, fury and magic wreathing her like smoke. "Dorian," she hissed, "I said stop them!"

He raised one hand. "Let them breathe. Just for a moment." He looked back to the pair standing defiant amid the debris.

"You came all this way," he said quietly. "Might as well see what's being born. The Lord of Bones returns," he murmured. "The veil between worlds collapses... and from the ruin, a new order will rise."

Chase's eyes narrowed. "Remade into what?"

"A reflection of the Withering Veil," Dorian said. "A realm of structure. Of purpose. One where the living understand their place... as vessels."

Diego spat. "You're insane, man."

Chase drew breath through clenched teeth. "You're not creating paradise—you're paving a road straight through hell."

Dorian's expression chilled. "You think this is madness. But all your world offers is chaos. The lord offers a design."

"You're not God," Chase replied. "You're a butcher with a secondhand prophecy."

The smile vanished. He raised his wand. "Enough."

A burst of arcane force erupted from Dorian's palm—slamming Chase back into a crumbling pillar. Stone cracked. Runes flared painfully across Chase's chest. He stayed down only a heartbeat.

Diego dove left, rolled through rubble, flung a die mid-motion—

Black Mark.

The jinx flared. Dorian's next spell warped sideways, detonating with a whip-crack of backlash. He staggered, cloak torn.

"Charming trick," he muttered. Threads of razor-thin arcane filament spun outward from his wand.

Chase surged up, tommy gun blazing, tearing the spells apart with burning rounds. Dorian shielded. Countered. Sidestepped. They moved like two storms colliding—Chase a blaze of infernal fury, Dorian a surgeon of precision and cruelty.

Makalith watched. Breathing shallow. Bleeding steadily. Unable to move. A shackle sparked against the pillar as he strained silently—hopelessly—trying to break free.

The chamber thundered with spellfire and ricocheting hexes.

Diego's next die fizzled in a canceling field.

Dorian whispered, cold: "You fight like men." He lifted his wand, sigils forming like frost. "And I don't believe in men anymore."

Makalith clenched his jaw as another tremor ran through the ritual circle. He could feel it—his own power, sealed under his feet, choking him. His allies slain. His vengeance stolen.

And yet he watched. Because even chained, he knew the tide had shifted.

———

Skye stepped through the archway and into hell. The air inside Von Epp's ruined lab was thick with smoke, blood, and the chemical bite of preservatives gone rancid. Vats once filled with arcane ooze and glowing rime had burst—their contents splattered across the floor in slick puddles that hissed against the broken sigils beneath them. The scent of decay was suffocating.

Half-formed Rotmourned twitched in their ruptured tanks, their bodies caught mid-transformation—fused with metal, bone-stretching enchantments, or necrotic grafts. One rasped, eyes blind, jaw fused shut, a sound like a dying flute escaping its throat.

Skye tightened her grip on her arcalam, its miniature rapier form glowing with blue-white light as it cast sharp shadows along the stone walls. Shell casings littered the floor—dull brass scattered like the aftermath of a gunpowder storm. Chase's work. He'd come through like a reaper.

She stepped past a shredded Mourned slumped against the wall, its head barely attached by a stretch of sinew and spell-scarring. Another was split open, burnt from the inside, a signature flare round still smoking near its ribs.

Her boots crunched over glass and bone.

This wasn't a fight. It was a purge.

She moved cautiously through the wreckage, her light catching the edge of a shattered operating table, blood dried black along the clamps. She paused. Closed her eyes.

Please let them be okay.

She didn't know where Chase or Diego were. But this trail—they'd left it for her. Whether they meant to or not.

A sound.

Skittering.

She opened her eyes.

The lab wasn't empty.

Something moved overhead—too fast, too light for a full-sized creature. Her gaze snapped upward.

A vial tipped off a shelf behind her and shattered.

She turned—just in time to see the blur.

A blur dropped from the darkness.

She twisted aside—barely.

Claws raked her shoulder as the first Homunculus landed, grinning up at her with needle-like teeth. It was a miniature version of Von Epp—stitched flesh and mechanical sinew, patchwork limbs wrapped in runic threads. Its voice chirped like a child's toy soaked in blood.

"Replication... complete."

It lunged again—but this time she was ready.

Skye jabbed the Arcalam forward and barked, "Jahna kree!"

A bolt of white-hot arcane light lanced from the wand and exploded against the Homunculus mid-leap, slamming it into the far wall. It screeched, flailing in the rubble.

Then—A second one stepped out from behind a toppled cabinet. Slightly taller. Slightly wrong. One eye lower than the other. Its gait uneven. The copy had copied itself.

It hissed, then raised a tiny scalpel-hand and fired a stream of corrupted ichor from its wrist. Skye stumbled back falling over a fallen chair, the stream slicing into the ceiling above her, sizzling. It jumped landing perfectly on her chest.

It reached out sinking smalle clawed fingers wrapped around her throat.

Not claws—surgical blades. Bone and brass, fused into fingers. They bit into her skin, warm blood trailing down her neck. With her free hand she slapped it away.

She gasped, legs kicking, boots skidding against the wall for leverage.

A face leered down at her—too small. Too familiar.

Another one.

Crawling from beneath a shattered examination table—twisted, deformed, incomplete. Its limbs were mismatched—one arm swollen with warped muscle, the other a flopping, half-stitched stump. One eye glowed bright; the other was a dangling optical tube, swinging loosely as it clicked.

It clapped wet hands together like a child. "Replication... failed... correction in progress."

"Ferren luxa!"—and the floor erupted in a burst of violet flame beneath the malformed creature. It howled and leapt toward her.

Too slow.

She pivoted, wand raised—and sent a searing arc into its chest. The malformed Homunculus crumpled, convulsing.

The first one was already climbing again—scuttling along the wall like a spider. Skye turned and thrust her wand up just as it pounced —"Kalrex!"

The blast hit it midair.

It shattered into burning sinew and bone, landing in a twitching heap.

Breathing hard, Skye approached the remains, neck bleeding from shallow cuts. One of the Homunculi spasmed, twitching fingers curling toward her boot.

Then it whispered, sparks crackling in its ruined throat:

"Resurrection... protocol... active..."

And died.

Skye didn't wait to see what that meant. She grabbed her wand, wiped the blood from her cheek, and stepped through the rear exit, deeper into the tunnels. Her boots echoed through the dim stairwell below. Arcane light danced on the stone.

Whatever Von Epp was planning... it wasn't done.

And she had a feeling these were just the test models.

She followed a spiraling staircase down past jagged bricks and collapsing rune-stones.

She pressed forward. Her boots hammered down a spiraling staircase, the stone narrowing and slanting as if the tunnels themselves were shrinking away from what lay below. The walls broke into jagged bricks and collapsing rune-stones, old wards sparking as she passed.

Above the hum of residual necromancy, voices rose—shouting, bone against steel, spells cracking off walls. Skye broke into a run.

She rounded the last bend and froze just long enough to take in the scene.

A Gravecaller stood in the center of the corridor, robes torn, hands drenched in violet light. He wasn't commanding the Mourned, he was killing them.

A Mourned child lunged toward him, jaw distended in terror. The Gravecaller thrust a sigil forward and vaporized her midair.

Skye's chest tightened. Fury replaced fear. She didn't hesitate. Her arcalam snapped up, blue-white arcane force slammed into the necromancer's spine. He staggered, twisting, ribs visible through smoldering robes.

He hissed. "You again—"

He didn't finish.

A second Gravecaller materialized behind Skye, glyphs blazing along his left arm. "Die, little lawyer."

His curse struck the wall where Skye's head had been a second earlier, splintering stone, showering her with debris.

Skye rolled, came up on one knee, wand forward. The second Gravecaller flicked a blade of necrotic force at her—she countered. Her arcalam spat a beam of sapphire light, slicing the hex in half, scattering sparks across the floor.

The first Gravecaller recovered and fired a bolt of shadow directly toward her skull. She spun aside—felt the heat of it scorch her cheek.

Two-on-one. Claustrophobic hall. Dead children around her. She didn't panic. She got angry.

The second Gravecaller snarled, raising both hands—the ceiling above her cracked, runes glowing as he began collapsing the entire tunnel on top of her.

Skye dove hard to the right, her shoulder slamming into a support arch.The ceiling buckled a rain of stone obliterated the spot where she'd been. Her arcalam clattered away.

She reached for it and paused. One Gravecaller stalked forward, bone mask tilting. The other circled left, wand raised, necrotic sigils flaring. "Bind her throat," one rasped. "We'll take her tongue after."

Skye's hand slid into her coat pocket. The Gravecaller fired first. A jagged bolt of black-green death shrieked down the corridor—Skye threw herself sideways, felt it sear past her cheek and detonate against the far wall.

Her fingers closed around cold steel. She drew her revolver and fired. The round punched into the lead Gravecaller's thigh, staggering him, bone mask jerking down as he collapsed to one knee with a choking hiss. His wand clattered across the stone. Skye crumbled on all fours, pocketing her revolver and summoning her arcalam to her hand. She spotted the Gravecallers wand. Skye stretched out her free hand."Come to me."

The wand shivered. Then it ripped off the floor and snapped into her palm. Both Gravecallers froze. Skye rose—slowly—one wand in each hand. Her Arcalam thrummed with sapphire fire; the stolen bone wand pulsed with sickly white.

Her breath steadied. Her eyes hardened. "You hurt these children," she said. "That was your last mistake." They fired in unison—two deathbolts spiraling toward her like screaming serpents.

Skye stepped forward crossed both wands in an X

"Varma Belit"

A radiant shield formed in front of her blocking the blasts at the last minute. Skye rotated her arcalam drawing a sigil in the air and with a quick slashing motion, abeam of sapphire and bone-white magic roared outward, intertwining into a single devastating column of force that swallowed both curses whole.

The corridor exploded with light. Masks cracked. Robes ignited. Wards shattered. Both Gravecallers were ripped off their feet, slammed against the walls hard enough to crater the stone, and dropped in burning heaps.

When the flare faded, silence followed except Skye's ragged breathing. Her hands shook. Her eyes shimmered—wet, but burning Her chest heaved. Sweat mixed with ash on her brow. The corridor still crackled with the fading echo of her spell. Both Gravecallers lay in smoking heaps against the stone.

Skye stood over them—two wands in her hands, breath sharp and uneven. Slowly, she looked at the bone wand in her left grip. The thing still pulsed faintly. Hungry.

She let the necrotic wand fall. It clattered onto the floor. She stepped forward—deliberate, almost ceremonial—and brought her heel down. The wand split in half. Another step. It shattered completely, splintering like brittle bone under her boot.

Only her Arcalam remained in her hand—clean light, honest power, her own. Chase was below. Diego too. Aspen was still alive. And Skye Anderson had no intention of being late.

———

Dorian's spells came like hale—ruthless and unrelenting. Chase ducked beneath a lashing arc of necrotic chainfire, his coat scorched and his arm bleeding. Diego flanked wide, weaving between hex-laced columns as curses detonated around them in bursts of green light and spectral flame.

"He's toying with us," Chase snarled, deflecting a cursed bolt with a flare from the Searing Aegis.

"No," Diego yelled from cover, dice clattering in his palm, "he's calculating."

Dorian's wand spun—unleashing a spreading ring of null-gravity. Both men lifted a half-foot from the floor, momentum shoving their attacks wide.

"You're clever," Dorian said, voice steady despite sweat, "but I've bled sharper men than you."

Diego smirked. "Not me." A glyph flared beneath his feet. The Die of the Black Mark flashed between his fingers.

He whispered: "Flickerswitch."

Dorian blinked—And Chase was suddenly where Diego had been, already mid-lunge, his arm outstretched, the sigil on the back of his hand flaring molten red.

The Infernal Lance screamed from his fingers—a spear of white-hot hellfire that carved toward Dorian's chest. It struck home.

Not fatal—but enough. The blast ripped through layered wards, burning cloth and biting deep. Dorian screamed, staggered, drawing breath like he'd inhaled razors.

"You bastards," he gasped.

With a sharp, pained flick of his wand, he unleashed a kinetic shockwave—hurling both Chase and Diego backward in a thunderous blast that cracked stone and rattled ancient sigils.

Chase rolled. Diego skidded. Both rose.

Dorian Blackwell wiped the white spit of blood from his mouth, wincing as he clutched his side. Every breath knifed through broken ribs, every movement sent pain lancing down his spine. Across the ritual chamber, the Crown of Mortem pulsed atop Aspen's brow, feeding the cavern with a heartbeat of grave-light. He convulsed inside the sarcophagus, runes boiling across his skin.

And Makalith Ravenwind hung chained to the rune-pillar—bound in necro-steel, suppression sigils burning beneath his feet, magic smothered to embers.

Dorian swallowed the copper taste in his throat.

"Ravenwind," he called out, voice strained and urgent. "This ritual cannot be interrupted. Help me stop these intruders, and your life is yours. Walk away from this with power intact."

Makalith lifted his head slowly, shadowed eyes burning through him.

"My life," he rasped, "was never yours to promise."

Dorian's jaw tightened. "We had an accord. We can forge a new one.
"

Makalith laughed—a raw, bitter crack.

"I protected Adriana.I brought you a new host.I secured the Crown. And in return—" His voice turned sharp enough to cut stone. "—you butchered Fae children. You let Sirus bleed out on the floor while you hid behind your sister. You betrayed everything you promised."

Dorian flinched—just once.

"No honor," Makalith whispered. "No justice. Only rot."

Dorian wiped more blood from his lip, something cold and vicious settling in his eyes "Then you're useless to me now."

He snapped his fingers at the last surviving Gravecaller. "Kill him."

The masked necromancer stepped forward, claws rising toward Makalith and a Thompson burst ripped through the chamber.

Chase Cassidy stormed through smoke and bone-dust, sigils guttering and flaring across his forearms. The Gravecaller staggered under the hail of inferno-tipped rounds; its wards cracked, its mask spiderwebbed.

"Diego—move!" Chase barked.

Diego Salazar sprinted past him, sliding across the stone to Makalith's side. He jammed a pry-spike into the glowing necro-lock. The rune pulsed like a venomous heart. Diego rolled the dice across his palm, breath catching. "Come on... be kind to Daddy."

He slammed them into the lock.

MASTER DIE: The Black Mark

PIPS: 6 + 5 = 11

Effect: JINXED CIRCUIT

The necro-lock flickered—snarled, then blew apart in a rain of ruptured sigils. The chains split wide. Makalith collapsed to one knee, gasping as magic surged violently back into his limbs.

"You're free!" Diego shouted. "Now fight with us!"

Makalith staggered upright, leaning on the pillar. "You don't understand. Adriana is ascending. And with Von Epp at her side—there is no victory. Together they are—"

"Von Epp's dead," Chase said flatly.

Makalith blinked. "What?"

"And the mourned assassin's dead too," Diego added. "Mr. Scissor hands. Chase burned him to pieces." The fey mage froze—shock, then realization, then quiet hatred flickering across his features.

"Utilis..." Makalith whispered. "The betrayer deserved his fate. Coco always warned me... and I ignored her." His voice hardened. "But if Von Epp is truly gone..."

Chase nodded once. Something inside Makalith shifted—grief calcifying into purpose. "Then Adriana stands alone," he said. "Ascended, yes—but weakened without the Second Seat feeding her. She can be stopped."

He lifted his wand. Black fire spiraled up its length like a living brand. "For Sirus. For the murdered children. For the boy bound in that coffin. Perhaps I can help stop what I helped create."

He stepped beside Chase and Diego. "I will fight with you, Spellbound."

Silence fell. Dorian stared across the chamber at the three of them—Spellbound, Dice Mage, Fallen Archmage—standing together.

His pupils shrank. "No," Dorian whispered. "No, no, no—this is not the shape the ritual was meant to take."

He turned desperately toward Adriana. "Lady Mortem!" he cried. "Assist me! Your ascension is in jeopardy—help me stop them!"

But Adriana did not turn. Her eyes were rolled white, body suspended inches above the dais, runes spiraling around her in a cyclone of deathlight. The ritual consumed her completely. She could not hear him. Or chose not to.

Her voice—deep, ancient—echoed through the chamber: "I walk the path of gods. I am beyond you."

Dorian's expression collapsed into horror.

The Gravecaller at her side hissed, "Master, we must—"

"Silence!" Dorian snapped, staggering backward. "She's locked in the rite. She won't—she can't—help." He looked again at Chase, Diego, and Makalith advancing slowly toward him. Three predators closing in. Panic cracked through Dorian's mask of poise. He spat a curse, reached into his coat, and tore free a black mirror—slick as obsidian oil.

"Not like this," he hissed. "I will not die here." Glyphs erupted around him. The mirror split open like a wound in reality. Dorian leapt backward into the rift—vanishing in a swirl of shadow and contempt. The mirror snapped shut with a thunderous crack, leaving only the rising screams of the ritual and the three men facing Adriana's apotheosis.

Adriana Mortem Ruthven hovered a foot off the ground, arms stretched wide, crimson tendrils of arcane power writhing around her like serpents. The altar behind her pulsed with a steady thrum. Aspen floated above it, unconscious, skin etched with glowing runes that seemed to breathe.

Chase stepped forward, bare-chested, blood still streaked along his ribs. The drum-fed Thompson in his hands felt too light—one mag left. He leveled it anyway.

"Let the boy go."

Adriana tilted her head, bemused. "That's the voice you use when begging? Pity."

A flicker of magic shimmered at her fingertips.

Chak-chak-chak!

Chase opened fire.

The Tommy gun roared in the closed chamber. A stream of arcane-laced bullets cut through the space between them—but Adriana moved with inhuman grace, tracing a ward in the air that bent the rounds off-course with a burst of red force. They pinged and sparked harmlessly against the stone columns.

With a flick of her other wrist, she retaliated. A lance of fire-threaded energy—bright and fast—screamed toward Makalith.

He barely raised his wand in time. A spiral deflection shield burst to life, catching the bolt and ricocheting it skyward, where it exploded against the ceiling in a shower of molten stone.

Makalith grit his teeth. "She's fast."

"Fast?!" Diego shouted from cover. "She's a damn nightmare."

He rolled one of his enchanted dice—sleek, black, etched in faint silver runes—and whispered a charm over it as it spun through the air.

Click-click. Big Red
Double ones. Snake eyes.

Time stuttered.

Adriana smiled. She reached out and twisted her fingers mid-air—she had frozen the dice mid-roll. Manipulated the outcome.

"Snake eyes, little cheat," she purred. "Snakes always bite back."

The die ignited, and a *crimson rebuke sigil* pulsed where it fell.

A geyser of flame erupted beneath Diego's feet.

He dove instinctively, rolling away just as the stone floor erupted behind him. His jacket caught fire—he ripped it off mid-roll and came up behind a pillar, coughing.

"Dios mío...!"

Adriana floated downward now, her bare feet touching stone. Her expression was composed—calm—but there was fire building in her irises. She was enjoying this.

"You're out of tricks," she said to Chase, her eyes flicking to his almost-empty drum. "Out of toys. Out of time."

Chase grimaced. He racked the bolt, feeding in the last rounds. "Still got lead."

He fired.

She didn't even blink. A flick of her wrist, and the rounds deflected again—but this time the kinetic force forced her back a step.

Makalith seized the opening. He surged forward, wand a blur as he sent a volley of kinetic slashes her way. Arcane blades rippled in the air, blue-white with Fey fire. Adriana raised a shield of blood-mist that absorbed the first two—but the third cut through, raking across her side.

She hissed. Her eyes snapped to him, and she extended both hands.

A concussive blast sent Makalith sailing across the chamber, crashing hard into a pillar. He slid down, coughing blood, his wand still clutched in one hand.

Diego, seeing him fall, stood from cover—hands trembling. "Damn it…"

He extended both palms, fingers glowing faintly. Direct casting. Something he rarely did.

A shimmering ripple of chaos magic coiled toward Adriana—wild, unpredictable, shaped by his will alone. A trickle of sweat fell down his temple.

Adriana didn't counter it. She *stepped through* it, like smoke through sunlight. Her form distorted, her body unraveling into mist, and reappeared just behind him.

"Cute," she whispered.

Diego turned—but not fast enough. She backhanded him with a wave of raw energy that sent him sprawling.

Chase caught her movement and pulled the trigger again. Empty.

His jaw clenched. He dropped the gun and drew Effie and Pearl, the twin pistols gleaming with runes—but he didn't fire.

Not yet.

Adriana, breathing heavier now, turned to him fully.

Blood ran down her arm, and a chunk of her shoulder smoked from Makalith's strike. But she still stood.

Still powerful.

"You'll die," she said flatly. "But not before watching me complete the ritual."

Chase raised the pistols.

"We'll see."

They squared off again—wounded, exhausted, outclassed.

But not backing down.

Chase fired, unloading both pistols in an attempt to overwhelm her magical shielding. Circular impacts rippled across the surface as the shield absorbed the arcane rounds.

"Pathetic" she smirked as Chase slide behind another piller to reload.

Makalth moved wide to her flank, wand flashing as he launched a trio of razor-thin spell slices.

"Jahna kree!"

Three arcs of cutting light tore through the air—fast and jagged as broken glass. Adriana raised her left hand—no words, no breath. Just a flick of her fingers and a ripple of pale energy hardened in front of her like frost forming on glass. The first arc shattered against it. The second bent mid-air. The third struck wide, missing her cheek by an inch.

Makalith rolled left. "*Sileth no'bar!*"

Black vines erupted from the ground at her feet, barbed with obsidian hooks. She stepped back—and without casting, stomped once. A pulse of necrotic energy burst outward, searing the vines to ash before they touched her.

He ducked low. "*Torun vek'kal!*"

A concussive blast roared from his palm. Adriana was flung back, just slightly, her gown snapping in the wind. She skidded, feet dragging, but didn't fall. Her fingers twisted again—this time forming a circle in the air.

A crackling tether of violet thread leapt from her hand and wrapped around his shoulder—pulling.

"*M'fala!*" he barked.

A cold-fire spear shot forward—but Adriana was already gone, displaced in a silent flicker. The spear struck her afterimage, burning a hole through empty air.

From behind him, she reappeared—no sound, no smoke—just the shifting of shadow.

Makalith snarled. "*Deru sa'tor!*"

He spun mid-air, hurling a fan of bone-thorns from his outstretched hand. They struck her arm, her side, her thigh—but each thorn hissed and dissolved, swallowed by her graveward armor—a necromantic construct of spirit silk and marrow plating.

She didn't retaliate immediately.

That was worse.

"*Ni'korae val!*" he hissed.

Invisible glass shattered above her—sleeting down in a storm of razor-shards. This, finally, made her flinch. One hand rose to shield her eyes. Blood lined her cheek.

"Yaneh do'fe," he whispered, planting a trap ward beneath her feet as he landed. Adriana landed across from him, blood on her brow, smile like a knife.

She stepped directly onto the trap.

It pulsed.

Then fizzled.

Her barefoot rose, revealing the charred remains of the ward.

Makalith's eyes widened. She'd overwritten his magic. Silently. He hadn't even seen the counter.

Then Adriana grinned.

She drew her hand back and released what looked like a simple stun bolt.

Makalth raised his ward, prepared—but the bolt split midair into five separate streaks, fanning out like a predator's claws.

He twisted, deflecting four of them in sequence with masterful wandwork.

The fifth clipped his right flank.

His body stiffened.

Makalth froze in place, eyes wide, wand trembling in a locked grip. "Damn it—"

Adriana stepped back from him, smirking.

"Clever mage... but I've played this game longer than your bloodline's been walking upright."

Across the room, Diego raised his pistol and his palm, dice suspended in the air again as he channeled raw chaos. "You really oughta be more polite—"

Her eyes flashed. She spoke one word.
"Come."

A glamour.

It struck him like a wave of perfume and memory. His limbs slowed. The world dimmed. She didn't walk—she pulled him.

Diego's boots scraped across stone as he was drawn toward her outstretched arms, her mouth parting slightly—fangs glinting.

"No—no no no—" he snapped, trying to resist. His pistol hung limp. His dice glowed but remained stuck above his head.

Chase, bleeding, wards flickering, moved.

He surged forward, pistol out, trying to reach Diego—trying to break the spell. Adriana flicked her wrist.

A blood sigil burst under Chase's boots, sending him flying backward.

He hit the ground hard—right beneath Diego's hovering dice.

For a breath, all was still.

Then Chase gritted his teeth and punched upward, knocking the dice with the flat of his palm.

The dice hit the stone floor and spun—then stopped.

Double sixes.

Big Red.

Adriana's glamour flickered.

A deep *thrum* pulsed beneath the chamber. Her eyes widened.

From under her feet—

BOOM.

A pillar of infernal fire erupted, engulfing her in searing heat and molten air. She screamed, this time in real pain, the flames lifting her off the ground and hurling her into the far wall.

Her robes were gone. Her skin blistered and peeled. Blood ran down her sides where old flesh met new ruin. Still breathing, still furious—but hurt.

She staggered upright, body shaking.

Chase crawled to his knees, eyes glowing faint gold from the rebound. Diego, now free of the glamour, sucked in a deep breath and retrieved his dice with trembling hands.

Makalth stirred, breaking free from the stun lock with effort, leaning on his wand. "That… was new." The three of them formed up.

Adriana swayed, her hair wild, her eyes burning with unholy light. Her voice cracked as she spoke: "I must finish the ritual…" She flexed her hand—and the blood-magic flared again.

CHAPTER 11

Roll the Bones

— *A Conversation Between Chase Cassidy & Diego Salazar*

"So... the Lord of Bones. What the hell is that supposed to be?" Diego muttered.

"Some necromancer who should've stayed dead," Chase said, rolling his shoulders. "Lucky us—we get to remind him."

The burnt scent of ozone and blood clung to the stones as Skye ascended the winding stairs, heels echoing with purpose. Her grip was firm on the arcalam, the wand's rapier-like form humming faintly— attuned to the chaos unfolding beyond the heavy chamber doors.

But it wasn't the doors that made her pause. It was the woman dancing.

Coo Coo Le Fey.

She spun on bare feet in a circle, humming a haunting waltz off-key, twirling like a fractured music box ballerina around the blackened remains of the Mourned Chase had slain earlier. Her tattered dress floated around her, patched with lace, blood, and stitched-up memories. One hand gripped a parasol that served no purpose except madness. The other held a single yellow daisy—plucked and stripped of petals.

"He loves me... he loves me not... he loves me... he—"

Skye stepped cautiously forward, arcalam raised. "Step away from the body. Now."

Coo Coo pirouetted, then bowed in dramatic curtsy. "Ooooh, darling lawyer girl... you're right on time for the grand finale." She cocked her head with a porcelain smile cracked across one cheek. "Tick tick tick, and the curtain's about to fall."

"I won't ask again."

"Oh, you won't need to."

Coo Coo leaned against the corpse like a lounging diva, twirling the daisy between two fingers.

"See, Maky—dear Makalith, with his good cheekbones and bad

morals—always keeps his ace tucked real close. Right next to his heart." Her voice grew suddenly clear. "But even he doesn't know the full hand he's playing."

Skye lowered the wand an inch, wary. "What ace?"

Coo Coo grinned wide—too wide. "Why, *me*, silly."

A thunderous crack from beyond the chamber shook the walls. Dust rained down. Skye flinched, eyes darting toward the double doors. The fight inside had escalated.

Coo Coo twirled again and whispered as she passed, close enough for Skye to feel the chill off her breath.

"You're gonna want to watch this part. It's where everything *beautifully* falls apart."

And then she skipped ahead, stepping between the columns, arms stretched like a dancer taking the stage. Her bare feet left behind faint smears of blood. She didn't enter the chamber—but she was headed right for it.

Skye remained where she was for just a second, the image burned into her thoughts:
Coo Coo, the ace in the heart.
The chaos they hadn't counted on.

Then she moved. Fast. Arcalam in hand, lips whispering a spell of shielding as she chased the madness into the jaws of war.

The doors shuddered in their frames, scorched and cracked from the battle raging beyond.

Skye skidded to a halt, breath catching—Coo Coo Le Fey stood still at the threshold, her arms wide, spinning one final time as if basking in the chaos through stone and soul.

And then—she shrunk.

No incantation. No gesture. Just a shimmer of violet shimmerdust as her form collapsed inward like a folding star. In her place hovered a delicate sprite no bigger than a teacup, wings twitching like hummingbird glass, eyes wild and thrilled.

She zipped forward with a mad giggle and shot under the door.

Skye cursed and surged ahead, kicking the battered doors wide.

———

Firelight flickered off broken stone and melted sigils. The chamber trembled under the weight of battle.

Adriana Mortem Ruthven bled from her side, her elegant clothing scorched, hair disheveled, skin blackened in patches—but she was not down. Not yet.

She moved like a wounded predator—grace and gore in equal measure—her arcane energy now drawing back from the ritual. The protective barrier around Aspen shimmered violently, weakening as her focus broke.

Across from her in the midst of battle was Makalith, breathing heavy, wand burning bright, coat torn and hanging off one shoulder like a war banner. Chase, shirtless, sigils glowing dim and angry along his forearms, spent of grenades, the last drum of his Tommy gun loaded but nearly dry. Diego, face smeared with soot, one hand crackling with raw chaos magic, the other steady on the grip of a battered silver revolver, its cylinder already half-spent.

"She's pulling power from the boy," Makalith growled, his voice hoarse but firm. "If we keep this up—"

"She can't finish the ascension," Chase finished for him, stepping forward, flame licking from the base of his sigils.

Then the chamber exploded in red.

Adriana raised both hands—her eyes glowing with bloody light—and unleashed a hexstorm of blood-crafted sorcery, sharp as glass and just as cruel. The ground cracked with arterial glyphs. Magic tore through the air like barbed wire, slashing wide arcs across the room.

Chase dove left, lighting his Searing Aegis, the shield flaring just in time to intercept a harpoon of sanguine power. It still drove him backward in a slide of sparks and ash.

Diego dove right, hurling a die mid-roll—a single six. "Flame Veil," he hissed, and the fire from Adriana's volley curled around him instead of through him, dancing like hungry wolves.

Makalith dropped low and rolled, then snapped his wand up mid-motion and fired.

His blast wasn't at her.

It struck the base of the ritual dais—an enchantment-breaking curse, anchored deep and dirty. There was a resonant *snap*, a howl of ruptured sigils, and then—

The ritual shield collapsed.

The floating lattice that protected the boy—Aspen Willowbark, now limp, barely conscious—flickered out like candlelight.

Adriana turned, eyes blazing with hatred. "NO!" She screamed, and her power answered.

A beam of jagged crimson burst from her palm and smashed into Makalith's chest, sending him spinning. Bone cracked. His coat smoked. He struck the altar with a sickening crack and crumpled down its side like a marionette with its strings cut.

Skye was there, already sliding across broken stone to catch him. She grabbed his collar, pulling him against her lap.

"Chase!"

His name, shouted in her voice.

He turned—Tommy gun rising instinctively—then froze.

Skye. Alive. Bruised, bloodied, but alive.

For a second—just a second—the noise fell away. The ritual chamber, the death magic, the smell of burning blood—it all vanished under the sight of her moving, breathing, here. His gut twisted. She didn't smile. Didn't blink. Just held Makalith and nodded once—eyes locked with his. Focus. They'd talk later. If they survived.

Chase turned, stepping between her and Adriana as the next wave of death magic flared. She was already casting again. Blood pooled fast. Makalith gasped. Still alive. Barely. But above them—the ceiling had changed.

The glyphs Adriana etched in blood across the ceiling began to twist, peeling reality like wet wallpaper. The air warped. Winds from nowhere blew inward. Every candle in the room snuffed as if afraid.

And then came the sound.

The shriek of something ancient clawing back from beyond.

Ribbons of black mist poured from the breach. Whispers grew louder. Symbols stitched in bone and hex began to pulse on Adriana's arms as she chanted the final syllables of the rite.

She turned toward the portal—not the boy.

"My Lord" she screamed "I am your descendent, you most loving servant, welcome to back to the world"

"She's ripping open the tear!" Diego yelled, eyes wide as he read the arcane geometry bleeding into the sky.

"Then we stop her now," Chase growled, stepping forward again, flame coiling down his arms. But they were too late. Above them all, the Withering Veil ruptured.

———

Above the cathedral, the streets were unusually quiet. Most civilians had cleared out at curfew. Those that remained huddled indoors behind locked doors and closed blinds—everyone felt the pressure in the air, even if they couldn't name it.

Captain Whitman stood just outside the patrol wagon, coat collar turned up against the wind, gloved hands twitching as he watched the others fan out. Four officers. None of them knew why they were here. He did.

"Perimeter sweep," he'd told them. "Standard routing."

Bullshit.

He was here because he wasn't allowed to help Cassidy. Because Colonel Robert Langely had told him to stay out of it. Because Senator Wilder wanted thing to play out so he can lock down the zone even more.

So he brought his boys as close as he could get without breaking orders.

The cathedral loomed ahead—dark, cracked, and wrong in ways no building should be.

"Cap," said Officer Pirelli, squinting up at the clouds. "You see that?"

Whitman followed his gaze.

And his breath caught.

The sky was turning red.

Not the natural kind. Not sunset or flare. This was a bleeding light.

A sickening, pulsing hue, like the afterimage of staring into an arcane detonation. And it wasn't just the color.

Glyphs began forming—slowly spinning circles of burning script, etched in languages no man should know. One hung low like a crown of thorns above the spire. Another pulsed wide over the southern stretch of sky like an enormous, unseen gate.

They weren't just forming. They were remembering something.

Reactivating a design long buried in the bones of the city.

Whitman's stomach dropped.

He'd seen this before.

Passchendaele. 1917.

The trenches screaming. The sky catching fire with infernal sigils. A young soldier—Chase Cassidy—his body glowing with wards, eyes lit like hellfire, dragging wounded men through dirt that melted under their boots.

Back then, the sky broke open, and things came through. Things that didn't bleed right. Things that whispered in the dead men's voices.

And now?

Now it was happening again.

"Sir?" another officer asked, voice small.

Whitman didn't hesitate. He yanked his service revolver from its holster and snapped the cylinder open. Full.

He looked at the cathedral.

Then at his men.

"Boys..." He shoved a fresh cigarette between his teeth, struck a match with his thumb, and took a long drag.
"...we're going in."

———

Reality cracked. The chamber tore like wet canvas—edges bending inward, then outward, then folding into impossible geometry. The Withering Veil strained against its boundaries, its surface pulsing as something inside it clawed outward.

The first of them slipped through. A Veil Wretch—a multi-limbed, skinless nightmare shaped from broken thoughts and discarded hours—dragged itself from the rift. Its joints bent wrong. Its mouth split too wide. Its fingers were too many.

A second Wretch pressed against the tear behind it. Adriana didn't turn. Her eyes were locked on Aspen Willowbark suspended above the altar, his veins blackening, shadow-crown almost formed.

"Contain them!" she shrieked. "They seek to stop the ritual!"

The first Wretch sniffed the air and lunged for Makalith.

Gold fire rolled from Makalith's wand in a sweeping arc—sharp, precise, devastating but the Wretch only staggered and twisted, its body reforming inside the flame as if it had been expecting to burn.

"These things aren't from our plane!" Makalith shouted, blood thick on his cheek. "They don't obey your rules, Ruthven!"

Adriana stood behind the ritual dais, eyes glowing with predatory calm. She didn't even look at him when she answered: "They obey hunger."

The first Wretch lunged.

It hit Makalith like a collapsing building—jointed limbs splitting into more limbs, stabbing and curling around him in a lattice of impossible anatomy. Makalith braced, grounding himself, blasting another wave of gold fire straight into the creature's core—but the Wretch pushed through it, shrieking.

A limb scythed across Makalith's ribs. His breath hitched—blood spilling down his coat.

"Maky—!" Coco shrieked from the rafters, voice cracking.

He responded with a wordless snarl, trying to force himself upright —but the Wretch's next strike knocked him to both knees. A jagged bone spur punched into the side of his torso.

Makalith's wand slipped from his hand. His face went pale. He sagged against the stone pillar, breath rasping.

A second fissure tore open in the Veil above them. Something huge, starved, and wrong dropped through—limbs folding and unfolding like blades. It locked onto Chase instantly.

The Wretch crashed down where he had been standing, claws

sparking against stone as Chase slid aside and came up with his Colt drawn. He emptied three rounds into its exposed flank—each one etched for arcane penetration—but the creature devoured the damage, flesh reknitting as fast as the bullets tore it.

The Wretch shrieked. Charged again.

Chase brought up his forearm—sigils along his forearm pulsing once. The aegis formed, a silent hard-light shield, catching the Wretch's limbs just long enough for Chase to pivot under its mass and slam a knee into its jointed underframe.

It faltered. Barely. Then recovered instantly.

Diego hurled a die toward Chase's feet, wild luck flaring. The sigil triggered beneath the Wretch—its limbs buckling for a heartbeat, spine twisting in confusion.

"Don't die yet!" Diego yelled. "I owe you money!"

Chase didn't answer. He was already moving.

The first Wretch, the one mauling Makalith, shifted its entire ribcage into a bone cage and drove three limbs into Makalith's back. He choked. Collapsed fully. Eyes glassy. He tried to raise his head—but the creature's limb closed around his throat, cutting off breath. Cutting off magic.

"Maky!" Coco screamed. She dove, wings blurring, tugging desperately at his coat collar, trying to drag him away—but she had no leverage. She was too small. Too panicked.

Diego threw another die—Black sparks erupted under the monster — It jolted aside, confused for a fraction of a second. Enough time for Coco to yank Makalith sideways by sheer desperation. He slid across the stone, unconscious, gasping shallowly.

Coco clung to him, trembling.

Chase pivoted around a column as the second Wretch barreled past him. It hit the wall hard enough to crack stone. He felt heat blooming beneath his skin—his sigils responding to danger, pulsing like molten circuitry.

His gloves steamed. He lifted two fingers—Hellfire snapped out, shaping itself into a spear of white-hot force—

Infernal Lance.

It punched through the Wretch's shoulder, searing bone and shadow alike. The creature recoiled, screeching, half its limbs collapsing into slagged ash before reforming in jagged convulsions.

It lunged again.

Chase slid under it and used its momentum to plunge the lance upward, pinning the creature's torso to a shattered column. The infernal heat pouring off his arm traveled down the blade—burning the Wretch from within.

It spasmed— shrieked— then imploded into black dust. Chase slowly stood and exhaled once—hard, sharp, pained. The Wretch attacking Makalith reformed its limbs and scuttled toward Chase, screeching in a pitch meant to break human sanity.

Chase lifted his arm again—but the sigils along his forearm flickered. He was overheating. Too much infernal output. Too fast. The Wretch sensed the weakness.

It lunged—but Diego was already moving. He appeared at the Wretch's flank, boots skidding across blood-slick stone, the old Winchester 1897 braced against his shoulder. He popped the action open with a shuck and dropped all three dice directly into the shotgun's open chamber.

The dice pulsed violently, glowing like tiny dying suns. Diego snapped the breach shut. The shotgun shook in his hands, runes crawling across the barrel that were not there a second ago. "You wanted odds?" Diego growled. "Count em"

He FIRED. The shotgun didn't fire a shell. It fired pure fate. Three dice screamed from the barrel like meteors, spiraling midair in molten arcs of probability magic. They struck the Wretch square in the torso— and detonated into three simultaneous effects:

BLACK MARK — a hex ripping through its internal geometry

WILDSHIFT — twisting its limbs in impossible directions

CRITICAL CASCADE — forcing every mutation it carried to collapse inward at once

The Wretch seized— Convulsed—Folded in on itself like meat collapsing into a singularity. Its limbs bent the wrong way. Its torso twisted into an angle no mortal thing could survive. Its head imploded like wet paper. The monster hit the ground in a trembling, broken tangle of limbs.

Diego blew smoke from the shotgun's barrel. "Load of crap dice," he muttered. "Finally pulled their weight." The shotgun crumbled apart in a shower of brittle ash.

Chase and Diego hurried to Makalith's side. The Fey mage was slumped against the shattered pillar, bleeding badly, breath bubbling weakly.

"He's alive," Chase said, checking his pulse. "But he's out."

Coco hovered inches above Makalith's chest, tears streaking her glamour. "Fix him. Fix him. Fix him—"

"Coco." Chase's voice cut through her panic. "The ritual isn't finished." The sprite froze mid-flight.

As if on cue, Adriana's voice rose from the dais, shimmering with power and malice.

"My lord awakens." Aspen screamed, Not human. Not mortal. Something caught between worlds. The air vibrated. The Veil pulsed like a beating, rotting heart. Chase stood.

Diego reloaded. Coco wiped her face with the back of her hand, fury shaking through her wings. They turned toward the dais—

A third Wretch dropped through—bigger than the others, its frame stretched by Adriana's ritual, limbs spiked and dripping with shadow-rot. It landed between them and the dais with a sound like bones being wrung out.

Chase stepped forward automatically. Diego peeled left, shotgun raised low.

Adriana lifted both hands above the ritual circle, arcs of violet magic whipping outward.

"KEEP THEM FROM THE VESSEL!" she screamed.

Bolts of shadow erupted. And then— A wall of shimmering sapphire energy rose in front of Chase and Diego. Skye Anderson staggered into view behind them, both hands locked around her Arcalam wand, runes blazing along the shaft.

Her voice cracked with effort.

"KEEP—PUSHING!" Another blast hit her shield and skidded off in sparks.

Chase didn't look back. Didn't dare. The Wretch screeched and charged Diego first, drawn to weaker blood. Diego rolled beneath it, dice scattering in a spray of glowing pips.

He slapped the floor. Probability warped. The Wretch tripped mid-lunge, spine bending at an impossible angle before snapping back.

"HEY! OVER HERE, PUTO!" Diego barked, sprinting toward a column. The Wretch leapt on him, crashing into the dice mage and pinning him to the floor before Diego could react. Its mouth opened and rage and hunger bore down towards his throat.

Skye dropped her shield and shouted " "Kudur-Lagaš". Stone chained formed out of arcane light lashing to the creatures head, preventing Dieog's death by inches.

Thats all that was needed. Chase was already moving. Sensing his approach the creature spun back towards him, limbs blade-long and dripping. Chase planted one foot into the cracked stone and pushed off—sigils along his forearm igniting like a furnace.

The searing aegis snapped into existence along his forearm. The Wretch shrieked and leapt, a tangle of claws and rot aimed straight for Chase's throat.

Chase braced and THREW the Aegis down the beast's centerline. The shield spun out from his arm with brutal momentum, burning and cutting a perfect vertical line through the creature's chest. The Wretch split in midair, torn in two halves—black ichor raining across the dais.

Chase didn't stop. The moment the Aegis left his arm, he triggered the next sigil—

INFERNAL SURGE.

Heat exploded through his muscles. He ran straight THROUGH the collapsing monster, bursting through the cloud of dissolving flesh and shadow-rot, fire trailing behind him like comet tails. The blast of momentum carried him forward directly into Aspen Willowbark.

Chase SLAMMED into him shoulder-first, driving the boy off the ritual plinth. They crashed to the stone hard enough to crack it. The impact knocked Aspen's head sideways and the Crown of Mortem flew off, clattering across the floor like a kicked skull.

Aspen convulsed, choking on breath and shadow. Chase pinned him with one burning hand across his sternum, leaned in, and almost apologetically whispered—

"Infernus."

Hellfire flooded from his palm, not to burn the veil but to destroy the boy. Aspen screamed. The ritual screamed with him. Above them, Adriana shrieked in fury as the flames engulfed her as well. Her wards buckled but held under power of the infernal flame, singing her clothing but keeping most of the damage away from her flesh.

"NO! YOU BURN WHAT YOU DO NOT UNDERSTAND!"

Chase didn't even look up. The Crown lay abandoned. The ritual's heart had finally been shattered. The Wretch's scream dissolved into smoke.

Adriana staggered, wards struggling to reform, the Veil fraying behind her like torn canvas. The ritual was breaking apart—the chamber trembling with the force of it.

Chase dragged his burning arm across the runes, as the hellfire expanded. He concentrated all his infernal energy into the casket.

"That's the idea!"

The sarcophagus became to glow red, pulsing and warping at the sides, and then it detonated, sending out a wave a necromantic force. Chase was blown clean off the altar. Adriana crumpled to one knee, skin peeling, eyes wide with disbelief. "No… no—no, my Lord—." She raised her hand to curse the defenseless hexbreaker.

A streak of fae light shot across the chamber. Coco Le Fay. Full sprite. Full mania. She grew mid-flight, slamming into Adriana's chest like a comet.

Adriana choked, flailing. "Get—OFF—ME—"

Coco kissed her violently, laughing into her mouth with that unhinged brilliance only the half-mad could wield. "I'm crazy, honey," she whispered against Adriana's lips. "Now, you you will feel what its like to be bitten." Then Coco sank her teeth into her throat. Adriana screamed —more in psychic backlash than pain—as the bite tore through glamour, blood, and shadow-magic in one shocking pull.

Her wards buckled. Her flesh blistered. Her power flickered like a failing lantern. Adriana staggered backward, gasping black mist, her body breaking apart in sheets of ash—

Her eyes—wide, hateful, impossibly bright—locked onto Chase, Makalith, Diego, everyone still standing.

"You will not have me."

Her body convulsed and exploded into mist.

Teleportation magic stuttered violently, unstable from the broken ritual. The Veil fissure behind the dais buckled inward, collapsing like a dying lung—

And Adriana, desperate and furious, lashed out with one last spell. A whip-crack of violet lightning snapped from the imploding fissure—and wrapped around Coco's waist.

Coco twisted mid-air. "M A K A L I T H—!" she shrieked, reaching for him, her fingers inches from his—

He dove after her, shoulder slamming into the floor as the Veil's suction raked across his skin, shredding his glamour, cracking the stone beneath him. Their fingertips brushed air.

The Veil tore closed. Coco's last glimmer—pink, blue, gold, frantic—snapped out of existence. A faint echo lingered for a heartbeat: "...Maky...?"

Then nothing. Silence swallowed the chamber. Aspen was nothing but ash..

Diego coughed smoke. Chase steadied himself on a pillar, ribs screaming.

Makalith stared at the sealed fissure, face empty, eyes hollow. Coco Le Fay was gone. Dragged into the Withering Veil. And Adriana Ruthven—shredded, weakened, but undeniably alive—had escaped into the dark.

Dust drifted from the ceiling as Chase spun—just in time to see Diego's try top stand but his knees buckled. The wound Lilidan carved across his ribs finally split open under the strain of the last spellshot; blood darkened his burned shirt as he collapsed sideways, hitting the stone with a wet gasp. Chase sprinted, sliding the last few feet on broken floor, catching Diego before his head struck the ground.

"Diego! Diego—stay with me!"

Diego's eyes fluttered, unfocused, breath stuttering in and out.

"Ah... hell," he wheezed, trying and failing to smirk. "Guess... the house finally... collected."

Skye reached them an instant later, dropping to her knees so fast she nearly fell. Her hands glowed a faint, trembling blue as she pressed them over Diego's wound, voice cracking: "Hold still—just hold still—Diego, look at me." Her breath hitched when she felt the depth of the cut, but she didn't flinch. She leaned over him, shielding him from the raining debris, her wand shaking in her fist as she drew a protective circle around all three of them.

"Don't you dare pass out on me!"

Diego forced a smirk. "I would never. Not with you yelling."

Chase pressed two fingers to the side of Diego's neck. Pulse—thready but steady. He exhaled, shoulders sagging in relief. Skye did the same, one hand brushing Diego's hair back from his forehead.

"You're gonna be fine," Chase said.

Diego opened one eye. "Yeah? 'Cause everything hurts. Even the parts I didn't know were parts."

"Then you're fine," Chase said, patting his cheek—half-gentle, half-brotherly smack.

Boots thundered above them—then down the stairwell. Blue-coat First Arcane officers poured in, wands raised, guns drawn, expressions freezing as they took in the horror:

Captain Whitman led the charge, eyes wide and white. "What... the hell... is this place?"

He took one step in—then stopped dead as he spotted Chase.

"Cassidy?"

But Chase didn't look at him. He was staring toward the altar—toward the thin smear of mist where Adriana Mortem had vanished. His jaw locked.

"It's not over," he said, voice low, steady... dangerous.

Whitman blinked. "What are you—"

"She's alive." Chase rose slowly, one hand gripping the pillar for support. "She didn't die. She fled."

Skye straightened too, still keeping one hand on Diego's shoulder. "How do you know?"

Chase turned—eyes burning with recognition.

"She's a vampire. An old one. They don't just vanish unless they're retreating. She'll need to regenerate…"

Skye's eyes widened as the memory hit her. The heavy crates of earth. The massive vats sealed with rune-wax. "…from her homeland," Skye whispered.

"A vampire can only heal inside soil from where they were turned."

Chase nodded once. "And the only place we found that kind of soil…"

Both said it at the same time: "The docks."

Whitman snapped out of his shock. "Wait—you're telling me she's trying to escape the city?!"

"Yes," Chase growled, shoving a fresh drum into his Thompson that he took from a pass patrolman. "Remember the soil we saw Whitman. That will heal her."

Whitman nodded understanding the gravity.

Skye rose, already summoning her arcalam into her hand. "No more running. Not for her. Not for us."

Diego coughed a weak laugh, wincing. "Go get her… don't leave any pieces big enough for her lawyer to argue with."

Skye leaned down, kissed Diego's soot-streaked forehead. "You stay with Whitman. If you try to get up, I'll break your legs myself."

Diego tried to salute. Failed. Settled for a thumbs-up.

Whitman barked orders over his shoulder. "Medics! Stabilize him! You three—secure this chamber! And someone get me a damn map of the harbor!"

Chase slung the Thompson, the weight of it familiar and righteous.

"Whitman," he said without turning, "keep your men out of the docks until I'm done."

Whitman stared. "I will, but what're you planning?"

Chase's voice was ice wrapped around iron. "Finishing this."

He started toward the outer tunnels. Skye fell into step beside him, jaw set, wand glowing faintly. It was only then did they realize that Makalith Ravenwind, leader of the Twilight Collective and ally of convenience was gone.

———

Adriana Mortem crashed through the wooden floorboards, her body plunging into the vat of blood beneath the abandoned warehouse.

The impact sent a violent ripple through the thick, crimson pool, the viscous liquid slopping over the edges as her charred, torn body sank beneath the surface.

For a long moment, she remained motionless.

The pain was unbearable.

Her once flawless skin was now blackened and blistered, her limbs twisted with damage, her once-immaculate clothes burned and shredded from the infernal fire Cassidy had unleashed upon her.

That hex-breaking bastard.

She sucked in a ragged breath, her lips parting beneath the thick, stagnant blood.

She could feel the arcane properties within it—a supply gathered from the sacrifices of fey-blood children. It was meant to sustain her in times of great wounds…

But something was wrong.

The magic in the blood was old. Stale.

Most of its potency had been spent to help her recover from her long trip.

Adriana emerged, gasping, dragging herself over the side of the vat, her hands leaving streaks of red across the dusty floor. Her wounds closed —but not fully.

The fire-scorched flesh still ached, her body far weaker than it should have been.

Her lips curled back in rage.

Damn that Spellbound. Damn Makalith and curse Dorian Blackwell.

Her hands clenched into fists, nails digging into her own palms. She had trusted him, allowed him into her circle, let him stand beside her in the ritual—

And he had abandoned her.

For what? Power? Self-preservation?

Adriana staggered to her feet, her body shaking.

She needed her sarcophagus. It was the only thing that could restore her properly. But it had been used for the ritual. A now it was molten slag thanks to the spellbound.

Her sharp, bloodshot eyes darted around the room. Two bodies lay on the floor. Their suits marked them as mafia men, the hollow out eyes marked them as consumed. Her wards did their jobs.

She stumbled forward, her movements weak, unsteady. The world tilted around her, the aftershock of the hex-breaking flames still rippling through her blood.

She reached a heavy iron door, rusted at the edges, marked with sigils of protection. With a grunt, she pushed it open, revealing a small chamber beyond.

The air was thick with the scent of old earth and dried herbs.

At the center—

A coffin.

Not the grand, ornate casket she had prepared for the ritual, but a simpler construct. Its wood was darkened with age, the etchings along its surface primitive yet potent.

She brushed her fingertips along its edge.

The soil of her homeland rested within, gathered in secret, imbued with the last remnants of her ancestral power. It was not perfect. But it would do. For now.

Adriana leaned against it, her breath ragged.

She would heal here. Slowly. Painfully.

But when she awoke—

Dorian Blackwell would pay with his life.

Adriana's lips curled into a snarl as she lifted one trembling hand.

A single arcane symbol burned at her fingertips, searing the air with necrotic energy.

"Come," she commanded.

The shadows in the room trembled.

A figure materialized.

A vampire—one of her own. A loyal servant, clad in tattered crimson robes, his fangs dripping with fresh blood.

His pale eyes glowed, locked onto her with silent obedience.

Adriana's voice was low, powerful.

"You will protect me as I sleep."

The vampire bowed his head. "As you command, Mistress."

She raised her bloodstained hand, chanting in a language far older than the city around them. Dark energy swirled.

The vampire's eyes widened, his body convulsing—

As his flesh began to twist.

His skin bubbled, reshaping. His limbs elongated, bones cracking, twisting, his body growing grotesque.

Fangs extended into jagged protrusions, his once humanoid face morphing into something monstrous—something inhuman.

He let out a guttural, agonized wail, but Adriana never flinched.

She watched as he became a true nightmare.

A guardian. A beast. A protector of her slumber.

When it was done, the creature slumped forward, its massive clawed hands pressing against the stone floor, its breathing ragged, low, animalistic.

Adriana smiled faintly. "Good."

With the last of her strength, she climbed into the sarcophagus, the soil of her homeland embracing her body like a shroud.

She let out a slow, shuddering breath. This was not the end. It was only the beginning. As she closed the lid above her, her final words echoed in the darkness—

"Let no one disturb me."

————

Return to the Present – Adriana's Death

The scent of blood, salt, and gunpowder thickened the air at Warehouse 24.

Chase Cassidy stood over the ancient sarcophagus, his Tommy gun gripped tight in his hands, the weight of the drum magazine a familiar comfort against the tension curling in his gut. The moonlight cut through the high bay windows, streaking silver across the cold, concrete floor.

Two drained corpses lay sprawled beside him—children. Their hollowed-out eyes stared into nothingness. The sight gnawed at him, twisting something deep inside, but he forced it down. He had a job to finish.

A slow creak echoed through the warehouse.

The lid of the sarcophagus shifted.

Then, Adriana Mortem emerged.

She rose like a specter from the grave, her skin pale as moonlight, her black dress slick with the blood she had stolen. Red eyes gleamed with unholy hunger, sharp fangs glistening in the dim light.

Despite the massacre she had left in her wake, she smiled.

A sultry, beguiling thing. A predator's smile.

She took a step toward him, moving with an unnatural grace, her voice dripping with dark seduction.

"Put the gun down, Chase."

The words slid over him like silk, wrapping around his mind, pulling him into her orbit.

His grip on the Thompson loosened.

His body swayed, just slightly.

Then—his wards flared to life.

A golden sigil ignited across his skin, his spellbound protections snapping him back to reality. The charm shattered like glass, his mind clearing in an instant.

Adriana's smile vanished.

Faster than thought, she lunged.

Her clawed fingers latched onto him, pushing him hard against the side of the sarcophagus. Her strength was monstrous, unnatural. The Tommy gun nearly fell from his grasp as her lips parted, fangs hovering just above his throat.

Then—his wards flared again.

An arcane shockwave burst from his skin, knocking Adriana back with a scream of pain.

Chase didn't hesitate.

He lifted the Tommy gun.

And pulled the trigger.

The warehouse exploded with the roar of gunfire.

.45-caliber rounds ripped into Adriana's body, punching through her ribcage, staggering her back. Some of the bullets slammed into an invisible shield, sparking against her magical defenses—but enough got through. Enough to make her bleed.

Dark ichor spilled down her dress, her beautiful features twisting in rage and agony.

Still, she tried to stand.

Still, she tried to fight.

Then—Skye Anderson stepped into the room.

Her presence was commanding, her arcane power humming in the air like a storm waiting to break.

Chase caught a glimpse of her—cinnamon-colored skin glowing under the moonlight, wavy hair framing sharp, intelligent eyes, her blazer still dusted with the grime of battle.

She raised her arclame, its metallic rapier-like form gleaming in the darkness. She touched Adriana's sarphocas. The tether.

Adriana, sensing her death, gurgled, her voice hoarse. "A life for a life—"

Skye didn't let her finish. "Esto es tu fin. Ahora, arde en el olvido."

"This is your end. Now, burn into oblivion."

She lifted her wand, arcane fire spiraling at her fingertips, forming a brilliant blue glyph of power.

Her voice was steady, sharp, and final.

"Exilium Exsurgo" *A banishment spell struck.*

A chilling, inhuman wail erupted from Adriana's throat—a sound not of pain, but of erasure.

Her flesh withered, her bones cracked, her very soul being torn from the mortal realm.

She clawed at the air, trying to hold herself together, but there was no escape.

The spell took hold.

And Adriana Mortem ceased to exist.

Her body crumbled into ash, dissolving into the wind, leaving nothing behind but the scent of burning evil.

Chase exhaled, lowering the smoking barrel of the Tommy gun.

The dock was silent.

The storm was over. For now.

CHAPTER 12

...Hope You Enjoyed Your Stay

On Men Who Rarely Smile

- by Captain James Whitman, 1st Arcane Police Department

Former Company Commander, Harlem Hellfighters

Men like Chase Cassidy don't smile often. Not real ones. Not the kind that reach the eyes. Back in the 369th, he kept to himself—polite, capable, deadly when he had to be, but never close to anyone. You see boys form bonds in war, but Chase... he carried his distance like armor. I figured it came from his upbringing. Or his blood. Or the spellbinding that carved half the softness out of him.

Then one day in France, I saw a young legionnaire walk into our camp. Skinny, bright-eyed Puerto Rican kid with dice hanging from a bootlace. Diego Salazar. And damned if Chase didn't light up the moment he saw him. First time I'd ever seen the man smile. A real one. Whole-faced. Human.

I didn't see that look again for years. Not until Skye Anderson came barreling into his life like a storm in heels and silk and stubbornness. Funny thing, watching a man who's been carved by fire remember he still has a heart.

You don't forget moments like that.

The sky over St. Brigid's Cemetery was the color of pewter—flat, cold, unmoving. The kind of winter sky that swallowed sound and turned breath into ghosts.

Black cars lined the gravel path. Hushed voices drifted on the wind. And the two coffins—one oak, one mahogany—rested side by side beneath a great weeping willow.

It should have been impossible. A Negro man and a white man buried together in 1924. But love—and secrets—sometimes bent the world.

Father Patrick Albright stood between the coffins, eyes red from exhaustion. Silver-rimmed spectacles fogged with each breath, but his voice was steady.

"We gather today," he said, "to honor two men who lived their lives in service to others—whose kindness shaped this community in ways many will never fully understand."

Skye stood between Nadine and Tommy Dixon, wrapped in a black coat far too big for her. Her hands trembled despite the gloves. Her eyes were hollowed from nights without sleep.

Chase stood a few feet back, beside Luther, Benjamin, and Captain Whitman. Clusters of mourners gathered—clients, neighbors, shopkeepers, children Donald had defended pro bono, families Thomas had helped in matters nobody else would touch.

No one said the truth aloud. But several eyes lingered on the two coffins touching.

On the closeness no one could quite explain. Father Albright cleared his throat, glancing at Skye.

"I was asked," he said softly, "to make no mention of anything beyond friendship and partnership. And so I won't."

He looked from one coffin to the other. "But I will say this: these men were good. They loved deeply. And the world is lesser without them."

Skye's knees nearly buckled. Nadine wrapped an arm around her waist, steadying her.

Tommy Dixon cried openly. Benjamin's small hand slipped into Chase's. Chase didn't move—but he curled his fingers gently around the boy's.

A hush fell as pallbearers moved forward—six men for each casket. But when they lifted Henry's coffin, Skye stepped forward, voice breaking.

"Stop."

Everyone froze. She placed both hands on the polished oak, forehead resting against it.

"Daddies..." she whispered to herself. "I—I'm sorry I wasn't there. I'm sorry."

Her breath caught.

"You always told me I was too stubborn. Too loud. Too much. But you made me believe I could be something." Tears slipped down her cheeks. "I hope I made you proud. You she whispered. You taught me how to fight. How to stand. How to choose what's right even when it hurts." Her voice cracked like breaking glass. "I hope I made you both proud."

She pressed a hand to her mouth, shaking. Chase stepped forward then—not touching her, not saying a word, just standing behind her like a wall she could lean on if she chose to.

She didn't turn. Didn't acknowledge him. But she didn't step away. The coffins were lowered. Earth thudded softly against wood.

Father Albright recited a final prayer. "Bless these men with peace, with rest, and with the reunion of souls."

A long, heavy silence followed. Skye inhaled sharply, wiped her cheeks, and stepped back. The moment she turned away from the graves, her eyes met Chase's. Something inside her shattered.

She walked past him without a word. Chase didn't follow.

Benjamin gripped his coat tighter. "Are we going home?"

"Soon," Chase murmured, staring at the two fresh mounds of earth. "Soon, kid."

Captain Whitman placed a hand on Chase's shoulder before he left. "Cassidy, come with me. Travers is waiting."

Chase exhaled once and nodded. They stepped away from the cluster of mourners. Father Albright's voice drifted over the grass, low and steady, offering hope for souls Chase wasn't sure ever found peace.

Chase glanced back. Skye stood near Nadine and Luther, her gloved hands folded at her waist, her eyes hollow from grief and exhaustion. The wind lifted a strand of her dark hair. She didn't see him being led away.

Whitman guided him behind a row of cypress trees—out of sight, out of earshot. Governor General Travers waited there. His posture was immaculate, but his eyes were rimmed red with sleeplessness. He gave Chase a curt nod and motioned for him to step closer.

"Detective Cassidy," Travers said quietly. "Let's make this brief."

Whitman let go of Chase's shoulder but remained at his side like a wall.

Travers cleared his throat. "In light of recent... events—namely the exposure of the Court of Bones beneath the city, unexplained civilian casualties, and diplomatic pressure from half the arcane committees on the Eastern Seaboard—certain decisions had to be made."

Chase's jaw tightened. There it was. He knew the sound of a guillotine being raised.

Travers continued: "You're to be placed on immediate administrative discharge from the First Arcane Police Department. Effective today."

Chase didn't blink. Didn't breathe. Didn't give them the satisfaction of surprise.

Whitman spoke through clenched teeth. "This is political. You know that."

"Of course it's political," Travers snapped softly. "A supernatural cabal nearly destroyed Manhattan on my watch. Someone must answer for it."

"And that someone is the man who stopped them," Whitman growled.

Travers ignored the jab. His eyes returned to Chase.

"Your badge will be suspended pending formal termination. Captain Whitman will send Sergeant O'Leary to collect your weapons— The colt's and the Thompson included. Sullivan Act nonsense. But the law's the law. You'll receive written notice by week's end."

Chase swallowed once. Effie and Pearl—he had purchase them with Skye when he needed more firepower. Now they were headed to a property locker.

Travers hesitated before his next line. That alone told Chase how scripted this was. "There is... another option," Travers continued. "Governor-elect Landon intends to expand the State Hexbreaker Division. Your combat record and... unusual talents qualify you for immediate placement."

Whitman muttered, "Don't do it, Chase."

Chase kept his eyes on Travers. "No," he said simply. "I'm not being turned into an attack dog for Albany."

Travers exhaled through his nose. "Cassidy, if the world discovers what happened beneath this city. If they know magic is out of control. There will be crackdowns—curfews—registries. We need trained arcane combatants. This is your chance to serve again, properly, and now not as local enforcement. Something with teeth using your dog metaphor. The teeth of the State of New York."

Chase's gaze sharpened. He thought of the tunnels. The burning. Benjamin. Skye's trembling hands.

"I serve people," he said. "Not committees."

Travers 'expression tightened. "There won't be many men willing to sign up after what happened to you. After what the public saw. You're making this harder—for everyone."

Chase shook his head. "You want hunters?" he said. "Then make 'em independent. Let them answer to themselves. Not to politics. People will trust that." He shrugged. "State goons? Nobody's signing up for that."

Travers stared at him, unreadable for a long moment. Then he adjusted his coat "Governor Landon will do as he sees fit. My term is ending, Cassidy. I intend to leave this mess with as few open wounds as possible."

He offered Chase one last nod—formal, strained, almost regretful. "Good luck," Travers said. "You'll need it."

He turned and left through the trees to an awaiting car. Whitman remained. His voice dropped. "Chase... I'm sorry."

Chase forced a breath. "Not your fault."

Whitman's eyes softened. "I'll stall O'Leary for as long as I can. Give you time to... adjust."

"Thanks."

Chase glanced toward the building, where mourners drifted inside, but Skye still waited solely near her father's tome stones.

Whitman clapped his shoulder once. Firm. Loyal. "Whatever happens next... you're still one of the good ones."

Chase didn't answer. He walked back towards the thinning gathering.

Skye barely heard a word of the conversation between the

Holloways. Nore did she pay attention to Benjamin's Zorro story. The boys was trying to brighten up her mood and his sweet heart couldn't realize that he was failing.

Her fathers were gone. Both of them. And she felt hollow in ways she didn't know a person could be hollow. She felt Chase approaching the mourners with Whitman. He didn't speak. Didn't breathe much either. He stayed close only in case she reached for him.

She didn't.

The coffins lowered. The earth thudded. The final words were spoken. And then people began to drift—quiet condolences, handshakes, murmured prayers. Some touched her shoulder but she didn't feel a thing.

Nadine tried to guide her toward the car. "Skye... come on, sweetheart."

Skye didn't move. Not until a soft voice behind her said: "Miss Anderson."

Isabelle Monceau had just stepped out of a car, the long hem of her mourning coat brushing the gravel path. George, ever the dutiful machine, held the door open in silence. She paused before stepping inside and turned, her gaze sweeping past Chase to land on Skye.

"Ms. Anderson," she said. "A word, please?"

Skye exchanged a glance with Chase, then stepped away from the others, heels crunching softly on loose stone. They stopped beneath the crooked arm of a dying tree, just far enough for their voices to carry only to each other.

"My condolences," Isabelle began, tone smooth, eyes unreadable behind the veil. "For the loss of your father. And Mr. Pierce."

Skye gave a small nod. "Thank you."

"I've been watching," Isabelle said. "You and Chase. The way you move around each other. The way you hold him up when he's too proud to ask. It's admirable. Dangerous, too."

Skye frowned faintly, folding her arms.

"I'm not here to pass judgment," Isabelle continued. "But I want to offer you something. A warning, if you'll take it."

Skye didn't answer. Not yet.

Isabelle leaned in just a fraction. "Whatever future you're imagining with him... it won't be easy. Not because of who he is, but *what* he is. I'm sure you've noticed it by now—when he draws on his spellbound gifts. That amber light? That heat? That isn't just arcane war-forged magic. That's blood. Old blood. Twisted and corrupt."

She paused.

"You've felt it, haven't you? When you're close. When he's on top of you."

Skye stiffened but said nothing.

"There are things in this world," Isabelle said softly, "that walk in shadows but wear a persons skin. Chase is a good man. One of the best I've ever known. But he's not just a man."

A beat passed. Then another.

"I once carried his child."

That stilled Skye.

Isabelle's voice was low now, threadbare around the edges.

"It...She, was born wrong. Twisted. Cold. She breathed smoke and screamed in silence. And then... stopped breathing alltogether."

A crack ran through her composure, a flicker of grief that burned hot and fast before vanishing behind iron restraint.

"He never knew. He still doesn't. And I pray he never finds out. But you should know, before you let him any deeper into your life—into your body—that what's inside him *will not die in him.* Be careful what you create in love, Ms. Anderson. Not everything born of it comes out whole."

Isabelle stepped back. Straightened. Smoothed her gloves.

"I've said what I came to say."

Without another word, she turned and disappeared into the car. George shut the door, and the Rolls-Royce ghosted away down the winding lane, its engine fading into the hush of dusk.

Skye didn't move right away.

The sound of the car engine faded into the distance, swallowed by the trees and gravestones, but Isabelle's words clung like frost to her skin—cold, invasive, lingering in the places she didn't want to look.

She stared at the patch of gravel where the woman had stood, back ramrod straight, voice so damn calm as she spoke of *screams in silence* and a child that never should've been born.

Beneath the thin, dying branches overhead, Skye wrapped her arms around herself.

Damn her.

Damn her for planting that seed and walking away like it didn't matter. Like it wasn't going to grow roots and dig down into Skye's thoughts and twist around everything she was trying to build with Chase.

Because it had always been a risk—being with him, she knew what spellbinding did to the body, how unstable that kind of magic could be. She'd read the reports, seen the wards carved too deeply into the skin. There were reasons for concern. Reasons to hesitate.

But this... this wasn't about sigils or infernal enhancements.

This was something older. Something darker. Something *inherited.*

And Skye—brilliant, driven, rational Skye—had suspected it. In the quiet moments, when Chase lit up with more than arcane fire. When his eyes flashed amber in anger. When his body thrummed with heat that didn't belong to the world of men.

She had seen it. Felt it.

Now her suspicions were true. Her lover was a Cambion.

She exhaled slowly, tried to steady herself. Chase stood a few paces away, watching her with mild confusion, one hand on Benjamin's shoulder. He didn't know. About Isabelle. About the child. About what it meant.

And if she had anything to say about it... he never would.

Skye straightened her spine. Wiped the thought from her face. And walked toward him, her footsteps measured, her expression composed—but Isabelle's words followed close behind, whispering in the spaces between each breath.

———

The chamber was still. Dead magic clung to the air like cobwebs spun from ash and sorrow, thick with the copper tang of blood and scorched stone. The ritual circle was shattered—sigils cracked, chalk and bone dust blown across the floor like the aftermath of a storm. Faint torches guttered in their sconces, their fire too afraid to burn bright.

Dorian Blackwell stood alone.

Aspen Willowbark's broken form had been removed days ago. The vessel was ruined. The soul, fractured.

The Crown of Mortem—the final key to dominion—lay cracked on the floor, pulsing faintly like a dying heart. Veins of black-red light seeped from fractures along its silver edges, each glow a silent scream. Without the gift of arcane sight, the agents sent to cleanse the scene had missed it entirely.

But something remained.

The veil shimmered behind the altar. A ripple in the fabric of reality. And through it… something stirred.

A presence, vast and skeletal, pressed against the border between death and now. A towering form of bone-mist and hollow light loomed, its limbs indistinct, its face a ruin of crown and fang.

The Lord of Bones had not claimed flesh. But it had not left. It lingered—unfinished. Watching.

Dorian bowed.

His coat was in tatters. Blood dried along his temple. His sister was dead. The ritual, broken. The Mourned had failed them. The Gravecallers scattered or slain. Von Epp—mutated and slain by his very experements. Still, he endured.

"You failed," the voice whispered—not spoken, but breathed through the marrow of the walls. "And yet you remain."

Dorian raised his head slowly. "We lost everything. Mortem. Von Epp. Linden. The boy couldn't hold your soul."

"No," the Lord rasped. "They were too weak. You are not."

It drifted closer—hovering inches from the stone. Wherever it passed, the floor blackened, and broken sigils flinched like wounded animals.

"You understand loss," it hissed. "You understand hunger. Von Epp clung to past glories. Adriana to her vanity. But you… you see what must be done."

Dorian's jaw clenched. "There's nothing left."

"There is always something left," it whispered. "You will burn away the rot. And take the First Seat."

The words struck the room like a bell tolling in a mausoleum.

Dorian stood taller. His eyes burned. His voice dropped low. "There are supposed to be five. Five fingers to make a fist."

The Lord did not respond—only watched, silent and vast.

Dorian paced once, then bent to retrieve the broken Crown of Mortem, holding it as though cradling a child. "I'll rebuild the Court. Piece by piece. And when it stands, when the throne is mine, then I'll find Makalith. I'll end him myself."

The veil rippled, and the Lord's skeletal presence leaned in, its voice like frost on bone.

"Good. Find the lost. Gather the strong. And when the time comes... punish the faithless."

Dorian's voice was cold iron. "And Cassidy?"

The torches dimmed. The air seemed to still. The name echoed like a curse through the bones of the chamber.

"Not yet," the Lord of Bones whispered. "Not until the Court stands unbroken. Not until the crown is whole. When that time comes—he dies. Screaming."

Dorian nodded once. A dark smile curved his lips.

"Blood and betrayal," he murmured. "It's always been the currency."

The Lord's form faded, its parting words curling like smoke in his ear:

"Then spend it well, Dorian Blackwell."

———

The funeral hall had mostly emptied. Chairs were scraping. Voices were low, quiet, respectful in the way people get when they've run out of words. Evening light spilled through the stained-glass windows, cool and blue, settling like frost along the floor. Chase stood beside one of the tall pillars, collar tugged loose, feeling the exhaustion settle into his bones like sand.

Thomas and Donald were in the ground. The case was closed. The blood was washed away—but not gone. And he was out of a job.

He saw Skye down the hallway. She'd gone to the powder room to fix her face, but her eyes were still swollen. She walked toward him with quiet precision—measured steps, hands clasped in front of her like she was holding something fragile inside.

"Chase," she said softly. "Can we talk?" The room around him muted into a distant hum.

He nodded.

She lead him to a back room. A private room meant for family needing a moment of peace. She closed the door behind them.

"Site please." She asked. Chase removed his overcoat and sat crossed legged quietly wondering what the secrecy was about. Skye stopped a foot away, close enough that he could feel her warmth, far enough that he couldn't touch her.

She stood there.

Her silhouette was backlit by the dim floor lamp, her coat gone, hair loose, the funeral dress hanging like a shadow around her frame. She looked fragile—but her movement was deliberate as she slid of her shoes.

"Skye…" It was barely more than breath.

She didn't answer.

She unbuttoned her dress. Golden brown skin shimmered in the sunlight. She turned for him as she removed her veil. He could feel the heat of her skin. Close enough that if he raised a hand, he could touch her cheek.

She didn't let him.

Skye reached down and placed his hands on her breasts. Her fingers brushed his jaw—soft, trembling, reverent in a way that shattered him instantly.

"Are you sure?" Chase whispered, voice low, rough. "Skye, We don't —"

"I want this," she said. Her voice cracked. But her actions didn't. She unbuttoned the top clasp of his shirt and kissed his chest.

He caught her wrist gently. "You don't think this is too soon?"

She closed her eyes, just for a second. "I want to remember you…

without the blood. Without the fire. Without everything else."

His throat tightened. She stepped closer, and her fingers went to the rest of his trousers—slow, deliberate, almost ritualistic.

"Skye..." He wanted to ask her why she was shaking. Why she wouldn't look him in the eyes too long. Why her breaths came ragged between words she wasn't saying. But she pressed a finger to his lips.

"I need you," she whispered. "Just... be here. With me."

He nodded. Her hands slid up his chest, around his shoulders, guiding him down as she kissed him—soft at first, then desperate, like she was memorizing him one last time. She lifted her dress and straddled him as she inserted the magic soldier inside her. They moved together slowly, quietly, almost reverently.

It wasn't passion; it wasn't heat. It was grief. It was goodbye. When it ended, she stayed on top of him for a long moment, head resting on his chest, her fingers curled into his hair. Her breathing was calm... but distant.

Chase gently brushed her back with his hand. "Skye... talk to me. Please."

She sat up. The tenderness vanished from her face. And what replaced it wasn't anger, it was a decision. She slid off him, buttoning and smoothing her dress calm and businesslike, like she were preparing for court instead of stepping away from the man who loved her.

Chase sat up, chest still bare, shirt tangled around his waist. "Skye... what is this? What are we doing?"

She didn't look at him as she retrieved her shoes. Or her coat. Or her lipstick retrieved from its pocket. She applied it with steady hands. Then finally—finally—she turned to him.

"I want to thank you," she began. Her voice was steady—not strong, not trembling. Just... controlled. "For everything you did. For saving Benjamin. For fighting for me. For trying to keep us whole."

He waited. Something in his chest twisted.

"But," she continued, "I can't stay in this with you. Not anymore." It hit harder than any spell or blade he'd taken underground. Skye swallowed, shoulders trembling.

"Every path around you is fire," she whispered. "Death. Loss. Enemies I didn't even know existed until I stood too close. And I kept telling myself I could survive it. That we could survive it."

A tear slipped down. She brushed it away quickly. "But I can't live in a war, Chase. And that's what your life is."

He opened his mouth—But she lifted a hand.

"Please," she said. "Let me finish."

He fell silent. She reached into her coat pocket and pressed a folded card into his hand.

"My real name," she said softly. "My true name. I've never given it to anyone else."

Chase didn't open it. He couldn't. His fingers trembled around the paper like it might burn straight through him. She took a step back, shoulders rising as she wiped her face—once, twice—rebuilding whatever strength she had left.

"I love you," she whispered. "I always will. But love isn't enough to survive your world. And I'm not willing to lose myself trying."

She turned. The doors to the hall opened in a gust of cold air. Nadine stood there waiting, jaw tight, eyes damp. Luther farther back in the hallway, hat in his hands. Diego lingering near the corner, unsure if he should look at Chase or the floor.

Skye paused at the threshold and looked back at him one last time.

"Goodbye, Chase."

Then she stepped out. The doors closed behind her with a soft, final click. Only then did Chase unfold the card.

Isla Esperanza Ortega.

Not Skye. Not the mask. Her. The truth sat small and warm in his palm while the rest of the room felt colder than winter stone. He didn't chase after her. Didn't call her name. He just sat there, staring at the letters until they blurred.

Because some endings aren't loud. Some endings are just... quiet.

And final.

———

Rain tapped against the steel shutters of Red Row, soft as coins striking tin. Chase pushed open the door to his room, shoulders heavy, coat damp from the walk back across the district. He had just come from the children's home—Benjamin's new reality. A ward of the state. A lonely bed in a quiet wing. A boy who didn't understand why the adults who loved him couldn't stay.

Chase understood too well.

And it sat like lead behind his ribs.

He tossed his keys onto the table. The burned photograph of Elijah Cassidy lay beside them like a wound that refused to close. He stared at the charred edges for a moment—grateful that at least something of his past had survived, even if it hurt to look at.

But the tiny photo of his mother—once tucked into the corner of the frame—had gone up in ash.

Just like the memory of her name.

The room was small, barely big enough for a cot, a chair, and the war-locker at the foot of the bed. But it was his. And tonight, like every night, the silence pressed too close.

He reached for the trumpet resting on the windowsill.

The brass was dull, dented along the bell from years of being carried through moves and battles and nights he didn't want to remember. He lifted it, attached the mouth piece, breathed once, and played.

A low, aching note spilled out—steady, unpolished, honest.

A second followed. Then a third.

Somewhere between the breath and the sound, something inside him loosened. Not healed—never healed. Just… loosened.

He didn't even notice the footsteps in the hall until the knock landed softly against his door.

Three taps. Even. Deliberate.

Chase lowered the trumpet, wiped the condensation from the bell, and opened the door.

A woman stood in the frame—coat dripping from the rain, hood overshadowing her face. Not a vamp. Not a monster. But not normal, either. Her presence hummed faintly, like static behind glass.

Her eyes lifted.. "You're... actually pretty good," she murmured. Then, after a breath:

"I heard you used to be a copper."

Chase didn't confirm it. Didn't deny it. He simply waited. She swallowed, voice trembling at the edges. "You still help people? Even if they... can't go through the police?"

A faint pulse throbbed under his skin—his wards stirring not in warning, but in recognition. A Siphon. A fragile, frightened one. The air around her bent in that subtle way only they carried, emotions humming off-key, tugging at the edges of his own pulse. Siphons didn't cast spells; they didn't need to. Their voices, their fear, their very breath could sway the human heart—nudge a room toward calm or panic without ever meaning to.

And this one... she was leaking terror like a cracked lantern, enough that his wards tasted it before he did. Chase straightened, suddenly far more alert.

This wasn't just a woman at his door. This was someone whose world had just gone very, very wrong.

"I can pay," she added, voice trembling despite her posture.

Chase stepped aside. "Come in."

She crossed the threshold.

"Start from the beginning."

The woman took a shaky breath as she crossed the threshold. Chase closed the door behind her. Down the hallway, a radio blared to life.

"... And now we return to The Grim Truth with Walter Grimsley, brought to you by WBC Radio—New York's finest voice in news, patriotism, and purity.

"For those just tuning in, you're hearing it here first—confirmation out of the Arcane Licensing Committee. Effective next week, the Governor-General has authorized a brand-new initiative: the Independent Hexbreaker Registry.

"That's right. With the First Arcane Police Department outgunned, and the Bureau of Arcane Enforcement tripping over their own boots, Albany's solution is to let freelancers take the reins. Their word, not mine."

"They're opening the doors for privately licensed Hexbreakers—arcanists, warlocks, spellbound oddities—to hunt the things prowling the Madhatten Zone. And they're paying bounties to do it.

"Imagine that, folks: the government hiring sorcerers to police sorcerers. Letting the wolf guard the henhouse because the shepherd nodded off. And while they're at it? Curfews.

"Mandatory. Citywide.

"Because nothing says 'public safety' like locking honest families indoors while the creatures that thrive in darkness get more excuses to roam it.

"This is the world they're building: a world where the devil polices his own. And they expect you to trust it.

"Remember, folks—when the state starts deputizing the damned... they're not protecting you. They're protecting themselves."

—static crackles—

"Speaking of protecting themselves. The brass suits up in Albany have declared it official: as of this week, the borough once known as Manhattan will be renamed and redrawn, into something new. Something they're calling 'necessary.'

"The Madhatten Containment Zone."

"I've said it before, and I'll say it again—when you let arcanists run free, the gutters flood with blood. Vampires masquerading as socialites. Demons walking in men's shoes. Hexbreakers given the authority to kill without trial. And now? Children with glowing eyes running wild while parents are too afraid to discipline them."

"But not me. I remember a better Manhattan. Before the sigils. Before the wards. Before you had to wonder what walked beside you in the dark."

"So while the soft-handed senators toast their containment protocols, and while bleeding hearts cry for magical rights—I'll be right here, telling you the truth, my fellow Americans."

"Because it ain't just about safety. It's about blood. It's about knowing who's pure—and who's pretending."

"Signing off from the ashes of a city that once knew better... this is Walter Grimsley, bringing you the voice of reason."

"…This is The Grim Truth."

THE END

EPILOGUE

Blackwell Island

A cold wind swept over the East River as the ferries docked against the cracked stone pier. Floodlights cast long, sterile cones of light across the asylum grounds, illuminating broken windows, collapsed wards, and the eerie stillness of a place abandoned by magic and men alike.

Today, at last, Blackwell Island was being emptied.

BAE Containment officers guided shivering patients down the steps one by one—blankets draped over shoulders, wrists still bearing old restraint marks, eyes hollow from months of neglect. Some cried. Some stared. Some simply shuffled forward, too numb to do anything else.

Dr. Rahm, the newly assigned medical supervisor, waited with a clipboard thicker than his forearm.

"Name?"

"...Serafina Polk, I think."

"Step aside, please. Next—name?"

"...I... I can't remember."

He marked each name with a heavy sigh.

"So many lives lost in paperwork," he muttered.

"Next!" an officer called.

A woman stepped forward.

She wore a simple gray patient's dress. Barefoot. Her hair spilled down her shoulders in a dark curtain—wild but clean, as if no filth dared cling to her.

She moved with an effortless quiet. Almost graceful. Even exhausted, she carried a presence the others lacked—something old, patient, and watchful.

Dr. Rahm looked up from his clipboard.

She met his eyes. Her irises glowed faintly—gold, like candlelight behind glass.

Rahm blinked and steadied himself. "Ma'am... your name?"

She tilted her head, as though the question amused her. A slow smile curved her lips, soft and knowing.

"My name," she said calmly, "is Marrowwyn."

The pen fell from the doctor's fingers. A hush spread across the line as though a chill had swept through all of them at once. Even the wind seemed to pause, listening.

Marrowwyn stepped off the final stair of the asylum. She inhaled deeply—her first true breath as a free woman in a decade. Behind her, frost crept across the railing where her hand had rested.

The BAE officer cleared his throat nervously. "Right this way, miss. Transportation is waiting—"

"I know," she whispered, almost kindly. She walked toward the ferry with slow, deliberate steps. The floodlights flickered overhead—not broken, not faulty—simply reacting to something powerful waking up inside her.

And as the ferry pulled away from Blackwell Island,

Marrowwyn stood alone at the bow, hair streaming in the winter wind... watching Manhattan rise in the distance. Watching his city.

Waiting.

ABOUT THE AUTHOR

Charles Draevyn hails from the vibrant streets of Harlem, NYC, where his early immersion in Dungeons & Dragons, anime, and manga laid the foundation for his storytelling. Diving into these realms before they gained mainstream popularity, Charles developed a deep appreciation for intricate narratives and complex characters.

A dedicated military professional, Charles served with distinction in both the U.S. Marines and the U.S. Army, completing tours in Afghanistan and Iraq. His experiences in these combat zones have profoundly shaped his perspectives, infusing his writing with authenticity and depth.

Beyond his military career, Charles is a devoted family man. Married to his teenage sweetheart after 26 years apart, they have built a blended family of five children and share their home with their loyal dog, Creed.

In his debut series, *Wands & Tommy Guns* based on an original award winning short film screenplay, Charles masterfully intertwines his rich life experiences with his passion for fantasy and noir, crafting a narrative that resonates with both realism and imagination.

ACKNOWLEDGEMENT

To Charles Steffen Haskins Payne Sr.
A writer. A revolutionary. A father.
Your words lit torches. Your spirit still marches.
Gone too soon—but never forgotten.

To My Wife
Thank you for enduring the countless rewrites, midnight ideas, and every "just one more hour" assurance.
Your patience, strength, and unwavering support kept me grounded.
I love you. I honor you. You will forever be my muse.

To My Sister, Akiya
My first baby. My first audience.
Thank you for listening to every story I ever told and for always believing in the worlds I dreamed up.

To My Daughter, Kiana
Thank you for your loyalty, your understanding, and your love.
You've always made room for your old man's madness—and I'm endlessly grateful.

To Phoenix, Alyssa, and Justin
"So let me run this idea by you…"
Thank you for your ears, your feedback (even the brutally honest ones), and for never shutting the door on a rambling 50-year-old RPGer with too many plot twists.

To My Beta Readers: Teel, Kevin, Amber, and Ed
Your time, insight, and honesty were vital to shaping this book.
Your notes pushed me harder and helped this story become what it needed to be. Thank you—truly.

APPENDIX

APPENDIX I — CHARACTERS

The world of Wands & Tommy Guns is shaped not by kingdoms or courts but by individuals—scars, gifts, wounds, and choices bound together by circumstance. What follows is a record of the central figures whose actions formed the events of the Madhatten Affair.

Chase Corvin Cassidy - Once fought as a Legionnaire before joining the United States 369th Infantry, the Harlem Hellfighters. His body was carved with infernal sigils during the military's doomed attempt to bind hellfire to mortal flesh. A soldier, detective, and reluctant weapon, Chase moves through the world carrying the weight of ruined wars and ruined loves. His instincts are sharp, his loyalty unyielding, and his capacity for violence both feared and desperately needed. Recently became aware that he is of partial infernal heritage.

Skye Anderson-Pierce - born Isla Esperanza Ortega, is a brilliant duelist-mage whose sharp legal mind and sharper integrity set her apart in a city drowning in corruption. A survivor of prejudice both magical and mundane, she remade herself through discipline and brilliance. Her heart is fierce, her boundaries hard-won, her magic a razor of light in dark places. An advocate of the people she takes on an ever growing case load of pro bono work at her patterers dismay.

Diego Salazar - Child hood friend of chase Cassidy. Grew from a Legionnaire arcane-sapper into a dice-mage whose strange, probability-twisting magic is equal parts genius and madness. Charismatic, loyal, and wildly resourceful, he masks trauma with humor, gambling instincts, and a deep devotion to the few he calls family.

Benjamin Bright - Is a young Fae-blood runaway whose gentle nature conceals a lineage others covet. He is the quiet heart of this story, a reminder that innocence is a currency far too often spent by the wicked.

Makalith Ravenwind - Half-blood dusk-born Fae and battle-mage, is a creature of twilight and sorrow. Bound by honor yet twisted by grief, his alliances are fragile, but his resolve is absolute. His companion and chaos-twin, Coco Le Fay—Miriam Le Fay—shines with manic brilliance, her sprite-shifting form masking both unbearable trauma and unbreakable hope.

Adriana Mortem Ruthven - vampire aristocrat and the architect of the

Court's ascension, stands as the embodiment of power without restraint.

Hermann Von Epp - necromancer and warmonger, forged his empire through bone, science, and the broken bodies of the dead.

APPENDIX II — RACES

Humanity remains the dominant population of the known world, though "dominant" is a fragile word in an age when magic has returned with teeth. Humans encompass the full range of arcane potential: some mundane, some Bloodlined, some trained into dangerous sophistication. Their adaptability makes them both prey and predator in equal measure.

The Mourned are the failed and forsaken results of necro-alchemical experimentation—men and women warped by Von Epp's sciences into tireless, often mind-shredded revenants. Some retain fragments of awareness; most are tools fashioned from agony. Their bodies are mechanical grafts and marrow-forged constructs, powered by unstable necrotic essence. They are not truly alive, nor fully dead, but something left shivering between.

Automata—called automations by the public—are arcane-engineered constructs, forged from brass, gearwork, and runic induction coils. These machines are not sentient in a human sense, though some exhibit eerie approximations of instinct or preference. Most serve as laborers or guardians, but some have wandered the world long enough to develop quirks, personalities, and dangerous unpredictability.

The Fey (or Fae)

The Fae were never merely creatures of magic—they were magic given bone and breath. Long before the rise of human sorcery, they shaped forests, storms, rivers, and dream-paths, changing shape as easily as a mortal draws breath. All Fae are natural shapeshifters, though their forms differ: the females bear wings and can collapse themselves into delicate sprite-bodies no larger than a hand, a state humans foolishly labeled a separate species. The males are wingless, bound more to the earth than the air, heavier of presence but no less wondrous. Once, the great Seelie and Unseelie Courts ruled over them all, radiant and terrible, the twin poles of order and ruin.

But when the Fae Wars tore their realms to ash, the Courts sealed themselves away from the mortal plane—closing the gateways, severing the leylines, and abandoning those kin too wounded or fractured to retreat. These forsaken became the Dusk-Born: Fae of twilight, sorrow, and in-between places. Neither Seelie nor Unseelie, they were left stranded in the waking world, forced to root themselves among humans who barely understood them. Today, nearly a third of all Fae who remain on Earth descend from these exiles. There are no purebloods left; even Coco Le Fay, as close to true lineage as any living Fae, carries the mingled marks of survival and loss. The Dusk-Born endure with fragile brilliance—winged women who shrink to protect themselves, wingless men carved from shadow and longing—nature spirits who remember a world that no longer remembers them.

Dusk-Born Fae represent the largest surviving branch of Fae-kind. Once shapeshifters of limitless expression, the surviving Fae have settled into forms the mortal world understands: winged women capable of collapsing into sprite shapes, and wingless men bound to dusk, sorrow, and earth-magic. They remember realms that no longer remember them. Their abilities involve glamour, limited shifting, emotional resonance, and an ancient understanding of life between light and shadow.

Other Fae-descended hybrids exist across the world, though none are pureblood. Centuries of exile fractured the lineage, leaving only echoes of what the ancient Courts once created.

Stunts

No one uses their old name anymore—Dwarrow, Stoneborn, Deep-Forged. In the modern age they are simply Stunts, a human misnomer that stuck out of mockery and ignorance. They were once the master engineers of the ancient Fae realms, natural geomancers and arcane smiths whose minds were built for metal, runes, and leyline architecture. It was the Stunts who first revealed the existence of the Fae to humankind, attempting to forge an alliance that could break the stagnation of the Seelie and Unseelie Courts. Instead, humanity turned on them—stealing their works, razing their forges, and hunting their clans. The betrayal ignited the long fall into the Fae Wars and left the Stunts abandoned when the great Courts sealed themselves away.

Today, the Stunts survive as scattered remnants—small in number, fiercely private, and still unmatched in engineering or arcane tinkering. Their stature belies a dense physical resilience, and their craftsmanship remains coveted by arcanists, artificers, and industrialists alike. Though often misjudged as insular or dour, they carry the memory of two betrayals on their backs: the humans who used them, and the Fae rulers who deserted them. A dwindling people, yes—but one carved of stone, pressure, and endurance, whose forges continue to burn in the forgotten places of the world.

APPENDIX III — ORGANIZATIONS

The First Arcane Police Department stands as the city's first attempt at structured magical law enforcement. Underfunded, overwhelmed, and often politically constrained, the APD represents an imperfect shield against arcane crime.

The Bureau of Arcane Enforcement—the federal arm—is larger, more rigid, and frequently incompetent. Their agents are well-funded but poorly trained for the eldritch realities of the Madhatten Containment Zone. Their bureaucracy consumes more resources than their actions justify.

The Hexbreaker Guild stretches back centuries, an order of sanctioned hunters operating independently of traditional government bodies. Their job is simple: find magic that goes wrong and stop it. Their methods vary wildly, their reputations stranger still, and until recently, the Guild refused all government interference. With the new registry of independent Hexbreakers now operating in New York, the Guild's presence will only grow.

The Arcane Society is the academic and political powerhouse of magical education. They regulate wandcraft, magical research, sanctioned dueling, and most wizard certification. Their neutrality is a myth, but their influence is undeniable.

The Court of Bones—the necromantic cabal responsible for the events in the Underwalk—sprawls through the criminal underworld like a cancer of bone and shadow. Though Von Epp and Adriana were its greatest architects, its networks remain embedded in ports, orphanages, black markets, and forgotten tunnels.

Other factions—vampiric families, fae enclaves, mortal guilds—watch from the margins, waiting to see what the Containment Zone becomes.

APPENDIX IV — LOCATIONS

The Madhatten Containment Zone, once Manhattan, is now an island half reclaimed by arcane disaster. Quarantine wards, collapsed infrastructure, and roaming entities from the Veil have turned it into a no-man's-land of danger and opportunity. Portions of the city remain habitable. Others are lost forever to nightmare logic.

The Red Row: Where the city put everything it didn't want to see. A narrow stretch of neon rot wedged between the river and the elevated rails, the district thrummed with the business of the desperate—brothels behind velvet curtains, back-alley gambling dens, potion runners, washed-out arcanists selling tricks for coin, and every flavor of body-for-hire work that the law pretended not to notice.

It wasn't a refuge so much as a holding pen for the forgotten.

Veterans haunted the corners with thousand-yard stares, spellbinders whose talents had burned them hollow drifted from vice to vice, and men and women with nowhere else to go survived behind rusted steel shutters and flickering red lamps.

People didn't come to Red Row to live.

They came because everywhere else had already cast them out.

And Chase Cassidy—tired, half-broken, carrying scars no one could see—fit the place a little too well.

THE UNDERWALK

The Underwalk is the true underbelly of Madhatten—an endless, unmapped labyrinth of abandoned rail lines, sealed transit tunnels, collapsed stations, half-built arcane chambers, Prohibition-era smuggler routes, and ruins far older than the city itself. No official agency admits how deep it goes. No map has ever been complete.

Everything that cannot survive in daylight survives in the Underwalk. The Feralborn roam its arteries. Necromancers bury their secrets in chambers carved from old stone. Black markets thrive in its blind spots. The Arcane Police enter only when absolutely forced, and never without backup.

The Underwalk breathes—the city's grief, its history, its monsters—and the Hollow is its deepest wound.

THE HOLLOW

The Hollow is not the Underwalk. It is a pocket within it: a cavernous, echoing breach where the boundaries of stone, shadow, and old magic collapsed into one another. It is where the Veil thins without warning. Where echoes last too long. Where the air feels wrong even when still.

Every faction knows of the Hollow, but none claim it. Too many died trying. It is the perfect ground for rituals, ambushes, disappearances—and the place where the Court of Bones carved its throne in secret.

Two major sub-districts feed into it:

- **ASHEN ROAD**

Ashen Road is the main corridor leading into the Hollow. Named for the persistent gray-black ash that eternally falls—ash with no fire, no smoke, no origin—this long passage is lined with charred brickwork and scorched arches. Footprints linger in the ash long after their makers leave, and sometimes appear when no one has passed at all.

For spellbinders, Ashen Road is a transit route. For monsters, a hunting ground. For everyone else, a warning.

• THE MARKET MACABRE

Near the Hollow's western wall stands the Market Macabre—a shifting bazaar of illegal magic and forbidden trade. Merchants rearrange themselves constantly, as if following rules written in a language the living no longer remember.

Here, buyers can find essence vials harvested from the Mourned, Veil-tainted relics, soul-bound curios, hex-cages, cursed organs in preservation fluid, and artifacts scavenged from the Court of Bones after its fall.

The Market Macabre offers everything—except safety.

The Hudson Highlands Reserve and the **Catskill Restriction Zone** remain under heavy federal control, remnants of earlier magical disasters that reshaped entire landscapes.

Other boroughs—Brooklyn, Queens, the Bronx, and Staten Island—have become semi-lawless arcane slums, operating as unofficial restriction zones where magic thrives without oversight.

APPENDIX V — MAGIC

Magic is older than empires and deeper than blood. It is the breath of the world—the force that once shaped forests, storms, dreams, and nightmares—and in the modern age it manifests through the inheritors of ancient Bloodlines. These Bloodlines are five in number: Fae, Draconic, Arcane (sometimes called the Magi line), Infernal, and Celestial. Every human carries traces of them, but only a few are born with enough arcane potency to wield their power.

These are old legacies—genetic and spiritual inheritances mark a family as touched by supernatural ancestry. Every mage, warlock, arcanist, or sorcerous prodigy draws their strength from one or more of these ancient threads.

The Fae Bloodline is the most common, a residue of intermingling between mortals and the Dusk-Born. It grants heightened intuition, glamour resistance, emotional resonance, and the potential for illusion-craft.

The Draconic Bloodline is rarer, associated with internal power, elemental force, instinctive spellcasting, and territorial will.

The Arcane or Magi Bloodline arises when generations of spellcraft refine human potential into something cleaner and sharper. These individuals demonstrate extraordinary control, precision, and the capacity to learn complex spell structures.

The Infernal Bloodline is controversial—descended from pacts, demonic influence, or ancestral corruption. Infernal practitioners wield volatile power tied to destruction, heat, entropy, and emotional extremes.

The Celestial Bloodline is the rarest of all, characterized by healing, light, sanctification, and the ability to manipulate spiritual harmonics. Celestials often become priests, exorcists, or miracle-workers whether they want to or not.

An Arcanist is any human born with a Bloodline strong enough to manifest minor talents. Not all Arcanists become spellcasters; many live ordinary lives with only flickers of power that surface under stress.

A Sorcerer is an Arcanist whose bloodline burns so brightly that their talent manifests without training. They are raw power given direction only by instinct. Their spellcraft is limited in variety, but overwhelming in potency—burst-magic, emotional projection, elemental surges, and destructive feats that defy the more structured methods of the Mages. A sorcerer may know only a handful of spells in their lifetime, yet each one is mighty enough to rewrite a moment, a battlefield, or the fate of a small room full of enemies. They are feared and revered in equal measure, for they represent magic before discipline—wild, unpredictable, and often astonishing.

A Mage is an Arcanist who has received formal education in the Art. Mages train in structured spellcraft, runic theory, wand techniques, and the foundations of dimensional understanding. They operate within approved channels—dueling colleges, universities, guild-sponsored programs.

A Spellwright is an Arcanist who abandons incantation in favor of runic engineering. Where a Mage shapes ephemeral forces, a Spellwright binds magic into matter—steel, wood, gemstone, fiber, circuitry. They create enchanted weapons, arcane cartridges, warded armor, spell-cores, rune engines, automaton glyph-matrices, and sigil-stacked devices capable of rivaling spellcraft. Spellwrights are the artisans of the arcane world: half engineer, half mystic, translating magic into tools that endure long after the caster is gone.

An advanced Spellwright who completes the Trial of the Forge earns the title Artificer.

A Wizard is a mage who has passed at least one of the Three Great Trials. These trials test what no classroom can teach:

- **The Trial of Flesh** examines resilience, pain discipline, bodily endurance, and the ability to survive raw magic passing through a mortal vessel.

- **The Trial of Heart** tests emotional fortitude, moral clarity, compassion, and the capacity to wield power without letting it wield the practitioner.

- **The Trial of Veil** challenges perception, metaphysics, and the ability to navigate spaces where reality grows thin.

Most mages complete one or two. To complete all three is to become a **Magi,** one of the rare few whose mastery crosses body, spirit, and mind. Their authority is recognized across all magical institutions.

The Artificer is the spellcraft equivalent of a Wizard. An Artificer's creations are singular, potent, and often soul-bonded—able to channel enormous power, resist decay, and sometimes exhibit a kind of sympathetic consciousness. Where a Wizard wields magic through will and knowledge, an Artificer wields it through creation and permanence. Both are elite. Both stand at the apex of their respective paths.

Most mages complete one or two. To complete all three is to become a Magi, one of the rare few whose mastery crosses body, spirit, and mind. Their authority is recognized across all magical institutions.

A Magi stands at the summit of the formal mage's path. Whereas a Mage is one who has learned the structures, laws, and disciplines of spellcraft, a Magus is one who has proven mastery over those laws through ordeal. The title is not granted lightly, nor is it ever inherited. It is earned through the Arcane Trials, rites older than most nations and feared even by those who administer them. Only a small fraction of Mages attempt the trials, and fewer still survive them.

When a Mage completes all three trials, they are recognized as a Magus. Their spellcraft gains a fluidity and depth that lesser casters cannot replicate. They manipulate magic not merely by memorized sigils but by grasping its living intention. A Magus can bend a spell's shape mid-cast, weave multiple workings simultaneously, or fold their will through ambient energy with little more than breath and focus. They stand among the highest authorities on the theory and practice of magic, often becoming master instructors, arcane strategists, court sorcerers, or solitary scholars whose names become whispered legend.

But the title carries weight. Magi are held to stricter expectations, for the power they wield could topple cities or stabilize kingdoms. It is said that a Magus is not simply a master of magic—they are a guardian of its boundaries, one entrusted to understand where power must be applied, and where it must be withheld.

The world remembers Magi not for their spellcraft alone, but for the consequences of their choices.

Magic in this world is as diverse as humanity itself: wands, sigils, hellbinding, glamour, necromancy, pyromantic sigils, probability dice, and arts yet unnamed. Power is rarely the problem. How it is used is the story.

www.ingramcontent.com/pod-product-compliance
Lightning Source LLC
Chambersburg PA
CBHW081127020726
47505CB00010B/2268